PARRISH

A Novel by

Mildred Savage

Simon and Schuster · New York

PUBLISHED BY SIMON AND SCHUSTER, INC.
ROCKEFELLER CENTER, 630 FIFTH AVENUE
NEW YORK 20, N.Y.

To E.S. and B.L.S.
and
to Sue and Duke

CONTENTS

BOOK 1

1948: *Spring, Summer*

1

THE BATTERED station wagon was filled with a strange, sweet smell like incense. Parrish had noticed it when he stepped into the car in Hartford and here on the unshaded concrete highway, with the noon sun beating down, it grew heavier. Breathing in sharply a couple of times, he pressed himself to name it and was about to ask his mother if she knew it. But he checked himself. He didn't want her to think he was complaining. As long as he had given in to her and come along, in spite of not wanting to and believing that he should not, as long as he was doing this, he wasn't going to gripe.

It was getting hot in the car and he leaned over the cracked leather seat to talk to the driver. "What's your name?" he said.

The driver puffed his pipe and scratched a four-day growth of red whiskers while he seemed to consider the question. "Call me Teet, kid."

"Listen, Teet," Parrish said. "Do these windows work?"

Teet aimed some tobacco juice at the ribbon of straggly grass up the middle of the highway. "Nothin' in this car works, kid, exceptin' the motor. An' I keep that goin' with spit 'n' a prayer."

Parrish grinned and settled back, shifting his long legs to where they didn't bump the luggage. He was a tall boy of eighteen, with dark hair and eyes and a wide mouth, and a look to his body of bones stretching out so fast no amount of eating could put meat on them. Reflectively now, he considered Teet, letting his eyes rest on the crease of dirt between the scraggly red hair and the frayed shirt. In the railroad station in Hartford, where Teet had met their train, Parrish had seen that his feet were stuck into filthy ankle-high shoes, laced every third hole with knotted strings, and that a piece of rope held up his dirt-blotched jeans. Remembering, he winced a little.

Not that he minded the dirt himself. But Sala Post, whatever he turned out to be, could not have sent a more discouraging man to meet Parrish's mother at the train—even though she had not shown it in the station and didn't show it now.

Parrish glanced over at her, sitting next to him, looking fragile and beautiful and serene as always, and still seeming too young at thirty-seven to be his mother. Smiling a little, he thought, not for the first time, that you had to admire the way she insulated herself. Ellen MacLean saw everything, heard everything, but nothing ever got through to disturb that eternal calm, that lovely, untouched, deceptively dependent look. With her pale-blond hair and bright violet eyes, she looked like some kind of Dresden doll you had to be careful not to break.

Turning away, he let his eyes take in the Connecticut countryside through the dust-caked window which, he had on good authority now, would not open. He could see that they were leaving the prosperous-looking fringe of the city, moving into a shabbier rural area. Off in the distance the land rose a little into pale-green hills, but here along the highway it was very flat, with field after field of strawlike weeds stretching a long way, broken only by plowed patches of dirt that seemed dry and starved. Even Parrish, city-bred, could see it wasn't much.

He leaned forward again. "Is all the land around here like this?" he asked Teet, motioning toward the brown countryside.

"Like what, kid?"

"Scrawny-looking, kind of."

"Can't say as I ever noticed, kid."

"Doesn't seem to grow much," Parrish said.

"Depends on what you're growin'," Teet said. "This is tobacco country."

Parrish told himself he should be thinking more seriously about all this. Not so much what it would mean—pulling up stakes in Boston, where he had lived all his life, and moving up to a tobacco farm, or, as Ellen preferred to call it, a plantation—but more about whether he had done right letting her give up a good job in Boston to take this one with Sala Post, letting her make him the reason for it.

Another sorry little patch of tilled land came along, set with rows of small plants. "How about that, Teet?" he said. "Is that a tobacco farm?"

"Broadleaf." You'd think it was garbage, the way he said it.

"What's Broadleaf?" Parrish said.

"Don't know much about tobacco, do you, kid?"

"Up in Boston we smoke tobacco. We don't grow it."

"That's a riot, kid."

"O.K." Parrish laughed. "What's Broadleaf?"

"Tobacco."

"Is that what Sala Post's farm looks like?"

"We're in Shade," Teet said contemptuously. "That crummy stuff is Broadleaf. We're in Shade."

"I'll bite. What's Shade?"

"Kid—" Teet's voice was strained—"you grow it under cloth that shades it, so it's Shade."

Ellen looked amused. "What do you do on Mr. Post's farm, Mr. . . . uh . . ."

"Howie, ma'am." Teet's voice changed. "Teet Howie. I drive tractor."

"I thought you must," Ellen murmured, just the proper admiration in her soft voice.

"You spotted it, eh?" Teet said, pleased. "I can hit a row within half an inch—best tractor driver on any farm in these parts. Farther, even. I worked farms from Canada to Florida, never seen a better driver 'n myself."

"I can tell by the way you handle this car," Ellen said.

Well, the guy was not handling the car so terrifically, Parrish told himself. Just like anybody else handled a car—stayed where he belonged on the road. Already he was doing better, exhibiting his skill, holding the wheel as if it were a wafer that might break off.

"Any big outfit around here would hire me in a minute," Teet told Ellen. "Take Raike, for instance. I could go to work for Raike this afternoon if I wanted."

"And do you want to?" Ellen said.

"Nah. Too big. Give me a smaller outfit, where nobody tells me what I can do with my tractor. Big outfit like Raike just complicates things."

Parrish listened, fascinated, in spite of the fact that he had seen this kind of thing before. It was uncanny how his mother could always put her finger on what made a man tick. Give her about five minutes and she nosed it out like a bug nosed out a lighted bulb, and from then on she had him eating out of her hand, like Teet, and loving every minute of it. That was how she handled everybody, sure and easy. Himself included. Why else was he here?

"Now, them are tobacco sheds." Teet pointed to two brown barnlike buildings constructed out of loose-looking vertical boards. They were in very poor condition. "'Course, them are pretty crummy. Old Sala wouldn't have sheds lookin' like that. Barns, maybe. But not sheds."

Old Sala. Parrish let his thoughts wander ahead a little, speculating again on what they were coming into, what this Sala Post would be like. What kind of man, he asked himself, sent to Boston for a combination governess and social secretary for a seventeen-year-old daughter? Why Boston? According to the employment agency, Ellen was to keep an eye on this girl as well as get her through a debut in the fall. Ellen loved that stuff and whenever Parrish laughed at it she told him that he wouldn't always feel that way, that he just laughed now because he was wild and full of rebellion, and when he calmed down and became civilized he would see that it had its place in the world. Parrish always wanted to ask how he was wild and uncivilized, but he never did, knowing ahead of time that he wouldn't agree with the answers. What kind of seventeen-year-old girl, he asked himself now, still had to have an eye kept on her?

They passed another shabby farmhouse, dirty white, with two or three dull hemlocks clutching close to the ground. "You should have seen the time I came up to Connecticut with Milky," he said. "It wasn't anything like this. Nothing but trees for miles and miles—thick and green."

It was the only time he had been in real country, the time his Uncle Milky had taken him to Connecticut for three days on a construction job. "And so quiet you never heard a sound but our hammering. And a couple of birds, maybe."

Ellen smiled her bright smile but didn't say anything and Parrish knew it was because she didn't intend to waste much time talking about Milky. Ellen and Milky had never seen eye to eye, the whole time they had lived in Milky's house. And when you came right down to it, that was the real reason they were here in the back seat of a dirty station wagon with its odd sweet smell and a sign on the door saying THE SALA POST FARM, and both of them wondering, he knew, what they were riding into. That was the real reason and not because Ellen had walked in on him last week when he was in the living room with Milky, drinking beer.

"There's more sheds, ma'am." Teet's voice interrupted his brooding. "I bet you thought they was barns."

"I would have if you hadn't told me," Ellen said.

"You can tell by the loose boards," Teet said. "They're loose so's you can open 'em for air."

One of the sheds bore a sign advising that you would get a square deal from somebody named Tower at his used-car establishment. Apparently Tower was the local tycoon. Already they had passed Tower's Texaco Station, Tower's Dine and Dance, Tower's General Store and Apothecary Shop, which looked like two old barns joined together by a narrow passageway. The tobacco sheds seemed to mark the start of an area even poorer than before. An old cemetery came along, with thin slanting stones, and then a shack that offered chickens and eggs for sale. Parrish doubted that even a hen could scratch out a fat living here. It didn't seem that other living things could, with the scrawny shrubbery and the trees against the wires thin and scarce.

At a traffic light Teet drew to a stop behind three cars in a single line. Then he said suddenly, "There he is! There's the big man now!"

"Who?" Parrish looked up quickly, thinking he meant Sala Post.

"Raike. Judd Raike. Like to get a look at him?" Abruptly Teet swung out of line. "This guy is the biggest grower around here. Owns half the farms in the Valley. Judd Raike."

Teet squeezed the station wagon in between the line of cars and the strip of grass with scarcely six inches to spare on either side until he pulled alongside a long black chauffeur-driven Cadillac with a gold "R" monogrammed on the door. He jerked his head and Parrish looked over, but the man sat deep in the corner of his car. All Parrish saw was the large hand that held a cigar. Then the light changed and the hand flicked impatiently, as though urging the chauffeur to leave behind this obscenity of the highway.

Teet, who had been bent over the wheel like a racer, shot the old wreck ahead first, amid a great rattle and clatter, but the Cadillac rolled past and left them far behind.

"It kills that guy," Teet said, "that I don't work for him. He's sent around askin' me maybe half a dozen times."

They passed Tower's Liquor Store and at last the previously heralded used-car establishment, where they turned off the main highway. Suddenly it was fragrant and cool. A shaded country road wound around, rose and fell on small hills, narrowed down to just room enough for a car, and went over a little bridge. Below, a stream gleamed and splashed against rocks in its bed, its banks thick with fresh-tipped green, and beyond, thick woods rose, dark with tall, lush trees. You could smell damp earth and hear the silence. Then, abruptly, the road rose in a steep hill and at the top, crowning the Valley, set back on a knoll far off the road, Parrish saw a house, wide and white, fitted as if it had been there forever to a rolling green lawn and tall elms, and he knew they were at Sala Post's.

Teet stopped and turned carefully into an entrance cut in a high stone wall. Over the cool drive elms joined branches, shutting out the sun, their trunks wider than the circle of a man's arms, with light playing on the outer fringe of leaves. Then Parrish smelled it again, the odd sweet smell, not so overwhelming here, but heavy and fragrant, striking the senses sharply, like the sudden smell of spring at the first thaw.

At last, reaching the house, they passed under an ivied arch to one side and stopped and Parrish saw it, the thing called "Shade."

From the crest of the hill, acres and acres of land, covered with white cloth, stretched as far as the eye could see. A continuous tent, propped up with posts, looked in the glaring sunlight like an endless field of tree stumps in a countryside of snow, rising and falling with the contour of the land—a white ocean, ending at the horizon against the harsh brilliant blue of an unbroken skyline. And in the whole white expanse there was no hint of motion, not of tree or of man. Only the eye moved, following the cloth stretching out over the land.

2

PULLING HIS eyes away from the white sea of cloth, Parrish looked slowly around him, taking in the house and grounds and a large garage that he could see had once been a stable. Then, in the driveway, he noticed a queer-looking car, high and stately, shiny black, with the unreal look of something out of another age.

"Whatcha lookin' at, kid?" Teet hitched the rope that held up his jeans. "That crazy car?"

"What is it?"

"Rolls Royce, kid. Family heirloom—left over from better days. John tells me Sala's had it eighteen years now and the head ain't never been off." Teet looked at the old car admiringly. "They's times I'd give a week's pay to drive it, but that Rolls is like a live baby to old Sala. Don't let nobody touch it but hisself."

Parrish looked at the old-fashioned high cab and short hood, thinking that it didn't look like so much, and then a door opened behind them and he turned to see a light-skinned colored girl in a blue maid's uniform approaching from the house.

"Teet," she called.

"Hullo, Hazel Anne, my lil sweetheart."

"Teet," she said, "John was in. Says a tractor is stuck in the mud and for you to get on out there. But first you drive over to the garage and take them bags up to the apartment."

"Jesus Christ, who got my tractor stuck in the mud?"

"Mind your tongue, Teet. Mr. Post's to lunch right there in the dining room with the windows open." She eyed Parrish with what seemed to be an unuttered question on her face. "And don't forget the bags."

"I ain't cartin' any bags. I'm gettin' back to my tractor."

"Now you know Mr. Post don't like things out of place and I don't want him riled by them bags. Things are bad enough for him today."

Ellen followed the girl into the house and Parrish nodded toward the old stable. "Is that the apartment?"

"Yeah. You get to share it with the Rolls. Don't belittle it. Like I said, that car's like a live baby to old Sala." Teet frowned toward the tobacco fields, in the direction of his beloved tractor.

"Well, go get it out of the mud," Parrish said. "I'll carry the bags."

"So get 'em out of the wagon," Teet said. "Ah, leave 'em be. John's comin' in the truck. I'll ride out with him."

A gray Ford pickup truck came along a path next to the white cloth, two colored boys sitting in the back. The truck stopped and the driver, a man of about forty with a rugged tan face, stuck his head out the window. "So you got back?" he bellowed. "Thought maybe you was takin' off the week."

"Hey, Gladstone," Teet called out. One of the colored boys looked up.

"Hello, mon." He spoke in a strange Calypso rhythm.

"You get my tractor stuck in the mud?"

"I do eet, mon." Cheerfully, Gladstone jerked his head toward the driver. "John he tell me drive eet," he said in the Calypso accents. "Cannot wait, he say. No time. Hurry, hurry. Teet too slow."

"You real slow mon, Teet," the other colored boy said, grinning.

"O.K., get the lead out of your feet," John barked. "I'd like to get the tractor out of the damned mud before the day's out."

Now Teet did a switch. "I gotta carry some bags," he said, not budging an inch.

"You can carry bags later. Hop in. Let's go."

"Gladstone—" still Teet lazed against the station wagon—"you're one lousy, stinking tractor driver."

"I am that," Gladstone said cheerfully. "Too much mud. Rain too much. Do not rain all week, I do not get stuck. That ees eet, mon."

Teet thumped Parrish on the back. "Well, good luck with Sala, kid," he said, and moved at last toward the truck, hopping into the back with Gladstone and the other boy.

Watching the truck disappear around a corner of the white cloth, Parrish smiled, wondering about Teet. Maybe he had just affected concern for his tractor to get out of carrying the luggage. Or was there, maybe, some spark of beautiful human dignity beneath the filth and scraggly beard that pushed back against being pushed against, even when the pushing was in a direction he wanted to go. Or maybe, Parrish thought, the guy just hated work. A man could do a thing for any number of reasons, many times not knowing himself what the real reason was.

The sound of the truck died and it was quiet. Except for the cry of a pigeon perched on the garage, there was absolute silence and Parrish listened a moment, his mind slipping off to old questions. Reasons, he thought carefully, because today this seemed important, reasons were funny things. And many times what seemed to be the cause of an act was only the match that sparked it off, the real cause being a thing you maybe never put your finger on, although it was there nonetheless, beneath the surface, growing and getting more urgent until the time arrived for it to explode. Then it was set off by a little prick, a little episode, like the incident of Milky and the beer, and the little episode was called the big reason. And a person could act on it, and maybe never know what, underneath, had been the real cause.

With Ellen and Milky the dynamite had been there, quiet, for years. Parrish had known it long before he and Milky talked about it last night in his room, bringing it out into the open.

"We both know it wasn't that lousy can of beer," Milky had said, his big face going red as he looked at the open suitcase on the bed. "Don't we?"

Parrish laughed. "Hell, yes."

"Parrie," Milky said, "you oughtn't to go. You ought to put your foot down."

It was what Parrish had been thinking. "I figure it's only temporary, Milky. I'll get drafted. Or maybe join the Navy."

"Be the best thing could happen to you." Milky settled his bulky frame in a chair. "You know, Parrie, your old man came from a fancy Boston family, a lot fancier than me. But when he was killed ten years ago, he left your ma with you and one thousand bucks' insurance."

"Yes."

"Now, Ellen's a smart woman. She sees everything anyone else sees and a lot the others miss. She came to live with Mae and me so she could work and Mae could keep an eye on you. Only thing she could do. She didn't come because she wanted to."

"Probably didn't think too much then about wanting or not wanting, Milky."

"Last place she'd have picked by choice, Parrie. Mae and Ellen ain't much alike. You'd never know they was sisters."

Neither from looks, Parrish thought, nor from what went on in their minds. Aunt Mae was a simple sort of woman, plain and good and trusting, who worried that Parrish was too thin and why Ellen didn't get married again, and leaned for everything on Milky's broad shoulders. Ellen could have had the broad shoulders, too, had she wanted them, but this particular type of shoulder was not what Ellen had in mind. Less brawn and more wealth and grace would be closer to Ellen's liking. Mae was simple and satisfied. Ellen was subtle and ambitious.

"She never figured on staying this long," Milky said.

"Well, I'm glad she did, Milky."

Parrish grinned and blushed a little after he said it, but it was the truth. With Milky, he had never felt the lack of a father. In his blunt, honest way, Milky had taught Parrish a lot. Milky was a real man and, insofar as one person could do it for another, allowing that in the end each had to do it for himself, he'd tried to make a man out of Parrish.

"You're eighteen, Parrie, finishing school this month, and Ellen counted on you going to college."

"If I went to college, I'd be leaning on her another four years. Her and you."

"It'd be all right with me, boy. You know that."

"I don't want to, Milky."

"I know. I know. But soon as Ellen saw you meant it that you wouldn't go, she had to do something. Ellen knows if she don't get you out of here, you're going into construction with me. Not just Saturdays and summers, but steady. That don't suit Ellen."

"Well, it suits me, Milky. Just because I'm leaving now doesn't mean I won't be back."

"Parrie, it don't matter. You work in construction or you work at something else—long as you pick it and it's what you want. Not Ellen. Fella, if it hadn't been the beer, it would have been something else. It's not just that construction ain't such a fancy job. That's important, but more than that, what's eating Ellen is she's afraid she's gonna lose you. Why else would Ellen be goin' to a farm? She's a city girl, for God's sake. Likes things fancy." Milky stood up and came over to the bed. "Parrie, you gotta break away."

Parrish knew it was true. And it made him feel worse instead of better to hear it from Milky. It was as if, until now, he had been hoping he was wrong, and now that it had been said aloud, it was final and could not be taken back and was true. "What about her, Milky?" he said. "Don't you think it's time I started looking out for her, instead of the other way around?"

"If she wanted it, I'd say yes. But she don't want it, Parrie. Ellen don't need lookin' after, for God's sake. Not Ellen." And then, before Parrish could agree or deny it, Milky said, "O.K., fella. I made my point. No need to beat it to a pulp. Just remember it when you get there, Parrie. She's bound she's gonna run your life. Don't let her."

He left, but all night in bed Parrish had thought about their talk, and this morning coming up on the train—assuring himself first that he was doing the right and manly thing and then feeling, with sudden misgiving, that he was being a traitor. Then he would ask whether the treachery was to himself or to Ellen. Knowing she was coming here only to hold on to him, was it kindness or cowardice to humor her, to let her uproot her life, thinking she had a chance to succeed when in the end, he knew, he had to break away? If not now, then soon. A man had to be what he had to be.

Now, at Sala Post's, he looked at the pigeon on the garage, and with a sudden longing he wished he could make his mother understand how it was with him, explain that there was no place special he wanted to go, nothing special he wanted to do, that he just wanted to get going at it, that there was a churning up inside him to get moving—to turn where he wanted to, even if it was the wrong turn and led to nowhere. But it was a feeling in him so strong he couldn't put it into words. Words fenced it in, cut it down to the size of ordinary things. He couldn't explain it because it wouldn't make sense to anyone but himself.

The pigeon flew away and Parrish wondered whether Sala Post was through with lunch yet and talking to Ellen. He walked to the side door and went in. Carefully he shut the door, hearing the click loud in the quiet of the house, and walked down a dark hall to where a shaft of light from a single open door streaked across the thick carpeting. He looked into the room and saw that Ellen was still waiting.

"This place is like a funeral home," he whispered, sitting on a stiff chair. "Only gloomier."

All the furnishings—heavy draperies, straight-backed chairs, deep carpeting—were in a dark, dreary red. On a table he noticed a couple of tintypes in gold frames, and he looked at them closely, wondering whether any of these fine-featured, humorless faces was Sala Post or his daughter. He decided against it. The pictures were too old, of another era, like the house itself. "They must call this the Rose Room," he said, noticing again the monotony of color.

"The maid called it the sunroom."

"Must be a standing joke of the house."

"It's all windows behind those draperies."

Carefully, Parrish lifted back a heavy drapery. "Wonder what would happen if I pulled 'em all back. Probably wake up the dead. Looks like they'd have a lot of dead hanging around—tucked in corners here and there."

"Parrish, be quiet. Somebody will hear you."

Parrish laughed. He wondered whether Ellen had been dragged up here because Sala Post looked one day at his daughter, brought up in this ancient atmosphere, and figured something had better be done about her before it was too late. If that was it, he'd picked the right woman. Ellen MacLean could coax a dry turnip into a blooming rose. It occurred to him that she was the one who ought to be anxious, not he.

"You want me to come with you when you talk to this guy?"

"No," Ellen said quickly. "You stay here."

"Well, don't let him throw you. Remember, if he gives you a hard time, the trains are still running."

"Parrish—" she laughed—"don't be silly."

He threw himself down in the chair again.

"And don't fling yourself around like that. You'll break something."

She was right. He was being silly. Ellen didn't give up so readily. As Milky had said once, with tempered admiration, "Making Ellen little and delicate like that was just nature having a big laugh."

The maid's voice interrupted his reverie. "Mr. Post will see you now. In the library."

Then Parrish saw a tall, thin man pass in the dark hallway. He looked to be about fifty and walked very erect, his head high, looking straight ahead, not even glancing in their direction. Making no sound as he passed the door, Sala Post seemed so spare and quiet he could have been the shade of one of his ancestors instead of flesh and blood.

Parrish smiled at Ellen, but inside his stomach tightened. He had seen these cold, tense men before. "I'm coming with you."

"No, Parrish," Ellen said firmly. "You stay here."

Then he knew that Sala Post had not gone by without seeing them, because he was back. He was wearing riding breeches and knee-high boots. He had a sharp face with a thin nose over a straight line of a mouth—an unpleasant-appearing man, not so much from a look of meanness as because it seemed impossible that he could smile. He did not smile now as Ellen introduced Parrish.

"Your son!" Sala Post turned to Parrish. "It was quite unnecessary for you to come along. My man would have taken care of everything."

Parrish stared. Instantly he realized that he was a complete surprise to Sala Post. In taking this job Ellen had seen no need to disclose a son, whose presence would automatically disqualify her. She had counted, rather, on her ability to handle Sala Post once they were here.

"We can't drive you back to Hartford!" Sala Post bit off his words like a man ready to explode. "This is our busy season. We're planting. You can wait until four-thirty for a lift to the bus line. Or else walk." He turned away, dismissing Parrish.

"I'm not going back," Parrish blurted out.

"Parrish—" Ellen cautioned him softly.

"I didn't just bring my mother up here," Parrish said, his resolve clear for the first time. "I'm staying."

Sala Post's cold blue eyes went from Parrish to Ellen, demanding an explanation, his mouth tight, his thin nose high. Parrish gripped his hands into fists, telling himself that if Sala Post didn't lower that nose to Ellen, he'd do it for him.

"We didn't realize my quarters would be so close to the house," Ellen said. "Of course, we wouldn't think of having Parrish stay here now."

"I find all this distasteful and an imposition," Sala Post cut in. "You were told I have a daughter who is at a vulnerable age."

Suddenly Parrish smiled, thinking that Sala Post might be solving his problem for him. With all his figuring and worrying, this hadn't even occurred to him.

"Young man, if you find this amusing, I'll ask you to take your amusement out of my home."

The smile vanished. "I'd like nothing better!"

Sala Post turned to leave. "I'll speak to you, Mrs. MacLean, after your son has gone."

Parrish began to shout, "You don't think I'd dump her here and walk out! Not after seeing you!"

The man paused in the doorway, his shoulders seeming to sag a little. "In that case," he said, "we have nothing more to discuss."

Parrish started to shout a retort, but he felt Ellen's restraining hand on his arm and when he whirled about to protest he saw her catch Sala Post's eye, a little understanding smile playing on her lips.

"My son has just turned eighteen," she murmured, "and is taking very seriously this business of being a man."

Parrish looked from Ellen to Sala Post and saw him, almost imperceptibly, ease up. Openmouthed, Parrish stared at Ellen, a slow flush of embarrassment creeping up from his jaw to his hair. Ellen met his look squarely, silently commanding him not to say another word. He bit back his protest, his lips tight, and jammed his hands into his pockets.

"Perhaps in the library," Ellen suggested, "as you had planned. Without Parrish's help."

"I will be in the library," Sala Post said. "If you can bring your son under control, I'll be glad to discuss the situation with you, although only with the distinct understanding that he does not remain."

"If I leave—" Parrish forced himself to speak quietly—"she leaves, too."

Sala Post inclined his head and closed the door.

"You're becoming quite a man." Ellen smiled at Parrish indulgently. "Now all you have to do is learn to control your temper like one."

"Let's clear the hell out of here."

"Parrish, go take a walk. This is a fine job—"

"You can't work for that guy. He's not human!"

"Mr. Post is now a ruffled wet hen." Ellen was still calm. "And the sooner we dry him off and smooth his feathers, the better. Of course, with his daughter here and my apartment so close, you can't stay with me now. We'll have to find a place for you until I can bring him around."

"His daughter, for God's sake!" Parrish snorted. "He can wrap his daughter in cellophane and pack her in mothballs for all I care. Tell him for me I don't want any part of his daughter—or him, either."

"I'll do that, Parrish." Ellen laughed. "I'll tell him."

She went across the hall to the library. She would calm Sala Post down, Parrish knew. She would tell him he was absolutely right, that she wouldn't dream of having it otherwise. She would speak softly and a little flatteringly and with great dignity. But most of all, she would agree that he was right. Parrish had no doubt about it: Ellen would calm him down.

Scarcely noticing where he was going, Parrish wandered down the dark hall and found himself in a large living room, dark and quiet like the others, heavy draperies tightly closed against the sun, somber, luxurious furnishings in the shadows, ornately framed old portraits of people you knew were long since dead. In the fantastic quiet he heard a muted clink from another room and, guessing it was the maid washing the luncheon dishes, he followed the sound down another short hall.

As he entered the big old-fashioned kitchen Hazel Anne was putting a platter of chicken into the refrigerator. She looked over and smiled. "Mr. Post didn't take much lunch. Day Miss Alison is due home is always a bad one, till Mr. Post eases into having her here." She held out the platter. "You want some chicken?"

"You sure he won't slit your throat?"

"Mr. Post ain't so bad. You get used to him."

Parrish sank his teeth into a chicken leg. "I'm not staying long enough to find out, according to Mr. Post."

"He don't want you?" It sounded more a statement than a question.

"It's his daughter. He feels it's not fitting for me to live in the same house, practically, with his daughter."

Hazel Anne nodded knowingly. "How come they didn't straighten it out before?"

Parrish restrained a smile. How come, indeed? It was a long and complicated story. Aloud he said, "Agency told my mother she'd have her own cottage on the grounds."

"Well, she does. That's a real nice apartment up there over the garage."

"She figured if she had her own place, I could live with her." Parrish bit off the last of the chicken and fell silent, reluctant to continue the pretense even in his own mind.

"Mr. Post get mad?"

"He was mad."

"I guess she couldn't know how Mr. Post'd feel about it." She put a few dishes on the drain rack. "Your ma get mad, too?"

"My mother never gets mad," Parrish said. "What's the matter with the daughter?"

"Ah, Mr. Post has a hard time with Miss Alison."

"That her name—Alison?" Parrish said. "What's wrong with her?"

"Ain't nothin' wrong."

"Then what's wrong with him?" he asked, answering it in his own mind —plenty.

"Nothin'."

Loyalty or discretion was getting the upper hand here and Hazel Anne was clamming up.

"Then why don't they get along?"

"They get along—after a fashion. They're different, that's all. Folks can be all right and be different." Hazel Anne changed the subject. "What you gonna do about yourself?"

It was a good question and one which he was not particularly happy to consider. Until now he had not wanted to stay; now that he had seen Sala Post he wanted it even less. But going back to Boston and leaving Ellen behind was out of the question. "You know any place around here I could get a room?"

"Well, sure you can get a room! Tell you what you do." She walked over to the window. "See that there brown shed over by the tent cloth— the one says number three? Wait there and Teet'll come by with the water barrel. Tell him and he'll find you a place. And if one of the Jamaicans goes by instead, have him tell Teet you're lookin' for him."

"Is that what they are—Jamaicans?"

"They come up from Jamaica to work in tobacco. Couldn't you tell from their talk?"

"I could hardly understand them. It sounded like Calypso. I thought maybe Trinidad."

"Well, they're Jamaicans. Now go along or you'll miss Teet and he won't be back again for some time."

Near the shed it was hot and dusty. In spite of the rains he knew had been here, the path was sandy dry, showing distinct tractor and truck tire marks and heavy shoeprints, with clumps of tough, stringy weeds pushing through. Also the peculiar sweet smell he had noticed before in the station wagon and near the house was here, heavier and sharper still, and by now Parrish realized that this was the smell of tobacco. Not the smell of cigars or cigarettes, but the smell of growing tobacco.

In a few minutes Teet came along in an orange tractor with a water barrel on a two-wheeled trailer hitched behind. "What you doin' here, kid?"

Parrish smiled. "Teet, I hear you're a pretty good renting agent."

"What's on your mind?"

"You know any place I can rent a room?"

Grinning his lewd grin, Teet scratched his red beard and leaned closer to Parrish, as if he were about to tell a dirty joke. "Ole Sala don't want you hangin' around, eh, kid?"

It struck Parrish that Teet had known this was going to happen. "How'd you know?" he said sharply.

Teet ignored the question, turning his attention instead to the housing problem. "Tell you what I'll do, kid. I'll ask John Donati, the fellow you saw before. He's got a room and that'd be a good place for you. Lives right over there." Teet pointed to a small white cottage down the hill.

"He won't rent out a room."

"Kid, you never know till you ask."

"Then ask," Parrish said. "But start your mind working on another possibility, too, what do you say? I need a room for tonight."

"O.K., O.K.! Soon's I fill this water barrel I'll shoot back to number seven and find John. So we got time, kid. Don't get excited."

Ten minutes later Teet was back, riding his tractor, and Parrish could tell from the grin on his face that Donati had refused.

"Kid, how'd you know John'd say no?"

"I could tell. He's got that look on his face that says he wouldn't want to be bothered."

Teet nodded. "Says do you want a job?"

"Well, sure I want a job, but first I have to find me a goddam berth."

"Wish I could take you, kid." Parrish thought wildly what that would be like. "I can't even put you up overnight. It's my wife and me and three kids in the littlest damn trailer you ever seen."

"Well, if I find a place, I'll let you know."

"Stick around, kid," Teet said. "We ain't through. I'll find something."

He bumped off and Parrish walked over toward the tent cloth, thinking that, for lack of something better to do, he would take a look at what was inside. I'm getting a little sick of this whole deal, he said to himself. Slightly fed up. I'm getting a helluva lot fed up.

Reaching the cloth, he picked up the side, seeing that it was a coarse net sewed with rope onto heavy wires held up by the posts. He could see that under the cloth the glare of the sun was less, and, expecting it to be cooler, he stepped inside. He felt the change instantly. But it was not coolness. Under the cloth it was at least ten degrees hotter. The air was damp and tropical and artificial to the senses, like hothouse air, and heavy with the sharp, sweet smell of tobacco.

For as far as he could see, the posts stood at regular intervals of about thirty feet. On the ground were even rows of tiny emerald-green plants, about four inches high, on straight thin stems. The regularity, the even repetition of poles and plants, and the artificial air, heavy and sweet-scented, combined to give an atmosphere of unreality to the place. Parrish bent down and touched a small leaf and felt that it was thicker than a tree leaf, and when he took his hand away it felt gummy. He touched another and it was the same. Then he heard the tractor coming back, and, rubbing the sticky stuff on his hand against his pants, he stepped outside and walked back to the number-three shed.

"Kid—" Teet aimed a little tobacco juice at a scrawny patch of weeds— "you're all set. I got you a real sweet berth."

"Good."

"I want you to know, kid, I didn't stick you just anywhere. I looked out for your interests."

Parrish smiled and waited. By now he realized that Teet was immune to urging. Teet scratched at the red hair on his chest and got that wicked look in his eye. "Kid," he said, beaming, "I got you in with Lucy."

Parrish realized that some sort of enthusiastic response was expected. "Wonderful!" He clapped the sweat-matted back of Teet's shirt. "Great! Who's Lucy?"

"Lucy's Lucy Ballow. Kid, I wish I coulda done it for myself, but, like I said, I got a wife and three kids." Teet looked gloomy. "Twins on the way."

"That's a lot of kids."

"Probably have a dozen before I'm through."

Parrish gestured uncertainly. There wasn't much he could say to that. Then Teet brightened again, taking vicarious pleasure in what was in store for Parrish. "Lucy says you can go on down or wait for her at four-thirty."

"Where's her house?"

"About a mile down the road. Maybe a mile and a half."

"I'll wait."

"John says start tomorrow morning." Teet pulled the gas handle of the tractor. "I pick up Lucy in the truck, quarter to seven."

"Teet," Parrish said suddenly, "how'd you know Sala wouldn't want me living near his house?"

Teet's mouth went into that lewd grin. "You tole me, kid."

"You knew before that." Parrish pressed him. "How?"

"Kid, you're a good-lookin' fella. You got a kinda wild look about you, like you don't exactly sit home nights. An' that kinda shy grin women go for. That fools 'em, don't it, kid?"

"Get on with it."

Teet leaned closer and flipped his hand lightly against Parrish's chest. "Sala's got enough headaches already. He don't need you to mess around with his hot-pants kid."

"Oh, quit kidding!"

Then he saw that Teet meant it. The slow-starting grin spread over Parrish's face. A picture of Sala's daughter had already formed in his mind, but not that one. Thinking of Sala Post, he told himself it just couldn't be.

"Kid," Teet yelled over the noise of the tractor, "that Lucy is a real doll."

Watching him go the way he had come, Parrish struggled with the idea of Sala Post's daughter. Another pigeon lit on the barn and cried and flew away and Parrish stared over at the barn where the pigeon had been. It was very much an eyesore of a barn, an old faded monstrosity, of no specific shape because of many additions, half green, half dirty gray, with a carelessly patched roof and a doghouse of windows on top for light.

Everything about this place, he thought, is either very good or very bad. The house is magnificent, if very gloomy, and the barn is a mess. The Rolls Royce is polished to a high shine and the station wagon is thick with mud and dust. And Sala Post seems colder than is human. And his daughter . . . The thought stopped him. It didn't seem possible that Sala Post could have sired a warm-blooded daughter. It didn't seem possible that Sala Post could have sired anything.

Parrish kicked at an old rag of tent cloth and stirred up a little cloud of dust. At least he had found a room and that was something good. And then he thought, Don't kid yourself. This isn't going to work. This Sala Post is going to be a tough baby to get along with and nobody's going to enjoy it. And the sooner you persuade her to clear out, the better all around. The better for her, and the better for you.

You were weak in the head, he told himself, to have come. But he knew he couldn't have refused her. He was crazy to act as though there had been a choice, because the power was not in him, now, to deal Ellen the kind of blow a showdown would bring. Maybe it was a feeling of responsibility, maybe something more. Just love, maybe. Hell, it was nothing to be ashamed of. She was his mother. For all his big talk, he knew he would stay here as long as she did. Or until the Army got him. Or the Navy.

Then he saw Ellen coming out the side door, her lovely face calm, certainly not looking as though she had been through an ordeal.

"Mr. Post will find you a room, Parrish," she said as he came up.

"I found a room."

Relief came so quickly to her blue eyes that he knew she had been worried. "Wonderful, Parrish! Where?"

"Teet found it."

The smile died. "Parrish, are you sure it's all right? With nice people?"

Parrish laughed. "I haven't seen it yet. It's a mile and a half away and I didn't want to go down there until I got you settled. But it'll be fine." He picked up Ellen's luggage and walked with her to her apartment.

"It's temporary anyway, Parrish. Just until I can persuade Mr. Post to let you move in with me."

Parrish smiled to himself, wondering whether Ellen knew what he knew, and still could not believe, about Sala Post's daughter.

"Parrish," she said, "this is going to work out all right. Mr. Post isn't a happy man—"

"That's plain, even to the naked eye."

"But he's not a mean one, either. He's just not a happy man."

Ellen unlocked a door to the left of the garage. A wide stairway, walled off from the car area, led up to her apartment. Setting down the bags in her living room, Parrish felt a little better for the first time today. He had to admit it was pretty nice. There were four rooms—a living room, two bedrooms, a small kitchen and a bath—and there was nothing cheap or careless about the way they were furnished. Much brighter than the house. Parrish speculated that the stuff that had proved too cheerful for Sala Post's gloomy personality had been sent over here. When Ellen raised the window shades and let in the sunlight, Parrish had to admit it was a mighty fine-looking apartment. In his mind he felt a little easier about leaving her when, at four o'clock, he went back to the shed to wait for Teet and Lucy Ballow.

The truck stopped in front of Lucy's house and she got out of the cab and came around, carrying her lunch box and an old leather jacket, and waited while Parrish climbed out of the back.

"So long, fellows," Lucy said to the Jamaicans.

"Goodbye, Lucee," Gladstone said. "Tomorrow you do not pull so many plants, make me work so hard."

Lucy laughed. "Ah, Gladstone, you don't even know what work is. All you do is set on the setter and go for a ride. If you was pulling plants all day you'd never live through it."

"Oh, that ees not true," Gladstone said mournfully. "I am one very hard-working mon, Lucee."

Lucy laughed, and as the truck moved off Parrish picked up his suitcase and took a good look at her. She couldn't be more than fifteen—sixteen at the most—still showing baby lines in her clear, sun-tanned face. She had bright dark eyes that danced when she smiled, heavy lashes, and dark curly hair, unshaped and snarled, tied back at her neck with a blue kerchief. A blob of lipstick was carelessly applied to full round lips that looked, at the same time, very young and very knowing. Parrish let his eyes go down to the tilt of the well-developed breasts and to the round hips that filled out her jeans. Smiling, he understood why Teet felt he had done so well by him.

"You sure this will be O.K. with your folks, Lucy?" he said.

"Oh, sure. We got a lotta room." She motioned toward the house. "You can see for yourself."

It was a big house that, years ago, must have been rather fine. But now a few clapboards were ripped off and the windows sagged and the slanting sun hitting them showed thick dirt and a few panes broken. But most startling of all, Parrish saw, was the absence of front steps. A stone walk, overgrown with weeds, led up to a big front door, painted green. But there was no porch and no steps and the door was six feet off the ground.

"Frenchy's been fixing them steps for years," Lucy said, friendly and unembarrassed, her jaws working at a piece of chewing gum. "But we got the back door."

"Who's Frenchy?"

"He's Rosie's husband. Rosie's my sister. They live here, too, them and their daughter, Celeste. And Mamma and Gramma and me."

"And you've got room for me?"

"Oh, sure." Lucy motioned with a large, generous gesture that suited her personality. "We got lots of room."

They entered the house by the rear door, going into a kitchen where a wrinkled, unpleasant-looking old woman was investigating the contents of an old-fashioned icebox. She poked at her white hair under a faded kerchief. "I'm real pore today," she complained. "I'm so pore the preacher's comin'."

"Oh, Gramma, not again!" Lucy said.

"You'll go to hell, sure," Gramma said in a matter-of-fact voice. "Get out the lace tablecloth so we can give the preacher tea."

"O.K." Lucy chewed her gum. "Soon's I get Parrish settled."

"What's Parrish?" Gramma said.

"Mamma," Lucy called, going into the next room. "Rosie."

"Yer Mamma's gone down to Tower's for sweet cookies for the preacher. An' Frenchy's still plantin'—so the field is where Rosie is."

Lucy walked back into the kitchen. "Come on upstairs, Parrish. I'll show you your room."

He followed her up a narrow flight of stairs off the kitchen, watching her bottom wiggle with each step, and down a hall past several bedrooms with unmade beds, past a bathroom with brown-stained plumbing and dirty towels, and up another flight of stairs to the attic, where they entered a small square room with a low ceiling. The room was dark now, with the yellowed shades down.

"O.K.?" Lucy said.

Parrish set down his suitcase. "Fine."

"I'll bring you some sheets and stuff and put a clean towel in the john. Anything else you want?"

Parrish found himself looking more at Lucy than at his new room—at the dark eyes, the tangled mass of black curls, the wholesome baby face with its look of having been born wise, especially in the ways of men. "This is fine," he said again.

She smiled at him, almost as though she knew what he was thinking. "Come down when you want." She worked her gum, starting out of the room. "Come take tea with the preacher if you want."

She left and Parrish was alone. All the way over in the truck his arm had been itching and now he pulled off his jacket to rub it. After a moment he went over and raised the shades, upsetting a lining of dust, and opened the window and looked around. It was a dreary room with a cracked, yellowed ceiling and faded yellow and red flowered wallpaper. In one corner stood a big iron double bed, the mattress stained and lumpy. Across the room was a brown dresser with a round wavy mirror. On the dresser was a chipped china pitcher, next to the dresser a brown kitchen chair.

He opened his suitcase and put his shirts into a drawer and found a bar in the closet he could use for ties. He was practically moved in. He sat down on the lumpy mattress, absent-mindedly rubbing his itchy arm. A kind of sadness filled him, a little shrinking in from all this that was new and strange, a little longing for what was familiar and loved. The arguments leading up to this seemed long past, Boston and Milky a million miles away—and this strange room, for a while, anyway, was to be his.

Then all at once it struck him, through the strangeness and the loneliness, that this was what he had been asking for. This was his room—to pay rent for and live in, alone, to come home to when he pleased and go out of when he wanted to. And nobody ever asked a boarder where he had been or why. A little surprised, he lay back on the mattress, examining this new idea. It was as if for weeks he had been flinging his weight in vain against a bolted door, and all of a sudden it had squeaked open. Nobody ever told a boarder what was good for him or what he should do.

"All my life I been in tobacco," Frenchy said. "An' you wanna know somethin', I couldn't tell you why I bother."

A short, heavy-muscled man, he was squatting down on the floor, trying to expand a table, while Rosie rested her great bulk on the other end. From where he sat Parrish could see Frenchy's head getting pink from exertion under the thinning yellow hair.

Frenchy tugged at the table. "Rosie, I t'ink dis ain't movin' cause you weigh so goddam much."

"Aah," Rosie said good-naturedly.

Parrish scratched at his arm. The itch had grown worse and spread to his chest and he was getting worried. "Can I help you, Frenchy?"

"Nah." Frenchy struggled to his feet. "Ain't nothin' wrong except after plantin' all day I ain't got the strength to move the table and Rosie, too." He slapped Rosie's bottom and her flowered dress rippled over her flesh. "Let's go, Mamma."

"Don't you have any cloth, Frenchy?" Parrish said. "That stuff I saw over at Sala Post's?"

"A little fella like me can't grow Shade!" Frenchy stared. "Shade! Just gettin' that cloth up costs you maybe five hundred bucks an acre—you ain't even got a plant in the ground! I grow Broadleaf—right out in the sun like corn or anything else."

"So are we opening the table?" Rosie said.

"Broadleaf's bad enough." Frenchy heaved at the table. "Every fall when I got the crop in the shed, I says to myself, never again. Next year I'll lease to Raike. But comes spring, where am I? Back in tobacco. I'm nuts. Good thing I got a few chickens."

"Raike?" Parrish remembered. "We saw him today. Big black Cadillac."

"Raike's the big wheel around here. An' I got good tobacco land, too. Raike'd lease it in a minute." Then, as if offering an excuse for his foolishness, Frenchy said, "Ah, tobacco gets in your blood."

Lucy came into the room, wearing a white lace blouse and black peasant skirt. She was carrying a coarse tablecloth, and Rosie's daughter, Celeste, who was nine, followed with a tray of pink and green cups and saucers.

"You figure you got tobacco land, you might as well use it," Lucy said.

Itching badly now, Parrish tried to keep his mind on the conversation. "Isn't any land tobacco land?"

"Are you kiddin'?" Frenchy said. "They's a little stretch, starting about here and going up to Greenfield, Mass., both sides of the river, and that grows good tobacco and other land don't."

"Why not?"

Frenchy shrugged. "Nobody knows. Just something about the land and the air right here along the river makes good tobacco. Only place around."

"'Course, they got it down South," Rosie said. "Virginia and down there. They grow for cigarettes. This here's cigar tobacco."

"Tobacco, tobacco. It's a curse one way and it's a curse the other." Mamma, who was fat like Rosie and wearing a twin to Rosie's flowered dress, came in to inspect the room. She shook her head as her eyes settled on a broken window. "Honest to God, Frenchy, I wisht you'd fixed that window before the preacher come back."

Frenchy shrugged. "It's summer."

"All the same. He noticed it last time."

"So he'll notice it again. He'll live."

Gramma peered into the room from the kitchen. "Frenchy, you ain't got the proper respect for the preacher. You'll go to hell, sure."

"Just gettin' in trainin' for the preacher, eh, Gramma?"

"You be more respectful, Frenchy," Mamma warned. "We got enough troubles without askin' for more."

"Who ain't bein' respectful?" Frenchy demanded. "I'm here, ain't I?"

"Yer a heathen!" Gramma yelled in from the kitchen.

"Listen," Frenchy yelled back. "You can it or I'll go upstairs and to hell with the preacher."

"Frenchy," Rosie cautioned, "you better be careful. You'll jinx yourself talkin' like that about a preacher of the Lord."

"You'll get hail and bugs fer sure," Gramma cackled. "Bugs'll eat you out by mornin', talkin' that way. You'll get a plague, sure's God."

"Ah," Frenchy said, making his apologies to the Lord. "I didn't mean nothin'. It's a good sign the preacher comin' on plantin' day."

"Sure." Rosie backed him up. "Frenchy's glad the preacher's comin'."

"This Montague—" Frenchy winked at Parrish—"come here to work because tobacco's a sin and growin' it's a double sin. Addin' to the general evil of mankind."

"Frenchy, you'll burn in hell, sure," Gramma said.

By the time preacher Ezra Montague arrived, Parrish was really worried. His arm and chest were itching so intensely that it took great effort to refrain from digging his nails into his flesh. He was about to escape to his room when he heard a cultured voice in the kitchen.

"Repent!" the preacher announced himself. "Repent your sin before it is too late!" He came into the room, a slight, bespectacled young man with a soft mouth that he pursed primly as his eyes inspected each member of the family. "So you planted today?"

Frenchy nodded and introduced Parrish, and the preacher turned to him with a fiery eye.

"Have you come to work in tobacco?"

"I'm going to work for Sala Post," Parrish said.

"Then pray for your soul! The sins of man are great. To give the sweat of your brow to grow tobacco which contributes to the sins of the flesh increases your sin ten times."

"You'd better pray, boy," Gramma cackled. "You'll go to hell, sure."

"You're working for an evil man," Ezra Montague said. "An arrogant sinner who has turned his back on God. Obstinacy in sin is a double sin."

"Ha-a-a!" Gramma rocked wildly in her rocking chair.

"When he is scorching in flames, God will laugh!" The preacher slobbered a little on his lower lip. "His saints will sing and rejoice that His power and wrath are made known." He slammed the table in front of Parrish.

For the first time that day, Parrish found himself on the side of Sala Post. "Maybe he'll repent," he said.

Feeling his arm itching furiously now, Parrish turned up his sleeve and saw faint red blotches rising all over his forearm, swelling up even while he watched, and growing darker. Hastily he rolled down his cuff.

"I came to this valley because these people are sinners," Montague preached on. "They were miserable creatures and they suffered and knew not why they suffered. Now they know and they suffer gladly."

This guy is crazy, Parrish thought. He's crazy and I'm sick and I'd better get out of here. I'd better go upstairs and figure out what in hell I've got.

"They know that they suffer their miserable poverty and pain because of their sins and the sin of Adam and the individual sins of each man and woman and child."

"Amen!" Mamma was getting into the spirit, too.

The itch burned furiously, eating into Parrish's arms and chest until he couldn't sit still. "Excuse me," he gasped, rushing out into the kitchen, tearing off his shirt as he ran up the two flights of stairs to the attic. He hooked the door closed and threw himself on the bed. His arms were great swollen blotches now and his chest was covered and he could feel it coming out on his face.

He heard Lucy's voice at the door. "Parrish, what's the matter?"

"Go away, Lucy. I'm sick."

She tried the door. "Maybe I can help you. Open the door."

It was all over his face now. He could feel it everywhere. He tore at his chest.

Then he heard another voice—the preacher's. "What's the matter with him? Can't he bear the thought of his own guilt? You're a miserable sinner, boy."

"Please, Mr. Montague," Lucy said. "He says he's sick."

"You're damned, boy. You'll go to hell. Pillars of flame and thick smoke will scorch you and lick at you like fiery snakes. You're doomed!"

"Get out of here," Parrish yelled. "Get back where they need you!"

"Eternal damnation!" the preacher screamed.

Parrish didn't answer. He covered his swollen eyes with his blotchy arm and tried not to scratch. He heard the preacher's footsteps going down the stairs. Somehow, he thought, he ought to get to a doctor.

"Parrish, open the door." Lucy was still there. "Come on, honey."

He stood up and lifted the hook, and then backed away to the window. Lucy crossed over to him and touched his chest and arm, her hand feeling cool on the hot rash.

"I'm sorry, Lucy," he said. "Coming to your house and getting sick."

"Parrish—" she raised her dark eyes—"you touch any tobacco plants today over at Sala Post's?"

He nodded, remembering the sticky feeling they had left on his hand.

"You got tobacco poisoning, Parrish."

"What in hell is tobacco poisoning?"

"I'll go down to Tower's and get you some calamine," Lucy said. "It'll help some. It'll kill the itch."

"What's tobacco poisoning?" he asked again.

"Kinda like poison ivy," Lucy said. "Try not to scratch too much until I get back, Parrish. It's best to just let it be if you can stand it."

After she had gone Parrish hooked the door again and alternately paced the floor and flung himself down on the lumpy mattress, the half hour until she returned seeming an eternity. At last he heard her step and rushed to open the door.

She came in carrying the bottle of calamine and a roll of cotton and some clean sheets to make up his bed. She put down the sheets and poured calamine onto a wad of cotton and reached up, patting it lightly on his face and neck.

"It's sore, ain't it?" Lucy's voice was soft and sympathetic and the lotion felt cool on his flaming skin. "But it'll only last a day. You'll be better in the morning and by tomorrow night it'll be all gone. One day is all it lasts." She smiled up at him, her dark eyes shiny. "Bet you was real scared, wasn't you?"

Sick as he was, looking down at her smooth young throat and the rise of her breasts under the lace blouse, Parrish felt his stomach tighten. He could swear all he had to do was move his arms toward her and she would be in them, calamine and rash and all. He held back and stood rigidly still. She doused his back, giving a final caressing little pat to his shoulder blades, and turned to making up his bed. Parrish watched her smooth the sheets, looking so much like a little girl, but moving with the quick, sure confidence of a woman. Feeling his eyes on her, she flashed him that friendly unself-conscious smile, and it struck him that Lucy was the most completely natural person he had ever seen.

She fluffed the pillow. "You're all set now. Keep yourself doused with calamine. You can call me to do your back if you want."

She paused at the door. "Once is all you get tobacco poison," she encouraged him again. "After this you can work and you won't have to worry."

It was dark now and he lay on the bed, caked with calamine, hearing cars shooting past on the highway, watching blades of light from their headlights flick across the wall and vanish.

He thought of his mother, wondering whether she was having a hard time with Sala Post. Probably she would be alone, now, in her apartment over the Rolls Royce. It was pretty nice, that apartment. She would go crazy if she knew he was in a place like this. He smiled as he thought of how she would look if she could see Rosie and Frenchy and Mamma and Gramma. Next to them, Milky would seem like a prince.

Then Milky was in his mind again. Milky, standing in the bedroom, telling him he was being owned, that it was more than the beer incident. Licking his parched lips, Parrish wished he had a beer right now. His mother never knew about the other times Milky had given him beer, starting when he was ten years old.

He thought of them now with sudden yearning. Milky, sitting in his brown leather chair in the living room after work, Aunt Mae bringing him the beer. Always Milky would hold out the bottle to Parrish first and say, "Just a sip, Parrie, no more'n one. It'll stunt your brain."

Parrish remembered how he would laugh and make sure the sip was a big one, running his tongue over the bitter taste, wondering if his brain would really be stunted—not that it worried him, because he didn't intend to do brain work. He intended to be a construction man, like Milky.

It was all a long time ago, he thought, feeling the itch flaming up again. A long, long time ago. He turned over on the bed toward the calamine, and his burning eyes, already swollen, stung with tears.

He itched, and, more than the itching, he felt terrible in an oppressed way he had never known before. Sleep was impossible. He got out of bed and walked over to the wall, groping for the light switch. The wavy mirror on the dresser lit up in front of him and he bent down to look at himself—seeing the swollen eyes, the blotchy, puffed face, caked with calamine all the way into his hair.

"You poor bastard." He shook his head at himself in disgust, considering his misery, while the oppressed feeling, so much more than an itch, took on new meaning. "You poor, miserable bastard, you know what's wrong with you!" He could hardly believe it. "You're homesick!"

3

AN EARLY-MORNING mist moved over the Valley, drifting and swirling close to the ground. In the truck the Jamaicans sat huddled against the cool dampness, collars turned up to meet their hats, but to Parrish the slight chill felt good against his skin, no longer itchy this morning but still hot and raw. Gladstone peered up toward the dim ring of the sun.

"I theenk this weel be a fine day," he said. "I weel ask John to send me to Hartford. Teet say somebody must go for Mr. Post's daughter's luggage."

"I theenk, mon, he weel not send you," Cartwright, another Jamaican, said.

"I weel ask him."

"What's she like, Gladstone? The daughter," Parrish said.

"Since I have been here, I have not seen her, mon."

"Nor have I," Cartwright said.

At Sala Post's the mist shrouded the tent cloth and made gray outlines of the house and garage, but the truck had barely pulled to a stop when John Donati, the foreman, emerged out of the whiteness. "Gladstone, Cartwright, Willis—get over to the seedbeds and carry off them tops. Mac-Lean?"

The foreman moved closer. He was a stocky man of medium height with the ruddy, weather-beaten face and clear eyes of a man who worked outdoors. "MacLean, I'm gonna put you straight right now. In tobacco you got just so much time to grow your crop and no more. You get behind, you never make it up. It costs you money. We're behind right now on account of too much rain, so if you stick around, plan to work."

"John," Gladstone said plaintively from the truck, "you are a very tough mon. I do not know what make you so tough."

"Gladstone, take MacLean with you to carry off tops."

"What you theenk, John?" Gladstone hopped gracefully out of the truck. "You theenk I can have me a ride to Hartford, pick up Miss Post's luggage?"

"Get them tops off, Gladstone, and water down them beds or you'll be goin' a lot farther than Hartford." John turned back to Parrish. "After them tops are off get over and pull plants with the women. When Gladstone's done waterin', give him a hand puttin' 'em back on. Then go back to pullin'. And don't stop workin' in between."

"John," Gladstone said, "eef I ever find out what make you so tough, I weel let you know, mon."

"You do that," John said. "Let's go now. Pick up your shoes."

Uncertainly, Parrish followed Gladstone toward the woods that bordered Sala Post's property. The seedbeds turned out to be long wooden frames, built on the ground, with slanting glass tops, beady now with dew and glistening in the shots of sunlight reaching through the thinning mist. Nearby, in the woods, birds talked and Parrish caught the smells of damp earth and leaves mixed with the smell of tobacco. At this early hour the farm had a lonely look, wet and desolate and a little shabby. He bent down with Gladstone to lift off a top and saw, inside, a thick emerald carpet of tiny plants, so close together you couldn't see the earth that held them, and seeming too green and lush in the morning mist to be real.

"You take these off and put them back every day, Gladstone?" he said.

"Many times a day, mon," Gladstone said. "Whenever these little plants require water to keep them fresh. Also when these girls pull them out, the earth must be very much wet. Otherwise, they weel break the little stems. I can tell you, I weesh somebody would take care of me one half so finely as I care for thees tobacco. I am very experienced mon."

Parrish laughed. "How long you been in tobacco that you're so experienced?"

"I am here three years, mon."

They carried the glass top off to one side and came back for another. "What do you do, Gladstone—rent a room around here?"

"We all live together, mon, the workers from all the farms—Raike, Holden, everyone. We have barracks at Bradley Field, which ees an old airplane field. Except some farms are far away, have their own barracks on the farm."

They moved quickly back and forth, piling up the tops, and when the last one was off Parrish hurried down to the first bed, where the women were crouched over, pulling plants—seeing them start to look him over as he came near. They were an odd assortment, all ages, ranging from Lucy, the youngest, to Mary, a wrinkled old woman who had ridden with them in the truck that morning and who looked about eighty. Most of them had bad teeth, and they all wore blue jeans except Mary, who wore a house dress down to her ankles, with a mustard-colored kerchief tied under her chin.

"This here's Addie, Parrish." Lucy motioned to a fat girl with very large breasts, exaggerated in a tight-fitting shirt. Addie giggled. "And that there's Eileen." Lucy pointed to a skinny young woman with a bad complexion.

Addie giggled again, while Lucy introduced the rest. "I hear your ma's the new nursemaid," she said. "You gonna work in tobacco long as she gets along with Alison?"

"Guess so," Parrish said.

"Wonder how long that'll be."

"You big fella." Mary's spotted old hands moved swiftly in a patch of plants. "You smart, you'll look for somethin' else. Ain't nothin' in tobacco for big fella like you."

"Get started, Parrish. Pull easy." Bending over the bed, Lucy grasped a plant low on its stem, drew it carefully out of the dirt. "Just take the big plants. We come around again in a couple of days, after the little ones got a chance to grow more."

"Gotta get big ones out of way, give little ones chance," Mary muttered. "Just like people. Get big fellas out of way, give little ones a chance."

"What's the matter with you today, Mary?" Lucy laughed.

"Nothin's the matter," Mary said. "I'm an old woman and I know it's the truth."

Wincing a little as he thought of the rash, Parrish pulled out a few plants.

"I guess we won't see Sala today." Addie's tone smacked of gossip. "With Alison home."

"Does Mr. Post come out here?"

"Sala comes every day," Lucy said. "Usually before his breakfast."

Parrish couldn't have said why this surprised him except that he couldn't imagine Sala Post in the sunlight, walking in dirt paths that raised dust to the ankles.

Mary jerked her head. "He's a good tobacco man, Sala. Lives on his land. Ain't many Shade growers do that."

"I thought all farmers lived on their land."

"These ain't farmers," Lucy said. "They're big companies. American-Sumatra, Consolidated, Imperial. Nobody even knows who they are. The other big growers, Raike, Holden, live in Hartford. They got foremen. They don't know anything about tobacco. Not growin' it, anyways. Ain't around it enough."

"Tobacco's like a kid," Mary said. "You gotta know your own kid."

"Old Sala knows," Addie said. "He's got the touch. Even more'n John."

"What's that?" Parrish said. "The touch?"

"Ah, knowin' your crop," Lucy said. "When to irrigate, when to pick, take down. You can't know too much about tobacco. And even then you get it in the neck, often as not."

"In this business, anything can happen." Addie lit a cigarette and looked at the match. "Like once I saw a man drop a match near tent cloth. Burned up the side and over three acres before the firemen got it under control. Any little thing can grow into big trouble."

Parrish dumped a fistful of plants into a box on the ground. "Why do they start these plants here in beds?" he said. "Why don't they just plant right out in the field?"

"They'd die, Parrish. They're very delicate."

"Tobacco like a baby," Mary said again. "Grow inside until big enough." She sat up, looking withered and resigned, as if remembering past troubles. "Then you get it out and it's the boss. Gotta keep it warm. Keep it sheltered. Water, hoe, sucker. All the time, care. It never leave you alone and you can't leave it alone. All the time work for it. Worry about it. Too hot, too wet, too dry. Hail, bugs, disease. And it grow fast and in the end give you nothing but trouble."

Parrish looked over at Mary. This seemed very much like Frenchy's attitude toward tobacco and he wondered whether it was always that way and why. Then Gladstone called him to help carry back the tops and a few minutes later John returned.

"All right, a little speed here," he greeted them. "I need a couple of you out in the field."

While he talked, John worked his way along the beds, leaving empty boxes near the women and taking the filled ones over to the truck. In spite of his abrupt, driving manner there was warmth and good humor in John's sunburned face. It was, Parrish thought, the face of a man you could like, although he suspected John Donati wouldn't care whether you liked him or not. He would be a tough man to know or make friends with.

"MacLean, you think you could find the railroad station?"

"I could find it."

"You go for the luggage. Not now. Later. Stop at the house and get the checks. Pick up your shoes, Gladstone."

Gladstone quickened his pace a little and Parrish looked at him apologetically for getting the assignment to go to Hartford. "Eet does not matter, mon." Gladstone smiled. "I know he does not send me to Hartford. I am too highly skilled mon. I only ask to make conversation. But I am theenking eet ees better sometimes not to know too much."

Carrying back the tops, Parrish could hear the women still chatting steadily and he wondered where they found so much to talk about. Half an hour later, when he came back to pulling, they were still at it.

"I always said—" Addie flicked some dirt off her fat red face—"with all Sala knows, you wouldn't think he'd a got it in the neck so hard. Just shows—you can't beat tobacco when it turns on you."

"Ah," Mary said. "It was his wife brought it on."

"Mary, you ever see her—Sala's wife?"

"Very beautiful. Half-Spanish girl. Very rich. Very beautiful."

"You wouldn't think that'd be the type Sala'd pick."

"She only stayed a year," Mary said. "Maybe two. This life wasn't for her. They said she had lotta men."

"Boy," Eileen said. "If I went out even once, my husband'd slug me so I couldn't get up for a week. I even go to the movies with a girl friend, I gotta give him a big accountin'. I got a whole big deal on my hands."

That seemed to give them private thoughts and they fell silent for a moment. Then Addie started again. "Honest to God—" she scratched at one huge breast—"would you think Sala'd pick that type, hey? And be sucker enough to let Raike get all his land?"

Mary shrugged. "Nobody know for sure what happen. Sala was the big grower and Raike started comin' around. Then she left and all of a sudden, it's all Raike land—all but this."

"How about the Holdens, Mary? They always had land?"

"The Holdens always had land. Them and the Carrs was cousins. Ain't no Carrs left, only that skinny one married to Edgar Raike."

Now Parrish realized this gossip was for his benefit and, covertly looking them over, he saw that it gave them a sense of importance, making them feel somehow bigger for knowing and passing it on. Then he saw Addie give him a broad wink and he grinned because she was so horrible.

A sleepy mood settled over the little area. Across the bed, Gladstone and Cartwright began to sing in remarkably mellow voices, an American song in Calypso accents. They sang lazily, not together, but responsively, one echoing the other.

"May-bee, you'll theenk of me—"

                                      "May-bee, you'll theenk of me—"

"When you are all a-lone—"

                                        "When you are all a-lone—"

"I don't know what he saw in that Carr girl," Addie said. "Built like a stick!"

"Not like you, eh, Addie?"

"Some men like 'em skinny, I guess," Addie said tolerantly.

"For lookin' the skinny ones is all right," Mary said. "For bed, the fat ones better."

Addie shrieked. "You know that too 'cause you're an old woman, Mary?"

Mary shrugged. "Also it matters the man. Man who is man take a fat woman to bed. Man of small guts take skinny woman to bed. Weak, droopy, no pep. Is good enough for man with no guts. What would man with no guts do in bed with woman like you?" Mary looked up at Addie.

"Just what all the others do, wouldn't he, Addie?" Eileen screamed. "Ain't you funny!"

"Couldn't handle her," Mary said. "Damn near kill him. Ain't that right, boy?" She turned to Parrish.

Lucy looked up and smiled at him, friendly and unembarrassed. Parrish laughed without answering.

"What's the matter, boy, you no like talk about sex? What's the matter, eh? You big fella."

Parrish laughed out loud. It wasn't exactly the subject he would have chosen, but as long as they had picked it, it was all right with him. "Long as they're women," he said. "I love 'em all."

That seemed healthier to Mary than modesty and she was satisfied.

It was getting hot. Unnoticed, the mist had burned off and the sun beat down on the dusty paths and the tent cloth. Parrish could feel perspiration starting to irritate his raw skin and he took off his shirt and tossed it aside, and then, the way the women looked at him, he was a little sorry he had. Then he grinned. This was certainly different from construction. In many ways.

A few minutes later John was back and, from the direction of the house, Teet came along in the truck. "Hey, John," he yelled. "I got news. You're gettin' company today. Lewis Post. Comin' for plants."

"Oh, Christ!" John's face went red.

"Ought to be a big day." Teet's evil grin widened. "He's bringin' his boys. Sala says they should pull their own. Three acres."

John stopped. "We didn't figure him when we planted the beds. We already gave a bed to Oermeyer with his blue mold. We get an emergency, we'll be short ourselves."

"I tole Sala. Sala says Lewis wants to work this year, give him enough for three acres."

"Goddam it!" John exploded. "Sala hangs onto that old bum like—" He broke off.

Addie's beady eyes gleamed. "Ain't it sump'n, the way Sala puts up with all that crap from Lewis Post?"

"Ah," Mary grunted, looking out across the fields, "you gotta understand how it is with Sala. That old drunk is a Post, too. The Posts been here a long time."

"Girls," John yelled. "Lewis Post shows up, he don't get none of your plants. He pulls his own. Y'hear?"

"O.K., John," Lucy said.

"Lazy, drunken bastard," John said. "MacLean, you get up there to the house now."

Parrish put on his shirt and started across the beds. "Ah, Mary," he heard Addie shriek, "don't talk so much about sex. You're too old."

"Only sex I know, now," Mary said, "last year I plant corn, I plant five rows female corn, one row male corn."

Addie laughed very hard at that and over her laughter John barked, "Pick up your shoes, men. Let's go."

Sala Post lingered in his library and lit a thin cigar. It was cool in the house but outside the morning mist had burned off, and, seeing the sun glitter hard on the cloth, he knew the day was warm. Upstairs Alison was still asleep and he told himself he ought to send for Mrs. MacLean and talk to her before Alison came down, but he sat still and broke the ash off the end of the cigar.

Through the open window he could smell the warm earth and the wild blackberry flowering at the edge of the woods and most of all the sharp sweet smell of tobacco, not as strong in the young plants as it would be later drying in the sheds, but strong enough to cut into his senses and remind him that the crop was going into the ground and that soon the leaves would be pushing up to the cloth, spreading to meet, plant to plant and row to row. The cloth never seemed so bright as in these days of early June, as much for the contrast it made to the bare fields he looked out on most of the winter as because it was new and clean, not yet dusty or rain-soaked or flecked with tree pods that would cling to it later. He ought to send for Mrs. MacLean.

Others in tobacco, he knew, said the best time was the fall when the cloth came down and the crop was safe in the sheds, and not much could happen any more. No worries, then, about mold or worms or rot. No anxious eye cast at the sky in a prayer for rain or a prayer for dry. No more sudden thunderstorms or hail to rip your cloth or tear your plants. When the crop was curing in the sheds was the best time for other tobacco men because they lived in the city, away from their land, and to them tobacco was only a business.

Sala walked over to the window. Off to the right, in the distance, he could see the Black Angus on the rise of the little hill, the part of his land that he leased out, where the soil was clay and not suitable for growing tobacco, and beyond that, over the hill, he knew the land dropped off again into the Ridge lot, where the soil was lighter and there was always trouble in a drought—except that he didn't have the trouble any more because it was no longer his land but belonged to Judd Raike, who worked it every year and got a pretty good crop, but never the quality Sala had coaxed out of that field.

It was a long time since he had worked the Ridge lot and the nearly three thousand acres beyond. Thirteen years. But it seemed like yesterday and when the cloth went up and the earth smelled alive and young pheasant appeared in the woods, his imagination couldn't stop at the ridge but soared beyond, out over the entire valley. But Sala was a disciplined man and he didn't let himself think about it often.

He had held on to the home lots, the best hundred acres in the Valley, and he had turned his back on a world he could not understand. He lived in this quiet house, where Posts had always lived, and he prided himself that Post land still turned out the best—if no longer the largest—tobacco crop in the Valley.

Sala pulled his thoughts back to Alison, feeling again the bewilderment and the guilty resentment her coming home always churned up in him. Alone, his days were uneventful, but undisturbed. When Alison came home she wrenched him out of his careful peace and plunged him into a sea of problems.

Upstairs an old board creaked, telling him she was awake. He hoped things would work out with Mrs. MacLean. He had intended to have somebody here long before Alison came home from school, but finding the right person had not been easy. Mrs. MacLean was the fourth who had come from out of town, to say nothing of the countless numbers from Hartford whom he had interviewed. Two from New York had not pleased Sala and one other from Boston would never have understood Alison. Picking up the telephone he called over to the apartment, hoping he was right and not just telling himself, because he was weary of the whole thing, that Mrs. MacLean seemed satisfactory.

Alison's green eyes darted toward Mrs. MacLean and back to Sala, questioning. Small and erect, she sat near the window in the breakfast room, wearing a white peignoir with a green velvet ribbon that matched her eyes, the sun playing red lights on her heavy black hair. Watching her, Sala felt again the rush of bewilderment and inadequacy. As always, when he came upon her in some part of the quiet house, after she had been away, he felt a disturbing shock at her vitality. Alison could sit perfectly still, as she was sitting now, sipping her coffee, and to Sala she was restless, tempestuous, sparking energy.

He saw it in the green eyes that glowed or danced or stormed, depending on her mood that could change without warning, and in the way her thick black hair sprang in curls from her temples before it fell to her graceful shoulders. Even when he looked with pride at the way she held her back straight and her head high and he thought she was every inch a Post, Sala could feel the unexpectedness of her, the dammed-up energy that could overwhelm him. He felt it now, as she watched him, wary, carefully exploring this unexpected situation.

"You forgot to tell me," she said, softly, "about Mrs. MacLean."

"Mrs. MacLean arrived only yesterday."

"From where?"

Sala couldn't have said how he knew she was about to explode. Miserably, the fear of her and the fear for her clutched at him and he told himself it was just that she looked so much like Margarita—that fire, that bewildering maturity at seventeen. He told himself he had raised her to be a Post. But sitting across from him at the same table, with the same heavy black hair and the green eyes, first darting and restless, then steady and accusing when things were not going her way, it could have been Margarita all over again.

Margarita, whom he had married when she was seventeen and lost by the time she was twenty, bored with him and bored with the farm. Sala didn't think of her any more except from the shock of seeing Alison. But he knew now, years later, what he had refused to see then, that in her own way Margarita had tried. She had begged him to move to New York or at least to Hartford, but he had insisted that a man had to live on his land. So she had left him with his land, a little while at a time and then altogether. And after he had lost her, he had hated the land. Then he turned to it for comfort. For four years he drove himself, working every acre he owned. For four years, when he should have cut back, he produced to the hilt, for a steadily declining market, and he lost two million dollars. When he came out of it with only a hundred acres, he had learned to live without her and had found peace again in the quiet house and in the land.

Alison was waiting, sitting straight and composed, only the eyes hinting of anger and suspicion.

"Mrs. MacLean came from Boston, Alison," he said. "To help you come out."

"All the way from Boston!" she said.

"There was no one suitable in Hartford."

But she was putting things together quickly, understanding that more was involved than a social function. Eyes too steady now, she sipped her coffee and picked up the silver bell and rang it.

"That bell hasn't been polished in a month," she murmured, and when Hazel Anne came she said, "May we have more coffee, Hazel Anne? And hotter, please."

She was seething, Sala knew, picking on trifles while her mind whirled about the greater problem.

Hazel Anne picked up the coffee pot. "Lewis Post's been out there past ten minutes," she said. "Says how come he has to pull his own plants."

"Oh, no!" Alison seized on it. "Don't tell me you're still bothering with that old bum!"

"I'll be out directly," Sala said. "Tell him I want him to wait right here at the house."

"He's got his boys," Hazel Anne said.

"Is he sober?" Alison's eyes were wide and questioning, as though she really cared. "And the boys—are they sober?"

"I didn't notice they weren't." Hazel Anne left the room.

"Wouldn't that be remarkable!" Alison said. "If they were all sober at the same time! That would be truly remarkable."

"We won't discuss Lewis Post, Alison."

"This is the family bum, Mrs. MacLean. Father's sixth cousin, four times removed. A real derelict."

"Alison—"

"Just shows what can happen to these old families." She smiled brightly. "That's all that's left of us, Father and me and our cousin, Lewis, who lives in a shack up in the hills and gets drunk so he can forget he's a Post."

"Alison, I will not have this!"

"And I will not have a watchdog!"

Her eyes, meeting his, were dark with anger. "What are you expected to do, Mrs. MacLean? Manage me or just spy and report to headquarters?"

"Possibly," Ellen said, "help you?"

"Alison, you're assuming things!" Rage mingled with embarrassment as Sala strained for control.

"Assuming! I'm not assuming a thing. I know!" Like a highbred cat, she was still elegant but all anger, preparing to attack. "You can't hold me down yourself any more so you've brought in help!"

Mortified, Sala stole a glance at Mrs. MacLean. He was relieved to see that she seemed neither shocked nor discouraged but was only cautiously studying Alison, who was too angry to notice.

"You think with help you can chain me down here—away from everyone and everything, with all the creaky old furniture and musty portraits. Well, you can't!"

"This is your family home—"

"It's a prison. Not even a decent way to get into town. A choice between an old relic so people know you're queer right off the bat—or a broken-down station wagon you're not even sure will last the trip. Family home!" Her eyes blazed. "Why don't you think of what I want just once instead of your precious family monument?"

Sala gestured helplessly. How could she feel that about the house where Posts had lived for more than two centuries? "It's just that you're so young." And then he murmured, "There are so few places like this left."

"You're happy here. You don't want to live. So you think nobody else has to live, either." A toss of her head was more defiant than if she had clawed at him. "This place is a living death and you can't jam it down my throat. And you can't hire somebody to. I'll do what I want. And I'll get what I want. So send your spies home. Send her home!"

Abruptly Sala stood up. "Alison, we'll discuss this later. Perhaps tonight—"

"Tonight I have a date."

Sala paused. "With whom?"

"You can't stop me," Alison warned. "I'll tell you, but I'm going—whatever you say!"

"Alison, who—?" Sala's hand pressed the table.

All rebellion and defiance, her eyes flashed up to him. "Wiley Raike."

Slowly the fingers on the table closed into a tight fist. "You know I won't permit it! Judd Raike!"

"The date," Alison said archly, "is with Wiley."

"This is something we won't discuss, Alison," Sala warned.

She shrugged, sipping her coffee again. "You do business with Judd himself. You sell him your tobacco. I think that's worse."

"He pays my price."

"He lets you stick him," Alison laughed, "to soothe his conscience."

"I grow the best tobacco in the Valley. This is the best hundred acres—"

"Raike has thousands."

"He stole it! You know he stole it!"

"All right, he stole it, but he's got it. Maybe the Posts stole it from somebody, too—way back when they fenced it in and said it was theirs. Maybe once we were a bunch of thieves, too, and common as Judd Raike. Anyway, we can't steal it back. But there's more than one way to skin a cat."

"Alison, you're a Post!" Sala clutched the chair until his hands hurt. "You're not going to stoop to associating with a Raike."

"Oh, really!" Alison said. "Names! Today the name Raike is as good as Post."

"Thirty years ago, Raike wasn't even here!"

"Well, he's here now. With about twenty million dollars. And with that, nobody cares where he was thirty years ago." Abruptly she put down the cup, giving way to anger again. "I'm going, and you're not going to stop me. And neither is your spy. Nobody is going to stop me!"

Hazel Anne was back.

"Well?"

"The boy's been waiting for the checks to get your luggage."

"In my purse." The restless eyes, angry at the interruption, dismissed the maid with a quick glance.

"Do you want me to get them?"

"Oh, I'll get them myself." She moved toward the door. "We can't have a boy wasting time. Not this time of the year."

Hazel Anne turned to Sala, undisturbed. "Lewis Post's getting sort of impatient, Mr. Post. You know how he gets."

"He's drunk," Alison flung at her father.

Bewildered and hurt, Sala looked after Alison, knowing he was defeated. She was too much for him. He couldn't understand her, he couldn't control her. He couldn't keep her from going out tonight with Judd Raike's son. Embarrassed, Sala saw that he was still gripping the chair and he took hold of himself and released it and went outside to see about Lewis Post.

Waiting in the kitchen Parrish tried to look as though he were not eavesdropping, but when Alison said she would get the baggage checks he was alone, so he stepped over toward the hall to catch a look at her.

Even without listening he would have known something was wrong, the way she came bursting out of the room, her head high and defiant, and strode to a hall table for her purse. She stood there, impatiently pushing back the heavy black hair that fell forward over her face, and then, instead of the baggage checks, she took out a comb and ran it through her hair, furiously at first and then more slowly. Lips parted slightly, eyes intent on a mirror above the table, she combed it back from her forehead and twisted it into a knot high on her head, looking, in her loose-hanging white robe, like a Greek goddess suddenly breathing life. While she studied her reflection she seemed to change. A little smile played on her lips, a glow came into her eyes, and she seemed to bring into the somber room a radiance as though curtains had been thrust back, windows opened to sun and air. Dreamily, she turned away from the mirror and was starting to look for the baggage checks when she saw Parrish. The smile vanished and a mask settled over her face, except that, as in a mask, the eyes remained bright.

"Who are you?" she said.

Suddenly self-consciousness crawled over Parrish as he realized that he was filthy, his skin raw and perspiring, dirty shirt hanging out over his dirtier jeans. He jerked his head toward the breakfast room. "She—" he cleared his throat violently—"she's my mother."

"Do you want to see her?" When she wasn't angry she had a low soft voice, making you feel you had to pay attention.

"No," he said. "No—I'm here for the baggage checks."

"Oh. I didn't realize—I thought it was one of the Jamaicans. Here—" She held out three checks. "Wait a minute. There's one more."

She looked into the bag again and then snapped her head up and stared. "Do you live over the garage, too?"

Parrish shook his head. "I—uh—I live—" he felt himself going clammy —"down the road a way."

Repressing a smile, she looked down again into her bag, and Parrish thought she could probably imagine that Sala had objected. Obviously she had her own troubles and he suspected she understood Sala pretty well. Then the smile broke through, and, seeing it, Parrish laughed and their eyes met and she laughed, too. Parrish relaxed and leaned against the wall while she looked for the other check.

"She's pretty easy to get along with," he offered, nodding toward the breakfast room."

"That hardly concerns you."

"It does. It looks like I—we—might be back in Boston tonight."

"Here's the other check."

"If you have to have a watchdog, it's better to have one who knows how to close an eye once in a while." He grinned, trying to recapture that flash of understanding that had passed between them. "I don't know why I'm giving you all this good advice. I'd like nothing better than to be back in Boston tonight."

Her eyes danced up to him. "Well, get my bags before you go," she said, laughing softly, and started back to the breakfast room, walking more slowly, he noticed, than when she had stormed out. It struck Parrish that this was a girl the likes of whom he had not known in Boston, and that he had just found the best reason yet for liking tobacco.

Ellen sat in the living room and watched Sala pace around and around in the near-darkness, pausing at the stairs and looking up them with helpless anger. Upstairs she could hear the little noises of Alison moving about dressing to go out, and she wondered how much the girl cared for the young man and how much it was a deliberate issue she was creating to establish her rights. Ellen could tell better after she had seen him, this Wiley Raike.

Her eye followed Sala across the room. Tonight she had set the table with fine old linen and silver that hadn't been used for years and had taught Hazel Anne to serve properly, and she knew without being told that for Sala, eating in his own home in this grand manner again was reliving days he had held on to only in memories. In his pale-blue eyes was a light that didn't come often, and though he was not a man to show his feelings, he seemed relaxed, almost happy. It was a shame Alison was spoiling it now.

He had stood behind Alison's chair tonight at dinner, pouring brandy, and Ellen had caught a portrait of them, together—so unlike, as different as lightning and gaslight, and yet with a sameness to them. They were not like other people she knew. It was more than this house, alone and set apart as it was, although that was part of it. She felt that they were set apart, too—from life. Life and the world of people. The one apart and afraid to be caught up in it, more at home in the past; the other apart, restless and hungry, wanting to devour it.

Now she looked at Sala again, standing at the window, where the last brilliance of the sun inflamed the sky through the lower branches of trees, the upper already dim against the darkness, and she thought that, standing against the dark and the flame, he looked like a primitive god of wrath, nursing his ancient hatred.

"Is the boy so bad?" she asked softly.

"He's nothing," Sala said, and Ellen wondered whether he meant it on a social or a personal level. "But he's Judd Raike's son, and I have no use for Judd Raike."

"Is Wiley like his father?"

When Sala answered, his voice was sharp. "Breeding tells, Mrs. Mac-Lean. A rotten streak shows up. You get it in plants and you get it in cattle. Superior strains and inferior strains and you breed accordingly. You get it in people, too."

Now the trees were all dim and crickets cried, and sitting here, waiting, with dusk settling in, Ellen's thoughts slipped off to her own problem—to Parrish, half man, half boy, attached to her and longing to be free, who had come with her, not wanting to, and was trying to make the best of it.

It was for his own good that she had forced this break with Milky, who influenced him too strongly and in a direction Ellen didn't like—

away from her and into a lack of ambition. Common labor on a farm certainly wasn't what she wanted for Parrish, but she would handle that in good time. For now she had taken the most important step. She had taken him away from Milky before Milky took him away from her. Still, Ellen thought, however much Parrish resented this, there would never be the gulf between her and her son that existed between Sala Post and Alison.

Somewhat calmer, Sala came away from the window and picked up a book that lay on a table, opening it in a familiar way—the way, Ellen thought, some people might open a Bible to comforting passages in times of stress. He looked up after a minute. "Thoreau," he said. "*Walden.*"

Ellen searched her memory for some scrap of information about Thoreau. She smiled and shook her head.

"He was a naturalist." Sala idly turned the pages. "I can't agree with him on everything. He didn't believe in large farms, and—" he looked up with a little smile—"he never touched tobacco. But on the whole his values are simple and dignified. The more I see of people today, the more I'm drawn to Thoreau."

He looked down at the book, but Ellen saw he wasn't reading, and soon the anger boiled up again and he went back to his stand at the window, jerking the cord, opening the draperies wide. For an instant Ellen felt she was being drawn into the hatred, too. Then she heard a car in the driveway and saw the fine line of Sala's jaw go rigid and she knew young Raike was outside.

He bounced into the room, a gay-looking, good-natured young man, red hair cropped short, impeccably and expensively dressed in dark pants, white jacket, and bow tie. Hand extended, he walked quickly over to Sala, who turned reluctantly to greet him and to introduce Ellen.

"How's the crop, sir?"

Wiley remained standing while Sala stood.

"We've had rain," Sala said.

"It's the same all over the Valley. Everybody's behind."

Wiley seemed friendly and very much at ease. If he knew how unwelcome he was here, he didn't show it. Ellen asked herself if such hatred could exist unbeknown to the hated.

"Hope it doesn't mean a drought later." Wiley was serious while he talked about the crop.

"Not necessarily."

Every word Sala spoke seemed an effort, and Ellen tried to divert Wiley's attention. "I find all this such a surprise, Mr. Raike," she said. "In Boston we didn't even know there was such an industry here."

"So few people do," Wiley said. "I can never understand it."

Then Alison came downstairs, and it struck Ellen that, for all the girl's protests, Sala's training had not fallen on totally deaf ears. In a simple white linen dress she looked elegant and unattainable, and in her manner toward Wiley there was just a hint of an air that said she was a Post and he was a Raike.

After Alison and Wiley had gone Ellen waited a few minutes. She was eager to get back to her apartment, hoping that Parrish would be there, but she didn't want to appear to be escaping. "Will you want to discuss anything more with me tonight?"

Sala seemed to have forgotten she was there. "Oh, no. You're free to go back."

"If there's anything more I can do—" Ellen hesitated. Then she said, "It's only a stage she's in. They reach an age when they must do the things we object to most. It makes them feel their identities more." But even while she spoke, Ellen knew she was oversimplifying. With Alison it was more than that. "Good night, then," she said.

She was at the door when he stopped her. "Mrs. MacLean—dinner was very pleasant tonight."

"I'm glad you enjoyed it."

"Please don't feel you have household duties," Sala said.

"There are such lovely things in this house," Ellen said. "It's a shame not to use them."

A smile crossed Sala's face and disappeared as quickly as it came. "Good night," he said.

When Ellen reached the apartment Parrish was waiting, and she asked him to stop in a bookshop one day when he found one and buy her a copy of Thoreau's *Walden*.

4

PARRISH TOSSED his pay envelope onto the dresser. There was something about a first week's pay that settled you down, made you feel you were beginning to know what the job was all about. In his attic room, with the late afternoon sun still warm, he moved about, peeling off his dusty clothes, thinking that, with a week behind him, he wasn't worrying so much about how he could leave and how soon. His mother was getting along fine, both with Sala Post and with Alison, and though for Parrish Sala would be impossible, he'd be glad to try with Alison, if he could find her. But in the week since she had given him her baggage checks he hadn't set eyes on her, not even coming in or going out or walking around her own back yard.

He reached for a towel. On the whole he had to admit this was working out better than he had expected. If Sala Post was too cold and strait-laced, Lucy's family were warm and free as rain, and he liked it here and he had a week's pay and after dinner, he decided, he would ask Lucy if she wanted to go down to Tower's Dine and Dance.

Going downstairs to wash, he heard Lucy's voice and Rosie's giggles in the bathroom and found Frenchy waiting in the hall.

"I think they're campin' down in there." Frenchy wore a long-suffering look. "Boy, it ain't easy, livin' with nothin' but women."

Parrish sat down on the bottom step. "You always lived here all to-gether like this, Frenchy?"

Frenchy nodded gloomily. "I musta been nuts. But Rosie and the kid was here already, so when we got hitched, I just moved in."

Parrish smiled. A week ago he would have been—maybe not shocked, but a little startled, at Frenchy's statement. But if he had learned any-thing this week, it was that standards were different with these Valley people. Sex they could afford, and they were for it, there were enough problems without making that a problem, too.

"When'd you get married, Frenchy?" he said.

"Couple weeks after the kid come. I give Rosie a chance to get on her feet." Frenchy grinned. "Besides, I didn't want to be rushed. Marryin' is a lot different from jus' climbin' in bed—you know? You don't get off on the right foot, you're sunk."

In spite of trying not to, Parrish had to laugh. He was glad Ellen couldn't hear any of this. "A simple God-fearing people," he had told her. They were God-fearing, all right, thanks to preacher Ezra Montague, but fearing God had little direct effect on their lives. Parrish figured they pretty much accepted the idea that they were going to hell, but having reduced their lives on earth to the simplest possible terms, they'd ap-proach hell the same way.

You're probably just a natural-born bum, he told himself. You know they're just a bunch of degenerates. You shouldn't get such a helluva bang out of them. But he did.

"Lucy," Parrish said, coming into the kitchen later with Frenchy, "you like to go down to Tower's tonight?"

"Gee, Parrish." Lucy looked up quickly. "I don't know."

"Take the truck," Frenchy put in generously.

"I'm not sure yet I can go," Lucy said. "I gotta wait and see."

"Why can't you go, for God's sake?" Frenchy demanded.

"Frenchy," Rosie warned from the living room, "you know damn well why maybe she can't go."

Frenchy changed the subject. "Payday, eh? Boy, you don't know when you're well off. I get paid once a year. Maybe. When I sell the crop. What I wouldn't give to see a pay every Friday, regular and solid."

Then Rosie came in, unwrapping a bulky object which turned out to be a big blue piggie bank with pink ears and snout. "Anybody in this family gets outside work this year, every payday puts fifty cents in this pig. We're gonna buy a refrigerator—electric. One thing I'm sick of, it's that crummy icebox." She put the pig on the table and stood off to admire it.

"O.K., Rosie," Lucy said cheerfully, taking fifty cents out of her pay envelope. "That's a good idea."

Parrish had to smile because Lucy was the only one who worked outside regularly. He reached into his pocket for a half-dollar. "There's mine."

"Ah, Parrish," Lucy said, "you don't have to."

"A dollar already!" Rosie beamed.

Lucy took out another quarter. "Here's your allowance, Gramma."

Gramma's skinny brown hand came out and snatched the quarter. "New icebox, eh?" She peered at the pig. "Ha! I heard that before."

Parrish waited until after dinner to ask Lucy again. "How about it, Lucy, you want to go to Tower's?" He sat next to her on the back steps. On the highway, traffic was still steady, but the farm was quiet, the chickens still, the sun red over the shabby barn. "This pay's burning a hole in my pocket."

Lucy raised her dark eyes. In her yellow skirt and low white blouse she seemed almost too young to be out after dark, but the look of the eyes and mouth drew a man to her, and not as to a child. "Gee, Parrish, thanks a lot. But I don't know."

"You mean somebody beat me to it?" He twisted a lock of her hair on his finger.

"This fella said he'd call last night if he could, and if not he'd try tonight, and I promised I'd wait."

"O.K.," Parrish said, easily. "Maybe he won't turn up."

Lucy reached down and pulled a weed to suck. "We could go tomorrow, Parrish."

"All right."

"Only you're in the mood tonight, ain't you? I could tell the way you didn't eat much at dinner."

"Maybe I just wasn't hungry."

"When a fella ain't hungry," Lucy said, "it's usually 'cause he's got something else on his mind."

Parrish laughed. "Maybe the mood will keep."

Now the sun was sinking below the pointed roof of the barn, glowing purple over the tobacco plants, and in the pond frogs were starting their night talk. Parrish ran his hand under Lucy's soft hair and across her bare brown shoulder.

"Parrish, I wouldn't wait for this fella, only I promised."

"It's O.K., Lucy."

"Honest, if it was anyone else, I'd just go. But this particular fella—well, he kinda has a hard time getting out."

"And you promised."

"I did." Then she said, "I could go for a walk while I'm waiting, Parrish. Out around the barn and the apple trees."

"You feel like walking?"

"Rosie could call me. I could hear her from there."

Over the fields dusk had settled in and the heat of the day was gone. Pale light showed through the apple trees. "I'll only wait a little while," Lucy said. "And if he don't call, we can go."

Parrish turned her face to him. "Lucy, are you in love with this guy?"

"No!" The laugh came so quickly he wondered why she was waiting at all. "I hope he don't call."

"We could go now and you just won't be here."

"No, I better wait—a little, anyways."

Under the apple trees the ground was damp and Parrish looked around for something they could sit on and saw some old cartons he could knock flat.

"It'll be nice tonight," Lucy said. "Just a quarter-moon."

"The nights around here are always nice," Parrish said. "You don't realize because you've always had them." At night a magic descended, blotting out the shabbiness, and the countryside looked abundant and mellow. He sat down and drew Lucy down beside him.

"You like it out here in the country, Parrish?"

Touching the smooth skin of her neck and shoulders, Parrish felt his stomach tighten. "I like it fine, Lucy."

"I'd think living in the city would be really swell."

He could smell the faint odor of tobacco in her hair, mixed with the cheap perfume she used. He could smell the warm young smell in her neck that was peculiarly hers. "Country's nice, too."

"There's better country than this."

"I know."

Lying in his arms, Lucy was very young, but very knowing, more knowing than he was. She moved with sureness and Parrish could feel the eagerness in her round body, moving close to his, and the tremor when he touched her, and the wanting in the full lips that sought his, firing his own wanting, as he smelled her hair and the tobacco and the dampness under the apple tree.

Like the screech of a hawk, Rosie's voice split the sweetness. "Lucy!" she yelled. "Lu-cee."

He felt Lucy jerk away as he reached to hold her. "Don't answer."

"Lu-cee. It's him, Lucy."

"Don't answer."

But already Lucy had pulled away. "Parrish, I gotta."

"No. Lie still. Don't answer her."

"Lu-cee, it's him."

"Parrish, I have to."

"You don't have to."

"You don't understand, Parrish. I gotta." Lucy stood up, smoothing her skirt and her hair, as if the other man were already there looking at her. "I gotta go, Parrish. I'll go down to Tower's with you tomorrow night. Honest."

Before Parrish could stand, Lucy was running toward the house. He leaned against the apple tree and watched her go, staring for a long time after she had disappeared into the darkness, with his blood pounding and the smell of the apple tree teasing his senses. Slowly he started back to the house and then turned and strode across Frenchy's field to the road.

When he reached the highway the first stars were just coming out over the narrow band of dying daylight and by the time he slowed down, face and neck damp with perspiration, the sky was showered. What had happened, he asked himself. What did the man have? What pulled her so hard? Not love—she had told him that. Then what? He walked on without direction and then came to the road that crossed the bridge to Sala Post's and turned in.

Through a parted curtain Parrish could see Sala alone, reading in his library, and he wondered where Alison was tonight. Wherever it might be, it wasn't around here. She was never around here.

Walking past the house, Parrish headed for Ellen's apartment. Beyond the garage the outline of the old barn had a kind of majesty, dark against the woods with the "doghouses" on top rising into the sky like ancient parapets. Nearby, in an even row, the sheds stood black, and beyond them stretched the cloth, covering plants Parrish had helped to set. Plants that were only two inches high a week ago now had eight inches' growth. The ones they had put in today in the number-eleven field would be limp now from the shock of transplanting; but overnight, except for the few you always lost and had to replace, they would catch hold and be on their way.

Parrish put off going upstairs a minute and walked over to the cloth. This farm was becoming familiar to him and he was beginning to feel an affection for it, and yet, he thought, it was different from construction. These people in tobacco didn't work relaxed, sure of the outcome. Filled always with uncertainty, they did what they could, the best they knew how, but the crop was a whimsical tyrant that might favor you one day and turn on you the next. It was the center of their lives. They liked Lucy here not because she was cute but because she worked quickly. They respected Mary, not because she was old, but because she knew tobacco. Half-apologetically, like Frenchy, they said that tobacco got in your blood; but it was true that it did, and it ruled everyone it touched.

Parrish started for the garage and then stopped when the driveway was suddenly flooded with light and the door to Ellen's apartment opened. A moment later Alison stepped out.

She hadn't been expecting to see anybody here any more than he had, and she stopped abruptly and took a half-step back. Then she recovered, and while he was still staring she smiled. "Hello, there!"

Parrish could see the smooth outline of her hair and her head tilted up the same as that day in the hall, giving off that same radiance, that feeling of aliveness.

"Hello." He said it at last, hearing it sound strained in the silence around them. He ought to say something more.

"Have you been out in the fields?" Alison said, puzzled.

"I was just noticing how it looked in the moonlight." Parrish felt a flush creep up him because it was one of those things that sounded right in the head but wrong when it came out in words. Now he realized that for a week he had been looking for her. Every day at lunch when they sat near the number-three shed he had looked for her, and late afternoons, passing the house to go home; and he had come back here evenings to see Ellen and he had been looking for her then. He had looked for her tonight.

"How does it look in the moonlight?" Alison said.

"Take a look."

"I've been looking at it all my life," Alison said. "It's just more desolate at night than in the daytime."

She brushed her hand under her thick black hair and he noticed how perfect was every detail about her—the even part in her hair, the line of

her eyebrows, the curve of her lips. Then it struck him that she was staying here, talking to him, not moving away as she might have. Fences he
had built between them crumbled. Tension left him a little. Caution left
him more.

"Where've you *been?*" He grinned, and wondered wildly at this impulse
that was pushing him faster than he ought to go. He knew—he knew
clearly—that this was one relationship he should keep the brakes on. But
knowing was not enough. "I've been looking for you."

"I don't stay here any more than I have to." The thick lashes moved
over her wide green eyes.

You couldn't blame her, Parrish thought, for wanting to get away, with
the kind of dreary life Sala had set up for her here. "Maybe if you took
a fresh look at it," he said, "it'd seem different."

"You'll have to show me sometime."

"I'll show you now."

Alison laughed a little, but walking next to him she fell quiet and Parrish felt there was something in her silence directed more to the fields
and the cloth than to him—a resentment, as if they were the things that
stood in her way—and he wanted to tell her he could understand the feeling and had known it, too, but the wanting stuck in his chest and couldn't
find words.

They had drifted now, out of the glare of the bulb, toward the edge
of the cloth where only the pale moonlight etched blocked shapes out of
the darkness.

"Do you like it here, Parrish?" she said.

He nodded, burning that words wouldn't come. "I do."

He took a quick deep breath and maybe he would have managed to
say what he felt if he hadn't heard the footsteps then, very close on the
gravel driveway. Even before he turned he knew they were too close, and
together they whirled about to see Sala Post standing almost next to
them.

Guilt flooded through Parrish as though he had been caught in a sneaky
act, and then it changed swiftly to anger—anger that Sala should make him
feel guilt in innocence. Impulses to protest, to explain, to fight back swept
through him, and while he was still struggling to speak out Sala put a
hand on Alison's elbow.

"Good night, young man." They were the only words he spoke but his
look said that Parrish had not heard the end of this.

Furious, Parrish watched Alison and her father walk away. All his
original bitterness toward Sala Post rose up again, and he stood a long
time in the shadow of the sheds until gradually it gave way to thoughts of
Alison—how she looked, how she hated it here. Actually, he knew, there

was no meaning in the fields or the cloth to hate, or to love, either, except what a person gave to them in his own mind. Sala kept Alison here because he'd tied himself to them, and her along with him, so she hated it instead of him, maybe because it was easier.

He went up to Ellen's apartment, still thinking about Alison. You couldn't expect a girl so full of living to accept imprisonment without a fight. One way or another she would break out.

"Just a little longer, Parrish—" Ellen's words brought him back sharply —"and you can move in here. I know I can arrange it."

Parrish stared. "I don't want to move in here!"

"Now, Parrish, you know you can't stay there with those terrible people."

"I like it there!"

"Parrish, they're barbarians!"

"They're not barbarians. No more than we are—or Sala Post. They're just—" he groped for the word—"a lot freer."

Ellen regarded him with that look that made him feel like a frog under a microscope. She sighed. "Parrish, you're letting this sudden urge to be free of everyone run away with you. It's fine to be able to do as you please, but you can't live your life all alone. You need people."

"I don't mean free of people, exactly. I mean—" He knew so well, but it was hard to catch it and put it into words. "They're more natural. They don't waste a lot of time on—well, on conventions, stuff that doesn't mean anything and doesn't do any good."

Ellen shook her head. "You've got to get over this idea that you can break all the rules and get away with it."

"I'm not breaking any rules. What rules am I breaking?"

"Parrish, you live in society with other people. That society sets standards for itself and it's much more practical to conform to them."

"Just doing the things you feel like isn't breaking any rules," he said stubbornly.

"If you try to live your whole life as a rebel, you'll only make things hard for yourself." Ellen's voice was soft, but serious. "Parrish, following the rules is the easiest way to get along with people. Rules may seem silly to you, but they're important to some people. Besides, if they're so trivial, there's little to be gained by breaking them."

What rules, he thought. What rules are we talking about? "You talking about laws? Or just manners?"

She laughed. "I know you're not going around breaking laws."

"This is just a lot of talk about nothing, anyway. Sala Post doesn't want me here."

"I can bring him around."

With the scene that had just passed! "Not him."

"He's easy to get along with once you understand him."

Parrish tried a new approach. "Why stir up trouble? You're getting along fine. And I stop in every day."

"Parrish," Ellen said, suspiciously, "what's happened down there?"

"Nothing's happened. I just hate to see you stir up a hornet's nest. You like it here."

Ellen stopped arguing. "We'll see. There's no hurry."

A few minutes later he left. When he walked past the house he looked for Alison, but all he saw was Sala sitting in his library alone, reading. The rest of the house was dark.

During the night it turned cold. Waking up when Lucy came home, Parrish felt the chill in the air, more chill than just the heat of the day dying out. In the morning a heavier-than-usual mist hugged the Valley and the Jamaicans arrived bundled up to their ears. "I am an icicle for sure thees morning," Gladstone said. "I am frozen through."

Reaching the farm, the truck bumped along the sandy path to the number-twelve field where they were to plant today. They passed the number-ten field, planted early this week, where already the plants had a few inches growth, and came up to the number-eleven field, planted yesterday. Suddenly Teet slammed on the brakes and the Jamaicans fell silent.

Puzzled, Parrish peered into the gray mist, swirling like smoke on an uncertain wind. Next to the field the small truck stood blocking the path, and then he made out John, just inside the cloth, down on his knees clawing at the plants. Parrish turned back to the Jamaicans, huddled silent and sober in the truck. "What's happened?"

"I am afraid," Gladstone said, softly, "that we have found worms. Or worms have found us—whichever you like, mon."

Following Teet, Parrish got out of the truck and ducked under the cloth and then he saw it. Plants that had been set in yesterday, fresh and green, that always drooped a little with transplanting, had not picked up overnight. They stood in hideous patches, dark and wilted. Every night you lost a few and replaced them by hand the next day, but in the number-eleven field not just a few plants had failed. Whole patches were dead. For a few yards there would be a stretch of good plants and then, plant after plant, limp and dark. Slowly it came over him that this was one of those tricks of nature they were always half expecting here in the Valley— the quick, sudden reversal, unreasonable, unpredictable, from favor to wrath. Overnight something, without warning, had turned healthy, carefully nurtured plants in carefully prepared fields into sick and drying rot.

Silently he looked down at John and saw him pull a dying plant out of the soft earth, the frail roots hanging limp. He split open the thin stem and ran his finger along it. The split stem was just a thin crust, hollow, eaten away, but on John's finger a worm moved.

Parrish looked over at Teet, who was holding out both hands to show him. In one hand lay another dying plant, stem split, in the other, the worm, about an inch long, with white rings around a hard brown body. Teet dug his dirty nail into it, splitting it in two.

"Wireworms." He flung the severed worm out to the path.

On his knees, John tore at the soil with both hands, searching the mound from which he had pulled the dead plant. "Sonovabitch!" He pulled out two more worms, split them, and grubbed back in the same mound. Finding no more, he moved to the next dead plant.

Teet found his tongue. "I knowed it," he said. "In the middle of the night I felt it gettin' cold, I says to my wife, 'If the goddam temperature don't stop droppin',' I says, 'all them worms in number eleven we had two years ago is gonna come up. Little bastards'll have one helluva feast on them plants we set today,' I says."

"Oh, Christ, shut up!" John tore at the earth.

"Well," Teet said, "they had it."

"Goddam right." John turned to the Jamaicans, still sitting silent in the truck. "Well, what the hell, you nailed down in there or something?"

Slowly, the Jamaicans climbed down and drifted to the edge of the field.

"You." John yelled to Parrish. "Take the truck and go get the women. Leave Mary and Addie pulling plants and bring the rest. And bring up all the plants they got pulled."

"What you do, John?" Gladstone said. "You harrow under or restock with hand?"

"It ain't bad enough to harrow under," John said. "It's spotty. Here's a mess of 'em, but there's a couple of yards ain't hardly any."

"It's lousy with 'em over here," Teet called from a section alongside the cloth.

"We'll restock by hand," John said.

When Parrish pulled up beside the field again with the truckload of women he saw the station wagon in the path and Sala a little way inside the cloth, with John. Uneasily, Parrish remembered last night. He ought to stay out of Sala's way today. Then he saw Sala's face and he felt small and ashamed for his thoughts. He got out of the truck and walked into the field near them.

Sala moved up the row. "Is the other end the same?"

John nodded. "Just about."

Sala turned away. "It's not bad enough to harrow under." John nodded his agreement. "You have a full crew this morning?"

"Practically." John shrugged. Saturdays and Mondays there were always a few who didn't show up, for too much drinking the night before.

"Let's not waste time," Sala said, abruptly, in a manner John might have resented but didn't because of all the things it left unsaid—that restocking by hand was slow work, and even with a full crew they would be lucky to finish today; and that the only extra help for hire were the bums that wandered through, and on the weekend you couldn't even find them; and tomorrow being Sunday, you wouldn't even get all of your own crew, and it was bad to be restocking on Monday in a field set on Friday. And that it was the middle of June, time the plants set earlier were fed nitrogen, and you had to start hoeing and cultivating and there was no time to waste on worms. You couldn't spare another day. You couldn't even spare today but you had to or lose your field.

Sala walked down the path, past Parrish, hardly seeing him, and Parrish knew Sala wasn't thinking this morning that last night he had kept Alison too long in the moonlight in the shadows of the sheds.

"Well, what the hell!" Donati turned on the Jamaicans and the women standing in little clusters, waiting. "You know what you're here for."

The clusters dissolved, the Jamaicans taking up trowels and water and fresh plants and moving silently across the field.

Pull the dead plant and split the stem and kill the worm. Grub in the soil for more. And dig a hole in the dirt, pour in a cup of water, stick in a fresh plant, "shoe up" the earth into a little mound around the stem, and hope for the best and move on. Nobody chatted or laughed this morning. Nobody sang. A hush lay over the field like the mist, all hands silent and respectful, as was fitting in the presence of a superior force sending evil, while they split worms in half, one by one.

Working down a row with Teet, Parrish yanked out the dead plants. "Not as many worms here," he said.

"They's as many dead plants, kid."

"That's true." Parrish stood up to take off his jacket. Now that the sun was up, it felt like summer again.

"That's why they ain't as many worms now, kid," Teet said. "Gets hot the little bastards goes down in the ground."

"You mean they just disappear when it gets hot?"

"What'd you think brought 'em up last night? They wasn't celebratin' a birthday. It was cold was what brought 'em up. Now it's hot, they're goin' under."

Parrish moved on to the next dead plant and yanked it out and got the worm and threw them away, dead plant and dead worm. Only yesterday he had set these plants, healthy and fresh, riding the automatic setter that made furrows and fed the water and shoed up behind, so that a man had only to put in the plant. In a day four men and a tractor driver could plant a whole field. But a machine didn't know bad plants from good, so today it stood idle, still hitched to the tractor, while nearly three dozen human beings slowly and painfully pulled up and restocked by hand.

They wouldn't finish today. It was nearly noon and all you had to do was look around and you could see they weren't going to finish today.

"Seems it would be better," he said to Teet, "to turn them all under and reset with the setter." Time was precious and plants were cheap.

"It ain't that simple, kid," Teet muttered. "You disturb the ground, you bury the fertilizer too deep."

"So?"

"So the plants don't get no fertilizer until the roots get way down deep and that's a helluva long time. Get a lousy crop. Sometimes you gotta do it, but it ain't good."

"Can't you fertilize over again?"

"Fertilizer's gotta set ten days before the plants go in or you get fertilizer burn. You wait ten days from now to set this field you might as well wait till Christmas."

There seemed to be no answer.

"Besides," Teet went on, "when you harrow under, you just bury the little bastards. You don't kill 'em." He brought his thumb down and split the hard brown body and chucked it away. "I like killin' the little bastards."

"We don't get them all this way."

"Hell, kid, we get another cold night tonight, we'll have as many again tomorrow."

Pull the dead plant and split the stem and kill the worm and grub for more. Dig a new hole and spill in the water and set the plant and shoe up the soil around it. Hope for the best and move on.

"In that sweet—"

"In that sweet—"

Gladstone was starting a hymn, his rich voice slow and plaintive, singing a line and stopping while Cartwright picked it up.

"Bye and bye—"

"Bye and bye—"

"We will meet on the beautiful shore."

The plants were beginning to slant small shadows on the earth and Parrish's back was starting to ache and his legs felt cramped from crouching all day and he could taste the dirt. He could feel it in his nose and mixed with sweat on his face and gritted into his nails and creeping down inside his coarse woolen socks.

And you could ache and be gritty with dirt and tell yourself to push on (you were slowing down, they were all slowing down), and even so not be here at all. Not here but back last night in the darkness of sheds and trees, with Alison, and all of you was there—all your thoughts and all your feelings, all rushed together like streams swifter than you had thought possible. You were there, cool and clean, and she was only an arm's length away, and you didn't feel the ache or taste the dirt.

And you could pull out a plant, set yesterday and dead today, and split the body of a hard brown worm and not see its insides squash out on your finger because you had moved time ahead and it was tonight and you had walked back to the farm, timing yourself to be walking up the winding drive as the last light of the sun faded and she was waiting for you, knowing you would be there, in the same way you knew she would be waiting, and she would be just a hand away. . . .

"In that sweet—"

"In that sweet—"

"Bye and bye—"

"Gladstone," Cartwright called, "what time have you, mon?"

"Eet ees a quarter past three, mon."

"We weel not finish. I theenk we weel have to come back tonight—work very many more hours."

"I weel come," Gladstone said. "I can use the money."

"Thees one ees always looking for more money," Cartwright said. "He theenk he would like to be a rich mon."

"When eet comes your way, I do not hear you say no."

"I do not make eet my chief conversation. Eet ees very greedy to wish to make money on these leetle worms."

"Eet was a slip of the tongue, mon," Gladstone said. "Many a tongue slip at times without breaking your neck."

Moving up his row, Parrish drew alongside Gladstone. "What you going to do with all that money, Gladstone?"

"He weel go to Hartford to see his bambine," Cartwright said. "He ees a real lover boy, thees one."

"I do not have so much money," Gladstone mourned. "Every week I make so much money. First they take out thees much to pay for room and board. Then they take out thees much for savings. I do not want to save it, maybe. Eet does not matter. I have to save, anyway."

"Who makes you save it?"

Gladstone shrugged. "The American government, the British government. I do not know. I theenk eet ees the British government who makes me save, but I do not know."

"Eet ees a deal they work out together," Cartwright said. "We are British subjects, have to do what they say."

"They put the savings in a bank in Jamaica and I am not there, but I am here. Three years I stay here and my bambine is here and all the time the money is there. Eet does not please me, I know."

"Didn't you have a bambine back in Jamaica, Gladstone?" Teet said. "You don't look to me like you'd get caught without a bambine."

"I theenk he have a wife and one dozen children in Jamaica," Cartwright said.

"Not such thing, mon," Gladstone sighed. "Thees government make me live poor and die rich and I would prefer eet the other way around. Live rich and die poor. But there ees nothing I can do about eet."

Parrish laughed and Gladstone fell silent, and a moment later John came up to them. "MacLean, you work tonight? Stay through dinner?"

"I can stay." He straightened up. Lucy wouldn't even expect him to keep their date, with work to be done. Here, he knew, the crop always came first.

"Keep working." John turned to Gladstone and Cartwright. "I'm keeping you an extra hour. We'll get you back in time for dinner."

"You want us back tonight, John?"

"Try gettin' a little work done now and a couple of us can finish up tonight without you. Time I waste gettin' you home and back, there won't be much daylight left to see by." He walked over to the women. "Anybody got a kick about workin' an extra hour?"

"Gee, John, I don't know," Eileen grumbled. "My husband don't like my comin' in late an' no dinner ready an' all."

"He'll live. Addie?"

"Gee, John, I got a date tonight. I gotta have time to get fixed up."

"Addie, you're gorgeous any time." But there was no humor in it today. "Anybody want to work tonight?"

None of the women did.

It was done. They had worked the last hour by the headlights of the truck, four of them, Parrish, Teet, John and Sala, to the end of the last row and now they dragged themselves out of the field to go home, three of them heading for the truck, Sala Post going over to the station wagon.

"You know where the damn worms came from in the first place, don't you?" John burst out.

"Yup," Teet said.

"Lewis Post." John spat out the name like bad medicine. "Damn beetles all over his cloth two years ago and him too drunk to see 'em. How can I run a farm with that old bum working even one acre across the way?"

From where he sat in the truck with Teet and John, Parrish saw Sala Post wearily lift one dusty boot into the station wagon and drag the other one in after him. Just looking at him you could tell he was worn out, and Parrish thought there was no accounting for people. Who would have expected Sala Post would work right in the fields with them, sticking to the end? While he watched, Sala backed the station wagon onto the path, the headlights flashing on the automatic setter, and seeing the man and the machine Parrish was struck by the thought that you judged the one too much by the other. Knowing what to expect from a machine, you got to thinking about people the same way, figuring you could know what they would do; and when they surprised you, you asked yourself where you had been wrong. But if you thought about it, where you were wrong was in thinking of them as machines—expecting you could know what to expect. He guessed he had a thought there, but he was too tired to pursue it further. He'd probably forget it by morning.

At the house he saw Sala stop and brush the dust off his boots and then, by the light she had left on for him, Parrish saw Ellen come to the door and Sala straighten up a little, looking less tired, and give her a smile.

Awaking in the night, Parrish felt the cold again. In the morning he was out of bed before the call came from John, and he dressed and went outside with Lucy to wait for the truck, remembering it was Sunday, and thinking that nature did not wait on church.

They were only half a crew today. Most of the Jamaicans were there but of the women only Mary and Lucy showed up. "Always excuses not to work on Sunday," John grumbled. "They gotta do their housework— their husbands complain—they ain't got no one to watch their kids. All right—let's go." At noon Mary left because she had family coming, and Lucy quit because there was no other woman working.

They moved faster today, maybe because they had killed worms by the thousands yesterday. Teet had told Parrish that two years ago they had thought they'd licked the worms in this field, feeding them a bait crop mixed with poison. The trouble was they lived more than a year in the grub stage and you found out about them only if you got a cold night right after setting the plants. Later, in July, Teet said, they turned to beetles and you saw them clinging to the side cloth.

Hot, tasting dirt again, Parrish pushed himself past healthy plants to the next dead patch. "What makes them pick on some plants and not others?" he said to Teet.

"Kid," Teet said, "I ain't asked 'em."

Parrish pulled a dead plant. "Now why'd some worm decide he wanted this plant for his dinner instead of that one?" He pointed to a healthy plant. "They're all the same."

"Should I happen to overhear, kid, you'll be the first to know."

"Maybe they stake out underground claims." Parrish grinned. "You think that some worm comes along and says this here yard of plants is mine and no trespassing and he considers he owns it in a kind of God-given way like Sala Post thinks this land is God-given his?"

Teet peered at him over a week's growth of beard. "I'd advise you not to let Sala hear you comparin' him to a worm."

"Maybe it's just luck," Parrish said.

"What ain't?"

It was probably just luck, the same as with people. He had always figured that a lot of what was called luck, good or bad, was a person's own doing, but there were times it came from nowhere, picking one person and not another, like the worms picked one plant, when they all seemed alike. Or maybe from a worm's point of view there was a big difference between one plant and another.

Parrish laughed at himself. Farming sure had a funny effect on a man —put crazy thoughts in his head. He could see Gladstone a few yards ahead, and he wondered what Gladstone was thinking. Did all men have the same kind of private wondering, there being just so many thoughts and sooner or later they all went through a man's mind in a lifetime? Private thoughts of his bambine, maybe, like his of Alison—seeing her standing there in the dark of the driveway and this time no Sala Post to interrupt and all you had to do was hold out your arm, not even all the way, and you could be holding her and, although you had held your share of girls in your arms, you knew if you had held twice as many there would never have been one like this. Maybe to a worm one plant looked better than all the rest, like one girl to a man.

Pull, split, kill the worm. Dig, pour, set, shoe up the dirt. Move on and hope. Hope. He was getting awfully sick of pulling out dead plants and killing these damned little worms. He was dirty, sticky hot in the humid air under the tent cloth, but he sure as hell hoped the heat was here to stay.

He dragged himself on to the end, seeing the Jamaicans leave again at five-thirty and Sala Post give it up an hour later, dirty and exhausted. The three of them, Parrish and Teet and John, worked until dark and then, hardly exchanging a word, climbed into the truck to go home.

Stopping at the barn to leave equipment, Parrish noticed that the Rolls Royce was out of the garage and he looked up to Ellen's apartment and saw that it was dark. His eyes went over to Sala's house.

"O.K., kid." Teet came out of the barn.

"Listen, Teet, you go ahead. I'm going up to see my mother."

"Get in the truck, kid," Teet ordered. "Your ma'll live without you."

"No—you go ahead. I'm not tired."

John opened his eyes. "My God! Youth, it's wonderful."

Teet started the truck. "Pray for a heat wave, kid."

Parrish walked toward Ellen's apartment, knowing she was not in. Persistently, his eyes went over to the big house. On the wide veranda he had seen a figure move. It moved again. He left his lunch box on Ellen's steps and walked toward Sala's house, surprised himself at his pounding pulse.

Stopping near the veranda, he peered into the darkness, not thinking what he would say if the figure turned out to be Sala. But he knew it wasn't Sala—nobody but Sala used the Rolls Royce. And without that, Parrish knew it wasn't Sala. He waited. He could have sworn Alison had been here. But she didn't speak and now he saw no movement, and yet he would swear she was here still. After a long moment he turned and walked back to Ellen's.

Parrish was lying on the living-room sofa when Alison came in. He had found some cold meat and cake and milk, and, after he had eaten, fatigue had hit him all at once. He heard the door open. Almost asleep, he forced his eyes open to find her staring at him.

"You look awful!" she said.

"Well." Parrish sat up, rubbing his dirt-inflamed eyes. "I'm not exactly in the pink."

He looked up at Alison, small, clean, every detail perfect as always, and then down at himself, filthy, lumps of damp dirt clinging to his pants, dirt caked in his fingernails, and he wondered with horror what he was thinking of, coming here like this. When she came near him he edged away.

Alison sat on the sofa, smiling, her head at that elegant angle, one arm gracefully over the back in a way, Parrish thought, that suggested that there would be no interference if his hand moved out just a little and touched her. He shook his head to clear it. She wasn't suggesting a thing. He was reading meaning into the simplest of gestures. Let your mind run away with you and it could convince you of anything—there were places for people like that.

But it was there, this two-way magnet between them, and Parrish felt it and he knew Alison did. It didn't make it any less because you couldn't say where it came from or how you knew. You just knew. You didn't make mistakes about things like that. He backed into a corner of the sofa.

"What's the matter, Parrish?" she said.

"Nothing," Parrish stammered. "I'm just—well, I'm pretty dirty." Clear out, he told himself. Go while you still can.

"Have you got the worms licked?"

"We don't know yet."

"I've never seen a wireworm."

Alison's eyes danced over to him and Parrish stood up and looked away from her. "What are they like?" she said.

He couldn't keep his eyes away from her any more than a man in a desert could keep his eyes off a mirage, even though he knew it was only that and nothing he was going to taste.

"They're brown little worms," he said, swallowing. "They're—uh—hard and shiny. And they have white rings around them—and they're about that big—" He marked the size on a finger. He sat down on the sofa again, not so far in the corner, and looked into Alison's deep green eyes. "You dig them out and split them in half and throw them away."

Alison shuddered, but her eyes flashed.

"Alison, you shouldn't be here," he blurted out.

She laughed, making his words sound weak and foolish. "Of course not."

Parrish put his head back against the sofa with a terrible feeling of being in over his head and covered his eyes with his arm. Even with his eyes shut and neither of them talking, he could feel Alison's presence, and when he looked at her again he was half asking for permission to touch her, to hold her, to bury his face in her thick black hair, not understanding why he was bothering to ask.

And then while he watched her, beyond turning back and only waiting for some signal from her, Alison seemed to come to her senses. She changed. She looked away, drew off, the fire going out of her eyes. That mask he had seen before settled over her face and when she spoke she was cool and distant.

"As long as Ellen isn't here," she said, as though that were the reason she had come, "I believe I'll go back now."

While Parrish was still reeling from the sudden change, feeling as though he had walked into a stone wall, Alison stood up and said good night, formal and condescending. Parrish watched her go, wondering if he had said something or done something wrong, asking himself if, from the start, he had mistaken polite friendliness for something more.

A few minutes later, while he was still wondering, exhaustion overcame him and he fell asleep.

When he opened his eyes, daylight was slanting in through a crack in the curtains Ellen must have closed when she came in, and he saw that it was six o'clock. Still dressed, he tiptoed down the stairs and opened the door and felt instantly that it was cold again. Nearby a blue jay perched cockily on a branch of an elm tree, his white breast gleaming in the morning light. It was a ten-minute walk to the number-eleven field.

He was still looking at the field, peering through the cold mist, when John pulled up in the truck. He looked at Parrish without speaking and ducked under the cloth. Parrish waited outside. When John came back he had a set look, his collar up, shoulders drawn in.

He glanced at Parrish. "You walk out here?" Parrish nodded. "All the way from Lucy's?"

"I slept at my mother's."

John shrugged, opening the door to the truck. "Let's go."

Parrish started for the truck, not asking what John would do. The field was far worse this morning. It was as if ten worms had come for every one they had killed. Then they heard a car and Sala came along in the station wagon, looking frail and white, bundled in his jacket, his thin nose red. He got out of the wagon and walked straight to the side cloth, raised it for a second and dropped it almost immediately. He looked at John, questioning.

"All the way down." John hunched his shoulders.

Sala's mouth set in a thin line, his jaw jutting out a little, and he said what they all three already knew. "Harrow it under."

Parrish was surprised at his own feeling of pain and defeat when he heard the words. He didn't want to look at Sala or the plants. He didn't know what he was doing here, anyway. Then he heard Sala say, "You come out here with John, Parrish?" He didn't think Sala even knew his name!

"I found him here," John said.

Parrish looked up. "I fell asleep on the sofa in the apartment."

Sala Post didn't exactly smile. Nor did he show anger that Parrish had stayed at Ellen's. It was more a look that seemed to have no reason—a look, if Parrish read it right, of understanding, almost of compassion.

5

"THREE HUNDRED pounds calcium cyanide."

The clerk at Tower's Apothecary Shop nodded as Parrish gave him the order. "Still got 'em, eh?"

"We harrowed under yesterday. You want a hand with the three hundred pounds?"

"I can manage." The clerk started for the back room. "Sala gonna sacrifice that whole field?"

"Just letting it lie for a change in the weather," Parrish said. "We're planting number twelve and we'll go back."

"You can't put new plants into cyanogas."

Parrish shrugged. "I only work there."

The clerk went into the storeroom. When the door opened again young Anson Tower—a tall, clean-looking young man with dark hair and bright blue eyes—came through, a sack of chemical braced against his shoulder. He eased it down on the counter and straightened up, flexing his arm.

His customer, a seedy-looking Broadleaf farmer, cackled a short laugh. "What's the matter, Anson? All that studyin' gittin' you in the muscles?"

Anson smiled. He knew these farmers. "Good thing I come home once in a while to get in shape," he said. Then he noticed Parrish and waved.

"Looks like," the farmer said. "I hear tell Sala Post's runnin' out of plants, what with his worms and all."

Anson bent over to write a slip. "Need anything else, Ben?"

"Nope." Ben addressed himself to Parrish. "I say, I hear tell Sala's runnin' kinda low on plants."

Parrish looked up. It was true. Sala had been out all morning looking for plants. Yesterday the women had pulled the last of their own, leaving the beds dry and empty, and last night Sala had borrowed enough from Tom Holden to finish number twelve. He had to find more this morning if they were going to plant number eleven again. Aloud, Parrish said, "Last I saw there was plenty."

"Jes' sayin' what I heard." Ben got a hurt look on his face. "I hear tell you're goin' back to that Harvard place to study again this summer, Anson."

Parrish watched a yellow jacket, its stripes butter-colored in the noon sun, circling near the screen door, making a hum like a buzz saw.

"I'm doing graduate work, Ben," Anson said. "One more year and they'll let me teach there."

"Ask me, Anson, you're gettin' too damn old."

"Isn't there anything more you'd like to learn, Ben?" Anson smiled.

"I get by." Then, to show he wasn't bull-headed, "Likely if I'd give it time, I'd think of sump'n, but jus' offhand, I can't say."

"What if you could learn ways to grow a better crop?" Anson's blue eyes regarded Ben thoughtfully. "Better ways to guard against bugs and disease, and all the other troubles a farmer has?"

"Can't learn to stop a drought," Ben said, "an' it takes money, not learnin', to irrigate. Can't learn to talk a hail storm into passin' you by."

"How about learning why the big growers are getting richer every day," Anson said, "and the poor farmers getting nowhere?"

Ben thought about that a minute, while he picked up his sack of chemical. "You know what they say—the rich get richer and the poor gets kids. God knows I got enough of them!"

Ben banged out the screen door, sending the yellow jacket flying, and Anson came around the counter. "Why do I bother to argue?" He laughed. "Parrish, what's the secret on the calcium cyanide? Lewis Post?"

Parrish grinned.

"Don't you know," Anson said, "in our little valley we have no secrets?"

"I'm finding it out," Parrish said.

Outside, Parrish saw Ben stop at Sala's truck to examine the equipment that was to be left at Lewis Post's along with the calcium cyanide. Later in the day John would send over a crew to drill the chemical into the soil to get rid of Lewis's worms once and for all. Lewis himself, after the first cold night, had retreated to his shack with his sons and a bottle, cursing Sala for giving him a worm-infested field. Now, four days later, he was still drinking. "Funny thing about Lewis Post," Parrish said. "How Sala is so proper and Lewis is such a bum."

Anson smiled. "It isn't really. Not if you think about it."

Outside, Ben finished poking around the truck and left. A wiry teen-age girl came pumping up on her bicycle and stopped. Dressed in blue jeans and an oversize man's shirt, her tanned face dusty, with a streak of grease, she could have been taken for a boy but for an incongruous pair of thick blond pigtails hanging down her back. Shoving her hands into her back pockets, the girl headed for Tower's General Store, and Parrish saw that she wasn't local stock. She moved differently. Even walking cowboy style, she held her back straight and her head high, a posture totally different from the slouching, loose-jointed wiggle of the Valley girls. Parrish turned back to Anson.

"You mean there's a long line of drunkards in Sala's family?" he said. "Like Lewis Post?"

"I mean Sala and Lewis are both the end of a long line that has grown weaker and more decadent with every generation. It's the natural result of too much money. Slow rot sets in. Sala is prim and strait-laced, bolstering himself with his fake standards about his ancestors, and Lewis is dirty and lecherous and stinking drunk most of the time. But they're both in a state of decay. And Lewis's sons are one step closer to the end. And just as well. Too much money will do it every time, Parrish. It's like a law of nature. Has to be."

"Maybe so," Parrish said. But still he wondered. "Doesn't seem it'd be that certain."

"I've studied them for years, the rich growers around here." Anson spoke as though he were talking about white mice. "The more money they get, the less they can think of to do with it and the harder they try to live their way through it. They're on a propped-up bicycle, pedaling like crazy, but not getting anywhere. And every year they go to pot a little more. I've watched them a long time. Objectively and dispassionately. I know."

Parrish wondered. Whatever name you gave it, it was pretty hard to put Sala in the same bracket with Lewis Post. And of one thing he was certain, it didn't fit Alison. If Alison was a line petering out, more lines ought to try it.

Anson read the look on his face. "Alison's not a Post. She's her mother's daughter. It's just a dirty trick on her that she lives with Sala. Lewis know you're coming with the cyanogas, Parrish?"

"No."

Anson gave him a quick look. Then the clerk came back with his order piled on a hand truck and Parrish followed him outside. The girl with the blond pigtails came out of the general store, eating a strawberry ice-cream cone not much pinker than her tilted sunburned nose, and went into the Apothecary Shop and a moment later came out again with Anson, laughing.

"Parrish," Anson called, one arm around the girl's waist, while she looked up at him with large cocoa-brown eyes, "come meet the love of my life."

"Oh, Anson, honestly!" The girl laughed and blushed and Parrish thought that she looked like a healthy young urchin, all brown and tan, brown skin, big brown eyes, and the fat blond pigtails.

When he came closer, Anson said, "This is Paige Raike."

For an instant the name didn't register. Then Parrish realized that Anson had said Raike and in amazement he took another look.

"Paige is on a tour of duty," Anson said. "She feels she has to visit every Raike farm at least once a year."

"Anson, it's not a tour of duty and you know it!" Paige laughed. "I do it because I like it."

Anson patted her head. "Deep down, where you're too young to look yet, you feel it's your duty. It's definitely a chatelaine-of-the-village complex. Very feudal. But on you, baby, it looks very sweet."

"Anson," Paige said, "you just say all those silly things because you know I've no idea what they mean and can't answer you back."

"Stabbed!" Anson said. "And by the fairest of women!"

"Anson, you're really insane!"

"And just when I'm trying to look out for you. Parrish, can you put the bicycle on the truck and give this madwoman a lift? She's headed for their Ridge farm. She's pumped ten miles already and I can't stand to think of her climbing back on that bicycle, even if she can."

Paige blushed. "Anson, that isn't necessary. I can make it perfectly well."

"Of course you can, baby," Anson said, and came over to help Parrish load the bicycle. "Don't take Paige to Lewis Post's, Parrish."

"Oh, Anson, I've seen old Lewis before," Paige said.

"Not on a four-day drunk, you haven't. I have and it's not nice." Anson turned to Parrish. "He's not going to like the cyanogas, Parrish."

"I'm hoping he'll be blind," Parrish said.

Driving up the highway, with Paige Raike beside him, Parrish thought about Anson's theory on Sala and Lewis Post. Anson was easy to like and you marveled at his knowledge, but listening to him you could get confused. Maybe he was right about too much money getting in the way of living. Parrish had never thought much about money, probably because he'd never had any. Or maybe because he'd never much wanted anything that lack of money stood in the way of having.

Then he thought, what about the wanting for Alison? The wanting that hadn't left him these four days, pushing in him harder than anything he could remember. It was a wanting that you couldn't talk yourself out of, or work yourself out of, or laugh yourself out of. He could be dirty, dog-tired, and still he wanted her. Or he could list all the reasons why he couldn't have her—the wanting went on, and the reasons didn't matter because deep down in those crazy, unthinking feelings of his he didn't really believe he couldn't have Alison.

In the distance somebody's lunch whistle blew and Parrish wondered whether Sala had come in with plants. Next to him, he saw Paige Raike watching him and he smiled over at her. She must be fifteen, he thought, not much younger than Lucy. And she was taller than Lucy, but Lucy was a woman and Paige was a little girl. A little tomboy with good speech and nice manners, her only pretty features her coloring and those big liquid brown eyes. He ought to talk to her.

"Why do you visit every farm once a summer?" he said.

Paige flashed him a smile. "I just like to. That's all."

"Why not pick one farm closer to home and just go there when you want to see some tobacco?"

"Well, they're really different in little ways. I like to see them all. I visit Sala Post's every year, too."

"I should think you'd keep pretty busy just visiting your own."

"We buy Sala's crop." Paige pulled her knees up to her chin and wrapped her arms around her legs. "I usually visit there later in the season."

"Check up on your own first?"

"No!" she said. "It's just that I like to go to Sala's late, when the crop is almost grown, to see how much bigger his leaves are."

"Bigger than the leaves on your farms?"

"Oh, yes! Sala's crop is always better than any of ours." Then, with divided loyalty, "Of course, it is the richest land." Her loyalty jumped the fence again. "But he does know an awful lot about tobacco, Sala Post does. And John Donati, too. It isn't easy to know a lot about tobacco. You just have to work in it. And they really know. Look, as long as you're being so nice and giving me this ride, I can go to Sala Post's today and go to our Ridge farm some other day. I can go to Lewis Post's with you, too."

Parrish laughed and a few minutes later, over her protests, he dropped Paige at Sala's and turned around and drove back to the side road that led to Lewis Post's. When the hard surface ended in a deep-rutted dirt road, Parrish was glad he hadn't brought Paige in here. Dust rose over the windshield, and scrawny brush reaching out snapped back as the truck passed. At last the road ended in a clearing and Parrish stopped and stared, unbelieving, at Lewis's shack. About fifteen feet square, it was half of an old tobacco shed with a window, a door, and a chimney, the rotting boards patched with black and green roofing paper and even sides of old Coca-Cola crates. Nailed to a tree about twenty feet from the front door was a battered Bull's Eye target and around the target on the ground was a wide circle of old beer cans and broken whisky bottles. Wildly, Parrish could imagine Lewis and his sons sitting in the doorway, aiming their empties.

Six generations ago, Ellen had told him, Lewis's and Sala's ancestors were twin brothers sharing the same room in the old Post house. And one of the lines had come to this. Six generations hardly seemed enough.

He saw no sign of Lewis Post. Nothing moved and nobody came out to investigate his presence, so Parrish started to unload the calcium cyanide. He was carrying the second bag over to the field when he saw a rag at the window move. He stopped an instant, then went on to the field. When he came back, Lewis Post was waiting for him.

Lewis stood shakily, his bloated stomach bulging in a stained shirt over his dirty pants. "What you think you're doin'?"

"Just leaving this stuff," Parrish said, easily. "Mr. Post sent it over."

"What kind of stuff?"

"Take a look."

"I could take a look." The bloodshot eyes swam around. "But I ain't cuz you can tell me easy as not."

Parrish pulled off the third bag. "Calcium cyanide, it says here."

"Lew!" Lewis Post bellowed toward the house. "Fred!"

Two sloppy, hulking boys in their early twenties lounged out. Parrish saw now that Lewis Post had picked up the broken neck of a whisky bottle. He got the third bag off the truck.

"Drop it." Lewis Post advanced toward him.

"My orders are to leave it at the field."

"Drop it, I say."

"I'll drop it at the field."

"Boy—" Lewis came closer—"you gonna be hurt."

Parrish put the bag back on the truck. "Now, look, Mr. Post—"

"Mr. Post!" the boys roared with laughter. "Mr. Post! Get that."

"Shut up!" Lewis screamed.

Parrish looked them over carefully to see how drunk they were. They advanced closer, each holding a broken bottle neck now.

"What was you sayin', boy?" Lewis said.

"Sala said to leave this stuff here next to your field. He'll send a crew over later to take care of your worms."

"Take care of my worms, will he!" Lewis sneered. "An' my plants, too, and then what I do for a crop? Come beggin' again to his high 'n' mighty?"

"You've got no crop now. Your plants are all eaten away." Parrish reached for the third bag.

"Don't touch it!"

"I got orders to leave three bags."

Lewis spat toward him and Parrish had to jump back to avoid it. "That for your orders. Who d'ya think you are, comin' 'round here with orders. The maid's boy! Don't you give me no orders, you dirty little—" He spat again.

Parrish picked up an iron bar that lay in the truck. He held it tight in his hand and walked up close to Lewis Post. "You spit near me again and this'll come down on your head."

Lewis looked at him. He got ready to spit again. Parrish's hand tightened around the bar. One of the boys moved and Parrish whirled around to him. "Stay out of this."

"You ain't sluggin' my pa!"

"He's asking for it."

"The maid's boy!" Lewis taunted.

"When I get through with you, old man, you won't be able to say that again or anything else."

Lewis's eyes slid to the bar and a look of fear flashed in them.

Parrish raised the bar. "Get back in your hole."

"I'll tell Sala how you talked to me, by God!"

"You do that." Parrish stepped closer. "Back out of my way."

Lewis stepped back. "Leave 'im be, boys," he mumbled. "Sala'll take care of him for us. We don't have to dirty our noses with trash."

The boys fell back a step. Tucking the iron bar under his arm, Parrish picked up the last bag of calcium cyanide and took it over to the field. When he came back Lewis and his boys were still there, regarding him with hatred. He stepped into the truck, the iron bar next to him on the seat, and backed around. As he started forward, he heard Lewis yell, "You tell Sala I'll rip open every goddam bag before he gets here, by God!"

A bottle crashed against the wheels as Parrish drove the truck into the ruts and tangled brush.

Alison awoke at a little past noon and stretched lazily in bed, slipping again into that strange lassitude that had hung over her these last few days. Ordinarily, when she awoke, her thoughts leaped eagerly ahead to her plans for the day at the Charter Oak Country Club. But yesterday and the day before she had lain abed for an hour, doing nothing, getting up only when Wiley Raike telephoned. Today she felt she could lie here forever.

Idly, last night's party at the country club drifted into her thoughts. It had been a wonderful party. Everyone was there. Dozens of people had said charming things about her new gown, and Wiley was properly jealous to find her so much in demand. It had been an altogether perfect evening, even though all through it she'd had that feeling that she was not quite a part of it, that she was waiting for something.

She reached for her robe. Today beside the pool there would be early cocktails, "the hair of the dog," and lovely post mortems, too good to miss. She hoped Wiley would come for her soon. Going downstairs she told herself that only her dependence on someone for transportation marred her perfect happiness, and before long that would be corrected. As soon as the crop was in the ground—her father had promised, at Ellen's urging—they would go into Hartford and buy her a car. Alison knew exactly what she wanted: a convertible, pale yellow, sleek and low, and when she had it she would fly where she pleased, the instant she wanted.

Feeling unusually agreeable this morning, Alison decided not to disturb Hazel Anne and went into the kitchen to turn up the flame under the coffee pot. Waiting for the coffee to heat, she slipped away again into that strange mood. The coffee was boiling over when Ellen came in.

"It was a divine party," Alison said.

Ellen handed her a cup of coffee.

"Even Judd Raike was there." Alison's eyes searched the fields but all she saw was the women huddled over their hoes. "With Maizie Holden. They say Judd is thinking of marrying Maizie, now she's divorced again." Her eyes went over to the garage, where a truck had stopped, and then moved on to the old barn. "Everyone says that would be more a merger than a marriage."

"Your coffee's getting cold," Ellen said.

Alison scanned the paths, hearing another truck coming. Then she saw Ellen watching her curiously and she said, "Every time I see those women I wonder how they can let their looks go like that. Do you ever wonder how women can just let themselves go like that, Ellen?"

"Frequently."

"Every time I see them I wonder."

"Your coffee's cold." Ellen took the cup and refilled it.

Suddenly Alison saw what she was looking for. He had stopped the truck near the garage and got out, and from the way her pulse pounded down to her fingertips, Alison almost admitted to herself the reason she had been in this dreamy mood since Sunday night. She summoned her rear-line defenses just in time.

Hastily she turned away from the window. "Won't it be delicious if Judd does marry Maizie?" she said brightly. "I know there's *something* to it. He's having her to dinner tonight with her brother, Tom. Wiley can't come out. They all have to stay home." She took a quick sip of coffee.

"Alison," Ellen said, puzzled, "is anything wrong? A minute ago you were dreaming and now you're all keyed up."

"Everything's wonderful, darling. There'll be lovely gossip at the pool today about Judd and Maizie. I'll keep you posted." Anticipating it, Alison felt better—more the way she knew she ought to feel, and strangely relieved.

"Alison," Ellen said, "why don't you stay home today?"

"And miss everything!"

"Your father is still out looking for plants. When he gets back he'd be pleased if you were home, waiting to see if he'd found them."

"Oh, he'll find them. I can hardly remember a year he hasn't loaned plants to others. Oermeyer or Tully or somebody."

Suddenly Alison saw Paige Raike out there talking to Parrish. Now how could Paige know him? Then Alison smiled; Paige Raike was nothing to worry about. Still—the smile died—all that Raike money; and Sunday night, alone at Ellen's, Parrish had been cool. Well, he was tired. But not that tired. Her armor felled by sudden jealousy, for the first time Alison admitted to herself that she cared about Parrish and instantly denied it. But she wasn't going to let Paige Raike have him right off her own farm. Paige Raike of all people!

Alison decided to talk to Paige to learn how far things had gone. It would be simple because Paige was really quite a ninny. People fussed over her only because she was a Raike.

"Alison," Ellen said, "your father looked worried this morning. Will you please stay home—for your own good?"

Suddenly it did not seem such a bad idea.

"He has a whole field at stake, Alison. His most fertile field. And you still haven't ordered the car."

"He wouldn't!"

"No, I don't think he would," Ellen agreed. "But it would help if you seemed genuinely interested in his problems, too."

"He'll never believe that," Alison said. "But I'll stay. I don't mind."

"He'll believe it," Ellen said, "because he wants to."

With Ellen curious now, Alison would have to wait a little before going out there. She idled through her bath and lingered nude before the mirror in her dressing room, approving of her flat stomach and small waist and the way her breasts had filled out this year. Her thoughts slipped back, pleasantly, to Sunday night, and then, suddenly, she froze. What an awful chance she had taken, going over there to see Parrish. If Sala had caught her it would surely have cost her the car. She must have been crazy!

Silly risks like that and you could end up miles from where you had intended. Look at all those women out there. Once some of them had been quite pretty—Alison could remember it—and they'd had lovelier plans for themselves than digging in dirt all their lives; but someplace along the way something—and usually a man—flashed a tin pan in front of their eyes and it looked like pure silver and blinded them so they lost the path to where they were going and never found it again. Not Alison.

She knew what she wanted and it was Wiley Raike, gay and untroublesome while he bought her her fondest dreams—not Parrish with that slow smile and those strong brown arms to wave a tin pan in front of her eyes.

Now that was settled, she went downstairs and put on some records to play and curled up on the sofa with a copy of *Harper's Bazaar* and reflected on a picture of a dark-haired girl very much like herself, dressed in pale mink, stepping out of a yellow Cadillac. Still . . . perhaps tonight, as it was getting dark, she might just wander over to Ellen's for a chat. No, she wouldn't. She put the idea out of her head. It returned. There was nothing to do but face it squarely.

Then suddenly Alison saw quite clearly what was happening. Her father, by forbidding it, had given the little flirtation an importance beyond all reason. Alison laughed out loud. There was an attractive man on the farm and she wanted him. What harm to have a little fun? Now that she saw it in its proper perspective, she felt better. Tonight would be an incredible bore after a deadly day and certainly a walk over to Ellen's would be practically a necessity.

When she looked out again she saw Paige Raike coming in from the fields. Parrish was still near the garage, replacing a canvas cover on the smallest truck. Alison slipped out the side door and headed for the group of lawn chairs in the back yard, taking the more circuitous path that passed closer to the garage.

"They're back from Lewis Post's," Paige said, sitting down on the grass beside Alison. "They've drilled him full of cyanogas and now everyone's just waiting around here for plants."

"Mmm," Alison murmured, only half listening, trying to watch Parrish while she appeared to be ignoring him.

"Everyone!" Paige sighed. "All the Jamaicans. Teet. John's been in about a thousand times to see if your father got back. And Parrish is right there in the drive so he'll see the minute he comes."

Alison hoped Paige would leave before Sala returned. Twice already Paige had said she ought to go because Maizie and Tom Holden were coming to dinner, but still she sat, buzzing on as steadily as a bug in the long weeds. Alison wondered whether she dared say a few words to Parrish while Paige was still there.

"It's like waiting for someone to die!"

Alison whirled to stare at her.

"Nobody wants to be too far away when it happens but they can't just sit around chewing gum or something. So they keep poking their noses back to see if it's happened."

Wincing at Paige's language, Alison felt a sudden annoyance. "Paige, you're dramatizing this whole thing."

Not bothering to argue, Paige flung herself into a lawn chair, practically sitting on her neck, and moaned violently. "That's such a rich field!"

Alison decided against saying a word to Parrish or even looking at him with Paige around. Paige noticed everything, including a lot that never happened, and anything that entered her head came out of her mouth. No telling what she might tell Wiley if Alison so much as flicked an eyelash in Parrish's direction.

"Alison," Paige sighed. "Doesn't it seem tragic that in the number-one field there the plants are so high and that in that beautiful, gorgeous, rich number eleven they haven't even been planted?"

I think she's crazy, Alison thought. I do think she is definitely a little daft—getting into trouble with her father by hanging around here, and moaning on about that field. She tried to recall whether there were stories of insanity in Judd Raike's family. How could there be? Nobody knew a thing about Raike's family or where he had come from or how.

"You know what Tom Holden always says about tobacco, Alison? He says it grows so fast you can see it if you watch it."

"I haven't been watching," Alison said. "I just came home from school."

"Lucky you!" Paige flung her legs over the arm of the chair and dropped her head back, so that Alison stared wide-eyed, thinking how the blood was rushing to her head. "My father would never send us away to school. He has to know what we're doing every minute. Even Edgar and Wiley just went to Loomis and commuted."

That was nothing new. Everyone knew the way Judd Raike ran his children's lives. "Paige, you ought to start back."

"Even to college they just went over to Yale where Father was always handy," Paige said. "He's always worrying about how we're turning out. You'd think we were arsonists or extortionists. Murderers, maybe."

"Perhaps if Evaline told him—" Alison said, absently, trying to follow Parrish's movements out of the corner of her eye.

"Evaline!" Paige gasped.

It was a silly suggestion, Alison admitted. Evaline was just about the mousiest creature anyone had ever seen. Since she married Edgar Raike and moved into Raike's house seven years ago, she hadn't once talked back to Judd or Edgar or even her own children.

Parrish had taken off his shirt and Alison looked, fascinated, at his sun-bronzed body. Tonight, just before dark, she would definitely walk over to Ellen's.

"Why are you watching him like that?"

Alison snapped back, "Sh-h, he'll hear you."

"Why are you looking at him that way?"

"I'm not looking at him. I was thinking about something else entirely. I was wondering if my father could have driven in before we sat down here and gone out to number eleven with the plants."

Paige shook her head. "No, they'd all be out there planting. Alison, wouldn't it be awful if he couldn't find any?"

Something akin to fear began to nudge Alison. "Of course he'll find some," she snapped. "Don't be ridiculous."

"I don't know," Paige said. "It's awfully late in the season. Most people have turned their beds under. I hate to say it, but I'm worried."

Furious, Alison glared at Paige. Paige was worried! What did she have to worry about? She could have anything in the world she wanted. Next year, when Paige turned sixteen, she'd sweeten up to Judd and she'd get a car—any kind she wanted.

But—Alison was really panicky now—if her father didn't plant his number-eleven field, he would surely back out on her yellow convertible. He couldn't afford it, he would say. She could just hear him. She could be driven in the Rolls Royce, he would say. Oh, that horrible Rolls Royce. If he said that, she told herself, fists clenched, feeling her eyes smarting, she would scream at him.

It wasn't fair, she thought illogically, when she was twice as pretty as Paige! Well, some day when she wanted a new car there would be somebody dying to give it to her. A new car and anything else.

Alison stared at Parrish again, suddenly hating him, seeing him as a threat and not bothering to ask herself why, shocked that she had thought of stooping to this minor flirtation with more important things at stake. Then she looked past him to the garage, toward Ellen's apartment, and she calmed down a little. Ellen wouldn't let Sala back out. Ellen had extracted the promise in the first place and somehow Ellen would talk him into keeping it. It would be all right. Ellen would see that she had her car.

Paige chatted on, oblivious of the fears she had aroused. "I just can't stay any longer. Evaline's never on time when Maizie and Tom come because they're her cousins so she thinks it's all right. And if I'm late, too—Alison, don't you think it's queer that Evaline and Maizie are first cousins?"

"Um," Alison said, deaf now to this gibberish.

"Evaline's so quiet, but Maizie—she's kind of, well, flashy, but she's so alive."

"Maizie can get away with being so flashy because she's got family," Alison snapped. "Good family." She felt nasty and she didn't care about restraining herself, but the barb missed its mark.

"I don't mind her being flashy," Paige said. "I love it. Maizie does just about anything she wants, I guess. I love it when they come to dinner. Tom's so sweet, you know—"

"Oh, Tom," Alison shuddered.

Paige looked up at her. "I love Tom."

"He's so ugly!"

"I don't think he's ugly," Paige said hotly. "He can't help it if his face got smashed—if some old horse kicked him. Besides, I don't even notice his face, he's so nice." She stood up. "I have to go home."

Well, who's keeping you, Alison thought. She had noticed John come out of the house and stop a moment to speak to Parrish and she wanted to run to ask what he knew.

Paige had her bicycle turned around and one foot up when she stopped. "Goodbye, Parrish." She walked over and held out her hand. "Thanks ever so much for the lift from Tower's."

So that was how Paige knew him, Alison thought. That was all there was to it. She didn't care now. Not a rap. Not even when she heard him say, "If you like, I'll drive you home so you won't be late."

"What if Sala comes in with plants?"

"He hasn't found any," Parrish said. "John spoke to him. He won't get any now until tomorrow."

Paige climbed into the truck and Alison watched it go down the driveway. Paige Raike was really impossible. She just didn't know a thing. She didn't even know any better than to ride in a truck with a common laborer, right out in public where anyone might see her.

6

WHERE'VE YOU BEEN, Paige?" Edgar called as she tried to reach the stairs without being seen.

Paige stopped. "Out."

"Out where?" He came out of the den, wearing that righteous, superior expression on his face.

"What does it matter? I'm home now."

Edgar looked at his watch.

"Edgar, I've loads of time so just don't work yourself into a snit."

"I'm not thinking of myself. I'm thinking of Father. God, you look a mess."

Wiley came into the hall, carrying his drink, looking handsome in a white jacket, his face tanned, his red hair brightened by the sun. Paige guessed he had spent the day at the country club playing golf. Then she looked back to Edgar, who'd always had that mousy hair and sallow complexion and now was developing a potbelly, not so much from fat as from softness and bad posture.

"Edgar," she said, "you ought to spend more time outdoors. You don't look healthy. In fact, you look awful."

Edgar flushed. "Thank you, Paige. But I think we'll save a discussion of my health for a time when you're not quite so late. If," he sighed, "that time ever comes."

"Where you been, Paige?" Wiley asked, smiling. "Greasing an axle?"

Paige turned and started up the stairs.

"And Paige," Edgar called, "for God's sake, get yourself presentable. Don't come down looking like a freak. Put up your hair—that'll please him."

Even in relaxation Judd Raike stood with his shoulders slightly hunched as if ready to attack. He was a big man, with heavy eyebrows and black hair going gray, and a look to his body of a bull in his prime, all power and drive. Hands thrust into his pockets, he stood now with his two sons in the wide white hall of his mansion, greeting Maizie and Tom Holden, watching Maizie start to hand his butler a pure-white mink stole.

Then she paused. "Judd," she demanded in her throaty voice, thrusting the mink toward him. "How do you like that?"

Smiling affably, Judd Raike shrewdly appraised the mink stole—five thousand easily—and considered Maizie's hands that were a mass of diamond and emerald rings, with two diamond bracelets and an emerald one, and a diamond watch with a diamond-studded band. Only Maizie Holden, Judd reflected, amused and a trifle perplexed, only Maizie Holden could get away with it.

"Well, how do you like it?"

"Magnificent." Judd kept his hands in his pockets, sensing that Maizie expected him to touch the fur in admiration. Standing next to him, Edgar extended one hand slightly and then, noticing his father did not, he drew back.

Maizie rippled the skins. "Present to myself. Ran into New York and picked it up this afternoon." She tossed it carelessly to the butler who materialized once more from the shadows. "How are you tonight, Maples?"

"Thank you, madam, very well."

"How're those mutts you're breeding?"

"Very healthy, madam."

Tom Holden handed Maples his hat and held out his hand to Judd, a smile on his battered face. "Maizie's in great spirits tonight. Celebrating."

Judd Raike motioned toward the smaller of his two living rooms. Maizie was always celebrating something, usually with a story to it, and if Judd had to listen he was going to have a drink and be comfortable. Edgar and Wiley stood respectfully aside to let him lead the way.

"Now, Maizie, what are you celebrating?"

"Cory Lessès got married today—the utter idiot—so I'm five thousand a year to the good. He can't collect alimony from me any more."

Judd laughed. Cory Lessès had been the fourth of Maizie's five husbands. Because of her many marriages Maizie and her friends found it simpler just to call her Maizie Holden, which had been her name for the first sixteen years of her life, the longest period she had kept one. There had been times in between that Judd had considered marrying Maizie, but he had never proposed it, having an uneasy, unexplainable feeling that she would laugh at him.

"Edgar, you knew Cory at Yale. He was a smart boy."

"I couldn't say, Maizie." Edgar smoothed back his thinning brown hair. "Seven years, you know." Maizie Holden, and especially her marriage to Cory, ten years her junior, had always bothered Edgar Raike.

"He was smart. Smart enough to get alimony out of me—the only one of my five husbands to do that. Well, darling, he married a baby-faced doll who dances in the line at some New York saloon and she hasn't got a dime. But I'm delighted to be saving the alimony. I couldn't be more pleased."

"That always bothered Maizie," Tom said, good-humoredly. "Not the five thousand, you understand. Poor Cory needed that. It was the principle."

"God, yes! I'd have given ten thousand a year to charity, to Tom's precious Children's Home—and yours, too, Edgar," she hastened to add. "Or to the church or even old hell-fire Montague, just not to have paid that alimony. Made me feel I was slipping."

"Not you, Maizie," Wiley said gallantly.

"Wiley, I love you," Maizie said.

"Some things never change," Edgar murmured. "Oh, here you are, Evaline." His voice sharpened a little as his wife slipped unobtrusively into the room, a black-haired, childlike girl with bangs and wide dark eyes.

Maizie and Tom kissed their cousin and Maizie stood off to look at her. "A little pale, dear," she said.

"Nonsense," Edgar protested. "Evaline's fine."

Maizie's eyes lingered another moment on Evaline. Then she said, "Where's Paige?"

"Paige is late as usual," Raike said tersely, and turned the conversation to his favorite subject. "Tom, Sam Coletti says you're not working your Broadbrook field. What's wrong?"

"Nothing's wrong, Judd." Tom smiled. "I'm just taking it easy this year. War's been over three years now. I want to see what happens to the demand."

Judd Raike looked at Tom sharply. Tom Holden was overcautious, a dreamer who had inherited his fortune and all you could say for him was that he had managed to hold onto it, which was more than a lot of them had done. Judd Raike had watched them all, had seen them millionaires one year and broke two years later. They weren't smart, the ones who inherited their tobacco businesses, and in this business you had to be smart to live. He didn't add that one reason you had to be smart was because your competition was Judd Raike.

He looked from Tom to Maizie and Evaline. Cousins they were, and all of them soft. "Edgar, you'd better get Evaline just a glass of sherry. You do look tired tonight, my dear."

Evaline blushed while Edgar put down the Martini pitcher and reached for the sherry. "I'm quite all right," she stammered. "The children were just a little excited at their dinner. Little Juddsy spilled his milk—"

"Don't call the boy Juddsy, Evaline," Judd said, pleasantly. "Call him Judd."

"What's the matter with you, anyway?" Edgar whispered to his wife. "You know Father hates you to call him Juddsy."

"It just slipped out." Evaline twisted her handkerchief. "I'm sorry."

"Perhaps you shouldn't even drink sherry if you're on a blundering binge."

Evaline raised her dark eyes to him. "I'll be careful, dear."

"See that you are." Edgar turned abruptly back to Judd and Tom.

Bursting into the living room just as they were about to go in to dinner, Paige rushed up to Maizie and Tom. Looking at Tom, Paige remembered how Alison had recoiled at the mention of him, and almost for the first time she saw how ugly was the damaged half of his face. For an instant she hesitated and then, flooded with self-reproach, she flung her arms around him and kissed him. Tom smiled down at her gently, almost as though he knew what had gone through her mind.

"Really, Paige." Judd laughed and turned to escort Maizie into the dining room. "We can never tell with Paige these days. Outbursts at the most unpredictable moments."

Paige flushed.

"It's the age, Judd," Maizie said. "You should have seen me at fifteen. Only my outbursts were different. I eloped at sixteen."

Seated at the table, Edgar immediately turned the conversation back to his father's favorite subject. "It's a crime what labor's getting an hour these days. Common labor. Time's coming when an expert will have you over a barrel. A good foreman will ask anything he pleases and get it." Edgar's thin mouth set in a straight line. "All started with the damn war plants."

Raike sipped his wine and smiled. "We don't have to match factory wages and we never will. The factory isn't in their blood."

"The good old stand-by." Wiley laughed, draining his glass. "Tobacco gets in your blood and you can't get it out. You can always depend on that."

"Well, now," Tom said, "it never bothers me to pay a good foreman a good wage. I'll admit a fellow who dopes off the minute you turn your back is another matter, but I'll go along with a good foreman any time. He's worth it."

Judd Raike sat back in his chair. "A man," he said, "is worth exactly as much as his nearest replacement."

"There's not always a replacement."

"Then he's worth more."

"How much then, Judd?"

"Five cents more than your toughest competitor will pay him."

Tom laughed. "I'll give your Sam Coletti or Sala Post's John Donati that extra nickel any time they want it."

Raike looked sharply at Tom Holden. "Nobody can take Sam Coletti away from me, Tom. And when I get Sala Post's man, nobody will take him, either. John Donati."

Judd Raike clamped his mouth shut. He didn't believe in letting competitors, however friendly, know what to expect of him, but there was a certain pleasure in reminding Tom Holden that Judd Raike was the biggest and knew more about the industry than he did. The Holdens had been in tobacco as long as Sala Post's family—a couple of centuries. Judd Raike had no idea what his own ancestors were doing two centuries ago and cared less. What he lacked in background, he made up in other ways.

"I saw John Donati today," Paige said. "He's all planted except—" She caught herself and stopped.

"Except for what?" Edgar said.

"Except number eleven." Paige wished she could eat her words. She had a vague feeling that this was betraying a confidence and now, uncomfortably, she saw all eyes suddenly on her, Judd's, Edgar's, and—in a different way—Tom Holden's.

"Why didn't he plant number eleven?" Edgar said.

"He's planting it now. It'll be done tomorrow."

Paige looked quickly about, hoping she had covered up, but she saw her father take out one of his cigars in an aluminum tube, not to smoke but just to toy with, the way he did when he was thinking, and she knew he would ask more questions. For a moment Raike held the sealed tube in front of him, lightly between his two forefingers. Then he said softly, "Why is Sala behind on number eleven, Paige?"

"Well, honestly, how should I know?" Paige spoke with exaggerated innocence. "I just rode out on my bike and came home again."

"What did you do there, Paige?" Judd snapped the seal with his thumbnail and Paige shuddered involuntarily at the moment it split.

"I just sort of said hello to everybody."

"Stop fidgeting."

Paige sat rigidly still and felt herself going red.

Taking out a gold penknife, Raike opened the blade and carefully scraped off the seal he had just split. He gave Maizie a helpless smile. "What am I to do with this little hoodlum of mine, Maizie?"

But Paige saw nothing amusing in it. She was all tight inside and hurt because she loved him and had been trying to behave well to make up for being late. "I am not a hoodlum!" she cried.

"How am I to make a lady out of her?"

"I think Paige is a very great lady," Tom Holden said, softly.

Paige threw him a grateful look and strained to hold back tears.

Maizie laughed. "Don't worry about Paige, Judd. Just wait until she gets her first crush. Some gangly teen-ager will throw her a toothy smile and he'll do everything in a minute that you've been trying to do all these years."

Raike was not a man who liked to think of anybody accomplishing anything that he could not, especially with his own children. "My dear, what made you go out to Sala Post's today?"

"I didn't start for there. I started out for our Ridge farm."

"I'm glad to know you at least started for one of our own farms. What made you change course?"

Paige hesitated. She felt she was being baited and couldn't tell how. Moreover, she resented having to account for her actions.

"Well?" Judd said.

She might as well get it over with. "I stopped at Tower's for ice cream," she said, rebelliously going into minute detail, "because I'd pedaled all the way out on my bike and I was getting hot. Was that all right, if I stopped at Tower's?" Her voice rose involuntarily. She saw Wiley draining his wine glass and Evaline staring, wide-eyed with vicarious pain.

"Certainly," Judd said. "Go on."

"And then I went over to talk to Anson Tower in the Apothecary Shop."

"Well, how's Anson?" Maizie said enthusiastically. "There's a handsome lad."

Judd smiled at Maizie indulgently.

"Anson's fine," Paige said, calmer. "He's just home from Harvard."

"And did Anson lure you away from the Ridge over to Sala Post's?"

"Oh, no!" Paige laughed. "You know old Anson. He doesn't like Sala Post any better than us. Anson doesn't like any owners. He says we're all robbers and exploit the poor."

Judd Raike dismissed this nonsense with a shrug. "That boy's gone to Harvard six years on money Tower makes from the owners."

"Anson's an idealist," Paige said.

"He's a fool, you mean," Edgar said.

Raike snapped shut the blade of his gold knife. "All right, Paige, if it wasn't Anson who diverted you from the Ridge farm, who was it?"

"The housekeeper's son. Sala Post's."

Wiley spoke up. "She's not a housekeeper."

Judd looked at him questioningly and Wiley went on. "She's for Alison. To help her come out. And she sort of keeps things running smoothly around Sala's house. Ver-r-ry smoothly." Wiley laughed and Paige looked at him reproachfully, suspecting that he was a little drunk.

Maizie was fascinated. "Now how did I miss that little bit of gossip?"

"She keeps Sala running very smoothly, too," Wiley added with a wink. "I haven't seen Sala Post this easy to get along with in years. In fact, never."

"Tom, did you know about this?" Maizie demanded.

Tom laughed. "Maizie, I'd know better than to keep such news from you."

"Old Sala!" Maizie roared. "The old son of a gun!"

"Maizie, I wish you could see her," Wiley said. "This Ellen is a real doll. Young, blonde—"

"Aren't you being a bit too enthusiastic over a servant?" Edgar said coolly.

"They don't look at her that way!" Wiley said.

"Naturally!" Maizie roared. "Old Sala! It's been years since I've called on Sala. And that's a rotten shame."

Wiley laughed again. "You won't know what a shame until you see her."

Judd Raike cleared his throat. "That's enough, Wiley," he said, and Wiley, still smiling, stopped talking and reached for his glass. Raike twisted the pieces of the aluminum tube and patiently resumed his interrogation. "How did this woman's child get you out to Sala's, Paige?"

"He's not a child," Paige said. "He works at Sala's. He's eighteen."

"Go on."

"He was at the Apothecary Shop while I was there, so Anson got me a lift."

"And you took it?" Raike twisted the tube. "What in?"

"Sala's truck."

"A complete stranger."

"Well, Anson introduced us."

Judd looked at Maizie. "You see what I mean?"

"To me," Maizie said, "the most amazing feature of this whole story is where Paige found the strength or the inclination to ride a bicycle out to the Ridge field."

Raike studied the two pieces of the tube. "So you said you wouldn't bother about the Ridge. You'd go to Post's, instead?"

"Yes." Paige looked down at her plate.

"My daughter—" Raike threw down the cigar tube—"not only accepts rides in trucks from complete strangers, but she can't even impose on them to take her where she wants to go. She goes where they want to go."

Paige bit her lip, not knowing whether to cry out or flee to her room. "It wasn't like that."

"How was it?"

"I told you."

"And I repeated exactly what you said."

"You put your own twist on it. You always twist things your way."

Raike brought his fist down on the table. "My daughter is not a common floozie to be joy riding—with pickups."

"I'm not a floozie. There was nothing wrong in it."

Raike gestured indulgently. "Your superior wisdom, Paige—at fifteen."

"You want me to say it was wrong just because you tell me it was. Well, it wasn't." The words spilled out, uncontrolled. "Everything has to be your way. Just because Edgar and Wiley agree with everything you say doesn't mean I will. And I won't. You only love people as long as they're doing what you want. Well, I don't care. I don't care if you don't love me. There was nothing wrong in it and I won't say there was. And if you want to know something else, he drove me home, too, in the truck because I hung around too long and I was going to be late. And there was nothing wrong in that either." Paige pushed back from the table.

"Stay where you are."

Paige sat rigidly still.

Raike picked up the tube, slowly separated the pieces. "If you stayed so long at Sala's that you needed a ride home, you did more than say hello."

"I talked to Alison."

"And what was wrong with Sala's number-eleven field?"

"Judd, for God's sake," Tom interrupted. "Sala had a few worms in his number-eleven field. Wireworms. He restocked twice by hand and yesterday he harrowed under."

Judd smiled. "That's no crime, Paige. Anybody could get wireworms."

Paige bit her lip and said nothing.

"Sala had worms in that field two years ago," Edgar said.

Judd nodded. "Did he have enough plants to replace them, Tom?"

"No, Judd, he didn't. Oermeyer had blue mold. Sala gave him some."

"What'd he do?"

"I gave him what we could spare. He picked up a few more here and there."

"Enough to fill the field?"

"It's pretty late. Everyone's turned under."

"You mean he's still short?"

"Couple of acres."

"Well, hell, I can give him plants. Tell him to give me a ring."

"I doubt that he'd do that, Judd."

"Then I'll give him a ring. You sure he's still short?"

"He's still short eight acres," Paige said, feeling better about her father because he was doing this thing.

"I'll call him in the morning," Judd said. "Or I'll drive out there."

Through unshed tears, Paige smiled at her father affectionately. "That'll be wonderful. John felt badly about those eight acres being idle. Number eleven is a very fertile field. Very heavy soil."

Judd reached over and patted her hand. "You can't beat Paige when it comes to tobacco."

Paige felt flooded again with love. Finishing her dinner in silence, she told herself that you really couldn't blame him. After all, he didn't know Parrish, or how it was, and she guessed when you told about it cold, just like that, it sounded worse than it really was. He was only trying to take care of her.

In the living room after dinner Raike smoked his cigar and let his mind toy with the information that Sala Post had wireworms. Here was a situation created by many factors, like a plant fed by soil and rain and chemical and sun. Remove a single factor and the plant changed. Take away the cloth over fine Shade and you had coarse Broadleaf. It depreciated in value, was worth less on the market.

Had the cold nights come earlier, there would have been no plants in Sala's number-eleven field to be eaten. Had Sala reached that field three days later, nothing would have touched his plants. Tonight was warm. But the cold nights had not come earlier; and Sala, late already, was not late enough, and had run through his own supply of plants and borrowed what he could and needed more. A week ago Sala could have found plants easily. But today, Raike knew, the only grower in the Valley, besides himself, who still had plants was a fellow near Greenfield named Thompson. He put an arm lightly on Paige's shoulder. "If you like, you can come out to Sala's with me tomorrow," he said. "In the car."

Then Raike left his guests and went into the den and telephoned to Thompson and bought his plants.

Judd Raike's office, located in his warehouse in Hartford, was a testament to modern design. It was a large room, paneled in light-brown mahogany, the color of cured tobacco. Air conditioning and lighting that simulated daylight enabled Judd to keep the heavy beige curtains closed against the noise and the steel and concrete ugliness outside.

At one end of the beige-carpeted room, on an eight-inch-high block of granite, stood Raike's desk, a half-circle, twelve feet in diameter, hewn from a single piece of California redwood. Into it were recessed all equipment and records that Raike wanted at his fingertips, made instantly available to him by push buttons which sent the desired drawer into position at his elbow. Another row of buttons summoned Edgar, Wiley, his secretary, or the warehouse foreman. On one wall hung portraits of his three children, a firmer-chinned Edgar, a stronger-faced Wiley, a tidier, lovelier Paige. On the opposite wall a mahogany board bore in gilt letters the legend of his empire, the name and acreage of every Raike farm. A space at the bottom allowed for future expansion. On a gleaming table lay a single "hand" of choice cured tobacco.

On the day after he had gone to Sala Post's Raike sat at his desk, thinking about Ellen MacLean. A good-looking woman. Charming, exquisite. Small. Judd Raike liked a small woman. A big man, he liked to feel his size and strength and maleness contrasted with a small fragile woman. He liked a small woman walking at his side, looking up to him when she spoke. He liked the feeling of helping a small woman into an expensive wrap that he had paid for, dropping it lightly onto her shoulders, knowing that his arms could encircle her and hold her immobile, almost more firmly than he could hold her with money. He liked a small woman in bed.

Raike opened his gold penknife, running his thumb over the blade. He admired this knife, its precision, its clear, clean lines, nothing wasted. It was very sharp, very expensive. He took a fine cigar from the humidor and laid it on the desk and moved the hair-edged blade over it, slicing it unhurriedly into shreds.

Raike's thoughts moved from Ellen MacLean to Sala Post. Thin, spare, tight-lipped Sala. He stopped cutting, the knife poised over the cigar. Yesterday he had offered Sala enough plants to fill his field. In a friendly gesture he had driven out there with his two sons—Paige had not gone—and offered to deliver the plants to Sala within the hour. Sala had refused the offer. Raike leaned back, his massive shoulders butting against his wide chair, and smiled. Sala had refused because he hadn't yet learned what Raike knew—that there were no other plants in the Valley. Raike was sure. This was his valley, more than any other man's or group of men's. He owned more land—his eyes traveled down the gilt-lettered mahogany board and rested on the unlettered space at the bottom—he owned more land and he would own still more, he and his sons. His glance swept over the firm-chinned Edgar, the strong-faced Wiley. They would own more than the Holdens, combined with their cousins, the Carrs, had owned in their heyday. More than Sala Post had ever owned, before he was reduced to a hundred acres. And one day they would own that hundred acres, too.

It didn't bother Raike that Sala had turned him down, had not even bothered to lie that he didn't need the plants. Raike had arrived just as Sala was coming in to lunch, walking across the driveway with Ellen Mac-Lean. The picture flashed across Raike's mind of Sala looking amused and contemptuous as Judd Raike turned back from watching her go on into the house. What was he looking so damned superior about? Raike flung his gold knife at the desk top and the tip bit in, quivering. He had the woman on his farm, didn't he? And he looked better for it, damn him! Raike pulled out the knife and snapped it shut. Well, what of it, he said, half aloud. He pressed a button, summoning his sons to go to lunch. What of it? He had taken more from Sala Post than a woman.

"Sala call yet?" Edgar asked, a thin smile on his lips as he slouched into the room.

"Give him time."

Raike would give himself two hours after Sala called to get the plants out there on a Raike truck. Then he would call Ellen MacLean. He stood up. Idly he wondered what her price would be.

"I thought he'd call by now," Edgar complained. "He must have known last night he couldn't get plants anywhere else."

Wiley grinned. "Maybe Sala was busy last night. How'd you like Ellen?"

Raike's hand closed over the knife in his pocket as he walked ahead of his sons to the door. "Wiley, when I have nothing better to think about than another man's servant, I'll let you know."

He pushed open the door and strode through the warehouse corridor. He had a feeling she would come high. But, he speculated, she would be worth it. Two hours he would wait after Sala called. He liked a small woman.

7

PARRISH LAY on his back and looked at the pale sky just slipping off the night. In the east a silver band outlined the far trees, the sun not yet up. A teaser of a breeze blended the smell of tobacco with morning dampness, a breeze that moved without cooling, warning before the sun showed itself that the hot spell would go into another day.

He lay still, thinking that sleeping outdoors a man saw and felt things he had not known before—the way the stars showered the sky when the moon was low, some bright and bold, some seeming shy and steady, as if content not to cause too great a stir, knowing they were there forever; the way the world lit up before the sun came up red, shining clean and soft on the grass and leaves of trees and the breasts of birds; the sound of bird talk that was different in the early morning. And most of all the feeling—a passionate feeling of self and of joy to be alive, a feeling half peace, half longing. The joy of aliveness—and woven into its fabric a thread of a hunger Parrish couldn't name. He didn't know what he longed for; he only knew the longing.

Now the sun was showing the top of its head, bouncing diamonds off Lucy's window and the one to his room in the attic where it was too hot almost to breathe, let alone sleep, and presently Lucy looked out and, a moment later, came down the back steps, barefoot, still in her little pink nightgown.

"I figured I'd take a look-see if you was still here." She sat down near him, her sheer nightgown concealing nothing of her full round body. "What you figure the temperature'll go today, Parrish?"

"A hundred, maybe."

"Higher—except in the shade." Lucy looked over at the pink mountains of clouds in the distance. "It's gonna rain."

Parrish laughed. "Snow, maybe."

"No kiddin'," Lucy said. "Them're thunderheads. We got a storm comin'." She wiggled her toes in the dirt and Parrish thought that if ever a person fitted into his feeling of freedom it was Lucy, with her brown bare legs and feet, the tips of her breasts showing through the flimsy fabric of her nightgown.

"Ah, work," she said. "Who wants to work? Standin' all day in that hot shed, stringin' lath. You want to go to work today, Parrish?"

Parrish knew she was only talking. People like Alison and the Raikes escaped to the seashore, but people like Lucy had a short earning season, and heat or frost, they worked.

"I'm your boy, doll." He took her hand. "What shall we do instead?"

Lucy laughed her warm, excited laugh, her hand on his chest. "You know what I'd like to do?" She tossed her head back so that her thick curls bounced against her bare shoulders. "I'd like to walk down into the woods and just get into the stream with nothin' on. Just float around—bare as the day I come." She smiled, her dimple deepening. "Ah, I can dream, can't I? Don't cost nothin'." She moved to stand up.

"You don't have to go in yet." Parrish played with her fingers.

"I said I'd fix breakfast. Frenchy and Rosie and Mamma want to get an early start suckering—try to beat the heat a little." She stood up. "Sittin' on the ground pickin' off them sucker shoots is gonna be like sittin' on a furnace."

Watching her go, Parrish thought that Lucy seemed different with Alison away. More like when he first came. It was a week now, although it seemed longer, since the heat wave had settled over the Valley. To Parrish it was a new kind of heat, different from that of Boston; but in the Valley they knew it and fled before it, those who could. On the second day Sala had sent Alison to the shore accompanied by Ellen. And then, Parrish had noticed, Sala had seemed like a lost pup, aimless, wandering around, and finally yesterday he had followed them. Uneasily, Parrish wondered whether it was only to escape the heat. The thought that a bond was unquestionably growing between Sala and Ellen disturbed him like a sour note. Because it was strange, it could lead to no good.

Parrish's mind came back to Alison. Just a week. Yet it seemed this morning as if it had never existed, that wanting her that had kept him from any other pleasure, that half-amusement, half-sting when she ignored him, so carefully and thoroughly that it was almost more notice than if she had been friendly. Now that she was away Parrish found he was relieved. It was like having his tobacco rash heal. For a couple of days it had itched, not painfully, but irritating enough to prevent his having enjoyed what he otherwise might have. Then it vanished and was forgotten.

Thinking about Alison now, and the not thinking about her except at odd moments like this, made Parrish wonder. The sudden change from wanting to forgetting. It made him question the wanting and ask what caused such desire to burn in a man and take focus on one special object, dictating that he must have it. He wondered if a man ever really knew what he wanted—if he ever knew ahead of time what would give him a good feeling. Maybe a man never knew until he had it. Maybe not even then. Maybe nobody ever knew.

Under the cloth the air was like a boiler room, the ground so hot that the Jamaicans, sitting on it to break off the sucker shoots, had burlap wrapped around their bottoms. Coming in to lunch they poured pails of water over their heads and settled down against the number-three shed, hats over their eyes, complaining.

"John," Gladstone called. "I theenk you should geeve us a present— say we do not work thees afternoon. Eet ees too hot."

"I'll give you a present, Gladstone. Fifty cents to get some Speedarene."

"I took my Speedarene yesterday," Gladstone said. "Eet ees all gone. John, you weel lose one very good mon eef I am burned to a crisp."

"What's Speedarene?" Parrish said to Teet.

"Only a joke," Teet said. "It ain't nothin'."

Parrish stretched out under an old oak and pushed away his lunch box, unopened. Under the tree the land was dry and stony as though it didn't dare to be good with no tobacco planted on it. Gnarled old roots lay naked and exposed, spread out over the ground like the fingers on an ancient hand, where the soil had long ago eroded down the incline to the field that was planted to tobacco. Presently Teet dropped down beside him.

"Times like this," Teet said, "I think the preacher's got the right idea. Everyone in tobacco's goin' to hell and the Lord is givin' 'em a taste of the kind of heat they're in for."

"Since when you getting religion, Teet?"

"Preacher comes to see my ole lady." Teet scratched at the red hair on his bare chest. "With three kids and twins comin' I figure she's gotta have someone to blame. He tells her she's sufferin' because of Adam and Eve, so she feels better."

"You wouldn't consider taking a little of that blame yourself?"

"Don't go lookin' for trouble is my motto, kid. Last night I give 'im an argument. 'How come,' I sez, 'if that's it, how come the big growers ain't gettin' a lick of this heat from hell? How come the Lord sends them down to the beach where it's maybe twenty degrees cooler? Ain't they gonna burn in hell, too?' 'Twice as hot,' he says. 'Flames like snakes. An' all the angels of the Lord is gonna be hangin' around laughin' and watchin'.' 'Doin' what,' I sez, 'to keep cool, bein' angels? Drinkin' beer?'"

Parrish laughed appreciatively. "What'd he say to that?"

"I didn't give him time. While he was still rollin' his eyes around, gettin' over it, I cleared out. By the way, kid, I hear you was at Tower's last night with Lucy."

"You heard it with your eyes, boy," Parrish said. "I saw you."

"I was gettin' worried about you, kid. A guy can decide to be President, but meantime he's gotta eat. What happened last night with Lucy?"

"That's none of your damned business."

"Yeah, yeah," Teet said, unoffended. "You looked pretty simple-minded if you wanna know, dancin' with your eyes shut."

Parrish laughed again. But the thought of Lucy produced a pleasant sensation that surprised him.

A caterpillar crawled up his side and Parrish flicked it off, watching it head for the field, where the cloth was down on all sides, glaring in the sun. Underneath, the plants stood knee-high now, big and healthy, the leaves starting to spread out over the immaculate, deep-furrowed rows, and Parrish thought how in a month he had grown to like farming and wanted to stay; although, possibly, liking farming was more a sign of not wanting anything much, rather than knowing what it was he wanted. God knew nothing went around in circles more than farming. How many times had he been over this land since he came? Planting, cultivating, spreading nitrogen, and now suckering, to say nothing of the times he had gone back and forth filling water barrels and moving the "office," which was the polite name for the transportable outhouses. He had been over the farm so many times he knew it like his own face. You couldn't say farming was setting up anything you wanted and getting it. Farming was getting no place.

He looked over at Teet, sitting against the tree, a week's growth of red beard on his face. "Teet, you ever think about what you really want?"

Teet's eyes slid over and studied him. "Best thing to want, kid, is what you can get."

Parrish grinned. "Just seems to me lately—a man thinks he knows what he wants and all of a sudden he wakes up and finds that wasn't what he wanted at all."

"Way I see it is what you want depends a lot on what you had lately."

Teet puffed his pipe, mentally examining the problem. "Like you take people always sayin' what a man needs is a good woman. Maybe there's a guy don't need a good woman at all. Maybe what he needs is a bad woman. Maybe had half a dozen women last week or so, then he don't need no woman at all. What you reddening up for, kid? My Gawd!" Teet stared at him. "You ain't a molly about talkin' women?"

"Hell, no." Parrish lay back against the root so Teet wouldn't see the blush mount high in his face and creep into his neck.

Teet gave his lewd grin. "Kid, when a guy goes red like that it's 'cause somethin's hittin' home. Which is it, kid? You had six women the past week or you find you're wantin' one bad?"

"Jesus Christ, Teet, how can one guy be so revolting?"

"It ain't easy." Teet grinned. "The look you had on your face last night dancing with Lucy down to Tower's, looked like what you wanted was right there under your nose."

John stood up to ring the bell ending the lunch hour, and the Jamaicans resumed their moaning. "Health is important, John," Gladstone called out after him. "Not money. You know how many men have bad health, try buy it with money. Sometimes mon get sick, don't get better."

"What are you, Gladstone," John said, "man or mouse?"

"That depends. When eet come to working, I am a mouse."

"When eet comes to his bambine ees when he ees mon," Cartwright said.

"Health ees important, not money," Gladstone called again.

"See what I mean, kid," Teet said. "Even Gladstone's changed his mind about what he wants." He glanced hopefully overhead, where dark clouds were beginning to push across the sky. The air was heavy with that stillness that was the overture of the storm. "If you really want to know what I'd want, kid, it'd be my own grease pit, where I can fool around. And the first thing I'd do would be to get the head off Sala's Rolls Royce and see what makes it tick."

Passing the house, Parrish could see the shades drawn, the look about it of no one home, and he thought of Alison and, puzzled, remembered the old wanting. Passing by again, an hour later, with rain beating rivers on the dust-caked windshield of the truck, he thought of it once more, feeling the wanting, still, but not sure any more it was for her. His eyes went over to Lucy beside him, and he caught her watching him, as if trying to find in his face the reason for what her instincts told her, that things were getting better between them.

Later, after dark, the rain stopped and it was cooler. Parrish lay on his bed in the attic, listening to the cars splash the wet road. A moth beat against the screen, wanting to come in, and once it got in it would beat the other side, wanting to get out. He reached up and snapped off the light to stop teasing it, and it beat harder, looking for what it couldn't find any more. He lay awake, his mind too restless for sleep. Maybe a man understood better what he wanted after he'd used up a few years finding out. Like Sala.

Did Sala know? People said Sala lived for tobacco. But he had turned down the plants Judd Raike offered for the number-eleven field, preferring to let the field lie empty. Maybe Sala wanted tobacco, but it seemed he wanted his hatred more. And now, Parrish wondered, now did Sala want Ellen—his mother?

How about John? All he'd ever heard John ask for was speed. All that ever pleased John was a man who knew tobacco and was willing to work for it. And what about men like Judd Raike? He had caught a look at Raike the day he came to offer Sala the plants. Surely you had only to look at Judd Raike to think there was a man who knew what he wanted and knew how to get it.

Well, the hell with it. He snapped on his light again, and the moth beat against the screen and maybe a man never knew anything more than a moth and maybe just as well.

A minute later the door opened and Lucy came into his room in the pink baby-dress nightgown. She stood at the bed, smiling down at him, her dimples deepening, black curls falling around her face, no pretense about why she had come, not asking if he wanted her. Her instincts were too sure for that. It was no accident that she had waited until tonight.

Parrish grinned and moved over on the bed and reached out a hand to her. Maybe you never knew ahead of time what it was you wanted, but you sure enough knew when it happened.

8

Now THE tent cloth was more gray than white and alongside the field were piles of empty canvas baskets, while in a shady spot filled baskets holding layers of thick green leaves of tobacco, were lined up, ready to be carted to the sheds. Under the tent cloth pickers moved quickly down the rows in pairs, "draggers" following with baskets to gather up the picked leaves. In the air there was a new feeling of production, a lazy farm

changed suddenly to an industry. The women were in the sheds sewing
the leaves onto laths to be hung for curing, but more men had been
added to the crew, more Jamaicans and some local boys, fourteen and
fifteen years old, small boys who moved easily and speedily among the
bushy plants.

Loading filled baskets onto the truck, Parrish watched the busy crews
hurrying down the rows, almost, he thought, like an organized colony of
ants systematically attacking an enemy bastion. New faces, new boys, so
many new people he had not yet heard their names—knew them only by a
number John gave each group to simplify keeping production records. It
struck Parrish that there was something indecent about working with a
man and not knowing his name, giving him no identity in your mind
other than one half of pair number seven or dragger number nine.

He could hear the familiar voices of Gladstone and Cartwright, sing-
ing as they picked a row together:
"Oh, my Cindy, she have religion,
She try that once before."

>   "Oh, my Cindy, she have religion,
>   She try that once before."

Even the song was different, no lazy, dreamy melody now, but a racy,
fast-paced Calypso rhythm.
"When she hear my ole banjo
She the first one on the floor."
"Gladstone," Cartwright interrupted. "You do not hurry, you weel not
be the first one through a row, I theenk."
"I am hurrying, mon."
"You weel not make very much money today, mon. And I weel not,
either, with you my partner. Eet ees a great injustice."
"Not such thing, mon. I have to make money for my bambine."
"Hurry, mon. Hurry."
Parrish loaded the last of the baskets and climbed into the truck.
Money, he thought. It's wonderful. It's magic. For weeks the men had
been paid an hourly wage, and John had pushed and yelled and all day
long it was "Pick up your shoes" and jokes about Speedarene. And then
suddenly it was picking time and everything changed. Pay by the hour
became pay by the bent picked, a bent being the distance between two
tent-cloth posts along a single row. And the battle for speed was over, won
by the simplest of human laws—economics.

Taking advantage of the magic of piecework, Sala had gone to the
beach again to be with Alison. Ellen, having been away for more than a
month, was coming home this afternoon for a few days. It would be good
to see her.

"That place agrees with you!" Parrish kissed his mother and stood back to admire her. She had a deep tan and with her vivid pink lipstick and pale blond hair she looked almost girlish. "You look wonderful!"

"You're looking fine, too." Ellen laughed, with an air of happy excitement. "Just fine."

"Well, there's nothing like the outdoor life to make a man healthy and—healthy." He grinned. "How's everything at the beach?"

"Lovely and lazy," Ellen said. "Except for a few arguments about that perennial thorn in our side, Wiley Raike."

"He still down there?" Through the window, Parrish could see Lucy waiting for him, lying on the grass against the number-three shed. Seeing her black tousled curls and the baby lines of her face, the familiar womanly lines of her body, he smiled, a warm feeling going through him. Then he saw his mother watching him and turned quickly away. "What's he do, stay there all summer?"

"The Raikes are all down there. They own the hotel."

"Sala must love that."

"He just ignores them." Ellen laughed. "But on the whole Sala's been very happy and relaxed these past few days."

"Well, that's nice."

"Parrish, you shouldn't feel that way about Sala. In some ways he's very fine. I'm quite fond of Sala."

Parrish looked at his mother carefully. "How long you here for?"

"Just a few days."

Ellen's eyes went over to the window for what Parrish thought was the second time and he began to get an odd feeling, like a small boy about to be caught. He was sorry he'd told Lucy to wait for him. He stood up. "Look, I'm pretty dirty. How about if I go clean up and come back and take you out to dinner?"

"Parrish, I'd love it." Ellen drew her slim ankles up onto the sofa. "But I have a date for dinner tonight."

Parrish looked around, surprised. "Who with?"

Ellen flushed a little and an excited look came into her eyes.

"Well, who is he?" Parrish teased her. "You haven't found yourself some crummy Broadleaf farmer you're afraid to talk about?"

"With Judd Raike, Parrish."

"Judd Raike!" Parrish stared. "How do you know him?"

"He's been at the beach off and on all month. Parrish, you don't mind?"

"Hell, no!" It wasn't that he minded. "I'm just surprised." Then a slow smile crept over his face and he said, "What's he like?"

"He's exciting, Parrish. Just tremendous energy. And he treats you elegantly!"

Parrish sat down again. He remembered Judd Raike from the day he had come out to offer Sala plants—a big man, shoulders hunched a little, who seemed to be all energy held in check. Towering over Sala, making him appear puny and weak in comparison, he looked like a man who did as he pleased and got it done fast. Parrish couldn't blame Ellen for finding him exciting. Then a new thought struck him. "What's going to happen when Sala hears?"

Ellen frowned a little. "I don't believe anything will happen."

"You'll get the sack."

"No, I don't think so, Parrish. But Sala would be hurt, and just when I'm beginning to make him happy. He needs me. And Alison does, too."

Parrish was unconvinced. Sala Post would be more than just hurt. He sprawled down in the chair, turning this over in his mind. "You have the right," he said, after a while, "to see anyone you want. But if Sala hears it, he'll be damned sore, and you'll be back in Boston before you know what happened. If you're smart, you'll keep the whole thing very quiet."

Ellen nodded, but Parrish could see she did not wholly agree. The sun slanted past the gold curtains now and cut a long path on the deep-piled carpet to the cherry-wood desk across the room, the room that Ellen had made so charming in a hundred little ways, and Parrish felt suddenly how much she would hate to lose all this.

"I suppose it would be best to try to keep it quiet," Ellen said at last. "Only I suspect that Judd Raike would like that, too. Quiet, private little meetings."

"You mean he's getting soft—doesn't want to hurt old Sala, either?"

"I mean," Ellen said, "he doesn't want to hurt Judd Raike."

It took several seconds for Parrish to grasp the incredible implications of his mother's statement. Then he understood. Thunderstruck, he sprang to his feet, a terrible rage bursting over him. "Well, what the hell—!"

"Parrish, dear, don't get excited."

"Don't you go near that guy again! Tell him to go to hell."

"Parrish—Judd Raike!"

"Who the hell is Judd Raike?" Parrish yelled.

Ellen sighed, patiently amused. "Parrish, he's an interesting, exciting man."

"O.K., O.K. Don't tell him." Parrish stormed about the room. "I'll tell him for you."

"No, Parrish, you won't. I'll change his ideas in time. The trick is to make yourself necessary before you make demands. Now demands would only spoil things—and I like him."

"The hell with that!" Exciting! Interesting! How could she be excited about a man who was ashamed to be seen with her? Then, suddenly, Parrish understood. It was no different from the Jamaicans getting interested in tobacco when they went on piecework. "You like his dough!"

"That's part of it."

"Why?" he shouted. His hair fell over his face and he pushed it back. "All money's for is to buy things. You for sale?"

"Oh, Parrish, please," Ellen said, indulgently. "Some day you'll learn money helps. Besides, I want to go out with him. I'm used to a big city and lots of people. I get lonely here and both Sala and Judd Raike help fill that loneliness."

"That's just an excuse. You're always making excuses, always compromising."

"Life is a compromise, Parrish. If you won't bend, you'll break."

Angrily Parrish strode to the window and stared out, surprised to see Lucy still waiting. In his anger he had forgotten her. She had turned over and was lying bottom side up now, head on her arms, face to the window, with a sweet, contented expression as though she hadn't a thought in her head except to wait for him as long as he wanted, and he wished to hell he'd sent her home.

"Parrish—" Ellen was looking out the other window—"aren't you compromising a little, too? With that girl out there?"

So she was going to change the subject by dragging Lucy into it.

"You look very relaxed these days, Parrish." His mother's eyes met his in a straightforward look. "You look like a man who has a woman all his own who thinks he is wonderful."

Parrish felt himself go red. "We're not talking about me."

"Is she really all you want—that girl?" Ellen said.

Parrish clamped his mouth shut. How could he explain Lucy or the way she made him feel? She was like the wild pheasant that flitted in the woods, brilliantly colored, free, laughing as readily as a bird sang, unquestioning—loving. And nights, when he turned over to reach for her and she moved into his arms, he had no questions, either.

"Parrish," Ellen said, "it's all right for you to move in here now."

"Move in here!"

"Sala is perfectly willing—"

"But I don't want to move in here!" He couldn't move in here! He had tasted the sweetness of freedom and he couldn't go back to fences. And he couldn't leave Lucy now. His need for her had become as natural as hunger.

"Parrish—" Ellen's voice was tight—"how far has this gone?"

You couldn't tell your mother to mind her goddam business, the way you could Teet. Parrish bit his teeth together and turned to her with flaming cheeks and eyes that answered for him.

Silently, Ellen turned and walked away from him across the room, and Parrish could feel her pain and her anxiety and he groped miserably for something to say. It was several minutes before she looked around. Then she came back, seeming quite calm again, and sat in a chair.

She smiled. "Parrish, when a father discusses these matters with a son, he tells him of the easy girls he knew in his youth, he advises him to watch his step, and it's a great bond between them. When I talk to you this way, you think I'm prying—invading your privacy."

"No—" Parrish protested, halfheartedly. "I don't think that."

"But I have to do this, Parrish, because you have no father. I must tell you that this girl isn't what you want. She's a first love. Everyone has a first love, every man and every woman. You're a man—or almost—and she's a woman. And she's there. She's available. She's not wonderful, Parrish." Ellen shook her head. "Only available."

Available! How could you call the thing that was between him and Lucy just availability?

"Move in with me, Parrish. See her if you want to, but don't live with her. She can become a habit, and just being a habit can be a very strong hold."

Parrish looked down at his mother, seeing how small she was, seeing the thing in her face so close to fear, and he felt he couldn't continue to hurt her. "It's nothing." He forced himself to speak lightly. "Only that, well, she—Lucy's so free, not tied to all the mean little things like—lots of people. She's free and natural and I like it."

"Nobody is free, Parrish." His mother's eyes, bright and direct, met his. "Everyone is tied to something."

He didn't answer because he was trying not to argue. He had only said as much as he had to offer some sort of explanation.

"You're in love with an illusion, Parrish. She seems free to you now, but she is tied, like everyone else, to somebody or some thing or some idea. The person doesn't exist who is not."

Then suddenly she stood up and came over to him. "I'm sorry, Parrish. I shouldn't insist on your moving in here when your freedom is so important to you."

Her sudden understanding made him feel rotten. He put an arm around her and said what he didn't mean at all. "Why not wait until you're back for good? And Sala's home again, and has Alison here?"

He started for the door.

"Parrish." He stopped. "Try not to get more involved than you can see your way out of."

He went downstairs and closed the door behind him. Watching from the window, Ellen saw him walk toward the station wagon with Lucy, an arm on her shoulder in a gesture of closeness, a kind of possessiveness that made her wince. He was a man, now. Still her son, but no longer a child, and he didn't need her any more.

Suddenly Ellen felt terribly alone. A feeling swept over her that she was alone in an unfamiliar room on a strange farm and that all around her people moved to and from each other, but she stood alone. Ellen knew this sensation—she had had it at other times. Often, at night, she had heard her sister and her sister's husband speaking to and answering each other in another room, and she would lie stiff in bed and feel the loneliness. She would lie there until the voices stopped and then she would get up and go into the room where Parrish slept and straighten his blankets and sit next to him on the bed, thinking how young and untouched he was and how much he needed her, and when the loneliness had quieted she would go back to bed and sleep. Now—Ellen stared out at the empty driveway and at the garden beyond, where a sprinkler turned water on the red phlox and white petunias and the straw-colored stalks of iris, dry and dead—now she was losing him.

She had always known the day would come when he would no longer need her. Now that the day was here, knowing didn't make it easier. Ellen thought of Lucy—the snarled curls around the sweet face that the years would make heavy and coarse, the well-developed breasts, the round hips in the dirty jeans—and a cold feeling swept over her. She was prepared to let him go. But not to this.

Slowly, common sense mastered Ellen's panic. Not need her! Parrish needed her now more than ever. For him these were critical years—years of rebellion for the sake of rebelling, of finding himself, of finding a meaning for himself; he would make mistakes and she must see that the results were not permanent, and that he learned by those mistakes. This girl was part of his learning and must be just that, and no more.

Perhaps, she thought, this would be the last time Parrish would ever need her. Her son was very much a man—in spite of her feeling of loss, Ellen felt a surge of pride—a man who wouldn't lean on her, or on anyone else, as some children leaned forever on a parent and stopped only to seek a substitute. Like Alison, who was racing passionately through life, looking for the chimney down which Santa Claus would come bringing everything on her list. Alison, Ellen knew, would need her much longer than Parrish. Alison would always need someone, and Ellen understood the need.

Ellen chided herself angrily. She could understand Alison and meet her on her own terms. And Sala on his. And Judd Raike. All these people on the fringe of her life. But with Parrish, who was the heart of her existence, she was filled with panic and held on too tight. It was what came of loving too much.

But if Parrish was the center of her life, Ellen knew that she could no longer be the center of his. Whether she liked it or not, she had better fill her life more without him. Thoughtfully she fingered the copy of *Walden* on the desk. She wondered what Judd Raike read, if anything. She put the book back on the desk and went into the bedroom to dress.

"Still frettin', Parrish?" Lucy came into his room and sat down beside him on the bed.

"Just thinking."

"Sometimes I think I never seen such a one for thinkin'."

He smiled and held out an arm and she moved into the bed beside him. "And other times?"

"Ah, don't worry about it. I'm crazy for you, anyway."

He played with a black curl over her ear. "Mostly I think about you."

Lucy laughed, pleased. "Ain't you the one!"

Sometimes there were things it was hard not to think about her, thoughts he would push away, telling himself that they were questions which would not occur to him at all if some of Ellen's properness hadn't rubbed off on him. In her generosity Lucy had taught him much and at times Parrish caught himself wondering who had taught her. Who and how many?

"Honest, Parrish, it beats me how just seein' your ma could get you so riled up. What'd she say, anyway?"

"She said I look better than ever. That's your fault."

"Ah—" Lucy stirred about. "You really think about me a lot, Parrish? When we're not together?"

"Sure. Don't you think about me?"

"Ah, you know I went for you right from the start." Lucy's hand moved down his chest.

"Not from the start," Parrish said. "Once you ran out on me."

"I never did!" Then her expression changed. "Oh, that!"

"What happened that night, Lucy? Was that other guy so great?"

Lucy moved away a little, her round body no longer touching his. "He wasn't so great."

Parrish told himself to drop it. It was just one night—one night compared to the many they'd had together since. "O.K.," he said. "I'm glad he wasn't so great."

But it nagged him and he wondered why tonight he was so pressed to find out. Other nights he had thought of it and had put it out of his mind. Maybe it was what Ellen had said about everybody being tied to something. What was so important about that guy to Lucy?

"I didn't mean his name, Lucy," he urged her. "I mean what was so damned special about him?"

"Ah, Parrish." Lucy dropped her uneasiness under his caress. "I think you're jealous!"

"Mmm-hmm."

"Parrish," she said simply, looking into his eyes, "you ain't got nothin' to be jealous about."

She was right. Slowly, Parrish reached for the light switch. What had happened before was past and the only thing that mattered was that tonight she was here and there was nothing of any importance to come between them.

"So how's every little thing, kid?" Teet said. "How's the family and all?"

Parrish turned over where he lay in his usual lunchtime spot under the old oak tree to look at Teet, propped against the tree trunk. "What's eating you?" he said.

"What's eating you is more like it." Teet puffed his pipe. "You ain't said a word all day."

Parrish shifted his position. Over against the shed the Jamaicans were figuring the morning's bents in terms of dollars and cents, and Parrish had been lying here, sore, listening to them while his mind fretted over thoughts that had plagued him since yesterday.

"Teet," he said suddenly, "what do you know about Judd Raike?"

"Like what, kid?"

"What kind of guy he is. You ever talk to him?"

"All the time." Teet scratched his stomach. "We play poker—regular."

"Ever hear anything about him?" Parrish pursued it. "Good or bad?"

"Hear good and bad about everyone."

"Jesus!" Parrish exploded. "How can one guy take so long to answer a simple question?"

Eyes closed, Teet explored his unshaven face. "Kid, Raike's got more dough than anyone else around here ever seen. And twenty-five years ago he didn't have nothin'. So he didn't get it by bein' so nice 'n' honest, you know what I mean?" He opened one eye to look at Parrish. "On the other hand, how many did?"

Parrish read curiosity in Teet's eyes and decided to drop it. A buxom pigeon landed on the roof of the shed and he watched it perch for a moment, proud and exuberant, deciding, maybe, whether this place suited its fancy.

"Now with women," Teet said casually, "he's the love-'em-an'-leave-'em kind. For a week he treats 'em like they was Queen Victoria. Then he moves on."

Guardedly, Parrish looked back to Teet.

"A-ah, that's what happens when you get a stack of dough. Maybe a hundred dolls Raike's had. Real dolls." Teet got a lecherous, dreamy look on his face as though reviewing a parade of Raike's former loves. "But a guy gets a tall stack of chips, nothin' suits him. Allers figures he can buy somethin' better."

A little knot of alarm was tightening in Parrish's stomach. He should have gone over to see Ellen this noon instead of lying here, thinking. Not even thinking. Moping, more. He wasn't using his head for anything or deciding what to do.

Teet aimed tobacco juice at a scrawny daisy. "You want a little advice, kid, don't go gettin' all lathered up, 'cause you'll just about work up a good head of steam an' it'll all be over."

Furious, Parrish whirled about.

"What you sore about? You want Raike should play around with her for a couple of years instead of a week?"

"Why don't you shut your goddam mouth?"

"Excuse me for breathin'," Teet said, elaborately. "I take it all back. Raike's a great man. The kinda guy you can't help but love. I'm glad you asked, kid, so's I got a chance to tell you. He don't drink, he don't smoke, he don't touch a woman from one year to the next except maybe to help old ladies across the street."

Parrish looked at Teet with a set, unsmiling mouth. Damn it, he should have gone over there this noon to find out what happened last night, even if there were other things he wasn't ready to discuss again.

"Practically a monk," Teet went on. "In fact, he makes Sala look like a bum. Now you happy?"

Angrily Parrish kicked at a tree root. "Sala—all of a sudden Sala says I can move in with my mother."

"So? Ain't that what you wanted?"

"Hell, no. I like it where I am. I don't want to go back to any ball and chain."

"Last I heard, you hated Sala's guts because he wouldn't let you hang around."

"I just don't like him because he's miserable and narrow-minded, thinking he's God Almighty!"

Teet shrugged. "Kid, ever occur to you that you're a little mixed up?"

"I'm not mixed up."

"First you're sore because Sala won't let you live here. Then you're sore because he will. And you're sore 'cause you're afraid Raike's buyin' up your private property and you're sore 'cause I tell you he ain't buyin'—he's only rentin' for a couple of days." Teet grinned over his pipe. "An' you ain't mixed up?"

Narrowly, Parrish looked at Teet sitting under the tree, as placid as the Black Angus that grazed on the hill, and told himself it wasn't Teet he should be sore at. "What I'd like to know is how you found out so goddam fast."

"Oh, kid," Teet said, pained. "You know they ain't no secrets in this Valley."

Abruptly Parrish turned away. Over against the shed, he could hear the Jamaicans still talking finance.

"One hundred and fifty-six bents," Gladstone was complaining. "I am sorry eet ees not more, but thees Cartwright ees a very slow mon."

"Not such thing, mon."

"You are very expensive partner. Cost me much money."

Parrish dropped his head back against the tree and closed his eyes. Why couldn't they just once—just once—talk about something besides money? Then the whistle blew, ending the lunch hour, and he pushed himself to his feet and started for the truck.

"Kid." Teet came up behind him. "Why not figure your ma can take care of herself? She ain't no baby."

Parrish told himself Teet was right. Probably when he got over there later Ellen would tell him that she'd found out herself all about Judd Raike. No one had ever made a fool of Ellen yet, and it wasn't likely anyone could start now. Besides, Ellen liked it here too well. She wouldn't throw all this away just for a few evenings with Judd Raike.

"Parrish—" The words of his mother's note leaped at him like flames licking off a log. "Off for the day with Judd Raike. Come tomorrow."

For several minutes Parrish stood staring at the note in his hand and then, unbelieving, he began to stride through the silent apartment, senselessly opening doors and looking into empty rooms. Then he came back to the living room and flung himself down in a chair. He should have come at noon.

Once again he read the note, then crumpled it and threw it down. The sun had come around to the west and flooded the room, playing on the bright yellow and gold of the fabrics, the rich tones of the cherrywood furniture. There was a lot of Ellen in this room. She had put her mark on it, in the arrangement of the furniture, in the cluster of plants where the sunlight touched, in the bowl of flowers on a low table. Things Parrish had never noticed before suddenly stood out sharply. The room looked like Ellen, warm, lovely, and serene, so much so that it spoke for her, even in the emptiness of her not being here.

Suddenly Parrish shook his head. You could get trapped by sitting too long in this kind of rich quiet. It was like taking a drink at Tower's and feeling it warm through you, numbing sharp edges, making everything around you look good for a while. Look a lot better than it was, either before you started to drink or after the drink wore off, when it looked even worse. To break the spell, Parrish stood up and began walking about. But while his eyes had been charmed by the opiate of the touch of Ellen in this room, slowly a new discomforting thought had been forming in his mind. He tried to ignore it, but it only pushed harder and at last he was forced to consider it.

What right do I have, Parrish asked himself and stopped still with the shock of the question—what right do I have to interfere? Why shouldn't Ellen see Judd Raike if she wanted to? Where was his right to say yes or no to Judd Raike when he denied her right to say no to Lucy? How was it different? Because he knew if he insisted, she would probably give in to him? It wasn't enough.

Soberly Parrish sat down again. In his pocket, he felt the key to the old station wagon and he took it out and toyed with it. He slipped the key off the metal ring and held it in one hand, the ring in the other. They were separate now. You separate one from the other and they are equally separate. He was the one who had sought the separation. He had demanded freedom. Now he told himself there was a catch to everything. When you freed yourself from someone, you also freed that other person from you. Equally free. You couldn't claim the other any longer or a role in the other's future or a right to make his or her decisions. Freedom worked both ways. He put the key back on the metal ring and took it off again, holding the two objects apart. Equally separate, Parrish told himself. To the same degree.

It was a long time before he stood up. The sun was lower, now, slanting long across the desk, and he went over and threw the crumpled note into the waste basket. It was nearly dinnertime. He might as well go home.

At the door he paused, thinking of the chaos of the Ballows' house compared to this, the smell of cooking grease, the sound of Rosie and Mamma shrieking with loud laughter. Maybe he would just stay here. Then a warning came over him that this was an important moment in time, that something too strong out of the past was pulling him back. He had better go. Quickly he walked down the stairs and closed the door behind him.

Passing Sala's house in the station wagon, Parrish noticed a shabby man who looked like a tramp at the back door, talking to Hazel Anne.

Then the man turned, waving to Parrish to stop, and he saw that it was Lewis Post.

"Something I can do for you?" He drew up next to him, wondering how much of their last meeting Lewis had remembered after sobering up.

"Hi, Buster." Over Lewis's bloated stomach a single button held together a worn brown jacket, and he tugged at a gray handkerchief tied around his red throat. "Sa-ay, you're comin' up in the world, ain't you! Them lettin' you drive one of the cars!"

"I'm sitting right on top," Parrish said. "What do you want?"

"Gimme a lift home, will ya? I walked all the way over here an' din't git nothin' fer my troubles 'cause my cousin's at a goddam beach somewhere. An' I'm a old man." The bloodshot eyes blinked.

Parrish jerked his head toward the door. "Get in."

Lewis climbed in next to him. "Buster." Lewis's hand crept over to Parrish's knee. "I want you to know they ain't no hard feelings."

"That's good."

"After we scared you off that day, me and the boys, I got to thinkin'. I siz to the boys—Boys, you shouldna done it. That nice little boy was only doin' his job, bringin' over that cynogas. You shouldna took on like that with him. I tole 'em." Lewis's watery eyes sought Parrish's. "Damn shame about my plants, wasn't it?"

"Yeah."

"I'd a had a good crop this year, too. Handled them three acres like a baby. I tried to get new plants after you plowed me under—I tried." Lewis's head bobbed morosely. "I went five or six different places. Tom Holden, American-Sumatra, Consolidated. After I heard Judd Raike had bought up every last plant in the Valley I even went to him. I wasn't proud like Sala. Even if Raike took all our land, didn't bother me none. I went there. Lemme see him, I siz to that girl in his office. I wanna buy some plants. I wasn't proud."

Something went cold in Parrish. He heard Lewis Post's voice running on plaintively. "What did you say?" he demanded. "About Judd Raike buying plants?"

"Well, Buster, everyone knows how Judd Raike bought up all the plants in the Valley an' there wasn't many left, bein' so late in the season—"

"Why did he buy them?" Parrish spoke so sharply Lewis edged back.

"He bought them to make Sala have to come to him for plants. Everyone knows that. An' Sala wouldn't go. But I went, by God. I went and din't get none."

"Why? Why did he want Sala to have to come to him? Would he have charged hell out of him for them?"

"He'd have given 'em," Lewis said. "He din't want no money. He just wanted to make Sala eat crow, fer Christ's sake. Just for the fun of seein' it!"

Parrish felt sick. He could feel the sick feeling going all through him; he was sick with disgust, sick with fear, sick with the hope that it wasn't true. He told himself Lewis Post was no man to believe, he could have had hallucinations in a drunken stupor. He pulled over and dropped Lewis at the entrance to his road, actually apologizing for not driving him to his door, and hurried down the highway. Lucy would know, or Frenchy, or Rosie. If it were true, one of them would know. As Teet always said, there were no secrets in this little valley.

He found Lucy alone in the kitchen.

" 'Course it's true," she told him. "Everyone knew it. You musta heard it, too, Parrish. You only forgot." She smiled up at him. "Go on up and get cleaned up. It's almost dinner."

"I don't want any dinner." My God! he thought, and I was sitting around thinking up fancy ideas about not having any right to interfere!

"What's the matter, Parrish?" Lucy stirred the stew that smelled sickeningly of garlic. "You mad 'cause your ma's seeing him?"

"Jesus!" he yelled. "What did they do—announce it on the radio?"

Lucy laughed and touched his arm. "She's human, too, Parrish. Just like us—like you and me."

He shook off her hand. "Don't go assuming things about my mother."

Puzzled, Lucy moved off and reached for some bowls in the cupboard. "Parrish, she's been seein' Sala, too. Everyone knows she goes out with Sala. Eatin' dinner here and there, an' drivin' and all."

"That's different."

Lucy set the bowls on the table and came back to the stove and picked up the stirring spoon again. "Parrish, lemme tell you somethin'," she said, patiently. "In a way you don't know very much, you know what I mean?"

She looked up at him and he glared at her without answering.

"You say it's different with Sala. Why's it different? 'Cause Sala's like a bird and Raike is like a bull?" Lucy laughed. "Parrish, birds do it and bulls do it. That's the one thing you gotta expect—that's one thing you can absolutely count on."

Placidly, Lucy stirred her stew and Parrish stared at her, horrified.

"Maybe men are different in lotta ways," she went on. "One man's a tightwad, hates even to buy you a beer. Another one'll drink like a sponge an' take it out on you later. You'll go with one fella wears clothes so flashy you're practically blind. Next night a guy'll come around, he'll be a real slob, not even bother to shave." Lucy turned around to face him, her big brown eyes serious. "But that way, Parrish, they're all alike. That they all want, some more'n others, some operatin' a different way, but they all want it. An' they all get it. An' that's 'cause women ain't no different, neither. Unless there's something wrong with 'em. An', Parrish, I don't think there's anythin' wrong with your ma."

She looked at him steadily, thinking only to teach him, and Parrish felt so sick he had to turn away. "My God, is that all you ever think about?"

Lucy looked puzzled, pained. "No, that ain't all I ever think about."

"Then don't think it about my mother."

"Parrish, I'm only tellin' you for your own good."

"Don't tell me any more. I don't want to hear."

"O.K.," she said. "O.K."

Lucy turned back to the stew and Parrish stood rooted to the spot, staring at her, at the round curves of her hips, at the curly black hair.

"Parrish," she said in a low voice, without looking around, "you think it's such a crime, what do you do it for?"

"I didn't say that."

"Only for your ma, huh?" She gave a low laugh. "Not for you?"

"I told you to stop talking that way about her. Just because you—" He stopped, but Lucy's eyes flew up to his and he looked at her for a moment, and then he slammed out the back door.

He went to Tower's and sat at the bar and ordered whisky and the place didn't look any better. He ordered another. After a while Anson Tower came over to talk to him. At least Anson didn't talk about Ellen and Raike. At least there was someone left who didn't know.

Anson talked instead about equality of opportunity and about mental starvation being as bad as physical starvation, and Parrish only half listened. His senses were numb now from the whisky and his mind was too busy racing over his own problems. Just as Anson finished with mental starvation, Parrish was asking himself about the real reason he was upset about Ellen and Raike. Is it just because he's a bastard? he searched himself. Or is it because you're afraid he can steal her away from you?

This was a great little freedom he had kidded himself into thinking he had. He was free, all right. He was a great big free boy, having a big time doing as he pleased, as long as he knew his mother was there waiting whenever he felt like running home. But what happened the first time it looked like his mother might be leaving?

"Anson," he said, "all the things you think about, you ever think about people being free or not free? Or anything like that? You ever think anything like that, Anson?"

"All the time," Anson said.

"Great," Parrish said. "Swell."

He guessed he was getting a little drunk. He decided to go home. He ought to say something decent to Lucy after talking to her that way. Thinking of Lucy, Parrish squirmed. Why in hell did he get so mad at Lucy? Just because he'd been itching for an argument? Because his mother had him all mixed up? Because, maybe, he thought Raike was too big for him? Or maybe because he was mad at himself. Lucy hadn't done a thing but he was sore so he had taken it out on the one person who was simple and uncomplicated enough not to give him a hard time. That was great. That was really being a great man.

They had all gone to bed by the time he came home. Walking down the hall Parrish could hear the double snoring coming from Frenchy's and Rosie's bedroom, the bedsprings squeaking as someone turned over in the room Lucy shared with Celeste. He went into the bathroom to wash, and when he came out he saw that the door to Lucy's room had opened a crack and he knew she had waited up for him.

In the near-darkness he whispered her name, motioning toward the door. The crack widened and moonlight poured through the room into the hallway. "Lucy," he said, "Lucy, I'm sorry. Believe me, I'm sorry."

"It's all right, Parrish." Lucy tried to smile, but her eyes were filling with tears.

For an awful moment Parrish stood there unable to say another word. He wanted to tell her to come upstairs—she stood there waiting for him to, and he couldn't. The words stuck in his throat.

"Good night, Lucy." He touched her arm without kissing her and went upstairs, fully aware of the hurt he had left behind.

He flung himself down on the bed, flooded with anguish and self-reproach. What had he done? He had created for himself another situation just like the one he had been trying to get out of. He had given someone a hold on him, someone he couldn't leave without hurting.

He tried to think of Lucy, tried to picture her in his mind, but all he could think was that she was probably down there, lying on her bed, crying. Other than that she didn't seem real to him. Had he ever loved her? Or had he only loved what was happening to him, with Lucy just somehow there?

Even as he brooded about her, thoughts of Ellen, and fears for her, pushed Lucy out of his mind. Thinking of Ellen, Parrish felt like a small boy who had been playing with matches and saw suddenly that the house was in flames. It was too late to stop, and there was nothing to do but stand helplessly by and watch it burn, seeing parts of it still intact, but knowing in a terrible way that it was only a matter of time before the flames swept it all away.

Ellen wanted to see Judd Raike because she was lonely. And if she was lonely, whose fault was that?

BOOK 2

1948: *Late Summer, Fall*

9

Preacher Ezra Montague made his way up the highway, feeling with high elation that the evening air was electric with a storm. The atmosphere was heavy, hushed. Cars that shot past made sounds that seemed to die where they were born, suspended in air. In the trees, birds talked.

Undeterred by the threatening weather, the preacher was starting on his evening calls. Since noon, with mounting excitement and a sense of righteousness, he had felt the coming of this storm—the increasing oppressiveness in the air, the slow darkening of the sky in the late afternoon, the swelling of tension. Dinner had been impossible—food repelled by the pounding of his pulse in his stomach, hunger dying, unfed, at his sense of exaltation. It was right and just that this storm should come, that it should wreak havoc in the Valley—sweep across it in destructiveness, the hand of the Lord showing His wrath and His will.

Cars streaked past on the highway and a bus came, the bus that would take the preacher sooner to his destination. He let it go by. Tonight he wanted to walk. To walk tonight with the coming storm was standing at an altar, his faith revitalized, rededicated. It was two long months now that faith alone had sustained the preacher, for this was the most bountiful of summers, with occasional light rains at night and sunny days, and no disease, no plague of insects to carry the torch of the Lord against the evil of this weed. Everywhere he looked, the tobacco plants were high and green, the crop more than half picked.

In the sheds the fires burned, drying and curing the leaves. For three days and three nights in every tobacco shed, fires burned, nursed and tended and watched by sinners, the final blasphemy, incense-burning to the devil.

He went to the people and told them that they suffered because of their sins and out of respect they listened, but in his heart he knew he was losing them because they were not suffering. When they felt the sting of nature's cruelty he held them tight because they were uncertain and afraid. When nature smiled with persistent favor in a rare summer like this, he could not speak of God's wrath and exhort them to repent.

He walked past the old cemetery with the slanting stones and then past Tower's Apothecary Shop. In the west, the sun died ominously under thick, fast-moving clouds. Lightning stabbed the sky. He came up to Tower's Dine and Dance, hearing passionate music inside. A young man came out and headed for a car and the preacher saw that it was the young man who lived at the Ballows'.

He was a wild one, that boy. The old woman had told him that he was carrying on with Lucy, but now she said it had stopped. Ezra Montague dug his nails into his palms. It sickened him to look at this boy—the muscles, the brawn of the lean browned body, the dark, passionate eyes, the sensuous mouth that showed it had tasted sin and loved it, the way he walked, even, the swagger, the bravado. No, the preacher told himself, those were not the words to describe it. Nothing so superficial, nothing so easy to preach away. It was something more terrible and basic. It was appetite. The preacher shuddered with revulsion. It was animal male appetite.

He walked on. He asked himself whether he should try to save this boy, whether he could. He had struggled with the question before and put it off, telling himself he would start with the mother. But when he called on the mother, he came away charmed and confused, disbelieving the stories he had heard about her entanglements with Sala Post and Judd Raike, telling himself they were vicious lies, the guilty judging others by themselves. But then, only two nights ago, he had seen it himself—seen her covertly stepping out of Judd Raike's car and into a taxi to go back to Sala Post.

The skies blackened over now and night fell early. In the distance thunder crashed. The first drops of rain spattered the road. A car shot past, racing like the wind, a yellow convertible with the top down, a black-haired girl at the wheel, her hair blown like the storm. She was the very soul of the devil, Sala's daughter. The thunder was nearer, the lightning bright and fast, and the preacher watched, enraptured. Cloth would be rent and plants torn and beaten to the ground and the hand of the Lord would stretch over the earth and His wrath would be made known.

Parrish turned into Sala's driveway and drove the station wagon into the garage, noticing that the yellow convertible was still out. Giant raindrops were beating a slow staccato now, while lightning skirted crazily across the sky, chased by soft rolls of thunder. It was the teasing stage of the storm, the few minutes of warning before the skies opened up.

He stepped out of the garage, heading for Ellen's entrance, when he saw the flash of yellow between the trees, and a second later there was a clap of thunder and Alison skidded around the curve of the driveway just as the skies opened up.

Parrish stepped back and threw open the garage doors and she drove in. He darted in after her, pulling shut the doors to a fresh clap of thunder while new rivers of rain poured against the glass panes.

She sat in the car for a minute, blotting rain off her face with a handkerchief, and Parrish made his way past the Rolls Royce and came up next to her. "You get wet?"

"Not very." Raindrops were clinging to her hair, to the little threads of ringlets off her brow. "What are you doing here?"

"I came in just ahead of you. I was going upstairs."

"Lucky for me." She gave her hair a quick final shake and smiled at him. "Aren't you still living down at the Ballows'?"

"Mmm-hmm."

"I can't think why you stay there, Parrish, when you can move up here now."

Parrish leaned against the Rolls Royce. "Sometimes I wonder, too."

"Isn't it an awful mess down there?"

"It's not too bad."

Alison ran her hand under her thick hair and leaned back against the seat. Her eyes darted over to him, wide and bright. "I know why you stay there."

"Do you?"

"So that," she said, "for a little while every day, there's nobody to tell you all the things you can't do."

Parrish smiled, surprised that she understood. "Or all the things I should do."

"That, too," she said. "We have a lot in common, Parrish, you and I."

"I didn't think you knew that."

She smiled. "I knew. But I don't think it's worth living like that. I'd rather fight it out another way."

"I didn't exactly choose it at the start."

"But now you can come back."

"Now it's like running back."

"But don't you want to get out of there?"

"Very much." She couldn't possibly know why. "Very much."

Outside the storm was in full fury now. Lightning split the sky and rain beat against the garage. In the near-darkness Parrish picked his way past the Rolls Royce to the window. Heavy branches of trees reached down, all movement, and through them he could see shaded patches of light from the house.

"You want to go in the house?" he said.

"I'd be drenched."

Parrish nodded. "I guess the best thing would be just to stay here." At the house, a slit of bright light appeared at a window where a curtain had been drawn apart. In the wide garage there was no sound now, except the storm, rain blown in gusts and the rumble of thunder. Alison was silent, but Parrish could feel her presence as if an electric current ran taut between them. Even as he had said the best thing would be to stay, something told him that the best thing would be to go. At the house a figure moved into the light.

"Your father's looking for you," he said. "He must have seen you come up the drive."

"I'm sure he did."

It was all dark now and her voice, soft and halfway across the garage, deafened him to the sounds of rain and thunder.

"He's not looking for me, Parrish," she said. "He's looking at the fields. He waits for the lightning to see if the cloth is still up."

Caked dust washed down the panes before rivers formed off the window heads, their erratic courses lit up by shots of lightning. At the house Sala remained a while at the window and left.

"Why don't you get out of the car?"

"Why don't you get in it, Parrish?"

He threaded his way back in front of the Rolls Royce and stood next to her again, barely able to distinguish her pale features in the darkness, his pulse beating with awareness of her, as if she were in a blazing light. A flash of lightning revealed her upturned face, the wide eyes, the clean line of her cheeks and chin, the elegance he always felt with her, and then it spent itself and the garage was dark again but he knew she had not moved away. A faint voice of discretion struggled and lost the battle. Without trying to speak, Parrish could feel that his throat was tight. As he bent toward her, the faint warmth of her breath coming to his face, his lips touched her hair, felt the dampness in it, and moved to her lips.

Fire lit fire. The warmth of her, the scent of her, the fierceness of her fingers in his hair sent a savage abandon through him, and while a tyrant in his brain tore his lips away from hers another closed his arms around her, holding her against him.

"Where were you?" Alison whispered. "Where were you?"

Parrish raised his head, not understanding.

"All week, since I came back—where were you?"

He released her and opened the car door as she moved over on the seat. The feel of the cold wet metal in his hand sent a stab of reason across his brain. This was Alison, Sala's daughter, Alison, the china doll, Alison, the witch who played cat and mouse, the precious, untouchable—then she was circled in his arms again, warm and wonderful, and she was Alison, too lovely to be real, and the obstacles fell before a heat he had not known a man could feel.

There was a sense of the smallness of man in the sheds that bothered Parrish. At the long narrow sewing tables the women went soberly about their work, wearing solemn looks, speaking infrequently—a muttered comment and then silence—the only sounds the slush of leaf sliding over leaf as it was drawn off a pile to be sewed onto the laths. This was their response to the storm, the hush of people feeling how little were man and his plans in the face of the superior force that smiled on him for a while and then stopped smiling, and in a single night swept over him with disaster. Always they half expected trouble, and when it came they didn't question it but only felt again their own inadequacy. Like death, Parrish thought, so final and unquestionable it made them feel small and afraid.

It had been a quick, fierce storm, giving way before midnight to clear skies and a full moon. Dawn was clean and quiet and wet over the battered Valley and they came out early to make their way through muddy fields, repairing the damage, doggedly propping up plants that had been beaten to the ground.

Parrish stood on the bottom board of the scaffolding that was erected in the shed for hanging tobacco, passing the laths, heavy with leaves, to Cartwright, balanced on another level halfway to the roof; and high up, near the top of the shed, Gladstone hung it across the uppermost boards. Every time he reached down Parrish saw Sala Post standing near the women, with dried mud on his boots halfway to the knee.

Finishing their own repairs at noon, Sala had sent John with a full crew to help his neighbors, Tully and Oermeyer, who had fared worse, and come into the sheds himself, keeping only three men to hang laths that the women sewed with leaves already picked.

From the scaffolding Parrish looked down at the women: at Mary, old and wrinkled, who long ago had made friends with storms; at Addie, blubbery and weepy-looking; at Lucy, whose mouth these days wore a look touched with sadness; and then he looked back to Sala and told himself you had to admit there was metal in him. Then, a little surprised, he realized he had known it for some time. He had felt it weeks ago with the worms and again this morning, after the storm, as they repaired their damage and went on, not taking a backward look at what could not be saved—in the same way that nobody ever spoke in front of Sala about the empty number-eleven field, as many times as they passed it to work in number twelve.

But in spite of his new grudging respect Parrish wished that Sala were not here today. While he was still spinning with the wonder of Alison, Sala's presence reminded him sharply of the barriers between them. For the first time Parrish was seeing the world as Ellen had told him it would be. He had his standards, and Alison and Sala had others that he had never been able to accept; but it was their values that were popular and approved, while he stood alone. Until last night Parrish had wanted this aloneness, had fought hard for it. Now he wanted Alison more.

For the second time in two weeks, the frustrating realization came over Parrish that there was a catch to everything. He had held his freedom and given Ellen hers and that had become his first doubt. Now he wanted Alison more than he had thought possible, and he had to recognize how far apart they were and how much he would have to compromise. Certainly the idea of compromise was nothing new to him. All his life he had heard of it from Ellen. What was new was that he was thinking of accepting it. Already he was bargaining with himself, asking how far he would have to bend, how much of the one he could hold on to without losing the other.

10

ELLEN SAT next to Judd Raike in the Mermaid Room of the Surf Inn, which was the large and expensive hotel that Raike owned, overlooking the Rhode Island shore. They had taken dinner in Raike's private dining room and then he had said they would come in here, which was unusual because he disliked crowds and this was the public cocktail lounge. Across the room a piano tinkled softly. A waiter stood nearby, ready to refill their champagne glasses.

Raike was restless tonight. He took out a cigar, one of the aluminum-tubed ones he always carried, and snapped the seal with his thumbnail.

Ellen looked at the painting over the bar, from which the room took its
name, certain that the model for the mermaid was a girl Raike knew
or had known in the past. Although, she mused, if a man owned a hotel
and wanted a picture of a girl he knew painted with bared breasts and a
fishtail—and if it was all right with the girl—

Raike interrupted her thinking. "I don't know why I keep coming here
every weekend," he said. "I used to come because once I worked here and
it gave me a lot of satisfaction to own it. Now it doesn't even do that."

"I didn't know you had worked here, Judd," Ellen said.

"I worked here all right. This was where I first heard about a tobacco
industry." He laid the aluminum tube on the table while he opened his
gold penknife. "All the tobacco people came here. Others came, too, but
the tobacco people always seemed to have just a little more of everything.
So I went into tobacco." He scraped the broken seal off the tube. "Later I
bought this hotel from a bootlegger named San Pedro, who had a great
deal of money. He was Sala Post's father-in-law and he bought the hotel
from Sala after Sala went broke—in case Sala never told you."

Discussing Sala made Ellen feel like a traitor, and there was nothing to
be gained by it. She nodded toward the cigar in Raike's hand and said, "Is
that cigar made of tobacco from your fields, Judd?"

Raike didn't answer, although Ellen knew he had heard the question.
He picked up the cigar, holding it between the tips of his forefingers,
studying it. "Why'd you come, Ellen?" he said.

Ellen hadn't been expecting the question and she found herself groping for an answer, although she maintained a serene smile, while Raike
searched her face.

He laughed. "Don't tell me you don't know why. Not you, Ellen."

"You asked me to come, Judd."

"And you turned me down, at first. And then suddenly you changed
your mind and decided to come. What happened?"

"I just changed my mind, Judd. Nothing more complicated than that."

"Where'd you tell Sala you were going?"

"Here to the beach."

"With me?"

"Of course not."

"Tell your boy?"

"No."

Smiling, Ellen took refuge behind her glass of champagne, seeing Raike
continue to study her. He had the look, Ellen thought with a little shock,
of a man who was not questioning ultimate success with a woman but
was only speculating on how the victory would taste and, possibly, considering the question of timing. Not will she or won't she, but only should

it be now or later? To be perfectly honest, she supposed she couldn't blame him for thinking it.

"You look at me, Judd," she said, "as though you were a horse dealer about to count my teeth."

Raike laughed and the restless look left him a little. "My dear," he said, "if I were dealing in horses, I wouldn't have to count teeth."

With the blade of his knife, he began to separate the outer layer of tobacco from the cigar and Ellen, watching, thought that the answer to his question was so simple. She had come because she couldn't continue to walk a tightrope between two men who hated each other. Where Sala was concerned she felt like a cheat; and with Raike—she looked at him now, at the deep-set, brilliant dark eyes under bushy brows, the lips jutting slightly over a strong chin that gave him an expression of determination and, she thought, a little of cruelty—with Raike, she wanted this man. It was as simple as that.

She wanted him and she knew, in her deep, certain sixth sense, that in their hurried secret meetings she was getting nowhere. Almost ready to end it, she had decided, because she wanted him, to make one final effort. During this weekend she would become important to Judd Raike if she could, and if not she would terminate an impossible situation and Sala need never know.

But even while she assured herself that it was the only thing to do, Ellen smiled a little. In the end, you did what you wanted to do and then found ways to justify it. Like a gambler, you considered the prize and you took the chance. How many women before her, Ellen wondered, had decided Judd Raike was worth the gamble and how much had they risked? Looking again at the mermaid over the bar, Ellen thought they were probably kindred souls.

Raike had the cigar completely unraveled now and had separated the tobacco into three piles on the table. "I'll show you something, Ellen," he said, pointing with the knife to the largest pile, a heap of dark shreds. "This is the filler, the inside of the cigar. It's a blend. Some of it is Connecticut River Broadleaf. Some is from my fields in Cuba. And this—" he touched the point of the knife to the next pile, a lighter brown, that Ellen could see was of curls of leaf—"this is the binder. It holds the filler together. This came from my fields in Puerto Rico. And this—" the blade moved to the last pile—"this lovely stuff comes from my Shade fields in Connecticut. This is the outside wrapper. See how light it is. These are perfect leaves. This is what gives the cigar flavor." He moved the light, almost blond leaves closer to her. "This is what sells the cigar."

Raike snapped shut the knife and slipped it into his pocket, motioning to the waiter to clean off the table. "Have you been thinking of the reason why you came, Ellen?"

"No, Judd," Ellen said. "I've been thinking of the reasons why I shouldn't have come."

"That's easy. One would be enough. The obvious one—Sala. I didn't think you'd come, Ellen. Why did you?"

"Let's just say that I wanted to, Judd."

"Is that all you could think of all this time?" He laughed. "Ellen, don't worry so much about Sala. At least, not on my time."

"I'm not worrying about Sala, Judd. Had I been worried, I wouldn't have come." But she was worried about Sala. She had taken this positive step as much because she was afraid of losing her job as for any other reason. That wasn't like her, Ellen thought sharply, and yet it was true. She wondered if she was reaching that time in life when one began to make decisions out of fear instead of hope. The thought startled her, and she put it aside for a time when she could ponder it undisturbed.

The room was getting noisier as more people drifted in, and the piano player was getting jazzier, and the mermaid seemed to shrink in size, although her face remained extraordinarily real.

"Did you ever notice," Ellen said, "that girl's face looks real enough to talk."

"She was better," Raike said, "when she kept her mouth shut."

And then, although it was still early, they were walking out of the Mermaid Room and across the lobby toward the elevator. "You don't have to tell me what made you change your mind," Raike said. "I really don't give a damn."

"All right." Ellen smiled, unperturbed. "Then I'll stop trying to find the answer."

As they walked from the elevator toward Ellen's suite, Raike started to talk about Sala again. "Did you know before I told you, Ellen, that Sala's wife was a bootlegger's daughter?"

"No."

"Don't you think it peculiar? Just a little improbable?"

"Yes."

"Margarita was the prettiest girl for miles around, black hair, green eyes, a very fiery girl." Unhurriedly, Raike walked down the corridor beside her. "Great vitality. To marry her off was a waste of talent. Can you imagine Sala appreciating anything like that? Sala!"

"I suppose he did." Ellen was only half listening because she was thinking more about what she was going to do about Judd Raike in the next half-hour than about what had happened to Sala twenty years ago.

"They say Sala didn't begin to hit hard times until the depression. I think he was tottering long before that. San Pedro wanted Margarita to marry into high society, and Sala saw a chance to save his land. They both got what they wanted—temporarily."

When Ellen looked surprised, Raike smiled down at her. "Don't misunderstand me. I personally don't object to what he did. I only say he's no better than the next fellow who needs money and sees a quick, if somewhat shady, way to get it. It's all on the same level."

Raike inserted the key into Ellen's door, glancing at her again with that appraising look. "So you see, my dear, if you overlook telling Sala a few details of what you're doing in your time off, don't let it worry you too much. He's had his moments, too."

Raike opened the door and, putting his hand on her elbow in a gesture of possessiveness, guided her into the room. For one of the few times in her life, Ellen began to feel nervous. She wished she hadn't come—it was an incredibly naïve thing to have done. Sparring for time, she walked toward the balcony overlooking the ocean. She felt Raike's hand on her shoulder and it shot through her that this man's touch could stir feelings she had thought she was done with. His arm at her waist could make her, more than she could remember, feel alive.

Ellen had been a widow at twenty-seven, and many times she had looked at a man and thought she wouldn't mind if she let it happen—it was only natural—and then she would look again and the man would seem weak or dull and she would think wearily, Oh, God, I would mind. I would mind terribly to settle for this. Now, and not for the first time with Raike, a swift feeling of desire surged through her. Standing close to him at the door to the balcony, Ellen had to keep reminding herself that with this man she was playing for keeps.

Raike's arm held her close while he bent over her, and suddenly Ellen thought that she was crazy to hold out for the impossible when she could take happiness tonight with only a whisper, a murmur, even silence. It wasn't the things you did that you regretted, it was the things you didn't do. He kissed her and warring choruses drew a line of battle in Ellen's brain. The things you didn't do you regretted; live tonight. But she *was* playing for keeps. She freed her lips from Raike's.

"Judd—please—"

He didn't take her protest seriously but bent over her again, his grip tightening, and Ellen knew that if she didn't stop now she wouldn't stop. A determination that hardly seemed a part of her wrenched her away. She pulled out of Raike's arms, feeling like a foolish schoolgirl with her ridiculous wrestling, more angry at herself than at him. "Please, Judd."

"Well, for God's sake!" he began.

"I'm sorry, Judd. I can't blame you. It was my fault."

Then he knew she meant it and anger burned in his face. "I'm not a well-bred man, Ellen," he said darkly. "I get what I want."

"Of course, my dear," she said, gently. "You should. When you can."

Raike grew silent and Ellen knew he was reflecting on how he would handle this situation, and all she could think was that she was sorry she had come. Terribly sorry.

Raike leaned against the wall. "Ellen, how long has your husband been dead?"

It was a good question and, anticipating the next one, Ellen turned away and looked at the ocean, where scattered lights of boats were blinking on. "Ten years."

"And you've had a lonely bed for ten years?" He said it exactly as she had known he would. Derisive and plainly not believing.

A feeling took root in Ellen that now, in this moment, answering this question, she would seal her fate with Raike. Strange, she thought, because he was hardly a man dedicated to conventional attitudes toward sex. And yet the feeling persisted. "Judd—" she met his angry eyes—"when you ask me that, you're not asking me about myself but only my opinion of you."

"Don't feed me that," he said impatiently. But he was listening.

"Before I answered you—if I were going to," Ellen said, softly, "I'd ask myself, what kind of man is this? And I would answer, a man with power. A man who has conquered an industry singlehanded and doubled, tripled it in a lifetime—who holds almost a whole valley in his hands, hundreds of lives."

She moved a step closer to Raike, who was watching her narrowly. "I'd ask myself—what does he want in a woman? Does he want one who hasn't given herself to many men just out of animal hunger? A woman who in ten years couldn't find an answer to her seeking?"

"A-ah." Raike turned away impatiently.

"Or does he want a woman who is experienced?" Ellen went on, doggedly. "A woman who has known many beds out of the need of the moment? Who might be very good because of that experience? These are two different kinds of women, different right down to the core. You're not asking about me, Judd—" Ellen paused—"because whichever woman I was, I would lie to you gladly."

Raike whirled around, face flaming. "Don't ever try it!"

"I would lie to you, Judd. I'd be the one I thought you wanted—telling you only what I think of you, really, of what your most personal standards are. That's why I won't answer your question, Judd."

Suddenly Ellen knew that it was over. She went into the bedroom and closed the door and took out her suitcase. You couldn't stretch this kind of thing out over a weekend when it went sour on Friday night. A moment later, Raike stood in the doorway.

"What are you doing with that suitcase?"

"I'm going home, Judd."

"The hell you are."

"Offer me friendship, Judd, or marriage." She might as well say it all. "I love you. I'll marry you if you ask me."

"Marriage!" he burst out incredulously. "What do I want to marry you for?"

Ellen turned away. "At any rate, don't offer me some weak mongrel offspring that only vaguely resembles either and hasn't long to live." She finished packing. "Will you send me home in your car, Judd?"

"You walk out on me tonight, Ellen, and by God—" Suddenly Raike roared with laughter. "At least now I know why you came. Good Lord, did you think you could trap me that easily? Take the car." The laughter died abruptly and he darkened again with anger. "Take it and get out."

He picked up the telephone and ordered the car and a bellboy and didn't even look as she went out the door. After she had gone he paced around the room, giving vent to his fury. The more he thought about her accepting his invitation for a weekend, and then welching, the angrier he grew. Probably she didn't welch on Sala Post, probably that was what had stood in her way, for all her talking. Words were cheap. She was quite a talker. Very smooth! Damn it—he banged his fist into his hand—he had wanted that woman! He hadn't felt so hot in a long time. And she had walked out on him because of Sala Post.

Fury burst in him and in a few short steps he was at the telephone and in another minute was talking to Edgar. "You know where I am?" he shouted.

"Of course," Edgar said meekly.

"You know who I came here with?"

"Yes."

"See that Sala Post hears about it."

"What!"

"You heard me. Tonight."

"How shall I let him know?" Edgar said, worriedly.

"Goddammit," Raike shouted. "Can't you ever think of anything yourself?" He slammed down the receiver and went out of the room and slammed the door.

In Sala's garage that Friday evening Parrish and Teet peered under the raised hood of the station wagon. "Ever see such a piece of junk?" Teet patted the radiator affectionately. "A-ah, whatsa matter now, baby?"

"Must be the battery," Parrish said. "She ran this afternoon."

Teet moved his unshaven face about, squinting at the motor. "What this poor heap of trash needs is rejuvenatin'—like them sex hormones. You ever read about them, kid, in the papers?"

Parrish laughed. "What do you need with sex hormones?"

He looked over toward Sala's house, seeking Alison, and saw instead the shabby figure of Lewis Post. "Now what do you suppose he wants?"

"Who wants?"

"Lewis Post. He just went in the back door."

"Ah, he's lookin' for a handout, as usual," Teet said. "You think them sex hormones work like they say, kid?"

Parrish laughed. "Now how in hell would I know?"

"I think it's a fake, but it's a helluva hot idea."

"Keep your mind on the car," Parrish advised him. "By the time you need sex hormones they'll be selling them at Woolworth's."

Teet grinned at the tribute and nudged Parrish with his elbow. "Wouldn't that be sump'n, by God!"

"You think it's the battery?" Parrish looked over Teet's shoulder at the motor of the station wagon. "You want me to try to start her?"

"What's your hurry, kid?" Teet's eyes shifted up to him. "You got a big date? I figured you'd just be settin' around with your ma."

Parrish didn't answer. Now that it was growing dark he wanted to get rid of Teet because tonight he was certain, although he hadn't seen her since the storm, that Alison would come out. "No hurry," he said. "I'm not going anyplace."

"That's what I figured." Teet patted Parrish's shoulder. "I want you to know, kid, I think it's beautiful—you and your ma."

Casually Parrish leaned against Alison's yellow convertible parked between the station wagon and the Rolls Royce. If he showed impatience, he knew, Teet would be curious and stay all the longer.

"Only yesterday I sez to John, 'It's one of the most beautiful things I ever seed.'" A soulful look came over Teet's face. "'The way that boy don't think of nothin' except his ma.' 'Beautiful!' John sez. 'Peculiar— more!' 'John,' I sez, 'how can you say that? It ain't every son'd drop a hot little package like Lucy—drop her like he bit into a apple and found half a worm—just because his ma says please. It's beautiful!' You know what John sez to that?"

Parrish didn't bother to answer. In these monologues Teet needed no encouragement.

"John sez, 'Rats!' 'John,' I sez, 'how can you talk so crude about—'"

"What about the car?" Parrish said.

"You don't have to stick around, kid," Teet said. "You can go up and see your ma."

"I'm not going up to see my ma," Parrish said irritably. "She's not even home."

"She ain't, huh?" Teet's face went into a slow grin. "Where'd she go?"

Parrish realized that Teet had been baiting him. He'd heard that Ellen was away for the weekend and was prying for information. "Boston," Parrish said. "Last chance she'd have with that crazy debut party coming up."

"She go up there all alone?" Teet said, casually. "How come you—"

"Look." Parrish began to get mad. "It's none of your goddam business, you ever think of that?"

Teet grinned. "I never been so insulted."

"Trouble with you is you're a psychopathic snoop."

"And what's the trouble with you, kid?" Teet turned his unshaven face to Parrish, not teasing now, trying to be friendly.

Parrish flushed. "There wasn't anything the matter with me until you started yakking about my mother. Whyn't you think some more about those sex hormones? You were enjoying that. You were getting one helluva boot out of that all right."

"It's a great idea," Teet said. "I gotta admit it."

"Maybe you need 'em after all." Parrish blew up. "There's something goddam old-womanish about someone who does nothing but snoop."

"You're startin' to handle yourself pretty good, kid," Teet said, approvingly. He slammed down the hood of the car. "Ain't enough light left to see what ails this wreck. We'll give her the once-over tomorrow."

"Suits me. I don't care if she never runs again." The side door of the house opened and Parrish froze and then breathed with relief when he saw it was only Lewis Post.

Daylight was nearly gone now, the sun firing the sky before dropping below the tent cloth, and Parrish walked out of the garage, hoping Teet would see that he wanted to be alone. He sat down against a tree, wondering why he had lied about Ellen and telling himself it was just that Teet's filthy, suspicious mind had started him building suspicions, too. It was contagious, like a rotten disease.

Teet came up beside him. "You like to go down to Tower's for a beer or somethin', kid?"

Parrish looked up. "I guess not, fella. Thanks."

Teet regarded him for a moment, perplexed. "You're all done with Lucy, huh?"

"That's a helluva way to put it. As if she were some kind of thing you borrowed or rented." Parrish picked up a couple of small stones and aimed them one at a time at a nearby tree. "Used a while and then returned when you didn't need it any more."

Teet looked at him thoughtfully. "Don't you need it any more, kid?"

Parrish felt his face go red and he was glad it was nearly dark. It was two weeks now and he had felt a need and then, when he thought of Alison, had felt coarse and ashamed of it and tried to push it out of his mind. He watched a little stone bounce off the tree trunk into the long grass.

"Then what's bothering you, kid?"

"I don't feel like such a great man about it."

"Whyn't you move out?"

"Because then I'm raising the whole damn issue of moving in here."

"You're here all the time. Whatsa difference if you move in?"

Parrish didn't answer and presently Teet said, "If you're through and you're so damn all-fired sure of it, what you eatin' yourself up about?"

"Look, I was feeling great until you started all this." But it was true that Teet had touched a sore spot. His treatment of Lucy and staying on there in the house were bothering him more than he liked to admit. "It's not that easy," he said. "I got myself into it. Now I've got to get myself out."

"What's to get out of? You're done. You're through. So you're out."

"Teet, you just can't do a thing like that. This wasn't just a pickup for a night. This was—" He looked away. It didn't seem right to discuss it. "I just feel I owe her something," he finished lamely.

"Like what do you owe her?"

Parrish gestured helplessly, and before he could form a reply an uncertain figure came weaving between the trees and Lewis Post lurched up to them behind a gust of cheap whisky. "Hi, Teet." He showed a few teeth.

"How's every little thing?" Teet said.

"Hello, Buster." Lewis uncorked his bottle. "Care to take a drink with me?"

"Pal," Teet said. "We're talkin'. Beat it."

Wounded, Lewis Post lingered another minute, then heaved his shoulders and wandered off.

"So what was it you thought you owed Lucy?"

Parrish threw another stone at the tree. "I don't know. Just maybe honesty, I guess."

"So be honest with her. Tell her it's over and you don't go for her no more—if that'll make you feel better. Me, I think she's got a pretty good idea without you spelling it out."

Parrish stopped throwing the stones. It was all dark now, the stars dotting the sky, the frogs starting up. Why was he getting into this discussion about Lucy now, when all that filled his mind tonight was Alison? That and this new worry Teet had planted about Ellen.

"You promise her anything, kid?" Teet continued with his crude but realistic logic. "You force yourself on her?"

Parrish laughed. If anything it had been the other way around.

"She was willing, wasn't she?"

Willing! Hell, she'd been eager. Parrish's mind relaxed, began to reach out for other arguments. He remembered the night out in Frenchy's fields and the telephone call from the unknown lover that had sent Lucy flying.

"You can take my word for it, kid, Lucy knows better than to expect anything. She knows it don't work that way." Teet stood up. "You change your mind, kid, come on down to Tower's."

Parrish watched Teet disappear in the darkness. Then the side door of Sala's house opened again. Parrish jumped to his feet, hurrying toward it, when a form moved into the doorway and he saw that it wasn't Alison, but Sala. Abruptly he stopped, disappointed. The door closed and he knew Sala was standing on the porch in the dark.

"Look at him!" a rancorous voice said at Parrish's elbow and he started and then saw that Lewis Post had wandered back. "Look at him standin' there in the dark."

Parrish groaned. He might as well go home. It was useless to wait for Alison with Sala over there and Lewis Post lurking around behind trees. "Why'n hell don't you go home?"

Lewis blinked at him, hurt. Tugging away at his pocket he produced, triumphantly, an unopened bottle. "You want a drink, Buster?" he said. "I'll let you have it from this brand-new bottle."

In spite of his irritation, Parrish grasped the sacrifice Lewis was making. "Thanks, fella," he said. "But why not take it home to the boys?"

"They ain't home," Lewis said, sadly. "Went off and I don't know where they at."

"Probably if you go on home, they'll—" He broke off.

In the quiet summer night a laugh had rung out, dimming the chirp of crickets in the long grass, warming the scents of night air and earth, racing his blood. A laugh and a low-pitched voice that said, "Wiley, how you talk!"

Involuntarily, Parrish took quick steps toward the house, desire rising up in him like a torrent, to mix with anger and resentment. With no clear purpose he raced on for several yards until the slam of a car door stopped him. Stunned, he watched the tail lights go down the drive and heard the sound of the tires die away on the road.

Baffled and hurt, Parrish stumbled across the driveway with no thought of where he was going, except to get away from here. Anger, welling up, wrenched inward, and, abruptly and clearly, as though he stood suddenly in a spotlight, he saw himself for a fool. He had been so sure she would come—but there was no reason for his sureness. It was all in his mind. Self-contempt and hatred flooded him, driving him on in the darkness past Sala's house. Then a voice spoke in the darkness.

"Who's there?" It was Sala, still alone on the porch. "Parrish—?"

"Yes." Parrish kept walking.

"What are you doing here?"

"Don't worry," Parrish said, bitterly. "I'm on my way."

On the porch Sala stood, thin and straight as a reed. "You know your mother isn't here."

Resentful at Sala's questioning his presence, which he had not done for many weeks now, Parrish turned around. "The station wagon broke down, if you want to know." His voice was scraping now with anger piled on anger. "And Teet and I—"

"Do you know where she is, Parrish?" Sala cut in.

"Yes," Parrish countered. "I know."

"Did she tell you, too, that she was going to the beach to visit friends?"

"That's what she said and that's where she is." Parrish turned away.

"Yes." Sala's voice was tired and strained. "She's there."

"O.K." Parrish moved off. "She's there. Then good night."

"Wait a minute, Parrish. You should know it all."

He didn't stop. "I know it all."

"The friend she's with is Judd Raike."

Slowly Parrish came back to the porch. "You're lying!"

"No," Sala said. "It's true and you know it."

"I don't know it!"

"You know she's been seeing him." Sala's hand gripped the rail. "Everyone knows it. And tomorrow everyone will know she's become his—mistress."

"Damn you!" Parrish was up on the porch and over the rail. "You're lying!"

But now Sala seemed to be talking to himself, murmuring, "I know what Raike is—better than anyone on earth, I know."

"You goddam sonofabitch liar!"

"Watch your language to me!"

"Language!" Parrish tore at his hair falling over his eyes. "You're a liar. You hear? Liar!"

But the anger seemed to go out of Sala, leaving him limp with tiredness and defeat. Raising his head a little higher, he moved to the door. "I wish it were a lie, Parrish. With all my heart I wish it were a lie."

The door closed and inside the house the light went out. Parrish stumbled down the porch stairs, telling himself that it wasn't true. He thought of his mother—small and fragile, the pale hair, the clear violet eyes, the cleanness of her. He told himself that she couldn't. It was a lie. He thought of Raike, big bull-like Judd Raike, touching her, holding her, and he clenched his fists. A lie—a lie . . .

"Buster." Lewis Post touched his arm, hesitatingly.

"Oh, God, are you still here?"

"Kinda scares you," Lewis whimpered. "Don't it kinda scare you?"

Rooted to the spot where Lewis had stopped him, Parrish raised his hands to cover his eyes, frustration boiling over in him, poisoning him, making him sore and hot and blind.

"Makes you believe in a living devil," Lewis rambled on. "Him standing there in the dark all that time, just standing there, his flesh 'n' blood out with Raike's son, his girl friend off with Raike hisself, off on a holiday. Raike's got all his land, 'cept this. An' he'll get this, too."

Slowly Parrish uncovered his eyes as he realized that Lewis, knowing the news, must have brought it to Sala.

"All his life, he's had Raike to plague him," Lewis whispered. "Always against him, an' every time Raike wins. It's like they was just the two of 'em to carve up the world an' Raike was gettin' every inch an' every livin' thing and Sala losin' it all, a thing at a time." Lewis took a long gulp from his open bottle, terrified at the thought. "By Jeez, it gives you the creeps."

Parrish stared at Lewis. "Who told you?"

"Edgar tole me." Lewis bobbed his head. "Down to Tower's. He struck up a chat and he tole me. I thought Sala ought to know, what with her tendin' to Alison and all."

Parrish sat down and buried his head in his arms, too sore even to cry.

Lewis nudged him with the unopened bottle. "Buster, you look like you ought to take a drink. I'll sell it to you—just for what it cost me. A dollar eighty-nine." Lewis pushed the bottle at Parrish. "It's a man's drink, by Jeez."

Parrish just stared at the bottle and Lewis expertly removed the cork. "I gotta ask you for the dollar eighty-nine," he apologized. "On account of I gotta replace it."

Parrish gave him two dollars.

"Go on, now—get it in ya."

The whisky tasted terrible, burned his mouth and his stomach, and he bent over, hiding his face on his knees, seeing before his eyes a picture of Raike's face and his shoulders hunched like a bull, and it sickened him. He took another long gulp of the horrible, raw-tasting, gut-burning whisky and swallowed it and forced down still another. Then he choked and gasped and uncontrolled sobs broke from his throat. When at last he looked up, numb and exhausted, he could barely distinguish Lewis Post, stupid and bleary-eyed, watching him.

"Take another drink, Buster."

Parrish stared wearily, the sharp edges of pain dulled now with tiredness and drunkenness.

"Go on, go on." Lewis closed Parrish's hand over the bottle and pushed it to his lips. "Time a man needs a drink is time he ought to have it."

Parrish allowed Lewis to pour it into his mouth. Then he gagged. "No more. No." He jerked his head away. "No more."

Lewis focused his own half-seeing eyes on Parrish. "You gonna get sick?"

"I don't know," Parrish groaned, while his head bobbed dizzily.

"You don't feel good you better walk." Lewis Post tugged at his sleeve. "Walk—walk around. You don't walk around, you'll puke all over the place, fer crissake."

Propping him up with one hand, Lewis took an eager gulp out of his own bottle and wiped his mouth on his filthy coat sleeve. "Walk—walk." Together they began to walk up and down the driveway.

"There," Lewis grunted, pausing when they reached the garage. "Feelin' better?"

Parrish nodded several times, hardly seeing who his companion was. "I feel great." He clapped Lewis on the back. "You're a real pal."

"Don't you think we been hanging around this dump long enough?" Lewis demanded. "It's goddam dark and gloomy, if you ask me."

"I'll say."

"Let's go someplace where they's a little action and he-man's liquor." Parrish nodded.

"I don't think we ought to walk, Buster."

"Don't have to," Parrish told him. "I got the station wagon."

Parrish climbed into the driver's seat and Lewis climbed in beside him and said, "We're off."

Parrish shook his head sadly. "I forgot," he said. "It's busted. Dead."

Lewis looked as if he were going to cry, and only his bottle saved him. Then his face brightened and he nudged Parrish, nodding toward Alison's yellow convertible. Simultaneously, they got out of the station wagon, solemnly closing the doors, and moved across the garage to the yellow convertible. Parrish climbed into the driver's seat while Lewis climbed in beside him. Then Parrish got out again.

"Damn near forgot to open the garage doors," he said, and he went around behind the car to open them.

Then Lewis got out and shut the garage doors behind the station wagon. "Don't need these for anything." He gave a loose grin. "We got a good car now."

They got back into the car and Parrish put his hands on the wheel and then let them fall dejectedly to his lap. "No keys."

"You mean we can't go?" Lewis whimpered.

Parrish dropped his head back on the leather upholstery, feeling terribly tired and dizzy, yearning for sleep. Around him the garage was spinning, and he pressed his hot face against the leather upholstery, feeling the coolness. From far away Lewis Post was tugging at his arm.

"We ain't licked yet," Lewis was mumbling. "Come on, Buster, we got one more to go."

"Mmm?"

"Don't konk out on me now," Lewis begged. "This one'll go."

"Where we going?" Parrish murmured.

"The Rolls'll go," Lewis blubbered with excitement. "The Rolls'll go."

With Lewis tugging at his elbow, Parrish stepped out of the car, weaving toward the Rolls Royce.

"This one ain't locked." Lewis darted ahead, excitedly. "I tried it. It ain't."

Parrish sagged heavily against the door of the Rolls Royce. "I can't drive this one—don't know how. It's all different."

"I can," Lewis screamed. "Don't forget I'm a Post, too."

"You're right," Parrish answered.

Opening the door, Lewis shoved Parrish in and scurried around behind the car, threw open the garage doors, and jumped into the driver's seat.

With a jerk, the car lurched back out of the garage into the broad driveway and Lewis jammed on the brakes, throwing Parrish against the door. Tires skidded on gravel and then the car lurched violently forward and tore across the driveway, past the garage, past the tent cloth, toward the barn and the sheds. Parrish sat up, confused. "Hey, where you going?"

Tent cloth shot past like sheets on a clothesline and Lewis banged into a post and backed up and shot forward again, the side cloth ripping off and dragging along, flapping across the windshield. His vision blocked, Parrish rubbed his eyes and groped for the windshield, and then saw that it was tent cloth across the outside that cut off his sight and that Lewis couldn't see anything, either.

"Slow down," he yelled. "Slow down."

He grabbed at Lewis's arm and Lewis waved him off and the car lurched so sharply that Parrish was thrown violently against the wheel and a moment later they crashed through the wall of the barn.

He just wanted to lie there and go to sleep. He had heard boards ripping out and breaking glass—he could smell whisky spilled in the car. Slowly he became aware of a throbbing in his hand. He opened an eye and, without emotion, saw blood oozing down to his wrist. Then he saw Lewis

Post standing a few feet away, surveying the wreck. In a daze, Parrish pushed at the door and dragged himself out of the car. Lewis sat down dejectedly and Parrish went over and sat next to him, and then he was startled to see that they were sitting on the setting machine, inside the barn, and that half of the Rolls Royce had crashed through the wall.

Lewis whispered, awesomely, "It's like it was the end of Sala. That Rolls was the last thing he ever bought when he had all the money they was to have." Then he snickered. "The end of Sala. An' I ain't sorry. Him with his high 'n' mighty ways."

Returning hesitantly to the car, Lewis found the broken whisky bottle, looked at it sadly, and threw it away. "I'm pretty goddam glad, you wanna know the truth. Lordin' it all over, with me beggin' and thankin' all the time. Yes, Sala. Please, Sala. Everything I ever had from Sala I had to beg for—an' me a Post, same's him." He clutched Parrish's shirt. "I'm a Post, same's him, y'hear? I got the same rights as him."

He jerked away, his voice rising to a wild, choked laugh. "By God, that's the prettiest sight I seen in years. I'm glad we mashed up his car and he's done with, 'cause I hated his goddam dirty guts. Sala's done with! Goodbye, Sala! So long! You're done now!" Feverishly, he scrambled up on the wreck, perched there like a bird, looking eagerly first at one part, then another, laughing until he was crying.

And then suddenly John was there, pulling the hysterical Lewis off the hood of the car, brutally slapping his face while Lewis began to scream. Then a light went on in the barn and Sala came in. And through it all Parrish sat still on the setting machine, as if in a nightmare, watching.

"I'll get the tractor and pull it out of here," he heard John say, and he saw Sala nod.

In a corner, Lewis Post cowered, trying to push himself out of sight, and Sala slowly began to circle the Rolls Royce, his hand half extended toward it as if wanting to touch it and yet not wanting to, three times around, four times around, and then there was the steady sound of the approaching tractor, stopping on the other side of the ripped barn wall.

Moving for the first time, walking unsteadily, Parrish followed Sala out the door and around the barn. With the headlights of John's truck turned onto the wreck, Sala was trying to help John with a chain when Lewis Post scurried up between them, shouting again like a maniac.

"How about if I drive yer tractor for you? Allers wanted to try one of them things. Never had a tractor." He whirled on Sala. "Sala, how come you can't see fit to lend me that tractor when you ain't usin' it? Make things a lot easier—I ain't so young no more."

Sala backed away, speechless with contempt and hatred, and Lewis began to whimper. "Your own cousin. Your own flesh 'n' blood."

Suddenly John threw the chain to the ground. "Get out of here, you filthy bum." He tightened Lewis's shirt around his neck.

"Sala!" Lewis screamed. "Whatcha blamin' me fer? Why me? It was him did it." He pointed to Parrish. "It was him."

John struck him a blow on the face. "Shut up and get out, or I'll wrap this chain around your neck and drag you all the way to the road."

John shoved him away and, still screaming, Lewis lurched off.

Parrish picked up the chain and tried to attach it to the Rolls Royce, but it slipped out of his hand. He was picking it up to try again when he felt John's hand roughly on his shoulder.

"Get out of here," John said tersely. "Go upstairs and sleep it off."

Parrish blinked and picked up the chain again.

"Get out, I said. You ain't no good to yourself or no one else, the shape you're in. Go sleep it off." John pushed him in the direction of the garage and Parrish kept going. "And hereafter, watch who you get mixed up with. You'll be better off."

Parrish stumbled up to Ellen's apartment and lay down, head throbbing, blood caked on his hand. Presently he heard them hauling the Rolls Royce into the garage, the tractor motor grinding, the chain clanking, then John's loud voice and Sala's murmured replies. He lay still in the dark until the noises below stopped and he knew they had left. Then, with the light on, he saw fresh blood still oozing out of his hand and he wrapped a handkerchief around it, drawing the ends between his fingers to hold it in place. The light hurt his eyes and he snapped it out. The farm was dark now, no light from the garage below nor from the house where, he knew, Sala couldn't have gone to sleep but must be sitting alone again in the dark.

Drunkenly, Parrish stood up and roamed through the rooms. Sleep it off! Here! He couldn't stay here at all. Even in the dark, Ellen was everywhere here: her pen on the desk, its gold clip shining in the moonlight; a thin vase with a twig of climbing roses; the scent of her everywhere. Parrish's hand closed around the vase of roses and suddenly he picked it up and hurled it across the room.

Downstairs he heard activity again, heard the garage doors open, and a light went on. Not thinking or caring who it was, he slammed the door of Ellen's apartment and went down the stairs and saw that Sala was back. Confused, Parrish started toward him and then stopped because on the other side of the Rolls Royce he saw Wiley Raike, clean and spotless in a white jacket, carefully examining the wreckage. And near him, between the Rolls and her own convertible, stood Alison, dainty, immaculate, and silent, a remote look on her face, as if she had drawn herself apart from this unpleasantness.

Brazenly, Parrish settled against the side of the garage, but Alison didn't even glance in his direction. Nor did Wiley Raike. The hell with him! Nor did Sala, who looked dead.

Then he saw it. Alison was laughing at him! A noiseless unuttered laugh, but there was no mistaking it. It was on her lips that she strained to keep steady, and in her eyes where she didn't bother to conceal anything. Parrish struggled to focus while the whole garage swam before his eyes. Alison was laughing and calling him the fool that he was. The garage and the car slid away from him and he steadied his head against the door, understanding suddenly that he had taken seriously what had been to Alison just an amusing way to wait out the storm.

When Lucy woke him the next morning pain stabbed at Parrish's head and eyes, shot through his neck and shoulders, down his back. His hand was stiff and sore, his mouth dry. With effort he moved his legs under the tousled sheets and tried to push himself up in the bed, only to sink down again. He buried his face in the pillow.

"Come on, Parrish." Lucy's strong hands on his back urged him gently and firmly to get up.

Opening one eye, Parrish saw the bloodstained handkerchief that had come off his hand, matted and dirty on the pillow. Sunlight burned at his eye sockets and he shut it out. The smell of Lucy was in the bed, an all-too-familiar sensation telling him she had slept the night there. He groped through the vague blank of his memory, trying to reconstruct what had happened.

"Come on, Parrish, you gotta get up."

Through barely parted eyelids he saw Lucy leaning over him, still in her short nightgown, breasts showing fuller than he remembered them, seeming swollen to his blurred vision. Breasts, he remembered, running his sticky tongue over his dry lips, breasts he had caressed brutally and hungrily last night, lying beside the back porch—but was it outside, or was it right here in bed? He buried his head deeper in the limp pillow, tearing at his mind to remember.

He had come home—he couldn't remember how, but he did remember trying to pull himself up the six-foot wall to the front door and slipping down, bruised, and dragging himself around to the back, where he had found Lucy lying in the hammock. Hunching himself in the bed, Parrish groaned. It *was* right there outside on the ground under the hammock.

Outside, under the hammock, and then they had fallen asleep out there on the ground and—he remembered now—he had awakened while it was still dark because he was sick, sick and chilled and stiff, and found that Lucy had covered them with a blanket and stayed with him. Remembering, shame boiled over in him. He'd gotten sick outside, and when he thought he was done they had come inside and he'd gotten sick again in the house, in the bathroom—and somebody had stood outside the closed door screaming at him. Not Lucy. Gramma. Outside the bathroom door, in the middle of the night, Gramma had stood, cackling and shrieking, "It's sin, boy!" He could hear it now. "Your sin's catching up with you."

"The hell with my sins," he had yelled back when he could.

"Ha-ha!" she had chortled. "It's the hand of God—plain as fire in the burning bush—sending you to hell-fire and damnation."

"Great, great!" he had yelled back between retchings. "Now will you get back to your holy-rollin' bed."

"You're doomed," she had screamed out in ecstasy. "Doomed, boy!"

Then he'd heard Lucy coaxing the old hag back to bed and he had washed and gone up to the attic and Lucy had come up and he had slept with her again, and she had kept saying over and over that she wasn't good enough for him but, if he'd have her, she'd live just for him and do for him and him alone and no one but him and he could do anything he wanted with her. The idea had revolted him then and it revolted him now. The last thing he wanted was her sacrificing herself to him or for him—Lucy, or anyone else. He didn't want anyone owning him or devouring him or sacrificing for him. He just wanted to be left alone.

"Oh, Lord," he groaned. "What have I done?"

"I don't know, Parrish," Lucy said.

He opened his eyes and looked at her quickly. "What do you mean you don't know?"

"I just don't know. You came home weavin' and reelin' and mutterin'. Honest to God, Parrish, you was pretty bad off."

With an effort Parrish turned over to look at her.

"My God, you was blind!" Lucy touched his face, her hand feeling wonderfully cool. "I ain't never seen anyone so bad off. Where'd you get it and what for?"

Parrish shook his head slowly, pulling her cool hands over his eyes, struggling to think.

"You was talkin' a mile a minute, hatin' this one, hatin' that one, all burnt up with your hatin'. Your ma, and Sala. And her—Alison, I figure you meant from your mumbling. All 'cept me." Lucy flushed and gave a little laugh.

He remembered.

In a sea of shame he felt himself sinking, sick, lost in the enormity of his deeds. There were blanks, but he remembered, the horror of the night sweeping over him now like a fire. And then he remembered farther back to the cause of it. He remembered Ellen and—he opened his eyes, unwilling even to form Raike's name in his mind. But his passion was spent and he could only suffer now with the misery of the knowledge. There was no strength left in him to translate his frustration again to the ravages of the night before.

Sick and shaking, Parrish tried to work. At ten o'clock, in the mounting heat under the tent cloth, he blacked out.

When he came to he was in Ellen's bedroom, cool and dark, with the shades drawn, and he realized he had awakened to hushed voices in the living room—Ellen's voice, calm and definite, and the other, he recognized, was Sala Post's, hardly audible. He wondered if Ellen was being fired because of him. His head was clear now and he knew well enough what he had done, and he lay in bed, facing up to it, asking himself what he ought to do now. The voices in the next room rose a little.

"It was no kind of thing to tell an eighteen-year-old boy," Sala was saying, his voice strained.

And Ellen said quietly, "I thank you for telling me. I thank you very much."

"When I saw the car coming up the driveway last night I thought it was John coming back, and when it went on to the garage and your lights went on—" Sala paused, and Parrish knew guiltily that he was listening to something not intended for his ears—"I knew it wasn't the wrecked car I'd been thinking about, sitting there in the dark."

Parrish got up to make his presence known, and Sala and Ellen stopped talking. Someone, probably Ellen, had washed his face and hands and applied a clean bandage to his cut palm, and his clothes had been brushed and folded on the chair. Raising the shade, Parrish saw by the sun that it was late afternoon.

A knock sounded on the door and Ellen's voice said, "Come out here when you're dressed, Parrish."

Parrish buttoned his shirt and rolled up the sleeves, working his cut hand with some difficulty, and opened the door.

"Feeling better, Parrish?" Sala's blue eyes sought his, seeming more tired today than accusing.

Parrish nodded. A little uncertainly, he moved into the room, wondering what he should say. He had never been in serious trouble before and he knew this was a situation beyond apology. He stood silently waiting.

"Your mother was here last night, Parrish." Sala's mouth worked strangely, showing guilt and remorse, and then suddenly widened into a smile and pulled Parrish into a smile, too. Embarrassed, Parrish sat down, confused by a sudden feeling of affection for Sala.

Then Sala said, "I'll go now," and left without saying more.

"Parrish," Ellen murmured, "what I have caused!"

With a hollow feeling Parrish walked over to the window. "What's everyone being so charitable about? I'm the one who did it all and the blame seems to be falling everywhere except where it belongs. On me."

Below, he saw Sala stop and take another look at his poor smashed-up car and then walk wearily across the yard.

Ellen came over and stood near him. "Sala says he drove you to it, Parrish—that he told you—"

He couldn't look at her. "Yes, he told me."

"He blames himself. It wasn't a thing to tell a young boy."

Parrish shrugged impatiently. "That doesn't change things."

"No." Ellen looked at him searchingly. "Parrish, Sala told me Lewis Post was driving the car."

Parrish searched his memory. Until now his thoughts had not even included Lewis Post.

"Were you driving?"

Parrish struggled to remember. He tried to picture himself behind the wheel of the Rolls Royce, starting it, releasing the brake, shifting gears. The picture didn't come. He didn't know how to drive it. "I don't think so," he said at last. "I don't think I was driving. But I was in it—there's no doubt of that."

Ellen nodded.

"What shall I do about the car?" he said after a while. He hated to ask, feeling small and dependent, but he honestly did not know the answer.

"What can you do?"

"Can it be fixed?"

"I don't think anybody has tried to find out."

"Maybe with Teet—"

"If you can, Parrish, you should," Ellen said. "If you can't, then I don't know. Parrish, how did Sala know Lewis was driving?"

Parrish shook his head. "He didn't know."

"They didn't find you still in the car—Sala and John?"

"No," Parrish said, positively. "We were out of the car."

Sala had lied about this to Ellen, Parrish thought, giving him a complete out if he chose to take it. Sala Post, the first man he had hated, had tried to protect him. "He was bluffing. He didn't know." Then he said, "He figure to do anything about Lewis?"

"Parrish, you know he can't. He knows what Lewis is. He knows better and with more horror than either you or I will ever know. But Lewis is a Post and if Sala acts to destroy him in any way he destroys something of himself."

The intensity in her voice belied Ellen's cool exterior. "But Sala's a man with great integrity, Parrish, and a great sense of justice."

Parrish looked at her, puzzled. "You falling in love with Sala?"

"No," Ellen said. "But he's the finer of the two."

"You mean Raike?"

Ellen nodded. "Sala asked me to marry him, Parrish. Just now."

"Did Raike?"

"No."

"That why you came home?"

Ellen nodded. Then she blushed, a rare display of emotion for her, and began to busy herself about the room. "But I hope he will, Parrish."

But she wasn't as confident as usual. Seeing the quick flush touch his mother's cheeks, Parrish thought of Lucy. That was how Lucy had looked this morning, sitting on his bed, telling him that he had sworn he hated everyone but her while he twice made love to her last night.

Responsibility hung heavily on Parrish today and he knew he had to leave Lucy's now. It was one thing when he had thought he loved her. Last night was a different thing entirely. To remain, letting Lucy hope it would be the same as before and wait each night and finally realize, after his many lame excuses, that he had come back only in drunkenness—to remain now would be to be less a man. Parrish's thoughts came back to his mother. "They're both too old for you, I think," he said.

"Parrish, no they're not!"

"You don't have to marry either one. You don't have to get married."

"Parrish, I want to get married," Ellen said. "I can't hold you much longer. You'll leave me."

"That's not a good enough reason to pick one of these two."

He felt strongly that they were both wrong for her, and then he asked himself whether he would feel that any man was wrong for her, denying it instantly and then wondering whether you could really be honest with yourself in a thing like this. He asked himself if he wasn't holding on more tightly than his mother.

Ellen was watching him, mistaking his silence for protest. "Don't worry, Parrish," she said. "I've waited ten years. I'm not going to rush into anything now without knowing what I'm doing. And besides—" she flushed again, embarrassed—"only one of them has asked me."

"If you want," Parrish said, surprised that he felt nothing as he said it, "I'll move in with you—until—"

Ellen knew better than to show how much she wanted it. She only nodded while she continued to fuss about the room.

Parrish went down and packed his things. There was nobody home and he waited a little while and when no one came decided he would come back later to tell them and to say something to Lucy. And then he stood in front of the house, waiting for the bus, looking at the sun hitting the dirty window panes and at the green front door, six feet off the ground, with no porch and no stairs.

He asked himself why he was going back. Was it because of his mother? Or to get away from Lucy? Or was it somehow mixed up with the one thing he had not admitted all day, although it haunted him and he knew that it had happened? Was it mixed up somehow with remembering that Alison had laughed at him—because he, and he alone, had so widened the gulf between them that he would have to bend far her way to bridge it again?

11

No MATTER how many times Parrish entered a shed at night when the fires burned, it always struck him, as he stepped through the door, that it looked more like a setting for some primitive African rite than a phase of a twentieth-century industry. Even the way they spoke of these fires, burning three days and three nights, was ritualistic.

In daylight it was not so bad. Though the sheds were closed tight, enough light filtered in to reveal the interior exactly as it was. The tobacco leaves hung close together, seven tiers high, the bottom ones so low he had to stoop when he walked to avoid damaging them. In daylight you could see the leaves, still green, starting to dry to a brown tinge at the edges, and the even rows of shallow pans every six feet along the dirt floor, burning charcoal—gray ash, red coals, and over them the black chunks you were adding. You could see the concrete blocks holding the upright posts of the scaffolding and read on them the names the women had scribbled with lipstick, the Jamaicans with charcoal, and here and there an obscenity that could have been written by either. In the late afternoon when Parrish took over the watch you could see it all for what it was, a shed of tobacco hung in tiers over pans of burning charcoal. At night it was different.

At night, as you made your way between fires, with the added light of a single lantern you carried, you saw only the patterned glow of red coals at your feet, evenly spaced in the blackness, and the shadows of the bottom leaves, hanging like something dying, over your lowered head. At night you didn't see the crudely scrawled obscenities or the half-eaten sandwich stuck in the dirt but only the red glow and the shadows, and you smelled the terrifically heavy smell of tobacco, more suffocating in the hot, close air than the sweetest, sickliest incense, and you thought again, as Parrish did now, that it looked like a setting for voodoo.

He picked up the lantern, pausing a moment to get used to the strong smell. In the distance he heard the whistle of the New York train that crossed Cortland Street at 8:53. Sitting alone nights, you noticed sounds, made friends with them as sharers of your solitude, as signs along the way to eleven o'clock, when Percy, the old man who sat up all night because, he said, he was too old to sleep, would relieve him.

Parrish walked down between the pans to the thermometer and recorded on the card nailed to the post that at 8:53 P.M., August 28, the temperature in this shed was ninety-six degrees. Tonight was the third night in this shed. Parrish would add coals now and again before he left at eleven, and Percy would add them through the night, and in the morning these fires would be allowed to die. Tomorrow night they would be at another shed. Parrish moved over to the side, where the bags of charcoal were piled.

Outside he heard the familiar sound of a pair of dogs tinkling past in the night and then, as he brought the lantern close to find the open bag, he heard the unfamiliar sound of a car approaching down the country road alongside the sheds. It was an old road, leading nowhere except around Sala's property and, except when they worked in these far fields and sheds, it was rarely used. Straightening up, Parrish listened for the car to go past. When it stopped, he picked up the lantern and went outside to see who it was.

"Parrish?" a voice called to him softly before he had the door closed behind him, and Parrish recognized it instantly. It was Alison. His hand dropped from the latch. The door squeaked open, swung uncertainly on its rusty hinges as he started toward the car.

"You'd better shut that door," Alison said in a practical voice.

He went back and shut it and propped a board to hold it tight and, still carrying the lantern, walked over to Alison's car. By the small glow he saw her smiling at him, friendly and quite at ease, as if it were the usual thing for her to come here, as if three weeks hadn't passed since he had seen her last, the night of the wreck.

"What are you doing here?" Parrish blurted out.

"I only heard tonight that you've been watching the fires." She looked over her shoulder and gave a little shudder. "Don't you get awfully lonesome out here?"

"I don't mind."

"Aren't you going to ask me to get out?" She gave a little laugh. "Parrish, you're not very happy to see me!"

Parrish opened the car door. He wasn't sure whether he was happy or not, or whether he wanted her to stay. "You're about the last person I expected to come riding up that road," he said.

"Who were you expecting?"

"I wasn't expecting anybody."

Alison tilted her head up. "Then if you weren't expecting anybody, I'm glad I came."

Parrish closed the car door, sensing that she was teasing him and wondering why she had bothered to come way out here for that.

"I thought after you moved in," she said, "we'd see something of you. Instead, you've disappeared as completely as if you'd fallen down a hole."

"I've been watching the fires."

"I know that now, but it took me a long time to find out. I can't ask direct questions—" Then she stopped. "Parrish, you're not glad to see me."

"I'm surprised," he said. "Yes, I'm glad to see you."

Alison smiled at him, speaking softly and intimately, as though they had known each other forever. "You should have let me know—I thought all this time you were working in the garage fixing the car."

"I was at first." Parrish edged away a little, talking rapidly. "But now I watch the fires until eleven, so Teet's working on the car alone. I wasn't much help, anyway. I don't know that much about cars, and Teet's a genius at it. You know Teet."

"No," she said. "I don't know Teet."

He looked at her, a little surprised. "Well, anyway, he knows all there is to know about it," he went on because it was a comfortably impersonal subject, "so he's fixing it. He's moving right along, now that we've finally got the parts. It wasn't easy, getting parts."

"I shouldn't think you'd have been able to at all, except possibly in a museum."

"For a while I didn't think we would, either. Tower finally found them someplace. For a helluva price."

"Is that why you're working a double shift—to pay for them?"

"Well—yes. Look, are you planning to stay here a while?"

"That depends on you, Parrish."

"I've got to feed the fires. I was just starting when you drove up. You want to come inside with me?"

She wrinkled her nose. "I despise that smell. And it's so much stronger inside."

"Then will you wait for me?"

Alison smiled. "Of course," she said.

Inside the shed, Parrish closed the door between him and Alison and stood still a moment. He had thought a great deal about this, the last few weeks, alone nights out here. He knew that Sala had been very decent about the car and about his moving in with Ellen the next day, and he knew, too, that letting him live on the farm was an act of trust. For three weeks he had made no effort to see Alison, telling himself that it was a matter of honor. Now he suspected that his restraint had been as much self-defense as honor. He had expected that he would be rebuffed. With a tacit invitation now, just outside the door, honor was wavering.

Holding the lantern, he made his way to the charcoal pile, filled a bucket from the open bag, and argued with his conscience. He had been honorable, he told himself. He hadn't gone to her. She had come to him— that was different. He started to fill the pans, adding a shovelful of coal to each fire. This had nothing to do with his living on the farm. Out here, he was as far from the house as at Lucy's.

It wasn't enough. A trust was a trust, not a halfway thing, subject to convenient conditions. There was nothing halfway about Sala's never mentioning the wreck. There were no conditions imposed when Sala said he could move in. His trust was implied, and Sala had not felt it necessary to spell it out.

The door opened and Alison came in.

"What's taking you so long?" she whispered, standing close to the door.

"Wait a minute," he called, his voice sounding strange and loud in the dark. "I'll come and get you."

"Just hurry up," she whispered. "I don't like it out there alone."

He picked up the lantern and went down between the glowing fires.

"I don't like it in here, either," she said. "It's so dark and hot."

She looked like a frightened child, and he reached out and took her hand, thinking that it would be better if she had waited outside. There was something about these fires and low shadows that made playing the gentleman seem thin and unimportant. "Walk along with me," he said. "It won't be long."

She stood close to him, moving with him from fire to fire, and each time Parrish stood up to move to the next he knew that he had only to touch her to have her in his arms, and it wasn't easy to keep reminding himself about honor and trust. By the time he had finished the last pan it had become very hard indeed, and he dropped the bucket of charcoal quickly and led her out of the shed.

"Ugh," she laughed, while he propped the board against the door. "I hate it in there."

Outside, in the clear cool night, it was better. Alison thrust aside her irrational fears and became herself again and it was easier than when there had been the added impulse to hold her to protect her. Parrish led her over to an old blanket that he moved from shed to shed to lie on after the ground grew damp. "Why do you hate it in there?" he asked, sitting beside her.

"Does anyone like it?"

"I do."

"It's awful. It's an awful smell."

"I like the smell, too."

"We can't all be the same, Parrish," she said lightly. "You don't mind if I just go right on hating it, do you?"

"No," he said quietly. "I don't mind."

The dogs tinkled past again and Parrish waited until the sound died, wondering what there was for dogs way out here that they couldn't find closer to home. Then he looked at Alison, puzzled, and wondered the same thing about her. What could he possibly have that would interest a girl like this, draw her out here where, if she were discovered, it could lead only to trouble. It was far, far more sensible for her to laugh at him as she had done that awful night of the wreck. Many a night since, that mocking unuttered laugh had torn at him, but it made more sense than this.

"I think, Parrish," she said, "that you would rather I hadn't come."

"No," he protested. "I'm glad you're here."

She looked at him narrowly. "You're not expecting someone else, some little thing who carries lath or something?"

"Of course not." She was changing her manner now, turning on that cool, remote style of hers that made her seem miles away and a different girl. But these sudden changes didn't surprise him any more.

"I mean, if you are, darling, just say so and I'll leave you."

"I'm not expecting anyone," he said. "I'm just, well—I just can't figure out why you came."

She gave a low laugh, tossing her head back. "Parrish, this farm is spoiling you!"

He looked at her clear, perfect profile, elegantly tilted to the stars, her heavy hair falling back, and the way he was beginning to feel he decided he had better think of some more work to do.

Her eyes came back to him now. "I thought, darling, that we were becoming rather good friends, or didn't it mean that to you?"

Parrish swallowed. "What," he said in a queer voice, "did it mean to you?"

"Why, Parrish," she teased, lowering her lids demurely. "I thought after the storm surely you would offer to marry me. Of course, I couldn't accept, knowing you such a short time, so you'd have been perfectly safe."

"That's what I want," he said. "To be nice and safe."

"I believe you do!" Suddenly she moved to go.

"Look," he said, heatedly. "I didn't think you wanted to have anything to do with me after the wreck—the way you laughed. You were disgusted and I didn't blame you, so I stayed away. What are you laughing at now?"

"Darling, darling—"

He wished she wouldn't be so glib with that "darling" business when he was having a hard time even finding the right words to use.

She said it again. "Darling, I wasn't laughing at you. I was laughing with you."

"I wasn't laughing. I felt pretty lousy about the whole thing."

"I know you did, Parrish." She touched his arm and he felt goose bumps. "But I was delighted to see what I thought was the end of that awful relic. It was always a nightmare to me. I'm sorry you're fixing it."

"It means a lot to your father."

"It means too much to him—just like this land and all this tobacco." She sat with hands clasped around her knees, looking at the stars again. "Parrish, you'll never know the agony I suffered over that car, just to be seen in it—and everywhere I went I was taken in it. I'd beg him to stop a block away and let me walk, I was so embarrassed, but he never would. I don't suppose you can understand. You think I'm wrong to hate it so, when my father loves it."

He wasn't thinking of the rightness or wrongness, but only of her intensity. She was sitting straight, wide-eyed, one hand clasped very tight over the other, and he could read her hatred and thought how acutely she must have felt the pain and he couldn't help but wonder a little why.

"Just like all this," she said. "The tobacco and the shed and the awful smell. I didn't always hate that smell. I actually used to play in the sheds, not way out here but close to the house. I used to watch from the day they started the seedbeds until the cloth came down and it was winter. I loved it."

"What changed you?" Parrish said. "Why did you start to hate it?"

Her green eyes traveled over to the cloth. "When I realized I had to live out here away from all the people I knew and all the fun, just because my father wouldn't leave his plants. Because he says a man has to live on his land."

"He probably has a point there," Parrish said. "It seems if you got too far away, you'd lose touch—"

"Judd Raike doesn't live on his land," she said.

"No."

"Judd Raike has never lived on his land. Need I say more?"

They were both silent, aware that Judd Raike had taken on a significance this past month beyond the fact that he had taken Sala's land.

"And he," Alison said bitterly, "can have anything he wants. Including your mother."

"He doesn't have my mother." But he said it quietly. He couldn't be angry at her.

"He has only to decide he wants her."

It was true, Parrish knew, but he went through the motions of denying it. "I'm not so sure. It's weeks since she's spoken of him."

"Maybe she doesn't speak of him," Alison said. "But she doesn't give my father an answer one way or the other. He'd marry her tomorrow." Suddenly she laughed. "I'll bet he never expected that when he hired a watchdog for me."

She fell silent and in the still shadows of the sheds, next to the deserted road that nobody traveled, Parrish could feel the wanting they shared as they sat inches apart, not touching. In the darkness he opened and closed his hands, examining palms he couldn't see, and then lowered his head to his knees, knowing that he could not hold out much longer.

Abruptly Alison stood up. "Good night, Parrish."

He looked up quickly. "Where are you going?"

"Back where I came from."

"Why? I have another hour here."

"I couldn't care less."

In a step he was at her side. "Now what's wrong?"

"This place has spoiled you, Parrish. I liked you better when you first came."

Now that she was leaving, he couldn't let her go. "What's wrong? What'd I do?"

"Probably it's these long hours," she mocked him. "Working this double shift saps your vitality. Probably you have no strength left for emotions."

"It's not that," he said angrily.

"Then what is it? Do you find me so unattractive that you can't bear to touch me?"

He caught her wrist to keep her from getting into the car. "It's all I can do not to touch you!" he cried. "And you know it."

She tried to move away. "Please let go of my wrist."

"Alison—" he pleaded, searching for words to explain, words that had no real meaning for him any longer. "It's just—just that your father has been very decent with me—"

"And you thought you'd be a gentleman."

"Yes."

"Then please be one and let go of my wrist."

"I don't want you to go."

"But I want to go," she said coolly. "I'm sorry, Parrish, but the world is full of gentlemen with more practice than you—when I'm in the mood for a gentleman. Now I want to go home."

"No."

"You're hurting me."

"I'm sorry," he said, without releasing his grip. "Alison—"

"Let go of me, Parrish, or I'll scream."

"Scream."

"You'll get thrown out." Her voice rose angrily. "You'll get fired."

He smiled into her blazing eyes. "What will you say you were doing here?"

A look of angry defeat crossed her face and for a moment she couldn't find an answer, but for Parrish it was a hollow triumph. Already his conscience was asserting itself. He had caused enough trouble around here. He released her wrist and silently opened the car door.

After she had gone, he felt empty. There was no surge of righteousness, no sense of honor. Honor was only a faint candle next to the fire that burned for Alison. All Parrish felt now was misery because she had come to him and he had let her go.

12

HEY, GLADSTONE."

"Hello, Addie."

"Hello, yourself," Addie giggled. "Who you takin' to the party, Gladstone?"

"You askin' him, Addie?"

"I was hopin' he'd be askin' me," Addie giggled. "Here I been dressin' up like a doll all week, Gladstone, just so's you'd ask me and you ain't even noticed."

Addie put her hands on her mammoth hips and walked down the shed a few feet, wiggling her bottom in the dirty tight-fitting jeans while the other girls screamed with laughter.

She was talking about the harvest party that was held each year in the old barn on the first Saturday night after the cloth was all down. It was considered a big event and the entire crew came, bringing husbands or wives, boy friends or girl friends. Since early morning when Teet had begun to take down the cloth, the girls had been talking of nothing else.

"Get back there, Addie," John ordered. "And keep your ass to yourself."

Unoffended, Addie wiggled back up the shed. "I ain't offerin' it to you, John," she yelled.

"Thanks."

"You comin' to the party, John?" Eileen called. "Who you takin'?"

"Ah, he wouldn't take anybody." Addie chewed her gum and giggled. "He's gotta go stag so's he can give all the girls a break. Be a great lover."

Eileen shrieked and John came over to where they were working. "You wouldn't like to maybe shut up and try workin'?"

Addie giggled. "O.K., lover."

"These keeds, they get on John's nerves," Gladstone murmured to Parrish. "Especially Addie."

"I don't know why," Addie said. "I just mind my own business and everything I do he yells at me." She thrust out her arms and wiggled again to tease John and then stepped back to work.

Perched six feet off the ground on the crossbar, Parrish laughed, thinking that Addie looked exactly like a fat pig, bundled up in a huge navy pea jacket she had probably acquired off the back of some sailor. Compared to the near-nakedness in which they had worked unconcerned all summer, the girls all looked different now, squat and dumpy in heavy woolen sweaters or jackets. Even Lucy, he thought, young as she was, looked dumpy in that old leather jacket. He let his eyes go over to her. He didn't remember that jacket fitting so tightly in the spring. Lucy was getting fat.

"Gladstone," Addie called again. "Are you here?"

"I am here," Gladstone said. "What ees not frozen."

"That's the truth," Eileen said. "Honest to God, would you think it could get so cold anywheres in September?"

"All right," John bawled. "Cut the bellyachin'. You got a lot more to take down and it'll be a lot colder yet."

"Ain't you cold, John?"

"How can he be cold when he ain't human?" Addie screamed with laughter while John went over to pull shut the door that had swung open.

Outside, Parrish could see, the sun was bright. It was hard to believe that just the layers of tobacco and keeping the doors shut could make the shed so cold and damp this time of the year. But they needed this dampness to take down the laths of cured tobacco. Without it, the leaves became too dry and broke when handled. Twice this month they'd had to stop taking down to wait for rain, and now, when the damp was right, they worked quickly just to get the tobacco down off the scaffolding, not stopping to strip the leaves off the laths. For now, they only laid it on the dirt floor, placing each lath tight against the next, building a box as they went, the laths forming the sides and top, with the leaves inside. It was airtight, and, packed like this, the tobacco would keep indefinitely without further drying out. Later they would come back and strip it off the laths and pack it into crates for shipment. Parrish thought he had never seen a business so full of little tricks as tobacco. There was nothing complicated about those lath boxes, but it was an ingenious idea and you wondered who had thought it up in the first place.

"What about you, Parrish?" Addie interrupted his thoughts. "Who you takin' to the harvest party?"

Parrish paused in taking a lath. He had not even thought about going to the harvest party. All he ever thought about these days was Alison. Clinging to his resolve, he hadn't seen her, but nothing could drive her out of his mind.

Addie giggled. "You ought to take Mary, Parrish."

Old Mary let her wrinkled face, tied in a brown shawl, crack into a sour smile. "Yah, yah," she said. "I gotta go alone, like John. Give all the boys a chance."

"You hear that, Parrish, you're outta luck."

"Mary, you're breaking my heart," Parrish said.

"Broken heart is good for you," Mary said. "Teach you something, maybe."

"Oh, my Gawd, she's at it again," Addie said. "You startin' your preachin' again, Mary?"

"Startin' nothin'," Mary muttered. "I just sayin' smart boy, but don't mean he know much. I'm an old woman and I know it's the truth. He got a lot to learn."

A silence fell over the girls, one of those meaningful silences when everyone was thinking the same thing. Parrish could see Lucy bent over, working quietly and steadily, placing lath tight against lath with the leaves inside; but her face reddened and he knew their thoughts had to do with Lucy and him.

Probably they were thinking he was a heel not to be taking Lucy to the party. Until now it hadn't crossed his mind, and now that it did he guessed they were probably right. The best thing you could say about the whole way he had treated Lucy was that he was a stinker. He knew how she felt—he had only to look at her to see how she'd felt since he left her, letting herself go like that, getting fat and droopy.

But it would have been worse to go on dishonestly. And it was crazy even to be thinking that way, as if he could ever touch Lucy again when all he ever thought about, working, eating, or sleeping, was Alison. He wasn't planning to go to that party at all. Even now, while he was joking with Mary, the picture of Alison lingered in his mind, the lovely, deep green eyes, the way she'd opened them slowly and they had glowed after he'd kissed her; and he could almost feel the way her thick hair had brushed his arm.

Then, down below, Lucy stood up from building the box and rubbed her back and moved. She turned sideways to him and walked over to get some more lath and he just happened to be looking in her direction when she did it; and suddenly he saw what he had not seen before, and he had to hold onto the next crossbar to keep from falling off the scaffolding.

Lucy was pregnant.

He stood balanced on the beam, holding a pair of laths heavy with leaves, and stared at her, horrified. Then he realized that Lucy was looking at him, and their eyes met while his cheeks flamed scarlet, and they exchanged a look that said everything.

Long after Lucy had turned away he continued to stare at her, and with every moment it became more apparent. He must have been blind not to see it before. He stood perfectly motionless on the beam until Addie looked up and said, "Well, lover, you gonna hand me them laths or not?"

Parrish bent over and handed the laths to her and automatically reached up for another pair. He would ask Lucy at lunch. But he didn't have to ask to know.

Hearing Lucy confirm it added little to his misery. He walked with her up and down the path next to the shed, a little away from the rest, walking so fast she had to take little running steps to keep up with him, hardly noticing that she was puffing for breath.

"Parrish—" she caught his arm—"slow down. I can't go so fast."

He stopped then and turned to look at her, and at last he forced himself to ask the question. "Lucy, is it mine?"

He knew it sounded terrible, as if he thought her a common slut, but he knew—he *knew*—there had been others. And even while he waited for her answer, looking down into the flushed, sweet face with the big brown eyes and the dark messy curls, he was only half thinking of her—that she was just a child and what a rotten break for her. The other half of his mind was on Alison, who never looked hot or messy but was always cool and immaculate and lovely, and he thought that never during these past terrible weeks had he wanted Alison so much as now.

He looked back to Lucy. Oh, God, he thought, she's going to cry. He reached out and touched her arm. "Lucy."

Lucy turned away. "If you wasn't so dumb," she blurted out, "you'd know. If you just wasn't so dumb!"

Sick with guilt, Parrish told himself that this was still Lucy, not just some tramp he had picked up for a night. Very unwillingly, he told himself that if it was his, he would do the right thing. "All right, Lucy," he said after a long silence. "You should have told me."

She whirled around, red-faced and defiant.

"I'll marry you, Lucy." He said it after much too long a wait. "Lucy, please don't cry."

She turned away again, not wanting to look at him, and he told himself he couldn't blame her. It was a fine proposal he had made. Great. Very gallant. Oh, hell! Who was he kidding? If he still loved her, he wouldn't have been avoiding her all these weeks.

"You don't have to marry me, Parrish." Her voice came small and tight.

"It's all right, Lucy. I will."

She turned on him as if she were going to leap at him and claw his eyes out. "It ain't yours," she screamed. The tears made rivers on her dusty cheeks. "It ain't yours."

Relief flooded through Parrish so that he could scarcely stand. His heart began to beat again and he had a wild, crazy feeling that he ought to rush out and thank somebody for sparing him.

"If you wasn't the dumbest one on earth," Lucy was sobbing, "you'd see I'm four months along, easy. My God, look at me!"

Parrish sat down on a rock and drew Lucy down beside him and held her hand.

"My God, Parrish." She started to laugh, and he thought she was getting hysterical and put an arm around her. "My God, it ain't funny but I gotta laugh. Count—count. It's September. August, July, June, May." She counted off the months on her fingers. "It was July before I started with you."

He loved her. At that moment he loved her more than anyone in the world, for the reprieve she had given him. He brushed her forehead with his lips and she smiled up at him, calmer now, and he thought suddenly that it wasn't so much the thought of having a baby, unwed, that bothered her. That wasn't uncommon here in the Valley. They had them, accepted them, and the family raised them as best it could. It was that she had thought all this time that he must know and hadn't cared enough even to ask.

"Lucy, is there anything I can do for you?" It sounded pretty lame and it was.

"There ain't nothin' to do," she pointed out, far more logical.

"Would you like to go for a drive or something tonight? I guess you don't get out so much now."

"Not much," she agreed. "But I guess not, Parrish. Thanks, anyway."

"How about the harvest party?" he said. "I could come down and pick you up for that."

The way her eyes shone you would think he'd offered her the moon.

"Yeah," she said, "you could do that if you want."

It had been quite a fright and it left its mark. Parrish knew now that he had never given Alison up but had only been looking for some way to reconcile honor and desire, and his panic in the moment he thought he would really have to give her up dispelled his final doubts. He had tried to stay away from her, but it was no use. His sense of obligation to Sala was strong, but not strong enough to stand indefinitely as a barrier to Alison. That night, seeing her car out, Parrish waited for her near the garage, but she only walked past him and on to the house. Two nights later he tried again. On the third attempt, Alison smiled and lingered, and when she finally left him to go into the house it was all right again between them.

Now he waited for her where he always did these nights, on the deserted country road where the bridge crossed the little stream. She was late and Parrish walked along the bank, feeling the soft earth under his shoes and hearing the run of the water and the night sounds of peepers and bullfrogs, and crickets in the grass. The smell of bonfires was in the air, touched with the chill of fall, and the meaning of fall this year disturbed him.

The crop was in, the cloth down, and the farm wore a desolate look, with rows of evenly spaced posts on empty land. Judd Raike had bought the crop and all that was left to do was to crate the tobacco for shipment to his warehouse and then the last little melancholy details—closing the sheds, storing machinery, a few repairs. Five weeks of work at the most. And only four until Alison's party, the party that Ellen had been hired to plan. And then what? In a week Alison would be going back to school and Parrish would see her only on those weekends when she could come home, in fleeting moments they could steal from Sala and the friends he thought more suitable. It was little to look forward to.

He heard the cautious sound of Alison's horn and hurried to the clearing where she always parked.

"I thought I'd never get away!" She came into his arms as he stepped into the car. "Darling, did you think I wasn't coming?"

Parrish smiled without answering, touching her face and drawing her close.

"Darling, what's the matter?" she said.

"I'm only thinking how I'll miss you."

Alison didn't answer but only moved a little on the seat, and Parrish saw that this was one of her restless nights. She was so changeable. One evening she would be as relaxed as a small kitten, and the next she would be restless, impatient at everything. He knew her now so well that he could detect the symptoms and he dreaded this restlessness, not because it tried his patience, but because he sensed in it, always, a passionate quality that didn't make things easier for him.

With Alison there was never any thought, consciously at least, of plucking her off the pedestal where he had placed her. Never did Parrish speculate on whether he could succeed if he tried. She was every lovely thing he had ever dreamed, but when she was this way, other instincts, stronger, created an involuntary war in him. He wished sometimes that she cared less. It would have been easier.

"I keep thinking." He played with her heavy hair. "I don't know what I'll do when you're gone."

Alison sat up straight and stared. "Parrish, what *will* you do this winter?"

"Without you?" He smiled. "I don't know."

"I mean where will you go? Where will you work?"

"Oh, that. I don't know. I suppose I'll go to work in some warehouse like everyone else, if we stay here."

She frowned. "I don't like to think of you as a common laborer."

"Then think of me as an uncommon laborer." He smiled down at her.

"It's nothing to joke about."

He saw that she was serious and something in him grew serious, too. He met her eyes. "Darling, that's all I am."

"That's not all you are."

"Then what am I?"

"Well, you won't always be."

Parrish withdrew his arm. "No," he said, carefully. "I have a trade. I'm a carpenter."

"Stop being nasty."

"I'm not trying to be nasty."

"Well, you're succeeding."

He didn't answer.

"Haven't you ever thought about what you'd do?" she said, after a while.

"No," he said, slowly and honestly, "I haven't."

"How could you not think about it?"

He spread his hands open on his lap, wondering how to answer her. He didn't know why he had never thought about it.

"Don't you want to amount to something?"

"I don't suppose I ever will," he said, slowly. "Not the way you mean, anyway."

"Well, don't you care?"

This night was starting badly and Parrish asked himself why he was letting it happen. He looked down at Alison, sitting close to him, shock and disbelief on her face, and he thought of how he loved her, so much that he scarcely had a thought that did not include her. Why, then, was he letting this night go so wrong, when he had only to reach out and take her in his arms and tell her that he would conquer the world for her and everything would be all right again? But his hands stayed at his sides and the words didn't come.

When he spoke, he said, "There are an awful lot of people in this world, Alison, who are never going to amount to very much—the way you mean—and I guess I'm one of them. No, it doesn't bother me."

Anger and then coolness flashed in the deep-set eyes, and when several minutes passed and she didn't speak he made a move to leave her.

Then she laughed. "Really, I don't know what we're arguing about or how this all started." She spoke in a voice that was half apologetic, half like an indulgent mother who knew she could handle her child.

Parrish hesitated, still frowning, but only for a moment; then he settled down again, their argument still churning in his mind but starting to quiet, and then the magic she had for him began to work again and he reached over to take her in his arms.

But it was a short-lived truce. Something was wrong between them tonight and it flared up again when he told her that he was going to take Lucy to the harvest dance.

"You can't!" she gasped. "You can't do that!"

"Darling, it doesn't mean anything—"

"It will mean plenty to other people! She's pregnant!"

"How did you know?"

Alison ignored the question. "People will think it's yours!"

Why did I say anything, he thought. What's wrong tonight?

"Well, is it yours?"

"No," he said, knowing they were starting all over again. "But it could have been."

"Oh!" Anger came from deep within her. She moved away from him. "Why did you have to say that!"

"You asked me."

"I think you've deliberately set out to argue tonight. What's the matter with you? Are you looking for a way to end this?"

She was right in one respect. He shouldn't have told her. He could see that. Even if she had suspected what had once been between him and Lucy, it had been nothing more than a suspicion until he confirmed it. He took Alison's hands in his, thinking how small and smooth they were, compared to Lucy's that were big and rough. "Darling, I'm sorry." He tried to explain. "It's just that I love you so, I didn't want there to be any lies between us. I wanted everything to be honest with us, because I love you very much."

Alison began to calm down. "If you love me, Parrish, don't take her."

"It has nothing to do with my loving you."

"How can you say that!"

"Because it hasn't. Try to understand. I love you so that I want to be with you every minute. I don't feel anything for Lucy, except right now I feel sorry for her and she needs a friend."

"Lots of people need friends. What are you—a charity worker or something?"

"This is different."

"Why is it different?"

"Because," he said again, "it could have been mine."

"Well, it's not yours."

"Only because of luck. Because she was pregnant already."

"Oh! How disgusting can you get?"

"I'm sorry."

"You're not a bit sorry."

"Look, I'm sorry about everything. I'm sorry I told you. I'm sorry I'm arguing with you. I'm sorry the whole thing happened at all."

"Are you sorry you asked her?"

"No."

"Oh!"

"I wish you could understand. It's so little to do for her. She's in for a hard time and this will make it a little easier for her."

"If you loved me, you'd be thinking of what you're doing to me."

"Why," he said, wearily, "do you have to put everything in the name of love?"

"If you loved me, you wouldn't go to that party at all—with those awful people."

Something in him refused to tell her now that he had not intended to go. Instead he said angrily, "You go to your party and I'll go to mine."

"That's not fair. You know you can come to mine if you want to."

"I don't want to. What would I do at that kind of a party?"

"What will you do at yours—or shouldn't I ask?"

He tried once more to explain. "I want to do this because I feel it's the right thing to do. It's the last time I'll take her anywhere or see her at all, except working. I know if I let her down she'll live through it, but I won't feel honest. Doesn't that mean anything to you?"

"No, it doesn't. You don't have to be honest about something you didn't do."

For a long minute he looked at her, asking himself if there was any way he could make her understand.

Her eyes met his. "Parrish, I'm asking you not to take her."

He might as well not answer. There was nothing else to say. He might as well leave her.

"Are you going to?"

He nodded.

"Get out!" The green eyes darkened with anger. "I hate you. Oh, when I think—oh, I hate you!"

Parrish got out of the car and closed the door behind him.

He didn't see her again. On Saturday night when he left in the station wagon to go for Lucy he caught a glimpse of her coming down the broad front steps with Wiley Raike. He drove on without looking back, but anger at her for not understanding had long since died before his longing for her, and he only went through the motions of doing what was expected of him at the party.

But Lucy had a good time. She threw herself into it, probably knowing that it was her last party for a while, and as he stood in the doorway of the barn, watching her, Parrish thought if she danced any harder she would probably lose that baby before it got born, and a good thing, too.

Alone, he went outside and stood in the dark, beyond the light from the lanterns they'd hung in the barn, listening to the tinny music and the crude screams and shrieks. It was late now and they were all drunk and shouting dirty remarks and obscene jokes to each other and, while he stood unseen, couples began to sneak out and disappear into the bushes. It was probably wrong, he thought, for him to feel that way about Lucy losing her baby, wrong to think that about a life about to be. A life that would be part Lucy and part—who else? And yet an individual, one who someday might amount to something—even, he thought bitterly, according to Alison's terms.

John came out of the barn and stopped and lit a cigarette and saw Parrish and came over. "Christ, what a bunch of dogs!"

Parrish didn't answer. This was what he had let come between him and Alison, this drunken brawl, knocking the loveliest thing he had ever known out of his life and leaving him a terrible emptiness that couldn't be filled.

"Well," John said. "I had all I can stomach."

"You walk over, John?"

"Yeah. Good night, Parrish."

"Mind if I walk with you a little?" Parrish said. He felt that for a minute he would like to talk to somebody who wasn't drunk and wasn't screaming and wasn't any trouble to him—just somebody he wasn't too close to, who would talk about unimportant things and keep him for a few minutes from being alone and missing Alison.

"Hell, no," John said. "I'd be glad of it."

They walked around the barn without speaking, not trying to raise their voices above the racket from inside, and moved along the path toward the driveway. When they were a little distance away, so that the noise from the barn began to die in the chilly night air, John gave a little sigh. "It's the best time of the year," he said, "when the crop is in, and yet I hate it. You know what I mean?"

Parrish nodded and thought that, yes, he knew what John meant.

Then they came alongside the garage and suddenly John stopped and then Parrish saw it, too. Standing in front of Ellen's door, gleaming in the moonlight, was Judd Raike's long black Cadillac. Parrish felt John's hand on his elbow and his mouth jerked into a crooked little smile of resignation.

"Don't go wrecking any more cars, Parrish, huh?" John said.

Parrish flexed his hands in his pockets. "Don't worry," he said. "I guess I'm not surprised."

On the door of the Cadillac Parrish could see the glimmer of the gold-monogrammed "R" reflecting the light from the door lamp, and he stared at it and thought that he had known all along that this was going to happen, even though lately he had not been thinking much about it.

"Well," John said. "Good night, then."

"Good night," Parrish said. "Good night, John."

He might as well go upstairs and find out what was happening, see what he was like—the great man, Judd Raike.

13

Now THAT the wedding was over Parrish was going back to Boston with Mae and Milky. All through the ceremony it had seemed unreal to him. Even standing up there with his mother's hand on his arm, even afterward when he drank too much champagne and looked hard at Judd Raike's family—at Edgar, who perspired all through the ceremony and spoke to no one except his frightened-looking wife; at Wiley, who smiled and smiled, and only reminded him of Alison; at Paige, whom he had forgotten until she turned up at the wedding, the only one to speak to him; even when he looked at all these Raikes, he couldn't believe it was really happening.

Not even the wide diamond wedding band that Raike had placed on Ellen's finger had made it seem real. But later, after it was over, and Parrish went into his mother's room to kiss her goodbye and saw her take the diamond shoe buckles that Raike had given her for a wedding present, each containing twenty square-cut diamonds, and slip them onto her pumps and stand up and smile with complete composure—then, with sudden sharpness, it became clear that his mother was Mrs. Judd Raike and, in her own mind, had been for some time.

In his own room in the hotel to which he and Ellen had moved immediately after Alison's party, Parrish put the last of his things into the same battered old bag he had packed so reluctantly in June to come here. Now, with some of the same reluctance, he was packing it again to go back. Ellen and Raike were going to Europe, and Ellen had extracted a promise from Parrish that when they returned he would come immediately to Raike's house and stay with her for a month so that, she said, no one would ever consider him only a guest in her home. Parrish did not find the prospect a happy one but his mother had promised, in turn, that when the month was up, if he wanted to leave, she would not try to stop him.

Her room was empty now, and, closing the door to his own, Parrish went downstairs to the street and took a bus to go to Sala Post's, to say goodbye to Teet and John and anyone else who was there. And, he guessed, to Sala.

At the farm they were still stripping, Parrish knew—cutting the string of leaves off the laths and tying them in bunches called "hands" and packing the hands in crates to go to Raike's warehouse. John had said over the telephone that they would probably be working in shed number fourteen. To save time, Parrish got off the bus at Tower's used-car lot, where there was usually a cab available, found one, and took it to Sala's.

At the number-fourteen shed he stood a moment and looked down the row to number twenty-two on the corner, where the dirt path ran into the old country road: the place where he had been watching fires the night Alison came. She had gone back to school and had come home for her party, and twice besides, but he had not seen her. He told himself it would be easier to forget back in Boston, where there would be nothing to remind him. He turned away and pulled open the door.

Inside the shed it was unbelievably cold and raw and the girls had a pot of coffee going on a charcoal fire in the dirt. They stopped working when they saw him and it made him feel good the way they all rushed around him, even John.

"Lover!" Addie screamed.

"Hello, boy," Mary muttered, and John and Teet clapped him on the back.

"Hello, Parrish," Gladstone said, with a broad grin. "Hello, mon."

"How's your bambine, Gladstone?" he said.

"So you're set to go, eh, kid?" Teet said.

Parrish nodded.

"Well." Teet scratched at his heavy shirt. "I guess you won't be back in a hurry, eh?"

"I guess not," Parrish said. And then, suddenly, he felt terrible and he got the goodbyes over and left.

He should have kept the cab. It was a mistake to walk back because it took a long time to get up to and pass that number-twenty-two shed and even longer to get past the number-eleven field, which reminded him of things about Judd Raike he would just as soon not think about.

Reaching Sala's house, Parrish hesitated a moment and then went to the side door and rang the bell. Presently Hazel Anne came, saying, "Oh, it's you," surprised, and told him Sala was in his library.

When he knocked on the half-opened door, Sala looked up from his book and seemed so pleased to see him he was glad he had come. "Come in, Parrish," Sala said. "Sit down."

Parrish came in and sank into a chair, a little nervously. "I just came to say goodbye."

"Good boy," Sala said. "I'm glad you did."

Parrish looked around the room at the rows of bookshelves, as if he were reading the titles, and wondered what he ought to say next. Sala was not an easy man to talk to. "You sure have a lot of books," he murmured. Then he thought it was a pretty stupid remark when he had come to say goodbye, but Sala didn't seem to notice.

Sala looked at the volume he was reading. "Do you know Thoreau, Parrish?"

"No, sir." That was the book, *Walden*, that Ellen had asked him to buy for her.

"He was a great man," Sala said, turning the pages. "Only he didn't believe in tobacco."

Parrish smiled.

Sala lifted his eyes from the book and the trace of a twinkle left them. "You should read more, Parrish."

Parrish nodded. "I guess I should. I don't read much."

"That's a mistake, boy. You're cheating yourself." Sala gave him a surprisingly human smile. "In reading, Parrish, a man learns that his problems are not exclusively his own. He learns that he is not the first who has had them." Then Sala shut the book and handed it to him. "Why don't you start with this? I can't think of a better beginning."

Parrish touched the book but didn't take it. "I'll buy a copy in the bookshop, sir. I don't want to take yours away from you."

But Sala pressed it on him. "Take it. You can return it some day when you come this way again."

A little later Sala walked with him to the side door and shook hands, and then the door closed behind him and Parrish was walking down the long driveway that wound between the trunks of bare trees, his collar up, the copy of *Walden* tucked under his arm, feeling the cold October wind and hearing it whistle through the cedar posts with only wire strung between them, holding no tent cloth now over the bare brown fields.

BOOK 3

1949

14

DAMP BENEATH his collar, his feet cold and wet, Edgar Raike irritably slammed the door of the vestibule against the March rain and stood a moment in the near-darkness before entering the house. "This is it," he told himself. "She's in there."

In four months Edgar had not been able to call her, in his mind, either his father's wife or by her given name, but had only labeled her, with festering bitterness, "that woman." Now Judd had come home with her. Today at three o'clock he had walked into the warehouse, back from his trip that had included Europe and then Puerto Rico and Cuba, where he had inspected his tobacco fields and factories. Judd was home and that woman was in his house.

Inside, Edgar removed his damp coat and hat and went into the den, noting that Wiley and Evaline were alone, following his orders not to fraternize with her. "Well," he snapped, "where is everyone?"

Wiley looked up from the bar built into a wall of oak bookshelves. "Father hasn't come home yet. Nor Paige. Everyone else—" He shrugged. "Like a drink?"

Edgar winced. Last night, just thinking ahead to today, he'd drunk too much. Otherwise a drink might have helped. Then he noticed Maples building a fire in the wide fireplace where no logs had burned as long as Raikes had occupied this house. "What's the idea, Maples?"

Maples straightened up, brushing off his hands. "Mrs. Raike ordered it, sir."

Edgar whirled on Evaline and then in the same instant realized that the butler was not referring to her. Openmouthed, Edgar stared at

Maples, as if, by that simple statement, he had turned fear into fact. He had called her Mrs. Raike, and very casually, too, damn him, and she had given an order, changing things around her way already, as though she owned the place. With hatred, Edgar regarded the fire. "Where'd you get the logs?"

"They've been in the cellar, sir, for years."

The butler left and Edgar pulled out a cigar without lighting it. He didn't particularly like cigars, but business was business. Besides, there was an air of authority about a cigar, in case the woman should join them. "A little touch of Beacon Hill, I presume," he muttered. "Didn't lose any time getting around the house, did she? Even down to the cellar. Guess she knows the bottom is an excellent place to start. You can go far."

"She didn't go down, dear," Evaline said. "She sent Maples."

"Evaline," Edgar groaned, "don't argue, do you mind? I've had a very trying day."

Wiley looked up, surprised. "What's the matter, Ed? You didn't stay with him?"

"No, I didn't stay." Edgar's eyes snapped over to Wiley. "Didn't you?"

"Couldn't. Cocktail date with Maizie." Wiley laughed. "Hell, I wasn't going to be handy his first day back while he found everything all wrong."

"Nothing's wrong," Edgar snapped. "And you should have stayed. You knew I had a board meeting at the Children's Home."

Now Edgar was really annoyed. As though the board meeting had not been miserable enough! The Valley Home for Children was Edgar's favorite project and ordinarily after a meeting he felt great, suffused with satisfaction at fulfilling his duty to the unfortunate. Not today. Today he had run into nothing but opposition, chiefly from Tom Holden, nagging, carping arguments, and with this other matter on his mind it had been too much. In the end he had walked out on them, and then, once outside, he found he had forgotten his umbrella and his rubbers, and, damned if he would go back in there, he'd come home without them and gotten soaked.

But he had counted on learning from Wiley what, if anything, had displeased Judd. Not that his ability or his management during Judd's absence needed defending. It was just that there were so damned many departments—the fermenting in the bulk rooms, the sorting and grading of the leaves, packing, storing, price deals. Edgar frowned. Price deals— that's where Judd would look first, where you made your money. Well, he'd done all right there, even if everyone had tried to take advantage of him because Judd was away. Chiselers! But he'd shown them. The only trouble was he hadn't sold as much as Judd usually sold by March. Still,

Judd would have to admit he'd gotten his price, and if he'd made concessions he'd have been put on the carpet for giving the stuff away.

Edgar found suddenly that he had wandered over to the fireplace, was
actually standing warming himself at it—at her fire! Deliberately he walked
away.

"Only thing went wrong," he said, with a quick nervous jerk of his
unlit cigar, "was those Sala Post bulks heating up too fast. And that
wasn't my fault." At last Edgar had admitted his chief cause for anxiety.

He wished now that he had never started the whole business of Sala
Post's bulks. If he'd stopped to think he'd have foreseen that it could stir
up a hornet's nest; but he'd had so much on his mind, and when he came
on them bulking Sala Post's leaves just the week Mig Alger, the foreman,
was out with flu, it had seemed a golden opportunity. Thinking only that
Judd would be delighted to have something on Sala Post at last, Edgar
had pulled out the thermometer of a bulk packed only the day before and
heating gradually as it should, had announced that it had heated too fast,
cursed Sala Post for sending in wet leaves, and ordered the astonished
Jamaicans to rebuild it. How was he to know that two of the Jamaicans
were Sala Post's boys who came into the warehouse in the winter—they
all looked alike to him, those Jamaicans—and that they would tell John
Donati, who of course had run to Sala Post.

"It was damn lucky I caught them," he snapped at Wiley. "Before they
started to rot."

Wiley nodded but didn't answer.

"Much you know about it," Edgar muttered. "You don't go into the
bulk room from one year to the next. When did you last go into the bulk
room?"

Wiley laughed. "You know I hate the heat."

Edgar sank into a chair. If that had been all, it wouldn't have been so
bad, but it didn't end there. When he went out to sign Sala's crop for
this year, as Judd always did, Sala wouldn't sign because, he said, he'd
heard there had been trouble with his leaves. Now a little fear shot
through Edgar as he wondered how he was going to explain that to Raike.
Maybe he could tell him he'd left Sala for Judd to sign because it gave
him so much pleasure. Well, that was true. Everyone knew Judd hated
Sala Post and really wanted his land but meanwhile loved the day each
year when Sala signed on the dotted line.

Sala's land and the three small farms in a row next to him. They were
all Raike needed to complete his ownership of that whole stretch of land.
The three little farmers were Prentiss, Oermeyer and Tully, and Judd
spoke so openly about getting their land that his lawyer, Max Maine, had
a standing joke, using their initials, saying Judd wanted the POT at the

end of Sala Post. And—Edgar smiled—he'd get them all right. Once Sala collapsed, his three neighbors wouldn't hold out a month. Sooner or later Raike would get them all. Just as, sooner or later, he'd get the story on Sala's bulks. Edgar covered his eyes with his hand and sighed.

"Well, don't worry about it, dear," Evaline said. "You did your best."

"I'm not worried. I just had a miserable meeting at the Home, that's all. Thanks to your cousin Tom." He looked at her accusingly. "Tom was complaining about the matron over there—and the servants. Of course, he didn't fool me. Not for a minute."

"Tom wouldn't ever try to fool you, dear."

"I knew why he was harping on servants today. It was a personal dig at me."

Evaline was miles behind him. "How is the maid problem—"

"Because today," Edgar cut in, "because, as of today, we've got Sala Post's maid as first lady of our household—supposedly."

Wiley smiled up from a cabinet where he was taking out another bottle of Scotch. "She wasn't exactly a maid, Ed."

"She was a maid."

Evaline was looking at him with that childish, puzzled expression and Edgar couldn't resist pointing out that she was partly to blame for his humiliation. "Tom's embarrassed. Now that our father has married a servant, he doesn't enjoy his connection with us. It's his way of publicly washing his hands." With a weary shrug he turned to Wiley. "Sooner or later we're going to have to do the same thing. My God, when I think of it! People will die laughing. They're having a field day already. I've heard, here and there."

"Well, here's some nice sherry. Like some sherry, Evaline?"

"No, thank you," Evaline said quickly. "Edgar dear, it may not be as bad as you think. Today she seemed rather nice."

"Evaline, this woman is smarter than you are and she won't find it hard to delude you into thinking she's quite pleasant. Let's face it, Evaline. You may have your virtues, but brains is not one of them."

"Little sherry, Evaline?" Wiley said. "Nice bottle here."

"Wiley, do be serious," Evaline pleaded.

"I'm serious." Wiley straightened up. "There's just not a damn thing we can do."

"Oh, we'll have to put up with her for a while," Edgar said. "Until we can buy her off. That's all she's after. And it'll cost plenty. But we'll have to pay."

A board creaked on the stairs and, thinking it was Ellen, Edgar whirled about, bruising his knuckles against a table. When no one came he sucked his hand and accepted the drink Wiley handed him. "Where is she, anyway?" he said. "In the kitchen?"

"She's upstairs. With her son."

"You mean he's here, too!" Edgar closed his eyes. "Tell me the worst. Are we being invaded by any more of her riffraff relatives? That sad-looking sister, perhaps, who resembles a chambermaid? Or her husband with the large red face? You remember those charming people at the wedding?"

Wiley laughed. "How could I forget?"

"If she upsets you so, dear—" Evaline laid a hand on Edgar's arm—"and if you're going to get rid of her, we could move into a house of our own for a little while, until she's gone."

"You would think of that! That's typical, if I may say so. The easiest way out, every time."

"It wouldn't be easy. You know I don't know how to run a house."

"Precisely. But you don't consider that. The burden would fall on me. Besides, if you think I'm going to let a scheming scrubwoman push me out—"

Edgar broke off, hearing Raike's voice in the hall, and then breathed with relief when he heard that his greeting to Maples was cheerful. Today, at least, Raike hadn't found out about Sala Post or his bulks.

Parrish thought that this was different from tobacco talk he knew. At Sala Post's they talked about growing the leaves; they worked in the soil and tobacco meant a crop. Here tobacco meant warehouses, factories, distribution. Judd Raike had started talking business at dinner, and now they had been here in the den for a couple of hours and he was still talking. Ellen sat at his elbow, his sons close by—Wiley nodding at regular intervals, Edgar making occasional remarks, trying to sound executive but careful to keep his comments brief. Only Paige showed signs of restlessness and boredom. Slumped in a chair, she had pulled a long strand of her hair over her forehead and was peering up at it with weirdly crossed eyes. Then she saw Parrish watching her, and she grinned.

"Tobacco is entering into the biggest boom the industry has ever known," Judd Raike said. "Anyone thinks we've reached the peak is crazy."

"Of course," Edgar said.

Raike pulled down his heavy brows and let a look drive home his point. "Anyone cuts back now is a coward. Or a fool."

"Tom Holden," Edgar murmured. "I heard Tom's letting his Westwood field lie idle this year."

"You heard!" Judd Raike said, sharply. "Don't you know?"

"I'm driving over tomorrow to check it," Edgar said quickly.

Parrish sat in a corner, only half listening. He was extremely uncomfortable and ill at ease in this house and he felt that nobody was particularly relaxed. All evening he had felt an undercurrent of tension—everyone on pins and needles—or maybe he only imagined it because he was so out of place here himself, and so unwelcome. Not that that worried him, because he didn't want to stay here anyway. Idly, he let his eyes travel over the room, looking at the high ceiling, the oak-paneled walls, the deep carpeting. Like the rest of Raike's house it was handsome and a little overwhelming, and Parrish slid lower in his chair, telling himself that he wouldn't even last here the month.

"Thing I noticed on this trip," Raike said, "was that more men are smoking cigars than ever before. You saw it, Ellen."

Ellen smiled up at him. "It was everywhere, darling."

"Everywhere. Only thing keeps more men still from switching to cigars is women. Overfastidious women. Have to educate them." Raike laughed.

"You couldn't help but notice," Ellen murmured, and Raike looked at her approvingly.

"Have to educate them is right," Edgar said loudly, shooting Ellen a look that accused her of elbowing in on his position as number-one cheerleader.

Frowning, Parrish looked at him. He had disliked Edgar at the wedding, had thought him a small and sour man, and nothing had happened tonight to make him change his mind. Under a bright lamp that showed up his thinning hair and sallow complexion, Edgar sat straight and proper, knees crossed, nervously jiggling his slender foot in a polished black shoe. Already it was clear that he resented Ellen. But Parrish couldn't imagine Edgar really liking anyone. He seemed permanently down on life, feeling superior even to his poor frightened-looking wife, who sat next to him bent over a handkerchief, picking out the embroidery.

Briefly, Parrish's gaze moved to Evaline, with her childlike, straight-cut bangs and wide dark eyes, and then on to Wiley, who must have drunk himself beyond pain by now but who still smiled, dutifully wrapped up in his father's words. Parrish wondered how he could ask Wiley about Alison or find out when she would be home.

"It's a great industry now," Judd Raike said. "But nothing compared to what we'll make it in the next ten years. By the time I fill in those gaps in my land—why, by the time young Judd walks through those doors to take his place in tobacco, Raike and Company will be twice as powerful as it is today." He looked at his family for appreciation of what this meant. Then his eyes rested on Evaline. "By the way, Evaline, I understand you have a new nurse for Judd and Judith."

Evaline's eyes snapped up, widening.

"German, I understand," Raike said.

The dormant tension in the room seemed to come to life. Evaline twisted her handkerchief. "No, I'm sorry, but she's a Norwegian."

"Does she have an accent?"

"Well—a little. Edgar hired her."

"I believe you'll find she's qualified, sir." Quickly Edgar defended himself, annoyed that Evaline had passed him the burden. "We got her through Robert Catton's agency as you always do."

"Edgar explained to Robert Catton that you were away and he assured us that he knew exactly what you wanted—"

Raike took out an aluminum-tubed cigar and held it poised horizontally before his face. "Of course, these children are not Catton's responsibility, now, are they, Evaline?"

Evaline dropped her eyes to her handkerchief.

"Answer him," Edgar spat out at her.

"No." Evaline's eyes flew up, briefly, and down again.

"Then I think we'd better look into the woman." Raike smiled. "I suppose—" he turned to Edgar—"you took the first person he sent."

"She was well recommended."

"I don't like the idea of an accent," Raike said. "I don't want my grandchildren talking like immigrants."

"She's the best we ever had," Paige put in, sitting up now. "Judd and Judy love her."

Parrish thought there was something heroic about the way Paige entered into the argument. Wiley, sitting next to Evaline, was pretending he was not present.

"Tell the woman I'll interview her tomorrow evening at five o'clock. If her accent is marked, she'll have to go." Raike turned to Paige. "With your simple values I wouldn't expect you to realize it, but we're molding young children and there are certain minimum requirements."

Edgar gave a humorless smile. "Simple values is an understatement. Anyone pleases Paige. While you were away she was running around with all kinds of people. Absolutely no holding her down."

"Oh, what a lie!" Paige cried. "What a disgusting lie!"

"You'd think she was a shopgirl, the standards she's got."

"You're just trying to get the heat off yourself!" Paige's brown eyes smoldered, wide. "You're throwing up a smoke screen. Oh, what a coward!"

"Paige—" Raike cut in sharply. "What's this all about?"

"Ask him. He started it."

"I'm asking you."

"She's been running around with Anson Tower," Edgar put in.

"That," Paige said, airily, "is just one large, smelly red herring! I went skating and Anson just happened to be there. What's wrong with that? Dennis even drove me and picked me up. I never felt so silly, turning up at a public park with a chauffeur, but Edgar insisted. You'd think I'd elope or something if I took a bus. Honestly, I wonder how he got to be part of this family, he's so queer!"

"I'll attribute that remark to your adolescence," Edgar said, "and overlook it."

Raike cleared his throat for silence. "When I want anything overlooked in this house, I'll say so." He brought out his gold knife, opened the blade. "Now, I'm not pleased at any of this. You were the head of the family. Mighty poor job you seem to have done. Mighty poor."

Edgar flushed and Evaline threw him a quick sympathetic look. Parrish felt her anxiety, with a sad kind of love in it.

The knot of tension in the room pulled tighter. Raike started scraping at the seal of the cigar tube. He scraped with slow, even strokes, letting the shreds of paper fall into his lap. Nobody spoke and Parrish, looking from one tight face to another, saw that this tension was a familiar thing to them and that they were waiting it out. He looked at Ellen, expecting her to begin gently to coax Raike back to good humor, but she, too, remained silent, making no effort to ease the strain. As always, her face was serene, but a small tightening of the lips told Parrish that she had seen this sudden anger before and probably had learned that silence was the way to handle it.

When Raike had the seal completely scraped off the aluminum tube he pulled it open and took out the cigar, lit it, puffed a few times, and then, surprisingly, stood up and said, "Well, it's getting late."

Everyone moved a little, as though a school bell had sounded, dismissing the class. Paige leaped to her feet and headed toward the door.

"Paige—" Raike said, and she stopped. "I want Ellen to take you shopping tomorrow for some new clothes."

"Oh, thanks," Paige said, "but I don't need anything."

"Nonsense," Raike said. "I want you to do something about Paige, Ellen. That's not what I want my daughter to look like. Now stop sulking, Paige. You can learn a lot from Ellen."

Parrish saw Edgar throw his wife a sour, superior smile, as though to say he doubted that.

"You might go along, too, Evaline," Raike said. "Try to find something a little more impressive than you're used to. Play up your good points."

"Now see here," Edgar burst out, indignantly.

"What are her good points, Ellen?"

"Why, Evaline is lovely," Ellen said. "She has beautiful eyes."

"Good," Raike said. "Fine."

He took Ellen's arm and walked out of the room. The instant Raike was gone Edgar turned, flung his cigar into the fireplace, and started pacing the floor, so much hatred on his face that Parrish paused, alarmed. He was starting to feel a certain uneasiness about Edgar. At least twice tonight he had seen on Edgar's face a hatred for Ellen that went far beyond mere resentment.

He stood up to go to his room, catching a final glimpse of Edgar throwing his wife a nasty look as though daring her to say something. Parrish felt again the smallness of the man and thought, What makes a man shrink up so? Edgar was young still, but with nothing young about him— tight as a drum, his miserableness so apparent that it saddened you to look at him too long, made you want to turn away and not see the pettiness.

15

A FLAGSTONE walk led from Raike's house through a garden and around a swimming pool with a statue near it of three nude women carrying pitchers. The pool was empty now, the blue concrete bottom covered with a winter's accumulation of dry leaves; the garden was brown and dead-looking, the trees still bare. But the first birds were back, their talk different from the talk of winter birds, and in the air was a smell of warming earth to give you a passionate restlessness, and with all the bareness, you knew it was spring.

Parrish sat on the edge of the empty pool, breaking the dry papery brownness away from the brittle veins of dead leaves. Only three days he had been here, and already idleness was pushing him hard. He didn't hear Paige coming up behind him until she spoke.

"What are you planning to do, jump in and drown yourself out of loneliness?"

"I thought you were out shopping."

"All finished. I held my nose and swallowed fast, like castor oil, and it was all over before I knew it."

Parrish laughed. "Don't you like pretty clothes?"

"Oh, sure. It's not that." Paige sat down and looked at him soberly, as he had seen her do before during these past few days, studying him much as he had been studying Edgar. "Parrish," she said now, her big cocoa-colored eyes growing serious, "I figure you're probably feeling absolutely great here, so I thought I'd tell you I'm glad you came." She grinned, the wonderful eyes lighting up. "I'm delighted!"

Parrish smiled with quick pleasure.

Paige turned and dangled her legs over the side of the pool. "What're you doing out here, anyway?"

"Just figuring when I'll be leaving."

"Leaving! Aren't you going to live here?"

"No."

"Why not?"

For many reasons too complicated to explain, Parrish thought, and one very simple one—he didn't want to. "If you like pretty clothes," he said, "why'd you fight so hard against getting them?"

"Oh, you know how it is. Nag, nag, nag." Paige lay down beside the pool in one of those abrupt, almost violent gestures of hers. "It gives me claustrophobia."

"Claustrophobia?"

"As though I were in a little room and here was my father, one wall—" she held up a hand—"and here's Edgar, another wall—and when they start nagging and criticizing, the walls start moving and they get closer and closer—" Dramatically, with a sinister light in her eyes, Paige moved her hands closer and closer until they met. "Smack! That's me in the middle. Getting claustrophobia."

She rolled over on her stomach. "How do you like that hideous statue? In the summer the girls pour water out of their pitchers into the basin. Isn't that great?" She sat up. "Listen, honestly, didn't you come here to live?"

"I just came for a month because my mother asked me to. But she seems pretty much settled—I thought maybe I'd leave sooner."

"What's your hurry? Where are you going?"

"Back where I came from, I guess."

"Don't you know?"

Parrish laughed. "About your claustrophobia, is Wiley one of the walls, too?"

"No," Paige said. "He just drops hints to keep the peace. I keep telling myself I'm lucky to have people who care enough to care. I mean if they didn't love me, it wouldn't bother them what I was like. Then I'd probably be moping around because nobody cared." She frowned. "Sometimes I feel very guilty about the whole thing. It's terrible to be so mixed up, isn't it?"

"You're not so mixed up."

"Ho! I guess you're the only one who doesn't think so. Look, if you don't know where you're going or what you're going to do, you should stay here. That's my opinion." She stood up. "I have to go change for dinner."

Parrish stood up, too, to walk back to the house with her. "What about Edgar, Paige? Does he bother you much?"

"What do you mean, does he bother me?"

That was the trouble. Parrish wasn't sure what he meant. It was just a feeling, vague but disturbing. Maybe the whole idea was silly, as much the result of idleness as anything. "Does he ever do anything mean to you?"

"'Course not. What could he do? He just nags. Look, Parrish, as long as you're a man without a purpose, I think you should stay. Those are my final words."

Parrish watched Paige race around the house and disappear. She'd been right about one thing, he thought—calling him a man without a purpose. When had he ever had a purpose? The only single fixed idea he had ever had was to get away from his mother, who had always taken care of him. To be free—free to get nowhere. And that was still it. And yet, with this uneasy feeling about Edgar, what good would it be to leave? A man wasn't free if his thoughts stayed anxiously behind.

At dinner, seated opposite Edgar, Parrish looked him over again, seeing the pale, nervous hands over the dish Maples held and the fussy look to his face, and he thought: What am I worried about? She's handled lots tougher than Edgar.

Maples moved along the table to Paige and while he stood at her side Judd Raike noticed the new dress she was wearing. "Now that's good," he beamed. "Has she something dressier for tonight?"

"She has everything, darling," Ellen said.

"What's tonight?" Paige said.

"We'll be having guests," Judd said. "Quite a few, I'm afraid. You'd better stay on, Maples."

Paige and Maples exchanged a fleeting glance. "Yes, sir," Maples said. But Paige protested. "Maples can't stay on tonight. He's showing his dogs."

Raike looked at Maples, amused. "Planning to show dogs tonight, Maples?"

"Only if the evening were free, sir."

"Don't mind missing it, do you?"

"Not at all, sir." Maples finished serving and went out into the pantry. When he had gone Paige burst out: "I think it's terrible. Maples is dying to show his dogs. They're wonderful now and he'd surely take a ribbon."

Parrish winced, anticipating Raike's wrath, and he thought, "Why doesn't she keep out of it? It doesn't concern her." Then his eye fell on Wiley, suddenly intent on sipping his wine, and he thought with a shudder, Good God! That's exactly the way he figures it!

"Nonsense," Raike said. "You heard me ask him. Doesn't care a rap."

"He just said that because he knew he'd better."

"If Maples is unhappy here, Paige," Raike said, "he can leave. It's a free country. He can walk out in the next two minutes. And Maples is a good butler. Any number of places he could go, where the demands would be less."

"You know he wouldn't leave," Paige said.

Raike smiled. "And why not, Paige?"

"Because," Paige said, grudgingly, "you pay him too much."

"Well, Paige! You've learned a valuable lesson. I didn't think you knew that. I pay for perfection. I expect to get it."

"I don't think it's very fair!"

"Paige," Raike said, "Maples has his dogs to show and we have Ellen to show. Maizie Holden phoned that she and Tom were coming to call. That means we'll have fifty people here before the night is over. Who will keep things functioning properly? The cook—from the kitchen? Ellen?"

Edgar's mouth pursed at that, and Raike saw it.

"Get that look off your face, damn you!"

Edgar paled and looked down and his eyes slid over to Ellen.

Raike turned back to Paige. "It's too bad for Maples, but it's his job. Now, Paige—stop biting your mouth like that!"

Paige flushed.

Raike turned to Ellen, his anger beginning to break out. "Why is it, with all I've given her, she still can't impose on a servant to the slightest degree? Now, Paige, you're no beauty and you never will be and if you're going to be twisting your face into ugly contortions and eating at your mouth, it's going to be just too bad."

Paige went furiously red, trying to straighten out her mouth and hold it still, and then she let out a single frustrated gasp and fled from the room.

"Come back here," Raike ordered, and when she ignored him he pushed back his own chair as if to follow.

"Darling—" Ellen had half risen, too, and then hesitated, and Parrish saw, astonished, that she was uncertain whether to go on or remain silent. She sat down. "Darling," she said, softly, "Paige didn't realize— You're right, of course, darling, and she's only upset because she sees how right you are, and that she was wrong."

Raike frowned and paused and then pulled up his chair and reached for his wine. Parrish stared at Ellen, puzzled not by her words but because she had hesitated to interfere, much as Paige had needed help.

Then Edgar said, "Only way to handle her. She's getting out of hand lately. Completely." Then he added nervously, "Big crowd tonight, you say?"

And Parrish stopped wondering about Ellen's hesitation and looked carefully at Edgar, asking himself again how so much misery could stay bottled up in a man.

By ten o'clock both of Raike's living rooms and the den were filled with guests—the air heavy with smoke and perfume, the noise of many voices mixed to a grinding hum. Parrish stood in a corner watching the glittering crowd, beginning to recognize some of them. There was Clayton Norris, a close friend of Wiley's, a dapper but pudgy young man with a soft mouth who kept darting past as though hurrying to meet a train, pausing here and there to tell a friend in a businesslike manner that it was a great party; and Clayton's wife, Melissa, a pretty girl with fluffy brown hair and a sweet smile that never changed. Melissa was wearing a very low-cut gown, and as Parrish looked at her now he saw a small and proper-looking man named Nulty Sims staring pointedly at her round bosom. Then Mrs. Sims noticed, too, and Nulty shrugged and took a last peek and turned away. Parrish watched them move across the room, the wife asserting ownership of her husband's eyes, the husband making little gestures of resignation.

Edgar stood in a far corner of the room, worried, eyes busy, with the look, Parrish thought, of a man who didn't dare turn away for fear someone would tell a dirty secret about him. He wasn't drinking and kept twisting his neck nervously and muttering to Evaline without looking at her, although she kept her eyes glued on him. You wondered what she saw. Did a wife see a small and sour soul the way others did, or did she find something more?

Clayton Norris came trotting back. "Melissa, love—" he rolled his eyes—"three beauties I heard!" Then he spotted a late-comer across the room. "Harris! Melissa, when did Harris Lowe get back from Cuba?"

"I spoke to Lorraine yesterday and she didn't say a word, Clay."

"Suppose she didn't know?" Clayton giggled. "I hope she was alone! Lorraine—Lorraine, lovely, when did Harris get home?"

"Hello, Clay." A tall girl with red hair ambled up. "Hello, Melissa."

Then Maizie Holden pressed down on them, her black hair cropped short, her snapping black eyes heavily darkened with green eye shadow. She wore a black satin dress cut low over her rather flat bosom, revealing a deep Palm Beach tan and great quantities of diamonds and emeralds. She pushed a round little man ahead of her into the crowd.

"Georgie, here are two girls who'll keep you fascinated," she said in her deep throaty voice. "Georgie Worthy, girls. Visiting broker. But watch him, he's a pincher."

"Maizie, that's libel." Georgie Worthy gave a toothy smile.

"My foot!" Maizie laughed. "Clay, I have one for you. It seems there was this man with a yacht and up the river was a whorehouse—"

"Clayton, you dog!" The circle swelled again as Harris Lowe pushed himself in next to Maizie.

"You'll have to come over here if you want to hear the rest of this," Maizie said, in a low voice. "Nulty Sims is eavesdropping and I loathe that awful fraud."

Parrish saw that Nulty Sims had shaken his wife and returned.

"I mean," Maizie said, "I think a man ought to take his choice. If you're going to go fornicating around, you shouldn't try to be a pillar of the church. It's not the fornicating I resent, of course. It's the indecision."

Nulty Sims nodded to Parrish. "Warm in here, isn't it?"

Maizie turned to see whom he was talking to and broke into a broad smile. "I've been wanting to talk to you, beautiful!" She motioned with her long jeweled cigarette holder. "How are you enjoying this setup?"

"Fine." Parrish tried to sound enthusiastic. "Great."

Maizie appraised him with narrow, clever eyes. "You're a liar," she laughed softly.

Parrish sipped some more champagne and smiled because there was something about Maizie you couldn't help but like.

"Maizie, darling!" Harris Lowe put an arm around her. "Did you hear the one about the whorehouse up the river and the man with the yacht?"

"I've just told it to at least thirty people. Do shut up, Harris. I'm busy falling in love. Haven't been in love for two months!"

"Very unwise. There's nothing so bad for a champ as breaking training."

"How witty you are, Harris! And here's Clayton looking for you."

"Maizie, did you know there was a flag on the whorehouse?" Harris said.

"How many stars?" Clayton giggled.

"In the house or on the flag?" Maizie said.

Harris Lowe wrapped an arm around Clayton and launched into a repertoire of dirty stories, and Parrish made his way across the living room and into the den, where he found Paige with Tom Holden bent over to talk to her, a smile on his scarred face. Paige was wearing a pale silk dress Ellen had brought from Paris and, with her blond hair drawn high on her head and her brown eyes shining up to Tom, she looked quite pretty. Parrish wondered whether Judd Raike was pleased, since it was so important to him. A moment later Edgar came up and Paige motioned Parrish away a little.

"Poor Tom," she whispered. "Edgar'll make him talk about that Children's Home for about eleven hours."

"The way I see it, Tom," Edgar said, "the matron is a little heavy on discipline, but she's trained and that counts for something."

"What'd I tell you!" Paige laughed.

Now Parrish saw Ellen and Raike across the room, Ellen radiant, Raike beaming with obvious pride. For several minutes Parrish watched, pleased, until he lost them in the crowd.

"She's a mighty sour individual," Tom Holden was saying. "Just not right for those kids."

"Trained help is hard to find these days, Tom. And somebody's got to do the job. You and I don't have time for oatmeal and undies." Edgar laughed at his little joke and then he bent closer to Tom so that Parrish almost missed his next words. "Tell you one thing, Tom. Wish the only servant problems I had were with *hired* ones. You hire 'em, you can fire 'em." He slumped his stomach forward and spoke in a low, confiding voice. "It's a lot tougher, let me tell you, when someone's gone and *married* one."

Paige gasped and put her hand over her mouth. Instant rage burst through Parrish and he hardly felt Paige's hand on his arm. "Don't pay any attention," she said quickly. "With Edgar, it's absolutely essential to ignore him. He's a fool."

Parrish took a step forward. He'd show Edgar it was a lot tougher when you didn't watch what you said.

Firmly, Paige held his arm. "Parrish, not now! Not here!" He turned and saw her anxious dark eyes. "But it's not easy, is it?" She smiled with great understanding.

"What's not easy?"

"To ignore him—Edgar."

In spite of his anger, Parrish managed a small smile, too. Paige had grown up this past year, in many ways.

"By the way," Edgar was saying with condescending amusement, "how do you like her? Our—uh—addition to the household staff?"

Tom smiled at him, questioningly.

"I mean—" Edgar laughed—"Ellen, I guess they call her."

"Oh!" Tom's smile broadened, lit up. "She's charming! Thoroughly!"

Edgar stared.

"Just delightful!" Tom said.

Edgar tried a weak little smile, failed, tried again. "Yes—" The smile died, finally. "Isn't she?"

Paige shook her head and turned away, laughing, but this was more than Parrish could laugh off. The feeling of alarm swept back over him and he tried to argue it away. Clearly Edgar was a coward; how quickly he had backed down when Tom Holden spoke a different opinion. And if Edgar wouldn't stand up to Tom Holden, how much less would he dare to oppose Judd Raike. And Raike was all for Ellen. Anyone could see that.

Across the room Parrish saw the two of them again and assured himself that Ellen could take care of herself, and he looked back to Edgar and repeated that one thing you could be absolutely certain of was Ellen's ability to take care of herself. And yet, he thought, as long as he'd agreed to stay here a month, as long as that was the plan, maybe he'd better put off talk of leaving sooner. It would keep—a few days, anyway.

During the next week Parrish watched for trouble that didn't come, while he counted the days until he could leave.

Edgar's manner remained unchanged. He was sore as a boil always, his irritation seeming neither to abate nor to erupt. It was evident in quick sour looks, in a sustained attitude of contempt, in small nervous gestures; but when it found expression it broke out, not against Ellen, but translated into an attack occasionally against Paige but more often against his wife, who seemed long ago to have accepted being the butt of his abuse as her function in life. His hatred for Ellen was a thing more felt than seen.

After a week of empty, idle days Parrish rented a car at Tower's used-car lot for the remaining three weeks he was to be here. It was a very shabby car that caused Edgar no small anguish, but with it Parrish could fill the time that hung heavily on his hands. He called on Sala and on John and saw Lucy one day with Frenchy and Rosie going into Tower's General Store. He had stopped and gone in after them and then, seeing that Lucy had had her baby, he had felt suddenly embarrassed, wondering whether or not to ask about it. He was still wondering when Lucy told him she had had a boy.

Several times he stopped at Tower's Dine and Dance for a beer with Teet. And then everyone began to get ready for the new season, testing soil, tuning up machinery, and Parrish took to just driving through the Valley, stopping at Sala's when they were working there, feeling the excitement of the farm waking up, starting anew.

On the afternoon that he returned from watching Sala steam his seedbeds he found his mother in her upstairs sitting room, alone for one of the few times in the ten days that he had been here.

"Out in the Valley again?" she greeted him, putting aside a list on which she had been making notes.

"Sala's been steaming beds." Parrish settled into a chair. He felt good today. During the afternoon, as each section of dry crusted earth was moistened and turned, the old affection he'd had for Sala's farm had grown sharper, and even now the feeling lingered. "I went out to watch. And to return a couple of books Sala lent me."

Ellen looked at him curiously. "Did you read them?"

"Well, sure!" Parrish smiled. "Sala gave me a couple of others."

"There are plenty of books here, Parrish," Ellen said.

That was true. The den was lined with bookshelves, all of them filled, but to his own surprise Parrish had found that he liked to stop in occasionally to talk to Sala. And sometimes, even, Sala mentioned Alison. "Well, Sala picks them out. And I think he sort of enjoys it. He's improving my mind."

"Parrish, if you want to improve your mind, why don't you go to college?"

It was the third time she had brought it up and Parrish didn't bother to answer. Surely she must know that he couldn't hang around for four years going to some college on Judd Raike's money. Even staying here for a month, idle, he felt like a parasite.

Ellen glanced at her watch and stood up. "It's time to go downstairs. Judd will be coming in."

Parrish followed her. At the top of the stairs they heard voices in the den and Ellen hurried down because Raike was home already and he liked her to be there, downstairs, when he came in.

As soon as they entered the den Parrish knew something was wrong. Raike was sitting on the sofa, scraping at a cigar seal, and the family sat around him with concentrated quietness and dull stares. When the cigar seal was about half shredded away Raike looked up and fastened his eyes on Edgar, then looked briefly at Wiley, as though weighing his guilt in the unknown crime, and back at Edgar.

"All right, let's have the facts." Raike cleared his throat ominously and Parrish sat down quietly in the nearest chair.

"I'm asking," Raike said sharply, "for the facts on Sala Post's leaves. In the bulk room. What was the trouble?"

At the mention of Sala's leaves Parrish looked up quickly. Edgar, quite pale, began to fidget. Wiley carefully studied the glass he had just drained, bowing out of the explanations.

"No real trouble." Edgar managed a little shrug. "Nothing serious. Heated a little too fast but I caught them."

"Or so it says on the card—that *you* wrote up."

"It's all there." Edgar took a cigar, jerking it from one side of his mouth to the other while he snapped a lighter that refused to ignite. Furtively Evaline handed him a packet of matches, for which he thanked her with a look of pure hatred. Parrish wondered what this was all about. He'd seen Sala and John twice and Teet four times and nobody had mentioned anything wrong.

"Nobody seems to know about those bulks," Raike said. "Except you."

"I caught them. And a damn good thing, too. Nobody else was on the ball."

"Mig Alger didn't know anything about them."

"Mig was out sick. And right at the busiest time, too."

"Mig looked mighty uncomfortable and said, 'It's all on the card, that's all I know.' 'You only know what you read in the papers, Mig?' I said. And Mig said, 'Yeah, that's all I know.' "

"Well—" Edgar gave a little laugh that didn't come off too well—"that's hardly my fault."

"Weren't you in charge?" Raike said softly.

"Damn right. And I kept at it, too."

Raike examined his gold knife and scraped off the rest of the seal and inserted the blade into the seam in the aluminum tube. He pulled a card from his pocket. "Now this is the card from a Sala Post bulk." He looked it over as though seeing it for the first time. "This card says that bulk was rebuilt eight times instead of four. A couple of thousand cubic feet. You know what that cost?"

Edgar flushed and Parrish knew that he did not know and had not even thought about it until now.

"Well, sure, I know it cost plenty."

"I asked for a figure—not an opinion."

"I'll figure it out, then."

"Nine weeks after it happened you'll figure it out. That's fine."

"That stuff must have been green as grass, if you ask me." Edgar licked his lips. "And if you ask me, Sala Post doesn't give a damn how he packs the tobacco he sells us. What does he care how wet it is, how many times we have to rebuild the bulk, or what it costs us?"

In his memory Parrish could see John and Sala feeling the leaves, feeling, feeling—some days every hour—while they were taking down. He could remember days the girls went home at noon because the leaves were too dry or too damp. He could remember John's explanation of the additional expense in the bulk room, where the leaves were packed to ferment, if they were too wet.

"Ask me," Edgar whined, "ask me, I think he sends it wet deliberately to make us spend money. It's his crazy way of getting even. Sends it wet and dies laughing."

"That stuff was dry!" Parrish burst out indignantly. "I was there when they packed it."

Edgar swung around viciously. "That is something we'd like to forget." He snapped back to Raike. "And that's another thing. Him. He's running around with all that trash he knew out there, all those bums at Sala Post's."

Raike turned to stare at Parrish and Parrish opened his mouth to protest that he'd see whom he pleased, but in that instant Ellen cautiously lowered one eyebrow, warning him not to utter a word. Then Paige said, "Edgar Raike, you know Sala Post would never pack a leaf too wet!" Raike stared at Parrish for another half-minute and then turned back to Edgar.

"Now. Nobody noticed the bulks were heating too fast?"

"I noticed."

"Did you fire the men who were supposed to be watching?"

"No."

"Why not?"

Edgar didn't answer.

"I'll tell you why not. Because you're a liar." Abruptly Raike sprang to his feet as though he could no longer sit still. "You're a goddamned liar and a goddamned fool!" Swiftly Ellen went to his side, half holding out her hand and then suddenly checking herself.

"Even your sister, who at times I think knows almost less than any human being alive, although she thinks she knows more—even she knows Sala Post never sends in anything but a perfect crop—perfect leaves." He turned suddenly on Wiley. "Did you go into the bulk room?"

"No, sir."

"No. You hate the heat."

"Yes, sir."

Parrish looked at the three of them, poised as if in battle, and it struck him how different in battle they would be, although they were father and sons, brother and brother. Judd, bull-like, would attack; and Edgar, nervous, thin, slumping, would reach out and claw; and red-headed, good-natured Wiley would dodge. Wiley would just smile and step aside. And then he looked at Paige and thought that Paige was kin to all of them. And to none.

Raike's face was red and heavy now. "Fool!" he yelled. "Idiot! I marvel that a man can be so brainless."

Now Ellen, a thin tight line on her forehead, touched his hand and said very softly, "Darling, this isn't good—"

Raike shook her off. "You stay out of this."

A malicious look of pleasure darted across Edgar's face.

"You're taking it out on yourself, darling," Ellen said.

"When I want medical advice from you, I'll ask for it," Raike lashed out at her. "I got along without you a helluva long time."

Instantly Parrish was on his feet and Ellen quickly held up a hand to stop him. The look of pleasure broadened on Edgar's face and then prudently vanished. Raike flung out his arms, almost involuntarily, as though permitting the still-pent-up anger to burst out through them, and strode toward the door. Halfway across the room he paused and turned.

"You get one thing straight," he said. "I don't lose any love on that high and mighty bastard, Sala Post, and before I'm through I'll teach him a couple of tricks he hasn't seen yet. But if you think this is the kind of thing I want to pull on him, you're a goddam fool." He picked up the telephone, dialed, and without saying hello or identifying himself he ordered his lawyer, Max Maine, to come to the house. Then he stormed out of the room.

Ellen stepped out into the hall after him. "Leave me alone," he yelled at her. "You give me enough trouble."

By the time Parrish reached the hall Raike had gone into the small living room where he was pacing the floor, up and down, up and down. Ellen stood alone in the hall.

"Don't let him talk to you that way," Parrish whispered angrily. "Don't let him get away with it."

"It's nothing." Ellen was quite undisturbed. "He doesn't mean anything by it."

"The hell with that!"

"Parrish, he's a high-strung man. Put yourself in his position. How would you feel to think your son had done such a stupid thing?" Anxiously and even tenderly Ellen's eyes went over to Raike in the next room.

Incredulously Parrish stared at her.

"You have to understand that when he shouts at me, it's nothing personal," Ellen went on calmly. "When he gets upset he snaps at whoever is handy and then it's over with and he's fine. It's good for him to have me because I understand it. It doesn't touch me. But he feels he's accomplished something—whatever it is he has to accomplish."

Now Raike had seen them in whispered conference in the hall and had stopped pacing and was watching them angrily, and Ellen said quickly, "You go back to the den, Parrish. Go on."

"Oh, no—"

"Parrish, for heaven's sake, do you think he's the only man who ever shouted at his wife because he was upset about something else? Now don't be ridiculous. Go back and don't get involved."

Confused and unconvinced, Parrish started reluctantly back to the den, feeling Raike's eyes following him. In the distance he heard the sudden gleeful shouts of Edgar's children, their gaiety seeming incongruous in this house—as out of place as he was. And Ellen, too.

In the den he was not surprised to find Edgar berating Evaline. "Can't you shut those children up?" he railed at her, his mouth in a thin, bitter line. "I've asked you a thousand times. For years we've had this dinner-time chaos—"

The sergeant kicked the corporal, Parrish thought, and the corporal kicked the private. He started to walk out, having no taste for this private dirty fight between a man and his wife, but Edgar stopped him.

"As for you," Edgar spat out, coming toward him, "I've got just one thing to say to you."

Parrish smiled. "Just one?"

"Great sense of humor," Edgar said. "Probably acquired from your gentlemen friends. Well, while you're living in this house, you be a little more careful who you're seen with."

"Don't worry, Edgar, old man. The places I go, nobody you know'll ever see me."

"The point is not who we know. The point is who knows us."

"Oh, Edgar!" Paige said. "How can you be so stuffy!"

"You stay out of this!" Edgar cried, and snapped back to Parrish. "Now understand this. We have a position to maintain, even in the eyes of the lower classes where you find your friends."

"I'll remember, fella." Parrish nodded soberly.

"Just pretend at all times you're the King of Siam, Parrish," Paige said. "If people don't bow down to you, knock 'em down. After a little practice you'll get the idea."

"Listen," Edgar shouted at her, "I think you're crazy. I think there's something wrong with you!"

"Ho, plenty!" Paige agreed.

Parrish moved to go, but Edgar grabbed his arm. "And another thing—that woman," Edgar snapped. "Break it off."

"What woman are you talking about?"

"That woman you used to live with."

It took Parrish several seconds to realize that Edgar meant Lucy. His first reaction was to laugh because he'd seen Lucy only twice since he'd come here, once at Tower's General Store and once at the Dine and Dance. Lucy was the last person he intended to start seeing again. Then he wondered how Edgar knew. "What are you doing, having me followed?" he demanded, angrily.

"Hardly," Edgar said coolly. "It's hardly necessary. People like you are conspicuous enough."

Then Maples came in to say that Judd was ready for dinner and Wiley put down his glass. "Knock it off, Ed," he said. "He's ready to eat."

Edgar paused, his finger still pointing at Parrish. Then he put his hand in his pocket and hurried out.

Parrish turned to wait for Paige, seeing her gazing after Edgar, on her face a look of great dignity and, Parrish thought, of sadness—of pain she had learned to accept. He held out a hand to her, wondering whether she felt the sadness for her father, or her brothers, or for herself.

After dinner Max Maine arrived, a resigned smile on the deeply lined face that seemed to say he had ulcers and wore them like a badge. "What's the trouble, Judd?"

"Max, I'm sick of the way my land's chopped up out there. Those three trashy farmers—"

"Ah, the POT again." Max Maine gave a long-suffering smile. "The POT and Sala Post. What's happened, Judd?"

"I don't need these headaches, Max. I don't want 'em." He motioned the lawyer into the den. "Now you know Tower's got the mortgage on Oermeyer's and last year Oermeyer had blue mold."

"Everyone had a little blue mold last year. You had it yourself. And Tower's a man who'll go along with a bad year—"

"That's your job, Max." Raike shut the door behind him, ignoring Edgar, who stood just a few feet away, hoping to be invited in.

Furiously, Edgar strode into the small living room to join the others, and Parrish, debating whether to go out, could see from the way he flipped open the evening paper that it was going to take only a pinprick to make him explode. A moment later Evaline provided it.

She was chatting with Ellen on the sofa and said, innocently enough, "The children were lovely and quiet tonight, Ellen. Thanks to you."

Edgar looked up sharply.

"Ellen went shopping today and bought them a little mechanical marionette show," Evaline explained. "With lovely soft music, and it's to be set up only at dinnertime to hold their attention and keep them quiet. It's an inspiration."

To Parrish this was just another small detail in Ellen's efforts to make

Raike's household run smoothly, but to Edgar it was the final injury. The rage, blocked up in him so long now, broke out. He threw his paper to the floor. "You're trying to take over everything around here, aren't you?" he said hoarsely. "Well, you leave my children alone!"

"Don't worry, Edgar," Ellen said, calmly. "I'm not interfering with your children."

"You're interfering everywhere." Edgar's voice rose. "My wife, my children, the servants. Paige—"

Paige laughed and flung herself down into a chair. "Don't blame me on Ellen, Edgar," she teased. "I'm just my little old awful self."

"You've got the whole place in an uproar, you've disrupted everything, made our name the laughingstock of the town."

"Edgar, you stop it!" Paige said.

But Edgar continued hysterically, "Nobody would bother with you if Tom Holden didn't pave the way—always going to bat for you. Ask me, that looks pretty suspicious. I think there's something doing between you two!"

In two steps Parrish was at Edgar's side, pulling him out of his chair. Edgar's eyes were wide, his mouth slack with fear.

"Parrish!" Ellen cried out. A shocked silence fell over the room. "Let go, Parrish." Pale, Ellen struggled to remain calm. "Edgar," she said, after a moment, "if you're so miserable here, why don't you take your family into a home of your own? You'd be much happier."

"Oh, no, you don't! You're not pushing me out."

"I'm not trying to push you out. I just hate to see you so wretched."

"Don't pull that on me! I'm on to you." Edgar's voice was rising steadily. "You're trying to get rid of me and my family. And next it'll be Wiley and then Paige and you'll have it all to yourself. Well, goddam you, you're not going to succeed!"

Parrish's hand wrapped around Edgar's arm, and Edgar slapped at it blindly and pulled to get it off.

"Edgar," Ellen said, "as long as you're in this house, don't you ever swear at me again."

"As long as *I'm* in this house!" Edgar laughed. "As long as I'm in this house! Well, I'll tell you something. I'll be here a lot longer than you will! And don't think you can push me around like the others. As long as *you're* in this house, any time you interfere with me, I'll make you plenty miserable."

"Edgar, you've upset your father enough for one evening. The way you're screaming, he can hear you. I don't think he'll like what he hears."

Ellen was quite controlled again now and, sitting very straight and calm, she looked unflinchingly at Edgar, meeting his eyes until he flipped up the newspaper again in front of him.

On the sidewalk in front of Judd Raike's house Parrish leaned against the iron fence. It was a mild evening with a star-shot sky, the smell of spring still in the air—not so much the smell of spring arrived and in full bud as a whispered promise of life about to be, of things stirring, getting started.

He leaned against the fence and thought, Who am I kidding? All along he had known this was coming. He had read it in dozens of looks and gestures, each unimportant in itself but all of them together adding up to the fact that he wasn't going to be able to leave here at the end of a month. For more than a week he had known it. He had only tried to tell himself it wasn't so.

He walked along the sidewalk to the corner and back and after a while he went around for his car and drove out to the Valley. On the highway he passed the preacher making his calls. The preacher, no doubt, would tell him he was suffering for his sins. Tobacco, the preacher would say. Or his times with Lucy. Or what other sins? Wanting to leave his mother? Or the sin of no purpose, when everyone knew a man should live with a purpose. Or just the sin of being different, of never seeming to see things as others did. Parrish guessed in everybody's eyes sin was different, but no matter whose eyes you looked through, you'd find sin in him.

When he came to Tower's Dine and Dance he stopped and went in. For the first time this year he saw Anson, probably home for the weekend; but he wasn't in any mood for Anson's philosophizing tonight. Then at the end of the bar he saw Teet.

"What do you say, Teet?" Parrish shoved away a dirty ash tray and sat down. "You think Sala'd give me a job?"

Teet tapped his pipe clean. "What gives, kid?"

"Nothing gives. Didn't you ever look for a job?"

"'At's a great answer, that is." Teet unzipped his tobacco pouch and took his time refilling the pipe. "Whyn't you go to work for Raike?"

"If Raike wanted me I'd be working by now," Parrish said. "Judd Raike doesn't wait around to be asked."

"My opinion, kid, is that kinda thinkin' could stir up quite a stink."

"Judd Raike doesn't know I'm alive. He hasn't talked to me since he said hello the night I came."

Teet lit his pipe and puffed it, showing his strong white teeth in his red-bearded face, and glanced over at Parrish and worked his pipe some more. "Thought you was only stayin' a month?"

"Whatever gave you that idea?"

With another quick glance at him Teet flicked out the match and lit another. "Sure, kid," he said, when he had the pipe going. "Sala'll give you a job. He's got a soft spot for you—for some nutty reason I can't figure."

Parrish wondered if Teet had heard when Alison would be coming home.

"Listen." Edgar bent over Raike's desk. "You know what that kid's gone and done?"

"Who's that?"

"That damned Parrish."

"Oh, him." Raike picked up a copy of an order he had just sold.

"He's gone and gotten a job, at Sala Post's!"

Slowly, Judd Raike tapped the order sheet on the desk and regarded Edgar with sharp, narrowed eyes. "How do you know?"

"Lewis Post told me. Parrish was out at Sala's day before yesterday asking for a job and Sala said he could come to work."

"I'll be damned!"

"Spite, that's why he did it! Pretty goddam low."

"The young squirt!" Half smiling, Raike leaned back. "Why spite?"

"To get even with us because no one notices him around the house."

Judd Raike considered this as a motive. That he had hardly noticed the boy—that much was true. Now he asked himself why he hadn't noticed him. Was the boy deliberately staying out of his way? And if so, why? Raike had expected that Parrish would ask for a job and had intended to stall him a bit, to show him he hadn't boarded a gravy train, and then find something where he wouldn't get in the way. But the boy hadn't asked. Why not? What had he overlooked seeing in that boy? Not bad-looking—no angel, he'd bet. Probably wouldn't be satisfied with a Children's Home for his hobby, nor Evaline for a woman. Raike was pretty sure of that, so maybe he'd noticed him more than he'd realized.

"Well, don't you care?" Edgar demanded.

"Not particularly."

"Ask me, it's not going to look right—him living in our house and working for Sala Post."

"Don't worry. He's not going to work for Sala Post." Raike tossed the order sheet over to Edgar. "You know, I'd have taken a lot less for that stuff. You left a helluva lot of junk around here for me to get rid of. What'd you do the whole time I was away, anyway?"

He wondered if that boy had gone to Sala for a job just to attract attention, get an advantage for himself. Fairly clever if he had.

"I see you got my message, Parrish." Judd Raike greeted him as he stepped into the tobacco-colored paneled office. "Come in, come in."

Parrish crossed the room to the huge half-circle of a desk and waited while Raike took out one of his aluminum-tubed cigars. He found himself watching for the gold knife, but Raike broke the seal with his thumbnail and opened the tube. "Thought we'd see you down here before this, Parrish." Raike looked up from lighting the cigar. "Sit down, boy."

Parrish sat.

"Now." Raike looked him over while he puffed at the cigar a couple of times. "Don't you think it's time you came in to work?"

Parrish swallowed with a dry throat.

"What's the matter?" Raike said, easily. "Figure you're not ready yet?"

"No, sir," Parrish said quickly. "I've been itching to get to work."

"Should have come to me sooner." Raike leaned back to enjoy his cigar. "Always find a place for a good man."

"Yes, sir."

"Well, what's bothering you, boy?" Raike laughed. "You worried about what we'll find for you? Or the pay, maybe?"

"Sir," Parrish said, "you don't have to give me a job just because you married my mother."

Raike chuckled. "Well, now, I know I don't have to, boy. To tell you the truth, I did think maybe you'd try to get a soft berth. It's refreshing to see I was wrong."

Parrish managed a weak smile, advising himself that he'd better take this job without argument because Raike's good humor would vanish like his cigar smoke if he turned it down. He was staying here for his mother's sake. Having offered him a job, Raike would probably take it out on her if Parrish went to work for Sala Post.

"What would you like to do?" Raike said, jovially. "Think you'd like the warehouse?"

"If possible," Parrish hesitated, "I'd like to be outside. That is, if it's all right with you."

"Fine! Fine!" Raike stood up, put an arm on Parrish's shoulder and escorted him to the door. "Let you know in a day or two, soon as I find the right spot for you. Like to send you out to work with Lemmie—best foreman I've got. You can learn a lot from a good foreman."

He pointed to the cigarette Parrish was smoking. "You get a little older, we'll have to switch you to cigars."

That evening, dressing to go to Maizie Holden's for dinner, Raike said to Ellen, "Did you know he went to Sala Post for a job?"

"Yes."

"And you let him go?"

"He didn't think you wanted him, darling." She turned to meet Judd's accusing eyes. "At least he went to Sala where you buy the crop, instead of to a competitor."

Raike paced the floor. "You're loyal to me all right, Ellen, but I suspect your first loyalty is still to your son."

"There's no conflict between you, darling, so I don't have to make a choice." Ellen was relieved to see Judd smile. "He jumped at the chance to work for you once you offered him a job."

Raike laughed. "You always know all the answers, Ellen."

Actually, Ellen was very uncertain about this development. She would have preferred Parrish to work this summer for Sala Post and then go to college. Knowing Parrish as she did, and knowing Judd, she was not eager to push the two of them together. At least not now. Now was the worst possible time. Ellen picked up her sable wrap. Judd, of course, would never change, but Parrish was young and right now, unfortunately, at the age of uncompromise. A few years earlier he would have been unformed and easier to bend to Judd's ways. A few years later, and he would have learned that life was not always easy; then he'd be glad for a connection like this. For now, all Ellen could do was try to keep them apart as much as possible until Parrish grew to appreciate all this. All this and everything else Judd could do for him. He would in time, she knew. Everyone else did. Why would Parrish be different?

"Anything special you want him to have?" Judd put an arm around her. "Good office job? Something plush?"

"Of course not!" The last place she wanted Parrish was in Judd's office. "What does he know about office jobs?"

"What do Edgar and Wiley know?" Raike said, with a touch of bitterness.

Exactly, Ellen thought. Someday, someone besides Judd would have to know enough to run Raike and Company, and already Ellen had seen enough of Edgar and Wiley to start her thinking. It was a wild dream, she knew, and a brave one. But Wiley and Edgar didn't know a thing about tobacco and never would. And in the end there was no substitute for knowing.

"Start him at the bottom, darling." She smiled at Raike. "You'll feel better that way. He doesn't want charity from you. And you don't want to give it to him."

16

No USE tryin' to sew cloth in this wind." Arthur Lemmie, the foreman at Raike's Eastbrook farm, climbed out of his truck and turned his square sour face into the squally gust blowing across the field. "Another day shot."

He glanced at Parrish sharply with that look Parrish was beginning to recognize, a look that dared him to argue, that said since he was a Raike, or almost a Raike, did he think he had to say something about this. It was a look that accompanied everything Lemmie had ever said either directly to Parrish or merely in his presence. Carefully Parrish refrained from consulting his watch, knowing that the gesture would be interpreted as an argument that at most they would be losing about two hours and not a full day.

Instead he looked past Lemmie at the field, plowed and harrowed and about one-third covered with tent cloth. He hadn't realized last year, arriving late, what a tedious job it was, sewing every inch onto wires by hand. A few bents down, the first pair of workers drew into sight, the Jamaican struggling against the wind to pin down the cloth for the woman to sew. It was clear that after this row they would have to stop, which meant that the men would switch to mixing fertilizer. The thought gave Parrish no pleasure.

He looked over at Lemmie, questioning. With John he would have gone down to help the Jamaican, but two weeks here had taught him to wait for orders.

"How about going in and giving the fella a hand?" Lemmie said, with elaborate courtesy.

Parrish started toward the field. "You want me to drive the women home after this row?"

"You got anything better for them to do?"

Passing next to Lemmie, Parrish caught a whiff of the fishy smell of fertilizer that the wind carried off his clothing, and then Lemmie called after him: "Get 'em home, and then you get back here. You can give a hand mixing fertilizer."

Parrish kicked at a clump of harrowed earth. Well, there it was. Now he would have to explain that he couldn't mix fertilizer today and tell the reason why—that all the Raikes had to go to the country-club dance to-night, the great, godalmighty dance with about a hundred cocktail parties before and new gowns for everyone, even Evaline, who'd had to exchange hers twice before Edgar was satisfied. And he had to go, too. And, natu-rally, he couldn't go smelling of fish, which was how fertilizer smelled. So today he was under orders not to mix fertilizer.

He came up behind a pair of Jamaicans moving one of the heavy wooden horses on which they stood to reach the cloth.

"These horse are too heavy, I theenk," one boy was complaining. "Last year I work for Tom Holden where these horses are not so heavy, I—" Seeing Parrish, he broke off, lest his complaints be reported to Judd Raike.

That was a laugh, Parrish thought. He could just picture Raike asking him for small complaints from the farm. Then he climbed up on the wooden horse and thought, I'm getting damn sick of this.

They finished the row and Lemmie ordered the Jamaicans to the shed to mix and bag the fertilizer, tossing a side glance at Parrish, almost as though he knew. Parrish met the look with silence. Maybe he'd just skip the explanations and claim he'd had a breakdown with the truck. It would be an easy way out.

"O.K., speed it up," Lemmie barked at the Jamaicans. "We ain't got all day."

Waiting in the truck for the women, Parrish thought that Lemmie would never be half the man John Donati was, for all he knew tobacco and barked and griped the same. John could say those words and make the men feel like a great crew. And Lemmie could use the same words and just the way he spoke them—just the little things that went with them, or maybe were left out—could make them feel like a bunch of bums. Lemmie wasn't a man who would ever understand, as John would, how it would gall Parrish to have to refuse to mix fertilizer.

On the other hand, Parrish asked himself, what was wrong with him all of a sudden that he needed so badly to be understood? That he was dreaming up stories about breakdowns? He switched off the motor and walked over to Lemmie.

"When I get back," he said, "I can't mix the goddam fertilizer because I have to be with Raike tonight and he doesn't like the smell." Even as he spoke he knew it was impossible to explain anything to this man. He knew, too, that they were all watching—the Jamaicans and the women in the truck—and he felt suddenly and deeply humiliated. He turned away without waiting for an answer, but not without catching the look in Lemmie's eye that mourned how much he had to put up with.

"Just drop the women," Lemmie said, pained. "And go on home."

Parrish knew that he would never again be told to mix fertilizer and that, when they spread it in the fields, he wouldn't be asked to do that, either. He kicked at an old rag of tent cloth in the dusty path and slammed the door shut and drove faster than necessary out to the road, thinking how he hated this spot.

Brooding and with mounting rebellion he made the round, dropping each woman in front of her house. Hell, he thought, why shouldn't he mix fertilizer? He'd done a lot worse and nobody'd ever had to make allowances for his work before, not even Milky, when he was nothing but a green kid. Not mixing fertilizer because he had to smell pretty for a round of cocktail parties and a stupid dance he didn't want to go to with a lot of stupid people he'd be just as happy never to see again. . . . This was what he was beginning to hate more than anything about living at Raike's—the unimportant little concessions to keep the peace, the little compromises, each trivial in itself, that added up day after day, making you feel you were living a lie.

His own choice would have been to mix fertilizer. His own choice would be not to go to the dance. And yet he had refused to do the one, and in a little while he'd be on his way to the other. And whose choices were these, anyway, and why was he doing this? His choice would be to go back to work at Sala Post's.

Back at the farm he exchanged the empty truck for his own car and headed for Hartford, his thoughts going back, as he drove in the thickening traffic, to the careful, defensive attitude of the Jamaicans and Lemmie's petty resentment because he was a Raike and had come to work in the fields.

The wind had blown gray clouds across the sky now, bringing a dampness to the air. At the bridge, traffic slowed to a stop for a moment and Parrish looked idly down the long white lines dividing the bridge approach into three lanes, and at the signs ordering drivers to stay in their own lane, and back to the authoritative solid white lines, and he thought suddenly that that described it exactly—the way it was with people.

These were the rules of the road. Pick a lane and stay in it. No indecision and irresponsible driving, no cutting back and forth from one lane to the other, snarling up traffic. And no straddling a white line, half in one lane, half in the other. You couldn't drive in two lanes at once.

And, it seemed, you couldn't live in two worlds at once. No matter how little you cared to live in one or how willing to let live in the other. Except maybe in his own eyes, a man could not be just a man, unattached. To others he had a label; he belonged somewhere and he should stay there. In an orderly manner, the traffic moved over the bridge, everyone staying in his own lane, and Parrish stayed in his until he turned off to head for home.

Pondering and confused, recognizing the existence of a condition he could not understand, Parrish entered the house, pausing in the elegant white and gold hall and thinking that here, too, it was the same. Here, they had resented his cutting into their lane, but once he was in it they resented even more his ever straying out. Stay in your lane, boy, stay in your lane. Impulsively, balancing himself, Parrish walked along the raised band on the patterned carpeting, careful not to step off.

"What do you think you're doing?" Edgar stood in the doorway of the den.

"I'm practicing," Parrish said soberly, "staying in my lane."

"What!"

Parrish stepped off the line. "Private joke. All mine."

Behind Edgar, Ellen said, "Parrish, come in here, please. Something rather serious—"

Parrish saw that Ellen was disturbed and thought that if Edgar had been needling her again, this time he'd do something. Today he was in no mood for self-restraint. He went into the den, where Wiley, as usual, was tending bar for himself.

"All right," Edgar snapped. "Tell him."

"Parrish, dear—" Ellen started and paused.

"What's the problem?" Parrish said.

"The problem is you." Edgar couldn't hold himself in any longer. "The problem is you're involving us all in a scandal with that woman."

"What!" Parrish looked at the three sober faces accusing him. "What woman?"

"That woman you lived with—that Ballow female!"

"You mean Lucy?" Parrish sat down. "Is that what this is all about?"

"That's plenty," Edgar snapped. "You've got the whole town talking about how you're carrying on with her—what a spectacle you made with her at Tower's."

Parrish laughed. "That carrying on amounted to one dance and one drink with her family."

"I repeat," Edgar said. "Carrying on."

"Listen, boy, when I decide to carry on, it'll involve a lot more than that!"

"Parrish!" Ellen sounded a warning. "Be careful."

"I don't want to be careful!" Parrish yelled.

At the bar Wiley gave a short, bored laugh. "Maybe he just goes for her, Ed," he said. "How about it, Parrish? She get your pressure up?"

Parrish ignored the question and stood up to go.

"We're not through," Edgar said sharply.

"I'm through."

Edgar stepped in front of him. "That woman has had a child. They're saying it's yours."

"That's a goddam lie."

"I'm not so sure."

"Get out of my way."

"You're still running around with her. You seem to feel an obligation."

"That's a lie and you know it!"

"I know it!" Edgar screamed. "How do I know it? The whole town—"

"Because that baby's too damned old. I didn't get here until June."

Edgar got control of himself, drew himself up primly. "If I'd been unfortunate enough to have any association with that kind of woman I wouldn't have had to keep track of dates to defend myself."

Parrish let his eyes travel down Edgar's unprepossessing figure and back to his face, seeing to his surprise that Edgar was flushing. He gave a short laugh. "I agree," he said. "You wouldn't."

"Parrish—" Ellen cut in. "You and I will discuss this later. Go upstairs now and start to get dressed."

"And stop seeing that woman." Edgar threw a final shot.

Deliberately, Parrish turned back to him. "I'll see anyone I please."

"Parrish," Ellen said, firmly, "we're due at Maizie's at six and you're supposed to go on to Clayton's and Melissa's at seven."

Suddenly Parrish was sick of the whole thing, his resentment hardening into stubborn resistance. "I'm not going," he announced. "I'm not going to Maizie's, and I'm not going to Clayton's."

"You're going," Edgar said.

"And I'm not going to any dance."

"Oh, yes, you are." Edgar walked up close. "There's enough talk about you now. You're going to show everybody that you can behave decently."

"Maybe I can't," Parrish said. "Maybe I'm not even sure what decent behavior is. Anyway, I'm not going."

He went upstairs and, still fuming, flung himself down on his bed. A moment later Ellen came in and he got up and paced the floor in silence until she spoke. "It's true." She looked at him reprovingly. "People are talking."

"Let 'em talk."

"Now, Parrish, you know it won't do you any good—"

"I don't give a damn. Just because a lot of people have nothing to do they've found a new topic of conversation for lunch or for cocktail party number one or two or three. Or should I say new victim—same old topic."

"Parrish, this is serious. Your reputation is important."

"The only opinion of me I care about is my own," he said stubbornly. "And I don't want to talk about it any more."

"Parrish, you must care. These are nice people. You don't want them—"

Parrish snorted. "What's nice about them? The way Clayton Norris tells his dirty jokes? The nice way Harris Lowe makes passes at somebody else's wife while his own wife begins her disappearing act?"

"Parrish," Ellen said, shocked, "where did you pick up all this?"

"Of course, they're all very careful—like Edgar—that everything looks fine. In public, Harris Lowe and his wife are practically a model pair. And I never heard Clayton Norris raise his voice telling a dirty joke. You know Clayton Norris is even thinking of running for the legislature? That's a fact. He told me himself."

"Parrish, you're exaggerating and you're terribly confused. I don't know where you get these ideas."

"I'm not confused, and you're not, either. You know as well as I do that they've got a great big solid-gold set of rules, what Edgar calls decent behavior—" he started to yell—"and if you follow all these rules and wear the right clothes and go with the right people and say the right words at the right times, which is the same thing as saying nothing at all, then everyone will have a very high opinion of you and even Edgar, with his ear to the ground, won't hear anything wrong about you, and when you die Gabriel will say to St. Peter, Open up all the gates—here's a man who followed all the rules. Made a great impression on everyone. Even stayed in his own lane."

"Parrish, what are you talking about?"

"Never mind." He turned away. "It doesn't matter."

"Parrish, everyone cares what other people think of him."

"You won't believe this, but there are people who do not."

"You won't believe this, Parrish, but there are no such people. In very normal or in very twisted ways, everyone cares."

But now Ellen was looking quite worried and Parrish told himself to calm down. He was only taking out on her what he felt against others. "You notice Edgar didn't ask what the truth was," he pointed out. "He didn't say, 'If, by any chance, it's yours, are you being a man and doing something about it?' No. He just wants to be sure no one knows."

"Parrish, in this case Edgar is at least partially right. You should be more careful about that girl."

"Edgar is never right. That's a flat, positive statement. Edgar is never right."

"In this case he is," Ellen persisted. "You're letting yourself get a bad name for nothing. People don't forget things like that. It's not practical to be so careless."

Suddenly Parrish felt unexplainably sad. He sat on the bed and looked at his mother, wishing he could make her understand. "It was like this." He spoke quietly now. "Everyone was avoiding Lucy—all the fellows who used to chase her. I felt sorry for her. So I danced with her to cheer her up. And it did. She felt like a human being again. It was a pretty cheap form of charity."

"No, Parrish, it was expensive because people are talking."

"People! People make me sick. If a mangy dog comes along and you fuss over it, that's fine. But you find a human being who needs a little kindness and you give it, that doesn't go. That's immoral. Great world! Full of great people!"

"Parrish, you can't change it."

"Well, it can't change me."

"Parrish, you'll have to change."

"Don't bet on it."

"You'll have to learn to give and take and—"

"I know," he said, wearily. "Get along. Follow the rules."

Ellen nodded, obviously worried, and he hated himself for causing her this pain. Then she looked across the room and he saw for the first time that she had laid out his formal clothes—his costume of respectability bought since he'd come here. He had never been so respectable before.

"Parrish, please," Ellen said. "Get dressed and come to the dance."

The only reason he was staying in this house was to keep her from being hurt and here he was, delivering the worst blows himself. Edgar, he knew, could never hurt her the way he could.

Capitulating, Parrish stood up and started toward the closet. And then he thought, this was the way a man began—this was how he fell into the trap. Wanting to avoid pain to someone else or maybe just to himself, he sold off the first little fragment of his soul—just a little, it went almost unnoticed. Because it spared so much pain it was worth it. The act was reasonable, sensible. It was adult and civilized and here he was, taking the first giant step on the road to that great wonderful cure-all, compromise.

"Maybe later." He tried to sound as though he meant it. "Maybe I'll turn up later."

But she knew he wouldn't and that she couldn't persuade him, and she loved him anyway, understanding, as always. She touched his arm. "Parrish, you're a fool."

Parrish sat stubbornly in his room until he heard them leave for Maize Holden's cocktail party and then he changed into a bright red sport shirt and a pair of slacks and went out to his car and drove in to the Valley. Passing Tower's Dine and Dance, he slowed down, his anger boiling up again, and decided he could come back here later. He passed the road to Sala's and wondered with acute yearning why Alison had not come home yet. Then he passed Lucy's house and thought, Why not? Knowing it was mostly spite, but also a little to get the bad taste of properness out of his mouth, he turned in.

He knocked and Lucy came to the door, looking astonished and then pleased when she saw him.

"Parrish!" she cried. "Well, what do you know!"

He caught the familiar smell of garlic as he stepped into the room and then Frenchy yelled out, "Willya look who's here!"

Lucy shut the door and stood beside him. "Gee, Parrish, what are you doin' here?"

"Get the man a beer," Frenchy ordered. "And me, too."

"Sit down, Parrish," Rosie said, while Mamma moved a chair for him.

"Hey!" he protested. "I didn't get this much attention the whole time I lived here."

"You're company now," Lucy said.

"How's the baby, Lucy?"

"That kid!" Rosie was back with the beer. "Weighed more'n nine pounds. An' Lucy had a time like it was nothin'. Now me, all my organs was tore. Doctor says he don't know how I pulled through—with my organs."

"Ah, her an' her organs," Frenchy said.

"Yah—well, you try it sometime, see how you like it."

Frenchy whacked her bottom. "I'll do that, kid. First chance I get. 'At's a promise."

Rosie shrieked with laughter and Parrish smiled, feeling better already. He'd forgotten how free and easy they were and how good it felt.

"Parrish, I gotta show you something." Rosie opened a package on the table and held up for his admiration a pair of very long black gloves. "Fourteen bucks."

Parrish stared. Then, realizing what was expected, he said, "Boy!"

Rosie nodded importantly. "I'm wearin' 'em to a big wedding. Knock 'em dead."

"Nuts!" Frenchy tapped his head, but you could see he was proud of them, too. "Well, let's move in the parlor."

"This is O.K.," Parrish said. "I spent a lot of time in this kitchen."

"Yeah, but it's different now," Rosie said. "You're used to better, with all of them. Go on in the parlor."

Parrish looked at the circle of beaming faces, seeing now that they were flattered at his visit, and he stopped protesting. They expected him to move into the parlor. Disappointed, he thought that they of all people should know him better. They should know it wasn't different now. Taking a last look at the terrible black gloves, he picked up his can of beer.

It was a greatly changed parlor. In a corner, Gramma peered at them from the old rocker, the only thing in the room that was the same. The drab overstuffed furniture and the heavy dark table that would never open were gone, replaced by a chartreuse sofa, a pair of orange chairs, and an awful grayish-white table with a hideous lamp. And in the middle of one wall, jutting out into the room, was a tremendous, shiny, streamlined electric refrigerator.

"Ain't it sump'n!" Rosie said.

Thoroughly bewildered, Parrish stared, asking himself how many paydays he and Lucy had dropped fifty cents apiece into the piggie bank.

"The whole neighborhood's dyin', they're so jealous," Rosie said. "That's why I bought the gloves—gotta keep up impressions."

"Watch out for the devil!" Gramma yelled in her corner. "They're all sinners, now!"

"Preacher's got Gramma thinkin' the devil got in Lucy account of the baby." Frenchy shrugged. "Now she thinks it's spreadin'."

Parrish grinned. That was one thing that hadn't changed. But he'd had enough—he wanted to get out of here.

Then the baby started to cry and Lucy insisted that he come upstairs. In the baby's room, Parrish's bewilderment increased. While he'd lived here, no bedroom in the house had had so much as a cotton mat on the floor; but here was a large pale-blue rug, as well as a roomful of expensive, ornate furniture. Coming after the evidence downstairs of new-found wealth, it was just too much.

"Lucy," he said, only half joking, "you haven't been in business?"

"Ah, Parrish! You know I wouldn't charge!" Lucy laughed.

Puzzled, Parrish looked at Lucy's child, a sturdy-looking boy with bright red hair, and he wondered more than ever who the father was. It was strange that, even living here, he had not picked up the smallest hint. Watching Lucy while she fondled the child, Parrish thought for a moment that the boy reminded him of someone, and then he dismissed the idea. All babies looked alike. Probably, with those big brown eyes and dimples, the baby reminded him of Lucy. Only no one in this family had red hair, and the chin was different. A prominent jaw line, not at all like the Ballows, Mamma or Rosie or Lucy.

"Sit down, Parrish," Lucy said, unbuttoning the top button of her blouse. "It's feedin' time."

By the time Parrish realized that she was going to nurse the child, Lucy had her baby at her breast. He blushed furiously and looked away. "I'll see you downstairs, Lucy," he stammered.

Still puzzling, he went slowly downstairs again and found Frenchy alone in the living room, taking another can of beer out of the well-stocked refrigerator. "You must have had a good crop last year, Frenchy," he said, although he didn't really believe that was the answer.

"I had a good crop. But I was robbed."

"You're pretty fixed up around here."

"Big deal." Frenchy downed the can of beer. "Ah, it ain't bad, I guess."

"Don't you like it?"

"I didn't buy it," Frenchy said, flatly, as if that excused him from deciding, and got himself another beer. He patted the refrigerator. "This baby's O.K. with me."

"That's a nice-looking boy Lucy's got," Parrish said.

Frenchy eyed him narrowly, but all he said was, "Like another beer?"

Parrish shook his head, noticing that Frenchy was getting flushed and that he spilled a little beer while opening the can. "That kid remind you of anyone you know?" Frenchy said suddenly.

"Lucy, a little. But not much."

"Not the chin, eh?" Frenchy laughed. "Or the red hair?"

Parrish shook his head, waiting, afraid that a direct question would discourage Frenchy, and at the same time asking himself why he wanted so much to know. Then Frenchy gave a short laugh and the moment of expectancy passed. Frenchy wasn't going to tell him.

Then suddenly he didn't have to. In one of those unexplainable flashes, Parrish knew who the baby reminded him of. He leaped to his feet and rushed upstairs to look again, but even before he reached the room he knew, and as he looked at the red-haired suckling child, he was certain. It wasn't the second look he needed so much as time to understand what he had seen.

Lucy adjusted the baby at her full hanging breast. "Who told you, Parrish? Frenchy?"

The hair was brighter, but there was no mistaking that Raike jaw. The baby looked like Wiley.

Lucy frowned. "He shouldn't have told. Edgar give us all the furniture and the refrigerator—"

The payoff. He could just picture it: Edgar coming into the house, acting as though it were contaminated, buying his brother out of trouble —prudish, sexless Edgar, learning that his brother had been fooling around with this kind of girl. And, Parrish thought, Alison had been furious at *him!* Alison had gone with Wiley instead.

"Frenchy's just sore because Edgar bought his crop last year and didn't pay high," Lucy was saying. "But I keep tellin' him, he more'n made it up when the baby come. He was real generous then."

That fitted. Edgar would prefer to cheat a man out of his proper price give him charity instead. The charity made him feel so great. "Edgar' like that," he said. "Especially if Wiley's in trouble."

"Wiley? It wasn't Wiley."

Parrish smiled. Let her deny all she wanted, now.

"It was Edgar hisself."

Lucy turned away to tend to the baby. She put him on her shoulde and tucked her breast into her pink bra and buttoned her blouse "Whatcha lookin' like that for?" she said.

The times he had wondered what the man had that attracted her since she had said it wasn't love! "Lucy, how could you stand him? Edgar!"

"Ah—" Lucy looked surprised. "Truth is he wasn't so much. Kinda mad it up in meanness." Parrish looked so shocked that Lucy had to laugh "Lotta men like that, Parrish. They just figure men are better than women They gotta show you they got the upper hand."

"You ever think you didn't have to stand for it?"

"I don't mind a man havin' the upper hand. I kinda like it. You wa always that way."

"Never! I was never mean to you!"

"You was always the boss. He was a big boss, too, but not much good After you come I'd have stopped but it wasn't that easy."

"Why not? Why wasn't it easy?"

"Well, you know how it is, Parrish—"

"No, I don't know. How is it?"

"Parrish, him bein' a Raike and all—"

And he said it was mine. His sour mouth, and looking down his nose with his pale unhealthy skin, and his satisfied slump, knowing all th time, in his spineless sneaky soul, and saying it was mine. . . . The dam highway slushed under the wheels and the lines of the bridge approac gleamed white off the dark road and all the traffic moved in an order! fashion over the bridge. Waiting for me in the hall, a great, holier, pure cleaner-than-anyone, don't-touch-me look on his pasty, proper face. "Th whole town is talking about you. You're involving us in a scandal." Th soft lights of the country club came through the fog. The white stones the drive wound around to the parking circle. The music beat wit determined cheerfulness in the drizzly night air. *And he said it was min*

He sat hunched on the railing of the club veranda. A light patterning rain was falling, cold against the skin but smelling of spring. At his finger-tips dark branches of hemlock glistened in the lamplight.

He hated to step into that awful gaiety. Through the window he could see the ceaseless motion, the glitter and brilliant color, and hear shrill voices and practiced laughter. Over the persistent beat of a drum a piano tinkled, sounding thin and isolated, filling him with a feeling of his own aloneness. In front of a half-lowered shade he watched a tiresome little performance of a man's manicured hand, a star sapphire in his cuff, moving intimately along a slender feminine back. He turned away and walked down the veranda to a side door and entered the cocktail lounge.

Instantly, shocked glances skipped through the crowd as people began to notice his slacks and loud shirt, and Parrish told himself he didn't care about that, either. After a quick look around for Edgar he sat at the end of the bar. He was staring at the pyramid of bottles over the bartender's shoulder when Paige came up behind him with Tom Holden.

"What'd you have in mind," she greeted him, "coming here like this?"

"I just happened to be in the neighborhood," Parrish said belligerently, "so I thought I'd drop in." His eyes went up to Tom Holden, challenging, but Tom only stood with his arms folded, smiling patiently.

"Well, don't snap at me. I don't care." Paige waved away a cloud of cigar smoke. "It's a horrible party. Same old junk. Gol-lee, look at them looking at you!"

Parrish laughed in spite of himself. "Paige, you're wonderful!"

"Beautiful, too." Tom Holden ran his hand over her shiny hair. "And too young to be standing at the bar. It's against the rules." He smiled at Parrish. "You, too."

Parrish shrugged. "That's my career—breaking rules."

In the next room the orchestra was starting a rumba. He scanned the crowd again for Edgar, deciding that he'd probably have to go find him.

"Paige," Tom said, "will you dance with me two dances later, so that now I can have a drink with this career man?"

Watching while Tom walked Paige to the door, Parrish told himself he wasn't going to make any excuses to Tom Holden. But Tom only settled down on the next bar stool and took his time getting himself a drink.

"I've always thought, Parrish," he said after a while, his eyes friendly, "a man should pick his rules to break as carefully as his mistress."

The unexpectedness of the words produced a crack of a smile that quickly died.

"They'll both demand so much energy."

Parrish shrugged.

"It's bound to be harder work, swimming against the tide. I always figure it ought to be worth it."

Parrish took a quick look in the mirror over the bar for Edgar. Probably, he decided, he wouldn't have to go look for him. The way people were looking at him, Edgar would get the news and would soon be in here to speak his piece. "Tom—" Parrish ran the point of a swizzle stick along a seam in the bar, feeling irritation at the terrible rumba music grinding on—"you ever wonder what makes a man so miserable, like Edgar?"

"Oh, Edgar's all right," Tom said. "He just has his moments."

"Well, that's a sporting thing to say." While he talked Parrish wondered why he didn't just come out with the whole pretty story and show what a good fellow Edgar was. Edgar would have had it out already and added to it, too, had things been the other way round. Instead, he said, "You ever get moments like that, Tom? When you feel like grinding someone under your heel like a worm?" Tom smiled, creasing the scar on his cheek, and Parrish snapped the swizzle stick in two. "So it's more than moments."

"Is that what's behind this, Parrish? Some thought to even the score with Edgar? A glorious revenge?"

Parrish frowned, not sure of himself. In a way that was true, although it stung him a little to think it and until now he had not. But it was more. He was sore at the world tonight. He was sore at this crowd and at Lemmie and at the injustice and unreasonableness of people, the foolish importance they tied to things that made them so. He felt cheated, bitter because Lucy and Rosie and Frenchy had failed him. And yet that wasn't true, either. They hadn't failed him. They had always been as they had showed themselves tonight. Proof of that lived in Lucy's child, conceived before he had come here. The fault was in him, for not seeing them as they were. He was sore at himself.

"Parrish," Tom said, "did you ever meet my mother?"

Parrish nodded.

"Well, in twenty years my mother has not missed church on Sunday."

"Maybe she likes church."

"Not particularly. But she goes every Sunday. And I go with her. You see, Parrish, we have the money. Whatever we do we're conspicuous. Whether we like it or not, people watch us and we set standards."

Parrish looked at the frantic, half-drunken crowd. He saw Clayton Norris whispering to his buddy, Harris Lowe, and he knew he was passing along his latest sex story. He saw Lorraine Lowe edging toward the door and he'd bet a bag of the fertilizer he'd refused to mix that in ten minutes she'd be in the back seat of somebody's car. "Great standards."

"I mean public standards," Tom said. "So when Edgar fusses about how you behave in public, he's infuriating, but he's not entirely wrong. You're a Raike now and you can't get away with as much as before. You may not like it, but it's a fact. And you have a right to ignore it, but you ought at least to understand what you're doing—consider the cost as well as the winnings."

Parrish smiled. Tom Holden knew more than he had suspected. "Where'd you find out so much, Tom?"

Tom laughed. "They say out in the fields that in our little Valley we have no secrets. It's the same with us. We're a clan. You might almost say we've fenced ourselves into our rich little pasture. It's hard to get inside the fence. And not much gets outside the fence, but in the pasture we seem to have few secrets."

Tom stood up. "And now here comes Maizie to claim me. I should tell you, Parrish, that Maizie is in complete rebellion against everything I've said. Maizie would say, Don't worry about the rules you *break* but choose with supreme care the ones you *live by*, because they'll demand so much love."

Parrish grinned as Maizie came up beside Tom. "Maizie, I'm with you," he said.

"And I'm with you, precious," Maizie said.

And yet he wondered whether complete rebellion was the way. Lately he'd been rebelling against everything, raising one hell of a fuss, and right now he couldn't feel worse. A man could get so caught up in rebellion that he no longer knew clearly what he was fighting for—or against. Like his striking out against proper clothes and polite talk and manners, and thinking the Ballows so free because they lacked them. Now he saw that he was as wrong as the rest. The rest attached undue importance to these little things, but so had he, at the opposite extreme—both seeing only the manners and clothing, neither giving thought to the man inside.

"And now that I've given you all this good advice," Tom said, "would you care to join us at our table?"

Parrish shook his head. He thought maybe he would leave before Ellen saw him. What he had to say to Edgar would keep, and suddenly he wanted time to think. But it was too late. Already he saw Edgar hurrying up to him, brushing aside people who blocked his way, scarcely nodding to Tom and Maizie when they passed.

"Get out!" Edgar threw a quick nervous look around the room. "What do you mean, coming here like this?"

The anger Parrish had pushed away flooded back on him and he could only think that Edgar was here, right here; and he looked down at his fist, knuckled tight and trembling, and forced it half open, and it clamped tight again and he heard the orchestra pounding to a frantic pitch and thought he could hit him just once and everything he felt would go with that single blow to Edgar's face.

"When I talk to you, look at me!"

Edgar grabbed his arm and Parrish shook him off, and he grabbed again, his hand feeling like a hook in the flesh, while Parrish, his blood pounding as hard as the drums in his ears, thought blindly that he wanted only to hit Edgar and hit him again and again. Then a trumpet screamed a long note over the final crash of the drums, and the orchestra stopped. The room was quiet.

And Parrish thought, What for? What good would it do if he hit Edgar once or twice or a hundred times? Which of these confused, betrayed, mixed-up feelings would it help or explain? "Go away," he said, shaking him off. "Leave me alone."

"You get out of here—"

"Edgar, shut your goddam mouth and leave me alone."

A new thought was forming in Parrish's mind, a possibility that had not occurred to him before, more important than his hatred for Edgar, and he didn't want to talk. He wanted time to examine it.

"Why, you young delinquent! I'm going to have you thrown out."

Parrish swung around so quickly that Edgar backed away. "Look, Edgar, I know what the score is. I found out a lot about you tonight, so stop pushing me around."

Wariness flashed in Edgar's eyes. His lips twitched and, watching, Parrish pictured those thin hard lips devouring Lucy, and then it became clear to him that this was the least important of his feelings. That Edgar had made love to Lucy didn't matter (even while he thought the word *love* he knew it didn't apply, was used only out of habit to politely describe an act), that anything had existed between Edgar and Lucy didn't bother him in the least. He didn't know, even, whether it was still going on. He didn't care.

Edgar recovered a little. "Damn you! Shall I tell you the truth? They're all laughing at you—and at us. I'm having you thrown out."

"Edgar," Parrish said, "I was out at Lucy's tonight and I found out. So that's that."

An awful fear sat in Edgar's eyes. "I don't know what you're talking about."

"You know."

"It's a lie!" Edgar's tongue jabbed at his lip and the hand that held the bar trembled. "Parrish, did you tell anyone?"

Parrish stared at Edgar, seeing the sickening look of a cornered man, thinking that he ought to let him suffer awhile. He'd asked for it.

"You were talking to Tom Holden. I saw you. What were you talking about? *Answer* me!"

"Quit yelling at me, Edgar." Then he thought, Tell him. Tell him his secret is safe. "No," he said. "I didn't tell Tom. Or anyone."

"They wouldn't believe you, anyway." Little wet beads glistened on Edgar's pale face. "They think it's yours. They'll say you're trying to squirm out."

"Maybe."

"I have more friends here than you. They'll never believe a low character like you against me."

"You want to take that chance?" Parrish was almost sorry he'd started this here. Edgar was collapsing fast.

"Don't think you can blackmail me!"

"Damn right I think it!" In his mind he wasn't calling it blackmail, but the idea was growing, the pieces fitting together fast. "Damn right!"

"Now, Parrish, there's nothing to be gained by letting this get out— spoiling our good name." The words spilled out, wheedling, slimy. "After all, you're one of us now—"

"Oh, God, Edgar!"

Edgar licked at his lip. "What do you want?"

Now that it was becoming clear, Parrish was shocked that he had been so slow to see it, that anger had almost made him throw away this chance. "What I want, Edgar," he spoke slowly, examining the bargain even while he offered it, "is for you to be the most decent guy in the world to my mother. At home and in public, both. I want you to be so courteous, so considerate, that all your friends will think you're a very great gentleman."

Edgar gaped. "That's all?"

"That's all."

"But after they've said it's yours!"

Parrish gave a crooked smile. That was his choice—his reputation or his freedom. Even as he thought it, he knew there was no real choice. His eyes met Edgar's, and the bargain was made.

He was free. He ought to feel great.

Edgar moved down the bar and gulped a drink and Parrish watched him. Here, he thought, was a serious thing and nobody could bear to touch it. A son actually existed because of this man, a baby who was a Raike, looked like a Raike, and yet wasn't, because of the rules of civilized people. And Edgar was drinking, not out of guilt, but out of fear that others would learn a dirty thing about him, a thing that to Edgar became dirty only when it became knowledge in others. There was no rottenness in the act nor its consequences nor in him until someone could talk about it.

And Lucy told herself she had been privileged to sleep with him because he was a Raike and the greatness of money was on him. Not for the money, but because of it. Even though her instincts had told her Edgar was not much, still, illogically, she felt honored. And the family didn't face up to it for a bad thing because there were long black gloves and new furniture to impress the neighbors—and cold beer. Everyone was pretending, to others and to himself.

Parrish shook his head, wishing he could understand it, but knowing only that he felt terrible and that seeing the Ballows as they were was part of it. He had been a fool about them, painting a picture all rosy innocence, seeing in them only what he had wanted to see. He had been so sure of them. And he had been wrong.

Miserably, he stood up. The orchestra was starting again and he picked his way past people standing up to dance and at the door glanced back once more at Edgar and saw that Raike had joined him. Then Raike moved aside a step and Parrish, standing with his hand on the door, felt his heart leap to the ceiling and then sink, because standing next to Raike and looking across the room at Parrish with disgust were Wiley and Alison.

Parrish stood perfectly still. In his brain something warned him that there was nothing he could do now and the best thing would be to go, the sooner the better; but still he stayed and stared at her, seeing her heavy hair brushing her shoulders and her fluffy white gown trimmed with green, and everything about her immaculate and perfect as he remembered, and the tilt to her chin and that cold look that could never conceal her fire to anyone who had held her.

He wanted to go to her, to explain, to tell her what had happened, but even as he took a single step back into the room he knew it was no use, that it couldn't be done this way. He tore his eyes away from Alison and turned and bolted out onto the veranda.

The miserable feeling returned and Parrish walked down the steps into the rain, thinking of the number of times he had privately called Wiley a fool. Wiley did only a few simple things that were expected of him—he always managed to be pleasant and charming, he wore the clothes he was expected to wear, he said what he was expected to say, he never argued. And Wiley was inside dancing with Alison in his arms, and Parrish was out here alone. And who was the greater fool?

He made his way across the parking circle.

"Parrish?" He heard the voice from his car and recognized it as Paige's before he could make her out in the dark. A little annoyed, he stopped, not wanting to talk to anyone any more tonight, not even Paige.

"I figured you wouldn't last long in there," she called through the window. "Come on, Parrish, it's pouring—dope!"

Slowly, Parrish moved on to the car and got in. "What are you doing here, Paige?" he said, not too cordially.

"All that junk! I thought I'd ride home with you." Then Paige stopped, sensing that she was not entirely welcome. "Parrish, would you rather I didn't?"

"It's O.K." But he had nothing to say and he couldn't make small talk tonight. He leaned back on the seat of the car, crossing his arms over his face, and it came on him that the real soreness in him was having to face up to his own wrongness. Even to himself—least of all to himself—a man didn't like to admit that he'd been a fool. A sick feeling was taking root in him that perhaps he was wrong about everything.

"Paige," he said suddenly. "You ever find out that you were wrong about something? Something important?"

"Me!" She laughed. "Ho! All the time."

"You take something you really believed in—" Inwardly, he was crying out for answers, and speech was choking him. And yet he felt that Paige could sense what he was trying to say. "When you find out you're wrong where you were positive you were right, how can you be sure of anything then?"

"Parrish, mostly I don't think you're wrong about things," Paige said.

"Maybe all your ideas just add up to a bag full of holes, that won't hold water at all when you try to use it."

Hesitantly, Paige touched his arm. "I think quite often that you're right, Parrish."

"What'd I come here tonight for—dressed like this, making a big scene? I don't know." He stared gloomily at the rain-streaked windshield. "Slugging around at everyone and everything like a punchy fighter."

"Who?"

"Me. Wild man."

Paige's eyes widened. "In there?"

"No! No, I mean that's the way I've been lately. I can see it now. Last couple of years. A one-man lunatic rebellion, that's what I've been."

It was true. Rebellion for its own sake in the name of nothing. His mother had said he would find out, but he'd been so sure. He had been a very wise, very smart, very cocksure man and he had taken a look at a baby's jaw and red hair and suddenly realized he had been wrong about maybe a hundred thousand things.

Puzzled, Paige looked at him soberly. "Well, Parrish, if you're talking about rebellion," she began uncertainly and then went on, determinedly cheerful, "you've come to the right person. I'm an expert. I'm going to write a book on the subject. How to Get into the Greatest Possible Trouble over Absolutely Nothing with Your Eyes Wide Open. It'll be such a great book it'll live forever."

Parrish glanced over and saw Paige giving him a hopeful smile and he had to smile a little, too, in spite of his soreness. She was a crazy kid, but smart.

"I don't even know why I do half the things I do," she went on. "Take my father, for instance. I don't really want to make him mad all the time. He's my father and I love him. And I want to get along with him."

Parrish looked at her, interested and surprised at this unquestioning statement of her love for Raike.

"And I know how to, too. You know something, Parrish—I know perfectly well what he wants me to do and how he wants me to be. I could make you a list. And I could do all those things and give in to him on little things—"

"Like Edgar?" And, he thought, like Ellen.

"It doesn't keep Edgar out of trouble just because he's so dumb, but with me, it's some terrible mysterious thing." She sighed. "It just seems that he's him and I'm me and we're two separate people. And I'm the one who has to decide, a little anyway, the things about me. Otherwise it doesn't seem I'm me."

In spite of his being completely miserable Parrish felt himself drawn by Paige's intensity, and he was suddenly glad that she was here.

"And besides," she said, "I don't think it's right for him to love me just when I'm doing what he wants and then turn against me when I'm not. I don't think that's the way you're supposed to love people at all. I don't believe love is something you should have to bargain for." Then she flung up her arms. "O-oh, how'd I ever get on this weird subject? Parrish, you're having an awful time with us, aren't you? Are you going to stay?"

Suddenly Parrish felt he couldn't answer that. He was free and nothing held him now but his own self-doubt. But something in him shrank from walking away without re-examining all this that he had shunned, heatedly and unreasonably. Now it seemed like slamming your door in the face of a stranger without hearing what he had to say.

Besides, now Alison was home.

17

WHAT ABOUT Sala Post, Max?" Judd Raike said. "Is Oermeyer borrowing from him, too?"

Max Maine looked up from his little notebook and shook his head. For fifteen years, on Tuesdays and Fridays, Judd Raike had lunched with his lawyer, and always the little notebook had lain open on the table for Max Maine to make notes, a habit that had annoyed Raike until he learned that Max never consulted the little book later. The notes were a form of doodling, a compulsive orderliness. The details were firmly planted in Max Maine's brain, where they belonged.

"Not yet, Judd," Max said. "Just Tower. He gave Tower a six-month note to cover a cash loan and a season's credit. He's cut his acreage a little, that's all."

"Less profit."

Max shrugged. "Less risk."

Raike laughed while his mind worked at the problem of Walter Oermeyer. Today Max had supplied a complete report, including the present figure of Tower's mortgage on Oermeyer's property and the size of the emergency loan. Based on his reported acreage, Raike mentally estimated Oermeyer's gross and then his costs, including amortization and interest at six per cent. He frowned. With an even break, Oermeyer could pull through. And this was the first crack in that solid stretch of farms out there that broke up his land from Lemmie's to the Ridge—Oermeyer, Prentiss, Tully and Sala Post.

"Tell Tower you'll discount the note," he said. "Without recourse."

"I'll tell him, Judd. But right now he's not interested."

"What's his attitude? Would he go another year?"

"Now that I doubt." Max cheered at being able to give a little encouragement. "He might give Oermeyer a partial renewal on this note, but I don't think he'd make another loan."

"Then Oermeyer is down to the wire."

"Unless," Max said, cautiously, "he can find other financing."

"Make him an offer, Max. Twenty-two hundred dollars an acre."

"He's not interested, Judd."

"I am. Make Prentiss and Tully the same offer."

"They're all right, Judd!" Max protested. "All they had last year was a touch of blue mold in the beds and Sala Post filled them in on plants. And then ran short himself. Remember?"

"Don't get excited, Max. Just make your offers."

"If anyone's your man, Judd, it's Oermeyer, not Prentiss or Tully. They won't even listen."

"I can wait," Raike said easily, "until their hearing improves."

Max closed his little notebook and dropped it into his pocket and accepted the cigar Raike handed him. "Judd," he said, breaking the seal. "What about Ellen's son? He going to give you trouble?"

Raike looked up sharply. "Not me, he isn't."

"That was quite a show he put on at the club Friday night." Max frowned. "Boy like that spells trouble."

"You just worrying, Max, or you got some particular trouble in mind?"

"Judd, that boy's the I-don't-give-a-damn type. Wild." Max tapped his pen on the tablecloth. "Edgar and Wiley you've trained. They stay out of trouble. Even with a couple too many, they know what's expected of them. Same with my boy. God knows he doesn't do much else, but he stays out of trouble. Not that one. I'm thinking of the legal liability, Judd."

Judd Raike looked hard at Max before answering. For a few weeks now he had been taking more than cursory notice of Ellen's son—ever since the sudden realization that Parrish was neither trying to gain his favor nor coaxing cash out of Ellen. Raike didn't like it because it didn't make sense. A man didn't strike oil and then not bother to pump the well.

"Well, we'll change all that fast enough, Max. I've got him coming into the office this afternoon."

"Changing that one won't be easy," Max mourned. "You'll never know what's going on in his head. You don't even know if there's anything going on at all. Maybe just one hot crackpot notion after another."

"He'll fall in line when it pays," Raike said easily. "Like the rest of them. When there's enough at stake, he'll know what's expected, too."

"Not that one. He's not for sale."

"Everyone's for sale. The only difference is in price."

"That kid doesn't give a damn about money."

"The world is full of people who think they don't give a damn about money." Raike settled his big frame back in the chair. "Twentieth-century propaganda. Lasts exactly as long as they haven't got any. They play with a lot of noble substitutes—art, humanity. Well, all the noble substitutes crumple up like paper dolls once that dirty stuff becomes available. In their special hands, suddenly it's clean."

"Judd, last Friday night there was a hundred million dollars represented at the club."

"Well, I don't know what the damn fool thought he was doing last Friday night, but this I do know. With money you can absolutely count on it—everybody likes it and everybody wants more. You start with that premise, Max, and things will happen exactly the way you figure them." Raike puffed a cloud of smoke. "I'm going to make the boy a timekeeper. What do you think would interest him as a figure?"

"A buxom lass of about seventeen without too many scruples."

"For that matter, I think his taste runs higher." Raike laughed. "Judging from the look he gave Sala's daughter Friday night, during his spectacular performance. But I'm referring, of course, to his salary."

"Timekeeper pays about sixty-five a week, fifteen more than he's getting now," Max said. "What's that going to accomplish?"

Raike laughed again. "Well, you know, for a good man you up it a little."

"Throw in a snappy car, Judd," Max advised gloomily. "Judging from my own son, and yours, too, that would help. And if it doesn't work, in the summer you can try a speed boat. Or maybe a plane. These restless, reckless kids are crazy for speed." Max pulled out his notebook nervously. "Bribe him if you can, Judd. That kind of bribery is legal. And cheaper. Believe me."

Raike stood up to leave. "You got all your notes on Oermeyer in there all right, Max?"

"Oermeyer at least I can understand," Max said.

"And don't forget Tully and Prentiss."

Two hours later, when the boy sat opposite him, Raike thought that Max was right. He was listening politely enough, but his attitude was wrong. Twice Raike had paused, taking a cigar from his humidor, fussing with the seal so that Parrish might ask what a timekeeper was paid. After twenty minutes he still had not asked it.

"I've been watching you, Parrish," Raike said. "You're a good man and we like you. We'll make you a better man and we'll like you more." He smiled. "And we'll pay you while we do it. Pay you well."

Parrish sat still, hands in his lap. Raike took out his gold knife and placed it on the desk, unopened, waiting.

"This is a responsible job," he went on. "You go to every farm in your section every day. You get there, you check the time book, you ask if they have any emergency needs, and you leave. No horsing around with the fellows. No flirting with the tramps in the sheds looking to get laid. You keep moving."

Parrish didn't answer. That detachment was like Ellen's—and a good act, too, because he'd heard enough about this boy to know he was no monk. Raike picked up his knife. "Now, I'm a fair man, but I expect effort from people who work for me. Not just a nine-to-four routine performance with time out for cigarettes and coffee and hangovers. I expect production. I pay for it."

"Yes, sir," Parrish said.

Raike snapped open the knife blade. He was definitely getting the same impression as Max—that the boy would take this job and do it, but that he really didn't give a damn. Well, that attitude was going to change. He pointed the knife at the mahogany board on which, in gold letters, were listed the Raike properties. "Turn around and take a look at that board. Walk over where you can read it better."

Obediently Parrish walked over to the sign.

"That's the list of Raike farms in the order I acquired them. That sign means that Raike and Company controls more land and more dollars and pays more people than any other firm in the Valley ever has. More, even, than firms built up over generations." He pointed to the empty space at the bottom. "And when we go into another generation, it'll be bigger still."

He scraped a couple of shreds off the cigar seal, watching to see whether Parrish read the list or only looked at it. He read it.

"Now that's the kind of firm you're working for," Raike went on. "You're going to be one link in a chain that starts in the ground and stops with net profit. Every dollar you make in tobacco starts in the soil and that means there's plenty of trouble, unavoidable trouble: nature. That's the only kind of trouble I stand for. There's no room for any man-made trouble in my business and that includes your department. Now. It's a man's job. You think you can handle it?"

"I can handle it."

He said it simply, with no trace of self-doubt, and Raike pulled down his eyebrows. "A farmer can tell in a minute if he's got a fool for a time-keeper."

Parrish nodded and Raike thought this boy had learned at an early age the value of keeping his mouth shut. You couldn't be sure how little he knew. "Now, about the other night. I don't know what you were accomplishing, but you'll have to knock off that kind of stuff." Raike saw that he'd hit home on that and he felt better. The boy looked pained. "When you represent this company, you look like a gentleman and you behave that way. Nobody's going to put any higher value on you than you put on yourself. You look like a bum, you act like a bum, that's what you'll get called—a bum. People see what hits 'em in the face, no more. You'll be representing one of the greatest companies in a damn big industry.

See that you represent it right." He stood up. "Now, you'll need a car to get around. There's one downstairs we can take a look at. Let's go down."

Raike led Parrish downstairs and around to the back lot where there was a new red convertible he'd had sent over. Watching Parrish's face, Raike saw for the first time the kind of reaction he was looking for. Hell, the boy was just a kid! Opening doors and looking at every inch of the car like a damned idiot. Raike wondered what he'd been worrying about. These kids were all the same. Never stopped to figure out that if the new job paid him even twenty a week more, he could go out and buy the car. No head at all. He was beginning to think this boy's reaction to the new job was confident because he was too stupid to worry. Never asked what it paid at all.

"Tell me about Lemmie," he said. "What's he doing today?"

"One crew harrowing, another couple of days there. One crew sewing cloth, and a couple of boys mixing and bagging fertilizer."

Raike's eyes narrowed. He knew something. "Tomorrow morning you report to work here."

"Which car shall I drive home?"

"The new one," Raike said. "It's yours as long as you work for the company. Get an 'R' engraved on both doors, same as the other cars have."

Parrish reached for the car door, eager to try out the convertible, and Raike thought this was going to be so easy it hurt. Still he couldn't resist asking, "By the way, don't you care what this job pays?"

"Yes, sir. I do."

"A hundred and a quarter," Raike said, shaving twenty-five off the figure he had originally intended. The boy had cost himself twenty-five dollars a week with his stubbornness, and someday Raike would let him know it.

Sitting alone in a corner of the country-club bar, Parrish reflected that a man's thinking could play him strange tricks. For months it could lead him like a pied piper into tangled confusion, letting him believe he was thinking logically. And then in a few hours it could change.

Like his thinking about Alison. He'd thought about her so much it seemed there was nothing that had not gone through his mind. Only this afternoon he had been dreaming up wild, impossible schemes to see her and make up, this week while she was home from school, and he had rejected each scheme in turn as he found sound reasons why it wouldn't work. Only this afternoon he had gone into Judd Raike's office, still nursing his self-mistrust, dedicated since the dance to open-minded re-examination (he wasn't quite sure of what). Then he had been told he was to be timekeeper, he had been given a new car, his salary had been doubled and more. And suddenly all his thinking had changed.

Now, sitting here, he could look back and see what had been happening, as suddenly as if a man put on eyeglasses and blurred images snapped into focus. The trouble had lain not in the schemes, but in himself. He could see now that every plan had been knocked down by the fear of failure, a fear born of comparisons with Wiley. Offering nothing but himself had not seemed enough. But that was a fact with a bad taste and he had named a hundred other reasons instead. When the truth was unpleasant a man had no trouble finding substitutes. Only now, with the scales more evenly balanced, was he owning up to his own lack. It made you wonder if a man ever used his head at all for straight thinking.

He sat watching the club fill up slowly. Alison wasn't here yet, but he knew she would come before the night was over, with Wiley. Presently Maizie and Tom Holden came in and saw him and beckoned.

"Have a drink with us," Maizie said, as he came up to them. "I must say you look vastly better tonight, Parrish. I adore that wild primitive approach, but there's a certain charm in seeing you this way. Don't you think so, Tom?"

"Hello, Parrish." Tom offered his hand. "Pay no attention to her. She adores you anyway."

"I do," Maizie said. "Hello, the party's growing. Good evening, Clayton."

"Maizie, darling." Clayton Norris came hurrying up to the table. "Hello, Tom." He turned to Parrish, a look of fascinated disbelief on his face. "Man, have you got courage coming here! I didn't see the whole thing. I could kill myself. But I heard it was good. Good show! Man, where do you stow that courage?"

Parrish smiled. "I didn't think of it that way, Clay."

"Man, I tell you it's raw courage," Clayton insisted. "Maizie, love, it's wonderful to see you. Tom." Exuding good will, Clayton scurried off to greet someone else at the bar.

Tom laughed. "Clayton Norris is not quite sure whether you're a villain or a hero. Furthermore, I suspect the uncertainty worries him."

Parrish took a quick look to see whether Alison and Wiley had arrived with Clayton and saw that they had not. "If you hadn't calmed me down, Tom, he'd have seen an even better show. I was pretty sore."

"Did Tom do that, really? Tom, you are gallant—you didn't tell me! Parrish, what in hell were you running amuck about? Of course, I know I'm prying quite shamelessly."

"Quite," Tom said.

"I was just sore, Maizie," Parrish said. "Mostly at myself, I guess."

"Worse still," Tom said. "To accept oneself reluctantly is poison. The seed of a bad crop that grows as tough as cactus and bears no fruit."

"Can't you tell he's a farmer, though!" Maizie said. "Such an agronomical simile."

"Individual man's lowly opinion of himself," Tom said, "is one of the greatest afflictions of mankind. Maizie believes this even more than I do. You have only to speak to her five minutes to see it."

"More prevalent than the common cold," Maizie said. "Parrish, dear, in words of one syllable, what he means is, if you don't like what you are, you damned well ought to change into something you can like. Not you personally, of course. Man in general. Otherwise you begin to get in your own way."

"It's one of the simpler truths," Tom said. "Only a small segment of the larger problem of the freedom of man and the joy of living, both of which are becoming extinct, giving way to group allegiance and the psychiatrist's couch."

Maizie fitted a cigarette into a long holder. "Tom is a twentieth-century Patrick Henry, Parrish. His hobby is the freedom of man. Of course, all men do not want to be free—they would be terrified at the idea—and that has made it hard. He discovered one day that people are a bunch of cowards and frauds—"

"The one a direct result of the other," Tom said.

"So he doesn't work on just anybody, but every now and then he thinks he's found a recruit—in this case you, Parrish—and then there's no holding him. That's the real reason for all this talk that has you speechless, pet. You are speechless. You haven't said a word since he started."

"I'm listening," Parrish said, smiling.

"Do you understand a word he's saying?"

Parrish grinned. He did not.

"Of course not. He didn't lap this up in a single evening, either. He brooded and observed and mourned—and loved. It took years. I know, I was there. Well, Clayton dear," she looked up. "Back again. Won't you join us? We're talking about freedom."

"Man, I'm for it," Clayton said. "Liberté, égalité, fraternité, I always say."

"This is more the pursuit-of-happiness variety."

"Now, Maizie, it's hardly a year since I swore to love, honor, and stop pursuing."

"Clayton, love." Maizie eyed him narrowly. "Just as an academic question, do you believe man is born free?"

"Communist!" Clayton giggled. "Well, I'm on my way. Man, I repeat it, you have real courage. Why not have a drink with us later?"

"He's made up his mind," Tom said to Parrish. "You're a hero."

"He must have discussed it with someone at the bar," Maizie said.

"My point exactly."

She was here. She was just coming in, going over with Wiley to join Clayton and Melissa. With difficulty Parrish made himself sit still. Half an hour, he decided. He ought to wait about half an hour. Then he'd go over and ask her to dance. He turned back to Tom. "I used to worry about that a lot, Tom. Being free, and all that."

Tom smiled. "I confess that's why I brought this up. After you left Friday night, we talked about you, Ellen and I. Ellen says to you freedom is a kind of wanderlust—to be free of her. Her and the rules of society that she stands for to you."

Parrish blushed a little to learn that his mother had understood so accurately. "Well, partly. It used to be, anyway. I'm not so sure any more." He would like to talk to Tom about this, but at some other time. Right now he didn't know what he thought. And—he stole another look across the room—his mind was on other things. "Lately it seems more complicated."

Tom leaned toward him. "Freedom is more than just not submitting to commands of others, Parrish. And it's more than just cutting away—it's not just subtraction. It's something positive—it's addition, too."

"Well, something like that."

Tom nodded. "For years after a highbred horse gave me a boot on my fine highbred face I did my share of wandering, didn't I, Maizie?"

"Indeed."

"Then one day I saw that it didn't solve anything. Wherever I went people had eyes to look at an ugly face and see that it was ugly. People with eyes are almost as common as people with rules, Parrish."

"And a pox on both their houses," Maizie said.

"So I came home and looked elsewhere for the solution. Now I know that a man is free because of something in him, not because he has no boss or is footloose to roam the planet. A free man can choose to stay absolutely put and entwine his life completely with other lives, and still he is free."

Maizie put a hand on Tom's arm. "And that," she said firmly, "concludes our lecture for tonight. Question period to follow at a later date."

Cautiously Parrish stole a look at Alison and saw that she was watching him. Meeting his, her eyes lingered a second too long to be indifferent, and when she turned back to Wiley her smile was bright and mechanical. Parrish looked at his watch. With old misgivings, he thought that he should wait a little yet, that it wasn't time. And then he thought, of course it was time. It had been time long ago.

"Parrish," Alison said when they reached the dance floor, "you haven't changed a bit."

"Yes, I have. I've changed. I'm taking life seriously now. Developing great character. Ask anyone."

She tilted her head. "I hadn't heard. When did this change take place?"

"Today. It was a gradual change, started this afternoon and ended this evening. Now I'm a new man. You're one of the first to behold this new man."

Alison studied him carefully. "It seems quite a change at that."

"You bet."

"And for the better."

"Of course," Parrish assured her. "New job—great promotion. Great stuff. New car."

"I know. We saw the car outside. And Wiley told us about the promotion."

He shouldn't feel a tug of disappointment that she knew. All that naïve idealism of love-me-for-myself-alone was past and he'd been counting on the new situation to make a change. But it took time for old habits to die, even bad ones. They were like scars. You touched them and for a while, anyway, they hurt.

"Clayton Norris says you came here tonight to prove you dared. He considers it a great act of courage."

"In his spare time, Clayton Norris is quite a fool."

"Why did you come? You hate it here."

"And he has nothing but spare time."

"Why did you come here?"

"I love it here."

He drew her closer and bent down to her, brushing his chin on her hair, and she turned her face up to his. Parrish looked down into it, at the line of her hair that he used to touch with his hand, at the smooth, delicate bones of her face, the clear, deep green eyes, and while he searched her face, questioning, the green eyes changed and became questioning, too, and answering at the same time, and he understood that the strain was over. The glib chatter was no longer required. He touched her cheek.

"Parrish," she said, "why didn't you ever write me? Or come back?"

"Can you get rid of him?" He nodded toward Wiley. "Make him take you home."

"How can I do that?"

"Think of something. How long will you need? I'll meet you."

"That's an awfully mean trick."

"Mmm-hmm."

"Parrish, did you come here tonight looking for me?"

"Of course I came here looking for you. What would I be doing here without a damn good reason?"

"What was your reason last Friday night?"

"I must have had one. How much time do you need?"

"Parrish, calm down. People are looking at us. Go back to the bar. Have another drink. Have two." Her hand brushed his neck. "Give me an hour."

In the quiet night he waited, all waiting. The moon slipped down, a white sliver, toward a tree that was still only a winter silhouette until you drew close enough to see the red buds, swelled and ready to burst, full of life, a throbbing expectancy; a tree never dead although it had seemed it, but with its mysterious life sealed in, waiting for the time to open again to sunlight and moonlight and starlight and rain.

She came now.

A thread of strangeness, of separateness, rose up between them, each as though restrained by some inner guard protecting against the complete giving up of self to the other, an embarrassed drawing back from so bright a light.

His hand moved hesitantly, as though not to touch and be burned, and then it closed over hers and she moved into his arms and he knew there was no answer to anything for him anywhere except her, feeling the completeness of her coming to him as his to her, and he thought over and over, What was I thinking of, what was I thinking, to stay away so long.

Parrish lay in bed, too full of wonder for sleep. Already the white sky of daybreak was coloring and he stirred, thinking that a feeling of peace in a man could be as torrential as any storm. He was filled this morning with a sense of the rightness of things that reached out, because he was in love—reached out not only to Alison but to everything about him. Suddenly, for the first time, he saw this room as something he could like, this house now as a place he could live in, this new job he was starting today as an exciting beginning. Now, because of Alison and for her, he wanted this job—wanted to do it well and get a better one and a better one still.

Outside his window a bobwhite called and waited and called again, although there was no answer and none was needed, because the answer was in the bird itself; and presently Parrish got out of bed, although it was still early, and started to dress.

A few minutes later his mother came into his room. "I waited up for you as late as I could," she whispered, closing the door. "I want to talk to you."

"What's the matter?"

"This new job, Parrish—I don't know."

In the pale light Parrish looked at his mother, her robe drawn high around her throat, her eyes heavy, showing she had slept little. He saw that she was more than a little worried. "What's the matter?" he said. "Don't you think I can handle it?"

"The job, yes. Judd, no."

Parrish opened a drawer and took out a new shirt. "I know it won't be any bed of roses, but I'm figuring to make a go of it," he said.

"Why?"

She knew him too well, he thought. "I figure I've kicked up enough fuss for a while. I'll try getting along for a change."

Ellen's face showed she didn't believe him, but she didn't press him for the reasons. "Parrish, Judd is different from anyone you've ever known. He's brilliant and powerful and nobody has ever stood in his way."

She's proud of that—that's pretty special and important to her, for some reason. Thoughtfully, Parrish pulled out the cardboard and shook open the shirt.

"When he's calm, he's the most reasonable man in the world," Ellen said. "When he's upset, he's the most unreasonable. You've seen for yourself how upset he can get."

"I figure I'll do a good job and we'll get along."

"He expects perfection."

"He'll get it."

Ellen was silent a moment but Parrish knew he hadn't reassured her.

"Parrish," she said presently, "are you doing this because you've decided there's something in it for you?"

He turned to stare at her. "Well, that's a great question!"

"It's an important one."

"Why?"

"Because it's the only way you'll make it your business to get along with Judd. You have to feel terribly that it's worth it. And if you don't feel it now, I don't want you to be anyplace near him. Go back to Lemmie's. Because you'll just spoil things for yourself for later. Someday you'll realize that there's a great deal here for you, although right now, I suspect, you do not."

Silently Parrish continued dressing, putting on his shirt, rolling up the sleeves.

"Parrish, the only way to handle Judd is not to argue."

"Well—you ought to know."

"I do know. I've tried every other way. Nothing works. You have to keep absolutely silent until his anger spends itself. Like a string of firecrackers—once it starts you have to let it explode until it's through. The only defense is not to let it touch you. Trying to reason with him is just pouring on gasoline. When it's all over, he's fine. In the meantime, whatever happens, don't argue. Is that clear?"

"I'm getting the picture."

"Forewarned is forearmed, Parrish." He didn't answer. "He's a brilliant man and he's built up a great business singlehanded and it's his, not yours. If you work for him, you do it his way."

Parrish grinned. "You're rough this morning. Really reading the riot act."

"For your own good, Parrish," Ellen said. "And mine."

Now he looked at her carefully. "You're not afraid of this guy?"

"He's not a guy, Parrish. He's my husband. I chose to marry him and I'm not afraid of him. I worry about you, not him."

"I have to go or I'll be late the first day. Stop worrying, I'm a reformed character." He bent and kissed her and went downstairs.

"It's a big day for you, sir." Maples lingered while Parrish ate his breakfast. "And you're starting at a good time. The crop just beginning, the pressure not as bad as later."

"Even at the start there's pressure, Maples."

"Yes, sir, but later it builds up," Maples said soberly. "I always say it's like a conditioned reflex. The plants get off the ground and the nervousness starts and grows right along with them. We all breathe easier when the crop is in."

Parrish finished his coffee. "You always work for tobacco people, Maples?"

"All my life," Maples said, and he straightened up as Raike came into the room.

"Now," Raike said, seeing that Parrish was leaving, "you understand where to go?"

"Yes, sir. Mr. Gilliam's office, next to Edgar's."

"Right. Now keep your eyes open. Anything you don't understand, ask and we'll explain it. You'll be out all day with Gilliam. Report to me when you get back. I'll want to know where you were and what you saw when you got there. Any questions, any problems, I want to hear them." Raike looked him over carefully. "Going to have a good tobacco man here, Maples."

"Yes, sir," Maples said, and Parrish left.

Mr. Gilliam was an untalkative little man who methodically took Parrish to each farm, introduced him to the foreman, and showed him the time book. Between farms he spoke little. They returned to the ware-house at a quarter to five and Parrish went directly upstairs to Raike's office.

When he entered, Raike looked up from a stack of papers, pointed sharply, without speaking, to the chair in front of his desk, and did not look up again for twenty minutes. Parrish took out the notebook in which he had written his route as they followed it, along with the name of the foreman of each farm, and read it through and slipped off into reveries of Alison until the click of Raike's humidor brought him back and he saw that Raike had pushed aside his papers, taken out a cigar, and was watch-ing him. He sat straighter in the chair.

"All right," Raike said. "Where'd you go today?"

Parrish turned back a page of the notebook. Raike jerked the cigar to-ward it. "Don't you know where you were unless you read it out of a book?" Parrish glanced up, surprised, because Mr. Gilliam had used a list all day in directing him. Uncertainly, he closed the notebook.

Raike smiled tolerantly. "All right," he said, before Parrish had a chance to get started. "I see you need help. Take it off the board."

"I think I know it all right."

"Not good enough." Raike shook his head. "Around here we don't *think* we know. We're one-hundred-per-cent sure. And until we're one-hundred-per-cent sure, we keep the facts in front of us. Go over to the board."

Checking a protest, Parrish stood up. Every time he was in this office he seemed to end up in front of the gold-lettered list of the farms. "We didn't go to all of these, sir," he said. "And we went to some farms that aren't listed here."

"Now don't try to jump ahead of me," Raike said impatiently. "Right now I want you to read the names on the board. I want you to tell me which farms listed on that board you visited. I want only names listed on that board and I don't want any names not listed on that board. Is that clear?"

"Yes, sir." Obediently, Parrish picked out the farms he had visited.

"Now let's have it without looking." Parrish recited the list. He omitted one farm. "Take it off the board again."

Parrish looked back at the board.

"Memory." This time Parrish named them all. "Once again." Hoarsely he named them again. "Now come over here and sit down." He sat.

"Those farms," Raike said, working at the seal of the cigar case, "are the farms Raike and Company owns. Outright. We own the property. We put our man in to run it. Now understand this. There's nothing says our own man won't cheat us if he can get away with it. The reason he probably won't try is just this: He's been with us a long time and he damn well knows he won't get away with it."

Parrish squirmed a little in the chair.

"Now," Raike went on. "You went to other farms. Do you know why you went to them?"

Cursing the close-mouthed Gilliam for withholding this information, Parrish shook his head.

"You spent a whole day going to farms," Raike said, softly. "But you don't know why?"

Parrish nodded unhappily. He knew Raike was being unfair to him and the knowledge ate into him. He had seen it before with the others, had watched them try to shrink small and speak inoffensively, coasting until Raike's irritation was spent. And here he was doing it, too, and feeling less a man for it. Firmly, now, he said, "Sir, I went with Mr. Gilliam and noted where he stopped because you told me he was showing me my route."

Raike ignored this. He allowed a few minutes of silence while he took out his knife to work at the cigar seal. "The other farms you stopped at," he said, at last, "—now listen carefully, because around here we explain a thing once, and only once—the other farms fall into two categories. Some we lease outright. Our man goes in to operate them. We don't own them yet—someday we will. The others, the smallest ones, the farmers own 'em and run 'em. We carry each one's expenses, we take his crop. We give him back a share of the profit. That farmer—now get this straight and don't forget it—that farmer will cheat us every chance he gets. He likes using our money. He likes us to take his risks. But he doesn't like our being there. That farmer is basically a cheat. He considers it his duty to cheat us. He works at it. Whenever you look at him, regard him as a man who is cheating you. Now. Give me the names of these other farms. Take the leased ones first."

They both knew Parrish could not know one from the other. He said, "I can tell you the names of the other farms but Mr. Gilliam didn't tell me which were leased and which were farmers working their own land."

"Why didn't you ask?"

A little desperately Parrish said, "I didn't know about it. I didn't even know you didn't own them all."

He saw at once it was the wrong thing to say. Raike flushed angrily, thrusting his cigar toward the mahogany board. "There's more room there!"

Another tight silence followed. Raike scraped again at the cigar seal and Parrish sat still in the chair, twisting his notebook, his heart pounding. Raike broke the silence without looking up from scraping the seal. "I'll give you a couple of suggestions, and if you ever expect to get anyplace around here, you'd better take them." He dropped the knife and his eyes came up sharply. "You'd better start keeping your eyes open. And you'd better start asking questions about everything you see. And you'd better ask questions about what you don't see. Now you've seen that board before. You knew you were going to farms not listed on that board. You should have asked questions, questions, questions. Plenty of them. You're being paid a hundred and a quarter a week for being on the ball."

Parrish nodded while Raike thrust the cigar into his mouth and lit it. "Now are you going to throw yourself into this job or are we just going to get a routine forty-hour-a-week performance out of you? Burn up gas and make a few marks on paper?"

Parrish cleared his throat. Always, he thought, Judd Raike had a way of twisting things around to make himself look reasonable and logical in the end, until you no longer knew who was right or wrong. "I'm sorry, sir," he said. "Now that I know there are leased farms and the—the other kind, I'll find out which is which."

"Suppose you do that." Raike puffed a cloud of smoke. "Suppose you learn that much and come back and then I'll talk to you. And consider yourself lucky to be getting this second chance. When I was your age nobody had this kind of charity for me. I made one mistake and I was out. So I didn't make any mistakes. And I don't make 'em today."

Raike picked up his papers again as a sign of dismissal and Parrish stood up. "One more thing." Raike stopped him at the door. "Did you notice out Lemmie's way that you stop at every farm for a solid stretch of land except that patch between Lemmie and the Ridge?"

"Yes, sir."

"I don't like that break in my land. It's not practical. But it's there and it has to be watched. Any trouble there, I want to hear about it—fast. You'll hear in the area if anything is wrong. Do you know the names of the men you're watching?"

"Yes, sir. Oermeyer, Tully and Prentiss. And Sala Post."

"All right. We buy Sala Post's crop and we have to know what's going on. Raike and Company doesn't buy a pig in a poke. The others, sometimes we buy 'em and sometimes we don't, depending on what they turn out. But they're too close not to be watched. Trouble spreads fast in this business."

Before he went home Parrish made up a complete list of the farms on his route and asked Mr. Gilliam which were leased and which were financed. He double-checked the list with Mig Alger, the warehouse foreman. He took it home to memorize.

Away from Raike, Parrish tried to think calmly. It was Raike's way, he told himself—no surprise, nothing he had not known. These were the terms on which you came to work for him, and the trick was—as Ellen had said—to let the little annoyances slip past without touching you, without making you feel small. But to Ellen, Raike was a highly charged genius who had to let off steam, and to Parrish he was just bad-tempered and unreasonable. It was funny how different a man could look to different people. Still, if he could get past this first hurdle, then he would be at the farms all day and Raike would be in his office, and it would be better. He told himself to forget this afternoon. But the bad taste lingered.

Not even later that evening, sitting close to Alison in the small clearing near the bridge, could he leave it entirely behind. For a while he would forget it and then it would steal back.

"What are you thinking of so much tonight?" she said once.

"Only of you." Parrish smiled. "Just wondering how I'll live until you come home again in June. That, and how I'll suffer."

"Will you suffer, Parrish?" Alison laughed, sure of herself, and brushed his face with the back of her hand and even her fingertips could set him aflame. Then her mood changed and with sudden intensity she said, "Parrish, we were fools to stay apart so long. We'll never do it again."

"Of course not. I love you." He brushed his lips over her hair. "You notice how easily I say it now. Last year I used to blush every time I said it. You never noticed because it was dark. But now I say it easily."

"Last year we were both fools," Alison said. "This year we'll be much better for each other. Everything is better. Last summer—" She shrugged, leaving the sentence unfinished.

Last summer. Parrish could see moonlight on the rail of the little bridge and hear the stream below, lapping rocks and tree branches bending into it, and last summer was suddenly sharp in his thoughts again—Gladstone and Cartwright, and Teet and John, whom he never saw any more, and "Hurry up, man, take your Speedarene." Not "Hurry from farm to farm and watch to see who's cheating me, and know what I own, know it by heart—or at least by memory."

Well, a man couldn't have everything. That was done and over and it was different now. And this would be all right, too, if he would let it.

"Alison," he said, "does your father know you're with me tonight?"

A little defiance showed in the tilt of her nose and chin, and he saw the pulse-beat in her throat and the quick rise of her breasts, and while he waited for her answer he thought that her face had a delicacy all its own, but that her breasts and the blood racing in her throat were kin to her eyes.

"I told him we were going to a movie," she answered.

"Why'd you tell him that?"

"Because he asked what we were going to do," Alison said, petulantly. "I have to handle him carefully, you know. And I don't have Ellen any more to help me. I'm alone now."

"Then it was all right that you were going to be with me?"

"For the longest time he didn't say anything. I don't know what he was thinking about, because to him almost anyone is better than Wiley. And I'm surprised to find that suddenly he's fond of you. That makes me terribly suspicious, because he never likes anyone, you know. And no one likes him."

Parrish thought that wasn't true. Little memories crowded back, memories of Teet and John and Lucy and their respect for Sala, their defending him when he, himself, had felt otherwise, and the nostalgia started up again. Then Alison moved close again, with a childlike, clinging quality, and Parrish felt, along with his love for her, a sudden protectiveness that made the nostalgia for the happier, easier way seem weak and petty.

He drew her to him and she came eagerly and he could feel the small firm breasts move, just barely move against him, and a wildness rose up in him and beat back all thinking from his mind, and he put his hands on her shoulders and gently pushed her away and sat upright, leaning back on the seat, and rhythmically stroked her hand while he stared at the moonlight on the bridge, waiting out the wildness that refused to quiet.

The next morning when Parrish reported to the warehouse he found an envelope for him in Raike's handwriting. Apprehensively, he opened it. It was a "Memo from the Desk of Judd Raike" and attached to it was a complete list of the farms divided into the three categories, exactly as he had prepared it with Gilliam's help. The memorandum suggested that he memorize the lists and reminded him to report again to Raike personally after work.

All day Parrish went over the list in his mind. He memorized the name of the foreman at each farm and the number of people employed. He looked carefully at Oermeyer's from Lemmie's, and at Tully's and Prentiss's as he passed. He tried to think of something else Raike might grill him on but could not. At a quarter to five, hoping he was prepared, he headed for Raike's office. He wasn't afraid of Judd Raike. He was only afraid he would get sore at the needling and get himself fired.

But this afternoon Raike was in a fine mood. "Go better today?" he greeted him jovially.

"Yes, sir," Parrish said, wondering, better than what.

"How's the car running?" Raike said. "Get the company 'R' on it yet?"

"The garage said if I brought it in today after work—"

"Fine," Raike said. "Then go over there and get it done."

As Parrish got to his feet Raike came around the desk, walked with him to the door. "Glad to hear everything went better today. Now just remember to keep your eyes open and ask questions and it'll stay that way. Report in again tomorrow."

"Yes, sir." Leaving the office, bewildered and astonished, Parrish told himself he'd passed the first test, although he didn't quite know how, and that the worst was over. Probably, he decided, Raike had made his point yesterday and was satisfied.

18

ON A SATURDAY afternoon late in May Parrish sat in a booth at Tower's with John and Teet. This year during the usually wet period the rains had been light, but now, when everyone was geared up—two or three operations going at once—now it had rained steadily for five days. The crowd at Tower's had the gloomy, listless air of people with nothing to do and too much that couldn't be done—restless and discouraged.

Parrish watched John pull aside a curtain and stare morosely out the streaked window. It was the universal gesture these days. A moment ago a seedy-looking Broadleaf farmer had done the same thing. And afternoons at his office and evenings at home Judd Raike paced the floor endlessly, stopping only to look out at the rain, while frustration piled up in him, making him pick on everyone these days, sore as a boil. Parrish had come in here to delay a little longer going home.

John dropped the curtain and, next to him, Teet glanced up and said, "Ah, can't last forever."

"Damn near," John muttered. He looked over at Parrish. "So how's it going, being timekeeper?"

"It's O.K."

"Better'n Lemmie's, anyway, eh?" John said. "You hitting it off all right with Raike?"

"We get along."

"I'll tell you something," John said. "Don't sell Raike short. Just because he's got a mean streak, it don't get in the way of his knowing tobacco. Got a late start, but he caught up fast."

"I know that," Parrish said. "He can tell you everything about every farm he's working—how many acres, how much help, what kind of trouble it's likely to run into. I've seen him come out to a farm that's lost time and he'll stand there, sizing things up, and then he'll tell you how many man-hours it'll take to catch up and he's always right—that's how long it takes. You have to hand it to him."

John nodded and lit a cigar. "And as much as he knows, that's how much them idiot sons of his don't know."

Teet scratched his beard. "I bet things is real merry at Raike's these days, with the rain."

"I don't get any closer there than I have to," Parrish said.

John drank his beer, more because there was nothing else to do than because he wanted it, and nodded toward a man at the bar. "Tully there's thinking he could use this water later."

"Tully," Teet called over, "here's your irrigatin' water."

Tully shrugged. "Wish I could bottle it. Going to stop tonight, weather station says."

"Be another day before anyone can work. Be nothin' but mud." John stood up. "I'll see you later. This place gives me the creeps."

Teet, placidly puffing his pipe, watched him go. "Ask me, it's his sex life," he said.

"Ask me, you're nuts!" Parrish burst out laughing. "It's the rain."

"Kid," Teet said, "it's the whole damn business. Every year it's the same. Everyone's like a guy walkin' along a street figuring someone's waitin' to get him behind every house. Go faster and maybe nothin'll happen, and if nothin' happens, how come it ain't happened? By the end of the season, good or bad, everyone's all tied up in knots, eatin' his own guts out. I think I'll retire and go on relief."

Parrish laughed. Then he said, "If John's like that, you can imagine what Raike is like!"

All Saturday night the rain continued and a high wind blew, and then toward morning it stopped. By eight o'clock the sun was shining. Raike considered it a personal affront. Almost a week of work days had been lost and now on Sunday it cleared. It was just too much.

Belligerently silent, he strode into the dining room where the others were waiting for him for breakfast, only young Judd and Judith eating. On weekdays the children ate in a small room off the kitchen, but on Sunday mornings they were dressed for Sunday School and permitted to join their grandfather in the dining room. Today Evaline had come down early to urge them to finish before Judd arrived. Carefully, now, she motioned to them to continue eating. "Drink your milk, Juddy," she whispered.

Raike's eyes snapped up from his grapefruit. "Don't call him Juddy."

Evaline started, nodded silently, motioned again toward the glass of milk while Raike stared accusingly. "Why is he taking so long to drink it?"

"I'm sorry, Father," Evaline said. "He'll drink it."

"Drink your milk," Judd ordered. The child sat stubbornly, his mouth on the glass, letting the milk play over his lip but not drinking a drop. Evaline watched, motionless, agonizing. "Drink it!" Judd waved at the glass. "Get it down."

The boy stuck his tongue into the glass and looked resentfully at Judd.

"Take it away from him. Right now. Take it away."

Evaline froze. Paige reached over and took the glass from the boy and set it on the table. Young Judd slipped down out of his chair.

"Stay where you are." Judd turned to Evaline. "Don't give him any food in the morning for five days."

Evaline looked horrified. Young Judd reached for the milk.

"Get away from here. You can't have it now. Get out of the room."

The boy left, looking at his grandfather with silent disapproval. Raike tapped the tablecloth. "Now that boy has got to be disciplined. And he's not the only thing around here that has to be disciplined. There's no discipline around here of any sort, anywhere, at any time. Everything's running poorly—very poorly." He glared suddenly at Parrish. "What are you doing here? Why aren't you out on your route?"

"I'm just leaving, sir," Parrish said hastily. He knew nobody would work today because of the mud, but, leaving his breakfast, he hurried out anyway.

On his route he found he was right. Nobody was able to work, but at a few farms they had tried and, as a result, had trucks or tractors sunk deep in the mud. Several times, using hints he'd picked up from Teet, Parrish stopped to help free the tractors, and after he'd finished his round he went back to Colebrook, where two trucks were stuck fast, noticing as he passed Oermeyer's that Teet was doing the same for him.

On Monday he helped with two more tractors and four trucks. He telephoned the office that he would be late and was a little alarmed, on reaching the warehouse, to find Raike still there.

"Sorry, sir." He hurried in, conscious of his muddy clothing. "I stopped to help with some equipment that was stuck."

The week of frustration showed in Raike's face. He looked very tired but today not so sorely irritated. "Where'd you learn so much about mud?"

Parrish thought it would be as well not to name Teet. "It was wet last spring, too, when I worked at Sala's."

"It's wet every spring," Raike said.

If he knew that, Parrish thought, why couldn't he accept it and wait it out, but even while he thought it he knew that wouldn't be Raike.

"How many does that make it you've pulled out these two days?"

"About a dozen, sir."

For a moment Raike gave his attention to a note on his desk. Then he looked up at Parrish. "You like to have a boat?"

"A boat?"

"Would you like to buy a boat to have at the shore this summer? Everyone else has one. Wiley and Paige. Not Edgar. He gets seasick."

"Well—gee!" Parrish said, surprised. "I'd never thought about one—"

"Max Maine's had one offered him at a pretty good price. Sixteen hundred dollars. Nice little power boat. I figure hauling a dozen tractors out of the mud is worth a bonus, say six hundred dollars. If you want, I'll pick it up for you and take the thousand out of your pay, twenty-five a week."

Alison would love it, Parrish thought. She'd be crazy about it. And he wouldn't exactly mind, himself. "Gee, sure!" he said. "Thanks."

Raike laughed. "All right. Go on home now and get yourself cleaned up."

Well, what do you know about that, Parrish thought, walking through the empty warehouse. Maybe Judd wasn't so bad. Last week everyone had been irritable because of the rain; and besides that, maybe the trouble with him was nothing more than his sons. Show him you were willing to work and maybe knew a little something that he didn't expect you to know, and he showed you another side in return.

But a starlit night gave way to a gray morning. By ten o'clock a slow drizzle had started that turned into a steady rain before noon. When Parrish came in, soaked, at quarter to five, he learned from Miss Daley, Raike's secretary, that Raike had gone home early.

"Anything wrong?" he asked. "Besides the rain, that is?"

"Edgar." Miss Daley sighed. "Colebrook has to put in a bait crop for worms. Edgar ordered the chemical—about ten times too much." She showed him the bill.

"What'd he do that for?"

Miss Daley shrugged. "My own opinion is that he doesn't know better. By the time Mr. Raike found this, Edgar'd gone. Wiley, too. Wiley always leaves if Edgar leaves. He doesn't take chances."

Lounging against Miss Daley's desk, Parrish wondered whether to go home now or put it off awhile. He was wet and covered with mud, and there would be a letter today from Alison, but maybe it would be wise to delay.

"Mr. Raike wasn't happy," Miss Daley said, as though reading his mind. But the information could be interpreted either way, and Parrish decided it would be better not to be any later than he was already.

The entire family was assembled in the gold and white hall when Parrish came in. In front of the mail table Judd Raike stood holding a sealed envelope and looking angrily at Paige, who still wore her wet raincoat and was obviously equally angry. Ellen stood at the foot of the stairs and Edgar near the den, apparently only a spectator. Parrish saw Alison's letter on the table but held back from taking it.

"That letter's mine," Paige said hotly. "It's addressed to me."

"Who do you know at Harvard?" Raike demanded.

"Anson Tower."

"And you've been corresponding with him?" Raike examined the envelope. "Secretly—behind my back?"

"There was nothing secret about it," Paige said. "The letters came here."

Raike looked up darkly. "Am I going to need a spy system to keep my daughter from sinking to the level of a common tramp?"

Nobly, Paige raised her head and held out her hand. "Are you through with my letter?"

"Ellen," Raike said, "can you tell me why I wasn't told about this?"

"I'm sorry, Judd. It didn't seem a thing to bother you with—only an innocent correspondence."

Raike tapped the letter on his palm. "One thing I'm going to make clear right now is that anything that happens in this house is something I should hear about. And anything that my children do outside it I want to hear about, and anything that they are even thinking of doing is something I want to hear about. And I'm going to hear about it. Is that clear?"

Ellen nodded. "All right, Judd."

Raike turned back to Paige. "If you'd realize that I've had just a little more experience than you, it would save us both a lot of trouble. But since there's no telling you anything, I've no choice but to discipline you. In the end you'll thank me."

"I'd like my letter, please."

Judd Raike examined the envelope a moment, tapped it in his hand and then deliberately walked into the den and over to the fireplace. He opened the screen and, while his family stood in the doorway watching, threw Anson's letter into the fire.

"All you want to discipline me for," Paige cried out, "is so you'll think you own me! Like Edgar and Wiley. And Ellen. Just to do everything you say. You just want to own everyone—for miles and miles and miles. You don't love anyone—you just own them!"

Raike came back. "Now, you are not to write to this man and if any more letters come from him—" he turned to Ellen—"they're to be handled the same way."

Paige flushed, furious, and turned and bolted up the stairs.

"Judd!" Ellen began, "she's only—"

Raike cut her off. "Furthermore, any phone calls for Paige, she's out. Unless I'm home, when she can talk in my presence. We're not going to have a repetition of this."

Paige stopped on the stairs. "Go ahead!" she cried. "Burn them if it makes you feel so great. The only time you feel great is when you're lording it over your victims."

"Oh, Paige!" Ellen said.

Edgar shook his head. "It's the only way to handle her. She's getting pretty out of hand lately."

Raike turned on Edgar and jerked his head toward the den. "You get in there," he ordered. "I've a few things to say to you."

Startled, Edgar backed into the den and Raike started in after him. A sudden gust of wind threw rain against the window and Raike spun around, more unspent anger pushing itself out. "Ellen," he snapped, "you're getting entirely too sure of yourself around here. When I issue an order, what I expect from you is obedience. Not arguments. Absolute obedience."

"Of course, darling."

"You seem to think you're a great little manager, but we don't share our opinion. You've only been with fairly inferior people. You don't know as much as you think you do."

"Of course, darling. That's why I always ask your opinion."

"Lately you've been giving opinions more than asking, and you're causing a lot of trouble. When I want your advice on Paige I'll ask for it. When I don't ask, it's because I don't want it. Is that clear?"

"Yes, darling."

"Now, you—" Raike turned and strode into the den after Edgar.

"What the hell!" Parrish snatched up his letter from Alison and turned to Ellen. "Let's get out of here!"

"What!" Ellen said, astonished.

"You don't have to stand for that!"

"Don't be silly, Parrish. It's only the rain."

"Edgar's the one he's mad at. He pulled a boner on ordering chemical."

"So that's what started it." Ellen nodded.

"Only, Paige gets it on the chin."

"It's easier to burn a letter, Parrish," Ellen said sadly, "than to contro' the rain. And Edgar will never be anything but what he is."

"And that doesn't bother you?"

"If you could just learn that the time to argue is not when he's upset He's perfectly reasonable when he's not upset."

"You're blind! You're blind to what he really is!"

"Parrish," Ellen said, "if you love someone, you love him for his good points and try to help with his weaknesses."

With disbelief, Parrish searched his mother's face, seeing that she meant what she said, and then he turned away. If she wouldn't see, he couldn't make her. He went upstairs to his room and read Alison's letter feeling a little better as he reflected that in four days she would be home Then he went down the hall and knocked on Paige's door.

After a long moment she opened it, her face still angry.

"Let's get the hell out of here for a couple of hours," he said. "Go someplace."

"You don't have to feel sorry for me. I can take care of myself."

"I'm not sorry for you. We can eat out, go to a movie. How about it?"

Then Ellen came up to Paige's room, too. "Don't worry about it, Paige, she said. "We'll straighten it out. You'll be able to write to Anson when ever you want to."

"I intend to," Paige said, hotly. "And I don't care if he never get straightened out."

"Yes, you do. He's your father," Ellen said. "And in a way you're ver much like him, Paige. The stronger the resistance, the less you give in So don't complicate things by resisting for its own sake."

"It's not for its own sake," Paige said. "It's a matter of principle."

"Of course it is. And you're right and we'll straighten it out. Beside Paige—" Ellen smiled—"you're getting so pretty that if he's going to b upset about every young man that phones or writes to you, he's not goin to have time for anything else."

Paige laughed.

"So don't force him to set up a battle line over this issue that he doesn really want to fight about. Now get dressed and come down to dinner

"We're going out to dinner," Parrish said.

"No," Ellen said. "Go out after dinner."

When Ellen had gone downstairs again Parrish said, "I just want i go on record saying I don't think you're at all like him."

"If we go out," Paige said, "I'm not going to tell him."

"'S O.K. with me," Parrish said and went back to his room.

Later, driving in the Valley with only a light rain falling now, Paige grew more talkative. "He didn't care that it was Anson. It was just that I hadn't asked his permission. If I had, he would probably have said yes."

"Why didn't you, then?"

"I didn't see why I should. What's so terrible about it, writing to Anson or anyone I please?"

"Nothing's terrible about it."

"It's my time, and if I want to spend it writing letters to everyone I know, what's wrong?"

"You don't have to convince me, Paige." Parrish patted her hand. "I'm in your corner, one hundred per cent."

Paige smiled. "With all the trouble I cause?"

"Hell, I'm in trouble most of the time, myself. You know that. When I stay out of trouble, I've been working at it, full time."

Paige laughed and Parrish drove on slowly through the Valley, where the smells of a country spring filled the damp night air. Presently she settled back on the seat and he knew she was feeling better.

"Isn't it nice out here?" Paige said, after a while. "On these beautiful spring nights, or in early summer, the world seems so wonderful in the Valley I can hardly bear it. Once I got up at five o'clock and came out. I got here just as the sun was coming up over the tobacco fields and the mist was moving around and it was so unbelievable I just lay on a stone wall for a couple of hours watching."

Parrish looked at her and thought that he had never seen anyone who could get so starry-eyed and wrapped up in life as Paige.

"I loved everything I saw—the trees, a couple of old cows, even old Lewis Post who came stumbling down the road, probably just getting home. Me, even—myself—just for being there and seeing it all. Isn't that crazy?"

Parrish smiled. "It's not crazy."

She laughed. "I guess it's crazy, all right." Then after a few moments she began to talk about Judd again, but not so passionately now. "What do you suppose makes him that way, Parrish? Makes him have to own everyone for miles around?"

Parrish shrugged. "I don't know. Habit, maybe. Used to running things."

"Lately I think about it a lot. I get very mixed-up feelings. One minute I feel guilty because he's my father and then other times I don't feel guilty at all because I don't think he's right. I don't think he should try to own everyone and make them jump around like trained animals because he gives them things, and not love them if they don't. I don't think that's right in anyone and I don't think I should say it's right in him just because he's my father."

"I don't think it's right either, Paige. But that's the way he is. We aren't either of us going to change him."

"I even hate to see someone make a dog sit up and beg for food or a pat on the head. If you're going to give him something, give it to him, and if you're going to pet him, pet him. But I don't think he should have to beg for it. Or people, either. If I were a dog and someone made me do that I'd just bite 'em or foam at the mouth or something and go away."

Impulsively, Parrish took Paige's hand and raised it to his lips and kissed it lightly.

"Hey, what'd you do that for?"

"Because you've got a rebel streak a mile wide and I think it's great."

"Ho, I guess it's not so great!" She laughed, pleased. "I didn't think all that up myself—about his owning people. Tom Holden told me. Tom talks to me about everything."

Parrish whistled softly. He had wondered where she had learned so much. "I wouldn't spread that around, Paige," he said. "Don't let your father know Tom tells you that stuff."

"Ho, I know that!" Paige laughed. Then she said, "Anson is coming home soon and I know he'll ask me out. I intend to go."

"How you going to work it?"

"I don't know," she said. "Maybe I'll break down and ask his royal permission."

The rain stopped at last and after a few days of drying out the Valley began to catch up. The women were kneeling by seedbeds, pulling plants, Jamaicans were riding setters, and crops were going into the ground.

Daily, Parrish traveled his route, the farms along it familiar now. He knew the old weather vane at Colebrook's and the snapped birch branch that hung to the stone wall at Lemmie's, and then on along the road past Oermeyer's and past Prentiss's and Tully's and past Sala's, where every stone was as familiar as his own hand, and on past the field where the Black Angus grazed, to Raike's Ridge farm where a hollowed-out tree trunk lay next to the entrance and often a chipmunk sat. He traveled it automatically now, seeing things along the way, the wild blackberry flowering white, the green of early trees deepening, the hemlock emerald tipped.

This morning, through the open window of his room, he could smell spring warming into summer. Although it was Sunday, he was up early because a few farms were working, still trying to catch up. He dressed quickly, thinking that he would finish by eleven o'clock and then this afternoon he and Alison would go to the shore and she would lie on

the deck while he worked some more on his boat and then, later . . .
Quietly he opened the door to go downstairs. To his surprise, he found
Ellen in the hall, just coming to get him.

"Parrish," she said, "come downstairs. Judd wants you."

As he went down the steps Raike came out of the den, a black look
on his face, and motioned them into the dining room, where Paige and
Evaline and her children were already at breakfast. "Now don't argue,"
Ellen whispered as she walked past Parrish. Perplexed, he went in and
sat down.

For several minutes, without speaking a word, Raike looked him over
very thoroughly and then called out sharply, "Maples!" Maples opened
the pantry door. "Where are my sons, Maples?"

"They're not down yet, sir."

"Wake them. And tell them to be down here, dressed, in five minutes." Maples started to leave. "And you can tell them, Maples, that for
every minute they're late they'll be fined one hundred dollars. For inefficiency."

Maples nodded, the door closed, Raike ate two sections of grapefruit
and fastened his eyes again on Parrish. "You see, I've heard the news."

Bewildered, Parrish met the look with one of stunned surprise, remembered Ellen's repeated warnings, and said nothing. Raike finished eating
his grapefruit, gulped down some coffee, impatiently pushed the cup away
and said to Ellen, "Your son's quite an actor. I think he belongs in the
theater, not the tobacco business."

"Darling," Ellen said, gently. "Don't make it any worse for yourself."

"No advice this morning, Ellen, please. *Please*. And don't give me any
trouble. Your son does well enough at that."

Edgar came hurrying in, still fixing his tie. "What's the matter? What
happened?"

"Sit down," Raike said. "Blue mold, that's what happened. At Lemmie's. Lemmie just phoned."

"In the beds?"

"No," Raike yelled, "not in the beds. In the fields—number three. And
I'm trying to get to the bottom of it." He turned back to Parrish. "Now,
why didn't you report this to me yesterday—when you saw it?"

"There wasn't anything wrong at Lemmie's yesterday!"

"Well, you can try to squirm out if you want to. But you won't succeed.
My opinion is you forgot."

"I didn't forget anything!" Parrish burst out. "Nobody said a word at
Lemmie's yesterday about blue mold. Nobody was even working in the
number-three field."

"Nobody said a word—nobody said a word! Don't you have eyes? Can't you look around? Ask questions?"

"Darling," Ellen put in, and Parrish knew it was to draw off Raike's fire. "What is blue mold?"

"Tell her," Raike said to Parrish.

"I don't know what blue mold is. I never heard of it until now." But he had, somewhere. He tried to remember.

"It's a fungus that looks like mildew," Paige said quickly. "Usually it's in the beds and it's a sort of bluish color. But this attack is in the fields and out there it's yellow spots on the leaves. The heavy rains must have brought it out."

"Is it serious?" Ellen said.

"Of course it's serious," Edgar snapped. "It can ruin your whole crop if you don't control it."

"Stop asking foolish questions," Raike said. "A spotted Shade leaf is worthless."

Then he looked up as Wiley crept into the room, his eyes bloodshot, his skin pale beneath his tan. It was obvious that he had been awakened before he'd slept off the Scotch he had consumed last night. Blinking, he rested his forehead on his hand.

Raike looked at him coldly. "Will you sit up! I've got a farm rotten with blue mold. I've got a man who saw it and either wasn't interested enough to ask what it was or else deliberately withheld the information—"

Parrish threw down his fork, saw Ellen motion quickly to stop him, and ignored her. "I didn't report it because I didn't see it. And neither did Lemmie himself. Because yesterday there was nothing to report."

Raike stared. "I'm beginning to think you weren't even there yesterday. I'm beginning to think you're not even making half your calls. I think you're doing something else on my time." He looked back to Wiley. "Now get something in your stomach so you won't pass out. We're going out to Lemmie's." Abruptly, he left the table, turning in the doorway to Parrish. "You, too. This is your problem now."

The instant Raike was gone Ellen motioned to Parrish and he pushed back his chair violently and followed her out of the room. "What did you gain by arguing?" she whispered. "You just antagonized him."

"He knows there was nothing wrong yesterday."

"What difference does it make? Let him have his way."

"It makes a lot of difference!"

"Not really, dear. Not in the end." She touched his arm. "Go along, now, and please hold on to yourself."

"What's the matter with you?" Parrish shouted, and abruptly lowered his voice as Ellen hushed him. "Can't you see what he is? What's happened to you?"

"Parrish, get along with him. It's not as hard as you think. And there's so much here for you, if you will only take it. Don't be a fool and throw it away!"

In silence they rode to Lemmie's in Raike's Cadillac—Raike deep in thought, letting the ash burn long on his cigar, Edgar gloomy, Wiley slumped in a corner, his collar open, his skin a little green. Raike threw away his cigar, took out another, snapped the seal with his thumbnail and lit it. Then he spoke to Parrish, sitting in front with Dennis. "When you're at Lemmie's," he said, "what do you see over at Oermeyer's?"

"When I can see him, he's doing about the same thing Lemmie is."

"How many men does he have?"

"About ten. Men and women together, that is. No Jamaicans."

"What do you mean, no Jamaicans?" Edgar scoffed.

"He's working tobacco bums this year," Raike snapped. "He didn't get that loan from Tower on time to contract for Jamaican labor. Does he work himself—Oermeyer?"

"Always," Parrish said. "When I see him."

Lemmie was waiting for them at the seedbeds, a couple of Jamaicans with him, his sour face glum, shoulders hunched. Raike lit up a fresh cigar, passed one to Edgar and to Wiley, who looked sick but bravely lit up.

As they got out of the car Lemmie came up. "It was that lousy rain—"

"What are you doing?" Raike said.

"I'm waiting like you said. Mr. Raike, I gotta tell you it's in the beds, too. I seen it after I called." Lemmie pulled his battered hat lower, squinted toward the seedbeds. "The number-three field, Mr. Raike. And one bed."

Raike walked over to the beds, two Jamaicans hastening to lift off a couple of tops. He bent down to examine a few plants, walked along the bed and examined a few more. Edgar and Wiley drifted over, standing useless. Parrish bent down and looked at the underside of a slightly shriveled leaf, as he had seen Raike do, and saw a thin bluish mildew.

"We oughta knock this bed out right away, Mr. Raike," Lemmie said, "and start sprayin' the others and the fields. I got a little formate here and I'll get Tower to open up and give me more, and some formaldehyde."

"Hold on, Lemmie. Quit rushing me." Raike walked slowly around the bed and then looked at a couple of other beds.

Lemmie shuffled his feet. "It'd be best to knock out a couple of beds."

"The hell with that. You pulled that on me last year. I'm not even sure I'll knock out this whole bed." He looked over at the number-three field that ran along the fence that separated Lemmie's from Oermeyer's and noticed Oermeyer working at his beds. "What's he doing?"

"Ah, he putters around on Sunday, catches up on little things."

"If you ask me," Raike said, "that's where this came from. Oermeyer. He had it last year."

"Everyone had a little last year," Lemmie said, morosely. "Mr. Raike, we oughta be dousin' this bed with formaldehyde right now and sprayin' the rest, and the fields, too."

"Knock it off, Lemmie," Raike said impatiently. "It's the bunk, this lousy fear of blue mold that's spread through the Valley these past few years. The minute you hear blue mold you want to start killing every plant I've got. You can knock out this bed and that's all. Spray the others with formate and you'll be all right. You'll have to cancel out that number-three field this year. But here's what I want you to do. Way off to the side by the fence, where it won't bother our other fields, I want you to leave four rows from this bed, healthy-looking plants, no touch of mold on them yet."

"Jeez, Mr. Raike. What for?"

"Because I said to," Raike snapped. "Because I want an experiment. Once and for all I'm going to find out how much blue mold has to cost us every year. Used to be we sprayed beds. Then we started destroying plants. Now you want to spray all the fields." Raike thought a minute. "On those four rows—and be sure they're away from the rest—spray two and leave two absolutely alone. Don't spray them, don't touch them. Leave 'em alone and let's see what we find out. And—" he kicked the board of the infected bed—"put with them two rows more out of this bed. No touch of mold on them yet."

"Mr. Raike," Lemmie mourned, "do experiments have to be with my crop?"

"You're my only field that's got it, Lemmie, so you're elected. If it means a little extra work, I guess you'll live through it."

"It won't work, Mr. Raike. It's askin' for trouble."

"It'll work," Raike said.

He started to leave, with Edgar and Wiley falling in behind him. At the car he turned and looked narrowly at Lemmie and then suddenly jerked his head toward Parrish. "Was he here yesterday?"

Lemmie looked up, surprised. "Sure he was here yesterday."

Furious, Parrish stepped up to Raike, with no clear idea of what he would do if Raike started in again here; but Raike wasn't watching him. He was watching Lemmie, whose faced cracked into a sour grin as he realized that Parrish was somehow in trouble because of this. Then Raike, without another word, stepped into the car.

All the way home Parrish went over this in his mind, covertly watching Raike, puzzled. Had Raike really talked himself into believing that he hadn't called here yesterday? If not, what was he trying to accomplish? And if he had, how could so confused a man have achieved so much? But, Parrish reminded himself, from those who knew—from Sala, John, Teet—he had never heard anything about Judd Raike's confusion. All he had heard from them was advice never to underestimate him.

That night Parrish lay on the ground below a broad flat rock where Alison was sitting. "What's the use?" he said, chewing absent-mindedly on a stem of wild blackberry. "I can't get along with him."

"Parrish, don't say that even as a joke."

"I hate him."

"Of course, darling. Everyone does. You have to master the technique of getting along with him, like everyone else. You have to be deaf and dumb, not listen to him. Think very hard about something else." Alison came off the rock to where he was lying. "Think about us."

"I can't forget about him when I'm with him."

"Then think how everything depends on him—for us."

"Why does everything depend on him?"

"Because it does. Because where else would you get another chance like this?"

"I don't think everything depends on him for us."

Alison smiled down at him. "Darling, I'm only asking you to try. Promise me you'll at least try."

"You know what I think when I'm with him? I think that somebody ought to paste this guy one—and that someday I'm going to do it."

Alison drew off, looking thoroughly frightened. Smiling, Parrish reached for her. "Don't worry," he said. "I only think it."

"Parrish, promise me you'll never think that again!"

"The great man doesn't read minds yet."

"Promise me that you'll think only about us. Promise." She ran her fingers along his face and kissed him until he drew her down beside him. "Is it a promise?" she asked again.

"It's a promise."

"Parrish," she said, "he's not all bad. It's a lovely boat. And he didn't *have* to get it for you."

By the time Parrish reached Lemmie's next day, Raike's orders had been carried out. The infected bed had been destroyed, the number-three field cleared except for four rows along the fence, plus the two new rows which had been set in. Lemmie was spraying the two nearest rows. His unhappiness temporarily overcame his dislike for Parrish and he looked up and shook his head. "We'll infect God knows what!"

Parrish pointed to the two rows of smaller plants. "Those from the infected bed?"

Lemmie nodded morosely. He finished spraying the two rows and looked longingly at the rest, moving his sprayer up and down in his hand. Then he scratched his thick neck and turned away. Orders from Judd Raike were nothing to take lightly. Parrish bent over to look at a few plants in each row. They all seemed healthy and fine.

But on Friday Raike stood in front of the experimental rows and looked at badly spotted leaves. Parrish watched him walk up one row and down the other and waited for the outburst. It never came. "All right," Raike said. "Now we know."

"I wanna spray in the next fields, Mr. Raike, where it ain't touched yet," Lemmie said. "And I gotta use formaldehyde on two more beds."

"All right," Raike said. "Long as we know where we stand."

He squinted across the fence to Oermeyer's, where there was no activity in sight today, and looked back to Parrish, walking beside him. "You know what blue mold looks like now?"

"Yes, sir."

Raike chewed his cigar. "I don't like the idea of your not knowing these things. On a job like this you ought to know everything there is to know."

"I'm trying to learn, sir," Parrish said quickly.

"How are you trying to learn?"

"Why—" Parrish fumbled for an answer—"by keeping my eyes open and asking questions, sir." He fed Raike's maxims back to him, and Raike recognized them and, surprisingly, laughed.

"Tell you what you do," he said. "After work today you drive over to the experimental station and get some material to study. They've got pamphlets there on anything you can learn out of a book. They don't go the whole way, but they're a start."

"Yes, sir."

"And study them. I'll expect you to know everything in them. If anything like this happens again, you won't get off so easy, failing to report it."

A few nights later Parrish was standing near his mother while they greeted Tom and Maizie, who had come to dinner. The Holdens were among the few people Raike enjoyed and tonight he was relaxed, free of tension for the first time since the start of the unseasonable rain.

"How's your crop, Tom?" he said.

"Good year so far."

"That blue mold reach your section?"

"We were lucky."

"We had it," Raike said, soberly. "Damn trash farming out there is getting more expensive every year. Take that old drunkard, Lewis Post, for instance. Last year worked three acres, lost 'em all to worms. He's got to be stopped."

"Well, you know how Sala feels about Lewis," Tom said. "But he usually keeps an eye on him."

"You can't let one crazy old man's sentiment ruin a whole area." Raike lit a cigar. "And Oermeyer. Understand he lost two fields again this year with blue mold. And it didn't stop there. He gave it to all his neighbors. Prentiss lost a field, Tully lost a couple of acres. Lost two fields myself, out at Lemmie's, and I'm going to feel it. Lemmie turns out a high-quality leaf. All the trouble picked up directly from Oermeyer."

Next to Ellen, Parrish turned quickly to stare at Raike, and Ellen said in a low voice, "What's the matter? Didn't you know the others had it, too?"

"No," Parrish said, feeling vaguely troubled by this news.

"Why are you looking like that?"

But Parrish only wrinkled his brow. He was beginning to wonder.

19

THE WHOLE American attitude toward sex," Clayton Norris said, "has to be re-examined. It's damned important."

Bored and fidgety, Parrish looked out at the empty beach and the darkening ocean. At dusk the people left and the sea gulls came, and now they swooped and dived and pecked along the shore, fat and cocky scavengers. In the distance the lighthouse beacon blinked.

"Europeans take the whole thing much more casually than we do," Harris Lowe said. "Not less seriously, you understand. Only more casually."

"Europeans are very serious about sex," Clayton said. "Very."

Parrish shifted about in his seat. Alison loved this outer-deck cocktail lounge at the hotel and always insisted that they come, for a little while anyway; and ordinarily he was willing enough to let her have her fun. But tonight she'd wanted to sit with Clayton and Melissa. Small doses of Clayton Norris, Parrish thought, were all a man should be asked to take.

"Let's get out of here," he whispered.

"In a little while," she said.

"I knew an Italian once." Clayton chatted on busily. "A fiery black-eyed devil, knew what he was talking about, too—said the reason Americans have strange ideas on love is because the women are so cold. Said American women are damned unnatural."

"Ha!" Lorraine Lowe arched an auburn eyebrow.

"It's a damned interesting point of view," Clayton said. "And I know a Frenchman who says basically all American women are businesswomen."

Harris Lowe laughed. "Has he been home lately?"

"I knew a Czech once who said love is for the birds." Lorraine applied a fresh coat of lipstick. "Add that to your collection."

Restless, Parrish stood up and walked over to where Ellen was sitting with Tom Holden, waiting for Raike, who was in the office with his manager. A moment later Paige came in with Anson Tower, who had driven down for the evening. On the matter of Anson, Ellen had established peace as she had promised, and Paige was permitted to see him once a week. Watching them now, Parrish thought how Paige had changed. One day she had been an adolescent and then suddenly she was not. Where she had been awkward and angular, she was suddenly graceful; the eternal blue jeans had given way to a wardrobe that had drawn comment even from Alison. As Paige crossed the cocktail lounge, her blond hair drawn back, walking in that wonderful tall straight way that was the first thing he had noticed about her, Parrish thought that Raike could stop worrying—Paige could hold her own anywhere now.

Tom Holden, too, was watching her, and he said, "You've worked wonders with Paige, Ellen."

"She'd have outgrown her tomboyishness without me, Tom. Girls change at that age."

"But not so quickly without a clever hand."

"She calls herself my Galatea. She's only half joking—in a way she resents it," Ellen said. "But Judd is pleased."

"You're good for her in many ways, Ellen," Tom said. "Especially persuading Judd to let her go to Wellesley in the fall. I thought he'd keep her in Hartford. And Paige needs very much to get away, if she's not to turn into a damaged human being."

Ellen looked shocked. "That's very strong, Tom."

Tom nodded but did not retract. Then Parrish saw Raike in the doorway and got up quickly and left to go back to Alison, stopping on the way to say hello to Paige and Anson.

"Sit down," Anson said, "and dissipate with us. We've joined the bicycle brigade. Temporarily."

"What's the bicycle brigade?" Parrish said.

"Wheels propped up." Paige smiled. "Going nowhere."

"But spinning. Spinning like mad." Anson busied himself lighting a pipe. "Look at her, Parrish. Isn't she fabulous?"

Paige laughed and said, "Oh, Anson—honestly!"

"Don't you love the way she says that?" Anson smiled over his pipe. "Say it again, baby."

"Anson, you stop it or I'll leave you and go join someone really fascinating, like Clayton Norris, maybe."

"You wouldn't. I'm your rock and your salvation."

"Anson," Paige said, "you're much too sure of me. I'll have to start giving you trouble."

"Isn't she marvelous—suddenly a real coquette! Although, in a way, I miss the blue jeans. Don't you, Parrish?"

Parrish laughed. "She suits me either way."

"Down, boy. No trespassing." Puffing his pipe, Anson looked at Paige affectionately. "It's completely unscientific, you know. Explodes all my theories. Living proof that a rose *can* grow in the sands of luxury in the desert of decay."

Walking back to Alison, Parrish thought that, as always, Anson puzzled him. Anson said everything so smoothly, with such assurance, you were never quite sure where you began to disagree with him. You felt only that someplace your thinking took a different road.

Back at the table Clayton Norris was still pursuing his examination with scientific thoroughness. "Even Europeans differ," he was saying. "I knew an Austrian who used to point a finger and yell, 'One woman is enoff for any man!'"

"You know the old saying," Lorraine said gaily. "He who can does. He who can't preaches."

"Hey, Parrish," Clayton said. "You're damned silent tonight. What've you got to say on this love business?"

Parrish grinned. "I'm a man of action. No opinions."

"Hey, that's all right," Clayton approved.

Once Parrish had said it, action seemed a good idea, and he whispered again to Alison, "Come on, let's get out of here."

This time she agreed and they walked slowly up the boardwalk, leaving behind the lights and the noises of the hotel, moving into darkness where the only sound was of the surf. They reached Raike's pier and walked out to where Parrish tied his boat and stepped in, hearing the quiet, unhurried whispering of the water, and Alison came quickly into his arms.

"Darling," she said, "have you really no opinions on love?"

Smiling a little, Parrish searched the face that had become the only meaning of love he could remember, and thought that when you were in love it was all, and beyond opinions.

"You—" he touched the face—"are my opinion on love."

The boat rocked gently under the light of a thousand stars. "Parrish—"

"Mmm?"

"Tonight when you were sitting with Tom and Ellen—the minute Judd Raike came over, you left."

"Mmm-hmm."

"It was terribly obvious. You know how he likes people to fuss over him and show that they think he's great."

Parrish twisted a lock of the black hair. "Well, everyone else does, so I guess he won't miss me."

"That's just the point, darling. With everyone else fussing over him, you have to do it even more. Would you like someone who deliberately avoided you?"

"Uh-huh," he said, lazily.

"Parrish, don't you want him to like you?"

"He doesn't know the meaning of the word."

"Of course he does! Look at all he gives Edgar and Wiley. And he's crazy about Ellen."

"He abuses them, too."

"Not Ellen!"

"She says he's sorry afterward. He usually gives her something like a sapphire bracelet or a sable stole."

"Then she shouldn't mind too much."

Parrish looked at Alison curiously. "She doesn't mind. But not because of the sable or the sapphires."

"Parrish—" Half worried, half coaxing, Alison touched his face. "You are trying, aren't you, to make him like you?"

"To tell you the truth," Parrish said, "lately I don't give a damn."

Alison stared. "I do believe you're serious!" she gasped. "What's the matter with you?"

Parrish propped his elbows under his head, seeing that Alison was deeply concerned. "Alison," he said patiently, "I take orders from Judd Raike six days a week. I account to Judd Raike for every minute of my time. When I come in from work I sit down there below his desk and get nagged and needled and catch hell for things I didn't do. And now he's got me studying pamphlets from the experimental station. I've got a couple of dozen pamphlets on everything about tobacco you can think of, and every night after work I have to answer questions about them. So on Saturday night I don't give a damn about Judd Raike, and I don't want to look at him or talk to him or act as though I think he's great, because I don't."

"Well, you've got to learn how to handle him if you expect to get any-place!" she exclaimed. "And you never will with an attitude like that. You have to flatter him and not talk back and stay out of his way—"

On the shore a fire for a beach party appeared and someone had a guitar and began to tune up and the fire flared orange and water lapped the boat and Parrish thought that this was not a night for arguments. "You just told me not to avoid him."

"Not so obviously." For Alison there was no night now nor water nor stars; there was only her worry. "Once you were there, you should have stayed."

"There are times," Parrish said, "when I think it would be better if I didn't stay at all. If I quit and moved out and got another job."

Alison sat up, cool and distant, moving out of his reach. "That's fine! I'm glad to know how you feel—how much you care about me, about us!"

A sweet, lazy melody came from the guitar on the beach. "What has this to do with us?"

"Because if you left it would change everything. You know it. You just won't admit it."

He knew she was right. Of course it would make a difference. But something in him balked at admitting it and his silence only irritated her.

"If you cared anything at all about me, you'd use your head the way everyone else does so you'd get someplace. How many people get a chance like this—to be practically adopted by someone like Judd Raike?"

"Did it ever occur to you that Judd Raike got someplace himself, without getting adopted by anyone? And so did a lot of other people. And maybe I could, too?"

"Make that much money?"

"I don't even want that much money."

The green eyes were angry and defiant, and he saw that she was deeply hurt, like a child unjustly slapped. On shore the guitar began a plaintive tune and someone started to sing. Suddenly Parrish wondered what he'd been thinking of. He reached over to take Alison in his arms to reassure her.

"Leave me alone!" She pushed him away angrily. "Don't touch me. I knew it was too good to be true."

"I'm sorry. Don't be this way," he pleaded.

"You started it," she burst out, moving to the side of the boat.

After a moment Parrish got up and stood silently behind her and stroked her hair. "Darling, I'm sorry," he said. "I'm not going to quit. I don't even know why I said it."

"You never think of anyone but yourself."

"Don't worry about it. I get along with him." He turned her around. "I get along with him fine."

He drew her down beside him, feeling her resistance at first and then that she didn't resist any longer. The thought of losing her sent a cold stab of fear through him and he knew it would be far, far easier to turn a deaf ear to Judd Raike than to her, and that he would rather learn to live with Raike than try to live without Alison. He knew, too, that—although it was painful—those were his alternatives. He held her close, sweeter in his arms for almost having been lost, and he felt his blood beginning to race and her quick response, firing higher his own. He thought again what he already knew, that her elegance covered a passion far stronger than Lucy's, and he wondered if she knew it and he cautioned himself again to be careful, to hold onto himself, not to even think— He wrenched away and put his head down on his knees and locked his arms around his legs and felt worse.

He dropped his hand into the water and brought it to his face. After a while he felt her hand on his cheek, cool and light, gently stroking back and forth. He raised his head and looked at her and she drew him close to her and held his head against her breasts, and it didn't help at all.

"Teet—" Parrish sat down opposite him in a booth at Tower's. "You know a woman named Dahlia Crouch out there at the trailer camp?"

"A real nothin'," Teet said. "Dumb!"

"She works for Lemmie?"

"Mornings."

Parrish sighed. Mornings, when he called at Lemmie's, Dahlia Crouch was always there; but a week ago, overhearing a snatch of conversation, Parrish had begun to suspect that Dahlia was working only until noon, while Lemmie was entering her into the time book for a full day. "Why does she just work mornings?"

"Her husband works a second shift, takes care of the kids mornings. She's got to get home for afternoons. What's the big interest in Dahlia Crouch?"

"Nothing important." Parrish wished there had been another way to check on this besides asking Teet, but Raike watched his time so closely that it would have been impossible to recheck Lemmie's every afternoon without an explanation. And with Judd Raike he couldn't give a reason like that without being sure. Now he was sure. "I was just wondering why Lemmie was willing to work a half-day girl. Charity isn't one of his strong points."

Teet looked at him narrowly. "O.K., friend. If that's what you're selling, I'll buy it. You still like being timekeeper?"

"Great job."

"Tight schedule, eh?"

"I make it without killing myself."

Teet puffed his pipe contentedly. "But no time to get back to check on anyone pulling a fast one, eh? What's Lemmie doin'? Puttin' Dahlia in for a whole day?"

Parrish leaned across the table. "Look, Teet," he said, emphatically, "nobody in the world is closer to a clam than you, when you want to be, so clam up about this. Forget it. If Raike ever hears you picked this up from me, it'd be very tough."

"Kid," Teet said, "what do you stay for?"

"It's a long story."

"Ask me, it's a short one. And an old one, too." Teet tapped his pipe into the ash tray.

"I figure it's a difference of about eighteen dollars a week in Dahlia's pay," Parrish said.

Teet nodded. "Startin' when they go inside to string lath. She don't sew cloth. She wasn't there when you were, was she?"

Parrish shook his head. "Does Lemmie split with her?"

"Nah, Dahlia don't know nothin' about it. She's too stupid. Lemmie fixes up her pay, gives her what's comin' to her, and pockets the rest."

Eighteen dollars a week, Parrish thought. "I didn't think anyone would dare try something like that with Raike."

"It's an old trick. Lemmie ain't the first."

"I'm surprised Raike hasn't gotten wise."

"Ah, every job has its own tricks. Even Raike don't know 'em all. What you going to do now that you know? Turn him in?"

"Raike'll kill him."

"Lemmie'd be no loss," Teet commented. "Ask me, he's a real crumb."

"I hate to crucify a man for eighteen dollars a week."

Teet lifted his muddy shoes to the next chair and leaned back to enjoy his pipe. "Why not think about it awhile, kid?" he advised.

The noon sun shone hard on Sala's cloth outside the library window. Alison was curled in a corner chair, and at his desk Sala sat erect, listening attentively while Parrish told him about Lemmie and Dahlia Crouch. Then he said, "I think you have to tell him, Parrish."

"Truthfully," Parrish said unhappily, "I hate to turn anyone in to Judd Raike. Even Lemmie. And I have no reason to like Lemmie."

"It's not a question of personality," Sala said. "You took this job. You let Raike pay you to check up on this sort of thing. Now you've found out something, it's part of the job you took money for to report it."

"I feel like a stool pigeon. Like some kid tattletale."

Sala nodded. "In a way, yes. But that's what you agreed to be when you took the job."

Parrish looked up. "I didn't think about it that way."

"It didn't become that until you found something. But it's inherent in the job, Parrish. If a man pays you to check up on certain details of his business, he expects to hear the results—the bad as well as the good."

"He hears them all right. He gets a blow-by-blow report!" He could see Alison's eyes dart up to his, anxiously. "But I hate to hang a man for eighteen dollars a week. Even Lemmie."

"Lemmie created the situation, Parrish. Not you. He was the one who decided it was worth stooping to this for eighteen dollars a week." Sala broke the ash neatly off his thin cigar. "Parrish, quite apart from the principle involved, Lemmie isn't worth the sacrifice. He's a good tobacco man, but he's a pretty low type. And for all you know, Judd may be aware of this already. He may be waiting to see how long before you find it out."

Parrish was startled. He hadn't thought of that.

"On the other hand," Sala said, "if he doesn't know, he may admit you did a good job finding out—ease up on you a little."

He hadn't thought of that, either. All he'd thought, for two days now, was that it was a painful situation, however you figured it. Watching him, Sala said suddenly, "Parrish, what does he pay you? I hope you don't mind my asking."

"A hundred and twenty-five dollars a week."

"Did you know that's nearly twice the average timekeeper's pay?"

"It is!" Parrish said, astonished. "No, I didn't know. I never thought to ask."

"A hundred and twenty-five a week and that car, Parrish. He's buying you. You ought to know it."

Parrish reflected a moment. Then he said, with a little smile, "If you'd told me that when I started this job it might have bothered me. But it doesn't now. I'd say I'm earning it."

"You probably are." Sala stood up. "About Lemmie, you have to tell Judd, Parrish. You have no choice."

Walking with him to his car, Alison waited until they were away from the house before she spoke. "Don't pay any attention, Parrish," she said. "About Raike's buying you. My father hates him so, he'd say anything."

"In this case he's probably right."

"What does he know about it?" Alison said, impatiently. "He's probably remembering what timekeepers made twenty years ago. When he still had one. Before he managed to hand everything over to Judd Raike."

"It doesn't matter, anyway." Parrish started the car. "I have to go. If I don't make up this time I'll be tossed to the lions. Then what'll you do?"

"Parrish," Alison said, "this is what we've been waiting for. He'll see now that you're trying, you're really doing well, and everything will be different. It'll be all right now. I know it."

At quarter to five, as always, Parrish knocked on Raike's office door and went in. Falteringly he got through his story about Lemmie and Dahlia Crouch and looked up when he finished, to see Raike's face red with anger. Raike's hand went into the humidor for a cigar and he snapped open the blade of his gold knife and slowly scraped off a shred of the seal.

Parrish slid down in the chair. Already he was feeling sorry for Lemmie and wishing he had handled this some other way.

"All right." Raike cleared his throat violently. "Have you thought of anything to say for yourself?"

"Me!" Parrish's mouth dropped open.

"You don't think you're going to get away with this?"

"I'm not trying to get away with anything! It's the truth!"

"I regard it as a confession of your inefficiency." Raike scraped off another shred. "A confession that you've done a mighty poor job. That you've fallen down badly."

Parrish gaped at Raike, too astonished to protest.

"How long—" Raike scraped the seal—"have you been timekeeper now?"

Already Parrish could see how Raike was going to twist this. "Three months."

"And for three months a man on your route has been cheating me on the payroll?"

"I think he was probably cheating you last year, too."

Judd Raike's face darkened with anger, seemed to puff up, jerked involuntarily a few times. "We'll confine ourselves to your career, if you don't mind. Your brilliant career. We did manage to get along before you came to us. I'm sure you can't see how, but we did manage."

Parrish let out a frustrated sigh.

"Does this bore you? Perhaps you'd like to leave."

Parrish glanced up, biting back a retort, reminding himself that, to Judd Raike, any threat to that which he possessed was dynamite.

"Perhaps you'd like to leave us altogether?" Raike said. "And go back to earning fifty dollars a week."

Parrish bit his teeth together to remain silent.

"Now this cheating took place where?"

"What do you mean, where? At Lemmie's."

"I mean how did Lemmie report this woman's time?"

"In his time book."

"And whose department is the time book?"

"Look—" Parrish leaped up onto the platform that held Raike's desk —"Dahlia Crouch was there every morning when I was there. How was I to know she went home at noon? She's been going home at noon for years and you never caught on. And if I'd been suspicious sooner—of Lemmie or every other foreman you've got—I couldn't have checked back because anyone who works for you has to do what you say and nothing else. Nobody can do a better job than you let him."

"That's enough," Raike broke in. "That's enough from you. Sit down."

"I don't want to sit down!" Parrish gripped Raike's desk and Raike stood up threateningly.

"Now. For three months you've been okaying a doctored-up time book," he shouted, his face alarmingly red. "What else have you been approving of? How much else has been going on that you haven't noticed? Has Lemmie been pulling this with more than one? Maybe he's been making thirty-six dollars a week on the side. Or seventy-two. You don't know."

"He's getting the work out. You know there can't be more than one."

"Don't tell me what I know," Raike thundered. "Tell me what you know. Who else is pulling this stunt on your route, do you know that? And how much are they taking? Do you know that?"

"I could only find that out by doubling back on the route and checking a few each day. If I'd done that you'd have had my head."

"If you could speed up enough to check back, you should have done it long ago. I think what we'll have to do is get someone to check up on you."

Parrish closed his mouth. It was useless to try to say anything. Quit, he told himself. Tell him you quit.

"Go over to that board."

"I know what's on that board."

"You don't know nearly as much as you think you know. That board represents the biggest cigar-tobacco business in the world. It didn't get that way through a lot of damn-fool mistakes, through taking three months to find out what was going on, and getting second and third and fourth chances. Now I'm pretty disgusted and I'm damned if I'm going to waste much time on you. I've done my best. I'm trying to make a businessman out of you. Maybe you think I'm tough. Well, this is a tough world and if you don't believe me just get out and find out for yourself. I run a big business and I run it right and I'm not having any weak links. Now you think about that awhile."

Parrish was hardly listening. He knew all this by heart. "All right," he heard Raike say, at last. "You can go now."

He stepped off the platform and walked out of Raike's office into the stiflingly hot corridor of the warehouse, past the empty offices of Edgar and Wiley, and past Gilliam's, noticing that the old man was still at his desk. At the stairs he stopped and sat down on the top step and leaned his head against the gray wall. He'd said everything but the one thing he should have said—that he quit. He sat there on the step, almost crying. Then he got to his feet and made his way downstairs to the door, where he found Mig Alger waiting for him.

"Where you been?" Mig said. "I been here ten minutes. Mr. Raike phoned down he wants to see you."

"I've seen Mr. Raike," Parrish said.

"Wants to see you again," Mig said. "Go on back up."

"I don't want to see him again." Parrish moved to open the door, but Mig blocked his way.

"Better go back," he advised. "The old man wants you."

Numbly, Parrish turned and dragged his feet back upstairs, asking himself whether, if he quit now, there would be any way to make Alison see that he was right, and knowing only too well that there would not. Gilliam's office was empty now and Parrish pushed open Raike's door and saw that Gilliam was in there, sitting over next to the wall. Raike was still at his desk, writing, and since he didn't look up or indicate the chair below the desk, Parrish sat down next to Gilliam, looking at him questioningly; but Gilliam only glanced at him and looked away. A moment later, to his surprise, Edgar came in.

Appraising the situation as tense, Edgar sat down across the room, under his own portrait, and Parrish's eye caught the two together and he wondered what tricks the artist had used to make the picture so much like the man and yet so different. The door opened and Wiley came in.

With a tug of alarm Parrish wondered if everyone had been summoned · back because of him. If Raike thought that, in addition to the private performance, he was going to put Parrish through a public humiliation, he was crazy. Warily Parrish sat up, looking from Gilliam to Edgar to Wiley and up to Raike. Just let him say one word to me, starting it over again, and I'll leave if I have to knock down all four of them to get out.

Wildly he looked at the door and considered leaving immediately, before anyone had a chance to stop him. Then the door opened again.

Uncertainly, Lemmie came into the room.

He closed the door behind him, tugged at the brim of his hat, and stood waiting. Raike let him wait. Edgar and Wiley sat motionless. Gilliam picked at a fingernail. Sensing what was about to happen, Parrish sat wide-eyed and horrified. At last Raike put down his pen, settled his frame back, and pointed. "All right, Lemmie." Lemmie was getting the inquisition chair.

Lemmie sat and Raike nailed him awhile with that hawk-eyed stare of his. Then he said, "Now, Lemmie, how's it going out at your place?"

Lemmie hunched his shoulders. " 'S O.K."

"No trouble, eh? Except the blue mold?"

"You can't blame me for that, Mr. Raike."

"No, Lemmie," Raike agreed. "Not for that."

He paused and Parrish knew he was going to take out a cigar and his knife. While he opened the blade everyone sat waiting, Gilliam still picking at his fingernail, Edgar smoking a cigar, Wiley just fooling with his hands in his lap. Raike started to work on the seal.

Lemmie fidgeted in his chair. "What's this all about, Mr. Raike?"

Carefully, concentrating, Raike scraped another shred from the seal and then another. "Suppose you tell me, Lemmie."

"I don't know!" Lemmie's voice rose nervously.

Another bit of seal fell to the desk. "Think about it, Lemmie."

"I got nothing to think about! I don't know what's up." Lemmie looked over to Edgar and Wiley for some hint, and then to Gilliam and Parrish.

"How are your costs this year, Lemmie?"

"My costs are what they should be," Lemmie spread his hands. "Same as before."

"Haven't gone up?"

"Not a dime."

"You watch them pretty closely?"

"You bet I do."

"They haven't gone down, either."

"Ah, how could they go down?"

"You tell me, Lemmie."

"Mr. Raike, you know same as I do, nothin' goes down these days."

The seal was scraped away now and Raike put down his knife and took out last week's time sheet from Lemmie's farm. Lemmie shoved his battered hat back and slid a little lower in the chair. Raike took his time studying the sheet and then, leaving it on his desk, he reached into his pocket for a roll of bills, peeled off a ten and dropped it onto the open page, eying Lemmie carefully. He then added a five to it and then, slowly, one at a time, three one-dollar bills. He shoved the sheet with the money on it over to Lemmie. "Count it."

Lemmie glanced at the money without touching it and up again to Raike.

"How much?" Raike said.

"Eighteen—" Lemmie cleared his throat and the understanding coming into his eyes was sickening to see. "Eighteen dollars."

"Think that's a lot of money, Lemmie?" Lemmie shrugged. "Come on, let's have your opinion, Lemmie."

"It is and it ain't," Lemmie said.

With Raike's eyes nailing him, Lemmie began to perspire and he flicked his eyes around the room and up to Raike and down to his feet.

"You ready to tell us about it, Lemmie?"

"Tell you what?" Lemmie staged a final defense. "I got nothin' to tell." He scratched his thick neck, gave a short humorless laugh. "I'm still waitin' to hear what I'm here for. I'm just sittin' here on a hot seat, waitin'."

"Just waiting to find out, are you?"

"H-yeah!" Lemmie tried to smile.

"We'll wait with you."

Ten minutes seemed two hours, before the silent waiting became too much for Lemmie. "We gonna sit all night?"

"Not I," Raike said. "But you might. In jail. If I swear out a warrant for your arrest."

"My arrest!" Lemmie turned white. "What'd I do to be arrested?"

"I'd hoped we could straighten this out among ourselves, but we don't have to." Raike looked at his watch. "You've used up forty minutes of my time, Lemmie. You can have ten more."

Sick, Lemmie looked wildly around the room, starting another protest and then collapsing completely. "What you want to know?" he said thickly.

"You tell me."

"Ah, you know." His hand jerked up, dropped to his lap. "Wit' Dahlia."

"Dahlia who?"

"Dahlia Crouch," Lemmie said. "I thought you knew!"

"I know, Lemmie. But the others don't—at least not all of them. Suppose you tell them."

"What do they have to know so much for?"

"I want them to know. In case we ever have a thief again."

"I'm no thief."

"What are you?"

"Well, for Christ's sake, all I did was—well, all I did—"

"A little harder to talk about the stunt than it was to pull it, eh, Lemmie? Now what you did was—"

"Ah, I fixed up her time."

"Whose time?"

"Dahlia Crouch's."

"Then say it."

"I fixed up Dahlia Crouch's time—in the time book."

"Now, how did you fix it?" Raike said. "Describe it."

"I fixed Dahlia's time in the time book because she didn't work a whole day and—"

"Wait a minute. How long did she work?"

"She worked till noon."

"Then say so. Now start over."

"I fixed up Dahlia Crouch's time in the time book because she only worked until noon and I put her down workin' a full day—"

"Until—?"

"I put her down workin' a full day until four-thirty, with a half-hour out to lunch." Lemmie stopped, thinking he was through.

"Finish your story," Raike said.

"I finished!" Lemmie cried. "That's it."

"No, Lemmie, that's not it! You haven't told us what happened to Dahlia Crouch's unearned pay."

"I pocketed it. What you think I did with it?"

"Then tell us so."

"I got Dahlia's pay and I fixed it up and give her what was comin' to her and I kept the rest."

Raike nodded. "And that amounted to—?"

"Eighteen bucks a week. Just under."

Lemmie slumped deep in the chair now, ash-gray, and Parrish thought he was going to be sick and felt sick himself.

"Now there's only one more thing."

"That's it. There's nothin' else."

"How long you have been doing this."

"Almost three years," Lemmie said dully. "Weeks she worked."

Raike fixed a hard stare on him. "Now suppose you give us the whole story from beginning to end instead of in pieces, so we'll have it straight."

Without moving in the chair, Lemmie covered his eyes with his hand.

"For three years—" Raike prompted him.

Lemmie's lips began to work mechanically. "For three years I've been changing Dahlia's—Dahlia Crouch's—time in the time book because she couldn't work all day, she could only work until noon, and I put her in a full day every day till four-thirty with a half-hour to lunch and I fixed up her pay 'cause she didn't work it and I give her what was comin' to her and I pocketed the rest, eighteen dollars a week just under for almost three years weeks she could work 'cause she couldn't . . . work a full day." Lemmie stopped.

Raike shoved a piece of paper at Lemmie. He put a pen on top of it. "Write it out."

Lemmie looked up as though he didn't understand.

"Write it out and sign it."

Slowly, Lemmie stood up and bent toward the paper. His hand shook badly as it closed over the pen. He wrote. The pen scratched over the paper in the silent room. He wrote slowly and painfully and twice stopped and ran his sleeve across his mouth. When he finished he put down the pen and sat down. Raike picked up the paper to read. Lemmie didn't bother to watch.

"Now," Raike said, "does anyone have any questions to ask this man?"

No one had. They waited until Lemmie stood up, dismissed, and made for the door. He stopped once. "Do I go to work tomorrow?"

"That's up to you, Lemmie," Raike said, locking the signed confession into a drawer.

Lemmie left, closing the door silently behind him. Raike turned to Edgar and Wiley. "All right, we're pretty late," he said. "Good night, Gilliam."

"Good night, Mr. Raike."

Raike looked at Parrish. "You coming?"

Parrish got up and trailed behind them into the hot corridor and then out of the warehouse and got into his car and leaned his head back against the seat, feeling too sick to move.

For a long time after the others had left, Parrish sat in his car. The sun dropped behind the tall buildings, sending long shadows across the warehouse parking lot, and traffic thinned and daytime noises died. Then he drove wearily out onto the street and headed for the bridge and drove through the Valley until it was dark. At last, still in his working clothes, he went to see Alison.

She knew at once that something had gone wrong and with a patience unusual for her she waited until they reached the clearing near the stream. Then she sat quietly on a rock, letting him tell her what had happened.

"I'm through," he finished. "I don't want to look at him again. Tomorrow I'll drive over and leave the car."

Alison reacted with surprising calm. "Parrish, it's not as bad as you make it."

"It was disgusting."

"Think about it a minute, darling," she coaxed, like a mother with a stubborn child. "He didn't fire him."

"This was worse. It was indecent."

"Lemmie has four children, Parrish. All he knows is tobacco. And who would hire him after Raike fired him for stealing? You wouldn't have blamed him if he'd fired him?"

"It would have been cleaner."

"Cleaner, maybe, but much more serious for Lemmie. Much crueler, too. And he didn't do that. Once Raike decided to keep Lemmie, he had to teach him a lesson. Now Lemmie will never try it again and neither will any other foreman because the word will get around and they'll all know."

Reasons, Parrish thought. Always there were reasons to explain why a thing was all right when everything in you except reason cried out that it was offensive. Half-breed apologies. A thing wasn't right or wrong—it was right because it could have been worse.

"Where would Raike's business be if he let everyone steal from him? If he hadn't taught him a good lesson Lemmie would try again and again until Raike would have no choice but to fire him."

Parrish sat on the ground next to the rock with his back to her and pulled at a clump of wiry weeds.

"Come on, Parrish," she coaxed. "Cheer up. Lemmie is nothing to take on about."

Parrish threw himself flat on the grass. In the air he could smell the first hint of the end of summer. It was almost mid-August and Alison would leave him soon, and, if he quit, once again it would end badly. All too well he remembered last winter, the long months without her or any word of her.

"I consider it a very good sign," Alison persisted, "that he kept you there during the whole thing. He kept only the family—Edgar, Wiley, and you. He's beginning to consider you one of them—it's a wonderful sign."

"Gilliam was there, too." Last year they'd argued over Lucy, and this year Lemmie. And yet neither time was it as simple as that.

"Gilliam's paymaster," she said. "Anyway, he's always there. He's been with Raike since Raike bought his first farm."

Parrish thought of Gilliam, a frail, self-effacing man, very much like Evaline, and he wondered what went into making people that way. How many times did they bite back hot retorts before the retorts stopped rising to their lips? How many times did they hang their heads before they stayed down? Was a man broken suddenly or was it a slow eating away at the soul?

"With people like Gilliam," he said, "I always wonder which came first, the chicken or the egg."

"What are you talking about?"

"Do people like Gilliam get that way because for so many years they're pushed around by people like Judd Raike, until they have no shape left of their own? Or are they spineless to begin with, and do people like Raike latch onto them because they can push them around?"

"Parrish, you're dramatizing the whole thing. You're enjoying self-pity."

"No. I'm looking into my crystal ball—trying to see myself about ten years from now and discover whether I'll be like Gilliam, or say like Wiley, after I've let him push me around."

"You're not being pushed around! Look at your car and your boat and your salary and the way you live! You call that being pushed around?"

He didn't answer and she said, "Anyway, what's so terrible about Wiley?"

"Don't you think there's something queer about being so agreeable all the time?"

"That kind of queerness is just fine with me. I wish you were queer like that. And don't you worry about Judd Raike pushing you around for ten years. He'll break both arms and his back trying."

He laughed at that and reached up and took her hand and thought again of the months he would be without her—months that he knew would be forever if he quit over this episode of Lemmie that he was telling himself was more than Lemmie.

"Alison," he said, "you want to get married?"

"Married!" She stared at him.

He nodded, a little startled himself at his suggestion.

"When a minute ago you were talking about quitting?"

"If I don't quit—"

"Would you promise to really stay with him?"

He nodded.

"You wouldn't stay." She turned away. "Twice in a month now you've threatened to quit. Every time he does anything you don't like you're ready to quit. You're like a child."

"Are you saying you don't want to?"

She sat still, staring at the stream below, and after a moment she shook her head sadly. "Darling, it wouldn't work. I couldn't live on what you make and you wouldn't make any effort to get along with him so he'd give you more. And I'd never know when you'd quit and lose even that."

"Do you want to?" He turned her face to his. "Just tell me if you want to."

The green eyes darted away, became at once vulnerable and fiercely defiant.

"Yes or no?"

"Of course I want to," she said bitterly. "You know I want to. Don't keep talking about it when it's so impossible." She buried her head on his chest, her fingers gripping his arm. He thought at first that she was crying and then realized that she was not, and in that instant he understood that she wanted him as fiercely as he did her.

"All right." His lips found her hair. "All right."

Alison raised her eyes. "If you'd only get along with him. After a while he'd get tired of picking on you and find someone else. And everything would be all right. The only thing standing in our way is you."

He nodded, drawing her down beside him. "All right," he said again.

But a peace with Raike, he knew, would not be easy or quick, and he wondered whether Alison would wait that long for him—and, holding her close as she lay beside him, he wondered whether he could wait that long for her.

On the way home Parrish stopped at Tower's to eat, ravenously hungry because he'd skipped lunch to talk to Sala and dinner because he'd lost his appetite. But with the food in front of him he still had no taste for it, hungry as he was, and he knew it was because the Lemmie business was still with him. He ordered a drink to relax and tossed it down, feeling it hit him immediately on an empty stomach. He ordered another and started to eat. Presently Anson came in and saw him and came over.

"How's the tobacco business?" Anson greeted him.

"Great," he said. "Great business."

Anson looked at him quickly. "What are you celebrating, Parrish?"

"My future," Parrish said. He finished his hamburger and ordered another and some coffee.

"Look good?" Anson laughed.

"Dazzling," Parrish said. "Brilliant."

"It probably will be," Anson said.

He shouldn't have had two drinks before he ate. He wasn't that great a drinker. "All I have to do—" he looked at Anson narrowly—"is figure out the answer to one little problem: which came first, the chicken or the egg."

Anson laughed. "Or the acorn or the oak?"

"Right."

"Or ignorance or poverty," Anson said.

"Hadn't thought of that one."

"Or money or corruption."

Parrish squinted. "What's that got to do with it?"

"Do you have to be corrupt to make a lot of money or do you just get that way afterward?"

"Close relation." Parrish nodded wisely. "Very close relation to the chicken and the egg."

20

HEAD ON a log, hat over his eyes, a Jamaican snoozed in front of Sala's number-twenty-four shed. The shed was closed up and gave off the smell of charcoal fires.

"Hey, Willis," Parrish yelled, "wake up. That shed's gonna burn down right over your nose."

The Jamaican started. "Not such thing, mon! I am very wide awake."

"Where they working today, Willis?"

"Eet ees not een the fields, mon. We have finished picking three days now. Eet ees shed number eleven, I theenk, or shed number twelve."

Willis blinked and stood up to tend his fires and Parrish drove on to find John. It was a brilliant, warm fall day and Sala's sheds, slats open, looked full and abundant, the leaves hanging seven tiers high, wrinkled and turned a light brown now, only faintly tinged with green. In the fields the stalks were bare, a few sucker shoots pushing out at the bottom, a few unpicked leaves left at the top, and the pink tobacco blossoms pressing against the gray tent cloth, the blossoms that were the completion of the life cycle, bearing the seeds of another crop but spelling the end of this one. He found John in the number-twelve shed.

"What you doing here in the middle of the day?" John was just opening up the shed; the crew had not yet arrived. Inside, strips of light from the open slats sliced across the dark floor, where a few fallen leaves mixed with the sand like old rags.

"Raike told me to stop and look around, John."

"What at?"

"Didn't say. He just said to stop and have a look."

The first truck arrived with the Jamaicans and the women, shrieking and laughing as usual, and John went outside. "Hey, Gladstone," yelled a skinny girl as Teet brought up the second truck. "You're two-timing me. You rode over with Addie."

"Not such thing, Viola," Gladstone said.

"O.K., Gladstone," Viola screamed. "If that's how it is—"

"Who's Viola?" Parrish said.

Teet scratched at his sweat shirt. "Little hot-pants bitch come over from Oermeyer's after he lost them two fields with blue mold."

Parrish nodded, without comment.

"He's snake-bit, that Oermeyer."

"He's washed up," John said. "He cut back this year, anyways, and the blue mold finished him. Sheds are half empty. He's done unless Tower kicks in again, and Tower's about had his fill." He bawled out at the crew to get moving and then turned back to Parrish. "So what'd you say Raike wants you to stop here for?"

"Nothing special, John. He just told me to look around."

"Have a look. I don't know what you're gonna see." John shrugged. Then he looked queerly at Parrish. "Say, Judd Raike don't figure he's buyin' this crop?"

"Doesn't he always?" Parrish said.

"Not this year he ain't!"

"Kid, this crop's going to Tom Holden," Teet said.

Parrish stared, totally confused. Only that morning Raike had spoken of this as his crop.

"What happened?" he said. "Why'd Sala change?"

John looked down the shed to make sure his crew was working. "You heard about the bulks in the warehouse last winter—Edgar makin' a big stink about them bein' too wet. Them bulks wasn't wet. It was just some hot-shot idea of Edgar's. So Sala wouldn't do business with him."

"But what about Raike?"

"Raike never come," John said. "So we sold to Holden. Me, I'm just as glad."

Teet touched Parrish's arm. "Kid, lemme give you a little advice. Don't you be the one to set Raike straight."

"Jeez, no!" John said.

Parrish looked from one to the other, knowing only too clearly what they were thinking. "He has to find out soon. He'll see nothing's coming in from here. I can't figure out how he's gone this long without knowing."

"Let him find out his way," Teet said. "You stuck your neck out about Lemmie, and all you got was a kick in the pants. This time let someone else carry the ball."

"Edgar's the moron brought it about. Let him break the news." John went down the shed and Parrish was tempted to follow him to get more information, but if Raike wasn't getting this crop he knew all he had to know. The rest was unimportant.

"If Raike asks you, kid," Teet said, "tell him you stopped in and everyone give you a big hello and no one told you he wasn't getting the crop. Play it dumb."

"He'll never believe it," Parrish said. "He'll say I should have asked."

"It's a question of self-defense, kid," Teet said. "If you're gonna keep leadin' with your chin, you're goin' down for a helluva count. If you keep quiet, maybe Edgar'll catch it, not you."

"How long you figure I've got? A month?"

"Not that long," Teet said.

Probably not, Parrish thought. A few weeks now and Raike would realize nothing was coming to the warehouse from Sala's. He would have to decide fast whether to tell Raike or keep quiet, and he realized he wasn't thinking this time of duty or honesty, but only, as Teet put it, in terms of self-defense.

All over the Valley, now, the crop was in, and Maizie Holden was giving a party, as she did every year, to celebrate.

"I never like to go to a harvest party," Paige said, as they gathered in the den before leaving for Maizie's. "You know the worst is over, but the best is over, too, for another year. The only day worse is the day the cloth comes down."

Edgar looked at her sourly. "Every year you go through this maudlin housemaid sentimentality. Why don't you spare us for once?"

While everyone else, and especially Judd Raike, was noticeably more relaxed this week, with the end of picking, Edgar alone was growing more tense and irritable every day.

Paige ignored him. "You know what always bothers me this time of year?" she went on. "The top leaves that are left on the stalk. The leaves that are picked are so precious and these are just left and worth nothing. It doesn't seem right."

"In the future," Edgar said, "we'll have to change industry procedure to spare you this agony." Edgar was sore as a boil these days and Parrish knew they were sharing the same worry, although Edgar was only waiting for the inevitable explosion, knowing that the fuse of time was burning short, while Parrish, knowing the same thing, was still deciding whether or not to act.

"Cheer up, Edgar old dear," Paige said gaily. "Another week and I'll be off to college. Who'll keep you busy then?"

At that moment Evaline, who suffered from hay fever, was taken with a sneezing spell and Edgar turned on her viciously. "Will you stop it?"

"I can't stop," Evaline burst out with sudden courage. "If I could stop it, I would."

"It's damned unpleasant having you around like this."

If this thing didn't come to a head soon, Parrish thought, Edgar might live through it, but no one else would.

Maizie's party, as always, was a gay and crowded affair, attended by everyone who was anyone in tobacco: the owners, their families, their lawyers, their doctors, their psychiatrists, their brokers, and the first crop of visiting manufacturers, making preliminary goodwill and reconnaissance visits to learn what kind of year it had been, even though the leaves were not ready to be shown.

Seeing Judd Raike in a conversation with Tom Holden, Parrish thought of Sala's crop and was caught by conflicting impulses to eavesdrop and to get out of sight. Apprehensively he edged closer just as Harris Lowe, bold with champagne, sauntered up to join them with a foolish grin. "Cuba this year, gentlemen?"

To Parrish's surprise, Raike answered him instead of just turning his back. "Very likely," he said. "After sales are over here."

Tom Holden smiled. "Harris, I think the only reason you stay in your father's tobacco business is his fields in Cuba."

"Don't tell him, Tom," Harris begged.

"Looks like a good sales year, Tom," Raike said. "You sorry you cut back?"

"No," Tom said. "I just bought a little heavier to fill the gap."

Raike eyed him narrowly. "Who'd you buy extra?"

Parrish held his breath, but the single-purposed Harris Lowe, draining his glass, broke in again. "You shouldn't wait too long, Judd," he said soberly. "Miss the best part of the year down there."

"Well, don't worry about us, Harris," Raike said, laughing. "We'll all be down this year. Edgar and Wiley ought to get the feel of those Cuban plantations. You, too." He placed a hand on Parrish's shoulder. "You'd better plan on coming, too."

"Lucky, lucky!" Harris said. "Look me up, boy. I have addresses."

Parrish picked his way across the room to a far corner and leaned against the wall, wondering what Raike would do if he found out tonight from Tom. Would he let on that he hadn't known? Would he make a scene in Maizie's living room? Would he . . . Parrish's mind played with the awful possibilities until he realized someone was speaking to him and looked down to find he was standing next to Mrs. Holden, Tom's and Maizie's mother, an alert, bright-eyed lady whom he hadn't seen since spring.

"Well, Parrish," she was saying, "with two seasons of tobacco behind you now, how do you like it?"

"I like it fine," he said.

"Never did anyone any good." The alert, bright blue eyes were sharp. "Makes them mean and hard."

"Doesn't seem it'd have to, ma'am," he said, mostly for something to say, still watching Raike and Tom.

"It's the uncertainty," Mrs. Holden said. "It's the ten-to-one odds against you. If the worms don't get you, a fungus will. It'll rain all spring and you wallow in mud with your roots going deep and then you'll have a two-month drought. You'll watch your leaves turn brown, wilting on the stalks, and finally you'll irrigate. You'll stay up every night for a week, irrigating, and then the next day it'll hail, for sure."

Parrish thought suddenly that this was Valley talk, crop talk. You didn't hear it in just this way from the owners, who worried unspecifically. Surprised, he turned to look down at her.

"And if you're lucky and happen to get rich," she went on, "it's worse. This town isn't meant for rich people. Not enough for them to do—not enough good, honest talent to teach them that money isn't the only test of a man's worth." She eyed him narrowly, and then she broke into a pixielike smile and leaned toward him. "But I've been in tobacco for fifty years, and I like it fine, too. Just fine."

It struck Parrish that she was a quick-witted and fascinating old lady and that Tom was much like her. Then he saw that Tom and Raike were coming toward them.

"You should have a good start learning tobacco," Mrs. Holden said. "You had a good teacher."

"Yes, ma'am." Thinking she meant Raike, he tried not to sound unenthusiastic.

"I mean Sala Post."

"Oh, yes, ma'am!" He agreed heartily.

"Nobody grows better tobacco than Sala. Or ever has. Of course, he has that wonderful heavy soil—that whole belt out there. But there's something about Sala—" Tom and Raike were here now. "I'm just telling this young man, Judd, he was lucky to work a year for Sala Post. I hope you don't mind."

"Not at all, Mary," Judd Raike said.

"Business is another matter," Mary Holden said, "but when it comes to growing, there's something about Sala—"

"Of course, Mary," Judd Raike said, "he's got the land."

"That's true," she agreed. "But Sala makes it sing."

And once again Parrish stood, panicky, while they talked all around the dangerous subject and still did not touch it.

Two days later it happened.

Even before Raike came home Parrish sensed that he had found out. Since five-thirty the family had been waiting for him in the den, and there had been no message that he would be late. Nor, for the past two hours, had he been in his office. At seven o'clock Maples came in to say he had called at last, issuing two specific orders: no one was to be served dinner, and no one was to leave the house. Ellen and Paige looked puzzled, but in Parrish's mind there was no question about what was detaining him. Looking at Edgar and Wiley, he thought there was no question in theirs, either.

At seven forty-five the car sounded in the driveway and Maples hurried to the front door. Judd Raike stormed past him, turned, and said, "Did Max Maine call?"

"No, sir," Maples said.

Raike came into the den, stopping ominously in the doorway. In his mouth was an unlit, chewed-up cigar. His face was red with anger. "Maples," he ordered, "no interruptions in here except Max Maine."

Maples nodded, retreated, and Raike came into the room. He threw his brief case down on a table and stood in front of the bookcase, shoulders hunched, head forward, glaring at them, each in turn.

After several moments he opened his brief case, snatched out a single document, and threw the case down on the table and the paper on top of it. Wrathfully he turned to Edgar. "Do you know what this is?"

Already Edgar was pale and perspiring badly. Raike tapped the back of his hand on the paper. "Well?"

"A—a contract," Edgar said in a low voice. "It's a contract."

Raike pushed the contract over to Wiley. "You see it? Do you know a contract when you see one?" Wiley nodded, rolling his empty glass between his palms. Raike turned to Parrish. "What about you? Do you even know what a contract is?"

"Yes, sir."

"Fine! Excellent! This is a remarkably well-informed bunch." Mute with rage, Raike paced about the room, stopping once to thrust a chair violently out of his path. Watching with a worried look, Ellen half rose from the sofa. He whirled on her instantly. "Are you planning to say something? Because if you are, don't!"

"Darling—" Ellen started.

"Shut up!" Raike yelled, and Ellen, shaking her head, sank back. "I don't want you to say a word. I want you to sit there for one hour and not open your mouth. Don't say anything because there isn't anything you can say that I want to hear." He pulled out his watch. "Now it's exactly seven fifty-seven."

Parrish jerked forward and Ellen's restraining hand came instantly to his. Already Raike had turned away and was waving the contract at Edgar. "Now—you see it? You know whose contract it is? You know what's wrong with it?" He threw down the contract in front of Edgar.

Gray-faced, Edgar picked it up, his mouth pressed thin, jabbing at his lip with his tongue.

"Well, can you read?" Raike loomed over him. "Can you see whose it is?"

Edgar opened his mouth, but no words came. Perspiration stood like blisters on his upper lip.

Raike's voice went shrill as he beat the contract on the table. "Whose is the contract?"

"Sala Post's." Edgar said, almost inaudibly.

"Louder."

"Sala Post's."

"You hear that?" Raike demanded of the others. Wiley nodded. Parrish nodded. Ellen nodded. Raike stared at Paige. "Well?"

Paige looked up, deep resentment in her eyes. "I heard it."

"Then say so."

"I said it." Paige's voice rose, and a look of horror came into her eyes. Miserably, Parrish told himself that he could have spared them this. He could have brought this to a head in the office, with just Edgar.

Raike dropped the contract onto the table between Wiley and Parrish. "Look at it. Look at it carefully." He left it a few seconds and then snatched it away and threw it down in front of Ellen and Paige, who bent forward to look at it. "Did anyone in this room see a signature on that contract?"

Ellen sank back against the sofa and half closed her eyes, as if to say, so that's what this was all about.

"Did you?"

Edgar opened his mouth to speak, shut it, his head falling back like a spastic's against the chair. Wiley shook his head, staring dully at his highball glass in which the ice had melted to sticky-looking water. Paige sank lower in her chair, staring at her father.

"Answer me!" Raike pounded the table.

"There is no signature on the contract, Judd," Ellen said, calmly and distinctly. "And you are killing yourself."

"I told you not to speak for an hour. You still have fifty-three minutes of silence."

"Judd, this is too much!" Ellen cried.

Raike stared at her as though he'd been stabbed. "Are *you* telling *me* what I can do?"

Ellen looked at him steadily, saying no more but not retreating, either, and Parrish sat on the edge of his chair, watching, and saw that Raike was the first to turn away.

Raike snatched out a cigar, tore off the aluminum case, and lit it. Then suddenly he said, "Where is Evaline?"

"Evaline is in bed," Ellen said. "She has been ill all day."

"Will you keep quiet?" He turned to Edgar. "Where is your wife?"

Edgar struggled to his feet. "I'll get her."

"Judd," Ellen protested, "the poor girl is ill. What can she do about Sala Post's contract?"

"Do you want to get thrown out of this house?"

Ellen's chin tilted higher as she met his gaze squarely and calmly. "If you continue to speak to me like this, I shall be forced to leave it."

"Keep quiet," Raike entreated her. "Just keep quiet, will you please?"

He paced in silence until Edgar returned and a moment later Evaline, looking pale and sick, crept into the room in a bathrobe and buried herself in a corner.

"Now." Raike looked at his watch. "While Evaline kept us waiting, you all had a good long time to think up your excuses. *Why wasn't I told about this contract?*"

Nobody spoke. Like six dummies they sat, staring dully at nothing.

"I said—" Raike flapped the contract up and down on the table—"why wasn't I told about this contract?" His eyes fell on Paige, sunk deep in her chair, looking shocked and resentful. "Sit up when I'm talking to you."

Paige bolted upright.

"You go to Sala Post's every year. Why?"

"Because we've always bought the crop."

"And have you been there this year?"

"Yes."

"Then why didn't you take it on yourself to let me know, when you came home, that this year we were not buying his crop?"

"Because nobody told me," Paige said, defiantly. "I didn't know."

"What about you?" Raike confronted Evaline, sitting huddled in a corner, head in her hand. "Did you know Sala Post signed this year with your cousin, Tom Holden?"

Evaline raised her head and looked totally uncomprehending. Raike waited. "All right, Evaline. We'll take it slowly. Is Tom Holden your cousin?"

Evaline nodded.

"Do you ever see him? Do you ever speak to him? Do you ever ask him a question, Evaline, from one year to the next?"

Tears spilled silently out of Evaline's eyes.

"I don't suppose it would occur to you to find out what he's doing once in a while, or to feel any obligation to your present family. What's the matter, Evaline? Aren't we good enough for you? Perhaps our line isn't long enough or genteel enough for you. Well, I notice our money is good enough for you. You find that useful enough, don't you?"

Evaline continued to weep silently, holding her head and facing him.

"Evaline, do you hear me talking to you?"

"Leave her alone!" Paige cried.

Raike whirled about. "I'll tend to you later. After I get to the bottom of this."

"Then what are you picking on her for? She doesn't sign any contracts."

Sick with remorse, Parrish saw Ellen put a hand on Paige's and Paige bit her lip while two red spots rose in her cheeks, and he thought, why— why hadn't he brought this up in the office? Always, it seemed, with Judd Raike he made the wrong guesses, never seeing clearly until too late what he should have done.

In his chair Edgar was looking thoroughly wretched, although Parrish doubted that it was because he had brought injustice on his wife. At last Raike settled down to sensible questions. "You were in charge while I was away," he said to Edgar. "You tell me why Sala Post wasn't signed."

"He wouldn't sign with me. I tried. He wouldn't. I thought maybe he wanted to wait for you."

"And why wouldn't he sign?"

"I don't know why he wouldn't sign," Edgar babbled. "You know Sala. If you ask me, he's crazy. I figure he likes to sign with you. He gyps you every year anyway, getting a price like that, and I figured he likes feeling he's gypping you and—"

"You're a liar."

Edgar winced, capitulated, almost in tears. "It was his bulks. He'd heard they heated up too fast and he wouldn't sign. Said a lot of stupid crap about its not being right at that price for us to have trouble. You know he was just getting even."

"For what?"

Edgar didn't answer and Raike yelled at him, "Do you know what we make on Sala's leaves? Do you know any other leaves that come up to his? Not that Sala's so great. Don't misunderstand me. Sala's not great. It's his land." He stopped, looked around for an argument. "Sala's so great, they say, no one grows like Sala. Sala makes it sing! Like hell! He's no greater than anyone else. It's just the land. It's that whole goddam belt of land out there. Oermeyer, Tully, all of 'em—and until we can get it—" He broke off. "When you couldn't sign him, why didn't you tell me he wasn't signed?"

"God, I thought you must know! How could you go this long without looking at the contracts!"

Furious, Raike stared, and Edgar, realizing what he had said, looked ready to die. Raike's rage climbed, his head stuck forward, and for a moment he seemed unable to speak.

Paige coughed.

Raike whirled about in blind fury. "Keep quiet. Don't speak. Don't say a word. Not a sound. First person makes a sound I'll kill you. I may very well kill you!"

Suddenly Paige burst into tears and, clapping her hand over her mouth, ran toward the door.

"Come back!"

"I won't."

"Come back, I say."

"I won't. I won't look at you this way. I can't forgive you."

"Who's asked you to forgive anything?"

"I have. I've asked myself and I can't!" With racking tears Paige fled from the room and up the stairs.

For a moment it seemed that Raike was going to follow her. In a single quick look Parrish saw Edgar cringing like a whipped pup, and Wiley, digging at a cigar seal with his fingernail, eying the bar but not daring to get up, and Evaline biting on a soaked handkerchief. He stood up.

"Where are you going?"

"I'm going up to see Paige."

"Stay where you are." Raike thundered, so loud that Edgar started in his seat. Suddenly Parrish felt that his whole life depended on this moment, on this decision—to go back or to keep walking. Firmly, he took another step toward the door.

"If you leave here now, stay away from me!" Raike warned.

Parrish walked steadily on to the door, forcing himself not to hurry, not to look back, half expecting this man who had lost all control to strike him from behind. He reached the hall and, once he was out of Raike's sight, raced up the stairs. On the landing he paused and saw Maples opening the front door to admit Max Maine.

A moment later Judd Raike strode out of the living room. "Well?"

Max smiled. "Relax, Judd."

"Did you see Oermeyer?"

"I said you could relax, Judd. Oermeyer's finished—kaput."

Raike thrust out his lips in a little shelf of satisfaction.

"I think," Max said, "we can safely say you've got the handle of the POT."

"Handle, hell. I want the whole POT and the fire under it, too. And

when I get it, I'm going to burn it under Sala Post's goddamned aristo-
cratic nose."

"Judd," Max said, "Oermeyer would sell out tonight for twenty-two
hundred an acre."

"Offer him eighteen."

"We offered twenty-two in the spring, Judd."

"Max, I don't have to start teaching you how to deal. Start at eighteen
hundred. Go up twenty-five at a time until you get it. He'll break. You'll
sweat him down."

"Whatever you say, Judd," Max said.

Standing on the stairs, Parrish had a wild desire to rush to the telephone and call Oermeyer, to whom he'd never even spoken, and tell him
to hold out for twenty-two hundred dollars or go higher, even. But it was
only a wild impulse, like so many others, and instead he walked down
the hall and went in to see Paige, who was still sobbing bitterly on her
bed.

"Come on, Paige," he said. "Snap out of it."

"I hate to see him that way!" she cried. "I just can't bear to see him
that way!" She was shaking all over now and Parrish felt truly alarmed at
the depth of her misery.

"It's rough, Paige," he said. "I know it's rough, but he gets over it. He's
not this way all the time."

"I think he is," she said. "I think all the time inside him he's mean and
vicious and full of hate. I think he goes around hating everyone all the
time."

"That's not so," Parrish said, in his heart agreeing with her completely.
"He's a pretty generous guy mostly. It's just these moods get hold of him,
and you have to play along until they pass—" He stopped. His own words,
an echo of Ellen's and Alison's, gagged him.

"And I'll tell you this," Paige said, fiercely. "Once I get away from him,
I'm staying away. I'm never coming home." She sat up, mopping her eyes,
and struggled to stop crying.

Parrish waited until she was calm again, with only an occasional shaking
gasp, and said, "You want to come downstairs now?"

Paige shook her head. "No, I don't."

Parrish stood up, not eager to see Raike again, but determined to talk
to Ellen tonight. At the door he stopped. "He got Oermeyer," he said. "At
least he's going to get him."

"He did!"

"Max Maine just came and told him."

Her reaction, he felt, was much like his own, pity for Oermeyer, and something more, a feeling of futility, a touch of terror. Judd Raike was too big to fight. He always got everything he wanted. And everyone.

Parrish heard Raike's heavy step on the stairs and, knowing that his mother would follow right away, hurried down to intercept her. "Come here." He drew her into the hall, away from the others. "I want to talk to you."

"Now, Parrish," Ellen said quickly. "Calm down. Tonight was dreadful, I know. But it doesn't help if we all lose our heads."

"You mean you still haven't had enough!"

"Parrish, tomorrow morning he'll be fine. Naturally he's upset about losing his best leaves. Especially this year, when he lost two fields at Lemmie's, who puts out a high quality, too."

"Listen to me," Parrish begged. "Stop finding excuses. That guy is crazy! Leave him. Get out of here and get away from him."

"Parrish," Ellen said, "you're excited and upset and you're talking plain nonsense. He loves me and he needs me. And he's going to need me still more."

"You don't need him."

"I'll tell you something else, Parrish—"

"You're not willing to leave him?"

"Of course not."

"There's nothing else I want to hear."

"Parrish, if you'll stop these idiotic adolescent outbursts, this foolish antagonism, and make peace with him, he'll need you, too. I've known it from the start. And one day he will even admit to himself that he needs you because Edgar and Wiley do nothing but commit blunder after blunder. They can't help it. They don't know anything. They don't even know enough to try to learn. And someday somebody here besides Judd will have to know tobacco and if you will stop fussing and learn and learn and learn, you will be the one—the only one he can turn to."

"I don't want him to need me," Parrish said. "I just want you to get out of here."

"You only feel that way tonight, Parrish." Ellen started upstairs. "In the morning it will all be different."

Parrish sat down, head in his hands, wondering how much more she had to see to change her mind. He heard his mother walk down the hall and enter her bedroom—bravely, he thought, and stupidly—and close the door behind her.

The next instant he heard her scream.

"Parrish—!"

Parrish leaped up, taking the steps two at a time, his one thought that Raike had struck her. When she appeared suddenly at the top of the stairs, he stopped short, looking at her for signs of injury and beyond her for Raike.

"Call a doctor, Parrish—"

"What happened?" he shouted. "Where is he?"

"Quickly, Parrish—call a doctor."

Parrish closed the distance between them and gripped her wrist. "Tell me what happened. Are you hurt?"

"Stop wasting time!" Ellen was very pale. "He's collapsed. He's lying on the floor!"

After he had telephoned to the doctor Parrish went upstairs to Judd Raike's bedroom. The door was closed and no sound came from within. Hesitantly he cracked open the door and then stepped inside. They were all in here now, standing around looking shocked and helpless.

Parrish looked over to Raike's bed. It was empty! Uncomprehending, his eyes went over to Edgar and Wiley standing back against a wall, and then traveled across the bedroom. Then he realized that nobody had carried Judd Raike to his bed. He was still lying on the floor. He must be dead!

Then he saw him, a heap on the rug near the dressing-room door. He saw Paige, teeth digging into her lip, tugging at his massive shoulders, trying to lift him. He saw Ellen trying to restrain her. He saw Judd Raike move. He wasn't dead! He wasn't even totally unconscious.

"Come on," Parrish yelled to Wiley and Edgar.

Raike's sons seemed stone-deaf. White and trancelike, they stood together, backed away from their father's prostrate form, still pressing against the wall.

Raike's face was fire-red. His eyes were open and glazed. Now he moved again and Parrish saw he was writhing, making an extreme effort to get up and that, in his semiconscious condition, he could not comprehend why his body did not respond.

"Give me a hand." Parrish waved impatiently at Edgar. "Get him on the bed."

Edgar seemed to shrink farther back against the wall.

"Come on," Parrish yelled to Wiley. Then, gratefully, he saw Maples push past them and together he and the butler raised Judd Raike onto the bed.

Slowly, unbelieving, Parrish straightened up and turned to look at Edgar and Wiley, still standing as though hypnotized. They had shifted their eyes to where Raike lay on the bed, but otherwise they had not moved. They stood, cringing and paralyzed. Their faces showed shock and terror and, Parrish thought, something more—something he had never seen before in a man's face. A look of a man witnessing something that his reason told him could not happen. Panic.

With Maples, Parrish went downstairs to wait for the doctor. Neither of them spoke, but they exchanged a glance that told him they were thinking the same thing. And yet, Parrish knew, in their own way Edgar and Wiley had been as unable to move as Judd Raike.

BOOK 4

1950

21

THERE WERE things seen only when there was time to see—snow lightly cupped in the branches of hemlock, the sunlight glittering on the white bark of a single birch in the gray-brown woods, a cluster of dry leaves caught out of some autumn wind and held fast all these weeks in the crook of a limb. And the way the house that used to be Oermeyer's looked desolate across the frozen mud ruts of the drive, with a single shutter blowing and snow at the doorway showing only the prints of a dog that had wandered past. Probably the new foreman, whoever he would be, would live here, but for four months now it had been unoccupied. An empty house was quick to take on an abandoned look.

Parrish turned away from the house, letting his eye come back to Oermeyer's barn where, for half an hour, he'd been waiting for the truck delivering tent cloth for the coming season. He looked at the rusty hinges and the sagging doors he still had not unlocked. It seemed a little like trespassing, entering what he had always known as Oermeyer's property, being the first Raike man to go in there—for all that the barn looked more rotten than whole, and not much loss to any man, nor gain either. And yet, along with the reluctance, Parrish felt a quick excitement. Even outside here, several yards away, he caught the heavy, sweet smell of tobacco soaked into the old boards. And after his winter in the warehouse, it made his blood race to smell it again.

Not that he'd minded the warehouse. He'd learned a lot there, the wetness or dryness of leaves taking on new meaning after he'd rebuilt about a thousand bulks, and talk about appearance making sense now that he'd seen how carefully the finished leaves were sorted for size and quality and the difference in prices they brought. The warehouse was all right. But it wasn't like growing.

Beyond the barn he could see Lemmie's in the distance, where so often he had stood with Raike, looking over here; and he let his eye travel across Oermeyer's fields, across the untented poles, evenly spaced like crosses on a battlefield, to Tully's farm on the other side. Over on Tully's property he saw a station wagon moving slowly along a path.

The sun was dropping low and evening cold settling in and Parrish wondered what had happened to the truck. He walked up closer to the barn and pushed at an old board and it gave an inch under his hand. He gave a low whistle, suspecting that nobody at Raike and Company knew what shape this building was in. Edgar, he was certain, hadn't found time to get out here. Edgar never found time for anything. Things piled up and he stumbled and blundered through them, every task a burden. Talk big, think small, do nothing, that was Edgar. But Edgar's empty posturing shouldn't bother him any more; he should be used to it.

Still thinking about him, Parrish's mind worked back to the night of Raike's stroke and he could feel again the hard core of disgust, as he always did when he remembered. Probably a hundred times now he had thought about it—about the way Edgar had gone to pieces, and Wiley as bad; and still it sickened him to remember, although they'd recovered quickly enough. Wiley began squiring about Raike's doe-eyed little day nurse, and Edgar acquired the airs of a great tobacco magnate; only—Parrish kicked at a loose board—in five months he hadn't found time to get out here to Oermeyer's. Never again during Raike's long, tortured recovery were they caught with their weakness totally bared, as they had been that night, but Parrish had noticed that they avoided looking at Raike and beneath their fixed smiles it wasn't hard to read the revulsion his condition stirred in them.

Whatever warmth had been in the winter sun was gone now, and, asking himself again what had happened to the truck, Parrish walked briskly around the barn, poking at loose and rotten boards. If they intended to store anything here this season, they'd better get started fast on repairs. He was beginning to wonder whether he'd find a spot inside where the cloth would stay dry. Still, Oermeyer had used the barn. Many times, from Lemmie's, he'd seen him going in here.

Now he saw that the station wagon at Tully's had come back and stopped on the path where, for a short stretch before it curved away, Tully's land lay close to Oermeyer's barn. Then he saw that two men had gotten out of the car and walked over to the fence and were watching him. Squinting over, he saw that one of them was Tully himself, and that the man with him was Prentiss. Parrish had never been close enough to either to get a good look, but he knew the small pious-looking man with rimless eyeglasses was Tully and the taller, fleshier one Prentiss.

Parrish waved and started over to them, although they didn't wave back.

"I'm waiting for a truck," he said, beating his arms to warm up.

The men stood silent, letting their eyes bore into him. He noticed that Tully, though a thin man, had a little mound of a potbelly that protruded more as he tilted back on his heels.

"Truck bringing in cloth," Parrish said.

Still the men didn't answer. They only stood close together, looking at him hard, and then, abruptly, they turned and walked over to Tully's barn. They stopped once, at the door, and sent him a look of cold hatred before stepping inside and pulling the door shut behind them.

Well, what the hell! Parrish thought. Fury flooded through him, fury at them and then at the sudden unreasonable rush of guilt in himself. You'd think it was he who'd done it! He, who had been the only one who had felt a moment's anguish over it besides maybe Oermeyer himself. They had no right to place guilt on him! Indignant and hurt, he gripped the fence while it came on him that hatred for Judd Raike was hatred for Raike and Company and included him because to others he was part of it—which, in fact, he was.

Still smarting, he walked back to Oermeyer's barn, pointlessly asking himself again where the truck was—it'd be too dark to unload if it didn't come soon—and he jammed the key into the rusty lock and yanked at it and the old door creaked open on its hinges. Blinking, Parrish stood in the doorway, looking from light into dark. And then he continued to stand there, staring, shocked.

The interior of Oermeyer's barn was a rubbish heap of junk and garbage.

Light filtered in through knotholes and rusted-out nail holes and rotten boards, some of them, Parrish saw, deliberately loosened. Machinery was strewn about, uncovered, overturned, caked with dirt. Tools were thrown everywhere and lay, bent and rusty, among piles of old sandwiches, wrappings, dirty papers, cigar butts, filthy rags and just plain garbage.

Talk about hatred! Here was the final outburst of a man wild with hatred.

Slowly, stunned, Parrish moved into the barn, picking his way through the colossal mess. He found a rake and then stood still a moment, surveying the only spot where it seemed the roof might not leak. He dragged aside the heavier machinery and started to rake clean a place for the cloth. Raking, he asked himself whether it could be that Oermeyer had just given up, knowing that he was through—or that, as Raike had always said, he was a poor and sloppy farmer. But he knew better; those were not the reasons. The reason was simple. It was hatred.

He cleaned a path to the door, and, gripped by the cold dampness in the old boards, threw down the rake and went outside again. The sun was etching long shadows now, and Parrish looked out over the darkening loneliness of Oermeyer's farm. Twice in the last few minutes, he thought, he had seen the hatred that still lived in this place for Judd Raike, a hatred as intense as once his own had been. And yet he wondered how they would feel, Tully and Prentiss, if they could have seen Judd Raike in October and in November. Or even now. Would they still label him a threat—read danger in a fallen, crippled man?

But nobody except his family had seen Judd Raike. For eighteen days after he suffered his stroke he had lain in bed. Then they had carried him to a chair, his right arm and leg paralyzed, and had given him a little ball to squeeze, and he had sat there and squeezed, concentrating all his tremendous drive, which once had grabbed all this land for miles around, on a little ball.

Later they had brought him a walker, a three-sided contraption he could stand in for support. And he had stood in it and tried to work a leg that dragged so hideously it seemed that two steps would be impossible. It was agony to see the huge body lunge into the walker and struggle to take three successive steps and then five and then ten and twenty. Slowly Raike had mastered the walker, and the agony eased and then returned when he discarded it to use only a thick cane. He used it still, a crude thick stick; and still no one except his family had seen him. And so those who had feared and hated Judd Raike feared him and hated him still. In his own mind a man was often a changing and many-sided self, but to others he had a label and the label did not change.

And yet, Parrish had seen Raike fallen and his own feelings *had* changed. There were things seen only when there was time to see—and thoughts seen clearly only when there was time for thinking. Relieved of the ceaseless irritation of Raike's nagging, Parrish's soreness had eased and he had strengthened his defenses. A man, he told himself, did not have to give way to blind rage or fear whenever another man chose to make him. A man's soul was his own; no other man could invade it, except as the man himself took down his defenses and delivered it up. No man could touch you if you wouldn't let him. Not even Judd Raike.

Now at last Parrish heard the truck coming, and he gave the driver a hand at unloading, working quickly in the biting cold, and he counted up the bales and locked up and left, involuntarily eying the closed door of Tully's barn as he passed.

Warming up somewhat in his car, Parrish drove on into the Valley to look at some of the farms, and when he finished it was dark. Winter quiet settled over the country road, the moon lighting the snow, the farms peaceful, and it was too fine an evening to think about hatred. The cloth was delivered and in another month the Valley would begin to stir. Then it would be summer, and Alison would be home for good. Parrish even thought, happily, that it wouldn't be long before they'd go down some weekend to have a look at his boat. After a while, feeling better, he turned around and decided to stop at the country club for a drink before going home.

"Hey, man!" Clayton waved as Parrish came through the door of the cocktail lounge. "Just in time. We've got a helluva good discussion going." They were all here, Clayton and Melissa, Harris Lowe and Lorraine, Wiley, and Judd's doe-eyed erstwhile day nurse. "This American theory of sex and marriage is just a lot of propaganda," Clayton was saying. "The people who've made really comprehensive studies of basic sex—"

"By the way, Parrish," Lorraine said. "We're throwing a pre-season stinker Saturday night. Don't forget to come."

"These people have come up with some pretty interesting theories," Clayton persisted. "Now take this fellow in my office when I was in the Army, did a helluva lot of reading on the subject, and he said—now get this—he said, tying up sex and marriage is nothing more than legal birth control, dating back to when they hadn't got the hang of the thing yet."

"Illegal in Connecticut, friend," the nurse said.

"You don't get the point, darling. I'm talking about marriage."

"That's allowed."

"Marriage, this guy used to say, is the greatest selling job ever pulled off on the human race. Look what they've made of it. Bridal consultants, *Lohengrin*—a whole battery of bridesmaids dressed up like a damned flower garden. Why? All because once there was no scientific agriculture."

"Clay, you just say that 'cause you're a farmer!"

"Don't call me dirty names!" Clayton giggled.

"What's scientific agriculture got to do with it, Clay?" Parrish said.

Clayton thought a minute, trying to remember the rest of his story. "That was why. Not enough food. So they thought up this legalized birth control. Couldn't have kids unless you got married and that kept the population down."

"Precious," the nurse said, "would you care to join me in obstetrics some day?"

Clayton laughed, but the little nurse was getting in his way. "This is a damned serious theory, scientifically accepted. But the fantastic thing was how this fellow put the theory to work. Just a little sawed-off runt with horn-rimmed glasses, and living with this big sexy-looking doll—fifth one he'd lived with in Washington. Used to tell these dolls that marriage was for relics from a prescientific age. Got them thinking a suggestion of marriage was an insult. No woman wants to be called a relic. Damn sound theory. Interesting as hell when you get into it. Hey?"

"And how!" Harris agreed.

Clayton leaned back, satisfied, having stated as much of the theory as he remembered. "Hi-ho. Don't forget the stinker, Parrish. Live while you can. Our cloth comes in tomorrow. The faint smoke of another season is rising on the horizon."

"Ours is in," Parrish said. "We delivered today."

He leaned back in his chair, Oermeyer and Tully and Prentiss forgotten now, feeling fine, thinking that the first step of the new season had been taken.

Arriving home, Parrish found Ellen alone in the den, writing at her desk, although, overhead, he could hear the familiar irregular tapping of Raike's cane.

"We're going to Florida," Ellen greeted him. "Day after tomorrow."

Parrish glanced in the direction of the heavy irregular tapping. "Is he well enough?"

"Of course he's well enough." Ellen smiled confidently. "Look how far he's come."

Parrish sat down near his mother, thinking that she had borne Raike's illness well; if anything, she looked better. And then, once again, his thoughts worked back to the agonizing days of the little ball and the walker. "You think he knew that night," he said, "that they *wouldn't* touch him?"

"I don't know, Parrish. I'll never ask."

"You ever notice," he went on, "how Edgar and Wiley never quite look at him? Be right in the room and look all over the place, anywhere except at him? I wonder if he notices."

"Do you think he's so changed, Parrish?" Ellen gave a short laugh. "He can still see."

"He's changed all right. Hell, he never gets mad any more, and right there is one giant-sized change."

"He can't get mad. His doctor has positively ordered him not to."

Parrish smiled. "I hope he remembers that."

Then they heard Raike starting down the stairs and Ellen hurried to meet him, fixing her face into a bright smile before she stepped into the hall. When she returned she walked beside Raike, very careful, as always, not to try to help. Slowly, leaning heavily on his thick, crude stick, he came into the room. A moment later Edgar hurried in, carrying a long, narrow package which he leaned against the sofa.

Raike straightened up, weighting himself on his good leg. "How'd it go today?" he said to Edgar.

"Fine." Edgar shifted his eyes a little to the right. "Great day."

"What happened?"

"Not much. Nothing I didn't call you about. But I have something for you. Georgie Worthy was in today. Asked for you and brought you a present."

While Edgar unwrapped the package, Parrish looked over at Raike, seeing the sagging flesh around his jaw and a roundness to his shoulders that formerly had given such an impact of bulk, and he thought suddenly, he's getting old. He's getting to be an old man. Sharply and more vividly than ever during Raike's illness, it struck him that his stepfather shared impermanence with other men. The markings of time were on him, more sobering and unanswerable than the more dramatic crippling of illness.

"Georgie wanted to come up, deliver it himself," Edgar was saying. "But I told him you weren't seeing anyone yet. Next trip, I told him." Edgar said it as though he didn't quite believe it. "There now." He got the package unwrapped and took off the lid. "Well!" Admiringly he took out of the box an extremely handsome black cane with a foot of gold shaft at the top and a massive, ornate gold head. "What a beauty!"

Leaning heavily on his thick stick, Judd Raike stood motionless, viewing the splendid cane that Edgar held out to him. For a moment he seemed not to see it. Only his lips moved, jutting slightly. Then, deliberately, using his injured right arm, he closed his hand over the gold head. Unevenly, but very erect, Raike walked to the fireplace. Raising the cane, he tried to insert the gold tip into the opening of the mesh screen and failed and tried and failed again. On the third painful, awkward attempt, he guided it in and with the cane he slid the screen apart, first one side, then the other, baring the blazing logs. Not bending an inch, Judd Raike heaved the magnificent cane into the fire. Then he turned away and smiled a little at Ellen, and Parrish saw them exchange a look of complete understanding.

Together they walked out of the room and Parrish, looking after them, thought that this was the only tender moment he had ever witnessed between them. And suddenly he believed what he had never really believed before, in spite of all his mother's protests—that she really loved Judd Raike and that, in his way, Raike loved her.

Later, standing in front of the fireplace, Parrish looked at the charred black stick, and at the gold head lopped over against an andiron, and his thoughts crept back to Tully and Prentiss. To others a man had a label and the label didn't change. And maybe, to himself, it did not change so much, either.

The big rusty smokestack belched black smoke, and out of hoses and pipes white steam hissed into the hard, dry earth of the seedbeds, escaping around the edges of the huge iron pans inverted over the beds to hold it captive. A Jamaican threw a couple of shovelfuls of coal into the open door of the furnace attached trailer-style to the truck that hauled it. Now the pipes were yanked free, hissing loud, the boys lost in the cloud of steam while they moved the iron pans down the bed.

Parrish turned to go. Back from Florida, Raike had immediately scheduled employee conferences, and his turn was coming up this afternoon. But they would work here until they finished, and Parrish would come back later tonight to check things again. In the beds that had been steamed the earth was rich and dark, but more than half still showed the winter's dry crust and he decided they'd be going until nearly midnight.

The last chill of winter still hung in the air, the sun cooled fast and early, but still, as he walked past the beds, the smell of steamed earth came warm and wet to his nostrils and inside him something stirred.

He went into Miss Daley's office just as Mig Alger came out of Raike's, and through the open door, before Mig closed it, he could see half a dozen foremen still inside. Mig lounged over to Miss Daley's desk with an uncertain little shake of his head. "Seems changed," he said.

"Calmer, some," Miss Daley agreed.

"Good shape, though," Mig said.

"Mig," Miss Daley said, "they could have carried him in on a stretcher and he'd have looked good to me—after Edgar."

"He don't come in the bulk room no more, Edgar don't." Mig grinned, meaningfully. Then he nodded again toward the closed door. "But there ain't nothin' wrong with the old man. I watched. People'll tell you anything. Everyone said his right arm and leg was shot. While I was in there he walked around the room three or four times. Don't limp any more than I do."

Parrish smiled.

"And he walked over and fixed the curtain with his right arm," Mig went on. "Passed out cigars with his right arm. Did everything with that right arm, good as ever. I watched."

And so, Parrish thought, had everyone else. And so had Raike intended them to. Raike was leaving no doubts in anybody's mind as to whether they might be working for a cripple or an invalid who would let that slack rein continue that they'd had all winter.

"Kinda gives you the creeps, though," Mig said, "to see him holdin' in like that."

Miss Daley pointed her pencil. "Don't let that fool you, boy. His doctor told him to keep calm so he's keeping calm. Don't make the mistake some of those boys did and think he's gone soft—because that's why they're in there now, hearing how wrong they were. Take it from me, he's as sharp as ever."

"That's what I mean," Mig said. "Some of those poor bastards don't know yet what's hitting 'em, he started so gentle."

Miss Daley looked at her watch and then over to Parrish. "You might as well go in," she said. "It's your time."

In his office Raike was still talking to the foremen. "Benway," he was saying, as Parrish dropped into a chair, "you still working here?"

Benway said, startled, "Sure!"

"I wouldn't have known from the time you put in this winter."

"Mr. Raike, I wasn't feeling so good this winter. I think it's my—"

"A crop can't wait on your pains and fevers, Benway. Now if you're not up to it—"

"Oh, I'm O.K. now, Mr. Raike. Now I'm in the pink."

"That's what I thought. Stepowicz—" He had finished Benway and was starting on the next. "You running the Ridge farm for Raike and Company or Stepowicz and Company?"

"Ahn-h?" said Stepowicz.

"Aside from your Jamaicans, Stepowicz, you ended the season with nobody working for you but your family. And your family's family." The other foremen grinned. "Now if your relatives want to work they can spread themselves around on other farms. You hire people who aren't your relatives."

"Whatsa difference so long as they work?" Stepowicz said. "My relatives, my wife's relatives, they work good."

"Because when you run my farm, you run it my way. You want your relatives, find another farm. Now, gentlemen—" This was the change, Parrish thought. No waste. He cut right to the heart of the problem. "I don't like to suddenly find a lot of holes in my system. If there's any man here who feels he's done his best and can't do any better, I want to hear it now."

A couple of men looked puzzled. This was a tricky question.

"Is there anyone here who can tell me why I should keep a man who isn't giving me his best work?" They looked a little more miserable. "Now I want a written report from each of you. Tell me what you've been doing and where there's room for improvement. And what's going to be done about it."

The men looked horrified but remained silent. Raike leaned back in his chair. "That's all, gentlemen. I'll expect your reports a week from today. If any man decides he'd rather hand in a resignation, it will be accepted."

He walked to the door and, with his right hand, opened it for them to leave. He came back, motioning Parrish over to the desk. "Now, your schedule—"

From his desk he took a copy of Parrish's route schedule from last year. Then he glanced up. "Gilliam says you're complaining about your salary. What's the problem?"

Parrish looked at him, surprised. "No, sir, it's not a complaint."

"Speak your piece. Let's hear it."

"He was still taking out twenty-five a week for the boat," Parrish said, "even though it's past forty weeks and the thousand dollars is paid. So I mentioned it to him. He said he'd talk to you about it."

"That's all?" Parrish nodded. "I don't remember the transaction," Raike said. "I'll look it up. Now, this schedule. You add Oermeyer's."

"Have you seen his barn?" Parrish said. "It's in terrible condition."

Raike frowned. "Bad shape, eh?"

"Practically beyond use. So is the machinery."

"I'll get out to look at it. Meanwhile Lemmie'll have to make it do. He can fill in where necessary on machinery."

"Lemmie?"

"He's moving up," Raike said. "Moving up to Oermeyer's."

There was a knock on the door and Stepowicz was back, standing nervously in the doorway, his face screwed up with worry. "Mr. Raike, I cun't write no report. I wun't know how."

Raike laughed good-naturedly. "Get one of your relatives to help you."

"I cun't just promise not to hire no more family—let it go at that?"

"Get me a report, Stepowicz," Raike said, easily. "That's the new procedure around here."

He turned back to Parrish. "Now you know Lemmie has to be watched. Keep a record of his new tools and machinery." He ran his pencil over the list of farms, wrote in Oermeyer's name between Lemmie's and the Ridge farm, tapped the pencil thoughtfully. "I want you to keep a close eye on Tully and Prentiss when you're out there. I want to know what those fellows are doing. They're too close to Raike property now for comfort."

He rolled up the list of names and handed it to Parrish. "Get up a tentative time schedule for yourself with this."

Again Parrish looked at him with surprise. The list, except for Oermeyer's, was the same as last year's; all he had to do was pick up fifteen minutes someplace for the extra farm.

"I want the list made up like this, in this order," Raike said. "Write the name of the farm here and next to it mark your arrival time and over to the right put your time of departure. Work it out carefully and then make up three copies—no carbons—one for me, one for Gilliam, one for yourself. Is that clear?"

Parrish nodded, puzzled.

"Do it now," Raike said. "Before you leave."

Parrish went down to Gilliam's office. The sensible thing would be to refer to his time sheet from last year because Raike would surely consult it and question any differences.

Gilliam looked up in answer to his request for the records. "Mr. Raike say it was all right?"

"It's Mr. Raike who wants this schedule made up like last year's."

Silently Gilliam went to his filing cabinet and Parrish thought that there probably hadn't been a man-hour spent at Raike and Company for twenty years that this meek, methodical little man couldn't account for. It was like reducing a man's life to a sheet of paper. Gilliam handed him the records soberly and then hesitated a moment and said, "He's changed a little—some—don't you think? Not quite just as he used to be?"

Parrish grinned. This seemed to be the biggest news of the Valley. Even Teet, this morning, had stopped him on the highway to get a reliable report on whether it was true and, if so, the extent of the change. Teet had been totally unimpressed. His only comment had been, "He's a pretty old dog."

"For better or for worse, Mr. Gilliam?" Parrish said.

But Gilliam was afraid he'd already spoken out of turn. "I wasn't passing judgment," he said quickly. "I was only commenting."

He took a thick folder out of the file and returned to his desk. As Parrish began to copy the information he needed, Gilliam glanced at his watch. About ten minutes later he looked at it again, fingered through his folder, and telephoned to his wife that he would not be home for dinner. Parrish looked up, mildly surprised to learn that Gilliam had a wife. He had always seemed wedded to Raike and Company.

"I know," Gilliam was saying. "But Mr. Raike has found a tremendous amount of work overlooked in his absence. No, it wasn't anything I knew about before or I'd have done it before. Now it has to be completed before the season begins."

Gilliam hung up and bent over his work.

After dinner Judd Raike sat in his chair in the den, head back, eyes closed, looking tired. Around him his family sat quiet, Edgar and Wiley reading the evening papers, Evaline in a far corner absorbed in a book. In a few minutes Parrish had to leave to go back to the farm that was steaming beds. He wondered whether Paige, home for spring vacation, wanted to drive out with him.

Raike opened his eyes. "I hope you're not planning to go out tonight, Wiley."

Wiley lowered his newspaper. "I was, but of course if you prefer—"

Raike closed his eyes again. "I think you'd better stay home tonight."

Wiley waited, expecting an explanation, but none came. He glanced at his watch and Parrish knew he was calculating how long until Raike went to bed.

"I want you both at the office tomorrow by eight-thirty," Raike went on. "Gilliam is organizing some material for me tonight. You'll have to look it over in the morning—there'll be a conference on it in the afternoon."

"I have a meeting at the Children's Home tomorrow afternoon," Edgar said.

"Business comes first," Raike said, evenly, scarcely raising his voice. Then, softly, "What are you reading, Evaline?"

"Evaline!" Edgar said sharply. "Father asked about your book."

Evaline flushed and crept out of her chair and without a word held out the book to Raike.

Raike examined it and smiled. "Where in the name of heaven did you get this trash?"

Evaline bit her lip and Parrish thought, Why does she always look as though she's been committing adultery and been caught in the act? Then Edgar got up with that proprietary attitude of his where Evaline was concerned. It was his dog and he was going to help whip it. He snatched the book.

"*Truly Saved!*" he said, in a strained voice. "Good God!"

"You don't want to waste your time on that foolishness, Evaline," Raike said. "There's a good library here. Find something better."

"What kind of True Saving?" Edgar opened the book. "Oh, Lord! Where'd you get this anyway?"

"I—that is—a friend of mine—thought I'd enjoy it. Someone gave it to me."

Raike took the book and put it on the table next to him. "That's not the sort of thing you should read, Evaline. Find something else. If you like, I'll make up a list for you of books that would do you some good."

"Thank you, Father." Evaline's eyes strained not to look at her book.

"As a matter of fact," Raike said, "I think you should all do more reading. Wouldn't do you any harm. Keep you home nights."

Wiley looked truly alarmed.

"This winter I had a chance to take stock of this library. It's a good library, but it's disorganized. Take you half a day to find a book in here." Raike let his eyes go to the bookshelves, two whole walls, ceiling to floor, holding thousands of books. Parrish had no idea where they had come from. He was sure most of them had never been read. Maybe they had come with the house, like the logs in the cellar, or maybe Raike had bought out a library or commissioned someone to collect them. Max Maine, maybe.

Raike's eyes settled on Paige. "That's something you can do for me, Paige. Get some kind of system into this library. Get it organized. Get it grouped by subjects—history one place, philosophy another, economics, literature. And then get them into alphabetical order."

"Authors or titles?" Paige said, undisturbed at the enormous task.

"Authors would be best," Raike said. "First divide it into subjects and then arrange each subject alphabetically. You can set up a file system in one of the cabinets. Make out a card for each book and indicate where it's located. Do that and maybe we'll be able to find a book when we want to read."

"I'd be delighted," Paige said.

"You can start now, while you're home, and finish during the summer."

"I'll start first thing in the morning," Paige said.

"Why not look it over now? Be thinking overnight how you'll handle it?"

"Certainly," Paige said. "I'll get a paper and pencil to make notes." Calmly she walked out of the room.

That was that. Parrish stood up to leave for the farm. In the hall he met Paige returning.

"You know where Evaline got that book?" she whispered. "From that crazy Valley preacher, Montague."

"What!"

"Anson told me. He's got hold of her and she goes there twice a week."

"Oh, no!" Parrish had a wild picture of Evaline rocking in a chair like Gramma and shrieking, "Sinners—you're all sinners!" "But maybe he'll be good for her. He'll tell her she's suffering for the sins of Adam and Eve, and because she lives off tobacco, and she'll think it's her duty to suffer and she'll be happy."

"How do you know so much, my lad? Are you sitting under him, too?" Paige waved a thick pad of paper. "Does this look as though I mean business?"

"That job'll take the rest of your life."

Paige shrugged. "If he hadn't thought of this, it would have been something else."

"Are you coming, Paige?" Raike called.

She hurried into the den and Parrish went out to his car. Passing the den window he saw that Paige was standing in front of the bookshelves and that Raike was talking to her, issuing instructions. Parrish frowned a little. Judd Raike had changed, all right. There was no question about that. All day there had not been a hint of his losing his temper. And yet Gilliam was working tonight before the season had even begun and the foremen were writing reports and now Paige was cataloguing the library and reading lists were to be issued. Wondering a little, Parrish reached the bridge and turned into the highway that led out to the Valley.

An hour or so later he sat with Sala in front of the fire in his library. He'd checked the farm where the beds were being steamed, had seen that they had three more hours to work, and had decided to come in here for a while and then go back. He shook his head at the brandy Sala offered, and Sala poured himself a little.

"When you've been in tobacco as long as I have, Parrish," Sala said, "you'll think working past midnight to steam your beds is a better reason for staying up late than New Year's Eve. In fact, in the tobacco business, it *is* New Year's Eve."

Parrish smiled. "I know what you mean. It's so raw out there you feel cold all the way through, but that wet earth smells wonderful."

"You sure you won't have a little brandy to warm up?"

Parrish shook his head. "Thanks. It's warm in here."

"Then have some to celebrate starting the new season. This was my father's brandy. He opened one bottle of this special stock every year, the night they started the new season." Sala poured a half-inch into a snifter and circled it a moment and passed it to him. "Now, tell me about yourself. I haven't seen you since—your employer's return."

Parrish grinned. "My employer has been keeping everyone pretty busy."

"Already?" Sala murmured.

"I guess the big news is supposed to be how he's changed. That's all everyone seems to be talking about."

"He touches a lot of lives, so a lot of people care," Sala said. "What about you? Don't you think he's changed?"

"What would be your guess?" Parrish said.

Sala laughed and sipped his brandy. "You remember that passage in Thoreau, Parrish, where he says beware of any job requiring new clothes?"

Parrish nodded.

"One of the implications being that a man does not change so easily, and the whole thing smacks of fraud. Well, a man doesn't change that easily." Sala regarded him out of clear, pale-blue eyes. "Judd Raike may have changed his suit for the new job of preserving a body that has developed an injured part. But I doubt that the change is any deeper than that. Just a new suit."

Sala took out one of the thin cigars he smoked and lit it, smiled over the smoke. "You smoke these yet?"

"No." Parrish laughed. "You think I should start?"

"It's enjoyable." Sala blew a thin column of smoke toward the fireplace and watched it widen and drift away. Then he said, "What's in a man has to come out, Parrish. It comes out one way or it comes out another, in a new form, thinly disguised, but surely and inevitably it will come out. Men don't change. And new suits don't matter."

22

KID, YOU'RE lookin' great!" Teet said sarcastically as he pulled up in front of the Ridge farm. "Maybe I seen you look better, but I don't know when."

"What's eating you?" Parrish grinned, blinking his eyes, which smarted with dust.

"But considerin' that I can't remember last time I seen you, maybe you been lookin' good like this for some time. You figurin' to die?"

Parrish walked across the dusty path to Teet's truck. It was a Saturday morning late in June, not yet eleven o'clock, but already the sun scorched with midday heat. In the month since the last rain the paths had become deserts of gritty dirt that rose into your eyes and nose and crept down into your socks. "What you doing leaning on your shovel in the middle of the day?"

"Ah—" Teet gestured at the cloth shimmering in the heat—"we knocked off."

"Nobody's working today. I can't even find Stepowicz." Parrish looked toward the empty Ridge farm. "I just have to stop at Lemmie's old place and Oermeyer's and I'm through. You want to meet me afterward—kill an hour?"

"Tower's?"

Parrish shook his head. "Somebody'll see me there."

"So?"

"The great man'll hear I'm loafing on his time." He pulled out a couple of dollars. "Pick up some cold beer and meet me in that clearing by the bridge."

Half an hour later he dropped down beside Teet at the edge of the woods, which still smelled miraculously damp, and let his burning, dusty face take relief from the shade. "You have to be crazy to move in this heat."

"This whole summer is gonna burn like the fires o' hell," Teet said.

"We always get this heat wave late in June."

"Not like this. Too dry. Everyone's still sayin' this early dry is good.

Sends the roots deep. Not me." Teet pressed an opener into a can of beer and it foamed up over the lid. "This is gonna be one bitch of a summer."

Parrish went over and propped the rest of the beer against a rock in the stream.

"So how come you're just sittin' around?" Teet said.

"Nobody's working. I'm through."

"Whyn't you knock off?"

"Too early."

"You're done, ain't you?"

"It's easier to go in at twelve and not have to explain anything." Parrish came back and stretched out in the shade. "So I'm just going to sit out the hour. If I show up early, Raike'll find something for me to do that'll take the rest of the day."

"What can he find if nobody's workin'?"

"He'll find something inside, then. And this is one weekend I'm going to have if I have to play hide and seek all over the Valley. It's damned hot and I haven't seen my girl in two weeks because she's at the beach and that's where I want to get, not spend the day doing some damn-fool thing he'll dream up if I check in an hour early. I haven't had a weekend off in a helluva long time. It's what you call self-defense, my friend." Parrish lifted his beer can. "To self-defense."

"That why you're lookin' so great? Bleary-eyed and fagged out?"

"Nothing that a day away from this heat and dust won't cure."

Teet lay back against a rock. "It's gonna be a bitch of a summer," he said again. "That Anson Tower says the other night, 'Summer come in this year like a certain conqueror with hardly a backward look to spring!' Ask me, he's a horse's ass, that Anson."

Parrish opened his eyes, surprised. The only people he knew who would agree with Teet's opinion of Anson were Tom and Maizie. For a few weeks now Paige had been bringing Anson to the club and a small group of disciples had formed around him, which always drew an acid comment from Maizie. "The master," she always said, "is holding court again."

"What's the story with him and Paige?" Teet said. "She always seemed like a good kid, y'know? What's doin' there?"

"You know as much about it as I do. In fact, knowing you, you probably know more." Parrish laughed, but he wondered what Teet had against Anson Tower and why Tom and Maizie felt as they did.

For that matter, Parrish asked himself, what did he himself have against Anson lately? Once he had liked Anson well enough, but almost without his noticing it his feelings had slowly changed, and now, when he saw him with Paige, he resented him. When he saw the way Paige looked at Anson, hardly knowing another man existed, Parrish actively disliked him. Why?

Even now, lying here thoughtfully sipping his beer, Parrish wondered. It just seemed as though Paige deserved a bigger man than Anson. It was as though Anson had found the way to steal off with the big prize without having to earn it—just because he'd seen it first.

Teet interrupted his thoughts. "How long since you had a weekend off, kid, that you got such a beef?"

"Couple of months."

Teet opened one eye. "You kiddin'?"

"Hell, no."

"What's so important that you can't get time off?"

"Long story, Teet." Then Parrish said, "Raike's changed his style. Very calm now. Never gets mad."

"That can't last. Like I said before, he's a pretty ole dog. A dog an' old, too."

Parrish went over and got two more cans of beer out of the stream and came back and sat down. "He's like an ocean, now. You know, like they say, a sea of glass. No disturbances—that you can see, anyway—only he swallows everyone up. There isn't a person around him has a minute to himself. No more big blowups, red face, screaming—none of that. But Gilliam works weekends, Maples hasn't had a day off in I don't know how long. Even Edgar and Wiley are hopping all day long. Paige has been home from college two weeks now—she's hardly been out of the house till he's gone to bed. Me, I not only get weekend work, I get night work, too."

"There ain't that much work around yet, for Christ's sake," Teet said. "What do you do nights?"

"I study." Parrish punctured the cans and handed one over to Teet. Then he said, "Teet, what you got against Anson Tower?"

"Ah, I don't know." Teet settled back again. "He's gonna make things great for everyone. Only his way. He's got it all figured out."

Parrish laughed. It was true. "Teet," he said, "you've got the makings of a great man."

"It's the truth," Teet agreed, without opening his eyes. "It's the goddam truth."

"It's all yours, Mr. Gilliam." Parrish tossed the time book onto the desk, seeing Gilliam regard him reproachfully with faded blue eyes.

"What kept you? Mr. Raike was wondering."

"He's not still here!"

"No, he left. Finally."

This was a bad sign. Parrish scowled, wishing he had taken clean clothes along this morning so that he could leave from here. He started for the door and then paused. "By the way, Mr. Gilliam, did Mr. Raike ever talk to you about that twenty-five dollars a week you're still holding out for the boat? It's two weeks more than a year, now. That's way over the thousand dollars it was supposed to be."

Gilliam bleated. "What can I do? I spoke to Mr. Raike last time you mentioned it. He said he'd discuss it with you. I can't bring it up again."

"No," Parrish said. "I'll do it myself, Mr. Gilliam."

"If you consider it worth it," Gilliam said.

He did. As a matter of principle he did—though he cared little for the money—and also because the suspicion had entered his mind that Raike was making a test of it, to see how he would handle such a situation. He considered it worth it—but not today.

Arriving home, Parrish saw Raike's car in the garage and decided to take no chances. He entered the house through the rear door and went up the back stairs to his room, drawing a breath of relief when he made it. But his relief was premature. He was just taking a clean shirt out of the drawer when Maples knocked and looked in.

"You're wanted, sir."

Parrish spun around angrily. "Who wants me?"

"Mr. Raike, sir," Maples said, apologetically.

Already the vision of cool water, of the boat drifting idly under the stars, of Alison lying close beside him, began to recede.

"In the den, sir," Maples said.

For a moment Parrish stood still, gripping the shirt, controlling the wild impulse to dodge past Maples and rush out of the house. Then, with an almost convulsive effort, he got hold of himself. He put the shirt back into the drawer and started out of the room.

Going down the stairs he wrenched his mind back to last winter, to the long and careful thinking he had given feelings like these, to the times he had talked with Tom Holden about them. *Man is least human*, Tom had said, *when in the grip of some ancient passion, like hatred or fear. Then he acts blindly, without using his mind, which is his exclusively human part*. Now Parrish told himself to remember that. Whatever happened, he would keep his head; he would not let Judd Raike arouse him, as he could the others, to fear or to hatred, either.

He paused a moment in the hall and told himself he was ready and went on in. In the den Judd Raike was alone, examining Paige's library file. While Parrish waited he looked through a batch of cards in his hand, put them back, and took out another. A few minutes passed and then, without looking up, Raike said, "All your farms work today?"

"Just half a dozen, sir," Parrish said. "Until noon."

"What took you so long?"

"I made the round anyway. See if there was anything new."

"And was there?"

"No, sir."

Raike returned the cards to the file. "What did you expect to find?"

Parrish felt that he could kick himself for having added that last phrase. Maybe someday he'd learn to keep his mouth shut. "I just thought I'd make the full swing."

Raike flipped through two more batches of cards without speaking. Minutes ticked past. Parrish looked at the clock and saw that it was one-thirty already. He determined to be firm.

"Is there anything else, sir?" His voice cut into the stretched-out silence. "If not, I'm going to the beach and I'd like to get started."

Judd Raike allowed more minutes to pass before he gave any sign of having heard. Then he slid shut the card file and looked at Parrish for the first time. "*This* weekend?"

Parrish met his stare. "Yes, sir."

Turning on the smile that had become a substitute for temper, Raike strolled unhurriedly around the room, as though here was a situation that demanded careful analysis. "I think," he said, "before we go any further, you and I are going to have a little talk."

"I only meant if there was nothing more—" Parrish hastened to explain, but Raike held up his hand.

"First," he said, and cleared his throat. "First I want to know one thing."

He'd done it now, Parrish knew. He should pin a medal on himself. He watched Raike walk around the room, giving him the silent treatment, and struggled to get a grip on himself. With Raike, he told himself, memory was your worst enemy. It was memory that made you his easy bait. Always you remembered the times before—you recognized the little signs, you felt the tension piling up, and you started to tremble inside, or clenched up with determination not to, which was worse. If there were no memory, if he had to work you up anew each time, he'd find it far tougher.

"Are you interested in learning tobacco?" Raike said. "Or not?"

"Yes, sir," Parrish said, outwardly calm. "I want to learn tobacco."

"How do you propose to go about it? Or do you consider that you know it all already?"

"No, sir. I don't know it all."

"Then don't you think you just maybe ought to do something about it?" Raike said.

"Yes, sir. I certainly do."

"Like what?"

"What would you suggest, sir?"

Judd Raike stopped strolling about the room and dropped into a chair, superficially very relaxed. "I'll tell you one way you won't learn it and that's lying around the beach."

"Sir," Parrish said, "I know that. I know I don't learn tobacco at the beach, but I haven't had a day off in two months and—"

Raike smiled. "Maybe if you'd worry less about your time off and more about the crop, you'd know a little more what it's all about. Ever think of that?"

Parrish felt himself tightening up. Relax, relax, he pressed himself. He can't work you up if you won't let him, he can't touch you if you don't give a damn, he can't—

"I could make a good tobacco man out of you. But I won't beat my head against a stone wall." Raike leaned forward now, tapping his knee. "On the spot—that's how you learn tobacco. You feel it, you see it, you develop a sixth sense from being there. At all times and under all conditions. And unless you do that, you're not going to know tobacco at all."

The sun slanted around and the room began to get warm and Parrish wondered where everyone was. Whenever Raike stopped talking there was absolute silence. "Sir, if you prefer, I'll go back to work on a farm."

"No good. Now supposing we let me make the suggestions." Raike lit up a cigar, looked out at him over the match flame. "One farm won't do. Every farm is different and if you're going to be any use to me, you have to know conditions at all of 'em. Now this is a dry summer. Hot and dry. That means irrigation. You know all there is to know about irrigation?"

"I don't know anything about irrigation."

"Why not?"

"Your farms didn't irrigate last summer."

"The plain truth is you don't know very much. You should be able to walk onto any farm I own now—this afternoon—and tell me whether that farm ought to irrigate today. You were looking for something new. Maybe that was new, but you wouldn't know it if you saw it." Raike pointed his cigar. "Can you tell me what it costs to give an acre an inch of water, or two inches? Irrigating is an extra step, and in this business anything extra is expensive. And anything that ought to be done and doesn't get done at the right time is more expensive still. So I guess, with what you know maybe you're not worth as much as you think you are, eh?"

"I never claimed to know anything about irrigation or to be able to say at what point a farm needs water."

"You can't even tell me which of my farms is the first to irrigate. Well I'll tell you. It's the Ridge and you'd better get out there."

"When?"

"Now. This afternoon. As it happens, something was new today. Stepowicz has to irrigate his highest field today."

Wearily Parrish stood up, feeling the grit from the dusty paths still in his socks. "What time?"

"You find out. You're the timekeeper, not I."

Parrish started for the door.

"Just a minute. I'm not through. Now these orders stand for the summer. If anyone is irrigating, you be there. They don't irrigate in the daytime on any large scale, so there won't be any conflict with your regular work. When they irrigate nights, you work nights. And—" Raike pointed his cigar—"if anyone stops working because of heat, you're to know why. I want you to see the slightest change instantly, the way a doctor has an eye for a patient's condition. You should see the first signs of wilt. You should know how the air feels when we have to slow down on picking because the girls won't be able to sew. There's only one way to learn, and that's experience. You get that experience and get it every day. I don't want a day to pass that you don't learn something."

Parrish nodded. He could go tonight. After Stepowicz was through, he could still get down there.

"Now, there's a room in the warehouse where day-to-day records of every farm are kept. A man could learn what to expect at the different farms under certain given conditions by analyzing those records over a long period of time—say five years. If there's anything you'd like to learn about irrigation—not today, because today you get out to Stepowicz, but tomorrow—you've got a free day."

Parrish raised his eyes to look at Raike, not bothering to conceal what he was thinking—that suggesting he study those records was something Raike had deliberately saved for a time like this, appraising very accurately the time when Parrish's need to get away was becoming pressing, and that Raike was thoroughly enjoying his power to block his stepson's plans.

Raike smiled. "Of course, it's up to you. But if there's no rain by next week there'll be a lot more irrigating than one field at the Ridge. Might be bad to see the timekeeper floundering, not knowing what he's doing and no time then to learn."

Parrish stood still, gripping a table until his hand was stiff. He turned and strode through the cool hall out into the hot sun and got into his car and headed back to Stepowicz's.

Later that night Parrish sat alone on the steps in front of Judd Raike's house. He shouldn't have let Raike see that he could make him mad. Over and over again this winter, when there had been no pressure, he had drilled himself on this. Raike was an expert at baiting a man. He enjoyed it. But there was no law said a man had to take the bait.

It was past midnight and in the distance Parrish could see the thinning lights of the city, not as many now as when he had sat down here an hour ago. Closer, between the trees, he could see the lights of cars moving along the avenue, and, overhead, pale stars that always seemed dimmer here than in the Valley. A man did not have to give in to blind rage or fear whenever another man chose to make him. The rage, the fear, were parts of his private self; however much someone else demanded them, a man did not have to respond if he chose not to. A man's soul was his own and he could make it a fortress. No other person could invade it, except as the man himself took down his defenses and delivered it up. No other person. Not even Judd Raike.

Now a car swung up the driveway and Parrish saw that it was Paige and Anson. They came up the steps, stopping to ask what he was doing here, and went on into the house. Again Parrish asked himself what he had against Anson. He wondered whether his reason was akin to the one Teet had named this morning and whether Maizie and Tom knew why they felt as they did. Still, Parrish thought, why should any of them resent Anson when Paige was so obviously in love? Even tonight, coming up the steps with pale light touching her blond hair, she had had that radiance that only Anson could bring out in her. Even now, on the other side of the door, he could hear them talking in low voices; and the occasional quick laugh she gave was pure joy.

Then the door opened, and Anson came out and left, and Paige came out, too, and sat on the step beside Parrish. Overhead an airplane drifted across the sky, lights blinking among the stars, and Parrish followed it with his eye until it got lost in the lights of Hartford.

"Paige," he said, "you serious about Anson?"

Paige looked at him, surprised. "Very."

"Do you know why?"

Paige smiled and the glow touched her face and eyes. "I don't care why, Parrish."

"Don't you ever think about it?" he said, even though he knew she would not appreciate advice on this particular subject. "Don't you ever wonder why you picked Anson instead of maybe one of a hundred other guys?"

"There haven't been a hundred others, Parrish."

"There could be."

"Yes, I guess there could, now. There could be lots because my father is so rich, and even, I suppose, some just for me."

"Plenty."

"I don't want them." Then she said, "Oh, I guess I have thought about it some, Parrish. With Anson it's not my father's money, because he hates people with money. And it's not a superficial thing—say, because suddenly

I grew up and, with the help of a lot of wonderful clothes and some good advice from Ellen, got to be rather good-looking. Anson liked me long before that."

That was true. Parrish had to admit it.

"I guess it's partly that he cares for me, just for me."

Parrish smiled. "It's not hard."

Paige laughed, pleased, and went on. "And I suppose partly it's because Anson is so terribly clever. You listen to our crowd gossiping for hours on end, never talking about anything except sex and golf, and then you listen to Anson, who really cares what's going on in the world, and you appreciate the difference."

"Do you agree with everything he says?"

"Parrish, he's so brilliant, how could I not?"

"What if you didn't?" Now, suddenly, Parrish felt he was getting closer. Anson *assumed* that everyone agreed with him. Whatever he said, he said it as though his were the final word on that subject.

"It wouldn't make any difference!" Paige hugged her knees. "Anson cared about me before I had any clear ideas about anything. This isn't a conditional kind of thing. We aren't either of us in love with only a yes-man." Then she looked up and said, "What about you, Parrish? Do you know what you're doing?"

"With Alison?"

"No. With my father."

Parrish said, "I figure he can't touch me if I won't let him."

"I'm not so sure, Parrish," Paige said.

Parrish leaned back against the iron railing. "You can kick a man, Paige, but you can't force him to say it hurts."

"I don't think a man should allow himself to be kicked. By what right does any man get to kick another?"

"Paige, if you hate somebody or if you're afraid of him, that gives him an advantage over you. He can stir you up until you're not yourself and then he calls the shots. If you can keep your head, no matter what happens, you have the upper hand. No man can touch you if you won't let him."

Silently, Paige considered this for a moment. "I think," she said carefully, "it must be a question of degree. I can't think it can be made to work under all circumstances."

"I intend to make it work," Parrish said.

A man's soul was his own; no other man could invade it, except as a man took down his defenses and delivered it up. Not even Judd Raike.

In the distance Parrish heard the sound of fireworks—some kids getting an early start on the Fourth of July, the explosion muffled on the heavy air—and after it died only the steady hum of crickets and buzzing of bees in the silent heat. He walked down the thirsty-looking rut of a tire tread, toward the row of sheds at Oermeyer's, feeling his shirt sticking to his shoulder blades, his face dirty and itchy-damp. Wherever you looked, at the soil, the plants, the trees, the whole world seemed to be thirsting for rain. Pinhead-size flies teased unceasingly at his face and neck, and a huge ladybug settled on his forearm. He shook it but it stuck to him and then he flicked it off and it buzzed away.

From here he could see the irrigation pond, yellow and still, the unlovely water hotter-looking than the parched sandy soil around it. The pond was down about a foot from last night's watering. Next to it stood the pumping machine, and on the ground lay the heavy four-inch hoses. Everything was quiet now, but last night they had worked here until well past midnight. Beyond the fence, Tully had brought out his pumping machine and hoses.

Parrish walked toward the shed. Last night—Sunday night—he had worked here. Saturday night at Colebrook's. Tonight two more. Every night for a week now somebody had irrigated. Tomorrow was the Fourth of July and so far every farm was taking the day off and only the Ridge farm was irrigating that one high field at night. Parrish had made up his mind that unless somebody else decided to work he was going to skip that one field and take tomorrow off. After tonight's irrigating, which would probably end as the others had, well past midnight, he was going to drive to the shore to see Alison.

Lemmie came out of the shed, his red face redder with heat, looking tired and irritable, as everyone did these days.

"I see Tully's got his equipment out," Parrish said. "He irrigate yet?"

"I got my own problems," Lemmie said.

"Let me know when he does."

"If I happen to notice."

"Notice," Parrish said.

Lemmie's temper flared. "Listen—" Everyone got sore these days over nothing.

"Calm down, Lemmie. I'm not the one you're finding out for. You working tomorrow?"

"Nah. I promised 'em they come in today after last night they could take tomorrow."

"Good," Parrish said. "That's great."

"What's great about it?"

"Because that makes nobody working and gives me the day off."

Parrish went home and packed a suitcase so that he could leave tonight from the fields. Raike and Ellen had left already for the shore, but as a final precaution Parrish sought out Maples, relaxing in his room with nobody home. "If anyone calls for me, Maples, do you think you could just not know anything? Or later, if anyone should ask?"

Maples had been here too long not to understand. "I'll do it, sir," he said. "But I can't say I recommend it, if you'll excuse my saying so."

"Thanks, Maples," Parrish said. "And you're right. You're absolutely right."

Maples nodded. He could understand that, too.

On the day following the Fourth of July, when Parrish came in from work at quarter to five, four people gave him the message that Raike wanted him. Mig Alger was waiting at the warehouse door, Edgar at the head of the stairs, Gilliam was in the corridor outside his office, Miss Daley was sitting on her desk, chewing a pencil, watching through her office door. "I don't know whether to tell you to go in or run away," she said.

"Don't worry." Parrish smiled. "I'll come out bloody but unbowed."

"My God," Miss Daley groaned.

Just keep cool, Parrish told himself for about the twentieth time. A man should be master of his temper and master of his tongue, especially when he knew ahead of time what to expect. No man can touch you, he told himself, if you won't let him.

Judd Raike was looking squarely at the door when Parrish stepped into the office. With Raike's eyes on him, Parrish came across the room and sat in the chair. The gold knife was open on the desk, lying next to a cigar, and for a few minutes Raike studied Parrish and then he leaned forward and began slicing the cigar into half-inch sections.

He sliced off three sections and then he glanced up briefly. "Enjoy your little vacation?"

"Yes, sir," Parrish said.

Raike sliced another inch off the cigar. "You know they irrigated the Ridge?"

"One field. The high one. Two acres."

"You knew it before you left. The foreman told you."

"I knew it," Parrish said, evenly.

With a quick, jerking motion, Raike began cutting across the sections he had already sliced. "I don't know yet," he said, "what I'm going to do about you. But I'm not pleased."

"Sir, if it had been any field but that one I'd have stayed, but I've checked that one so many times I know it cold. The pump pumps five hundred gallons a minute, thirty thousand gallons an hour. It takes thirty-three thousand gallons to give an acre an inch. Stepowicz always gives that field two inches at a time. It takes them two hours and twelve min-

utes to do the field. And I checked the book this morning and it was
O.K."

"And what if he had claimed a breakdown?"

"He didn't."

"What if the pump had overheated, what if a hose had broken?"

"Nothing happened."

"What if it had—what would you have done then?"

"I'd have had to take his word for it. I could have checked up on
whether it was true."

Raike dropped the open knife on top of the pile of shredded tobacco.
"Well, maybe those methods satisfy you, mister, but they don't satisfy
me. You have your standards and I have mine. And if you look at that
board, you'll see what my standards got me and I can't see where your
standards are doing much for you."

"You're right, sir," Parrish said, remaining calm. "I can see that."

"Now get this and get it straight. My crops don't wait on your being
fed up. Now or ever. The next time you decide to ignore one damn thing
about so much as one plant in my fields, you're out. Is that clear?"

"Yes, sir."

Raike fell silent and after a moment Parrish said, "Is that all, sir? Benway is working tonight and I ought to get back—"

"I'll tell you when that's all," Raike said. "Now, about this boat of yours.
What kind of trick do you think you're pulling, telling Gilliam it's paid
for?"

"It is!"

"I'm afraid not."

"That boat's more than paid for. It's five weeks more than a year he's
been holding out twenty-five dollars a week. That's fourteen hundred and
twenty-five dollars. Four hundred and twenty-five more than you said it
would cost me."

"That boat cost Raike and Company two thousand dollars."

"You said sixteen hundred!"

"Plus about three hundred and fifty dollars for delivery costs, insurance,
minor repairs."

"I paid the insurance and I fixed it up myself!"

"Now two thousand plus three hundred and fifty—" Raike jotted figures on a piece of paper—"makes twenty-three hundred and fifty dollars,
less what you claim you paid. You still owe me nine hundred and twenty-
five dollars."

Furious, Parrish stared at Judd Raike. He knew it was futile to argue,
but anger pushed him on. "You told me the boat cost sixteen hundred

dollars," he said in a tight voice. "You told me you would pay six hundred of it as a bonus—"

"Bonus! What did you do to deserve a bonus?"

"You said," Parrish said wearily, "it was for pulling so many trucks out of the mud last spring."

"Six hundred dollars for getting my trucks out of the mud!" Raike laughed. "It's a little like buying them back, isn't it? If you knew how many times trucks got stuck in the mud in this business!"

"I know how many times. I pulled them out this year, too."

"How come you didn't ask for another bonus?"

Parrish didn't answer.

"As far as I'm concerned," Raike went on, "you owe the company nine hundred and twenty-five dollars, which will have to be paid before the company turns over the title to you."

Parrish looked at Raike incredulously. "You mean I don't own it!"

"You didn't check very carefully on this deal, did you?"

Blind fury flooded through Parrish—and hatred, so that for a moment he could think of nothing but the wildness with which he hated this man, and that if it took forever he would find a way to get even. Then, from deep inside him came the faint echo of his vanquished resolution, and he said to himself, *Now*—what about *now*? Can you do it now? A man can kick you but he can't make you say it hurts.

Raike smiled. "Be a good lesson to you."

Parrish smiled back. "I took your word."

Raike flushed. Silently they stared at each other.

"You can cut the sarcasm!" Raike said sharply, the flush creeping a little higher. "And in the meantime, since the company owns the boat, the company should have a key."

"There's only one key. I'll have another made up if you like."

"Just leave that one. You can come and get it when you want it."

Resisting an urge to throw it at him, Parrish slowly took out the key and walked over to Raike's desk. For a second he held the key over Raike's outstretched palm, meeting his mocking eyes unflinchingly. Then he dropped the key into Raike's hand and turned and walked away.

"Now lately—" Raike's voice rose as he called after him—"you seem to think the world owes you a living. Well, I'll tell you something. If you want expensive things like boats, instead of pulling low tricks like this to get them, try tending to business and earning the money. With me or with any other company the only man who gets ahead is the man who has something the others don't have. The company comes first. Turn around when I talk to you!"

Parrish walked on to the door before he turned.

"Now you'd better change your ideas pretty fast, or don't make any serious plans for your future at Raike and Company. I pay for what I get. Not for what you think I ought to get."

Parrish shoved his hands into his pockets and leaned against the door. "You want me to get out to Benway's by the time he starts?"

"There's one more thing. Your reports haven't included what's happening on the neighboring farms. Have Tully and Prentiss started to irrigate?"

"Prentiss irrigated once, I believe."

"You believe!"

"Prentiss irrigated once."

"Tully?"

"No."

Raike considered this a moment. "Well, Prentiss has more water. Tully has to watch it. You sure he hasn't started?"

"I haven't seen him."

"Then you're not sure."

"I can't stay there and watch him all night. I haven't seen him irrigate or any signs that he has. His pump showed up two days ago for the first time."

"What about Sala Post?"

"I don't know."

"Find out," Raike said. "And get out to Benway. He'll be through before you show up."

Quietly Parrish left the office and closed the door behind him, forcing himself to walk slowly and calmly past Miss Daley, out into the hot, humid hall.

In the office a few minutes later Max Maine said to Raike, "I passed Parrish on the stairs, Judd. I have to hand it to you. I never thought you'd whip that one into shape."

"He still isn't in shape."

"Not bad, Judd."

"Not the way I want him. He's gotten used to the saddle some, but he's not past bucking."

Max zipped open his brief case. "Considering what he was, he's turned out to be a good man for you. I watched him this winter. He was the one ordered for Oermeyer's. I don't want to say anything against Edgar and Wiley, but—"

Raike gave a humorless little laugh.

"But when it came to ordering cloth and getting a soil test and chemicals, it was Parrish who saw they remembered Oermeyer's."

"He has possibilities, all right," Judd Raike snapped. "And he's a natural at tobacco. But there's still a helluva lot of resistance to be knocked out of him before I can give him any more responsibility. He has the damndest way of thinking I ever saw in my life."

"Maybe you need a couple of people to think around here."

"As long as they think my way." Raike offered Max a cigar and lit one himself.

"You supposed to smoke, Judd?"

"No." Raike puffed contentedly. "But he's come a long way in a year. I'll bring him around. I can use him, all right, once I can depend on him not to kick up at the wrong time."

23

Max Maine sank into a chair on the terrace, looking wilted and resigned, and accepted the drink Wiley offered him. "The hell with my ulcers," he said mournfully. "This heat will kill me first. The heat or Tully."

He looked over at Ellen, who nodded but didn't say anything, and Parrish read in the look that Max, who was invited to dinner, had come half an hour early to talk to her. Except for Parrish, who had seven farms irrigating over the weekend, they were all leaving for the beach after dinner. For once he was content, because Alison was coming home for a few days.

"If Tully just hadn't put up that sign, I'd be bearing this heat a lot easier." Max sampled his drink. "Ellen, when you get Judd to the shore this weekend try to keep him there a couple of weeks. Keep him there till it rains."

"I wish I could, Max."

"You'd be helping him—and me too. He can't do anything here, can't make it rain. In my business you learn if you can't do anything about it now, let it ride awhile. That's why I have ulcers." He sighed. "I'd sure as hell like to knock down Tully's sign."

Ellen nodded, but she said, "I doubt that it would change anything, Max."

Parrish thought that she was right, of course, but he knew what Max meant. Everyone in the Valley was hot and tired these days. Tempers flared over nothing. Hatreds ran close to the surface. A twenty-degree rise in temperature changed a man, or at least showed up some of what was inside him. Some, like Sala, were philosophical—it was all part of tobacco and you took the bad with the good, nursed your crop through trouble like a child through sickness, uncomplaining. They were like old Mary out there, who always said, "Tobacco like a baby."

Others, in their calmer moments at least, cursed the true source of their troubles, the heat and the lack of rain. In Judd Raike, all the hatred and irritation had taken focus on Tully. He watched Tully endlessly, questioning Parrish and Lemmie on the number of hours he drew water and noting the number of days between irrigations. Regularly, on evenings when Lemmie was irrigating and Tully, with heavy soil but an inadequate water supply, was trying to put it off another few days, Raike would send Max Maine around with an offer to buy the land. Then, on a day after Tully did irrigate, when the man had been up most of the night and half his crew had doped off and he was painfully aware that another two feet of brown weed showed at the edge of his pond, then Raike would send Max again with another offer.

On the day following Max's last visit, a scorching blistering day with a steel-blue sky, Tully had erected the terrible sign. Exactly on the property line between his farm and Oermeyer's he had raised it, unnecessarily large, with bold letters: THE EUGENE TULLY FARM. It was enough. Raike had taken it as a personal insult and a challenge.

"I suppose," Ellen mused, "in a way that sign was something Tully had to do—putting it up like that."

"It was damned spite, that's what it was," Edgar said.

Next to him, Parrish saw Paige smile a little. She was sitting near the fountain, one hand in the little pool. "The thing we all seem to forget," she said softly, "is that Mr. Tully had a right to put up a sign if he wanted to. Even a great big sign." She raised her eyes—eyes not blazing as they used to in the old days of throwing herself into an argument, but the soft dreamy eyes of a girl in love. "It's Mr. Tully's property. It has been for some time."

"It's his right, all right." Max said, philosophically. "But damned unpolitic."

"When did you develop this sudden passion for Tully, Paige?" Edgar said.

Paige smiled and ran her wet fingers under her chin, then reached over and, laughing, ran them under Parrish's. "Yes, Edgar," she said, without looking at him.

"I suppose," Edgar said, "if you lie down with dogs you get up with fleas."

"I'll tell Anson you called him a dog," Paige said. "He'll be so pleased. As to the other part of your metaphor, I'll pretend I didn't hear."

"I don't think the sign changed anything, Ellen," Max said. "Certainly wanting Tully's land predates the sign. But Judd's sore now about the heat and the dry—"

Now Raike's car sounded in the drive and Max broke off and said, "There's nothing to be gained by his being here, Ellen. Keep him at the shore if you can."

Automatically the conversation died while they waited for Raike. Parrish, too, dropped his hand into the pool, feeling the water lukewarm but still refreshing, and his thoughts drifted off to Tully. There wasn't much to like in him, a cold man and righteous-looking, proper; but still, as Paige said, he had a right to put a sign on his property, whatever he was.

Parrish hadn't seen the sign go up. It was there when he arrived at Oermeyer's one day and he remembered how, when he saw it, he had winced. Now he knew it was for the same reason Max and Ellen wished Tully hadn't done it. Judd Raike, he thought, was like the hub of a wheel with all the spokes going out from him. He entered the life of everyone around him and the way they reacted to a thing was not what they, themselves, thought, but what they thought he would think. Even Tully. Tully had never felt the need of a sign before, not until Raike had become his neighbor and a threat.

Raike came out onto the terrace and Ellen stood up to fix him a drink. "You're early, Max," Raike said.

Max Maine spread his hands. "My family's at the beach. Nothing to keep me home."

"Take care of that today?"

Max nodded. Raike waited, with a sharp look, and Max shrugged. "Same old story. Judd, you're pushing it. This isn't the time yet."

Raike snorted. "Any time's the right time to get rid of scum. What about the sign?"

"It's Tully's land, Judd."

"That's not the kind of advice I'm paying you for."

Max looked as though his ulcers were starting to hurt, but he didn't say anything.

"Get rid of that sign, Max, even if you have to take him to court."

"You can't take a man to court on a sign on his own property, Judd."

"And I don't pay you to tell me what I can't do. I pay you to tell me how I can do what I want to do."

Max's scowl deepened. "Any time you feel you're not getting full value, Judd—"

"Max." Ellen touched his arm.

Suddenly Raike smiled that automatic smile. "Anyone would think you were afraid of Tully, Max. If I ever saw a weak sister, it's Tully. He's a low type, conceited, self-righteous. I think he's learned the attitude from Sala Post. Imitates him. A worm leading a worm. Get him out, Max. I don't want to walk on my land any more and have to look at Tully." He took a long drink from the glass Ellen handed him. "And get rid of that sign. I don't care what it costs."

Parrish's hand had stopped in the water and so, he saw, had Paige's. Max lit the cigar in his mouth. "Judd, you're getting nervous."

Raike turned swiftly on Max.

"Now, Judd, before you get mad and fire me and tell me to get the hell out of your house, you ought to hear me out. You want to complete your land, round it out. You don't like those few scrubby farms in the way and I don't blame you. And in good time we'll do it. It's unfinished business and we'll finish it."

Parrish moved toward the door. It was time to go to work.

"Now about that sign," Max said. "I can get that sign down. Hell, I can buy it down, long as you don't care what it costs. But before I do, I want you to get away from here this weekend and think about it. Ask yourself if you really want to give Tully that kind of satisfaction. It'd be quite a horse laugh for Tully, knowing he could get under your skin that easily. Just a sign."

Inside the house, Parrish thought Max Maine had named it. Unfinished business. It was true that with the heat Raike had grown more nagging about Tully, but he'd been after him hard since spring. Ever since Judd Raike's stroke, or at least since his recovery, from it, you had the feeling—as Max did—of something pushing him, of unfinished business he had to complete. He's afraid, Parrish thought suddenly, that he might die before he gets it! Until now, Raike could wait for the right time, as with Oermeyer. Now he couldn't stand to think that he actually might not close that gap in his land. And, Parrish thought, it was possible that he might not.

"Not a thing moving," Alison said. "You wouldn't think you could see so far with nothing moving."

Parrish nodded. "The air's heavy today. Dead."

In Sala's house, with its thick walls and the trees that had had a hundred years to spread their branches over it, it was surprisingly cool. They were sitting in the living room near the wide window that looked out over the fields. The sun directly overhead cast short, sharp patterns on the grass, green in a little patch near the house where a sprinkler turned, the rest dried out. In the garden, dying flowers lopped over sagging stems.

While he watched, Hazel Anne came into sight, off to one side at the clothesline, looking as limp as the tablecloth she dragged out of a basket and hung to dry. A few Japanese beetles flitted onto the wet tablecloth and hovered back to a brown blueberry bush as if deciding which was the leaner meal.

"Parrish—" Alison said, leaning her head against his shoulder.

"Mmm?"

"I see you so little."

He moved his arm and she snuggled into it. Just the feel of her hair against his skin pleased him.

"This summer has conspired against us," she said. "With tobacco you can't let it make you a slave or it surely will."

"We should be married," he said, and he closed his eyes, thinking that tobacco did not demand a slave nearly so much as Judd Raike and that they should be married and away from Judd Raike, both. When he opened his eyes again, he saw that Sala and John had come into sight at the edge of the number-three field and were talking crop, motioning occasionally toward the plants that still looked good in Sala's heavy soil. He saw John shade his eyes and squint out over the field.

"Parrish, my father says you come often even when I'm not here."

"Every now and then."

"It's strange what has happened with you two. That you like each other."

"What's strange about that?" Parrish said, feeling lazy and just content to sit here, just happy to have Alison home.

"Are you falling asleep, Parrish?"

"No."

"He likes it—your coming to see him."

"Mmm-hmm. I like it, too."

"You don't realize that it's quite remarkable."

"Mmm—"

Something was going on outside. John, shading his eyes again, was still looking out across the field, and now Sala was looking, too.

"I think he wants me to marry you. I really think he wants it."

"That makes two of us."

"Imagine, after the start you two made. I'm sure nobody would believe it."

"People are full of surprises," Parrish said. "Have you talked to him about it?"

"No, but I can tell he's for it."

"Should I talk to him about it?"

"Not yet," she said.

Because he was resigned to her putting it off and because he had only a short time with her, Parrish didn't argue. John and Sala had stopped talking now and were just looking. Whatever they were watching seemed to have moved higher and Parrish squinted out in the same direction, but he saw nothing unusual. The leaves were moving a little and the tablecloth stirred on the clothesline.

Aloud he said, "I can stay with you until six o'clock. I have three fields working tonight."

"Oh, Parrish." She was annoyed a little, and disappointed. He should be glad for that.

"I'll come back for a little while tonight after I get them started. Do you want to stay here or go somewhere? A swim at the club?"

"That'd be fun." She laughed. "It'll be nice to swim without Miss Foster's eagle eye on me, waiting for me to drown." Miss Foster was the woman Sala had employed to stay with her while she was away at the beach. "The truth is I didn't come to see you. I came to get away from Miss Foster."

"I'll send Miss Foster flowers and ask her to try to be even more terrible next week."

"She couldn't be more terrible. She's reached the absolute most. I tell her that it isn't drowning she's supposed to keep me from, but a much more terrible fate, but it makes no impression. Come on." She reached for his hands. "I'll run up and get my things and you go tell Father we're going."

In the hall Alison paused a moment before the mirror, pushing back her hair, a little remote smile on her lips, and Parrish came up behind her. "The first time I saw you here I thought you were wasting time. You were perfect already. I still think it."

The smile grew radiant as Alison tilted her chin and reached up to him. "I believe I won't marry you after all," she said. "You say such lovely things now, and I know the minute I marry you you'll stop."

"You're right," he said. "Absolutely."

He kissed her hair and let her go and she ran lightly up the stairs, and Parrish watched her and thought it was worth it—the heat, the dust, the punishment, Judd Raike!

Waiting for her, Parrish went back into the living room to see if Sala and John were still just standing at the number-three field, looking up over the top of the cloth, and he saw that now they had come up to the house and were standing near the kitchen door. Whatever it was that held their attention, they were still watching it hard.

Then all at once Parrish saw it, too. The sky was filling up with clouds. Black clouds. Swiftly they pushed in, dark mountains in the sky, moving, rolling on overhead in a wide mass, while at the edges the sky was still blue, stenciled with an eerie unreal kind of light.

He raced through the hall to the kitchen and out the back door to Sala and John, who glanced at him and back to the sky without speaking. The air was heavy, oppressive, starting to move. Tree leaves became busy, the tablecloth stirred. The tent cloth was half cast in shadows that rolled toward them. Sala and John watched warily, with unspoken fearfulness, and Parrish, waiting with them and sensing their anxiety, wondered whether they worried that the storm would hit them or would not. The earth was thirsting for rain. But when these clouds emptied themselves, it would be a downpour.

He heard Alison calling to him in the house. For a moment he delayed, while clouds mounted on clouds, spreading over the still sky like a stain in the sea. Alison called again and Parrish turned to go into the house to tell her where he was.

While he was still in the kitchen, it struck. There was a tap against the window, like a little stone thrown, and he stopped and then there was another tap, and then tapping everywhere, sharp and quick. Then the storm threw off all restraint and struck with such ferocity that he whirled about, instinctively, to rush back outside. He was at the door when he heard a sharp ping inside the house and turned again, certain that something had hit the stove, bounced on the metal and fallen to the floor. Uncomprehending, he bent down to pick it up and saw that it was a piece of ice the size of a golf ball. Then he looked at the open window above the stove and realized that this had shot into the room from outdoors.

Hail!

Now it was peppering the house—walls, roof, windows. He called out to Alison and ran outside again, still clutching the piece of ice in his hand, to where Sala and John stood in the same spot, ignoring the hail pelting them.

Everything was movement and fury now. Branches of old trees reached downward. The tablecloth flapped and beat and tore off the line. Wind pulled at the tent cloth, sucked it upward and let it go and sucked it up again with a devouring possessiveness, and played with it and whipped it into waves like ocean breakers. Hail hit it and danced on the tops of poles and bounced off into the sag of the cloth and rolled and bounced on the hard earth like marbles peppered out of a shotgun. The tablecloth blew against the house, a piece of ice the size of a fist caught in it.

Now the wind whipped itself into a frenzy and cut and lashed at the tent cloth, straining it at the poles, beat it and strained it again—and won at last, pulled it from its wire, ripped back a single corner; and then the entire field of cloth seemed to lift off the poles at one moment and fall back and wrap itself crazily around poles. Cloth dropped over plants and fell to the ground. And hail peppered the leaves, ripped them from their stalks, and beat whole plants to the ground to mix with torn cloth.

Then it was over. It had lasted eleven minutes. But as far as the eye searched on Sala's land it found no cloth on poles, nor standing plants.

The sense of smallness again. In the quiet voices of men picking leaves off broken stems, in the unspoken fear, the unuttered questioning, there was that feeling of the smallness of man and his efforts, the weakness of his reasoned schemes, before the tremendous, carelessly destructive force that could sweep them away. The feeling like death that made them conscious of their own inadequacy—ants, strutting and posturing for other ants while the whole colony could be wiped out, actors and audience alike, by the step of even a baby's shoe.

It had been an extremely local storm, hitting Sala and only the fringe of Prentiss and, in a straight line, a few Broadleaf farmers beyond Lewis Post's shack.

Valley people came to help as they always did. Silent and bewildered, they had viewed the wreckage and begun to work. Sala was directing a crew farther out, and John another farther still. Parrish was working a crew near the house. He had no way of knowing how bad it was out there, but here the cloth was beyond repair and at least half the leaves were torn. All that could be done was to salvage what was possible by picking the undamaged leaves and getting them in. The plants had not yet reached their full growth. There were about four ripe leaves on each.

A full moon shone and they worked now by the headlights of cars and trucks. Parrish straightened up as Gladstone and Cartwright came down their row, and he told them to move his car down to the next to give them better light. Teet was hauling to the sheds, and Parrish heard him coming back now with the empty truck and went over to give him a hand loading the filled baskets, wondering if these leaves could keep until they were sewn. Soreness hung on him—the soreness of disaster and, deeper still, the soreness of the knowledge that Alison had urged him to shun it.

Parrish bent down and lifted a basket up to Teet on the truck. It tore at him, the memory of Alison. He wished he could forget it or believe that she hadn't meant it. But he could still see her face, pale and shocked, as she had stood beside him.

With a kind of horrified disbelief she had come out of the house to look at the fields. Already Sala was inside, telephoning to round up help, and John was backing out a truck to drive to Bradley Field for Jamaicans. Alison stood still, her fingers digging into Parrish's wrist.

"Where are you going?" she said dully as he started to move away.

"I'll take another truck to pick up help."

Slowly her eyes came around to him. "You can't do that."

"Why not?"

"You don't work here!"

He'd thought at first she simply wasn't thinking clearly, and he had kept walking toward the truck.

"Parrish!" The tone of her voice stopped him and he turned and went back to her. "Parrish, you can't get mixed up in this. Go home!"

"Go home!" He waved at the battered fields. "This is a disaster!"

"That's it," she said. "That's right. It's a disaster. There's nothing you can do."

"They're going to pick to save what they can. They need help!"

"Save what they can!" she burst out. "It's scrounging—scrounging for salvage. Beachcombing. And he'll find out. Parrish, go—get out of here. It's not worth the chance. There's nothing left here. He'll find out."

"Who'll find out what?"

"Raike. He'll find out you worked here and it'll be the end of everything. You have your own fields to go to. You have a good excuse not to stay."

Understanding of what she was saying had come slowly to him and in sick disbelief he had turned away from her and started for the truck; but she had caught up and walked beside him. He had gone on without speaking while she strove to keep pace, and he had noticed, of all things, how her thin white heels sank into the dirt.

"Parrish, please," she begged, "listen to me. I need you. And now we both need him. Parrish, think what Raike will say—"

"The hell with Raike!"

She stopped, stunned. "It'll be the end, Parrish. And we've counted on him so, and it's beginning to work out. And now we need him more than ever!"

"How do you know we need him?" he had yelled at her in disgust. "You never tried thinking we don't need him."

She had stared at him and wildly clutched his arm. He shook her off and stepped up on the running board of the truck and then stepped down again and said, more gently, "Alison, go back to the house and I'll come in when I can to talk to you."

"It'll be too late! Parrish, go. Don't stay here with Father. He's finished. This is the end for him. And Raike—"

"He's not finished, and he's a hundred times the man Raike is—a thousand times."

"I know you hate Raike, but he's a sick man. He's had a stroke. He can't last forever. What will you accomplish if you stay here, picking up the ruins?"

He had climbed into the truck and driven off. When he returned, he didn't see her.

"That's it," Teet said now from the truck.

Parrish bent down for another basket.

"Parrish," Teet said, "come out of it. We got a full load."

Parrish put down the basket and went back into the field. In the house there was a light in Alison's room and he looked at it, sadly and hopelessly.

He lay on a blanket on the ground near Sala's garage and watched the sun beginning to touch the sky. It was the time just before dawn when, even in the heat, a breath of coolness brushed the land, and Parrish lay here now, thinking how he had forgotten all this—what it was to awake outdoors to a day still untouched by man, feeling whole and untorn, at one with all the eye took in. He'd forgotten what it was to work on the land, and the meaning tobacco had held for him when he first knew it here on this land before it was part of a spy system.

He lay listening to sounds he used to know, and his thoughts went back to the early days here, days he had thought tortured, when he had wrestled to be free. Freedom then had been a word he used easily. He was so sure, in those uncomplicated days, of what he meant. Freedom had meant freedom from Ellen's orders, and if it meant anything more, it meant freedom to roam—just his body free, unchained, to go where he pleased when he pleased. He remembered his pain on the night it had become more complicated for the first time, when he realized he had delivered himself from one kind of bondage with Ellen to another with Lucy—the bondage of responsibility for his own actions, to Lucy, whose appeal had been that she had seemed free.

Free. Parrish rolled over on his stomach and spread out his arms on the ground. The word was a mirage on the horizon that only moved farther away—beyond a man's reach and beyond his understanding.

Down the hill he heard the sound of a car starting and knew that John was up. He lay still another minute. Dawn light brightened into daylight and bird talk softened and the smell of earth and plants changed and the teasing cool had gone, giving way to another hot day. By tonight they would be scorched, dirty and done in if they picked this whole day in the battered fields. Today would be the kind of day that convinced you this Valley and tobacco were hell. And yet, thinking ahead to it, with the warm smell of tobacco coming to him now, he felt clean. He stood up and went over to the truck to go out and pick up the help.

The whole family was sitting in the den when Parrish came in, and nobody had to tell him that they were waiting for him. Defiantly he stopped in the doorway and leaned against the side, waiting. Raike was sitting in his chair, smoking a cigar, Ellen nearby. He seemed relaxed as he looked Parrish over. He even smiled a little. It was in the other faces, not Raike's, that Parrish read a warning, but he was too tired to care.

Raike cleared his throat. "Now, helping neighbors in a disaster is a tradition of this business," he said. "It's quite permissible."

"Good." Parrish straightened up. "Then if you don't mind, I'll go get cleaned up."

"Just a minute," Raike said. Paige was standing with her back to her father, working on her library file, and Parrish saw her wince a little and stop sorting her cards. "I said it was permissible," Raike said. "But not on my time, without my O.K. Do you get the difference?"

"Yes, sir."

"Don't ever do it again."

"No, sir."

Raike took out his knife. "How much did he lose?"

"I don't know."

"I think you're lying."

"No, sir. I only worked in the fields nearest the house. I don't know what happened in the others. There was a loss, but I don't know how much."

"Why didn't you ask?"

"I didn't want to know."

Raike snapped open the blade. "Why didn't you want to know?"

"I knew you'd ask." He saw Paige turn and smile.

"What!"

"I don't consider spying on my friends is part of my job. You'll find out anyway, but not from me."

Raike pointed the blade of the gold knife. "When you work for me, anything I tell you to do is part of your job. When I tell you to do it, it's automatically your job." A flush was creeping up his face. "If I tell you to jump, you'll jump. And if I tell you to work all day and all night, you'll do it. And if I tell you to spy, you'll spy. Now get back there and find out."

Parrish leaned against the wall and shook his head, and saw Raike's face go crimson. "I'll do any kind of work that's tobacco," Parrish said. "I've worked days and nights when you've said to, and weekends, too. I've worked half again as many hours as I should, and sometimes twice as many. And no complaints. And no extra pay. And that's all right."

"You're paid plenty."

"Yes, sir. And you tricked me and cheated me on my boat so that when you deduct what you've taken off you haven't paid me much more than any other timekeeper gets and I've done twice the work."

Judd Raike had risen to his feet, his face thunderously dark, and Ellen stood beside him, hand on his arm, the other hand outstretched to Parrish. "Parrish, go upstairs," she said. "Right away."

"I don't want him upstairs right away," Raike thundered. "I want him right here where he is until I'm through with him."

"And I'll keep on working and doing the job and all the unnecessary extras you throw in to prove that you can make the people who work for you do anything," Parrish said. "But I'm not going back and ask Sala Post how much he lost."

"Goddam you!" Raike shook his hand, holding upright the open knife. He whirled on Ellen. "Goddam your son!"

"Judd!" Ellen's voice rose frantically. "Judd—Sala Post isn't worth your life to you. You don't care that much about him. Who wins if he kills you?"

Her words found their mark and abruptly Raike sat down, his face still darkly flushed. Ellen sat on the arm of his chair. For a moment he played with his knife, running it round and round the split in a cigar case. Then he glanced up at Edgar. "You get busy on it."

"Yes, sir," Edgar said quickly.

Raike looked over to Wiley. "You too."

"Me!" Wiley gasped. "How can I find out?"

Over Raike's shoulder Ellen motioned Parrish to go.

Raike looked up at him. "Yes—go. Go get Sala Post's dirt off you. And get some sleep. You're no good to me on the route with your eyes half closed." He chuckled. "What little good you are now."

24

Tom Holden recognized the little firming of Maizie's lips that betrayed annoyance. In the cocktail lounge of the country club, for the past half-hour, a group of sober-faced young people had been gathered around Paige and Anson Tower. Absent-mindedly sipping at her empty glass, Maizie fixed a speculative eye on them. "The master," she said, "is holding court again."

Tom nodded, motioning to the waiter.

"It's something of a phenomenon, really," Maizie said. "They worship at his feet, remaining reverently silent, while he talks to them about matters that have never crossed their collective little mind."

Tom smiled. "They're flattered. They consider him profound."

"Glib is more the word."

"It gives them the illusion of thinking without demanding real thought." Tom considered the little group. Each night it seemed to grow larger, old worshipers bringing new recruits, and Anson never seemed to tire, either of talking or of the adulation.

"How does he strike you, Tom?" Maizie said.

On Paige's face while she looked at Anson was the glow of love, and tied to it was everything Tom felt about Anson Tower. "I care for him less as Paige cares more. I feel he's not right for her."

"Of course he's not right for her!"

Tom turned away from the glow. Perhaps, wanting so much for Paige, he was overcritical of the man. "Although," he added, "who are we to say?"

"Don't be so painstakingly broad-minded, darling. It's only me, Maizie. You know perfectly well he's not cut from the same mold as Paige. I just wish there were something we could do to open those pretty, big, love-blinded eyes."

The eternal meddling of man, Tom thought, even while he, too, wished it. Who could say who was right for whom? What of Maizie and her many marriages? The men had been dismally wrong for her and, clever as she was, she had never seen it at first, any more than Paige saw it now; and then she had seen it all too clearly. Rude awakenings, Maizie called them. But were her disillusionments different from any other? The signs were always there, signs not seen, or seen but not believed, and then half-believed, half-forgiven; and ultimately the rude awakenings—in reality only final admissions—mixed with the sting of self-hatred for one's weaknesses of blindness and hope. And what of himself? The women he'd had—bought? Without guilt, he had come to accept the purchases as part of his situation, even while denying that this was their essence, only wondering occasionally how it would be if he had lacked money to pay for women who abundantly pleased his senses if nothing more. One saw other people's signs, not one's own, except in retrospect. Tom hoped but did not believe that Paige would have special vision.

"Since we agree on this, Maizie," he said, "shall we join them?"

"We'll only turn her against us, Tom, if we try to show him up."

Tom nodded and hesitated. He saw that Parrish had joined them now, alone, with that harassed look he wore these days. For a moment Tom watched him, remembering the wild, rebellious young man who had first come here, so bursting with energy and love of life and youthful indignation. But Judd Raike had made up his mind to take him over, just as he had the land, and it seemed he had succeeded. He said to the approaching waiter, "Peter, we'll have our drinks over there."

Tom lingered at the edge of the little group where he could listen, unnoticed, and watch faces, like Paige's, too painfully radiant, and Parrish's, that showed he was sunk in gloom, hardly listening, although occasionally he looked skeptical. And Clayton Norris's. Tom had to smile. After Paige, Clayton Norris was, possibly, the most worshipful of the disciples. In mannerisms he had copied Anson's indulgent smile and the tolerant twinkle of the eye that hinted at insight into final unquestionable truths. At this moment he was nodding vigorously and glancing at Harris Lowe to communicate his approval of Anson's remarks.

"That the individual is a thing of the past," Anson was saying, smiling as Maizie took a seat near him, "has been pretty generally accepted in mid-twentieth-century thinking."

Maizie adjusted a cigarette in her formidably long holder and flashed Anson an innocent smile. "By whom, dear?"

"Scholars agree, Maizie." The twinkle said this was not open to discussion. It was settled, an accepted premise from which one could proceed. "Scholars agree that the individual as such has pretty much given way to the overwhelming impersonal forces of the age."

"I," Maizie announced, "do not feel in the least overwhelmed. I do not choose to."

Anson smiled indulgently, as if to say ignorance was bliss. "What we used to affectionately call an individualist we now call a neurotic. And with somewhat less affection. He lacks the ability to adjust either to his own group or to society as a whole. He's out of tune with the times."

The battle cry—Tom sighed inwardly—the call to arms, or rather to pasture, of the herd. The great disease of the age—groupism—in which the greatest virtues were conformity and adjustment, giving up what you wanted to do for something somebody told you you ought to want to do. Give up your pleasures, he thought, looking at these young people around him, give up your passions, give up your beautiful free soul which, like a capricious mistress, makes no promises and may offer racing joy today and swift pain tomorrow. Give all this up and receive, in return, warmth at the tepid fire of mass approval.

"Man has become more civilized," Anson said. "He has relinquished his excesses, he learns how to minimize his weaknesses, where he differs from the norm—"

"But, darling," Maizie protested, sweetly, "the terms are not synonymous."

"Today they are considered so, Maizie."

"Oh, rot! The best damn people I know differ radically from the norm. By definition, any superior person is different from the norm."

"Superiority is in the eye of the beholder," Anson explained patiently. "Maizie, the weight of today's opinion is against you. Even schools recognize that the ability to adjust to the group is vital to happiness and that the odd duck today is headed for trouble."

"But what delightful trouble! Anson, dear, you are a love and perfectly charming." Now Tom knew she had decided to give Anson a bad time. "But this well-adjusted, normal *thing* you're glorifying is a damned corpse!"

Clayton Norris was indignant. "Honestly, Maizie, this is nothing to joke about. This is serious stuff."

"Clayton, darling. I am terribly serious."

Watching, Tom saw that Maizie had not lured them from their hero. Like Clayton, and like Paige, too, they were insulted vicariously by Maizie's wild protests, they triumphed with Anson at his clever answers. Paige, Tom thought sadly, was deaf as well as blind. Adoring Anson, she was hearing only words, not meanings.

"What Maizie objects to," Tom put in easily, "is this idea of running only with the pack. Taking only the direction the pack takes—only that path. There's delight, too, in breaking off from the pack and going where you please, poking a little into byways where no path has been broken. Maybe you'll find sweet berries or maybe you'll pick up a bad case of poison ivy, but you've had the fun of the adventure. You've lived."

And therein, he added to himself, lies the difference between man and man.

Tom saw that Parrish's eyes were on him now, watching him intently with a rather brooding frown faintly reminiscent of that old questioning rebellion that Tom had once applauded and had regretfully watched die, and he wondered suddenly whether he ought to talk to Parrish. He had been tempted to, lately, so many times.

Anson said, "You're talking about the offbeat character, Tom. The odd duck. Nobody wants him."

Tom smiled. "I want him! And he's becoming too hard to find. I get young men in, just out of college, who ask more about retirement plans than the nature of the job they're going to be working at most of their waking hours."

"It's something to consider," Anson said. "With longer life expectancy."

"At twenty-one!"

"It shows foresight, a serious-minded consideration of responsibility."

"It shows a lack of guts." Tom stole a glance at Parrish. "And a morbid preoccupation with security. They're selling their birthright for a lukewarm, mildly seasoned pot of stew whose only virtues are negative ones—it is uncold, unsharp, and unending."

"Their birthright," Anson said, "is to have the security they are demanding."

"Security is not the highest goal a man can dream of!"

"What is? Just for clarity, Tom, what would you say is the highest goal?"

Tom realized suddenly that they had become a tense little group, hanging carefully on the verbal statements of two opposing camps, and it occurred to him that, tragically, with all their playing, within their little bubbles, these young people cared. Consciously or subconsciously, big questions had bothered them. Anson gave them answers they could accept. His own were disturbing. He leaned back and took a moment to answer. "The joy of living?" he suggested, quietly. "I don't mean hedonism. Or busyness. I mean joy."

Anson looked so puzzled and surprised that Tom wondered whether he had expected him to say something like amassing a large fortune or perpetuation of the race.

"In this world!" Anson said.

"Sure, this world! It's your world—embrace it. Love it, hate it, blast it, adore it! But don't just nag it for three meals a day!"

Anson was smiling indulgently. Paige looked, at last, faintly questioning. And Parrish was grinning broadly.

"Come on, Maizie." Tom stood up. Between them they had thrown a damper on things and it was time to go. He held out a hand to her and she, too, stood up, in fine good humor, showing that she had thoroughly enjoyed herself.

"Anyway—" she fired a final volley as she picked her way out—"falling in love and an old-fashioned bellyache are still individual as hell!"

But, walking back across the room, she said, "I'm afraid we didn't do a bit of good. With Paige, I mean."

Tom shook his head. You couldn't fight young passion with philosophical phrases—which, he thought ruefully, to a man who had just been shouting about the joy of living ought to seem a healthy condition.

"He is handsome and articulate, though," Maizie said, "and quite contemptuous of us, you know. It's very bad manners for him to come here and tell us."

"Maizie," Tom said, "how does Parrish strike you these days?"

"Unhappy."

"Obviously."

"He's had a row with Alison. He's here alone and she's been here every night this week with Wiley."

Tom frowned. "Once I thought him one of the rare young men today struggling to be free. You know that."

"He was, then."

"Lately, I decided it was only youthful rebellion that had spent itself and been curbed. Now I don't know. . . . Maizie, you think I ought to talk to him?"

"Right now I think he's only lovesick," Maizie said. Then she smiled, with her marvelous understanding. "Talk to him if you like, Tom. But you can't spoon-feed a man a free soul. You know that."

No, Tom thought. The best talking could do was to put into words the thing already felt. And even there Tom wasn't sure how he would go about it. He'd never systematized his own thinking on the subject, considering that the purpose of knowledge was not catalogues but understanding. He'd felt no obligation to be orderly or even to be right, except to himself. And yet, with Parrish, he would want to be clear and right. *Sooner or later,* he might begin, *a man is faced with the choice between his self—*

"Talk to him if you get the chance, Tom." Maizie touched his arm. "You'll never feel right if you don't. Of course, if you succeed, Judd will hate you."

"Hatred comes easily to Judd."

"Ellen won't like it, either."

"Do you think that, Maizie? In the long run?"

They were back at their own table now and Tom toyed with a pencil he took absent-mindedly from his pocket. *Here is man,* he might say, *man born into a world of hurricane pressures, on trembling legs. Somehow he must gain the strength to stand—*Tom stood the pencil upright—*which he can do in one of two ways: Slowly, and painfully, he can strengthen his own muscles, drawing the strength from his own spirit. Or he can weather the hurricane by holding onto a pole. In the one case he is free, because it is his own strength that holds him up. In the other, he cannot leave the pole—can go no further away than he can reach back. . . .*

Tom leaned the pencil against a wine card on the table and the card fell over and the pencil, too. He let it lie there. How many men did he know, he thought, who did not have their own little poles? However dissimilar, the poles were there and the men held them fast.

Then he saw Parrish coming toward them and he smiled at Maizie triumphantly. How many men did any man know who built on their own strength?

25

IT SEEMED now that the days were all the same. The thirsting Valley settled down to toil and heat and dust and let the fearful word *drought* creep into its talk. Parrish tasted dust and dug it out of his ears. All day he checked his farms and every night somebody irrigated, finishing sometimes by midnight but usually later because, as the dryness continued, every farm watered every field. Nights he would fall into bed still hearing the sound of the motor pumping water into the hoses. Always his eyes burned from lack of sleep and the unrelieved irritation of dust.

On a Saturday in early August he turned into Lemmie's. One more after this and he'd be through, and it looked as though a miracle was shaping up, although he was almost too tired to appreciate it. Nobody was going to irrigate over the weekend. The truth was, he knew, that everyone had reached the point where a break in the unrelenting pressure was imperative. The foremen, worn out trying to keep daytime schedules and still irrigate nights, couldn't drive their crews any longer without a weekend off. The men were starting to "dope off," the women grumbled because the picked leaves wilted and they couldn't sew as fast and their pay fell off, and because some days it was too hot to pick at all, the leaves wilting on the stalks, and then there was no pay.

Someone was complaining now as Parrish came into Lemmie's shed. "What you earn these days, it ain't worth comin' in." He saw that they were getting ready to go home, dusty baskets lying empty on the floor.

Lemmie walked up to him, raising dust to the ankles with every step, and looked at him out of pink, swollen eyelids while he checked the time book in silence. There was only about half a crew today. "They're fed up," Lemmie said. "Everyone's fed up. Including me."

"You're not the only one." Parrish handed back the book. He knew Lemmie wasn't ready to irrigate again but he asked, anyway.

"You couldn't pay me to work tonight," Lemmie said. "And I couldn't pay a crew to. I couldn't round up three men."

Parrish nodded toward Tully's. "How about him? He's about due to water again, isn't he?"

"I got my own troubles. I don't need his."

Parrish looked at him sharply. The old enmity between them had settled into a quiet mutual dislike that flared up unexpectedly. "What's the dodge, Lemmie? Did he work last night?"

"I went to bed."

"How long did he work?"

Lemmie shrugged.

"Look, Lemmie, if I don't give Raike the dope he's looking for, I'll get hell, that's for sure. But when he gets through with me, he'll start thinking that I didn't have the answers because I didn't get them from you. He's no fool and you ought to know it."

"I heard his pump till midnight."

And so he had a weekend to see Alison, if she had time for him. He didn't really think she would have, and he debated whether to bother to telephone just to hear her say no. But he knew he would. It was a poor, strained kind of reconciliation they had effected. While she was home, Wiley had seen her more than he had and now she was back at the beach, where Wiley had been able to follow her and, until today, Parrish had not.

Away from Alison, Parrish was torn by conflicting feelings. In spite of all that had happened, he wanted her. He ached for her, and the aching was with him always. Nevertheless, he knew he could never forget that look on her face while she viewed Sala's torn and ruined crop. Nor could he forgive the things she had said, nor her panicky retreat into Wiley's arms. These were signs of something in her that Parrish could neither like nor accept, and yet he wanted her still and loved her. Now he told himself he could stay home this weekend and get some sleep. He could use it—he could go to sleep now and sleep until Monday morning—but he knew he was going to call, even though he was sure Alison would say no. He pulled into Tower's Texaco Station and went to the telephone booth.

He could tell by her voice that he'd awakened her.

"Darling," she said, "I'd love for you to come, but I'm busy tonight. Couldn't you make it tomorrow night?"

"Tomorrow night somebody will be working. You know I couldn't get two nights in a row."

"But tonight's Saturday night. You couldn't expect—"

He hung up. He went back to his car and drove away.

When he reached the warehouse there was a message to call her and he rushed eagerly to the telephone and then with sudden hatred of his weakness hung up, and then he changed his mind again and went out to a telephone booth to escape Gilliam's ears.

"Parrish—?" Alison's voice sounded small and lonely now. "Can you still come?"

Another shift, he thought. Another game. Games were all right when you were sleeping all night and half the day—and playing the other half—so there was plenty of time to think of maneuvers, but right now he had no taste for it. "I guess not," he said.

"Why not?"

Parrish leaned wearily against the wall of the telephone booth and closed his eyes, feeling the sting of his lids.

"Parrish, are you still there?"

"I'm here."

"Parrish, please come. I miss you terribly."

I miss you, he thought. It was such an easy thing to say and so hard to resist. Knowing he shouldn't give in to it, he knew he would—he wanted to. And he couldn't not give in because she was moving away from him and he had to close the distance between them.

"Parrish, I want you to come terribly. I've broken my date. I've said I have a cold so I'll have to stay in my room all day. Come up when you get here and don't—" she laughed—"don't get yourself seen by too many people. What time can you get here, darling?"

She was so sure, he thought, so certain that if she opened the door a crack any time of the night or day he would come rushing in. But why shouldn't she be sure? He would come, and they both knew it. He looked at his watch. "It'll be late afternoon," he said. "About five."

It took only the glimpse of Alison's face as she opened the door when he knocked, only the sight of it growing radiant as she rushed into his arms, to dispel his doubts.

"Oh, I've missed you so!" She clung to him fiercely and then backed away and said, a little breathlessly, "Come. Come over here."

She drew him over to a love seat in front of the balcony doors that faced the ocean and sat close to him, snuggled like a kitten in his arm. "You can't think how I've missed you," she said again.

The answer had to be here with her. With the warmth of her close to him, and the eagerness of her lips under his, Parrish knew the answer had to be here somehow, because there was no answer to anything away from her. Outside, sunlight shimmered a path on the water, and a breeze came in, and through the iron fence of the balcony he saw a gleaming gull rise off the water and swoop down and soar again, and he watched its unimpeded flight, feeling the joy of it, and bent over Alison and buried his lips in her hair and then found her lips again and stopped watching the gull.

"In broad daylight!" She laughed softly after a while, pulling away. "It's a disgrace!"

"Terrible," he agreed. "Come back."

"Parrish, have you missed me?"

He searched her face, wondering if she could possibly know how much. "Have I told you lately how lovely you are?"

Alison beamed but persisted. "Have you missed me?"

"I've missed you."

The words could not say what they were supposed to and he reached out to her and drew her close, and then, alarmingly, broad daylight or no, he felt warmth rising fast in him and he let her go and stood up. It wasn't good for them to be apart so much. A thing dammed up pushed harder. Outside the gull had found a fish and the sun was lowering onto the water.

"Come away from those doors," Alison said suddenly. "Somebody might see you."

Parrish came away. "Don't worry." He smiled, sitting beside her again. "I'd marry you and save your reputation."

"It's not just that," Alison said. "I broke all kinds of engagements to see you. I'm supposed to be sick."

"Oh." Parrish told himself it was unimportant that it worried her. The important thing was that she'd done it.

Alison looked at her watch. "If we want to go out we can go in about half an hour. Everyone'll be in at dinner and we won't be seen. Although to be safe we'd better leave separately and meet someplace."

"All right." Parrish tried to keep the edge of annoyance out of his voice. "Where is our hideout?"

"Well, don't be mad, darling."

"I'm not."

"You are. I can tell." She kissed him, and then with her sudden change-ableness, even while she was coaxing him she began to defend herself. "You can't expect me to break a date and then deliberately parade around in front of him. You can't expect that. It would be insulting."

"No," Parrish said. "I wouldn't expect that."

"You do expect it. I can tell. And you're being unreasonable."

"I didn't expect you to break the date in the first place."

"Well, I did break it. And it wasn't easy. And I just don't want to complicate things, that's all."

The people were gone from the beach now and the gulls were scaveng-ing, gray and white, waddling on their yellow webbed feet, pecking their sharp bills at the sand.

"A month ago," Parrish said, "you weren't making dates you had to break when I called."

He regretted his words instantly. He had never asked her not to see Wiley. He wouldn't ask it, however much he might want to. It seemed like asking for a gift. When she wanted to stop, she would stop.

Alison shrugged. "Wiley's an old friend. I don't like to hurt his feelings. Besides, you don't ever come down any more. You can't expect me to die of boredom."

"I don't expect you to do anything you don't want to do or give up anything you don't want to give up."

"Wiley's a much older friend than you are. I've known Wiley forever."

Parrish stood up again. "That's not the reason you see him."

Her eyes flashed. "It is."

"The reason is his money. Or his father's money. You think somehow some of it will fall into your lap."

Alison curled up in a corner of the love seat. "You're being tiresome."

"It's true!"

"Of course it's true. I admit it. All he's got is money but he has plenty of that. Oh, and maybe a certain charm. He's agreeable. Which you certainly are not."

Parrish fell silent, determined not to answer or to argue any longer. He hadn't come here to argue. He didn't know when he would see Alison again and all he wanted was to be with her and to hold her. She sat in stubborn silence and he sat equally silent and baffled, wondering how two people who had been so close only a moment ago could have let such a wall rise between them. Maybe if he made the first move—said that he was sorry for whatever had upset her, that he didn't want to spend this one precious evening any other way but the best. . . .

"Parrish, you're just stubborn. You brought all this about because you've just stubbornly, bullheadedly, refused to try."

Parrish gave her a tired, halfhearted little smile. "In your wildest thoughts you can't imagine how hard I am trying."

"Oh, on little things I suppose you are. You do work hard. You look terrible, darling." Her voice softened and she ran her hand over his face. "And then you spoil it all when it comes to something big. Those damaged leaves. What did you gain by staying there and picking them up? The crop was ruined anyway. So much was lost—what did a little more matter?"

"Your father considered it worth trying to save what he could, and that was good enough for me."

"But think of the harm you did. That was what started all this. It was so wonderful with us and you spoiled it. You just threw it away!"

"You keep talking about losing and throwing away," Parrish said impatiently. "I can't see where anything so terrible's happened. I'm still working there. Raike didn't fire me. I gave him every chance to. And maybe it would have been best if he had."

"You undid all the gains you'd made. Raike gave you so much. He was teaching you everything—more than all the others. It must have been for a reason. He even gave you that boat to show he appreciated how you were trying and—"

"He didn't give me any boat."

"—and now he's sold it."

Parrish looked up, startled. "What did you say?"

"Now he's— Didn't you know he'd sold it?"

In a step he was at the balcony door, trying to make out the boat, but the wharf was too far away to distinguish one among the little pleasure fleet bobbing in the dying light.

"Oh, Parrish, he must really hate you!"

Parrish stood rooted at the door. Unseeing, he stared up the beach while all his hatred for Judd Raike rose furiously and pounded through him. It wasn't that his boat had meant so much, he told himself, more feeling it than reasoning it. It was nothing he had asked for or needed or parted from with great regret. And then reason gave way completely to passion and he thought only how he hated Raike and how he must fight back, and that he didn't know how to. There was nothing he could do—yell at him that he'd get even with him, punch him in the nose, get a lawyer. He laughed at himself, without humor, while frustration seethed in him. It seemed immoral to wish a man dead because you could not hold your own with him, and yet it was true he could not, and he found himself wishing it.

After a while he looked back to Alison and saw that she was watching him in the dying light. She met his eyes. "Parrish, why have you spoiled everything like this?"

Parrish unclenched his fists, feeling that he had dug his nails into his palms, and flexed his fingers. Out of habit he started to say that nothing was spoiled, but the words didn't come. There were other things that had to be said first, things not clearly formed yet even in his own thoughts, but pressing to be recognized.

"Alison, I've tried all I can." It was too dark to see her face now. "It's not the extra work. Everyone's working harder this year and work doesn't bother me. It's the compromise. You believe in something and then you compromise and you give in and tell yourself once that it doesn't matter, and twice, and then again and again, but the time comes when that's it. You just can't back down any more. You can't let yourself sink any lower. You feel that if you give in once more and shut your eyes to what seems right and decent, you'll just never open them again. You'll be lost—dead. You'll never know what you think again. I've already given up way beyond what was easy."

"Easy! Do you think this is easy for me?"

Parrish gestured helplessly, turning again toward the boats lying peacefully on the quiet, darkening water.

"Well, it's not easy!" Alison's voice grew sharp. "And it's not pleasant."

"Maybe it'd be easier for both of us if you'd try to see it just a little my way—give me a little time."

"For what?"

"To see what I could do myself. Without him."

"And what do I do in the meantime—live with you in some hovel and never get rid of that sickening sweet smell?"

The lights were coming on now, dotting the shore and the water like fireflies. "We even differ there," Parrish said with a resigned smile. "I like the smell."

"You're just not being realistic. Raike is the answer and because it's not pleasant you won't admit it. And you know it won't last forever—he's a sick man and I'll count on Ellen to do right by you."

"You don't know that it wouldn't work my way. You won't even try."

Alison tossed her head defiantly and when she spoke her voice was positive and too loud. "I'm not interested in sacrifice or principles or nobility. For my whole life I've been fed ideals instead of fun, and now I'm going to live and have everything I want and do everything I want and get everything I want." Her eyes flashed and her mouth was set in a hard, determined line.

"From the highest bidder?"

"Put it that way if you like." She stood up and went over to her bed and snapped on a light and started to come back and changed her mind and sat on the bed instead, picking up a little white fur poodle off her pillow. She smoothed out a green ribbon around the poodle's neck.

Suddenly Parrish felt that there was nothing more he could say and that he couldn't stay here any longer. Blindly he got to his feet and strode across the room and pulled open the door. Looking back, he saw that Alison's defiance had not softened at all, had, if anything, set firmer.

He looked at the ridiculous little poodle on her pillow. "Why do you see me at all?" he flung out at her.

"That's a stupid question."

He thought she must sleep at night with the poodle curled in her arm.

"Because I love you," she said icily. "And you've only made me miserable for loving you so. It's never been anything but miserable. I hate you!"

Parrish shut the door and came back into the room. She watched him, her eyes blazing. "Oh, get out!" she said. "You started to go. Go ahead."

He came on and seized her fiercely and kissed her with a violence that even he did not understand and then felt her fists pounding on him and realized that he must be hurting her, and he let her go, inflamed.

Silently he stood over her, next to the bed. She snatched up the white poodle and fussed pointlessly with the ribbon again and flung Parrish a hard, bright-eyed glance that was close to tears. Then she dropped the little dog and threw herself down on the pillow. "Oh, Parrish! Why does everything have to be so terrible when I love you so?"

Parrish stood miserably still. He had never seen her weep before.

"Why do I have to give up everything for you? Why?"

He was down beside her, seizing her roughly again. "I don't want you to give up everything for me. I don't want you to give up anything for me. I just want—" His mouth bit into hers.

She began to cry more violently and wrenched away. "All day I think of you—all night. Every night I lie here, right here in this bed, and all I think about is you." She stopped crying and said bitterly, "It's like a terrible disease. Like a bloodsucker that you can't shake off."

Suddenly he was calm again. He smiled and touched her hair and pushed it back from her face. "Don't think of it that way. It's a better thing than that."

He stroked her neck under her heavy hair, feeling that she was warm, and bending to her he knew the scent of her hair again and felt that the bitterness was slipping away from her. Just touching her hand, he felt tenderness pass between them, and to touch her neck and her breasts was part of it and part of them.

She quieted from the agitation of tears and touched his hand where he possessed her breast. At his insistent caress she warmed and was all response while he sought her more and more, knowing that tonight there was no question, that it was already born and had to be, and she moved to him eagerly, fired under his touch so that there was no quiet in either of them. There was no sham of resistance when he moved beside her. There was no protest as he reached to the light. The room darkened, letting in the paleness of night and the sweet shower of stars.

He awoke once while it was still dark and became very wide awake. It was a quiet night with a quiet sea and a foghorn speaking far out on the water and he lay still in bed, filled with a sense of wonder and of peace and the feeling that they had found understanding at last.

Discord had burned off in a violent passionate night, and peace was born in the ashes—strong, urgent and alive. Parrish touched Alison's face beside him, feeling wholly at one with her, and thought that maybe when a man told himself he had to break his chains and wander to seek the unknown thing he couldn't form or name, he was searching only for what they had found tonight. Once his boat came to mind. Then he buried his face in her hair on the pillow and slept.

26

It was a week today since Parrish had learned that Raike had sold the boat which had never been his. For a week nobody at Raike and Company had said a word, but today as he was leaving the warehouse Gilliam had called to him and asked whether he knew. Why, Parrish wondered now, had Gilliam waited until today? By this time the whole question of the boat had receded in importance; the gift, the cheating, the taking and the selling had all become just another of the hundreds of little incidents that couldn't bother you if you didn't let them. Idly, Parrish wondered how far a man could carry the not caring if he set his mind to it. How much could you train yourself not to care—and could you not care equally about all manner of things? Perhaps in the end it could be pushed to a whole new way of living. Total nonparticipation.

It was five o'clock in the afternoon and Parrish lay on the stone wall of the terrace near Ellen's chair. Across the way Paige sat beside the fountain that gave the illusion of cooling. Inside the house he could hear Edgar and Evaline quarreling.

"What's the matter with them?" he asked.

"I don't think it's anything," Ellen said. "He's been picking on her ever since he came home. And suddenly she turned on him and answered back."

"Good for Evaline."

"She was really snappy," Paige said. "I applauded her."

"I suppose this summer is beginning to wear Evaline down the same as everyone else," Ellen said.

Inside, the angry voices quieted now and Parrish's thoughts went back to the scene at the office. When Gilliam had asked him about the boat, Parrish had scarcely stopped walking. He'd been thinking about Alison, that she was coming home tonight and that they had better make some definite plans to be married. He had just paused when Gilliam spoke, and he had smiled and said calmly that yes, he knew, and then had walked on, taking a perverse pleasure in showing how little he cared.

Now he could hear Edgar and Evaline again. Probably, Parrish thought, Edgar was picking on Evaline because Lemmie had irrigated last night, which meant Max had been sent to Tully again today. Tully's sign was still up and Parrish knew he still had water—plenty of water, if he was careful—and his crop looked good. This being so, Edgar undoubtedly had had a hard day with Raike and had brought his wrath home, as Raike, too, would do. The general kicks the colonel and the private kicks the horse. Parrish decided to eat an early dinner in the breakfast room with the children. He had two farms working tonight. Going back and forth he could stop in and see Alison.

"At least we know every day is a day closer to the end," Ellen said, and Parrish knew that it was beginning to bother her, too. "A better or worse crop, it will be picked, and it will hang in the sheds, and this will be over. Just a memory. A nightmare of fatigue and hatreds people didn't know were in them—"

Inside, Evaline's voice rose high above Edgar's.

"—and thoughts they didn't know they could think," Ellen finished.

"Did you ever consider," Parrish said, "that not caring could be a very great virtue?"

"I do not think so," Paige said firmly.

"About what?" Ellen said.

"About whatever you don't want to care about. It could be quite an art. It could even be taught in schools. Instead of writing 'I will be a good boy' five hundred times, kids could write 'I don't give a damn.' Come to think of it, it amounts to about the same thing."

"I believe," Paige said, "that in practice it could be quite a boomerang."

This time Parrish looked at her. He knew what she was trying to say, but he had no answer for her. To explain in terms of his new feeling for Alison since the night at the beach—not only of deeper love but of responsibility—was out of the question.

"I heard about your boat." Paige looked at him in her direct, honest way, and he knew she still hoped he would say something.

Parrish nodded and closed his eyes, and when he opened them again Paige had gotten up off the stone wall and was walking toward the door to go into the house. In the set look of her face Parrish could read that she was disappointed in him.

Going in, she passed Maples bringing out the cocktail things, and almost immediately Edgar came out and sullenly mixed himself a drink, then grudgingly handed one to Evaline when she joined them.

"Thank you," she said.

"Just see that it doesn't destroy what little self-control you have left these days."

Evaline put the drink down with a thud. "It's a wonder I have any at all—with you."

"You're incompetent, Evaline. And your children show it. At least until now you've had the redeeming virtue of self-control. Now that's gone and I can't see where things are going to improve at all around here."

Cheeks flushed, Evaline leaped to her feet, knocking her glass to the floor. Appalled, she stared at it as though it, too, had turned on her, giving proof to Edgar's words. "I'm not going to stay here any longer with you!" she cried out. "You're a cruel, sinful man. It's ungodly and sinful to be so mean, and I'm glad someday you'll burn in hell!" Mouth open, she stared at Edgar, hardly believing that the words had found their way to her lips. "I hate you and I'm going home to my father. Or I'll go to Maizie's or my aunt Mary Holden's or—or to anybody except you." She turned and ran into the house, leaving an astonished trio on the terrace.

"Edgar," Ellen said, "for heaven's sake, go comfort the poor girl."

"She doesn't mean it," Edgar scoffed, with a show of bravado. But he looked after her and got to his feet. Then Raike came out and he sat down again.

Parrish stirred on the stone wall but didn't get up. Twice before when Raike had seen him sprawled out that way he'd ordered him to sit up. Let him tell him again. But Raike only sat down near Ellen, took the drink she handed him, and sipped it reflectively. Once Parrish opened an eye and saw that Raike was looking at him and closed it again.

"Talk to Max?" Edgar said, glancing uneasily toward the door.

So Edgar hadn't been abused in the office. He had only been anticipating that he would be abused tonight when Raike got home.

"What about?" Raike said.

"Didn't he go to Tully today?"

"Not today. No point in paying him to go out there every week when he can't produce." But Raike wasn't in a bad humor tonight. "I pay only for what I get, and sooner or later everyone who works for me finds it out."

"My God, you haven't fired Max!" Edgar said.

"No." Raike laughed and Edgar took advantage of his good humor to stand up and work his way over to the door.

Parrish opened his eye again. What's he looking at me for, he wondered; what's he trying to figure out?

"I'm only saying that when a man produces I pay well, and when he

falls down on the job he finds out fast enough that I'm no Santa Claus."
Raike glanced at Edgar and then back to Parrish.

The boat! He's needling me about the boat, Parrish thought. He told
Gilliam to ask because I've spoiled his fun by not saying anything! Parrish
stood up, seeing Edgar slip inside.

"Who works tonight?" Raike said.

"Colebrook and the Ridge."

"Tully look like he's ready?"

"Another couple of days," Parrish said, and added, just to annoy him,
"He's spacing it carefully and he still has plenty of water."

Parrish went into the house and upstairs to shower and change before
going back to work. Walking down the hall to his room, he could hear
Edgar's voice and Evaline's answer even before he passed their door. Edgar
was apologizing! Edgar was actually apologizing and begging her to stay,
and Evaline was weeping, gradually giving in to his entreaties and his
promise to do better and his protest that he loved her. It was a strange
love and a sickening scene, and Parrish hurried on, not wanting to hear it,
feeling ashamed and embarrassed.

The pump at the Ridge farm pounded like an outboard motor and the
canvas hoses swelled, wiggling along the ground like snakes, and the water
shot into pipes and out in a hundred sprays rising twice as high as the
tent cloth, like a fireworks display. The water stood in little drops on the
ground and then slipped off into silver rivulets before the crusted earth
softened and drank it in. Parrish waited a moment to be sure things were
going all right here and then drove down to check Colebrook's.

At about ten-thirty that evening, returning to the Ridge farm, he
stopped his car in the path a little before he reached the pump. He had
trained himself during these long nights to take catnaps for about twenty
minutes, whenever he felt himself beginning to fight to stay awake. He
could hear the sound of the motor and he saw there was no change here,
so, with the faint smell of gasoline exhaust in his nostrils, he dozed off.

It was the shouts that awakened him—shouts heard over the pounding
motor. Drugged with sleep, Parrish sat up, blinking and shaking himself,
while a little alarm flashed through him that something had gone wrong.
At first he thought that it was morning, that the red light was sunrise for
all it was in the wrong place in the sky. Then the steady sound of the
pump came to him through the shouts and he knew they were still
working and saw that it was night. Then he realized that the brilliant
sky was fire.

Parrish stumbled out of the car, found his balance and rushed toward
the shouting men as the clang and sirens of fire engines came across the

tobacco fields; and then, abruptly, he stopped as his thinking cleared and he saw that the fire was not here at the Ridge. He ran back and started his car, raising billows of dust around him as he raced along the paths of sand. Choking with dust, he reached the highway. From here the flames looked so close it must be Sala's. But the clang of the engines was too far for Sala's.

Driving on, Parrish decided it must be Prentiss's. Then, passing Prentiss's, he saw that it was either Tully's barn or Lemmie's. By now the whole sky ahead of him was lit up, and cars were backed up bumper to bumper along the road out of Tully's driveway. Parrish pulled out of line, shot past them, and dodged into Lemmie's driveway as the rising whine of another siren cut through the crackling air.

He parked in Lemmie's driveway and ran across the yard, feeling the heat of the flames on his face and arms even here, and then he saw that the burning barn was Tully's. Leaping over the fence, he came up to where a swelling crowd pressed together, standing back from the flames. He saw Tully first, clad only in trousers he'd hastily pulled on, his half-naked, unprepossessing body incongruous with the properness of his face and the thin silver eyeglasses. Prentiss was there, and Lemmie, too, and Parrish saw that an argument was going on between them, Prentiss and Tully standing together, Lemmie facing up to them, while a cluster of firemen stood around uncertainly looking from one to the other.

"Let it burn, I say!" Tully shook a fist in the air.

"Not on your life!" Lemmie turned to the firemen. "Come on, get moving. Get those hoses hooked up."

"Not with my water!" Tully shouted.

"Get going!" Lemmie jerked toward the firemen.

"Don't touch my water!"

"It's his barn. If he wants to let it burn, he can let it burn." That was Prentiss.

"The hell he can! You're threatening my barn already."

"That barn'd be no loss."

"Get going," Lemmie yelled to the firemen. "You ain't burning my barn!"

Parrish pressed into the crowd. "Lemmie," he yelled, "that lousy barn isn't worth fighting for." Nobody seemed to hear him or to pay attention.

"Burn my barn and you'll hear from Judd Raike." Lemmie shot a warning at the firemen.

"That barn ain't worth a doghouse," Prentiss spat out, but the magic name of Raike had had effect. The firemen looked sympathetically at Tully but began to move hesitantly toward the path leading to the irrigation pond.

Lemmie urged them on. "I got valuable machinery in there."

"Get it out then," Tully yelled. "Get it out while you got time, because nobody's touching my water."

Heat mounted and the swelling mass of spectators, like a single wave, fell back.

"Maybe," the fire chief said, "we could go easy on your water, just try to control it, keep it from spreading to his—"

Parrish shouldered his way past the firemen, who were shuffling uncertainly while the flames mounted and time passed in arguments. "Lemmie's barn isn't worth anything," he shouted to the fire chief.

Lemmie whirled on him. "You crazy or something?"

"There's not enough machinery in there to worry about!" Parrish insisted.

"You guys!" Lemmie yelled at the firemen. "There ain't one of you won't have to answer to Judd Raike if you don't get movin'." Lemmie started to the truck to drive to the pond. "You comin'?"

One by one, the firemen fell in behind him.

Screaming, Tully rushed up to Lemmie. "Lousy, bastard stool pigeon!" He grabbed his neck. "Don't touch my water."

Lemmie whirled about and crashed his fist into Tully's face. Tully sank down and lay half-naked in the dirt, his glasses knocked off, sticking upright in the sand. The truck churned dust over him as it lurched forward.

It was only a suspicion nudging into Parrish's mind—a suspicion barely conceived, still without form. But again and again his eye came back to Lemmie's flushed, triumphant face. A section of roof sagged and fell, the old boards burning like paper, the flames coming down with them and leaping high again. All eyes went skyward with them, fascinated, as if drawn by a magnet. The firemen sweated in the heat and the crowd edged off again. Lemmie's eyes glittered.

Sala had arrived now, and John, and they stood together, off a way, John tight-mouthed, pointedly standing next to a hose, refusing to help, as Parrish had refused when Lemmie ordered him to couple a section of hose. Sala's face as he looked at Lemmie was stiff and disturbing, and in Parrish the embryo suspicion pushed closer to birth.

Lemmie leaned against the fence and lit a cigar and flicked away the match. His eyes shifted over the crowd and stopped in an instant of involuntary communication when he saw Parrish watching him. In that split second Parrish knew that Tully's sign was coming down. Tonight Judd Raike was getting Tully, surely and beyond all doubt. Getting him through his water, through Lemmie next door protecting his decaying barn in the name of Raike, the mighty, the powerful. In Lemmie's eyes, in that second was spelled out Raike's ruthlessness. Suspicion, conceived, refused to abort.

Leaving, Parrish passed him.

"Little mixed up tonight, eh?" Lemmie, still leaning against the fence, spoke out.

"Not tonight, Lemmie." Parrish raised his eyes to let them say what he thought. Not thought, any longer. Knew.

"You'll be a long time talking your way out of this one," Lemmie said. "Judd Raike don't go for his men forgetting who they work for. I guess a lotta people heard you tonight, boy, takin' the wrong side."

Parrish eased himself over the fence to Lemmie's side, the side that used to be Oermeyer's, where he'd parked his car.

Lemmie turned, resting himself forward on a fence post. "Mr. Raike's funny that way," he said, showing an unnatural exhilaration. "People workin' for him he likes them to remember which team they're on. You don't improve your memory you're liable to find yourself out of a job."

Parrish snapped around so quickly Lemmie straightened up off the post. "What're you so hysterical about, Lemmie?"

"I ain't hysterical, friend." Lemmie laughed, his mouth loose. "I'm only tellin' you."

"Save your breath."

Lemmie grabbed at his arm. "Like to make a little bet on where you'll stand after tonight? Like a little bet, boy?"

Parrish snapped the hot hand off his arm. "Save yourself, Lemmie. I know where I stand right now. I don't work for Mr. Raike any more."

Without looking back, Parrish moved away from the burning barn. He could hear the hiss of fire hitting wet boards and smell the putrid smell of charred wood half burnt and doused out. Across the fields he could hear the distant beat of Tully's pump, pounding out his ruin. Night closed in on him as he walked slowly across what used to be Oermeyer's back yard and the far sounds of a barn burning up and the steady, faithful pounding of a pump seemed like noises of the jungle where men ate men openly.

"You young fool!" Judd Raike stared at the car keys that Parrish held out to him.

Wearily Parrish waited for Raike to take them. A terrible tiredness gripped him, the tiredness piled on tiredness of the whole hot rainless summer and the numbing exhaustion of the fitful, wakeful night he had spent, accepting this decision he knew he had to make.

"I've made you!" Raike said. "I've made a man out of you!"

"I hope not," Parrish said steadily. "Not your kind of man."

"I've taught you lessons you should thank me for!" Raike snatched the keys and threw them down on the desk. Then he sat and studied Parrish carefully, narrowly. A little disdainful smile worked on his mouth and he nodded resignedly. "But they were tough lessons and you couldn't take them. You expected a fancy job on a silver platter—a nice soft berth with a fat pay check. Brother, you picked the wrong man."

"I didn't expect anything from you, ever. And I didn't get anything—"

"You got plenty."

"What? What did I ever get that I didn't work for? Oh, hell, what's the difference? O.K., I got plenty. Now you can save it—all this great charity you were throwing around—because I'm through. And I'm getting away from you. As far as I can get."

"Now I'll tell you something!" Judd Raike waved his aluminum-tubed cigar. "You're sore. You thought you were working for a hundred and twenty-five a week and it turned out you were working for only a hundred. You got stung so you're crying."

This touched a tender spot and hurt.

"Did you ever make a move to look out for yourself? Did you even once take the trouble to look at the figures on your pay envelope to see what you were being paid? No. You're still wet behind the ears—a snotty kid, crying because you didn't know how to take care of yourself and someone slugged you!"

Numbly, Parrish stared at the aluminum case moving up and down, up and down—feeling Raike's words like a whiplash against a body too spent to absorb more pain. "It's not that," he said.

"It's that, all right!" Raike whipped back. "And you're sore about your boat. You thought you bought a boat and it turned out that you didn't. But did you ever take the trouble to ask for any papers? Answer me that." Judd Raike leaned forward on the desk, nailing Parrish with sharp, hard eyes. He waved the cigar tube accusingly. "What you should have done with that boat was get the bill of sale and know you owned it. You should have given me a note for what it cost and paid off the note like a man, with interest. But that wasn't for you! The business details were too much trouble. You handled the deal like a two-year-old and you're sore because I showed you up."

Parrish *was* sore. He could still boil, knowing he'd been cheated, but aloud he said, "I forgot that damned boat the next day. I wasn't sore."

"You were sore all right." Judd Raike laughed, enjoying it. "You're still sore. But I taught you a lesson you'll never forget. Nobody'll ever put one like that over on you again. Next time you'll get it in writing. And you'll get a lawyer if you need one and you'll give a note if you have to and you'll pay interest because in this world when you use another man's money you pay to use it. The day will come when you'll thank me, because the next time there may be a hell of a lot more involved than a boat. You blundered, you got stuck, and you want to blame someone else. You'd rather call yourself a victim than a fool."

Judd Raike was too old a hand at this not to read the first hint of uncertainty in Parrish's eyes. "Now I'll tell you something else." He pressed his advantage. "As long as you're lazy and stupid and willing to be taken, there'll be someone around to take you. Only, thanks to me, nobody will ever take you this way again—because you learned a lesson you're never going to forget. You'd have preferred learning it the easy way. Brother, you learned it the easy way. The hard way is the easiest way there is. And all you had involved was a boat. It was the cheapest lesson you ever had. But you're sore! Your nose has been bumped, so you're running off yelping with your tail between your legs like a whipped bitch!"

Parrish stood very still in the middle of the office, knowing that everything Judd Raike said was true.

"I was bringing you along." Judd sounded almost paternal now. "I was building you up to a big place here. But you're sore because I pushed you, because I made you get off your tail and learn what it was all about. And when I expect you to work a little harder because there's work to be done, you cry foul and quit." He dropped his aluminum case on the desk and spread his hands, resigned. "O.K., quit. Get out in the nice soft world. Find yourself another job that has nice soft rules, and see how far you get. You'll find that as long as there's work to be done that'll pay, there's going to be someone with a little more gumption than you who'll do it. And he'll take home the gravy—while fellows like you sit around and whimper about fair play."

Parrish stood confused, and the sickness of a man doubting himself began to run through him. How much of this was true? How much was he sulking, looking for an out, scratching for an excuse so he could escape without having to blame his own frailties? Always a man grasped at reasons other than his own shortcomings—the hardest thing to blame was himself. He clenched his hands in his pockets, hating himself for his mounting uncertainty and his suspected weakness.

Judd Raike shoved the keys back across the desk. "Take these and get out. Get back to work, where you belong."

Parrish hesitated.

"You've got a man's job in a man's world. Try to grow up and fit it."

Parrish's hand moved to the desk, but still something held him back. He needed time—time to think where he'd been wrong or right, or clear or mixed up or weak. He turned away and threw himself down in a chair, and buried his head on his hands, feeling hot shame at showing his suffering to another man. Desperately, he tried to think clearly, to go back and re-examine, but it was no use. He might as well take the keys and leave. This had kept a long time; it would keep another day.

He stood up and walked past the gold-lettered list of Raike property to the desk and reached for the keys. And then suddenly the hand moving at Judd Raike's orders to Judd Raike's keys seemed like the hand of another man, and he stiffened and rebelled at the act. The hand stopped and lay on the desk and then came slowly back to his pocket. Relief swept through Parrish as though a terrible weight had been lifted away. He shook his head.

"You're crazy!" Raike gasped.

A hidden reservoir of strength had been released. Parrish raised inflamed eyes to meet Raike's. "I used to tell myself I didn't care what you said or did," he said, slowly. "I used to think you couldn't make me care if I wouldn't let you. I was wrong."

"Damn right you were wrong! You'll care plenty before I'm through."

The shame in him now was of another kind—shame not for his weakness of being unable to take Judd Raike's cheating and abuse, but rather for having taken it so long. "I went a long time thinking I could overlook everything about you and not care. I've seen you lie and cheat and steal and dish out meanness for its own sake to everyone around you—"

"Get out!" Raike yelled suddenly.

"Not just to me." Tiredness fell away. "I could stand you and learn your great lessons the hard way. But what great lessons are you teaching when you abuse women—my mother, Evaline, Paige? You're teaching them to jump to your commands because you get a great big charge out of it and that's all you're teaching them. Because who in hell else is going to come along to abuse them, that they need lessons in it?"

"Shut up!" Raike was on his feet now, gripping the desk. "Get out of here!"

"Lessons! What lesson are you teaching when you drive a man off his land? You want his land and what you're teaching is that you get what you want because you can fight lower and dirtier than anyone else and can always find a rat like Lemmie to take your filthy money and do your filthy jobs—"

"Scum! Trash! Go on—move! Get out!"

"You think that you're the only one who can do such great things? Anybody could play as dirty as you and get what you get. All he'd have to figure out was how to live with himself—"

Raike's face was purple now and Parrish thought with sudden alarm that he would have another stroke. He broke off and almost ran to the door.

"Get out!" Raike yelled. "You're so smart with your ideas—you'll hang with 'em—you'll see—you'll be crucified—" He began to press all the buzzers on his desk.

"Maybe I will," Parrish yelled back. "Maybe I'll hang. But if I do, it'll be for what I believe, not for what you do."

He slammed the door and glared at Miss Daley, who was rushing with alarm to answer the frantic buzzer, and he slammed her door, too, and walked out of the warehouse of Raike and Company.

An hour later, more slowly, Parrish turned away from Alison, too. "You won't wait?"

"Not a day. Not five minutes!"

He had thought by now he was beyond pain, but it cut through him like a razor. "How can you turn love on and off like this?"

"Love!" Her green eyes were dark with anger. "What's love!"

Once more, one last time, he moved to take her in his arms.

"Don't touch me!" she cried. "Don't touch me!"

He left.

He walked to the highway and took a bus that was hot and stuffy and went into Hartford. He had wasted precious time, he thought through his pain. Time had slipped away in compromise. In the two years that he had stayed here because of Alison he might have shown her he could do something. He might have made a beginning, even a small one, to be a hope to hang on to, a reason to give him a chance. He had taken the path of least resistance. In spite of Raike's persecution it had been the easy way. Plenty of time, except lately, plenty of money, and nearness to Alison. He had taken the good life, there was no denying it, and had postponed the day of reckoning.

And yet, in perfect honesty, Parrish knew he would not have done anything spectacular in those two years. He knew carpentry and he knew tobacco and he would have worked in one or the other and not forged very far ahead in either. Things would have been no different.

In Hartford he got off and took another bus to New London to join the Navy. Afterward, he thought there was probably someplace in Hartford, too, where he could have joined up.

BOOK 5

1953

27

THE FIRST yellowing willow threads and budding laurel bent with the sudden lick of March wind and then straightened again, shimmering in the brilliant morning sun that was as warm today as late spring. Walking slowly up the winding driveway toward Sala Post's house, Parrish let his eyes travel over the still farm, taking in the old landmarks, familiar and forgotten, the stately white house, the stout old trees, the terrible barn with its patched roof and the doghouse of windows on top.

Three years—almost. But it was all the same. A man made too much of time, expecting that change had to pile on change, just because he had been away three years. Here, the garage doors held the same heavy locks; the same curtains of the apartment above were drawn tight; it could have been the same pigeon screaming on top of the number-three shed and flying into the old tree with the bare roots where he used to lie at noon and talk to Teet.

He walked on up the hill. Three years. He had left here and gone halfway across the world to a sea off the island of Formosa. He had made new friends—the gloomy Streeter, who worried that they would go to Korea and die, and Miller, who was a good drinker and a good poker player and reminded him of Anson Tower when he said once a day that they were all victims of the international power struggle. And Conte. Conte would have made a fine tobacco man. He had been in the last war, he expected he would be in this one, he thought he would come out of it. He always figured tomorrow would be better, except when he was drunk, when he would yell, like a battle cry, "Live today—tomorrow we die," as though no one had ever thought it before.

Three years. Parrish looked at Sala's house, reminding himself that Alison didn't live here any more, that for a long time she had not lived here. She would not be back to live here again. She had left a month after he had, needing only as long as that to marry Wiley. Almost clinically, Parrish examined the familiar pain. It was an old ache now, the sharpness long since gone out of it; for a little while it would hurt, aggravated by this place that stirred memories, and then it would die as it had before. He had not come without asking himself whether he could return here, and answering that he could.

He reached the top of the hill. Now the whole stretch of land lay before him, evenly blocked with poles waiting for the cloth, and he could see the shaded side of shed number three where Gladstone and Cartwright used to lie on a hot day. Over on the rise of land just before the Ridge the Black Angus stood still, as though they had not stirred since he left. He turned and walked toward the side door. Nothing had changed. It was good to be back.

A girl he didn't know answered the door.

"Mr. Post in this morning?"

"He's in." She stood with that familiar slump of the Valley girls. "He's in his library. I'll get him."

"I can find it." Walking down the dark hall, Parrish could see the shaft of light come from the sunroom where he and Ellen had waited that first day, and, at the end, the living room with the old furniture and portraits, where he had passed so many hours with Alison. The door to Sala's library was open and Parrish saw him inside, writing at his desk, which had been turned facing the door now instead of the window that looked out to the fields.

Parrish knocked and Sala looked up and the stern face creased with quick pleasure.

"Parrish!" Sala came around the desk and shook his hand and touched his shoulder affectionately. "Come in. Come in. I thought you'd come this afternoon."

Parrish smiled, looking him over, pleased by Sala's genuine pleasure at seeing him. "I have to meet my mother for lunch. I haven't seen her yet. I thought I'd get out here first, look the old place over."

"You haven't seen her yet!" Sala said. "Where are you staying?"

"At the hotel. The Bond."

"You're not with them—at Raike's?"

"No."

Sala motioned him into a chair and sat opposite him. "Sit down. Tell me about the Navy." He took out one of his thin cigars. "You smoke these yet?"

Parrish grinned. "No." It was all the same. Except Alison.

Sala lit the cigar, beaming at him. "Now—how did it go? Your letters were good, even when you complained of the monotony. Wisdom can be born of monotony—but I wrote you that. Did you read any of the books I sent?"

"All of them," Parrish said. He had started to read them only because Sala sent them and then he had found himself looking forward to their arrival. "Some more than once. Parts, anyway."

"Some have to be read more than once. I thought you should know what you were fighting for."

"I didn't fight. We lay off Formosa, which is a long way from Korea; but I was glad to have the books."

"Good," Sala said. "And what now, Parrish? What are you going to do now that you're back?"

Parrish smiled. Through the window he could see the dry, crusted seed-beds that soon would be steamed and turned to show rich brown, and then, almost overnight, would be emerald green with young plants. "I want to come back here," he said. "I want to go back into tobacco."

Sala's smile faded.

"Not to him!" Parrish said, quickly. "Here—with you!"

"Here?"

Parrish nodded. Then abruptly his eagerness died out and disappointment swept over him. He had spent long hours thinking about this, had considered very carefully whether he could come back, weighing all the reasons why he should or should not, thinking of Alison and of Ellen and of Raike. He had looked at all sides of the question, it seemed, except the most important one. That Sala Post might not want him had not even crossed his mind. And yet, even before Sala spoke, Parrish could see that he was going to turn him down. Puzzled and hurt, he stared at Sala, speechless. Then he thought—he's living with his damn ghosts again, not hiring me because of Raike!

"You know I've left him!" he said. "And you know why. I saw your face that night. The night of Tully's fire."

"And I saw yours. Parrish, I'd hire you in a minute. You know that." Sala stood up and walked to the window. "But I don't work this land any more."

"Don't work it!" Then alarm caught at Parrish and he said, "He didn't—?"

"No, Parrish, he didn't get me, too. I just don't work it."

"But why?" Parrish asked incredulously. "What happened?"

"Nothing happened, Parrish." Sala sat at his desk and picked up a silver letter opener and fiddled with it. "I worked another year, after you left, and then suddenly I didn't want to work any more."

"Why not?" It seemed impossible! "Did you have a hard year?"

"No. Strangely enough, I had a good year," Sala said. "One of the best in a long time. I didn't even plan to stop. It just happened. Last year. We'd fall-planted to barley. The cloth was ready—fertilizer, chemicals. Then it was time to steam the beds and suddenly I didn't want to start another year."

Parrish's eye went over to the window, followed the pattern of poles to the horizon. He couldn't imagine those poles in summer without cloth or those fields without a crop. And he looked back to Sala and thought that he couldn't imagine him without a crop, either. "It's hard to picture your land in summer without tobacco." Parrish gave a little shake of his head. And then another thought struck him. "Or do you—you don't lease it?"

"No." Sala shook his head. "I have enough to live on. I don't have many expenses these days." There was loneliness in the words. Alison had been his expense and his reason—Alison, who had always accused him of sacrificing her for his land. "I didn't want strangers working it."

Parrish understood that. He couldn't imagine Sala sitting here in the house with a lot of other people tramping around on his land. But neither could he imagine him watching the cloth go up over other fields and being able to resist. It would be too strong a pull. Then he thought there could be reasons pulling the other way, too. He said, "Did Raike get Prentiss, too?"

Sala nodded. "The same day as Tully. Prentiss wanted to get out while he was healthy. He offered it to me first. They both did."

And so he is surrounded, Parrish thought. The vise is almost closed.

Sala touched the letter opener to some papers on his desk. "I'm writing a history of tobacco now—going way back before Shade, back to the Indians, when tobacco was a very different thing."

Parrish glanced at the sheets of paper, written in ink in Sala's small, neat hand. But they were not the reason for Sala's stopping; at best they were a poor substitute for his crop. "He give you a lot of trouble?" he said. "After he got Prentiss and was so close?"

"He didn't give me trouble."

"Probably would have," Parrish said. "Would have tried, anyway."

"He figures he doesn't have to," Sala said. "He expects to get my land through Alison."

"Then Sala looked at Parrish quickly. The name was out. It had slipped into their talk and he was afraid it was still a sore subject.

"How is Alison?" Parrish said evenly. "How is she?"

Sala bent over and threw another small log onto the fire, which didn't need it, and carefully replaced the screen. "I don't know how she is," he said. "She comes to visit me every Wednesday afternoon and I'm glad to see her but other than that I don't know anything and I don't ask."

"Look the same?"

"She looks like the rest of them, expensive, aimless, discontented." Sala was silent a moment and then said, "What will you do now, Parrish? Will you stay in the Valley anyway?"

"I don't know," Parrish said. "This was kind of a surprise. I hadn't thought any further."

Sala nodded.

"Tom Holden, maybe," Parrish said. "I'll have to think about it."

Then it was time to leave and Sala stood up and walked with him to the door. "Come again, Parrish." He held out his hand. "If you stay in the Valley, come back soon."

The door closed behind him and Parrish was out in the brilliant sunlight again. He lingered a moment, looking at the fields, where furrows still showed and poles were bare, and then at the barn and the garage. But they had lost their meaning now. In three years things had changed, after all.

All the way back to town to meet his mother, Parrish thought about it. It was hard to believe that Sala had looked at his fields one day and found he hadn't the heart to go on. But, Parrish suspected, it was probably not as simple as that. Was it only that Alison had been his reason and was gone? Or was it something more—for all he didn't blame Sala for not admitting it. No man liked to admit fear, not even to himself—but you couldn't infect a nonexistent crop, nor use its water, nor spread blue mold to empty beds, and there wasn't much to be gained burning an unused shed or barn. Land that was idle was harder to lose. Harder to steal.

Across the luncheon table in the hotel dining room Parrish looked carefully at his mother and thought that there were times when a man's reasoning and his emotions refused to walk hand in hand, and that this was one of the times. The three years had not touched Ellen. She looked marvelous and he told himself that it was proof she was happy, which was all he wanted for her, and that he should be delighted. But instead he was aware of a vague kind of let-down feeling that he couldn't accurately explain to himself.

"It's bad enough that you're in Hartford and staying in a hotel," Ellen said. "You can't keep away from my house entirely. And really, Parrish, a small party for a few hours isn't too much to bear."

Parrish frowned. He couldn't think of anything worse than facing Alison for the first time, or Judd Raike, either, at a party with a roomful of witnesses. "It would be terrible."

Ellen smiled, undisturbed, and Parrish reflected that it wasn't that he expected her to try to change Raike or argue with him, or, any more, that he hoped she would leave Raike or, even, that he wanted her to. What would that accomplish? It would only send her back to loneliness, and she'd had enough years of that. There was nothing about this situation that Parrish would change if he had the power to, and yet the feeling persisted—a little sense of disappointment in her that she found it so right. He wondered if she knew about Sala.

"Don't you see, dear?" she said. "With guests present there won't be any awkwardness because there can't be. If we were all alone the first time, just the family, we would try to make small talk and act as though nothing had happened, as though you and Judd had not parted in anger, as though there had never been anything between you and Alison—"

"Those things happened," Parrish said. "You can't pretend they didn't."

He didn't mind her accepting the bad with the good, he told himself. That was part of any choice. Maybe all he wanted was some sign of her awareness that the bad existed, some sign that there were a few things she accepted with at least an inner reluctance.

"Of course they happened," Ellen said. "And you are not the only one who remembers them."

"Did you know," Parrish said suddenly, "that Sala Post isn't working his land?"

"Yes," she said. "How did you know?"

"I went out there this morning—looking for a job."

Ellen studied him carefully. "Parrish," she said, "if you want to go back into tobacco—well, Judd would growl a bit and make a few speeches but he would be very, very glad to have you."

Parrish stared. "You never knew why I left, did you?"

"I knew long before you left that you would have to," Ellen said. "But now it would be different. Parrish, Judd isn't the man he was. He's not sick, but he's not well, and he needs someone like you. Now you could make very good arrangements with him."

"I don't want any arrangements with him."

"Parrish, even if Sala were working, what could he offer you? Here there's so much."

Parrish looked across the table and thought that here was something that hadn't changed. He was still trying to make her understand how it was with him and he still knew she could not accept it and it was still important to him, because she was his mother, at least to try. Patiently he leaned toward her. "Mother," he said, "during the past three years not very much happened to me—by most standards. I was across the street from a war I didn't get into. I only got close enough to think that I might, and to hear men worry that they were going to die. There was nothing big and dramatic. I didn't watch my friends die on battlefields, or be blown up, or drown—none of those things happened."

Ellen sat quiet, listening, and Parrish gave her credit for not saying she was thankful they had not.

"But I had lots of time to think," he went on. "And maybe someday I'll find my thinking is all wrong. It's happened before." Maybe, he thought, all a man's figuring was nothing more than temperature or a night or day watch, or knowing they talked Chinese on the nearest piece of land. "I had time and I thought this out, knowing that any day somebody might ship me into a war to get killed, so I tried to think honestly; and one thing I decided absolutely was that I don't want to go back to Raike. So that's the way I feel now, and let's not argue about it any more."

Ellen nodded. "All right, Parrish."

"If it's ever different, I'll let you know. You won't have to ask me."

"Parrish—" Ellen looked at him soberly—"did you think only about what you don't want? Or have you decided, too, what you will do?"

He gestured uncertainly.

"You can't just drift," she said. "That's not good. You'll find someone and want to get married—"

"I don't want to get married." Then he smiled and said, "Don't worry about me. I'll be all right."

Ellen looked unconvinced, but she didn't press him. "Parrish, about tonight," she said instead. "Try to look at it this way. If you delay, it grows in importance out of all proportion. In a crowd, it will be simple. You're back, everyone has accepted it, and life goes on. You can come again tomorrow, or not for a month. It doesn't matter. Believe me, in a crowd of strangers is the best way."

Parrish smiled at her, feeling better, with a sudden affection. "Is this something you really want or are you just asking because you think you ought to? Is it important to you?"

"Yes," she said. "I believe you should come."

"You didn't plan it this way?"

"No, it's for Georgie Worthy's wife. It's her first visit to Hartford. But it's terribly convenient, isn't it?"

"If you say so."

"You'll come, then?"

"You always win. You know that."

"No," she said, "I don't." Then the smile returned as she took out her gloves. "But we do understand each other, Parrish, you and I. We agree on nothing, but we understand each other very well, and as long as we have that we'll manage."

Parrish walked with her to her car and shook hands with Dennis, the chauffeur, and watched the car drive off. There must be moments, he thought, when she sees Raike as he really is. Or doesn't she let herself, because, once she saw that, where would it lead?

"Man, you picked a great time to come back!" Clayton Norris pumped Parrish's hand. "Three weeks ago there wouldn't have been a soul here to greet you. My God, what a homecoming that would have been—nothing!"

"Party's not for me." Parrish stole a quick look over the crowd for Alison. "It's for Georgie Worthy's wife, whatever her name is."

"Man, that's the way the ball bounces. Helluva party, though. Her name's Winifred."

"Who?" He was beginning to be sorry he had come.

"Georgie's wife."

"Oh." It was like Alison to be late, Parrish thought. And what am I doing here among fools, waiting for her? It no longer seemed simple.

"Man," Clayton said, "you notice before Georgie Worthy got so big, he never brought his wife to Hartford. Before, little Winifred stayed in New York and Georgie came alone and pinched bottoms. Now he knows everyone has to be nice to her so he drags her along."

"Even gets a party given for her," Harris Lowe said. "Damned opportunist, if you ask me. Otherwise you'd have had this party all to yourself. Rotten luck."

Suddenly Parrish saw Alison. She was still out in the hall. He saw that her hair was different, parted in the center, shorter—too short to lie on a man's shoulder—and that she wore emerald earrings to match her eyes, and he felt a long-forgotten warmth stirring in him and he turned his back.

"Are you current," Clayton Norris said, "on all information and events? Family disharmonies, who is affairing with whom—?"

From behind somebody kissed him and Parrish jumped with an instant shiver and then saw it was Maizie. "God, I'm glad to see you," he said.

Maizie held out her arms. "Darling, you look beautiful and I love you! Are you thinking this is a hell of a homecoming?"

"It's not a homecoming." Parrish could tell by the morbidly expectant look on Clayton's face that Alison was coming closer.

"I've missed you so," Maizie said. "You have been faithful to me, haven't you?"

"Staunchly." He jammed his hands into his pockets. "Your picture was over my bunk. You were the darling of the fleet. Fourteen men fell in love with you and had your face tattooed on their chests."

"Precious," Maizie sighed, "if you were ten years older you'd never get away from me."

Now everyone's eyes told him that Alison was here. He clenched his fists in his pockets and stood still. Out of the corner of his eye he could see only Georgie Worthy coming from behind him, and his wife.

"Maizie," Georgie boomed, "Winifred's telling about her psychoanalysis."

"I've only been in it for two years," Mrs. Worthy said. "In psychoanalysis, that's only a beginning."

Then Parrish heard Alison.

"Two years," she said in her controlled voice, low and clear. "How interesting."

"Damned competent fellow," Georgie said. "Says she loves me and hates me at the same time. Hell of a problem."

"Isn't that interesting?" Alison said.

"And then there's our daughter," Georgie said. "She sort of hates us."

"Perfectly natural, you know," Winifred said.

"Perfectly," Maizie said.

This is fantastic, Parrish thought. After three years, we are standing an arm apart, listening to an account of some idiot woman's psychoanalysis.

"The age of devaluation of the parent, you know."

"Don't be an ass," Maizie whispered in his ear. "Turn around."

"They think their parents are inferior."

"And are they?" Maizie said.

He turned around and Alison smiled at him immediately. "Hello, Parrish."

My God, he thought, what a spectacle! "Hello," he boomed heartily.

Alison held out her hand, showing no emotion at seeing him. She had been warned and she was very good at this kind of thing. "How nice to see you—and how well you're looking. Ellen showed us pictures, didn't she, Evaline? Three, I believe. Or was it four?"

Parrish hadn't even seen poor Evaline standing next to her. "Evaline!" he said. "You're looking fine!"

"You're looking fine, too, Parrish," Evaline bleated.

Alison was smiling dazzlingly and he felt that she was putting enormous energy into this restrained performance. It was an energy with an almost hysterical quality, the kind he had seen a dozen times. "My father will be so pleased to hear you are back," she said. "Do try to drop in on him."

"I've seen him already. This morning."

"Why, Parrish, what a nice thing for you to do! How very kind!"

"It wasn't kindness."

"And have you seen Father?"

She meant Raike! Parrish stared at her and then over to Raike, who had come into the room with Ellen. Raike was heavier, now, flabbier, and he looked tired. Maybe, Parrish told himself, with Sala it was tiredness, too. Not fear. He wished he could think so.

Evaline said, a little worried, "We try not to upset him, Parrish."

"We always tried that, didn't we, Evaline?"

She nodded.

"And not to let him upset us, too." He smiled. And what about the people whose land he has stolen, are they still upset? And what about Sala, who is afraid to plant? Damn it, he thought, you don't know that he's afraid.

"Paige was looking for you, Parrish," Evaline said, to change the subject. "Her train just got in."

"You haven't seen Paige yet! Now that'll be a surprise." Clayton rolled his eyes. "Oh, to have my youth again!"

Alison moved away now and as she passed him her hand brushed against his. Parrish froze and told himself it was an accident. The instant she was gone Clayton was buzzing again, watching him carefully. "Alison's a great hit with everyone."

"Naturally."

"It pleases Judd enormously. He'd give Alison anything and, brother, does she play him for it! She's bypassed the intermediary and gone right to the source, if you know what I mean. Which is one reason the poor slob of a middleman starts to drink at noon these days."

"I thought Wiley was a friend of yours, Clay."

"My best. That's why I'm worried about him."

"I think I see Paige," Parrish said, and he threaded his way through the crowd to her.

A few minutes later they had to shout above the noise as the thickening crowd milled back and forth through the room, so Parrish motioned to the stairs and guided Paige across the hall. Sitting gracefully on a step halfway up, Paige arranged her full, elegant skirt. She let her eyes travel over the frenzied crowd and settle on a little group gathering around Harris Lowe and Clayton Norris, who were offering the latest of their repertoire of jokes. A film of smoke hung at the level of the crystal chandelier.

"You must be so glad to get back to all this!" Paige smiled a lovely, meaningless smile that showed neither warmth nor relation to her light sarcasm.

Perplexed, Parrish studied her. Here was the biggest change of all—Paige. There was a new quality in her, an aloofness she had not even known the meaning of when he left, underscored by a vague defiance that seemed to have become part of her general attitude, not just saved for indignant outbursts as before.

"Are you?" he said.

"Oh, indeed. I love it. They work so hard and they do so well at the thing at which they are working so hard."

He changed the subject. "How has it been at college?"

"Great."

Still she watched the crowd below with eyes that were bright and aware and disillusioned. "The only things ever new are their clothes. Otherwise, it's the same people, the same ideas, the same luncheon places, the same old parties. Oh, yes, and their pet phrases. Last year they were all calling their wives brides—too bad you missed that. This year they're just old wives again." She smiled and shrugged. "On the other hand, I suppose, why not, if that's what they want?"

"What are you in a lather about?" Parrish said. "This was never your meat. How's Anson?"

"I presume," she said, carefully, "that he is great." Now the eyes came back to him, the same beautiful cocoa eyes, without the dreaminess and the stardust.

"Presume? Are you—is that all over?"

"Quite."

So she had had an unhappy love and that was what had left her cynical. "I can't say I'm sorry, Paige."

"Who has said anything about being sorry?"

"How long ago did you call it off?"

"Last fall. And you don't have to bite your lip, Parrish, wondering what to say, because we're having no hearts and flowers." She turned on the meaningless smile again. "What about you? Did you have a bad time of it?"

"No."

"Splendid! Not at all—well!"

"Hell, any yellow moon can pull memories."

"Can't it?"

"For that matter, any sun rising over the water can race hope and bigness like crazy in a man—for a little while, anyway."

"I'll have to try that."

"It doesn't last."

"Then I'll try it anyway and not expect too much, which is better still."

At the foot of the stairs Georgie Worthy, who was everywhere tonight, wandered by, a hand solicitously at his wife's elbow, a large cigar in his mouth. While Paige watched him, Parrish studied her. She was extremely chic now, the blond hair drawn back in a smooth, elegant style. She had matured and she had an air of confidence about her, and the brown eyes were lovely and alert, and the breathless embracing of life was gone.

She turned back to him. "Georgie Worthy has stopped pinching bottoms."

"That's a shame."

"Isn't it? Maizie told me. She has watched all evening, very carefully. You see the demands position makes of one. Now that Georgie has merged himself into prominence, he has an obligation to behave. *Noblesse oblige*. It's like the passing of a champion. Joe Louis or DiMaggio or somebody."

Or, he thought, Sala Post. He wondered how she felt about that and whether she still cared who produced the best leaves or cared about tobacco at all or about anything. She was a polished, beautiful woman now, cool and composed, with a shell about her, and Parrish thought suddenly that here, too, had been the passing of a champion.

He looked at the face, by most standards more beautiful now than then, with everything about it as it should be, including the fact that it revealed nothing except a sense of fashion, and asked himself how he would name it—the thing at which Paige had once been so wonderful. Just being human, maybe. Whatever it was, he missed it and had a sudden longing to find it again.

"Do you think—" he still searched her face, seeing no crack in the shell— "if you and I got out of here, we could find something to talk about besides the end of Georgie Worthy's career as an explorer?"

Paige laughed unexpectedly, for the first time, and for a moment she eyed him as though suddenly deciding to reappraise him. "We might, Parrish," she said with a trace of the old directness. "You and I just possibly might."

But then two young men Parrish had never seen before stood at the foot of the stairs and one said, "There she is!" And the other pointed and said, "We've been looking for you!" and they came and sat down, too. For a minute Parrish felt sure Paige was going to leave them and come with him. And then while he watched, waiting, she settled down behind her defenses and flashed around her meaningless smile.

A few minutes later Parrish quietly closed the door behind him and walked down the front steps. A late-season snow had started, large wet flakes, melting as they fell—the start of spring reaching halfheartedly back into winter.

"You went there last night?" Sala Post worked at the fire with a poker. It was a gray, cheerless day that promised rain or snow, and the spit and crackle of the logs seemed to speak only of the loneliness of the day and the place. Seeing the flat bare land, Parrish remembered the emptiness of Oermeyer's farm after Oermeyer had gone, and he thought that there was nothing so desolate, not even the sea, as a farm that no man was farming.

He looked away from the window, back to Sala. Early this morning Sala had telephoned him, asking him, with a touch of urgency, to come out again, and sitting here now he could feel the loneliness that had probably prompted the call.

"I suppose you saw Alison?" Sala said.

"Just for a minute. There were about a hundred people there." And then, because Sala seemed to expect more, Parrish added lamely, "She looked fine. Kind of settled down, happily married—"

Carefully Sala stood the poker in its stand and then went over and sat at his desk. "She could have had a real man. She settled for less than half."

She settled for what she wanted, Parrish thought, and at least she knew what that was, which was more than some people knew. He glanced up at Sala. "I guess it wasn't all Alison's fault," he said. "Mine, too."

"Why?"

Parrish pulled out a package of cigarettes and made a business of opening it, carefully tearing off a neat little square of paper. "I never understood her need for you—you know—everything she had to have. Security, I guess you'd call it."

"She had security."

Parrish shrugged, gave a baffled little smile. He was beginning to be sorry he had come back to the Valley at all. "We were just too far apart. She couldn't help it and I couldn't help it. But one thing I've learned —I'm the queer one."

Sala's eyes sharpened. "You mean you'd decide it differently today?"

"No," Parrish said. "I'd do the same thing again."

"Then what—"

"I spent a couple of years in the Navy with men who were young, able-bodied, and worried. One was going back to a job he hated because he had seniority and couldn't be fired easily. Another was staying in the Navy because it offered lifetime care, a job, and a pension, and in the next war you'd be as safe at sea as on land. Safer."

He paused, not certain that Sala was listening. He was tracing little squares on the cover of the tobacco manuscript. But when Parrish stopped talking Sala glanced up, questioning.

"So they weren't so different from Alison," Parrish said. "The whole world wants security today. I'm the one who's out of step. I don't figure to get into step, but I'll never ask anyone again to give up their great security the way I asked her to. If I'd known all this then, I'd have saved us both a lot of trouble."

Sala traced another neat square, stopped, went over the lines again, and for a few minutes he was silent. Then he said, "Judd Raike get to talk to you last night, Parrish?"

"He said hello and how was I—the usual stuff. And that I seemed more a man."

"Didn't make any offer?" Sala said. "Ask you to come back?"

Parrish laughed. "He knows when he's well off."

"I think he will ask you, Parrish. He'll offer you a good job—a position —with independence and responsibility. You ought to decide whether you'll take it."

"I've decided." His eyes met Sala's. "You know I couldn't go back to Judd Raike."

"You want to go back into tobacco."

"Not with him."

"I don't have to tell you that if you come back into tobacco now you'll probably stay in it."

"I've come back now."

Sala stood up and looked out the window toward the bare fields, and Parrish thought that the only thing that could make him lonelier than this cheerless day would be the smell of spring. "What happened to everyone who was here?" he said, suddenly remembering the others besides Sala who belonged out there.

"John still lives in the cottage," Sala said. "He's working for Tom Holden. The women and most of the Jamaicans are scattered on other farms."

"Teet?"

"Teet left. I haven't heard anything about him. Gladstone and Cartwright went home. Their three-year period was up. I don't think they came back."

Abruptly, Sala turned around and sat at his desk. "Parrish," he said, "against my better judgment—" He paused, obviously hesitant about what was on his mind, opening the manuscript cover, looking at his title page. Then, decisively, he shut it. "Against my better judgment, I'll make you a proposition."

Parrish waited.

"I'm not sure you should accept it, but you can take time to think it over. If you think you want it—" Sala looked squarely at him—"I'll lease you part of my land."

Slowly, Parrish sat up straight.

"If you want it," Sala said. "And if you can hire a crew, which won't be easy."

"Lease me your land!"

"If you can hire a crew—which won't be easy."

"Just like that? You're going to lease me your land—if I can hire a crew?"

"I must warn you that it won't be easy."

"What won't be easy?"

"To hire a crew."

"Why not? What's so hard about hiring a crew?"

Sala frowned. "There's a feeling around here that Raike is destined by fate to get all this." Sala waved a hand impatiently. "And that any independent will be unlucky—fate will be against him."

"Unlucky, hell!" Parrish burst out. "It's not luck."

"You and I know that. They don't. They stayed with me because they'd always worked for me. They'll feel different coming to you. They have to be with a farm that works a full season—a crop that succeeds."

"I'll succeed," Parrish said. Then suddenly he looked at Sala and spread his hands. "I haven't any money."

Sala lit up a thin cigar and leaned back. "I didn't expect that you would have, Parrish. Limit yourself to a small acreage this first year and I'll meet your payroll for you. The cloth is here, paid for. And the chemicals. They've been here since last year. Your only problem is your payroll, if you can raise a crew."

"And the lease."

"And the lease."

"I probably couldn't even pay you for the lease in advance."

"That much you could probably manage," Sala said.

Parrish shook his head. "It's your land, your money. Why give it to me? Work it yourself, and I'll work for you."

"No," Sala said. "You work it. You're old enough. I ran it alone at your age. Unless, of course, you don't want to—"

Want to! Already Parrish could feel his blood racing, could almost feel the dirt in his hands and smell growing tobacco and see the leaves. "I'll raise a crew all right."

"It will be harder than you think. But you can give it a try. If you can hire enough people to work it, I'll stand behind you."

"I'll give you a note," Parrish said, "for whatever you lend me. With interest."

"I don't want your note. If I didn't trust you I wouldn't be doing this. You can pay me back when you sell your crop."

"Sir, you're taking all the risk—"

"Tobacco is always a risk. It's a risk when I plant and it's a risk when you plant—when anyone plants."

And he had thought Sala was afraid! Suddenly Parrish was ashamed, feeling that he had betrayed Sala, even momentarily considering such an idea. "About the lease—" he said.

"Parrish, you think about it. Make sure you want to do it. It won't be all rosy. It will be a lot of worry and hard work and there are easier ways to make a living. But if you decide that this is what you want, come back and we'll go over the details. I'll show you figures on what you'll be investing, your cost per acre, how many men and women per acre you'll need, and then we'll see who you can hire and decide how much you should work. You can have the rooms over the garage and live with your crop."

"What about the lease?" Parrish said. "Maybe I could at least pay you for part of that."

"The lease will be one dollar."

Parrish stared. Sala smiled and came around the desk, touched his shoulder. "This isn't as one-sided as you think, Parrish. I don't like to look out on empty fields. It will be as good for me as for you."

28

It was a cold morning, still seeming at this hour more winter than spring, with the sun low and a raw dampness reaching out of the woods, but Parrish wandered happily past the seedbeds and alongside the number-three field, kicking the hard earth and every here and there testing a pole that looked as though it needed replacing. Last night he had moved into the apartment over the garage and already he felt as though he had never been away.

The first thing he should do, he decided, was line up a few men. He would need them when the boiler truck came to steam the beds, and meanwhile he could keep them busy here, working on poles that needed attention after two years, and tightening wires for the cloth. He had written to Gladstone, asking him to come and to bring Cartwright and anyone else he could find, but that would take time and before they could get here he would need help to get started. Also, last night, he had gone out to the trailer camp looking for someone who knew something about Teet. He'd talked to half a dozen people without any luck. Tonight he would go back and ask some more.

A raw wind whipped across the open fields and Parrish turned up his collar and walked back to the garage for the old station wagon that Sala had said he could use, and drove down to Tower's Diner for breakfast.

The diner, almost empty, was warm and smelled of steam. At one end two all-night truck drivers sat huddled over coffee. The morning news was coming over the radio. Parrish pulled shut the door, closing out the cold air, and sat down on a stool, and the door opened again and he recognized the Broadleaf farmer, Ben, who was apparently working a milk route now. Ben put a crate of milk bottles on the counter and sat on the next stool. Presently the counterman shuffled over, recognized Parrish, and jerked his head in greeting. "Back, eh?" he said.

Parrish nodded and ordered breakfast.

"Where you been?" the counterman said.

"Navy."

The counterman nodded and went off to fix his breakfast. Ben looked over at Parrish. "I thought I seen you someplace," he said after a while. "Raike startin' already?"

"I'm not with Raike," Parrish said. "I'm at Sala Post's."

Ben showed surprise. "Sala workin' again?"

"I am," Parrish said.

The counterman came back with his eggs and coffee. "You on the level?" He put down the plate and slid over a fork and knife. "About workin' Sala's?"

Parrish nodded, seeing Ben and the counterman exchange a look. He might as well start right now. "Know anyone wants to work?" he said. "Men to steam the beds and fix poles?"

Ben looked away, concentrated on a plate of cake. The counterman leaned on the cash register. "You're early. The bums ain't come into the area yet."

"Don't have to be bums."

"You got Jamaicans?"

"Not yet."

"Women?" Ben put in.

"I'm just starting."

The counterman handed Ben his coffee and Ben poured some off into the saucer and added milk from a pitcher. The counterman turned back to Parrish. "You got nerve, I'll say that," he said.

"Why?"

"Ain't exactly been lucky out there lately. You hear that?"

Parrish said, "I don't figure it's luck."

"Don't know what else you'd call it," Ben said. "One damn thing after another out there. Wouldn't catch me around."

Parrish shrugged.

"Snake-bit, that's what it is."

Parrish stood up to leave. "The bums still hang out around the Apothecary Shop looking for work?"

The counterman nodded soberly. "When they're around. There ain't any yet."

He was right. It was a slow morning at Tower's Apothecary Shop, too early in the season to be busy, and only one customer came in and none of the migrant workers that the Valley people called "tobacco bums." Williams, the clerk, came over to talk to Parrish.

"Lotta talk about that section out there, y'know," he said.

"I know."

"Just thought I oughta tell you in case you hadn't heard. Now, personally, it don't cut no ice with me, that stuff. But you know how it is with some—couple things go wrong, they say it's the jinx working. Still, you know, been nothing but hard luck out that way. Makes you wonder —almost seems it'd be smarter not to go flirting with trouble. Comes often enough without going out of your way to find it."

Parrish decided to leave and see how many he could hire among the Valley people. He needed men first, but he'd better start signing up women too, before they were all taken. Starting at the most logical place, he drove out to Lucy's.

"Gee, Parrish, you workin' Sala's land! Think o' that!" Lucy was fat now—as fat as Rosie and Mamma. "You'll be a real big shot, huh!"

Parrish leaned against the door, smelling the goulash she was getting started, which would stew all day. "Not all of it, Lucy. Twenty acres."

"Twenty acres! Pretty good!" Lucy's face was a little flushed, and fat had erased the winsome sweetness and given her a heavy, coarse look. She stood at the stove, a hand on one wide hip that threatened to burst her jeans, breasts bulging against her blouse, and Parrish wondered whether she still worked as fast, carrying all that fat, and he reflected, I'm thinking already like a man who's paying the bills.

"I'm trying to hire, Lucy," he said. "What do you say?"

Lucy's face changed and she turned to stir the goulash. "You gonna handle them twenty acres alone, Parrish?"

"What do you mean, alone?"

"What about John?"

"John's already signed a contract with Tom Holden for the year." He saw Lucy give him a quick look that said there was more to it than that. "I don't need John for just twenty acres. He'll come next year when I work more."

"Yeah?"

"How about it, Lucy?"

"Ah, Parrish, I don't know. . . ." Lucy lit a cigarette and put it down on the counter, the burning tip over the edge. "I don't know that I'll work this year at all."

"Why not?"

The cigarette sent up a thin column of smoke that wiggled as Lucy let out a sigh. "Ah, you know how it is, Parrish—same old grind, you get sick of it."

"Lucy, you know you'll work."

"Maybe not!" She met his eye, fleetingly, guiltily. "I ain't been feelin' so good lately. I even told Stepowicz—"

"That where you went—Stepowicz'?"

"Yeah, and he'll be expectin' me back. You know, if I work, that is. If I feel O.K."

"All right, Lucy." Disappointed and angry, Parrish turned to leave. He'd known he wouldn't get them all, but the one he had never doubted was Lucy.

"Ah, Parrish, don't be mad. You know how it is."

"How what is?"

"Well, you know—" She flushed, looking very uncomfortable. "Parrish, you got any Jamaicans?"

"No."

"Then how you gonna work it?"

"I'm going to hire whatever help I can get until I have enough."

"Who you gonna get, Parrish? You tried any of the others? Addie or Eileen?"

"You're my first stop, Lucy."

Lucy sighed and her cigarette started to burn into the counter and she grabbed it up and put it out and looked at him, miserably. "Parrish, what's the good of it? Look what happened to the others—them all in there. Tully. And before him Oermeyer." So now it was coming out. "It's jinxed in there."

"Jinxed!" Parrish came back into the room. "You don't mean jinxed."

"Sure it is. That whole section."

"Lucy—" he pulled out a chair—"sit down."

Hesitating a moment, grudgingly, she sat and Parrish took his old chair across from her. "Lucy," he said firmly, "you know it's not jinxed. Nothing happened to Sala."

"Sure it did!" she cried. "One year worms—"

"Worms can happen to anyone."

"One year hail—"

"Hail can happen to anyone."

"But it didn't happen to anyone—it happened to him, Sala, right there in that section. Same as Oermeyer got blue mold, same as Tully had a fire. Sure, they could happen anywhere, too. Only they happened there." She tapped the table. "Right there an' not just anywhere."

Parrish regarded Lucy, dumfounded. "You really believe it! You really think it's jinxed!"

"Everyone does. An' you do, too."

"I know better, Lucy."

"Ah, you was always a one lookin' for trouble. You'll see."

"How come Raike's Ridge farm doesn't get jinxed, where you worked last year, Lucy? How come Lemmie's old place on the other side isn't jinxed?"

She shrugged. "That's the way it goes. Raike's lucky. He ain't jinxed."

"He's driving them out. He drives them out and buys their land."

Lucy looked as if he were crazy. "He didn't give Sala worms. An' he can't make hail. Even Raike can't make hail. An' besides, even if it was true, it'd be worse. If he could get them, with all the time they had in tobacco, think what he'd do to you!"

"He's not going to do anything to me because I'm not going to let him." Lucy chewed her lip.

"What do you say, Lucy?"

"Ah, Parrish, I don't know." She bolted back to the stove and stirred the goulash furiously. "Luck's either with you or it ain't."

"Lucy—" he moved over to her—"have I ever let you down?"

"It ain't that you'd want to!"

Abruptly Parrish strode to the door and left. He was around the house and walking down the path when the front door flew open and Lucy stood on the threshold, below which there were still no steps.

"Parrish—Parrish," she yelled, and instantly she looked sorry she had stopped him. "Parrish, try someone else. Try a couple of the others."

He came back a few steps. "And if I do?"

Torn by indecision, Lucy picked at the seam of her jeans. "If you get anyone else, any of the old ones who was with Sala—I'll come, too."

For three mornings after Lucy had showed him what he could expect, Parrish waited at the Apothecary Shop until ten o'clock and then spent the rest of the day searching out the old help, without succeeding in hiring anyone. Then he began to work alone, replacing poles and tightening wire himself in the daytime, and calling on people at night.

Each evening as he walked toward the garage, seeing the sun darken over the fields and thinking of all that had to be done, he would struggle to beat down the bewildering frustration of trying to win against a formless enemy that couldn't be seen or named or pinned down. He would back out the station wagon and start up the road, telling himself each time that tonight he would surely find one; all he wanted, all he needed, was one, and he could use the one to get others. Four times he went back to the trailer camp where Teet had lived. But it was more than a year since anyone had heard of him. Although everyone remembered his leaving, nobody knew where he had gone.

He hired five transients to help steam the beds. Three showed up and he brought them out their lunch and dinner for fear they wouldn't come back if he let them out of his sight. They worked until nine o'clock and he paid them and never saw them again. The next day a letter he had mailed to Teet was returned, stamped "address unknown."

At the end of the week Parrish drove into Hartford to put an advertisement in the paper, even though he knew that was no way to get tobacco help. On the way home, passing Tower's General Store, he spotted Addie, her arms full of bundles of groceries, and wondered whether to even bother to ask her. Then he thought that he ought to stop, anyway, and pick up a new ratchet for tightening tent-cloth wire, and as long as he was here—even though he knew what she would say—he might as well talk to Addie. Without the smallest hope of succeeding, he pulled over and called to her.

"Parrish, lover!" she screamed.

"Where've you been, Addie?" He got out and came up to her. "I've been looking for you for two weeks."

She giggled. "I moved. I'm married now."

"That's great, Addie. Come on over and I'll buy you a beer."

"My husband'ud kill me—a han'some fella like you!" Addie screamed.

"Where you working this year, Addie?"

"Lucy and I went to Stepowicz'."

"You want to come back to Sala's?"

"Sala workin' again?" Addie affected surprise, stalling for time. Parrish knew it didn't take two weeks for news to get around the Valley, but he went along with her little act.

"I'm working it, Addie."

"You, Parrish!" she shrieked.

"No one I'd rather have than you, Addie."

"Ah—you! You was always a great lover!"

"You and Lucy are the two best tobacco girls in the Valley."

Addie looked at him over her bundles. "Lucy comin'?" she said, with disbelief.

"If she comes, will you, Addie?"

The beady eyes in the fat face were suspicious. "She say she'd come?"

"Why do you doubt it?"

" 'Cause it's takin' a big chance. If she leaves a Raike farm and comes to you an' anythin' happens, maybe he won't take her back."

"What's going to happen?"

Addie didn't answer. Parrish looked at her fat pig face over the grocery bags and thought, What was the use. "O.K., Addie," he said.

"Anyways, I wish you a lotta luck, Parrish."

Parrish watched her walk to the curb with her bundles to wait for a bus. Luck, he thought, angrily. Luck. Jinx. How could you talk down this kind of superstition? How could you beat a thing that made no sense but had such a grip on these people that he couldn't even make a crack in it? One was all he needed—just one—but there was no weakness anywhere in this wall of fear. No matter where he tapped, nothing yielded.

Parrish started back to the car. He was beginning to wonder whether there was any point in buying the ratchet, whether, in fact, there was any sense in trying to go on. Then he caught himself, angrily. He had made up his mind that he was going to do this, and somehow, somewhere, he would find somebody who would come to work for him—even if it was somebody no one else would take. Even if it meant transients and nothing but transients, and a different crew every day and sobering them up every night, he was going to work that land. Even if he had to cut down to ten acres or five or two. There was one way to end jinx talk and that was to prove the jinx had not worked. He turned around to go back to buy the ratchet.

"Hey—boy—"

Parrish felt a tug on his arm and turned and found himself looking down at an ancient figure in a long house dress and a sweater, the same old mustard kerchief on her head. It was old Mary.

"Well, Mary!" Smiling, he put an arm around the shrunken old shoulders. Her face was brown and wrinkled and looked a hundred years old, but the eyes were sharp. "Come on, Mary, I'll buy you a drink. Addie turned me down."

"I drink hot water and lemon," Mary said. "Whisky on Christmas."

"You look better than when I left, Mary."

"Boy—" Mary thumped his chest—"I come work for you."

"Ah, Mary, you're kidding!"

"When we start?"

He took her rough hand, almost covered with brown spots. "You don't want to work for me, Mary."

"You don't want me?" she demanded.

"Sure, Mary, I want you. But everyone else is afraid to take a chance." He nodded toward Addie, watching from the curb.

"Ah, her. Too fat. No guts. I'm an old woman and I know. Tobacco like a baby—sometimes little fellow make better baby than big fellow."

Parrish couldn't help laughing. He threw his arms around her and kissed her and she pushed him away, pleased and embarrassed.

"Ha—see!" Mary jerked her old head toward Addie, who had wandered back a few steps from the curb. "Now you give her big troubles. She don't know what to do. You big, sexy-lookin' fella, she think maybe she like better work for you than Stepowicz. Here she come, ask you coupla questions."

"Hey, Parrish," Addie yelled. "Lucy said for sure she wouldn't come?"

Parrish smiled at Mary with pure love. He had one of the old ones. Very old. "Lucy's coming, Addie."

"Ya—ya," Mary yelled at her. "Lucy an' me we work good farm this year."

Addie shifted her bundles. "How about if I talk to my husband and let you know, huh? He don't trust that Stepowicz. It's his cousin." Her bus came and she struggled up the steps. "I'll give you a buzz, Parrish. Maybe tonight."

Mary poked her elbow into Parrish's ribs. "Hey, boy, you know what job I do for you this year?"

"What you gonna do, Mary?"

She winked a bright eye at him. "How about I drive tractor, hey? Pretty good, hey?" She broke into a cackle of a laugh and trudged up the steps to Tower's store.

29

PARRISH switched off the tractor and sat still a moment, hand on the steering rod, feeling the grit of dust on his face. It was getting too dark to plow. With the tractor quiet he could hear the frogs talking in the ponds—the quick peeps and the deep rumble of bulls. In the last glimmer of reflected light he squinted into the field, cursing that he couldn't squeeze in a little more time and finish it. But it was no use.

It seemed that no matter how much he worked he never caught up. Every day, after he drove home his little nervous crew that was too small to work twenty acres, he came back and worked himself until dark. He was barely managing to keep the minimum pace, and soon the cloth would start to go up and he would need more help still. And, he thought, he would probably have less. Only today when he drove the crew home he could feel their sullen uneasiness. They had passed Prentiss's old place just as Lemmie was coming out of the driveway and Lemmie had looked hard at the women and they at him, with a silence that had said too much. One little setback, no matter how small—or one good offer from another farm—and someone would quit, and when that happened what could he do to hold the others?

Fighting off discouragement that he knew would break over him like a giant wave if he let it, Parrish climbed out of the tractor and went over to the barn to close up for the night. He was just sliding the bolt when he heard unsteady footsteps in the driveway and he turned and peered into the darkness to see who was coming.

"Buster?"

Parrish recognized Lewis Post's voice and smelled the whisky before he distinguished his face in the darkness and, with quick annoyance, he started toward the garage.

Lewis caught his arm. "Buster, I come for my cloth."

"What!"

"My cloth. Sala always gimme my cloth."

"My God, are you working that land again?"

"I allers worked." Lewis drew himself up. "Even when Sala din't, I worked. I don't give up easy—not what's rightfully mine. Now, how about my cloth?"

"Go ask Sala for it." Parrish walked on to the apartment. "It's his cloth."

Lewis hurried along beside him. "Buster—he gives it to me, you gonna let me have a truck to cart it over?"

"Ask Sala that, too. He owns the trucks."

"He owns everything around here, don't he?" Lewis brought his face so close Parrish could see the bloodshot eyes.

"That's right."

"An' it ought to be me workin' it, not you. I was the one oughta had the offer of it. I guess I got some rights."

Parrish pushed away the foul-smelling face. "Go ask for your cloth and leave me alone."

"An' maybe I will yet." Lewis sneered. "What I hear, you ain't doin' much."

"I'm doing great."

"Yeah? That why your help's lookin' around, gettin' ready to move on?"

Parrish froze.

"I see 'em—couple of 'em. Only tonight, talkin' to Lemmie—"

"Who?" he burst out and instantly regretted it.

"Now wouldn't you like to know?" Lewis lurched off toward Sala's house. "Wouldn't you just bust to know?"

Slamming the door behind him, Parrish went upstairs and threw himself down on the sofa, trying to ease out of the tiredness and tension. He was almost asleep when he started and forced himself up. Three times he had fallen asleep here on the sofa and awakened the next morning stiff and cramped. Tomorrow was Sunday but he had to finish plowing and begin harrowing.

He walked into the kitchen to look for something to eat and found a doughnut, dried out because he'd forgotten to wrap it up, and poured himself a glass of milk and leaned against the open window, feeling the cool night air on his face, looking moodily out into the darkness. The moon was just coming up, a sliver alongside the doghouse over the barn. He heard Lewis Post wandering down the drive and wondered whether Sala had given him cloth.

He wondered, too, if Gladstone and Cartwright would come and bring others as he had asked them to. Soon he would have to decide whether to plant the number-seven field and the number eleven, where the woods ended and the land ran right alongside Prentiss's, or play it safe and let those two lie idle. They were two of the best fields and he hated to pass them by. Discretion was the better part of valor, but he hated to give in. He wondered about Teet—where he had gone. He wondered which of his crew had been talking to Lemmie.

The night air was waking him up. The fresh smell of lilac came from below, stirring in him a restless wishfulness for something besides work and dust. He turned from the window and drank down the milk and threw away the dry doughnut. He ought to get out of here. Someplace he ought to find a girl and just get out, even if only for a little while—not necessarily one to go to bed with, just one to be with. A little breeze carried the scent of lilac into the room. He remembered that Ellen had said Paige would be home this weekend. Twice before when Ellen had said she would be in he had been tempted to call her and had not. Tonight, he decided, he would try.

They sat on a sofa in the small cocktail lounge of an old inn a few miles out of Hartford, a place with wide floor boards and unlit logs piled in a stone fireplace, baking ovens showing to one side.

"It's terrible," Paige said when he had finished telling her about his crew.

"Uh-huh."

"Just outrageous!"

"It exists, and I can't seem to do much about it," Parrish said. "Maybe my approach is wrong. Maybe I don't invite confidence."

"You're not giving up!"

"Hell, no!"

"Good," she said. "Good for you."

Parrish was glad he had told her. Paige had started out the evening almost as cool and aloof as the last time, but now she was mad and all that beautiful righteous indignation was breaking through. Seeing it, Parrish grinned like a kid who'd lost his pet dog and found it again.

"Don't the bums wander through any more?" she said.

"So far I've had an even dozen. They work a couple of days for bottle money and move on."

"Damn bums!" Paige said.

"Watch your language." Parrish grinned. "Bums are my favorite people these days. I haunt the back roads looking for them because I figure every one I sober up I can get two days work out of."

Paige frowned, looking straight ahead of her at the unlit fireplace, and Parrish noticed again how well she turned herself out these days and thought once more of his pleasure at finding her not so much changed, after all.

"Parrish," she said presently, "it's going to be awfully hard to do it with just bums."

"Paige," he said, "I'm going to farm twenty acres and if I have to do it with bums, that's how it will be."

Paige turned and looked at him a moment, the cocoa eyes shining the way they used to, and impulsively she leaned her head against his shoulder and said, "Parrish, it's good to have you back. I'd almost forgotten how impossible and stubborn you could be. And how much I missed you when you left. And how I cheered that you had gone."

He'd almost forgotten, too, Parrish thought, the feeling he used to have that nobody ever sounded so true a note as Paige.

"I *knew* something was wrong," she said, "when you called so suddenly."

"It wasn't that." Parrish stretched out his legs, feeling very much better already for looking at something besides dirt. "I'd just finished working and I bumped into old Lewis Post, who always riles me up, and suddenly

I felt it was spring and a nice night and I wanted to be with someone, so I called you."

Paige smiled a little. "Do you remember the first time I met you, Parrish? You were going out to Lewis Post's then. You gave me a ride."

"You and your bicycle."

"That's right." She paused. "And Anson was afraid you'd take me to Lewis's and he'd be drunk."

Parrish nodded, surprised that she had voluntarily mentioned Anson. "He *was* drunk. Potted."

"I was eating a strawberry ice-cream cone. I was so impressed—had a terrible argument about you with my family that night. Everyone was awfully upset because I was quite unruly. Then I calmed down and promised to behave and they patted me on the head and I was a good girl after all. One of my fondest memories."

"I was pretty impressed with you, too." Parrish grinned. "You kept hanging over the back of the chair with your legs. Talking to Alison on the lawn."

"You weren't impressed at all. You were all taken up with Alison, even then. And she with you. She kept looking over at you."

"Did she?" It was talking about two other people who had loved each other in another age.

Paige watched him for a moment and then turned straight again, her smooth blond head back against the sofa. "Well, anyway, that's a lesson everyone should learn, isn't it? Be a good girl and do as we say and we will love you. Everyone loves a good girl."

"Or is it just the opposite?"

"You mean everyone loves a bad girl?"

Parrish grinned. "Don't ask me. I can't tell 'em apart."

"That's just the brave talk of a craven lot. It sounds so reckless and fascinating. Bad girl! But actually nobody wants her."

"They don't?"

"Uh-uh. She's bad because she's disobeying the rules of the game and all the world loves obedience."

"Paige, dear." Impulsively, he took her hand. "Drink your drink. You're not a bad girl. You're a very good girl."

"It's a lesson that really should be taught in kindergarten," she said, letting her hand stay in his. "Life is a deal. Love traded for obedience. Shall we go, Parrish? Another drink and I'll start to consider who gets the worst of the bargain."

A fog had settled in and he had to drive back slowly. "When will you be home again?" he asked.

"I never know." Paige shrugged. "I'm through soon. Another month."

"What will you do then?"

"I don't know, Parrish. I should think about it, but I don't." She waited a moment. "I was going to get married the day after graduation, and since I've abandoned that idea I haven't found a good replacement."

As the land dipped into a little valley the fog thickened and he had to concentrate on picking out the road.

"I worked last summer in the Valley Children's Home," Paige said.

"Did you like it?"

"It was awful. I could never go back—I couldn't bear it."

"I suppose someone has to take care of those kids."

"Oh, there are plenty of people who are dying to do that. Plenty." She sat up, looking straight ahead. "You know what Anson said when he heard what I was trying to do for them?"

"What'd he say?"

"He said, 'You're wasting your time. I know those little monsters.'"

"What were you trying to do?"

"I don't know how you'd describe it." Paige gave a little laugh. "I guess you'd say I was teaching them to break the rules and live a little."

Parrish laughed.

"Parrish, it's all so damned regimented over there! The matron is a top sergeant. She's what Edgar calls a trained, disciplined social worker, and how she cracks the whip! She knows all about vitamins and calories and duty to the church and cleanliness and schedules, but she doesn't even know the meaning of the word joy. And the people who come to help! The wealthy doing their duty to society. Ugh! It makes them feel so superior."

Parrish grinned, both at Paige's intensity and because he recognized a lot of truth in what she said.

"Not all, of course," she said. "Some were actually very kind, but they're in the minority."

"Well, that eliminates the Children's Home," Parrish said.

"They wouldn't want me again anyway. Edgar almost died all summer with fear of what I'd do next." She laughed and then sobered and said, "Actually, that was the beginning of the end for Anson and me. It's funny how things work out, isn't it? I don't know whether it's all a cruel accident or a diabolical scheme."

Paige fell silent and Parrish hoped, now that she had started, she would go on and tell him the rest; but she remained silent. In the yellow beam of the headlights the fog swirled, lifting briefly to show clearly the damp white-lined road, and then settling in again, blanketing the countryside so that they seemed completely alone, just the two of them in the night.

No one passed them. The moon and stars were gone behind the fog, the only sound was the soft slush of the tires on the road. Parrish could hear Paige's soft regular breathing as she sat, head back on the seat, the way she always had when they used to ride around together years ago.

Suddenly he remembered those other times. Never, he thought, had it been just for pleasure, but always to escape something—the night he had crashed into the country club looking for Edgar, and Paige had gone out to his car and waited for him; the first night Stepowicz had irrigated, which had been the beginning of that long, terrible summer that had ended things with Raike and with Alison, too; that night, way, way back, when Raike had found her letter from Anson, the beginning of what she thought had ended badly but what Parrish considered had ended very well.

"How," he said, after a while, "was it the beginning of the end?"

"What end?"

"With Anson."

"We argued about it," she said. "Not so much during the summer as later. In October he took me to a faculty party at Harvard. There were a few practicing social workers there and a lot of theorists." She hesitated and then went on, "I just happened to say what I told you before, that more people do social work because it makes them feel superior than out of kindness. I don't know how it happened to come out. I wasn't looking for trouble. I was really trying to be agreeable. I said it quite without malice. Anson—" she let out a little sigh—"Anson was speechless with shock. It started quite an argument."

"Was it so important to him?"

"Yes! Isn't that a surprise?" Now Paige seemed to want to talk about it and not to mind so much. "He said I shouldn't have said it and I argued that I had a perfect right to, that it was no worse my saying that, there, than his coming to the country club and being so contemptuous of everyone around."

She slid down a little on the seat and looked at the wet windshield. "I was defending a lot of people I care nothing about. That makes sense, doesn't it?"

"It makes sense."

"We tried to patch it up," she said. "But to me he was becoming just a charming fraud. And after a while he wasn't even charming any more. He was trying to make me over into something he wanted me to be. And the more he tried, the more deliberately I went the other way. Poor Anson— he had some bad moments, too." She laughed. It wasn't bothering her so much now.

The fog was starting little streams down the windshield and crickets and frogs called out of dark hiding places. Parrish looked down at the face beside him and saw that it was quite calm now. Lightly his hand went over her smooth blond hair and moved across her cheek, and he thought that here had been a grease stain the first time he saw it.

"But I should have known better, Parrish. I learned at a very early age that love is a bargain. People I loved always loved me only sometimes, only when I behaved as they wanted, when I was the person they wanted me to be. And when I was not, they had to change me. Of all people, I should have known that the kind of love I imagined Anson and I had could not exist."

"You only picked the wrong man, Paige."

"No," she said. "Anywhere you look, it's the same. Love becomes a license to start changing. One changes and one is changed. But I couldn't love a man who would let me change him. And I couldn't let him change me. I'm just not cut out for that game, although it took me a long time to learn it. Do you ever wonder, Parrish, why that is such a hard lesson to learn? Why is it that grown people can be sensible about everything else and yet, when it comes to love, let themselves hope for miracles?"

Peering carefully into the fog, Parrish reached down on the seat and found Paige's hand and kissed her fingertips the way he used to, feeling them warm and firm against his lips, and he thought of how deeply Anson had hurt her, and that the hurting was Anson's fault, but not the depth of it.

30

A GUST OF rain blew against Sala's dining-room windows and involuntarily Parrish looked up. A moment ago the clouds had thinned and whitened and the rain had let up briefly, but now once again the sky was a heavy gray, the rain coming fast and fine, and it looked as though it would continue, for a while anyway.

It was only because it was raining that Parrish was taking off this time to have dinner with Sala. Otherwise he would have stopped for a sandwich when he took the crew home, and he would have worked until he couldn't see any longer, as he did every night because the work was increasing and his crew was not. Even while he sat here, his mind kept wandering off—to his crop, to his crew, to all the things that had to be done but that the rain was delaying. If it stopped, he could get out and pin cloth. And later tonight he had to try to fix the pickup truck. This afternoon it had failed to start and he'd had to transport the crew in the big truck, which was not good. Now that the cloth was going up, it *should* be necessary to use the big truck everyday, but it wasn't. The sad little group was lost in it, and it had had the effect of pointing up to them how painfully small was their number.

Remembering, Parrish stopped eating a moment and was staring at his plate when he realized that Sala had spoken to him. "I'm sorry," he said. "What did you say?"

"I said you should begin to make some arrangements for selling your crop," Sala said. "You should know where it's going."

Parrish nodded. "I will. As soon as I can hire a couple more people so I can take off the time."

It was brightening up a little in the west. Maybe if it stopped he could still get out and get some cloth up and work on the truck with a flashlight after dark. They were far behind on sewing—they were behind on everything.

"You still have time to cut back, Parrish," Sala said. "You don't have to work twenty acres."

Parrish knew Sala was right. If he didn't find more help soon he would have to do it. Aware of this, he was working the side next to Prentiss's last. He'd plowed it last and he still hadn't harrowed it or put up the cloth. Only today he had decided to go on just until the weekend, and if he still hadn't heard from Gladstone and Cartwright he would cut back. He would give up the fields on that side.

"Mary is going to bring in some kids as soon as school is out," he told Sala. "Two grandchildren and some others she's dug up."

"That's good as far as it goes, Parrish, but you can't run a farm with just children."

"I know." He let out a sigh that carried in it more discouragement than he had intended to show. He would never have believed superstitious fear could be such a powerful agent in keeping people away. It was as though the place were infected with a pestilence, quarantined, shutting others out and sickening the ones who were here. They were a silent, gloomy crew, working as though they carried weights on their backs. He understood now that John, with his yelling about Speedarene and his insults to Addie, had been keeping them happy and working better. A couple of times Parrish had tried it, but it had fallen flat. It took more than a few hollow words to break through fear.

"Why do you keep looking at the window?" Sala said.

"If the rain stops I can get some cloth pinned yet before it gets dark."

Sala sat back and considered him thoughtfully. "Parrish, I'm beginning to think I didn't do you much of a favor."

Parrish managed a cheerfulness he didn't feel. "Oh, you know anyone can work more than eight hours a day without harm."

"I never heard of anyone out there pinning cloth alone in the dark."

"I get ahead that way. The girls can sew it faster than I can pin it in the daytime. John came up last night and the night before to help me. Can you imagine—John! The way he always complained that he got his fill of tobacco during working hours."

"Don't worry about John. This farm is his baby. If he hadn't signed a contract and already organized the farm for Tom Holden, he'd have worked for you this year. He'll be with you next year."

Parrish knew Sala intended it as a statement of confidence. He wished he felt the confidence himself.

The maid came in to clear the table and Sala took out his cigars and with a smile offered one, as he always did, to Parrish, who always declined. When the maid had finished Parrish said, "How old is the battery in the pickup truck?"

"Why?"

"The engine didn't start this afternoon. I thought maybe the battery was gone. I'm going over a little later to check it."

"Call Tower's and have them send someone over," Sala said, firmly.

"It may be just some little thing—spark plugs wet from the rain or something."

"All right," Sala said. "But don't stay up all night working on it. If you don't fix it right away, call the garage in the morning."

The sky darkened again in the west, the rain coming harder. He might as well forget about working outside tonight.

"Parrish," Sala said, "if you contract with Raike for the crop, he'll see that you have a crew."

Parrish looked up quickly. "I don't want to contract with Raike."

"Your problems would be over."

"I'll sell to somebody else."

"Raike will put in a crew. He'll do anything to insure getting these leaves. And he'll pay you well."

"I'd like to think there's something he can't buy."

Then he thought suddenly that this might be Sala's way of pulling out —of telling him he hadn't raised a crew and that he couldn't invest any more in certain failure. There was no denying it, no one on earth could handle a crop almost alone, even working all day and most of the night.

"Do you want me to do it?" he said. "Do you want me to contract with Raike?"

"No."

Carefully Parrish looked at Sala to see if he meant it.

"I only want you to know that he pays the best price," Sala said. "You'll make money and it would be a way out of your labor problems."

"If I wanted his money I could go back to him and get it," Parrish said. "I'll sell it somewhere else. Tom Holden—"

"But it would be hard for Tom to help you with a crew," Sala said. "He's not in this area at all."

"I wouldn't ask him to. It would really be asking him to fight Raike, and why should Tom take on a fight for me? I'll sell him the leaves when they're ready. He'll pay a decent price and that's all I want. If Raike pays more, he gets it back one way or another. With Judd Raike you get nothing for nothing. I found that out."

Then Parrish stopped, not certain of what Sala had had in mind bringing this up. If Sala was asking for reasonable security, he would have to give it, and if he was asking for absolute assurance through a contract with Raike, that was his right. He had no business being stubborn with Sala's money.

Sala stood up, took a bottle of brandy and two glasses from the buffet and led Parrish into the library. While he drew the curtains and turned on the lights and then poured the brandy, Parrish watched him carefully and thoughtfully.

"If you're worried about your investment," he said, "tell me and I'll contract with Raike."

Sala smiled and handed Parrish a glass of brandy and sat at his desk before he answered. "I'm not worried, Parrish."

"It's your money tied up here," Parrish said. "If it will make you feel better, I want to know it and I want to do it."

"No, Parrish." Sala smiled again. "It would make me feel very much worse." He fingered his manuscript on the desk. It had grown thicker since Parrish last saw it. Now he turned a few pages thoughtfully. "Do you know, Parrish, how cigars first came to be made in this area?"

"I never thought about it."

"It was during the War of 1812. There was a woman named Sally Prout lived not too far from here. Her husband was a peddler. You've heard of the Yankee peddlers?"

Parrish nodded, feeling the brandy warm through him, relaxing him and at the same time sharpening thoughts of his unhappy little crew and giving birth to a melancholy feeling of discouragement. It was not the end of everything, he told himself—he could still cut back to half the acreage.

"The blockade during the war cut off Prout's supply of merchandise," Sala went on. "He had always sold manufactured products, clothing and household goods, from England and the Continent—France, Belgium. So Sally, who was an enterprising New England housewife, rolled up tobacco and made cigars and sent him out to sell them instead. Did very well, too." Sala raised his brandy glass. "People manage, Parrish. Things are rarely exactly as they ought to be, but people manage."

Parrish made an outward show of agreeing, but the story did little to relieve his depression. He finished his brandy. It was dark now and raining harder, but he still had to look at the pickup truck.

Closing the side door behind him, he stood a moment on the porch and watched the rain coming down in sheets, soaking the porch floor all the way to the door, glistening in the path of the light from the house. He watched and the melancholy of defeat grew. He might as well face up to the cold fact that he had a small, unhappy crew that wasn't getting any bigger, and that there was a strong possibility that discouragement and fear would win over these few, persuading them to quit and take more certain jobs. He wouldn't bet a dime that Addie would last another week. Pride was pride, and Sala was being more than decent, but Parrish had no right to pour money that was not his into something he knew he couldn't finish. A sheet of rain whipped against him and he turned up the collar of his raincoat and started down the steps. He might as well go look at the truck and call the garage if he couldn't fix it.

He was walking across the driveway when a pair of headlights came into sight down the road, slowed at Sala's entrance, and turned in, flashing between the trees. Parrish stopped in the driveway and stood in the rain, waiting to see who it was.

A terribly battered old car, making an awful racket, chugged and rattled up the drive, and Parrish squinted into the headlights, hoping it was another migrant worker ready to put in a couple of days for liquor money. Rain trickled down his neck and he pulled his collar tighter, waiting. At last the car made the hill. The motor rattled and died and the door groaned open. Taking his time, a bearded man stepped out. Parrish started to walk over to meet him.

"Christ's sake!" A voice came to him through the rain.

Parrish stopped, hardly believing his ears, and then started to run.

"Christ's sake!" the voice said again.

"Teet!"

"Christ's sake," Teet said a couple of times more. "You'd think if a man had work he'd look up his old friends!"

Parrish threw his arms around Teet and slapped his back.

"Chris', kid," Teet said, "I was workin' way the hell up in Greenfield—took a couple of weeks for the news to get up there that they was good jobs again down here. An' then I had to get my trailer down here—Chris', it takes me a week to even find all my kids. Figgered you'd be takin' down before I made it an' I'd miss all the fun. . . ."

Deep in thought, Parrish hurried alongside the seedbeds, putting down empty boxes and picking up those half filled with plants. Only Mary and two of the grandchildren she had brought in were pulling, and he watched Mary's brown hands moving swiftly in and out of the thick bed of plants, never stopping, and patted her thin shoulders affectionately. Mary looked up and bobbed her head up and down with a look that said she understood that he wanted to give her more help here at the beds and would if he could and that it was all right.

"Go," she said. "Go see in the fields. Be all right here."

Parrish picked up her box and put down an empty one and went back and climbed into the truck.

For a few days it had seemed that Teet's arrival was a turning point and everything would be wonderful. Word had come from Gladstone that he and Cartwright were on their way, bringing with them another Jamaican, the slow-moving Willis. Then they had arrived and for a little while there was enough help and the crew was cheerful and it looked as though the worst was over and things were working out at last. But the change and the optimism were short-lived.

All along, Parrish had told himself that when the crop was in the ground the crew would consider it a milestone and feel some sense of achievement and relax. But in fact, he now realized, it was working out just the opposite. In the ground the plants seemed more vulnerable, exposed at last to the countless dangers of tobacco, and his crew were growing more, rather than less, nervous. A little each day, Parrish saw the superstitious fear returning and beginning to touch the Jamaicans, too.

Now the crop was almost in the ground. Only the two fields along the fence were left, the two next to Prentiss's that he always worked last. They were planting there today, just starting number seven, and all morning the nervousness had been growing. Parrish told himself that he had to do something, but he didn't know where to begin.

Driving along the edge of the woods he came to the fence between the two farms, where the number-seven field began, and stopped, backing the truck up against the water barrels to refill them from the fresh supply he'd brought. The tractor was coming toward him, nearing the end of the row, the three Jamaicans and an old man riding the setter. Nearby, Lucy and Addie were setting the pole rows. Parrish got out and walked around to the back of the truck.

He was reaching up, one hand on the rail, when he stopped short. About twenty feet the other side of the fence he saw Lemmie, just standing there, watching his crew. Parrish stood still, one hand gripping the truck, staring coldly over the fence. It was the first time he'd been close to Lemmie since he'd been back, the first time since the night of Tully's fire. Since then Lemmie had done well, he knew. His reward had been a promotion to area supervisor in charge of the Prentiss, Tully and Oermeyer farms and the three beyond. He was stockier now and wore a better-looking shirt and a hat with a broader brim pulled down at a confident angle. He stood motionless, hands in his pockets, looking over at Sala's land.

Still Parrish gripped the truck body. He didn't like it, Lemmie's standing there, didn't like him watching his crew, or the look on his face. Fear ran through him. Lemmie knew how to make trouble. He was an old hand at playing dirty, and he wouldn't hesitate a minute. Then, abruptly, Parrish shook himself. He was getting as bad as the crew. Deliberately, seeing the crew coming close, he made himself climb up onto the truck and turn his back, unconcerned, to the fence.

He saw Lucy and Addie, planting the pole row, steal a nervous look over their shoulders and plant a few more plants and glance back again. Silently Parrish came down off the truck and stole another quick glance himself at Lemmie. When he looked back he saw that Lucy and Addie were watching him, tight-lipped. They looked away, letting their eyes creep over again to Lemmie.

"What you looking at?" Parrish snapped impatiently.

"What you looking at yourself?" Addie said.

"Not a goddam thing." He filled their buckets of water for them and reached onto the truck for a box of plants. "You're working on this farm, Addie, not that one."

Addie didn't answer, but her look said she wasn't sure she was working here much longer. The tractor finished the row, coming out into the path, and Gladstone and Cartwright climbed out of the setter and went over to the drinking cup and took a drink and then they, too, shot uneasy glances over at Lemmie.

Parrish watched angrily. They could say what they wanted about the place being jinxed and call it luck or lack of it, but deep down they knew, too, that it wasn't luck. Even though they didn't understand it, they realized the trouble came from Raike and felt that they were next. The sense of impending disaster was everywhere. It wasn't good. Futility bred poor work. And it wasn't good because they were right. He should have stayed away from this side.

The sleepy Willis, Gladstone's and Cartwright's friend, eased himself out of the setter, and he, too, looked at Lemmie with baleful, frightened eyes, and even Teet shrugged impatiently and met Parrish's gaze, unsmiling, to say this was something to reckon with. It was one hell of a crew, Parrish thought. Addie never laughed or shrieked, Gladstone and Cartwright hadn't sung since the week they arrived, Mary didn't grumble, Teet offered no philosophy mixed with colorful epigrams. It was a lost battalion, waiting to be blown up.

"Come on," he muttered. "Let's go."

Addie and Lucy wandered over to the next pole row. Parrish took the fresh boxes of plants to the setter. He'd have to do something, and again he asked himself where to begin. How could you break into this kind of fear, especially when there was good reason for it?

"Oh, Gawd!" he heard Addie mutter. "Will you look who's comin'?"

Parrish looked up in time to see Lewis Post emerging around the corner of the cloth, and he thought, Trouble never comes alone. Belligerently he leaned against the tractor, glaring, and waiting for Lewis to reach them.

"Hi, Buster!" Lewis Post wore a ragged coat buttoned over his bloated stomach, and no shirt, his chest showing below a dirty yellow handkerchief tied around his neck.

"What do you want?"

"I come for my plants." The loose mouth worked into a grin, baring the spaced teeth.

"What are you talking about?"

"My plants. Sala allers gives me my plants."

"Maybe Sala did, but I don't."

"You gotta, Buster. Sala'll make you."

The crew had stopped working and drifted back uneasily, coming closer to listen. "You go take it up with Sala."

"I can't," Lewis whimpered. "He ain't home."

"Then come tomorrow. He's always home on Wednesday."

Lewis's eyes narrowed to slits and his face took on a sudden mean look. "You watch yourself, Buster."

Now the crew had closed into a watchful little circle.

"I guess you kinda forget who's got rights here, more'n you."

"Go on," Parrish said. "Go on home, you're holding up work here. Come back tomorrow and tell your troubles to Sala."

"Now don't think you can tell me what to do!" Suddenly, Lewis Post threw a hard blow at Parrish's shoulder that sent him spinning backward because it was so unexpected. Recovering his balance, Parrish lunged forward, catching a quick glimpse of his tight-faced crew and then of Lemmie grinning. Lemmie had moved closer, he saw, and stood now about ten feet away from the fence.

"Just watch your step," Lewis Post yelled. "Watch it, Buster, because I got rights here an' I know plenty an' I can do you a lotta harm. I can do real damage, me an' my boys. They ain't exactly cripples, you know, my boys."

Teet stole a quick look over the fence and Parrish, following his glance, saw Lemmie, standing only five feet away now, light a cigar and flick the burning match toward the fence. It landed in the dirt and went out. He could do that any time! Any time, he could come here and do that, flick it just a little farther and the cloth over this whole field and a couple more would go up in flames before anyone could even get here. Any time at all, and no one would know. And so could Lewis or one of his boys.

In a wild burst of rage Parrish was over the fence, grabbing the startled Lemmie by the neck.

"Don't you ever do that again!" He pointed to the match in the dirt. "Don't you ever do that any place near here again."

"Hey!" Lemmie yelled, dumfounded.

Parrish tightened his grip around his neck. "And get away from my land. Get your eyes off it. And don't come back looking at it any more."

"Listen, you punk—" Lemmie tried to break out of his grip.

"You listen, Lemmie," Parrish yelled. "I don't want any trouble with you. Keep your eyes off this land. Stay away."

"Let go me!"

"And don't think you can pull any tricks on me, like you pulled on the others, because I know all about you!"

"Get your stinkin' hands off me!" Lemmie's face was purple as he pounded Parrish's hands.

"And I know all Raike can do, too. All the others, the poor devils you did in for him—"

"I can't hear you." Lemmie clawed into him.

"They only tried to buck Judd Raike—that's how they learned about playing dirty. I was trained by him. More than you. He just uses you because you're dirty enough and crooked enough to do what he wants—and because he's got enough on you locked in his drawer to keep you quiet. And you know who found it out for him? I did."

Lemmie whirled about with hatred. "So you was the one—bastard!"

"He used you, Lemmie. But he trained me. I was scheduled to be the bastard to take over using you."

"I'll get you yet, punk!" Lemmie yelled.

"You won't get me, Lemmie, because I know all the tricks. Yours and his. I know how he works, and if anything happens here I'll know where it came from. We got no mold here, no worms, no disease, fungus, blight, or any damn thing you can think of."

Lemmie shook so hard to break free that his broad-brimmed hat fell off, showing his face purple to the roots of his hair.

"Also—" Parrish stood over him threateningly—"no fires, Lemmie. Like Tully."

"You're crazy! Crazy with the heat."

"I saw you." Parrish lowered his voice. "I saw you do it that night. I was driving back and forth, remember? Between Colebrook and the Ridge. And that's known as arson, Lemmie. And people go to jail for arson."

Now there was real fear in Lemmie's eyes and Parrish let go of him and walked back to the fence. "This fence is between you and me, Lemmie. Keep it there. You stay ten feet on your side and if I ever catch you any closer I'll come over it and knock you across that field until you can't stand up."

He stepped back over the fence. He walked up to Lewis Post. "You got any questions?"

Lewis's eyes darted around nervously while he shook his head.

"Then get going. And if you're thinking of firing my cloth or burning my sheds, I know those tricks, too."

"You got evil in you," Lewis Post whimpered.

"Damn right."

"You got too much evil in you for one man—thinking things like that."

"Just don't forget it. I got more evil in me than any man you know. And I had training besides." He grabbed the front of Lewis's jacket. "So any low-down dirty vicious crime you can think of, I can think of worse and do it better. You're not fooling around with Sala now. Sala's a gentleman. Not me. I've got as much a criminal mind as you have."

Lewis's eyes swam around pathetically, and he drew in his shoulders and shuffled off, shaking his head and mumbling to himself. Parrish turned back to the crew, who were standing around like dummies.

"Jeez!" Teet broke into a grin of sheer delight. "I don't know as I ought to be workin' for a criminal-type character."

Lucy giggled and Addie shrieked.

"O.K., let's go! Come on, Addie!" Parrish whacked her mammoth bottom. "What do you say?"

"Parrish!" she shrieked. "You kill me!"

"That's not all I'll do to you if you don't get off your tail, Addie!"

"Parrish, you're a livin' doll!"

"Willis," he yelled.

"Hello, mon."

"Get up there, cowboy. We got no money around here for Speedarene."

"We are very poor, mon," Gladstone said. "Like they say eet, we are poor but happy, I theenk."

"I am not happy." Cartwright leaped onto the setter. "I am very onhappy, I am sorry to say eet. And nobody care for me." He threw Parrish a wide, happy grin, and the tractor rolled forward and the setter began to click out water for the plants to go into the ground.

Parrish went over that evening to tell Sala about the scene with Lemmie and with Lewis Post.

"You shouldn't have planted that field," Sala said. "It was asking for trouble."

"I know it." Parrish nodded. "I'll take it down, just to be safe."

"No," Sala said. "It's planted now. Leave it."

"What about number eleven? Shall I let it go?"

"It's all ready?"

Parrish nodded.

"Then plant it."

"It's taking an unnecessary risk."

"Parrish, if you had asked me before, early in the spring, I'd have told you not to plant it this year—to wait until your position was stronger. But now to let it go will be bad for morale and inviting trouble. Plant it. Have you any extra plants for Lewis?"

Parrish nodded.

"Then give him some."

"All right. I'll take them over tonight if you want."

"No. Let him come for them. He and his boys can pull them."

Parrish looked at him sharply.

"I'll go out there with him and see that he doesn't bother the girls or take too many."

Parrish looked away, a little embarrassed for Sala, and Sala motioned to him to get the brandy bottle and glasses and waited while he did. "Parrish, how do you feel about it now that you have a crop under cloth?"

Parrish grinned. "I feel great."

"I wish I'd been there to watch you with Lemmie," Sala said. "He's a very low type."

"Anyone in the Valley will agree with you there. Even Judd Raike."

Sala smiled over the brandy glass he was circling in his hand. "I'd have enjoyed seeing that."

"I'll do it again for you sometime when you're around."

Sala laughed out loud. Then he sipped his brandy, growing thoughtful.

"Parrish," he said after a while, "is your mind too full of this crop to talk about something serious?"

"No."

"It's nothing you have to decide right away. You shouldn't decide it until the season is over. You should give it a great deal of thought."

"All right. Tell me what it is and I'll think about it."

Sala took another slow sip of his brandy and put down the glass. "If you make out all right with your twenty acres, and if you decide when the season is over that tobacco is what you want to do—" Sala paused and motioned toward the window, toward his tent-covered fields—"I'll let you start buying this land—if you think you want it."

31

PARRISH opened the downstairs door to his apartment and stopped, his foot on the bottom step. Uneasily he glanced back out the door toward Sala's house, where he had already noticed Alison's car. He had seen it when he passed to take home the crew, and again when he returned, and he had thought only that she was visiting Sala on Tuesday this week instead of on Wednesday. But now something stirred uneasily in him. In the air here, there was a faint familiar scent. For a moment he had not been able to place it, but now he knew it and, a little troubled, he wondered what she had been doing in his apartment. Was it possible that Sala had come in here for something and she had come with him? Then he remembered that Sala was not home today.

Slowly he climbed the stairs and stopped again. He was certain now that she was inside. He pushed open the door and saw her, curled up in a corner of the sofa.

"Parrish—" Alison smiled as though it were a sweet reunion, warmly, innocently, confidently.

Parrish stood still in the open doorway. "What are you doing here?"

"Come in, darling, and shut the door." She came toward him. "I waited as long as I could for you to come to me, dear," she said. "I couldn't wait any longer."

Parrish closed the door and backed up against it, alarmed at the warring feelings already racing through him. His first angry impulse was to tell her to get out. Then, even while he thought this, he recognized all the old familiar feelings that Alison could stir up surging through him—all the desire, all the undeniable hunger, rising even at the scent of her, before the sight of her. Shaken, he stood rigidly still against the door.

She came up to him and touched his face. "Parrish, come in and sit down. I won't bite you."

He came in and sat in a chair, slid unhappily down on his spine, and stared at his shoes. They were covered with dust and there was dust on his pants up to his knees. "I can't say," he muttered, "that I was expecting you."

She smiled. "I'm here."

He moved his right shoe up over his left woolen sock and scratched at his ankle. A little film of dirt sifted out. "Look, Alison, you're married."

"Nobody knows that better than I, Parrish," she said.

"So you'd better go." The words did not come easily, or quickly.

"Parrish!" she said. "Do you really want that?"

What did you do when you felt this kind of desire for something that wasn't yours? You told yourself it was only habit and your heart pounded. You told yourself it was long dead and it pressed harder. But, above all else, you told yourself that it wasn't yours and, whatever wild crazy ideas were pushing their way into your head, that was the cold hard fact.

"You know you can't stay here!" he burst out.

Alison came over and stood next to his chair. "Do you really want me to go?"

"Yes, damn it!" Parrish struggled to his feet, feeling his face flaming. "I do."

"No, you don't!"

He looked down at Alison and turned away, striding over to the window. Next to Sala's house he could see her car, shining in the sun near a bank of roses just beginning to open small and pink, and he thought that any minute now Sala could return and there would be no possible explanation for this.

"Go on," he said, angrily. "Damn it, you're married. What do you want of me?"

"Parrish!"

"You're married," he said again, stubbornly.

"Please stop saying that. I know I'm married. I know it terribly, every minute of the day and night. I'm married to a man I loathe, I detest, I can hardly bear to look at."

"You picked him."

"He's a drunk."

"He was a drunk when you married him."

"And a weakling."

"That, too. Then as much as now." Parrish struggled to hold on to one clear, cold thought. "Leave me alone. You picked him, so now leave me alone."

"Parrish, I didn't marry him until you left me."

He sat down and covered his face with his hands. "Oh, no—not that!"

Alison was silent for a minute and Parrish kept himself from looking up at her. He heard her soft breathing in the complete quiet that could fill this place, and he caught the faint whiff of her familiar scent that by itself could fire memories. After a moment he lifted his head and saw that she was sitting again on the sofa.

"Alison, you know it's no good and you can't stay here."

"No, you're right. I can't stay here." Suddenly she was on the floor at his feet, touching his knees, touching his thighs, and looking up at him like an innocent child. "You're so beautiful, Parrish—so brown and lean—"

"You get as brown on a golf course as on a farm. It's all the same sun."

"Parrish," she whispered, her eyes pleading, "I'm so miserable! I hate him so—he's so awful! Parrish, I was such a child then and I've learned so much. Don't send me away. I need you."

Tears filmed her eyes. Gently, without thinking, Parrish raised her up from the floor, drawing her over again to the sofa.

"Parrish, there was never anything like us!" she said softly.

And then she was in his arms and her lips were under his and he felt all the familiar hunger in her that he knew so well, all the warmth, all the eagerness, and her breasts, fuller than he had known them, moved against him, and he knew that he could have her right here, right now, and he thought, how long? And, why not?

He wrenched away.

"Parrish," she whispered, "I knew we were still the same. I knew it the first night you were back—the first minute I saw you. Darling, I'll get a divorce. I was a fool—I admit it! But I've learned. I can get a divorce—"

Parrish reached up and lowered her hands from his face. "In a million years, Alison, it wouldn't work."

"It could now, darling. I can get alimony!" Alison's eyes narrowed. "I have enough on Wiley to collect a fortune."

"Alison, your father will be home any minute and this will be one hell of a spot—"

"You're right!" She got up hastily. "I'll meet you someplace, darling. Follow the highway for ten miles out—there are some motels. I'll find one and you can look for my car and we can be alone. Parrish, it's so terribly important for us to be alone."

Alison picked up her purse off the table and, leaving the door open, ran down the stairs. Through the window Parrish watched her get into her car and back around and speed down the driveway, supposedly to find a motel where he could join her and make love to her and have her again, as once he had.

Slowly he walked over and shut the door. He went into his bedroom and peeled off his dusty clothes and cursed himself for having held her and for having kissed her and it didn't stop the wanting. He took a hot shower and a cold shower and then he dressed and went downstairs. He told himself he was going for a drive to calm down.

Glancing at his watch, he saw that it was almost dinnertime. He wondered whether she would really go to a motel on the highway. Or would she think better of it once she was away from him, and go home? If she didn't come in to dinner, what would she tell them at home, Wiley and the others? She'd think of something good, he thought. You could be sure of that.

Parrish reached the main highway and turned away from Hartford, in the direction of the motels. Alison was married, he thought, but to a man she had never loved. She wasn't the only person, married, who thought of getting a divorce. How could you fight all your life against something that burned as fiercely three years later as on the day you had gone away? A divorce, she had said. But not a clean break. She would get alimony. She had enough on Wiley, she said, to collect a fortune, and then the three years would have been a good investment, a business. What was it Paige had said that night—he tried to remember—something about a trade for love. No, it was something else—obedience. He wondered where Paige got all those ideas.

Then suddenly Paige was in his thoughts, the memory of the smooth blond head back against the seat, the wide brown eyes. He had seen Paige often now that she was home for good, and the times he had stolen from work to be with her seemed, in retrospect, the only good spots in the whole terrible business of getting the farm started.

Suddenly Parrish saw that he was almost there, where the motels were, and he slowed down. What am I doing here? he thought. What if Alison is really waiting in one of those places? He could picture her, the studied effect of innocence, the knowing, restless eyes and mouth that were kin neither to innocence nor to the knowledge of Paige, who knew more but was all innocence. Is that all I want, he thought—innocence? And then: Not innocence only, and not this, either.

Then he saw Alison's car. He jammed on his brakes so hard the driver behind had to swerve left to avoid hitting him. Hastily, almost in panic, he backed off the road into a driveway to turn around and let traffic go by. She had come, and she was in there waiting for him, a few yards away—Alison, once the loveliest thing he had known, waiting for him now in a pink motel on a strange cheap bed. And he was going to stand her up.

Violently, Parrish turned the car around into the highway and pulled into the first gas station he found and put in a call to Paige. Maples said she was just driving in and Parrish told him to go and get her. He settled down in the telephone booth to wait, glancing uneasily out the window, hoping Alison would not start back and see his car before he got out of here. Impatiently he tapped his foot on the floor.

At last he heard a click on the telephone.

"Paige?" he shouted.

"Parrish, what's the matter?"

"Nothing. Nothing's the matter. Paige, can I see you tonight?"

"Parrish, I'm sorry—I have a date."

"Can you break it?"

"But I saw you just last night! Is something wrong?"

"No."

"If there is—Parrish, there *is* something wrong!"

"No," he said. "No. How about tomorrow night?"

"That'll be all right," Paige said.

Parrish hung up the telephone and hurried out to his car and drove very fast until he turned into Sala's driveway.

When he reached the garage he saw that Sala's car was still out. The breeze had died and in the evening quiet leaves reached down a little, signaling rain. Parrish started to walk. He wandered past the garage to the barn. He wondered whether Alison was still at the motel, or how late she had waited. He walked over to the number-three shed and sat on a log and put his head down on his arms crossed over his knees. And he wondered what she had thought and what she had felt when she left. After a while he raised his head and leaned back. The sun was beginning to sink behind Sala's house and nearby on a tree a vivid blue jay screeched.

Parrish was still sitting there when he heard a car come up the driveway. Realizing that it wasn't the sound of the old Rolls Royce Sala still used, he got up reluctantly, afraid it might be Alison, and walked around the shed—and then saw it was Paige.

As he came around the garage she stepped out of her car. She must have been coming in from playing tennis when he phoned, and she still wore sneakers and shorts and her hair was braided and wrapped around her head. She looked uncertainly toward the farm and then started for the door to his apartment.

"Paige—"

She stopped and waited for him to come up to her, and for a moment they faced each other silently on the gravel driveway. She looked at him, questioning, and he knew his face betrayed that something was wrong and he looked away.

Paige looked out at the tent cloth that, from here, stretched as far as the eye could see. "It looks fine!" she said.

Parrish nodded. To him it was the neatest, cleanest, most beautiful cloth in the world.

"Are you all planted?" Paige said.

He nodded again and took her hand and led her away from the driveway toward the number-three field. The luminous quiet of the end of day had settled over the fields, the sky darkening over high clouds in the east, flaming in the west, and they walked silently and unhurriedly along the dusty path, past the side cloth of the number-three field and past number four and number five. He thought that he had never known anyone else he could just be with—not saying a word and yet feeling, as he felt now, that so much was being said.

They reached the country road. Along the path there were a couple of wooden stringing horses that hadn't yet been stored away, and Parrish leaned on one and Paige stood looking around and after a while sat on the other. She drew two large hairpins out of her hair and her braids slipped down to her shoulders.

Parrish asked himself if there was the slightest doubt in his mind. He understood her now, and that there would be no offering love to Paige or asking for it and then backing out later, or making conditions, without hurting her deeply. He told himself to sleep on it, to search his soul, to be sure.

In the silence of the untraveled country road a faint bell sounded and brought an immediate smile to his lips.

"What's that?" Paige said.

"Wait till you see." Parrish stood up and moved over to the other wooden horse where she was sitting. "This is my girl friend coming."

The bell—several bells—continued and came nearer and presently she showed up, his favorite Black Angus from the neighboring farm. She had a strap of bells buckled around her middle. "She wanders," he said.

"Why is she wearing bells?"

"So the farmer can hear her and track her down. Here he comes."

Now they heard the farmer's angry call and he came along the road and whacked the cow and shouted to her and the cow just ignored him and ambled along at her own unhurried pace.

Parrish grinned. "Meanest farmer you ever saw. And he can't do a thing with her."

The bells tinkled and the cow meandered across to the other side of the road.

"Just wanders around—does as she pleases and he can't do a thing with her! I'm proud of her."

Paige laughed out loud.

Parrish turned and looked at her as she sat there, braids brushing her shoulders, smiling at the ornery cow. He was sure. He had been sure for a long time.

"Paige—" He turned her face back to his and took her in his arms. "I love you, Paige," he said.

32

THERE'S never anything halfway about Paige," Edgar said. "Before, everyone pleased her, and now nobody does."

Ellen glanced up at Edgar but didn't answer, and Parrish saw that she agreed with him, partly at least.

Edgar looked over at Parrish. "You sure she knew you were coming for her? I mean, did you make it clear that you weren't just dropping in, that you were coming for her?"

Parrish nodded, puzzled, and Edgar sighed. "She probably won't come downstairs."

"Why not?" Parrish said. It was true he had been waiting half an hour, and Paige had never kept him waiting before.

"How do I know why not? She saw you twice this week. She probably thinks you've had your ration. Come back in a few months and she'll give you another hour or so."

Parrish glanced at his watch, wondering uneasily if there was any truth in what Edgar said. Everyone was going to a party tonight in honor of Mary Holden's seventy-fifth birthday and he knew that Wiley and Alison had left an hour ago and that Ellen was waiting because he was here and Edgar only to see whether Paige would come down. Only Raike seemed in no hurry to get started. He sat across the room, reading the evening paper, taking no part in this conversation about Paige.

"You know what she's doing up there?" Edgar said. "She's deciding that she won't see you. Pretty soon she'll send down a message that she's not coming, won't even offer some flimsy excuse—"

"Edgar," Ellen said, "you're making too much of this."

"I am not making too much of it," Edgar said. "You saw what happened twice this week. Those were damn nice fellows, too."

"What happened?" Parrish said.

"Nothing nearly so serious as Edgar makes it."

"Took the trouble to call her a long way—one from Baltimore, one from Philadelphia, damned eligible fellows. She could do worse. Argued like a couple of fools over the phone just for the privilege of coming up to see her. She didn't have time for them. She was busy. I ask you—busy with what?"

"Me, maybe." Parrish grinned.

"You're just an excuse," Edgar said. "You're part of the family."

"Edgar," Ellen said, "she's had so many beaux—perhaps she just didn't care for those two."

"She never cares for any of them. Sure she's had so many—a hundred since Anson—but she's never seen any of them more than twice. The only reason we accepted Anson was because she was so queer we thought we'd better."

Ellen gave a little sigh. "We really ought to be getting over to Maizie's."

"It doesn't look right," Edgar persisted. "She's queer and she's going to end up being considered very odd. Damn it, she *is* odd." He stood up to leave. "We'll see you over there."

Ellen looked at Raike. "Are you ready, dear?"

Raike didn't answer. He was still reading the newspaper—still, Parrish noticed, on the same page. Ellen went over and touched his arm, lines of worry creeping into her face. "Mary Holden's party, dear. Are you ready to go?"

Raike put down the newspaper.

"I'll just run up for my things," Ellen said. "I'll only be a minute."

Frowning, Parrish looked at his watch, more than a little concerned now about Paige. Then he saw that Raike was watching him and he thought, a little self-consciously, that this was the first time they had been alone since their parting three years ago.

Raike heaved himself to his feet, pulling on the arm of the chair as though it was an effort, and heavily walked across the room to his humidor. With a little shock, Parrish thought that he was aging and failing every week—every day. He seemed terribly tired, with bags under his eyes, the flesh loose around his heavy chin and neck. Only the eyes, studying him now, showed any of the old fire. Slowly Raike fished a package of matches out of his pocket and concentrated on lighting his cigar. Parrish glanced out into the hall for Paige, and then walked over to the open window and looked out at the late twilight of the warm summer evening. He was beginning to believe, as Edgar had said, that Paige wasn't coming.

Raike snapped on a light and then another and Parrish turned around.

"How's your crop?" Judd Raike said.

"Everything's fine."

"Good thing you're doing. Best experience you could get."

In the shadow of the lamplight there was a curious gaunt look over Judd Raike's cheeks that spoke, even more than his heavy movements, of his failing energy. "Run into any of the usual pesky troubles?" he said.

"I've been lucky."

"Well, it's good land," Raike said. "How about money? You feeling the pinch?"

"No. I try to be careful."

Raike nodded. "You've got the idea. But don't skimp where you shouldn't. That can be expensive."

What's he driving at? Parrish wondered. He knows all this—he knows everything I do. Uneasily, he sensed that this was not a casual conversation.

"Anything you need, let me know," Raike said.

Parrish took a deep uncomfortable breath. "I think everything will be all right," he said. "It's only twenty acres."

"It's a good start. Twenty acres of top-notch leaves is nothing to sneeze at." Raike stood in the middle of the room, almost frail-looking in spite of his bulk, looking narrowly across at Parrish. "Like to have you drop in at the office one day," he said. "I've a couple things I want to talk to you about."

Parrish jammed his hands uncomfortably into his pockets but he met Raike's scrutinizing look firmly. "I'm sorry, sir, but I don't ever have any free time during your office hours. I don't have a foreman."

Raike regarded him sharply for a moment, puffing rapidly on his cigar. Then he walked over to the fireplace and sat in one of the deep chairs and motioned to the other. "Sit down."

Reluctantly Parrish started for the chair and, with considerable relief, saw Ellen come back into the room.

"All right, dear?" Ellen said to Raike.

"Leave us alone a minute," Raike said.

Surprised, Ellen stopped and then went back out again into the hall, pausing only to say, "Paige is coming, Parrish."

Edgar was right. Ellen had had to persuade Paige to come down.

"Now," Raike said. "I hear you're doing a good job out there."

"I'm trying to."

Raike cleared his throat. "I—uh—understand you're working out some kind of a deal with Sala to buy his land."

"No." Parrish wondered where he could have heard it.

"No buying arrangements?"

"The only arrangements I have with Sala are for this year's lease."

"And what are they?"

"I think I ought to ask Sala before I discuss them with you."

"That's all right," Raike said. "I like a man in business who can keep his mouth shut. Now, here's what I want you to do. You keep your mouth shut, to me and to Sala, too."

Parrish shifted uncomfortably in his chair.

"You handle that crop out there as carefully as a new baby—let Sala see you're going to be a great tobacco man. I'll buy it from you. Give me good leaves and I'll pay you a good price. A damned good price. You'll have plenty left, even after you pay Sala his lease."

One dollar, Parrish thought. There was something Raike hadn't found out.

"You make that deal to buy it, and you'll have a sizable chunk for a down payment. We'll do it again next year and you'll have more. When you own the place, you come into Raike and Company and work up to be manager. Prove your salt and you'll end up with a full share of the stock along with Edgar and Wiley and Paige. Prove your ability, son, and you get a long-term ironclad contract that will give you management of the company when you're old enough to handle it. I'll train you myself."

Raike had made his proposition. He drew a long puff on his cigar and slowly let out a line of smoke that came across to Parrish, the product of everything best of Raike's lands, the best of Cuba or Puerto Rico, the best of the Valley Broadleaf, the richest of the Shade; the best of an empire worth twenty million dollars, of which he had just been offered a one-fourth share and control. In return for coming back into slavery and a lifetime of bickering with Edgar and Wiley.

"The purchase price will be your land."

"In return for double-crossing Sala." Parrish stood up. "I can't pay the price. I haven't got it."

"You'll get it."

"I doubt it," he said. "But thanks for the offer. I appreciate your confidence. I probably couldn't live up to it."

Raike flushed. "See here, you fool, do you know what I'm offering you?"

Parrish nodded.

"Are you refusing to trade a miserable hundred acres for one quarter of Raike and Company?"

"I haven't got the hundred acres to trade."

"I told you how to get them."

"And I couldn't manage Raike and Company. I haven't the ability. I wouldn't know where to begin."

"Of course you couldn't manage it today, you idiot. I'd have to teach you. I'll train you. I'll have to work with you."

Parrish thought with horror of what that would mean. "You don't need me. The others know the business already. They grew up with it. Edgar and Wiley."

"You fool!" Raike yelled.

Ellen came hurrying in. "What is it, dear?"

"Your son's a fool!"

Ellen looked quickly over to Parrish to see what had happened, and he didn't bother to explain but walked out of the room and found Paige in the living room, and they left.

"We'll have to stop at Mary Holden's party," Paige said.

"Oh, no!"

"Of course we have to, Parrish. I wouldn't hurt Tom and Maizie for the world and neither would you."

"What's the matter, Paige?" he said.

"Is anything the matter?"

He was certain now that she had not intended to see him or to go to Maizie's either, until Ellen persuaded her, and he didn't want to waste the night at a party. He wanted to talk to her. They drove in silence to Maizie's and Parrish parked behind a very long line of cars. "How long do we have to stay?" he said.

"Parrish, you don't have to come in if you don't want to."

Parrish looked at Paige beside him. She wore a pale silk coat that was, in the dim light of the street lamp, the same color as her skin and hair, and she sat erect, with a remote look on her face that gave him a feeling that she was only a passenger, that she was not really with him tonight.

"Just tell me," he said, "how long we have to stay."

"Only long enough to seem glad we came."

How long is that, Parrish wondered, sensing that it would not be brief. Paige opened the car door and stepped out and started toward the house, and Parrish hurried to catch up to her while he asked himself what had happened. Only two nights ago he and Paige had parted the best of friends, more than friends, but tonight she was trying to be a stranger.

It was nearly midnight when he asked her for the fourth time to leave.

"You don't have to wait for me, Parrish," she answered with a meaningless smile. "I can go home with the family."

"I'll wait," Parrish said, doggedly.

"All right." She turned away. "I'll let you know."

"Paige—" he started, but now Tom Holden came up to her. Somebody was always coming up to her. He hadn't had her alone since they arrived.

"How about it, Paige?" Tom put an arm around her. "Can I lure you back to the Children's Home this summer?"

"Oh, Tom. You know how I feel about that."

Then Melissa and Lorraine joined them and Parrish clenched his teeth. "Paige, dear, do you want to meet us for lunch tomorrow at Rennie's?"

"Thank you, Melissa, but I can't."

"Melissa," Lorraine said, "why don't we make it the day after, this week?"

"I have to go to Sherry's school. She's reciting three lines in the year's-end exercises."

"Why don't we go?" Parrish whispered.

"In a little while," Paige said.

"Darling, we're all going to school. The whole damn place is having poems or worse. Could you make it more easily the day after, Paige?"

"No, I couldn't," Paige said.

Patiently Tom watched, amused, and when they had drifted off he said, "They can't get an hour of your time any more than I can. Parrish, how do you manage?"

"Tom!" Paige said. "You know I'd do anything for you!"

"Except the Children's Home," Tom said. "If you'd start there, Paige, you'd see that the two of us could get our way some of the time. Or have fun, anyway, trying."

Paige smiled. "Perhaps if I were going to be here I'd try it, Tom. Just to see how much trouble we could stir up this time."

"Where are you going?" Parrish demanded.

"I'm going to Europe, Parrish."

"What!"

"I'm going to study for a year in Paris."

"When did this happen?"

Paige shrugged. "I don't know exactly. I've been thinking about it for a long time."

"How long?"

"Oh, a long time."

Angrily Parrish stormed away, leaving her talking to Tom. He passed Alison, who turned her back as he approached, without even a nod. He walked over to an uncrowded corner. But it was too much to expect to be left alone, and a moment later Clayton and Harris came up to him.

"Man, you're an unprincipled dog." Clayton poised a pencil over a piece of paper. "We want your opinion. We're taking a poll—"

Parrish gulped his drink.

"On monogamy," Harris said.

"I'm for it," Parrish said.

"Both parties?" Clayton gasped.

"Why not?"

"You can't mean that!"

"Why are you for it?" Harris said, incredulously.

"Man, you're mad!" Clayton said. "But that's not our question. What percentage of modern marriages would you say are not monogamous? That's our question."

"How the hell do I know?"

"We're taking a poll. We have answers all the way from fifty per cent to ninety-eight per cent. What do you say?"

"I think Paige is ready to go." Parrish elbowed his way past them. "Let me know how you come out."

As soon as they were alone in the car Paige turned to him. "We can go right home, Parrish."

"Why?"

"Didn't you say you were working tomorrow?"

He looked at her and then drove in silence until he found a place where he could stop. He pulled over and shut off the ignition and turned to her, leaning back against the door, not touching her.

"All right," he said. "Now tell me what this is all about."

She didn't move or even turn her head from where she rested it back against the seat. "What is what all about?"

"You know what I'm talking about. You've been avoiding me all night."

"Parrish, I haven't been avoiding you."

"You kept me waiting an hour, hoping I'd leave."

Paige didn't answer. Her lips set in an obstinate, defiant line.

"Then you told me not to bother to come to the party, then to leave without you, and now to just go home."

"It's late."

"It's not that late. And all of a sudden you're going to Europe. Last week you weren't going to Europe. What's got into you?"

Paige shrugged. "Nothing's got into me. The boats are full of people going to Europe."

"Edgar was right. You're running away. You won't see the same man more than a couple of times."

"Edgar said that?"

"While you were upstairs deciding whether to come down."

"You should know better," Paige said impatiently, "than to pay the slightest attention to Edgar."

"It seems this time he was right."

"If you want to think so."

"Then give me a better explanation."

"Why? Why do I have to explain anything? I'm free and I've decided to go to Europe. I don't have to explain it. And now I've decided to go home."

Parrish stared at her angrily, hardly believing this was Paige. She slid a little lower on the seat, turning up the collar of her pale silk coat, although it was a warm night, and stared straight ahead. Parrish started the car and drove her home.

At the house she quickly stepped out of the car and was halfway up the steps when he caught her. "Wait a minute, Paige."

She turned.

"Paige, come back and let me talk to you."

"It's very late, Parrish—"

"How about tomorrow night?"

"No. Parrish, I don't want to see you any more."

He came up beside her. "Why not? What are you afraid of?"

"I'm not afraid of anything. I just don't want to see you. And don't stand here, shouting."

He lowered his voice to a whisper. "Paige, please come back and let me talk to you. Just a few minutes. Let's walk around or something."

She hesitated and then gave in and let him lead her down the steps and over to the walk that led to the pool. Parrish searched for words, hearing the light tap of her heels on the flagstones. If he understood what was wrong, he would know better how to begin. They reached the pool and Paige turned.

"Well, what do you want to talk about?"

"Paige—" he stood behind her—"don't put me off this way and say you won't see me. And don't go running off to Europe, because I'll miss you. Because I love you very much."

At his words, Paige moved quickly away to the ladder of the pool, running her hand over the iron rail. "Parrish, don't be silly. Since you've been back we've been together about six times, twenty hours altogether, at the most. You don't fall in love in twenty hours."

"We had two years that I lived here, when we saw each other every day."

"You weren't in love with me during those years. You were in love with Alison."

"Is that what's bothering you?"

"Why should it bother me? I don't have any claim on you."

He took her hand. "Paige, of course I was in love with Alison. How can I deny it? Everyone knew it. And you were in love with Anson."

He felt her tighten up.

"I don't love her now." He could see her face clearly in the moonlight, and that her eyes were troubled. "It always bothered me, Paige, that you cared for Anson. I didn't know why—then."

"Parrish, I don't want to hear this." Paige moved into the black shadow of a hedge. "I don't want any part of love."

"Why?"

"The idea disgusts me."

"You don't mean that!"

"You're just like all the rest. June! Moon! And you think you're in love!"

"Look, Paige, just because Anson let you down—"

"Not just Anson. It's always the same. Love! It's just a lucky accident —or a terribly unlucky one. You just happen to come upon a man in a rare moment when his soul is on a vacation—taking a plane trip, soaring high. And you think this is special and you're in love. But it's always a mistake. In a little while he finds the air is too rarefied up there for his frail little soul that was never meant for greatness, so he drops down to earth where it's safe. He gives himself first to all the right things that are expected of him, and if love fits in conveniently and isn't too troublesome, it gets the scraps that are left over."

"It doesn't have to be that way."

"Show me an exception. Show me one exception!" Her eyes flashed. "Tonight at Maizie's they were taking a poll on monogamy. Voting on what modern marriage is like."

"You wanted to go there. I couldn't get you away."

"Because I didn't want to be with you. I don't want to take any chances on falling in love again. It's too easy—everything works to tempt you. You feel all this terrible love in you and want someplace for it to go, but you get fooled. You don't get love. The world is full of careful little people who never give much of themselves to life or to love or to another person. There's no such thing as a whole love—it's just a cautious little trial. Don't invest too much. One per cent of me for one per cent of you. Nothing big or joyous or wonderful—just a small exchange."

"Maybe you've just been with the wrong people, Paige."

"No. Souls don't soar. They don't even flutter their wings, because it isn't safe and they learn it very young. Each time they try, they get a little prick and they shrink back a little and then a little more and pretty soon they're narrow shrunken things. No joy—but no pain. No questions, no problems. Everything is as it should be—very safe. It's never been any different. I learned at a very early age that love is a bargain, only I refused to admit it. My father and my brothers loved me when I was a good girl. I loved them unquestioningly, but I got love in return when I followed the rules they set up for me. Anson loved me when I thought the way he thought and agreed with everything he said and seemed to be what he wanted me to be. When I said the wrong things to his friends, he had to change me. He couldn't love me that way. No, Parrish, the wonderful thing that love could be never happens. And I don't want to be hurt again. I'd rather do without, altogether. I'm the coward, now. Don't touch and you won't get burned. Just like everyone else, I'm playing it safe. Only they take the one-per-cent kind of thing. I don't want a few crumbs of the loaf. I don't want any part of it. I'd rather starve."

Parrish shoved his hands into his pockets and stared at the smooth surface of the water in the pool and kicked a stone in and watched it send out little concentric circles.

"Paige, that's the damndest speech I've heard in a long time."

"Well, now you know, so let's go."

Paige started for the walk and Parrish reached out to stop her. "Not on your life." He drew her close and kissed her, feeling her fight against responding. "Paige, there's nothing one per cent about this."

She tried to move but he held her firm and she turned her face away. "Why are you doing this," she demanded hotly, "when you know I don't want you to?"

"The only thing you said that made any sense—" he kissed her hair— "was that you're afraid you might fall in love with me."

"I didn't mean that. I'm not afraid of that."

"Good."

"I mean I'm not afraid I'll fall in love with you. I don't intend to."

"I know that's what you mean." He turned her face so he could reach her lips. "Paige, will you marry me?"

"No."

"Why?"

"I don't want to."

"I think," he murmured, "you won't marry me just because you know I can't support you and you'll have a terrible life."

She tried not to laugh. "Parrish, how can I be serious with you!"

Relief flooded through him that she was feeling better again and he drew her closer. "You've been serious enough for tonight. In fact, this little lecture on all your terrible friends will last a lifetime. I'll never forget it."

"I meant it."

"Of course you did. Is it safe to go now?"

"Safe?"

"I mean, when I come tomorrow night will you see me?"

"You'd better sleep tomorrow night because tonight is practically over."

"Will you still be here the night after?"

"Yes."

They started back along the flagstone walk. "I won't wait an hour again," he said. "I'll come up and get you."

Paige leaned her head against his shoulder. "This is against my better judgment, Parrish."

"Your judgment is terrible."

At the door he stopped her, serious now. "Paige?"

"Have you changed your mind?"

"Paige, I could never come back here—to all this—or work for your father again. It's only fair to tell you."

She nodded, with a little smile, and touched his face lightly and went into the house.

33

HEY, PARRISH," Lucy yelled from the back of the truck as they passed the garage, "your telephone's ringin'."

Parrish slowed down to listen. During the lunch hour he and Teet had taken the pickup truck that was giving him trouble again down to Tower's and as he passed here then he had thought he heard the telephone ringing, but by the time he reached the door it had stopped.

"Hear it?" Lucy said.

"Must be one of your women, lover," Addie yelled. "Hey, who is she, Parrish? What's she like?"

Parrish stopped and got out of the truck. Ordinarily he wouldn't bother, knowing that if it was important whoever it was would leave a message with Sala. But today Sala was at the experimental station getting information for his book. Parrish was halfway up the stairs when the ringing stopped. He waited a minute and when it didn't start again he walked slowly back to the truck to take home the crew.

"Ah, don't worry, lover," Addie yelled. "You know it couldn't be me 'cause I'm here and who else matters?"

After he had dropped the crew Parrish was tempted to go straight home, but he needed the pickup truck so he took the time to stop at Tower's to ask when it could be ready.

While he was talking to the mechanic Lewis Post came wandering up the highway. He stopped about ten feet away and let his eyes swim over to Parrish, then closed the distance between them.

"Well, Buster," he mumbled, "big news, eh?"

Parrish glanced up, saw that Lewis was drunk, and bent down under the hood of the truck with the mechanic.

"Buster—" Lewis whined, tugging at his sleeve.

Parrish straightened up. "What's the matter, Lewis?"

"Used to be you called me Mr. Post."

"O.K., Mr. Post, what can I do for you?" Lewis hadn't caused him any trouble. He was farming three acres that Sala had given him with plants that Parrish had given him, and since he was leaving them alone Parrish was willing to keep him happy.

"Now, if I asked you something, you wouldn't, would you?" Lewis rocked a little.

"Come on, fella, get to the point. I've got this truck here."

Lewis shook his head. "Buster, I don't want nothin'."

"Great. That's great." Parrish ducked back under the hood. When he looked up again Lewis was still there, staring at him out of bloodshot eyes. "You still here?"

"I was gonna ask you the same question."

Parrish saw now that Lewis was pretty shaky. "Come on, I'll give you a lift down the road."

"I'm only goin' down a piece to Tower's." Lewis climbed into the front of the truck and took out two creased dollar bills which he clutched in his hand. "It's a wonder you ain't gone down there."

Parrish didn't bother to answer. He was wondering if perhaps it had been Paige on the telephone, calling from the beach, where she'd been for the past ten days, or, if not, whether there would be a letter from her.

"Big news, huh?" Lewis said again after a while.

"Mmm," Parrish said automatically. Then he said, "What news?"

Lewis's eyes focused on him. "News about Judd Raike."

"What news about Judd Raike?"

"'At's families these days. Not what they was."

Parrish stopped the truck. "Come on, Lewis," he coaxed him. "Keep your mind on your business. What's the news about Judd Raike?"

Lewis shook his head mournfully, getting his eyes steady on Parrish. "Dyin'," he said.

"What!" Parrish grasped Lewis's shoulder.

"Maybe dead already."

"What are you talking about?" Only last night Ellen had called him from the beach and everything had been all right.

"Happened this morning. Fell down in the middle of the lobby of his hotel. Fell right down on the floor. Collapsed. Right in the middle of the floor. He's dyin', too, I heard it at Tower's. Maybe dead already."

"He's a little better tonight." Ellen opened the door to the balcony overlooking the ocean. "He won't die. Not right away, anyway."

She came back into her sitting room and lay down wearily on the sofa. "The children are at the hospital now. They didn't want to go, I made them. The only one willing to go in was Paige. And Alison. Poor Alison." Ellen covered her eyes with her hands.

"Why poor Alison?"

"I only meant that at least she is kind. She's hungry and restless but when she isn't too driven by her own insatiable desire she can be kind." Ellen sighed, very tired.

"Have you eaten anything?" Parrish said. "Have you had dinner?"

"No."

"I'll order you some."

"I couldn't eat anything." Tears came to Ellen's eyes. "Parrish, he'll never be the same. He was failing even before this. He won't have the spirit or the strength to recover like the last time."

Parrish went to the telephone to order her dinner, feeling her despair, and thinking that she had never really seen Judd Raike, after all, as others had. Ellen who always saw everything in everyone, had never seen Judd Raike as cruel, ruthless, and unscrupulous, and a dictator and a cheat. She had seen only the energy and drive—and the fact that, in his way, he loved and needed her.

"He'd sit and stare for fifteen or twenty minutes at a time—just look into space or at the same page of a newspaper or book until I would think his mind was wandering. Then he would come out of it and be all right. Maybe his mind did wander at those times. I don't know. Maybe he was only brooding. He brooded terribly. He worried about what would happen to the company. Only last week he admitted for the first time that his sons were failures. Imagine what it took for him to say the words. And it bothered him so, because he couldn't do anything about it. Even this morning—that was what brought it on."

"What happened this morning?"

Ellen sighed. "I should have taken him home when I saw what was happening. This place brings out the worst in them. In Hartford they're bad enough, but there something holds them together. They have a loyalty to the industry—to Raike and Company because it's big and important. But here they just dissipate and it upsets him to see it."

"Not Edgar?"

"Wiley and Alison. In Hartford they hate each other as much as here, but there they keep up appearances. Alison goes to Red Cross meetings, church meetings, Wiley does his share—even stays sober for it. Last year he worked for the Boy Scouts and the Children's Home. Here—"

"What happened here?"

"Wiley has been having an affair with one of the telephone operators and hasn't been too discreet, probably because he was too drunk to think straight. The girl claims to be pregnant—I doubt that she is—and Edgar paid her off."

Edgar, Parrish thought, is experienced at that.

"The girl brought the check to Judd as proof of the affair and demanded more money. Judd called them in here this morning and told them both that they didn't amount to anything and were a disgrace. He was upset because Wiley was such a fool and because Edgar blundered and paid the girl with a check instead of cash and then still didn't get rid of her. It was awful—I've never seen him so wild. Then he told them that whatever they did he could guarantee it would be wrong, and that they didn't know anything about tobacco and he would send them out as field hands to learn—he was just so excited he said anything. Then he said he was going to sell out because they were incompetent."

Ellen was sitting up now, becoming more distressed, remembering. "Wiley just laughed and said that was nothing new and started to drink, but Edgar went completely crazy and screamed that if anyone was incompetent it was Judd—and told him he was crazy. And Judd ordered them out and went downstairs himself and collapsed in the lobby."

The waiter arrived with Ellen's dinner. "Mr. Raike is better, madam?" he said, while he set the table.

"Yes, thank you."

"Mrs. Raike came in a while ago," the waiter said. "Mrs. Wiley. She said he was better."

Ellen looked up. "Are they all back?"

"Mrs. Wiley came in alone, madam. Half an hour ago. Mr. Wiley came in a few minutes ago and is in the bar."

Ellen said no more. When the waiter left, she said, "I didn't hear her come in. Their room is right next door."

"What difference does it make? Try to eat something."

A moment later Paige came in.

"How was he when you left, Paige?" Ellen said.

"Awful."

"Worse?" Ellen put down her fork. "Why didn't they call me?"

"No, not worse," Paige said. "Just awful. This one is worse than the last. I can see it."

"Yes," Ellen said.

"Edgar and Wiley were great. Stood around looking at their fingernails. Then, coming back, Evaline started talking about the will of God and I thought Edgar would kill her. Wiley's down in the bar for a change."

She went out onto the balcony. It was dark now and the soft slush of the ocean on the sand came through the quiet night.

"I really can't eat, Parrish." Ellen pushed away the table. "I think I'll phone the hospital."

She had picked up the telephone when suddenly from the next room came an angry scream. She dropped the telephone and Paige came rushing in from the balcony. Now the voices became more distinct, were unmistakably Wiley yelling and Alison screaming an answer.

Ellen flew out the door and down the corridor. "Be quiet!" She pushed open the door to their room. "Stop it. We've had enough scenes around here for today."

Parrish was just a step behind her, and then Paige came in, backing off a little with distaste when she saw the scene. In the room Alison and Wiley faced each other, and near the door, red-faced and embarrassed, stood a bellboy who looked like a college football player working for the summer.

"Slut!" Wiley yelled.

"Shut up!" Alison brought her hand furiously across his face.

The bellboy tried to get to the door, but Wiley, weaving a little, yelled, "Stay where you are."

Miserably, the boy halted, and then Edgar and Evaline came in and crowded his path so that he couldn't leave. Ellen stepped between Alison and Wiley. "Stop it. Stop it this minute. Remember who you are. And where you are."

Wiley reeled toward the bellboy. "I ought to kill you."

"Wiley," Ellen said, "what is this all about?"

"Look—look for yourself and you'll see what it's about. Whore!" he yelled at Alison. "You're just a common lay."

"There's nothing to see," Alison yelled. "You're too drunk to see anything, anyway. You walk in here, yelling like a maniac! What's bothering you tonight? And what brought you upstairs so early? Your girl friend turn you down? Or is she too far along to look good to you now?"

"Alison, keep quiet!" Ellen said. "Don't say another word." She turned to the bellboy. "Are you the boy they sent?"

The boy stared, speechless.

"I telephoned for a boy. Are you the one they sent?"

"Yes, ma'am," he stammered, perspiration standing in beads on his forehead.

"You have the wrong Mrs. Raike." Ellen started for the door.

"What'd you want a boy for?" Wiley demanded, the first hint of uncertainty in his voice.

"To close a window," Ellen said. "The window was stuck and I was cold. Good night, Wiley."

"Wait a minute." Wiley jerked his head toward Parrish. "Why didn't he close the damn window?"

"Parrish has just arrived." Ellen opened the door and spoke firmly to the bellboy. "Go downstairs now."

"Did you?" Wiley turned to Parrish.

"Yes," Parrish lied. "I just came."

"Good night, Wiley," Ellen said.

Parrish stepped aside to let Paige go ahead of him and saw that she was standing still, pale with shock and disgust. "Paige, come on." He put an arm around her. It was a gesture of love that he made unthinkingly, and when he looked back into the room he saw Alison staring at him with a look of pure hatred, understanding what she had seen.

At the door to Ellen's room Paige stopped. "I'm not coming in," she said. "I'm going for a walk to breathe some clean air."

Parrish hesitated, nodding toward Ellen, who had gone back into the room. "I ought to stay with her a little while."

"I'd just as soon be alone, anyway," Paige said.

Something in her voice alarmed Parrish and he said, "Can't you come in for half an hour, and then I'll go with you?"

"No," Paige said again. "I'd rather be alone."

"Paige, where will I find you?"

"I'll be somewhere on the boardwalk. I'll just be walking on the boardwalk."

Inside, Ellen sank down on the sofa, gray with exhaustion.

"What will happen now?" Parrish said.

"Nothing will happen. They'll go on just as before. Hating each other in private, courteous and even affectionate in public, doing what's expected."

"You think he believed you?"

"Probably not. It doesn't matter, anyway. It's not the first time. This has been going on for years. At first I used to urge them to get a house of their own. Then I stopped because I thought I could teach her to use a little restraint."

Parrish felt sick.

"She's cursed with an insatiable craving. Before, she craved everything money could buy. Then she got everything money could buy, so she craves another kind of thrill. And she gets it easily because she's beautiful. Judd gave her everything because she was so ornamental, and men want her for obvious reasons. The day she went to you and you stood her up she came home and rushed up to my room in hysterics. She sat in front of the mirror grasping her face in panic because she thought she was losing her looks."

"She told you about that!"

"She tells me everything. She leans on me like a child." Ellen stood up. "I'm going to get ready for bed, Parrish. I'll be right back."

Ellen went into the bedroom and Parrish sank deep in a chair and closed his eyes while the ugly scene and all its meaning replayed itself in his mind. In the room next door he could still hear voices, lower now, and he supposed they were still quarreling. He stood up and walked out onto the balcony. Below, the ocean whispered in the night and on the boardwalk a lone couple strolled, hand in hand, off into the darkness. A moment later there was a knock on the door and Parrish came in to answer it.

"Ellen—" Edgar strode into the room.

Ellen opened the bedroom door.

"I came to tell you," Edgar said, "that we are moving out of the Hartford house. Evaline and I and the children."

"All right."

"It's not good for the children to be in the house with an invalid."

Ellen came into the room, wearing a pale-blue dressing gown. "I take it, Edgar, that you spoke to them at the hospital?"

"They said he could be sent home in an ambulance in a week. Naturally, he'll be a long time recovering at home."

"Naturally."

"We discussed it on the way back from the hospital, Wiley and I, and we've decided."

"Then Wiley is moving out, too?" Ellen said.

"We're both leaving in the morning to look for houses."

Ellen regarded Edgar silently for a moment and then said, "In that case, please ask Wiley to come in here. I want to talk to you both."

"There's nothing to talk about. It's all decided. You can't stop us."

"I don't want to stop you. You should have done it long ago. But I do have something to say to you. Get Wiley, Edgar."

Edgar hesitated, but Ellen said again, very firmly, "Get him."

Edgar left. Ellen sat erect in a straight-back chair, visibly drawing on her last reserves of energy. A moment later Edgar returned with Wiley, who still wore a flush of anger.

"I understand," Ellen greeted him, "that you are moving out of the house?"

Wiley nodded.

"That's fine," Ellen said. "You both owe it to your families to have homes of your own."

Edgar looked at her suspiciously, as though, if she was for it, he thought he ought to change his mind.

"But I haven't the slightest doubt about why you're moving out now. You find it unpleasant to look at your father in his crippled condition."

"It's hardly a healthy atmosphere for my wife and children," Edgar said.

"It was never a healthy atmosphere for your wife and children. So it's very wise that you're moving." Ellen looked at them sharply. "But I'll expect you to come to visit your father every day for as long as he lives."

"Every day!" Edgar gasped. "That's ridiculous."

"Every day," Ellen said. "Both of you. And you'll go into the room and sit near him and look at him, not at your feet and hands and the ceiling and everything in the room except him. And if he wants you to come back in the evening, you'll come, and if he wants you to have dinner with him, you'll have it. And don't plead another engagement because you can break it."

"The hell with that!" Edgar said. "It's time we stopped being slaves."

"No, Edgar. The time you should have stopped being slaves was long ago. But you didn't then because you didn't dare. Now you'll go on just as before, and give him the respect he's accustomed to."

"Why?" Wiley said furiously. "All he ever did was push us around like trained dogs—laugh at us, insult us, crack the whip to make us jump through hoops."

"And now that he can't raise his arm to crack the whip any more you're going to stop jumping?"

"You're damned right. I'm not taking any more of that crap. I've had it!"

"If you had said that when he was strong, I'd have applauded you, Wiley. I'd have helped you make a break for freedom. But you didn't do it then, so you're not going to do it now. Now you'll stay and you'll do as you're told."

"What about him?" Wiley jerked his head toward Parrish. "It was different with him, wasn't it?"

"He didn't want your father's money. You do."

"You weren't interested in making a slave out of your own son. Only us. When he broke away you stood by him."

"He made his break when your father had his strength. He fought on equal terms—as a matter of fact, against superior odds. Now the terms are no longer equal." Ellen's eyes blazed. "In his way he was a great man, and I'm not going to have him beaten in his last days by his own sons."

Edgar lit a cigar and puffed pompously a few minutes. "Well, this is a lot of foolish talk. I'll be glad to come when I can, but I have a big business to run now and that comes first. When I'm tied up I won't be able to get around and I don't think that's open to discussion."

"It's not open to discussion," Ellen said flatly. "You're going to dance as long as the fiddler plays, however weak the tune. And if you don't, I'll work against you for as long as your father lives. I'll do everything I can to deprive you of as much as I can. I'll have his ear all day, every day. I'll tell him that you're avoiding him and ignoring him and rebelling against him and that you care nothing for him, only for his money. I can do it. I'll be living with him and you won't, Edgar. You'd better come around to protect your own interests."

This found the mark, and Edgar and Wiley listened more carefully now.

"So you'll be just the same as before," Ellen said, "and do everything and anything he wants. For as long as he lives. Just the same as when you were afraid not to because he held the purse strings. And because he was your protection against the world."

"I don't know what you're getting excited about," Wiley said. "Nobody's done anything yet."

"That's fine," Ellen said. "Tomorrow morning before you go home to look for your houses, don't forget to stop at the hospital."

"For your information," Edgar said icily, "we intended to."

"And on your way back."

"We're not entirely sure we're coming back."

"If you knew he could recover completely, would you come back tomorrow night?"

Wiley chewed at his lip. "It's all right with me," he said. "I don't mind coming back."

"Good night, then." Ellen stood up and Parrish turned away and stood with his back to them until he heard the door close.

Ellen sank back into the chair, letting down all at once. "I couldn't do it, of course," she said wearily. "Judd's fondest dream is to start a dynasty like the old tobacco families around here. But I can scare them a little."

"You scared them quite a lot."

"I just want to see him get his money's worth. It's no bargain, but he bought it. And now, Parrish, I have a strong sleeping pill and I'm going to take it and go to bed. Go find Paige. And will you sleep in here tonight in case the hospital calls and I don't hear the phone?"

"Hello, Tom."

Parrish had walked the length of the boardwalk and back without finding Paige and then gone into the hotel to telephone her room. She had not answered. Now, coming out again, he ran into Tom Holden, leaning against the rail of the walk.

"I'm just enjoying the night for a few minutes," Tom said. "These summer evenings, when the moon is waning and every star is out, can bewitch me each time as though I'd never seen such a sky before."

Parrish leaned against the rail next to Tom, squinting into the darkness for Paige.

"Also," Tom said, "I've been thinking about Judd."

Parrish glanced over at him.

"He was a strange man," Tom said. "A tremendous drive and energy, all directed to a single purpose—ownership."

"He cracked up trying to own everything," Parrish said. "Even while I was there, I saw it—the first little cracks. He owned more than he could ever need or use and he killed himself trying to own more still."

"He worked tirelessly for possession—of people as well as things," Tom said. "Creatively, imaginatively, and then all the energy and imagination stopped in a dead end."

A warm ocean breeze came up. It was growing late and the boardwalk was almost deserted. Parrish wondered if he had missed Paige.

"There was a kind of greatness in him," Tom said, as Ellen had a little while before. "There was a grandeur in his dreams. There was no boundary of city or even country to stop his expansion. He was far ahead of the rest of us. But it all centered on ownership and on orderly, efficient management and there it stopped. He never used what it brought him to any great purpose."

"He used it for power," Parrish said. "Absolute power."

"But not in any broad sense. He made no effort to get the slightest political power, or social power, or even power over larger groups, through philanthropy. Large contributions of money to charity—hospitals, institutions—can undeniably buy power, but I don't think that ever interested him. He concentrated on more tangible control, even if the object was much smaller. Many times he worked for such control with a determination out of all proportion to its value. Like Sala's land and those other small parcels. And even you, Parrish. Aside from that, all he ever thought to do with his money was to beat his sons into being great men." Tom smiled, a little sadly. "And that was the one thing he couldn't do with it."

"If there was ever any hope for them, he beat it out of rather than into them," Parrish said. "Nobody could live in that house and call his soul his own."

"Paige did," Tom said. "In a way she is the stronger for it. She grew, resisting."

"Yes." Parrish decided to walk up the boardwalk again to look for her.

"I suppose it's not unusual," Tom went on, "this lack of balance, greatness on one side and emptiness and blindness on the other. It's what makes people what they are—human, not a perfect product of a machine."

"You're charitable to him, Tom," Parrish said. "More than I can be."

"Possibly because I never had to bear the brunt of his attack," Tom said. "This one-sidedness was Judd's greatest weakness. But still it was his strength."

"Tom, have you seen Paige tonight?"

"She's out on the pier," Tom said. "Good night, Parrish."

"Good night, Tom."

At the end of Raike's pier he found Paige, sitting on the top step leading down to the boat moorings, and he sat down beside her, resting his hand on her shoulder.

"Edgar and Wiley are moving out of the house," he said after a while. "They told Ellen."

"I know," Paige said. "They talked about it on the way home."

"Paige, it will go very hard on you being the only one there."

Paige shrugged. Parrish bent over and kissed the smooth blond hair. "Why won't you marry me, Paige?"

She leaned back without looking at him. "No."

Parrish fell silent. It was no time to press her. Raike was, after all, her father, and he had more than half died today. And then there was the other ugliness, which had disturbed her badly. "Are you still upset about that other thing?" he asked.

"Yes. Are you?"

"Deeply."

"Parrish—" Paige turned suddenly to look at him—"I'm not going to marry you, now or later. I'm not going to marry you ever."

Carefully Parrish looked at her, growing more disturbed as he saw the set of her lips, the clear seriousness of her eyes. "Why have you decided that now, Paige?"

"I never said I'd marry you."

"No," he agreed, "you didn't. But why have you suddenly decided that you won't? Why are you picking this moment to tell me? Now, tonight."

"Maybe I just think somebody around here ought to be honest with somebody else. There's no point in letting you think I might when it's out of the question."

Parrish saw now that she meant it, that she was completely serious. Slowly he stood up and walked down the steps to the boat landing. He leaned over a thick post and heard the water, rhythmically lapping the dock, and asked himself what he had done now. Bewildered, he turned back to where Paige was still sitting on the step. "Paige, if you'd tell me what brought this on, maybe I could explain."

"Nothing brought it on."

"Then why—"

"Nothing—just nothing. I've made up my mind, that's all. Now, please leave me alone."

"Is there someone else?"

"No."

Angry and discouraged, Parrish left her. He strode past her, up the steps, and walked swiftly down the pier. He was almost at the boardwalk before he slowed down. Something must have happened, he told himself. He was sure of it. Maybe if he went back— No, he decided. If this was going to happen every week, he might as well accept it. He went on to the boardwalk and then he turned and went back. About halfway down the pier he met Paige coming in. He walked beside her, a few feet away in silence. Then he stepped in front of her. "Tell me why."

"All right," she burst out. "I'll tell you why. Because of tonight. Because all that happened in there made me wake up and see something I'd almost forgotten."

"What's that?" he asked, furious. "That marriage can be rotten? Sure it can. So can mothers and fathers and children and dogs and apples. But they can be good, too."

"No," she said. "It has nothing to do with marriage. It has to do with you and me."

"Nothing happened in there between you and me."

"Yes, it did, Parrish. You lied for her."

"For who? My mother?"

"No. For Alison. And more than that, you were upset. You were terribly disturbed over the thing you saw there as a cold, hard fact you'd have liked not to believe. You're still upset."

It was true. It had hurt him to see what Alison had become. "I admit it. I was upset."

"I was upset, too. And sick with disgust. But I was jealous, too. And after a while I was more jealous than disgusted."

"You don't have to be jealous. She doesn't mean anything to me. I was just—oh, hell!" He turned away. "It's only natural that I was upset. Once she meant a lot to me. I put her up on a pedestal. I thought she was perfect, some kind of goddess, and it made me sick to see what I saw.

Even if I don't love her, it made me sick. I'm sorry if you can't understand that."

"She still cares about you. She was furious when you put your arm around me. You could have her back."

"I don't want her back."

Paige started to walk slowly down the pier again to the water and Parrish walked beside her, a little distance away. "Paige—" he made a final try—"don't complicate things. You don't have anything to be jealous about. And if you were, you must care—"

"Yes," she said. "I do. I care too much."

Parrish closed the distance between them.

"You have too much power to hurt me," she said.

"Why should I hurt you? Damn it, the last thing I want to do is hurt you."

"But you could. And it would only get worse. You could own me—"

"Oh, Lord, Paige, don't get back on that again! I don't want to own you, I don't want to hurt you. I only want to marry you because I love you. I want to live with you and take care of you the best way I can and that's all. Marriage isn't ownership."

"In the end it always seems to be, though, doesn't it?"

"No, it doesn't always seem to be. It's only some idea you've got because you had more than your share of people trying to rule you."

"Yes," Paige said. "They tried. And they never frightened me because I knew they couldn't. But now I am frightened because I love you. If I married you, I'd be tempted to give in just to keep your love."

"I haven't asked you to give in on anything."

"I would, though. I'd give in and give in because I'd be afraid to lose you. And in the end you'd have a terrible power over me. And that is something I'm never going to let happen. Nobody is ever going to own me again."

Parrish tried to hold her. "Paige, listen to me—"

But already she had broken away and she ran back along the pier to the boardwalk and disappeared in the darkness.

34

"WILLIS," Gladstone called.

"Hello, mon."

"You are very slow mon, Willis. That ees the truth."

"Eet ees very hot day to be moving too fast." Lazily, Willis dragged in a canvas basket full of leaves to the table where the women were sewing.

"Willis, we do not expect you to move too fast," Cartwright said. "Eef you would move only a leetle we would be satisfied, I theenk. Can you help us hang thees top row, Willis?"

Willis ambled down the shed to where Gladstone was perched on the top of the scaffolding, Cartwright a tier below. "I cannot refuse you, mon."

"Come on, mon. Come on."

Parrish walked down the shed. At the door he stopped a moment, watching the women sewing and the trio of Jamaicans hanging the lath, and then he hurried over to the shed next door where the fires were burning. Then he would have to get back to the field where the rest of the crew was picking. Now that they'd gone into production, he hardly knew where to put his time first.

Inside the dark shed he stopped a minute. This was the first shed filled and closed up to cure. But he had no time for sentiment and he hurried up and down, adding a shovelful of coal to each pan, and left. Outside, he saw Sala driving up the path in the station wagon and he stopped and waited for him. Parking next to the shed, Sala stepped out of the car and Parrish noticed that he was wearing the knee-high boots that he hadn't had out in a long time.

"You're chasing back and forth like a maniac." Sala came up to him. "I've been watching you from the house."

"I know it." Parrish grinned. "This is where I could use John one place or the other. Teet's doing the fields but that makes me short a driver."

"Stay there," Sala said. "I'll stay here."

Parrish wiped his face on his sleeve, feeling the layers of dust he'd piled on by chasing back and forth this way. "Thanks," he said. "I hate to have you do it, but it'll sure be a help."

"It won't be the first time," Sala said.

"I'm firing that shed next door. Will you keep Willis checking it?"

"Don't you have a man on it?"

"I can't spare a man just to sleep outside the shed when it's right next door. I'm trying to take them in order so I can watch from here."

Sala frowned, but he said, "I guess that's safe enough. How about at night?"

"The old man works ten to seven. I watch it myself until he comes on." Parrish started to leave.

"Parrish," Sala called after him, "I want to talk to you later. Can you get someone to relieve you watching the fires and have dinner with me tonight?" When Parrish hesitated Sala said, "It's a matter I want very much to discuss with you. I don't want to let it go any longer than necessary."

"All right," Parrish said. It was his night to go to Ellen's and he'd gone to great pains to get Teet to take over here early because Ellen had promised to keep Paige in until he got there. Maybe he could go afterward. "I'll come as soon as I take the crew home."

"You've got a first-rate crop there," Sala greeted him in the library. "Those are good-looking leaves I saw today."

"Are they?" Parrish was pleased. "I mean, they seemed good to me, but I'm not an expert."

"You will be," Sala said. "Yes, those are very good leaves."

"I've been lucky."

"Yes, you have. But careful, too." Sala led him into the dining room. "Parrish, I'll go into the sheds for you this year. You take the fields. You can't be both places at once."

"That's no work for you!"

"It won't do me any harm. Probably enjoy it. And next season you'll be able to arrange for Jamaicans and you'll have John. You'll be all set next year."

Parrish smiled. There was a pleasurable feeling of permanence, talking and thinking now about next year. He wondered if that was why Sala had called him in. "I was going to ask you to help me later when it came time to take down. There'll be borderline wet and dry days when I won't be sure whether to take down or not."

It was typical of Sala, Parrish thought, that however pressing his business he didn't discuss it at dinner. All through the meal he talked about the crop and Alison's new home and about his manuscript, which was almost completed. Then he stood up and poured the brandy and led Parrish into the library.

"Parrish," Sala said, "do you remember I offered to let you buy my land?"

"Of course I remember!" Parrish said. "How could I forget a thing like that!"

"Did you think about it?"

"Sure I did. I think about it all the time. I just haven't brought it up because you said to wait until after the season."

"Then you think you're going to want to go ahead?"

Parrish grinned. "You knew there'd be no question about it."

Sala was silent for a few minutes, sipping his brandy, thoughtful. "Parrish, it's most distasteful to me to pry into your private life—" He broke off, as though the indelicacy were repugnant to him, and Parrish was surprised and puzzled, wondering what Sala had heard about his private life. The truth was he was so busy he had no private life.

"Parrish, I don't like to ask you this—"

Alison! Parrish sat on the edge of his chair. Alison had been here three times in the last week. He'd seen her car and deliberately avoided her. Alison had told Sala some kind of twisted story. . . .

"Are you planning to marry Judd's daughter?"

Parrish sank back. It was Alison all right, but not the kind of story he had been expecting. He saw that Sala was waiting and thought that he could give him the answer he was hoping for, and it would be true. But not by choice. "No," he said.

Sala looked so relieved that Parrish was almost tempted not to say the rest of it. "I'm not going to marry her. But only because she won't have me."

Sala's face clouded over again.

"I would if I could," Parrish said.

Silently Sala stood up and went to the window and looked out at the cloth and at his land. Before he spoke, Parrish knew what he would say. "Parrish, I've always considered myself a man of honor. I have never knowingly done a dishonorable thing in my life."

A thing could lie quiet in a man forever without change, Parrish thought. If nothing happened to stir it up, it lay there so long that everyone thought it was gone—everyone except the man himself. He knew it was there and in his own way he nourished it and kept it alive and strong so that it rose up to serve him at a moment's notice. A man didn't change. His thoughts were habits. And hatred was the strongest habit of all.

"I offered you the land," Sala said. "You had my word for it and you accepted it in good faith, as I would accept yours. But if you were going to marry Judd Raike's daughter, I would have to break my word to you."

Parrish dug his nails into his palms. Keen disappointment and sharp anger mixed in him, and for several moments he didn't trust himself to speak. All this old hatred was making him sick; everywhere you scratched, it turned up. Why should Paige, who hated Raike's methods as much as he did, be made to suffer for them? Paige! She was so unlike the rest of them he never even thought of her as a Raike any more. . . . Sala was waiting, still hoping for the reassurance that Parrish couldn't give; he clenched his teeth together to remain silent.

"As long as you have said no," Sala said, "the arrangements can stand and we'll talk about it after the season."

"No." Parrish shook his head quickly. "I don't want it."

Pain came to Sala's face as he stared at him.

"Paige won't marry me, and there isn't any other Raike, but I don't want your land on those terms. Because I would marry her if I could. I'll do everything I can to marry her. I don't think I'll succeed, but I'll try."

"In that case," Sala said formally, "any discussion of your buying it is ended."

Parrish stood up. "It's your land."

It's your land, he thought, with sudden fury, and you're a crazy old man with your precious hatred that's grown to be the most important thing in your miserable, isolated life. Live out here alone with your land and your hatred that you feed and cherish like a baby! Then he checked his wild thoughts and set his jaw. Except for this, Sala had been more decent to him than anyone he had ever known and he wasn't going to say anything now that he would be sorry for. He started for the door.

"You can lease it as long as you like, Parrish." Sala gestured a little helplessly, as though there was more he wished he could say. "You can lease it and make a good living here. I want you to. But I can't enter into any arrangements for you to own it as long as such a marriage remains a possibility."

"All right," Parrish breathed. "All right."

"If things ever change, if you decide against it, or you marry someone else, or she does, then—"

Parrish pulled open the door to leave. He turned to Sala and said, with careful control, "You're hating a ghost. There's nothing left to him."

Sala sighed. "She's still a Raike. There would be children who would be one-half Raike."

Parrish walked out of Sala's house. In bitterness he strode across the gravel driveway and out to the fields, kicking at clumps of earth and weeds and at the few bushy plants outside the cloth. He walked up one path and down another, past all the fields he had planted, walking for more than an hour. At last he went out to Teet, watching the fires in the number-six shed, to send him home early. Perplexed, Teet waited for him to talk, but Parrish was unwilling to discuss this even with Teet, and at last Teet gave up and, scratching a bit, settled down next to him in silence to wait until the old man came on.

The next day Parrish saw Alison's car again and went up to the apartment and locked the door.

Four days later he learned that Paige had sailed for Europe.

The crop was hanging in the sheds, seven tiers high. In some, the bottom tiers had already been taken down and lay boxed on the sandy floors, waiting to be packed and shipped to Tom Holden's warehouse. In the fields the plants had gone to flower and had been cut down. The season was over. Today the cloth was coming down.

From where he sat near the number-three shed, Parrish could see Teet over in a corner of the number-one field, ready to begin. Near the barn the canvas baskets lay in the sun, dirty and spotted, a couple of water barrels beside them. Now the first corner of the cloth sagged and he knew Teet was starting, and understood, as a queer feeling shot through him, why Sala always used to go away the day the cloth came down.

He stood up and walked around to the other side of the shed and sat in the sun, letting his thoughts wander. It had been a good year. He couldn't have asked for a better one. Except for the shortage of help at the beginning, and later the lack of a foreman, there had been almost no difficulty; and then Sala had helped faithfully in the sheds. And already Parrish had started arrangements for more Jamaicans for next year. His relationship with Sala was friendly again, although cooler than before, and he forced himself not to think about the episode that had come between them. It was, after all, Sala's land. He hadn't had to make Parrish the offer in the first place.

Parrish's thoughts idled over to Judd Raike. Raike's right side was crippled and would remain so. He had barely recovered enough to go to his office again, but he went every day. It was no more than a desperate gesture of hanging on, because he could do almost nothing. Even his mind was impaired, clear one moment and dazed the next. In the end, Parrish thought, who had won? Raike or Sala? Sala was straight and whole and Raike was dying, but in the end Alison would have Sala's land and would probably sell it to Raike and Company.

The land, he thought, that could have been his but that he couldn't take—not, at least, as long as he could hope that Paige would come back. He had learned her address from Ellen and had written to her and yesterday, at last, an answer had come and Parrish had found some small hope in that. He picked up a stick and fiddled in the sand and presently took out Paige's letter and read it again.

There was nothing special about it. It was neither affectionate nor excessively cool. She wrote of her studies and her apartment in Paris and said she supposed that when he received this the cloth would be coming down and he would feel the way all tobacco men felt who lived on their land. She was delighted for him, she said, that of all the land in the Valley, this was to be his, because it was the best.

Well, it wasn't to be his, but he would still lease it and it was the best land. He didn't want to sit here and dwell on it. He got up and walked over to the barn and stacked the canvas picking baskets that had been tossed carelessly aside and went inside the barn and made room to store them. When he finished, Teet had come in for lunch and Parrish went over and sat near him.

His thoughts went back to Paige's letter. With an ocean between them, he thought bitterly, she felt safe—safe enough even to write a letter. Then suddenly he sat up. He pulled out the letter again and swiftly skimmed over the pages to the part he was looking for. "I was so happy for you," she had written, "when I heard that Sala had offered you his land. Surely it's the best piece in the Valley. . . ."

How could she have heard? He hadn't told her; he hadn't told anyone, not even Ellen. And when Raike had asked him, he had denied it. Parrish's mind worked back over those last weeks he had spent with Paige. He knew he hadn't told her. He hadn't wanted to say anything until it was settled.

"Teet—" he said.

Teet, sprawled on the ground, opened one eye.

"Did you hear that Sala offered to let me buy his land? Did anyone tell you that?"

"You telling me or asking?"

"I'm asking. The deal's off, but did you hear it during the summer? You know—no secrets in our little Valley. Did you hear it?"

"That's one I missed," Teet said.

"Then how—" Parrish frowned—"could someone else, farther away, have picked it up?" Only one way, he thought, but he wanted to be sure.

Teet shrugged. "Ah—I gotta get goin' again with the cloth."

"Nobody knew except Sala and me. And I didn't tell anyone."

Teet frowned and stirred. "Well, I'll tell you, kid. You didn't tell anyone and Sala ain't no town crier, exactly. You know, he don't hang around Tower's shootin' the breeze. An' he goes into one of the stores, he says good mornin' an' that about covers it. An' he don't sit gassin' over the telephone. An' he don't hang around no fancy clubs, no more'n Tower's. An' he don't get no callers—'cept one."

Parrish nodded. It had to be Alison. Alison had told Sala about Paige, knowing, as certainly she would know better than anyone else, what Sala's reaction would be. And then she had gone home and told Paige that Parrish was going to buy Sala's land.

Slowly Parrish got to his feet and walked toward the house. No, he thought, Alison hadn't told Paige that he was going to buy the land. She had told Paige that he couldn't buy it because of her. And so Paige had gone away. Then she hadn't gone away because of those crazy notions of his owning her! Now he saw it clearly. All along, Paige had had those notions but she had never left because of them. She had talked about them and had let him argue them away—even wanted him to argue them away. Even the last time, when she hated his having lied to protect Alison, she had stayed on for three weeks.

And when she left it had not been her own fears that had driven her away, but the knowledge that she stood between him and the land he wanted. He understood Paige now and he knew how she would have thought about this. Even if Parrish chose her now instead of the land, she would have told herself, someday he would regret it, and all their lives it would hang over them and become a wall between them. He could almost hear her saying it!

Stuffing the letter into his pocket, Parrish rushed on now to Sala's house and pushed open the door and strode down the dark hall to the library, where Sala was writing at his desk. "Come with me!" he said.

Sala looked up quickly. "What's the matter? What happened?"

"Nothing." Parrish calmed down. "No—no, nothing's wrong. Nothing happened." They would just have time to make it. "I just want to show you something."

"What is it?"

"I don't want to tell you about it, I want to show you. It would be a great favor to me if you'd come. I'd appreciate it very much."

Sala gave an uncertain smile. "All right." He came around the desk. "Where is it?"

"In Hartford."

"I'll get my hat."

Parrish drove Sala into Hartford, talking a great deal to ward off his questions, about the farm and the crop and his negotiations with Tom Holden. Sala sat straight on the seat next to him, naturally bewildered by the sudden mystery but willing to go along with it. Parrish couldn't help smiling as he glanced over at him, sitting so straight on the seat. I love him, he thought. Away from his house he looks even more like something from another age, as straight as a rod, and all that high principle written all over his face, with his dignified, outdated straw hat. I love him, even if this doesn't work.

He pulled up in front of Raike's warehouse, parking directly behind

Raike's car that was waiting at the curb. Dennis, the chauffeur, had already gone inside. For the first time Sala showed annoyance. A little flush came to his face as he turned to Parrish.

"What kind of a joke is this?"

"Just sit here one minute. Don't get out of the car. Just sit here."

"Parrish, I resent being brought here in this peremptory fashion. I resent it deeply."

"I'm sorry. I apologize, but there was no other way to get you here."

"I didn't want to get here at all."

The door opened and Gilliam stepped out to hold it. Parrish nodded. "Look, now."

After what seemed an interminable delay they appeared, Raike inching along, his huge bulk weighing heavily on a cane, Dennis holding him on one side, Mig Alger on the other. He came out uncertainly and stood outside the door, hunched over, moving his head as if on a pivot, to look around. His eyes fell on the polished sign outside the door that said RAIKE AND COMPANY. For a long time he stood in front of the sign, a look coming to his face like the old Raike in the office counting his farms on the gold-lettered mahogany board. But he looked too long. The look grew vacant. He stared, leaning on the two men who held him. Minutes passed. At last Raike turned his head and mumbled something.

"What's he say?" Mig Alger said.

"The sign," Dennis said. "He thinks it's spotted."

"We'll polish it," Mig Alger said.

While they were still standing there Edgar came out, ducked his head, and strode past to where his own car with chauffeur, newly acquired, was waiting. He didn't stop to speak or to ask whether anything were wrong. They got Raike into the car and Dennis came around and got in and drove off.

"That's what you're fighting." Parrish looked at Sala. "What harm can he do you now?"

Sala didn't answer and Parrish started the car. All the way home Sala didn't speak and Parrish remained silent, too, because there was nothing he could add to what Sala had already seen. He turned into the driveway and drove up the hill between the trees to the side door and Sala got out.

"I understand what you are trying to tell me, Parrish," he said. "But it doesn't change anything. Raike and Company is still big and powerful and I don't want anyone connected with it here on my land."

Parrish drove on to the garage and walked back to the number-three shed. The cloth was down. The fields were bare. Near the barn were the canvas picking baskets, dirty and spotted, that he had piled for storage, and beside them the rusty water barrels. After a while he went upstairs and wrote to Paige that he loved her and wanted her more than the land, and he asked her to come home.

35

A COLD WIND whipped across the street as Parrish came out of Tom Holden's warehouse, and a few early snow flurries danced between the buildings. For a moment Parrish stood and watched, feeling strangely empty inside. The last lath was down, the last leaf packed, the last crate of crisscrossed hands of tobacco delivered on the truck to Tom's warehouse. At home, empty sheds were closed until another crop would be ready; the fields lay bare. It was all over and winter was coming. Parrish had Tom Holden's check in his pocket and nothing ahead of him for three months.

Turning up his collar, he made his way to his car and started home. He thought he would settle up his account with Sala and take a couple of days to put things in order around the farm and then go away for a while. No place special. There was no place he wanted to go. He would just roam around for three months until it was time to come back here and get started again. He laughed at himself halfheartedly. How long since he had had thoughts like that? Nevertheless, it was a good idea and he would do it.

When he reached home he went upstairs for his records and then walked over to Sala's to settle his account. Sala's stern face lit up, pleased, as he looked at Tom's check. "Fine!" he said. "Excellent! For twenty acres that's a fine return."

"I brought my figures," Parrish said, "to pay back what you lent me. Will you see if they agree with yours?" He held out the list on which he had itemized his accounts, but Sala only glanced at it.

"Put it on the desk. I'll look it over later." Sala indicated the opposite chair. "Sit down, Parrish."

Parrish put the papers on the desk, moved a paperweight over them, and came back and sat down.

"Edgar Raike was here today," Sala said.

"Edgar! What was he doing here?"

"He's quite a fool, isn't he?"

"He's a fool," Parrish agreed. "He tries to be crafty, but he has a real genius for bungling things."

"That was my impression." Sala stood up to put away the book he'd been reading. "I'd never really talked to him before."

"What did he want?"

"He wanted to lease my land for next year." Sala tucked the book into the bookcase, lining it up with the others in the row. "When I refused, he asked me if it were true that I was thinking of selling the land to you. I told him that we had discussed it. He let me know that would displease him considerably."

Sala glanced over his shoulder with a small smile and Parrish grinned. He could just picture Edgar. He was so pompous these days, he was ridiculous.

"He said he was looking out for Alison's interests and that you have no right to this land."

Parrish frowned a little, wondering why Sala was bringing this up again. Nothing had changed. Then, with a twinge of alarm, he wondered whether Edgar had brought news of Paige, something he didn't know yet, that would remove her as an obstacle. He looked up at Sala, worried.

"We talked for quite a long time," Sala said.

"What about?"

"Just talked. I wanted to see what he was like. I don't think you'll ever have any trouble with him, Parrish."

"What kind of trouble?"

"With the land. I don't think he'll ever get the best of you, if you keep your eyes open. He's too great a fool."

"I don't ever intend to let him get the best of me," Parrish said, "as long as I'm here."

"I don't know how Judd Raike could raise two such fools." Sala busied himself straightening books in the bookcase while he spoke. "After he told me he was pleading Alison's case he tried blackmail."

"Blackmail! How could he blackmail you?"

"He told me that several weeks ago he hired a detective—"

"That sounds like Edgar."

"And he had Alison followed, watched—" Sala pulled out two books and moved them to another shelf—"and he feels he has some information that might embarrass Alison, spoil her good name, and unless I agree to leave her the land that is rightfully hers he intends to divulge this."

Shocked, Parrish searched for the right thing to say. Quickly, he reasoned that Edgar would never expose Alison because she wasn't a Post now but a Raike, and who cared more for the good name of Raike than

Edgar? Preserving it was practically a career with him. Probably it was true that he'd hired a detective. That was the way he worked. But if anyone were to reveal embarrassing information, Alison could embarrass Wiley, and, Parrish thought with a sudden inner laugh, he himself could embarrass Edgar!

"What did you tell him?" he said.

"That was when our talk ended. I asked him to leave."

"He's only playing dirty games," Parrish said. "Alison behaves herself. He hasn't got anything on her."

Sala looked away and Parrish thought with a little stab that he knew the truth and wondered who had told him or how he had learned it. "Don't worry about Edgar," he said. "He's all smoke and no fire."

Sala nodded. "Parrish, there in the desk, in the top drawer, there are some long blue papers, typewritten, clipped together. Get them."

Parrish opened the desk drawer.

"Read them," Sala said. "Those are the terms on which I'll sell you the land."

Slowly Parrish picked up the papers, holding them in his hand without looking at them. He raised his eyes to Sala. "There's only one condition you could make that would keep me from buying it."

Sala shook his head and then Parrish saw that the date on the memo was June 15, that it had been drawn up before Sala knew about Paige. Before he himself knew.

"What did Edgar tell you?" he demanded. "That made you change your mind?"

"Nothing," Sala said. "Nothing in particular. He only talked enough to prove to me that he's a fool and nothing to be afraid of, and to point up to me the fact that he's anticipating my demise. He kept telling me I had better leave it to Alison in my will. He wanted my word that I would. At least he was willing to accept that as enough."

Parrish looked at Sala over the blue papers in his hand. "If you're convinced that Raike is finished, and Edgar is nothing to worry about, you can give it to Alison."

"Then he will get it," Sala said. "Alison will turn it over the same day if the price is right. What does she care?"

"And you believe now that I won't?"

"I know you won't," Sala said. "And I know that that fool won't be able to make you."

"And Paige?"

Sala looked away and a tight, flushed look came to his face. "I don't like it, Parrish, but what can I do? What can I do with my land?"

Parrish looked down at the sheets of paper without seeing the words.

There was nothing he could say to make Sala feel better, not even to repeat that there was probably nothing to worry about.

"Are you reading the papers?"

Parrish looked up. "No," he admitted. "I was just wishing there were something I could say to you, but there isn't."

"Read them," Sala said. "It's a fair sale, but not an easy one."

"Whatever you decide is all right."

"You get the entire acreage at a stipulated price per acre. It's all in there." Sala nodded to the memorandum. "The price is set, not subject to change if the market changes, up or down. All money is paid into a trust fund I've set up for Alison. She's entitled to the land, or, in lieu of that, to the money it brings. She should have money of her own. If she ever comes to her senses she should be able to leave that drunkard and have the means to live without a scandal."

Parrish felt a deep sadness for Sala, knowing how deeply it hurt him to say these things.

"For five years you pay nothing toward the purchase price. That's to enable you to build up working capital. I don't want you to have to mortgage for capital. One bad year on borrowed money and some Raike will manage to get in. I hope you'll keep your profits and live conservatively to build up that capital. You have a good start now."

Parrish nodded. "Don't worry about it. I'll build it up."

"After five years you pay fifty per cent of your profit after taxes, or ten thousand dollars, whichever is less, every year until the purchase price is paid. That will take care of you in a bad year. If you don't make anything one year, you won't have to dip into working capital. That's all. Take the agreement along and read it over. If you have any questions, ask me. If there's anything you think is unfair, we'll discuss it. When you're ready, we'll go into Hartford to my lawyer and draw up the papers." Abruptly Sala stood up and turned his back. "I can't tell you whom to marry. I hope you won't marry Judd's daughter, but if you do, she was always a nice little girl. It's just that she's a Raike."

You have good and bad strains in tobacco, Sala had said once, a long time ago, and you have them in cattle, and you breed accordingly. And then out of nowhere you had Paige.

Sala had stopped talking and remained with his back turned and Parrish thought that he probably wanted to be alone. "You want me to leave now?"

"I think so."

Parrish hesitated. "You going to be all right?"

"Of course, of course."

Parrish walked quickly out of the house and stopped in the driveway, wondering how to send a cablegram, and then raced into Hartford to Western Union.

> TODAY I BOUGHT SALA'S LAND. NO STRINGS ATTACHED. PLEASE COME HOME. I LOVE YOU.

He wrote it out and then, for a minute, couldn't remember her address in Paris.

After that, with Tom Holden's check and Sala's terms of sale still in his pocket, he drove for two hours all over the countryside, too excited to stay still. Then, thinking about Paige, he could picture her getting the cablegram and sitting there, looking at it, thinking it over, and he went back to Western Union and sent another: COME. HURRY.

By the time he remembered the check, the banks were closed. He walked around Hartford for a while and went into a bar and had a drink all by himself to celebrate and then went back to Western Union again, noticing the clerk beginning to regard him strangely. He laughed and wrote out a third message: IF YOU DON'T I'LL COME AND GET YOU.

At last he calmed down enough to go home. Upstairs, he settled down to read Sala's terms. He wasn't used to legal language and he had to read it slowly and parts of it over again before he understood it. It was just what Sala had said it was, nothing more, and he had no questions.

The next morning they went in to Sala's lawyer to draw up the bill of sale. Afterward Sala asked him to come over for lunch and after lunch took out his usual thin cigar and then reached for another and handed it to Parrish.

"Light up, my boy." Sala's pale eyes twinkled. "You're an owner now."

Late that afternoon the cable came from Paige and he tore it open and read: STOP THROWING AWAY YOUR PROFITS. I'M ON MY WAY.